Helen Forrester was born in Hoylake, Cheshire, the eldest of seven children. For many years, until she married, her home was Liverpool – a city that features prominently in her work. For the past thirty years she has made her home in Alberta, Canada. She has travelled widely in Europe, India, the United States and Mexico.

Helen Forrester is the author of four best-selling volumes of autobiography and a number of equally successful novels. In 1988 she was awarded an honorary D.Litt. by the University of Liverpool in recognition of her achievements as an author. The University of Alberta conferred on her the same honour in 1993.

D0682503

HELEN FORRESTER

Liverpool Daisy
The Liverpool Basque

Grafton

HarperCollins*Publishers*
77–85 Fulham Palace Road,
Hammersmith, London W6 8JB

www.harpercollins.co.uk

This omnibus edition published in 2005
by HarperCollins*Publishers*

Liverpool Daisy
Copyright © June Bhatia 1979

The Liverpool Basque
Copyright © Helen Forrester 1993

The Author asserts the moral right to
be identified as the author of these works

ISBN 0 00 773414 X

Printed and bound in Great Britain by
Clays Ltd, St Ives plc

Liverpool Daisy

ONE

The morning of the death of Daisy Gallagher's mother, Mrs. Mary Ellen O'Brien, began like any other morning.

"And yet, you know, Mog," Daisy once remarked to her aged tomcat, "it was the beginning — the cause — of me slide. I didn't fall into trouble — I slid. And at times, Mog, it was pure mairder."

Moggie stared back at her with sad, unblinking eyes, as if to indicate that, if a woman imagined that life could be anything better than pure murder, she needed her head examining.

As if to mourn the passing of Mrs. O'Brien, the clouds lay low along the Mersey; and occasionally thin rain spread up the river, like a bolt of grey georgette being hastily unrolled, a wavering wetness hardly dappling the heaving waters. Through its dimming folds, freighters and ferry boats passed liked silent spectres, their lights unearthly in the poor visibility of the morning. Through the dockside streets, men clattered in worn out boots, cloth caps set low over their eyes, stained cloth coats already wet, as they went to sign on for work which did not always materialize in those hard days of 1931.

A spatter of rain swept over Dingle Point and across the Herculaneum Dock. It pattered softly on the slate roofs of the tightly packed houses, which faced each other across each street like courting cats about to spring. The house which Daisy Gallagher and her sailor husband shared with her mother was much older than the rest and did not return the stare of another house. It faced directly towards the river, and the rain struck its windowpanes squarely with a sharp pit-pat, as if it were trying to rouse the dead woman within. For a hundred years the rain and wind had been buffeting its grey stone walls and solid oak door, making the windows rattle in warning of bad weather coming up the river.

"Och, who cares about the weather," Daisy would sometimes say to her dearest friend and sister-in-law, Nellie O'Brien; and Nellie, who looked so frail that a puff of wind would blow her away, would nod her greying head gently in agreement, knowing that nothing as minor as bad weather would upset buxom, cheerful Daisy.

Daisy would push an old stocking filled with sand across the bottom of the front door to keep the draught out, and would say, without fail, "Me grandmother was born in this house — just after me great-grandma come from Ireland in eighteen thirty-six. If she could stand it, I can."

As yet unaware that her mother would never again complain of the draughts, Daisy looked out of the living-room window and clucked irritably to herself when she saw the overcast day. It looked as if winter was going to set in early.

She picked up a steaming mug of tea from the crowded table and tramped slowly up the worn wooden stairs to the front bedroom.

"Here's your tea, Mam," she announced, as she marched into the low-ceilinged, chilly room.

There was no reply. Cold, unmoving eyes returned Daisy's glance. Mrs. O'Brien would never need tea again.

Pure terror paralyzed Daisy for a moment. Then she quavered, "Mam," as if she hoped to waken her. "'ere, Mam."

Fearfully, Daisy approached the bed and tentatively touched the already cold hand on the dirty blanket. "Oh, Mam!"

"Oh, Jaysus Mary!"

She felt, as she gasped out this plea for Divine help, that part of her own body had been torn from her, the pain of separation was so intense.

She stifled a desire to scream for help; it was no use screaming if there was nobody to hear. With a trembling hand she put
down the mug on the mantelpiece. Then she leaned over
cautiously to cover Mrs. O'Brien's waxen face with the end of
the blanket. Her lips quivered as she sought to keep herself
calm.

She ran down the stairs and out of the house as if the devil
was after her. The street was deserted, the pavement heavy with
drops of mist. The damp pierced her tight-fitting cotton blouse;
and her heavy black skirt whipped uncomfortably around her
legs, as she sped round the corner and up the sloping side street
to the house where Great Aunt Mary Devlin rented a room. She
hammered on the door.

Great Aunt Devlin answered the knock herself, so quickly
that it seemed as if she must have been waiting on the other side
of the door for weeks for just such a call.

Half panting, half sobbing, Daisy announced her news.

"Me Mam! She's gone!"

She leaned against the door jamb to steady herself, while her
normally rosy face drained of colour and her eyelids drooped
over her deep-set blue eyes.

"I'll come, luv," Mary Devlin wheezed in reply, her wizened
face puckered up in sympathy. "You should have put your
shawl on, luv. You'll catch your own death."

With fingers mis-shapen by arthritis, she lifted her own black
shawl over her nearly bald head; then she stepped out and
closed the door softly behind her. Great Aunt Devlin spent most
of her time with the dead, and her quietness could be unnerving.

After viewing the body with experienced, rheumy eyes, Great
Aunt Devlin drew fourpence from her apron pocket and pressed
it into Daisy's shaking hand.

"Ask t' chemist, if he's open, if you can use t' telephone. You
got to tell the club man and ask him to bring the burial money.
Then phone Doctor Macpherson to coom and certify her."

Obedient and still tearless, though inwardly shattered, Daisy

delivered these two messages as fast as her fat legs and empty
stomach would permit her.

On her way home, she knocked at the door of the house of
her sister, Meg Fogarty. The house was one of a row of
dilapidated brick houses opening directly on to the pavement.
The door had long since lost its handles, but it did not yield
when Daisy tried to push it open.

She heard the bolt squeak as Meg Fogarty wriggled it out of
its socket.

"'allo, what you doin' here so early?" Meg inquired, her
black-rimmed eyes staring apprehensively out of a gaunt, tired
face, as she wiped her hands on a grey apron. "What's to do?"
Her children crowded behind her, eager to greet their dear Anty
Daise.

Meg drew in a quick breath, and her round, grey eyes with
their black circles seemed suddenly much rounder. Her hand
went to her mouth in a gesture of shock.

"God have mercy on us! Is it Mam?"

"Yes. I been for the doctor just now. Great Aunt Devlin's
with her." Daisy lifted a corner of her apron and agitatedly
mopped the sweat from her smooth, broad forehead.

Meg's toothless mouth quivered. "She's gone, is it?"

Daisy nodded, and the children gaped at her with open-
mouthed, jam-smeared faces.

Meg's whole body sagged and she clutched her eldest
daughter's shoulder to support herself.

"Now, Meg," said Daisy sharply. "Don't take on. Pull
yourself together. I need help. Get your little Mary to go and tell
Agnes and George and Maureen Mary — and Father Patrick
— and all the others."

Little Mary on whom Meg was leaning ran the comb she was
holding quickly through her lanky, shoulder-length hair. She
said eagerly, "I'd love to go, Anty."

Her mother was dabbing her eyes with the back of her hand.
Now she sniffed, and ordered, "Not now, you don't. You can go

after school." She said firmly to Daisy, "I'm in a pile of trouble
for keeping her home to help me last week." She shut her eyes
tightly, and added passionately, "Poor Mam!"

Daisy sighed. "Well, send her after school, then."

The whole mystery and the fearsome finality of death struck
her forcibly as she shivered on Meg's doorstep. She wanted to
scream out loud, "Holy Angels at the Throne of God, it was unfair to take her from me. Mike's been at sea for eighteen months
now, and there was only her and me in the house. You know me
daughter, Maureen Mary, and her husband is too stuck up to
live with me — and the rest of me children is lost to me. Dear
Holy Angels, it's unfair, it is! It's unfair! I'll be alone, I will!"

But Meg's children were there, so she must be silent; and Meg
was saying that she would have gone herself to announce the
sad news to the rest of the family, but she dare not leave her invalid father-in-law, old Fogarty, for fear he fell out of his chair
or suffered some other catastrophe.

"I'll come over tonight, I will," she promised. "As soon as our
John gets home."

Daisy clasped her hands over her aching, empty stomach, to
comfort herself, and sniffed. Surely mothers came before
fathers-in-law, she thought angrily. Meg could have asked her
sister-in-law, Emily, to watch old Fogarty. But she did not feel
strong enough to fight Meg this morning — and Emily was a
fool of the first water, she had to admit that.

She sighed, and turned away without another word, and
walked hastily homeward. From time to time, she would clap
her hand over her mouth, as if to keep inside her the scream she
longed to give vent to.

After her unusually subdued children had gone to school,
Meg sat down suddenly on a kitchen chair and allowed the tears
she had withheld while the children were present to burst out of
her. She swayed her skinny body back and forth and beat her
breast, as she wailed aloud, "Me poor Mam! Poor Mam!"

"What you making such a racket for? What's to do?"

shouted Mr. Fogarty, her irascible, crippled father-in-law. "Shut up that row and bring the pot. I want to pee."

Meg ceased her sobbing. For a moment she sat quite still as anger overwhelmed her grief. "Why couldn't it have been you, you old bugger?" she muttered furiously, as she seized a jam jar from under the kitchen sink and scurried to him.

Great Aunt Devlin laid out her niece and sat for two nights in the cold bedroom with the corpse. Two shawls were draped around her shoulders, and in one apron pocket she carried a bottle of gin; in the other one lay her rosary which she told from time to time. It was she who was paid first for her services from the money promptly brought by the agent of the insurance company.

It seemed to Daisy that in death her mother was more important and received more respect that she had ever enjoyed in life.

Father Patrick came to see Daisy and offer consolation. And the undertaker arrived on the dog-fouled doorstep before either Daisy or Meg had communicated with him.

"As if he could smell a passing on the wind," snorted Daisy.

The tiny house seemed to be full of clumsy, gossipy relations, who thankfully left all the arrangements for the funeral to Daisy, since she was now the eldest woman in the family; in this matter of hierarchy Aunt Devlin did not count because she was a spinster.

Daisy's lifelong friend and sister-in-law, Nellie O'Brien, though obviously tired and ill, sat for hours on one of the kitchen chairs and listened kindly to Daisy's impatient fulminations about the laziness of the rest of the family. She had brought her only son, iddy Joey, to say good-bye to his Nan, lying cold and white beside Great Aunt Devlin, who, he was certain, was a witch. And, of course, there were neighbours who loved to come to inspect a corpse.

"I been fair run off me feet," Daisy complained to Mrs. Hanlon of the Ragged Bear, when she went to buy two bottles of rum and four of cheap port wine for the wake.

Mrs. Hanlon commiserated and tendered her condolences, as she thrust the bottles through the narrow hatch of the Off-Licence Department.

Mrs. Donnelly, the grocer, whose heart it was affirmed locally was solid flint regarding extensions of credit, also politely tendered her sympathy while she weighed and wrapped up three pounds of her cheapest currant cake.

"That'll be a shilling," she announced, putting one hand firmly over the parcel until the coin should be produced.

"You'll have to put it on me bill," Daisy replied, folding her great arms over her bosom. "I haven't got the insurance yet," she lied. Mrs. Donnelly and she had been crossing swords for nearly forty years and she saw no reason to part with good money for Mrs. Donnelly's benefit. Let the old devil wait.

Mrs. Donnelly's eyes narrowed till they looked like a bunch of wrinkles with only a pinpoint of light gleaming from them. "You owe me four and tenpence already. Seeing as I cut the cake I'll keep it for you till later on. The agent should come soon."

Thwarted, Daisy drew in a huge breath, savouring for a moment the familiar odours of rancid bacon, ageing cheese and carbolic soap. She blew out her cheeks till she looked as if she might burst. She was not going to walk all the way down the hill to her home and back up again later in the day; yet she did not know how to retreat from the stance she had taken.

Slowly she exhaled, making a most satisfying rude noise. Mrs. Donnelly clamped her thin lips together and busied herself by putting some bacon into the slicer, having first removed the parcel of cake from Daisy's reach.

Muttering sourly to herself, Daisy reached into her skirt pocket. "I got some of Meg's money. I'll pay for it from that."

Mrs. Donnelly thrust out a hand deeply lined with blacking from the daily polishing of her fireplace. Daisy banged two sixpences into it so hard that Mrs. Donnelly's knuckles nearly hit the counter. Mrs. Donnelly silently put the money into her wooden till. Then she put the cake on the counter within reach of Daisy.

Daisy snatched it up, tucked it under her black shawl and stalked out.

Daisy's eldest daughter, Maureen Mary, a faded blonde, arrived in the late afternoon of the day of her grandmother's death, from her home in Princes Park. Carrying her three-year old daughter, Bridie, she had set out immediately upon receiving word from Meg's little Mary. Knowing the sad state of her mother's home, she brought with her a pair of sheets on which to lay the body, and two candlesticks with long new candles to light the death chamber until the funeral.

She agreed with Daisy that dear Nan looked really beautiful after the ministrations of Great Aunt Mary Devlin.

"She must have looked like that when she was young," Maureen Mary remarked as she dried her eyes with a flowered pocket handkerchief. "I mean, before she had eleven children — and lost six of them."

"Yes," agreed Daisy with a sigh. "We was all young once."

She went on to tell Maureen Mary how she vaguely remembered being taken to say farewell to her own tiny, Irish Nan in the same upstairs bedroom. Nan had been still alive and had blessed her. Three days later she had been carried out of the house in a big box by four of her grandsons, Daisy's cousins.

"Priest told me," she added with a little chuckle, "that Nan would soon be with God; and, you know, it bothered me for ages that people had to be delivered to God in a box!" She chuckled again.

Maureen Mary looked shocked; it was improper to laugh at such a solemn time.

Daisy was immediately sobered by her daughter's disapproval and she said despondently, "It's going to be proper lonely without Nan, seeing as how you don't live here." And she glanced accusingly at her daughter.

Maureen Mary flushed under her heavy makeup. Her bright

red lips trembled weakly. She bent over Bridie, to pull up the tot's knickers which had slipped down around her bare knees. Her leaving home after her marriage was a very sore point between Daisy and herself. Good daughters brought their husbands home to live with their mother, just as Daisy had brought her sailor husband, Mike, home; and they had children to cheer up the old house with their squabbles.

"Perhaps Dad could get a shore job next time he comes home," she suggested hopefully.

"Himself? Swallow the anchor? That's not likely. 'Sides I couldn't stand having him under me feet all the time."

Maureen Mary was timidly silent for a moment, then she said, "Well, our Jamie and our Lizzie Ann will finish doing their time and come 'ome one day."

"Humph," grunted her mother. "Lizzie Ann's got at least another eighteen months to do — and Jamie, poor love, has got about another five years."

Silenced, Maureen Mary picked up Bridie and went home.

After she had gone, Daisy thought about this conversation, as she sat in a sagging chair and poked the coal fire in the iron grate, which took up nearly the whole of one wall of her livingroom. From time to time she gave a great heaving sigh. Now she would replace her mother as the Nan, the grandmother to whom all the family would look for help and advice; but there was not much pleasure in that if nobody lived with you, she decided. And how was she going to survive sleeping by herself? The idea was scarifying. Whoever had heard of a decent Irish Catholic woman, who kept herself to herself, having to sleep in a house alone? It had been terrible when the district nurse had suggested that Mrs. O'Brien would sleep better if Daisy did not share her bed — Daisy had reluctantly removed herself to a bed in the landing bedroom, tucked against the wall of her mother's room. But to be alone was to invite the Devil to come close.

As she sat forlornly by her fire, her plump figure looking somehow deflated in the flickering light, she received the condolences of neighbours and more distant relations. They slipped in from the street, not waiting for a response to their knock, to stand for a moment silently and with pinched lips; then they would say how sorry they were.

"She'll be sorely missed, God rest her," they invariably said. "She was proper kind, she was." Then they shuffled their boots on the stone floor and examined the toes of them, and added, "Maybe it's a blessing, God forgive us, that she had no pain."

Daisy, her throat tight with misery and yet still unable to cry, nodded her head sadly and motioned them to go upstairs, where they would respectfully view the body, under the jealous glare of Great Aunt Devlin. They all came down again weeping softly into the corner of their aprons and assured Daisy, "She looks beautiful — so peaceful, like."

Thankful for their company, Daisy then invited them to the funeral service. They went soberly out, and then rushed up the street to tell their families all about the corpse.

All available members of the family, including Daisy's middle daughter, Sister Margaret of the Little Sisters of the Poor, who travelled from Manchester, came to the funeral. Afterwards, they crammed into Daisy's little living room with some of the neighbours, who had come to pay their respects to the family and get a free drink. Everybody clutched a glass of rum or port in one hand and held a piece of currant cake cupped in the other.

With their mouths full, the members of the family argued in muffled tones about the division of the contents of the house, that being all that Mrs. Mary Ellen O'Brien had to leave.

Daisy was ignored. She downed a welcome glass of rum and listened, hand on hip, to the subdued babble of voices.

Through the conversation, she heard with anxiety the steady coughing of brother George's wife, dear Nellie. She silently poured a bumper glass of port and handed it to seven-year-old iddy Joey, with the request that he pass it to his struggling mother. He winked at his dear Anty Daise, took a quick sip from the glass and passed it over to Nellie.

The argument between the relations grew heated and voices began to rise. Part of the contents of the house belonged to Daisy and her husband, Michael; and when Daisy heard some of these named she would shift her cake to the other side of her toothless mouth and shout, "You can't have that — it belongs to me."

Nobody listened.

She was not disturbed by this lack of attention. The excitement of knowing she held a trump card had dulled some of the gnawing unhappiness she had been suffering. Her son-in-law, Freddie, had been brilliantly helpful. For the first time since Maureen Mary had brought home a neat, pin-striped nonentity called Frederick Brown, an English Protestant, and had announced to her enraged mother that she had married him, Daisy was grateful to him. She would never forgive him, she thought darkly, for being a bleeding Prottie or for taking Maureen Mary from her mother's loving arms. He had put his pretty wife into a grand three-bedroomed row house near Princes Park, instead of coming to live with his mother-in-law, Daisy, as was customary; and this was unforgivable. Daisy had, however, voiced to Maureen Mary her fears of being left in an unfurnished house, if Mrs. O'Brien's other children claimed a share of the furnishings. Maureen Mary had consulted Freddie, who, she assured her mother, knew all about laws.

As she watched Freddie standing solitarily with a glass in his hand at the back of the crowd, Daisy began to console herself about Maureen Mary's desertion and to think that perhaps when Elizabeth Ann was released from training school, she would marry and bring her husband to her mother's home, and so make up for Maureen Mary's dereliction.

Grinning maliciously, she snatched up a tin tray and the poker, and banged them together like a gong. The shattering noise in the confined space shocked her relations into silence. Shawls remained half hitched over shoulders, union shirt buttons about to be loosened because of the heat of the room remained buttoned. Children about to shriek in the course of a game of tag round the legs of adults paused with mouths open.

She drew an old butter box out from under the table and stepped up on to it. It creaked threateningly under her weight but did not split. From this elevation she looked even more ferocious than usual to her relations; her head with its neat plaits round each ear moved from side to side like that of a cobra, while she flourished the poker at them.

"Na, then, you pack o' vultures," she addressed them. "Our Mam not more'n an hour in her grave and you wanting to break up her home!" Her handsome face was spoiled by a deep scowl and her blue eyes flashed menacingly.

Daisy's younger sister, Agnes, sniffled and rubbed her pug nose with the end of her shawl. "I never said nothin'," she whined.

"Oh, shut your gob, Aggie," ordered Daisy. "Always snivelling about somethin' ".

Agnes burst into tears and turned to her daughter, Winnie, a gangling twelve-year-old, to be comforted. The child put her arms round her mother and glared resentfully at Anty Daise.

Daisy's middle daughter, Sister Margaret of the Little Sisters of the Poor, murmured a gentle remonstration against her mother's sharpness. Daisy silenced her with a heavy frown.

Maureen Mary smiled encouragement at her hefty mother. The last thing she wanted was for her mother to be rendered homeless — she might demand to live with her daughter in Princes Park, something that even patient Freddie would not tolerate.

Daisy's frown vanished. She beamed suddenly at the gathering until her toothless gums showed, and iddy Joey was reminded of the turnip he had made into a jack-o-lantern last All Hallow's E'en.

"I want to tell, you that our Nan left a will!"

"A will!" exclaimed Agnes's husband, Joe, an unemployed

labourer. "Whatever for?"

Daisy's square chin jutted out belligerently and again she scowled as she replied scornfully, "'Cos she knew the likes of you. 'Cos I nursed her. 'Cos I'm the eldest daughter and she wanted to make sure I got me rights. 'Cos this's always been Mike's and my home, too." She pointed the poker at him and he flinched. "It's only right."

Meg folded her skinny arms across her flat chest, and asked crossly, "What's right? It was my home, too, remember."

Daisy smiled oversweetly at her sister. "Well, as of yesterday I been tenant of this house. Mam asked the rent collector to arrange it a couple of weeks ago, so it's been passed to me like it's always been passed down." She simpered irritatingly at the other woman. "She didn't mean me to have an empty house, so she left me everything." Daisy crossed her shawl over her chest and the poker waggled suggestively from underneath the garment. "So there, Missus!"

"She never," exclaimed Meg indignantly. "She promised her mirror to me — many a time she did."

Daisy replied primly, "Mirror's in pop. She left you her wedding ring. It's on the mantlepiece by the clock."

The news that the mirror was in pawn did not surprise anyone — so were most of the company's more prized possessions.

Agnes raised her wet face from her daughter's shoulder and asked plaintively, "What about me?"

"You got the photo of her and Dad on their wedding day. We had to sell the frame — but the picture's still good."

Agnes was shaken by a fresh sob. She again flung herself upon her daughter.

Daisy turned to her brother, George, Nellie's husband. "You and brother Gregory, who couldn't come 'cos he's at sea, as we all know, she didn't leave nothing to. She reckoned you could manage. You never came to see her anyway unless she sent for you. It was only your wife, our Nellie, what did." And she bent an approving glance upon her friend, who was looking a little flustered and unsteady after her large glass of wine.

George glowered sullenly at his bossy sister. From long unemployment, his mind and body had become equally flaccid, but he managed to ask, "Where is the bloody will?"

Daisy smirked in triumph. "Our Freddie's got it."

TWO

The company turned wondering eyes upon Freddie. Few had seen him before. As Meg bitingly remarked, in his neat ready-made suit and striped shirt, he stood out like a sore toe.

"Smells like a bloody whore," grumbled George.

Agnes remonstrated, "Now don't you be using such language before the kids!"

George's heavy red face returned to its usual sullenness. He did not reply.

Freddie coughed, partly with shyness and partly from the overwhelming stench of unwashed bodies catching at his throat. A path opened before him so that he could go to stand by Daisy.

Freddie's relationship with his high-smelling mother-in-law was an ambiguous one. He had early in his marriage discovered that it was no good trying to cut Maureen Mary off entirely from her mother; Maureen Mary seemed unable to function at all without the support of regular visits to her. Gradually, mixed with his horror of Daisy had come a reluctant respect for her, and he sought earnestly to please her in the hope of keeping his adored wife with him. Daisy regarded him with contempt mixed with curiosity. She was surprised that anyone could earn as much as he did without getting his hands dirty.

Daisy had only once visited Maureen and Freddie in their home — she had never been invited, and pride kept her from calling again without an invitation.

They had been married in a registry office, because she was a

Catholic and he was a Protestant. Neither family had been present, in Maureen's case because she had lacked the courage to inform them until after the fact; and in his case because his parents were outraged at his marrying a poor Irish Catholic girl.

Maureen Mary had been a pert little Nippie waitress at his favourite Lyons' restaurant; he was a traveller for a sweet company. Neither had considered what the other's family might be like.

Daisy beamed toothlessly at him as he turned and stood beside her. "You tell 'em, Freddie," she encouraged.

"Proper fancy pansy," George muttered out of the corner of his mouth to John, Meg's husband. John nodded agreement.

George drained his glass and looked round for another drink. Daisy had, however, whipped the bottles away while there was still something left in them, and they were now reposing under the huge kitchen fender which her great-grandmother had brought from Ireland.

Taking small breaths so as not to be overpowered by the stink from Daisy, Freddie drew a long, narrow envelope from his inside pocket, an envelope which appeared to his experienced audience suspiciously like a summons from the beak.

It was not a missive from the magistrate which he took out, however, but a penny will form from the local stationers.

Though the preamble was almost incomprehensible to Freddie's audience, the bequests were clear. There was a tiny gift for each of her daughters and for her daughter-in-law, Nellie O'Brien. In addition she left her rosary to her granddaughter by Daisy, Elizabeth Ann, who was at that moment scrubbing the dining-hall floor in the training home and was weeping into the grey soapsuds for her dear, dead Nan.

At the mention of Elizabeth Ann, Meg drew in her breath sharply. Her hollow cheeks darkened as she tried to suppress her rising anger.

"Why Lizzie Ann?" she asked. "Why not our Mary?"

Agnes lifted her woebegone face.

"What about our Winnie, if it comes to that?"

Freddie's eyes were watering and his nose was beginning to run from the incredible effluvia emanating from his stout mother-in-law beside him. He took a handkerchief from his pocket and dabbed his eyes before answering Meg.

"Mrs. O'Brien states in her will that Elizabeth always admired the rosary, and was allowed to carry it to her first Communion when she was seven." He thrust his handkerchief back into his pocket, and added with sudden enthusiasm, "It is very beautiful. The beads and the crucifix are hand-carved. I understand Mrs. O'Brien's grandfather made it as a gift to his wife. Perhaps Mrs. O'Brien felt that Elizabeth Ann would take special care of it."

"Humph! So would our Mary."

"Or our Winnie," echoed Agnes.

Meg pointed a thin finger at Freddie and prodded him in the waistcoat. "I don't see why Lizzie Ann should be the only granddaughter to get anything."

Freddie moved back a step. "Mrs. O'Brien did not have much to leave," he said conciliatorily.

Meg advanced and prodded him again.

"She could have thought of something for Mary," she said savagely.

Daisy here interposed wrathfully and waggled the poker at Meg. "You shut up, Meg, and stop poking Freddie in the stomach." She snorted. "You always was a jealous bitch!"

Meg threw off her shawl and turned angrily upon her sister, ignoring the threatening poker. "Don't you call me names, you fat sow!" she screamed. "Always so bloody stuck up. Now Nan's passed on you needn't think you can throw your weight around, 'cos I won't stand for it." She raised her fist to strike her sister in the stomach, and Daisy teetered on the creaking butter box.

"Meg!" warned her quiet husband, John, shooting forward a fist like a prize fighter and grasping her bony shoulder.

She turned on him like an infuriated ferret, while at the same time Daisy stepped heavily down from the butter box and surged purposefully towards her, eyes flashing, huge arms akimbo, poker still clasped in one hand.

"Na, Daisy, na, Daisy. Meg didn't mean nothing. She's just hot-tempered. Come on, now, you know her." John attempted to clasp his wife firmly round her waist to hold her back. He had a despairing feeling that he was going to be caught between two hellcats.

"Didn't mean nothing!" Daisy paused, and her great bosom swelled. She thrust out her chin and screamed into the face of her small but determined sister. "I'll fat sow yer, yer greedy bitch. Where was you when Ma needed help? Where was you of a night when I was up putting hot poultices on her? When our Lizzie Ann was home she was proper good to her Nan. She earned the rosary, she did."

Daisy dropped the poker, and Agnes squeaked as it hit her ankle. She raised her fist to strike Meg, while John did his best to hold back his kicking, yelling wife.

"Na, Daise," he cried, "Don't you hit her. She didn't mean it. Meg had to look after me Dad. How could she help you?"

The fascinated neighbours began to edge back to form a rough circle and give the combatants room. Iddy Joey climbed on to the table and stood with one foot on a loaf of bread to get a better view. But clear across the squawks of the women and the anxious murmurs of the rest of the family came Freddie's voice, full of long experience of dealing with difficult customers and pathetically anxious to curry favour with his mother-in-law.

"Dear Daisy, restrain yourself."

The crowd reluctantly made way for him as he came towards her with the calmness of the bishop himself. "You must be dreadfully tired. It is time people went home."

Daisy stopped, arm still raised, fist still clenched. Nobody but Freddie had ever called her dear, and it seemed to her that only Freddie, and, of course, Nellie, had her interests at heart.

Meg, who hardly knew him, stopped in mid-shriek as if switched off. For a moment she gazed at him in dumb amazement and then she began to giggle. The giggle became a laugh. She threw herself upon John and howled with laughter. The other adults began to snigger and then to laugh. The children joined in with uncertain tee-hees.

Dumbfounded at the unexpected hilarity, Daisy dropped her threatening fist. She looked at Freddie. Didn't he mind being laughed at? Apparently not, because he was calmly folding up the will and gave no indication that he was perturbed by the mirth he had engendered.

His wife, Maureen Mary, said with brittle brightness to the assembly, "Yes, it's time for home — and I'll take back me sheets and me candlesticks now Nan is laid to rest." A tear trickled down her cheek as she picked up the bundle of linen from the back of a chair and took the candlesticks, encrusted with grease, from between iddy Joey's feet on the table. She gathered up her little daughter, Bridie, a pretty picture in a pale blue satin dress and bonnet. She blew a kiss sadly to Daisy across the room and, her arms loaded with sheets and child, she nudged her aunt towards the door. "Come on, Anty Meg."

John opened the front door and a still giggling Meg was shepherded into the street. As the other visitors flowed out Maureen Mary turned and tried to get back in, but it was too difficult, laden as she was, and she shouted with a little catch in her voice, "I'll come tomorrow, Mam!"

Daisy who had been watching the sudden exodus with narrowed eyes, as she considered what she would like to do with Meg, smiled suddenly and nodded agreement.

When the crowd had thinned, Nellie get up unsteadily from the chair on which she had been sitting.

"Get down off that table, Joey," she said ineffectually.

Joey danced around, to the further detriment of the loaf of bread. A few odds and ends fell off the back of the table.

George reached forward and caught his son by the back of

his clothes. He lifted him bodily on to the floor and gave him a
sharp slap across the head. "Gerrout," he said.

Joey howled as if he had been shot and fled to his mother, to
hide his face in her black skirt and bellow like a young bullock.

"You didn't have to do that," Nellie reproached her husband.

"Och, he's spoiled rotten," retorted George. He picked up his
jacket and swung out of the house after John.

Nellie bent over to console Joey. "Never mind, luv," she said.
"Never mind."

Daisy, being more practical, reached over to the plate of cake
still on the mantelpiece. " 'Ere ye are, Joey," she said, as she
handed him a piece.

Joey's wails ceased immediately. He emerged from the folds
of his mother's skirts, stuffed the cake into his mouth and
danced over to the door, through which Daisy could observe
him skipping happily across the road to look out over the river.

Nellie embraced Daisy lovingly. "I'll come tomorrow," she
promised. Daisy smiled and kissed her, holding the tiny hands
with their terrible, broken nails as if she could not bear to let her
go. She led the frail little woman to the door, where Freddie
stood running his trilby hat uneasily through his fingers.

"Goodbye, Mrs. O'Brien," he said politely to Nellie.

"Goodbye, Freddie. Ta-ra, Daisy. See you tomorrow."

Daisy stood with one hand on the door jamb as Nellie followed the little procession up the street. Freddie watched her uneasily. He knew he should suggest that Maureen Mary stay
overnight with her bereaved mother; yet he feared that if he did
so she would never return to him. His friends had all warned
him how Irish Catholic girls had a tendency to go back to
mother once they had a child or two, expecting their husbands
to follow uncomplainingly. He knew that he could never live in
this rough, bug-ridden home, the very idea made him shudder.

Maureen Mary wanted to stay the night; she had said so over
breakfast, and only his argument that the house was so damp
that little Bridie might get a chill there had dissuaded her. He

had not mentioned that he had a horror of her bringing back
vermin from her mother's home. He had been careful not to sit
down during the wake, but he was convinced that he had
gathered an unwelcome visitor — he itched all over.

"Be all right?" he asked Daisy lamely.

Daisy sighed gustily. "Yes," she replied.

She stood outside the front door to watch the procession of
guests and relatives along the road until they turned the corner.
Then she stared glumly at the river for a moment. A shaft of
sunlight pierced the clouds and gave a soft sheen to the gloomy,
heaving water and lit up the Wallasey shore. Then the cloud
closed over and the wind nipped playfully at Daisy's loosely
pinned-up plaits. She shivered, and stepped back into the
deserted house.

Inside, she paused, reluctant to shut the door. The silence was
oppressive. For the first time in nearly a hundred years there
would be only one resident in the house; for the first time in her
life she would be alone overnight. Through the residue of her
anger at Meg and her annoyance that Maureen Mary had not
stayed with her, loneliness began to penetrate painfully. It
seemed to creep through her like a paralysis, and her softly
rounded cheeks whitened, making the mauve mottles caused by
sitting too close to the fire stand out like scars.

She stood, head bent, in the cold draught and breathed heavily, her shoulders drooping under her black shawl.

"I got to get used to it," she muttered, "till our Lizzie and our
Jamie finish doing their time." She did not consider that
Michael, her sailor husband, might also return. He was a vague
figure in the background of her life who was more nuisance than
help when he did have a spell at home. "And I got you, Mog,
you old devil," she added forlornly to the cat, which was sitting
on the mantelpiece between two dusty china dogs.

She slowly shut the weather-beaten door behind her. "I'm the
Nan now, Mog. Only the's nobody here to be Nan over. It's a
proper queer life, isn't it?"

THREE

Daisy rubbed her tired eyes and then stretched herself. Though stout, she was by no means unhandsome and as she clasped her hands behind her head there was a sensuousness about her, reminiscent of women of an earlier age pictured by Reubens.

She put another shovelful of coal on the fire, and afterwards plonked herself thankfully down on the easy chair her mother had bought at a sale half a century before.

When she was a little rested she took a pad of notepaper and an envelope from the table drawer. Then she hunted impatiently through the rags, paper and ornaments which were piled on the mantelpiece until she found a bottle of Stephen's ink and a wooden penholder. She put everything down on the big, brass fender and sat down again.

To ease the tension within her, she lifted her long black skirt and petticoats up over her fat knees to allow the comforting heat of the fire to reach her thighs, while she considered what she should put in a letter to her husband.

Mike's last post card had been from Accra and had carried his usual message, "Doing fine, love, Mike." It did not inspire Daisy in her reply. Michael had been doing fine as a ship's stoker on tramp steamers, in between bouts of unemployment, through a world war and twenty-nine years of marriage. Scattered through the house were numerous postcards from him carrying cancellation marks of ports all over the world.

Daisy nibbled her wooden penholder thoughtfully. Mike had seen so much and was so good at telling stories about his adven-

tures — after he had downed a couple of pints of bitter, of
course — that he had convinced their first-born son, John, that
there was no better occupation than that of seaman; and the
boy had run away to sea the day he was fourteen. He had never
been heard from since. The memory of him made Daisy heave
one of her mighty sighs. It was hard on a mother to lose a boy
at fourteen, just when he could be sent to work to earn a bit of
money.

Now, Mike had been sailing up and down the coasts of Africa
for a year and a half. Eighteen bloody cold months, thought
Daisy, without a man to warm you occasionally.

She stabbed the pen into the ink and scratched carefully
across the lined notepaper, "Nan died on Monday, God rest her.
She was laid to rest today — St. Michael's Day." Mike would
think his patron saint really cared about him, she reflected acidly. The nib spat suddenly and made a blot as she crossed a t.

"Blast!" she ejaculated, and dabbed the ink dry with the corner of her apron, which was already dingy from many washings.
The ink smudged. She clucked irritably and again dipped her
pen into the ink.

"The man from the Prue paid her burial money prompt and
O'Toole did her funeral real nice. Her burial money will be
enough for Bill Donohue to wallpaper her room as well." She
stopped and chewed the end of her pen, pressing her toothless
gums against it so hard that it cracked. She spat the small sliver
of wood into the fire. Mike would resent good money being
spent on the redecorating of the room. Slowly and firmly she added in scrawling round letters, "Like he always done it." "Bugger him," she murmured crossly.

She had a fixed belief, handed down through the generations,
that nobody should sleep in a room in which someone had died
without it first being redecorated. She sighed sadly. So many
people had died in the front bedroom of her home — the wallpaper must be inches deep. It was the only room in the house
which had ever had anything done to it, as far as she

remembered.

"Hope this finds you in the pink as it leaves me, Daisy." she added to her letter. Then she picked up an envelope from the dusty rag rug beneath her feet and put the letter into it. In large capital letters she addressed the letter to Mr. Michael Gallagher, Stoker, s.s. *Heart of Salford*, c/o the shipping company's Liverpool office. She never knew until he came home whether he had received her letters, but she supposed this one would catch up with him eventually. He had been away such a long time that she had begun to forget him; for weeks at a time she never thought of him.

She heaved herself out of her chair and moved slowly to the oilcloth-covered table. The roses on the cloth stared back at her through a greasy film, where they showed between dirty mugs, wine and rum glasses. Among the glasses lay the sliced white loaf on which iddy Joey had stood; its slices were half out of their wrapping and were scattered and squashed. Beside them lay their inevitable companion, a mangled open package of margarine.

Impatiently she swept the clutter to the back of the table and laid the letter in a prominent position, so that she would not forget to buy a three-halfpenny stamp and post it.

She removed the glass from a small oil lamp, struck a match and lit the wick. Carefully she replaced the glass.

The lamp's weak rays did little to cheer the forlorn room. The walls and ceiling, blackened by a hundred years of coal fires, made it seem even smaller than it was. Generations of spiders had spun thick webs, now laden with dust in every cranny. The window curtain of cheap lace was so tattered and so grey with dust that it looked as if the spiders might have spun it, too. An old chest of drawers stood in one corner, its surface piled with odd sheets of newspaper kept for lighting the fire, and bits of rag which Daisy thought might come in useful for lagging the pipes of the recalcitrant water closet in the yard. Two straight-backed kitchen chairs stood in the middle of the room where they had been abandoned earlier by her visitors, and mechanically she pushed them under the table. Then she stood in silent contemplation of a crumpled newspaper in the hearth on which lay a few lumps of coal. She knew she should get some more coal up from the cellar ready for the morning, but she felt too weary.

The silence and the hollowness of the house made her uneasy. She was normally a cheerful woman, though often aggressive, and her hearty laugh would make her great breasts shake in unison much to the amusement of the male patrons of the Ragged Bear. Deep-set blue eyes looked out at a tough world, but she feared nobody within the confines of the streets she frequented. As far as she was concerned, all wickedness lay outside her own district — where you never knew what might happen to you, she would sometimes remark darkly to Nellie.

But an empty house was a new phenomenon to her.

"Bloody ghosts in the place," she said to Moggie in a voice that trembled slightly. Then she shrugged her plump shoulders and added with forced firmness, "It's me nairves, Mog. Just me nairves." Even the home's single water tap in the scullery, which had dripped for weeks, had suddenly stopped its irritating tap-tap. A cinder falling from the miserable fire made her jump. There was not even the usual clatter of boots and vehicular traffic in the street; the poor weather must have kept everyone indoors.

She trailed over to the front door and opened it. The night had closed in and solid blackness met her; she could not even see the light at the top of the steps that ran down to the Herculaneum Dock. She peered the other way. The street lamp seemed almost obliterated by fine rain. The dampness carried with it a searing acridity; it caught in her throat and made her cough. Hastily she slammed the door and took her black shawl off the hook at the back of it. She wrapped the garment round her shoulders and tucked it across her breasts. She returned, shivering, to her chair by the fire. From time to time, she coughed and cleared her throat.

The cough bothered her. "Maybe it's T.B.," she thought fearfully, "like our Tommy."

Tommy had coughed himself to death, at the age of twelve, in the room upstairs. The memory still brought a tear to his mother's eye, though it was eight years ago and the cabbage roses on the wallpaper put on after his death, were blurred and torn in places.

She sighed lustily. She had had no luck with her boys and very little with her girls. John, born when she was seventeen, had run away. Little Mickey had toddled into Grafton Street when he was three, and had been trampled under the hooves of a pair of Shire horses pulling a wagon of beer up to the Ragged Bear. He was dead, his tiny body mangled and broken, before the carter managed to put on the break and shout to the rearing horses.

And then there was James, the pride of her heart. There was a lad! How she wished he was with her now. But he was doing seven years for stabbing an Orangeman.

The very thought of the Orangemen made her face darken with venomous wrath. Serve them right if they got stabbed. She reckoned they should know by now that to parade on July 12th was asking for trouble. A pack of bleeding Protties going over the river to New Brighton to celebrate the anniversary of King William winning the Battle of the Boyne, to the ruin of all Catholics. And they carried church banners and all. Enough to make a good Irish Catholic puke.

In a fight with the members of a homeward bound procession, James had broken a beer bottle and accidentally cut the throat of an opponent.

Daisy, a soggy mess of tears, went to see him when he came up for trial for murder.

"I never meant to kill him, Mam," he assured her. "Just a good scratch. But his throat got in the way."

Daisy had been sure that James would hang. Through the trial she had, until she was finally ejected, wept loudly in the

Court, beating her breast and exclaiming from time to time, "Jaysus Mary! Me poor boy! God spare him!"

In the depth of despair, she suddenly remembered St. Jude, kind patron saint of lost causes. She fell to her knees on the stone floor of the scullery, and prayed. She promised St. Jude a three-line advertisement in the *Liverpool Echo* if he would only save the life of her beloved son, James.

Apparently, St. Jude heard the impassioned plea, because the charge was reduced to one of manslaughter, and James did not hang. Two days after James went off to serve his sentence, there appeared in the Personal Column of the *Liverpool Echo* an advertisement, which read: "Grateful thanks to St. Jude, patron saint of lost causes, for help in great trouble, D.M.G." It did not make up three lines, but Daisy could not think of anything more to say, and she hoped St. Jude would understand. She would make it up to him some other time.

"Ee, Mog," she addressed the cat, as it climbed on to her knee. "I could use a bit of help now, I could. The house is so empty."

FOUR

The quiet of the house became a miasma which oozed out of the walls and wrapped itself around her. At times she would shiver uncontrollably despite the warmth of the fire. She crouched over the failing flames and wondered what she had done to deserve such desolation.

Despite her feeling of being deserted, she did not grudge Maureen Mary her fancy home with its shiny painted window-sills and brass-edged doorstep — at least the girl seemed to eat plentifully and have more clothes than her mother had ever dreamed of, proper coats instead of a shawl, and rayon stockings instead of cotton or wool. And she was proud that Margaret was a nun. Of course, Elizabeth Ann had been very careless in allowing herself to be caught while shoplifting in Woolworth's; but then all young people were careless, you had to expect it.

She fumed for a little while when she considered that her sisters had also deserted her. It would not have hurt one of them to lend her a daughter to stay with her, she thought bitterly. Winnie or little Mary would have been most welcome guests. But then she remembered that she had had a fight with Meg, which Meg would not easily forgive, and she had reduced placid Agnes to tears, and Nellie, dear frail Nellie, must have taken it for granted that Maureen Mary would keep her company for a few days.

Daisy gave a great trembling sigh, as she stared moodily at the massive collection of Woodbine cigarette butts tossed into the hearth by her guests. A beam in the roof gave a sharp creak and made her jump. She looked fearfully up at the dark shadows at the top of the stairs. Somehow, she had to get up enough courage to go to bed, to clamber into an empty bedstead without even the comfort of knowing that her mother was only on the other side of the wall. She shuddered.

Then she remembered the bottle hidden under the brass fender beneath her feet.

She leaned forward and picked up a glass from the top of the oven. The dregs had dried in it. She felt around under her feet, found one bottle and then slipped down on her knees to reach the three others. She drained all four of them into a tumbler and sipped the mixture of rum and wine. It tasted good to her and warmed her.

The cat cried to be let into the oven, where it usually slept the night. She leaned forward and lifted its heavy latch. Moggie leaped into its womblike darkness.

Daisy got up and lit a stub of candle stuck on a saucer among the debris on the mantelpiece. Then she blew out the oil lamp.

Glass in one hand, candle in the other, she staggered up the hollowed wooden staircase, which led directly from the living room to an open space above which was known as the landing bedroom. From it, a door led into the front bedroom which had been occupied by her mother.

Two double beds took up practically all the floor space in the landing bedroom. One had only a lumpy horse-hair mattress on it, heavily stained by generations of incontinent children; the other bed had lying in the middle of it a mixed pile of old bolsters, a discarded overcoat and an old, horse blanket. Daisy did own a pair of blankets but they were in pawn and looked like staying there, unless Michael came home with some money. She had been paying the interest on them to the pawnbroker for months — Michael could use a belt with good effect across her back when he was angry enough; and the loss of the blankets, with the consequential chilly nights he would suffer while home, would be quite enough to raise his Irish temper.

She stood looking round this noisome den while she drained her glass. The chamberpot under the bed had not been emptied for a couple of days and was adding a finishing touch to the stench. The silence was as absolute as that of a church on a Monday.

Slowly she trailed through the door to her mother's room. A shaft of moonlight illuminated the empty, stripped bed. Mixed with the smell of bugs was a faint odour of flowers and of death.

She walked almost fearfully round the bed and put the candle in its saucer down on the mantelpiece. In its dim light she stood looking down at the pillow which still showed the indent of her mother's head.

Suddenly a great bellowing wail came from the bereaved woman. She flung herself on to the bed and, lying spread-eagled upon it, she beat the thin mattress with her fists.

"Oh, Mam!" she shrieked, "Mam!"

FIVE

Daisy was awakened by a steady tapping on the front door and a bright, little voice shouting, "Mrs. Gallagher!"

Daisy opened her eyes slowly; the lids were swollen from weeping and felt sore. She became aware that she must have slept for a long time and she turned to look through the undraped window. Though overcast, the sky was light and a wind was rattling at the dormer window, which Great Aunt Mary Devlin had left ajar.

The sharp tap-tap on the door was repeated.

"Come in," shouted Daisy, "Door's open." Then she realised that someone was tapping with a coin or other metal, not with a fist, as would one of the family or a neighbour. "Be down!" she cried.

She rolled slowly off the bed and stood for a second shaking out her skirts and pushing her loosened plaits back from her face. She sighed with a slow sobbing breath and then stumped down the stairs, little jabs of pain going through her head at every step.

She stumbled across the room with its litter of bottles and glasses, opened the door a couple of inches and peered out.

"It's me, Mrs. Gallagher," announced the neat young woman on the doorstep. "I've brought the blanket for Mrs. O'Brien. How is she today?"

The lady from the Welfare! Daisy groaned inwardly, acutely aware of the bottles on the hearth rug. The sight of them would be enough to cut off, for ever, this useful source of creature comforts. The cool wind from the river hit her and she breathed in deeply to help her head to clear.

She longed for the warmth of the blanket in the arms of the Welfare lady. If she was not smart, however, it would be given to another invalid, she was sure.

"Och, she's not so bad. She's sleeping now." She opened the door slightly further, interposing her plump figure so that the Welfare lady could not see into the room, and held out her arms for the parcel.

The lady from the Welfare blinked behind her glasses and held her breath, as the stink from the house and its tenant flowed around her. She dumped the parcel into Daisy's welcoming arms, and stepped back a pace.

Daisy said with suitable subservience, "It's proper kind of you, I'm sure. Please thank the ladies for their help." She gave an old-fashioned half-bob which she had discovered from experience seemed to delight Welfare ladies.

The Welfare lady smiled and gasped in response, "It will be a comfort to Mrs. O'Brien. Since she's sleeping, I won't come in today. Now don't forget, will you, that you have an appointment today to get your teeth from the Dental Hospital?"

Daisy simpered. Jesus! She had forgotten it. "No, I haven't forgotten," she lied glibly.

"I'm sure your health will improve immensely once you have teeth," the kind little woman assured her.

Daisy sighed. The collection of her teeth was the culmination of a long battle between her and the Welfare lady. For such a frail-looking vixen she had a will of pure iron, Daisy had ofen lamented to Agnes and Nellie. She could press you into anything.

"I'll be there," Daisy promised resignedly. "What time is it now? Me clock's stopped."

The Welfare lady looked at her watch. "Five to eleven," she said brightly. "Your appointment is at four."

Daisy nodded. "Thank you. Me mother will be glad of the

blanket." She eased back into her room a little. She would tell the Welfare next week that her mother was dead. They would never take a blanket out of a bug-ridden house like hers once it was unpacked.

The Welfare lady was greatly relieved that she had not to sit in Mrs. O'Brien's fetid bedroom. She promised to come again next week, when she expected Daisy to have a perfect smile.

Daisy smiled faintly and ran her tongue round her gums. Nobody expected to have teeth at the age of forty-five, unless they were exceptionally lucky. She glumly closed the door as the Welfare lady started up her tiny car.

There was no room on the table, so she dumped the parcel on the floor and broke the string.

It was a good, thick double blanket. Daisy had never touched such a blanket, and it gave her almost voluptuous pleasure to run her fingers over it. She sat back on her heels looking at its spotless perfection amid the familiar filth of her room. Her head ached excruciatingly and her first thought was to carry the blanket up to her bed and go to sleep again under it.

Moggie leaped down from the kitchen oven and came to nose around the woolly pile. He climbed on to it and began to move languidly round to make himself a nest, while Daisy stared through him, thinking how much her mother would have loved to have such a covering.

In sudden rage she slapped the cat soundly and he went spinning across the room with a frightened yowl.

"Yer—jigger rabbit!" she yelled at him, "Gerroff and stay off."

She got to her feet and picked up the blanket.

"I know what I'll do," she planned. "I'll wait till Mam's room's been done out and then I'll put it on her bed. And I'll have that room, and I can lie in bed and think about her and watch the ships coming up the river."

She was just frying herself a bit of bacon and a leftover potato on the living-room fire when Meg swept into the house.

The glasses were still strewn around the room, but the bottles had been removed to the scullery to await a visit from the rag and bone man.

Meg had not bothered to knock. She marched up to Daisy and stood over her, a thin and hungry fury suddenly jealous of Daisy's bacon and potato.

"I come for me ring," she announced, her long thin nose held high, her shawl wrapped tightly round her skimpy frame.

Daisy paused in her cooking long enough to point with a knife. "It's behind the clock," she said. Then she took the frying pan to the table, slapped it down on the oilcloth and looked around for a fork amid the debris. There was a strong smell of sizzling oilcloth.

Meg stood on the fender and felt behind the clock, which was now ticking again. "You're burning the table-cloth, Daise," she reprimanded without looking round, as she searched with her fingers amid the junk on the mantelpiece.

Daisy had found a fork and she said sourly through a mouth full of bacon, "It's *my* table cloth." The bacon was not very crisp and was hard to masticate without teeth.

Her younger sister got down from the fender and turned. She put on the ring and looked at her hand thus decorated.

"You don't have to tell me," she said crossly as she watched the ring flash from the light of the fire. "Mr. Fancy Pants Freddie told us yesterday and our John's been telling me ever since." She swayed over to Daisy seated at the table.

"Think you're clever, don't you?" she mocked.

Daisy stopped chewing. She shook her knife at her tormentor. "You get out of here, Meg, before I throw you out." Her voice quivered with indignation.

"I'll go when I'm ready. This was my home, too, remember."

"It's mine now." Daisy's eyes gleamed with resentment.

Meg leaned towards her. "Pah! Big cheese, ain't you?"

Slowly Daisy collected the unchewable bits of gristle in her mouth and spat at her sister. Meg received it straight in her face.

She jumped back, wiped her eyes clear with her hand and then with a scream she leaped at Daisy.

"I'll marmalise you, you dirty bugger," she yelled.

Daisy rose swiftly from her chair and with one hand swung the piece of furniture between her and Meg. She pointed the paring knife she had used to cut her bacon at Meg's chest.

Despite her rage, Meg realized that Daisy meant business. The knife was coming slowly closer to her chest, while the chair was grinding painfully against her shins.

She backed a little.

"Get out," whispered Daisy, a world of menace in her voice. "Sling your hook, you bitch. Out!"

Meg was scared now. She backed slowly towards the door, felt the latch behind her and lifted it.

Daisy suddenly flung the chair and the knife away. With a moan of terror, Meg turned and pulled the door open. Daisy moved with the speed of an angry elephant, snatched up her sister by the back of her blouse and skirts and flung her through the doorway, heaving her forward with the toe of her boot in the small woman's buttocks.

Meg shot across the pavement and into the gutter, barely able to keep her feet. She wobbled like a spinning top, then turned and tore back at her sister, face contorted with hatred, hands outstretched like talons.

Daisy hastily slammed the door and shot the bolt, then leaned her hefty weight against its ancient timbers.

Frustrated, Meg pummelled on its heavy panel and shouted, "I'll larn you, you fat sow." She kicked at the door and Daisy could hear her sobbing. "John'll marmalise *you* for this — you wait till I tell 'im." Daisy grinned at the latter threat. Big John would keep well out of any fight between women.

No amount of screaming would persuade Daisy to open the door again. After a moment or two she went contentedly back to her frying pan. Finally, Meg wiped her face on her shawl, shook her fist at the window, pushed her way through a small group of interested passers-by and marched off home, sobs of hopeless anger mixed with tears of grief for her dead mother making her a small, grey bundle of woe.

As she ran through the back alley to her own home, she muttered, "I'll pay her back, I will. Thinks she's the Nan now, does she."

SIX

The row with Meg and the storm of tears the previous night had done much to alleviate Daisy's tense misery. A good fight with Meg was such a normal part of her life — she could not remember when they had not been at war with each other over some trifling detail — that she felt much better.

Fortified by her breakfast she felt strong enough to walk over to Nellie's house to ask her to come with her to the Dental Hospital. To travel such a distance from home without a companion was unthinkable; Daisy could imagine all kinds of terrible things which might happen to her if she went alone.

Nellie, however, was feeling far from well and was still in bed. Looking white and exhausted, she lay curled up on a lumpy mattress in the back, ground floor room which was home to George, Joey and herself.

"I had a bad night, luv," she explained, "Thinking of your dear mother an' all. Your mam was always proper kind to me — I'll never forget her, God rest her."

Daisy felt a lump beginning to rise in her own throat. She fought it down. She must not cry before Nellie; Nellie was sick enough without being reminded of death. Her chest heaved as she considered that she might lose Nellie, as well as her mother. She made the suffering woman a cup of tea and said she would ask Agnes to accompany her. Agnes, however, felt that the Public Assistance visitor might call at any time and that she had better be at home, in case he got the idea from her absence that she was working.

"He's worse'n a dose of salts, that man," she told Daisy. "Always wants to know where the kids are, even in school time. Always sayin' 'Where's Joe' as if labourin' jobs were two a penny and he must be bringing home thousands a pounds. Fair demarmalises you, it does."

Daisy sighed and agreed. "I'll ask Mary Foley what lives round the corner if she'll come," she said. "Only I always kept meself to meself, and I don't like asking the neighbours."

"What about Meg? Or Nellie?"

"I'm not speaking to Meg at the moment," replied Daisy primly. "And our Nellie's not well at all." She leaned towards her sister, and added in a whisper, "I got the intuitions something awful about Nell."

Agnes looked startled. "Ee, don't say that," she implored.

A tear welled up in Daisy's eye. She sniffed. "Well, I just hope I'm wrong."

"T.B.?" inquired Agnes, her voice hardly audible as she asked the dread question.

Daisy nodded, her expression lugubrious. The sisters looked at each other in silent horror.

"God have mercy on us," quavered Agnes, flinging her arms heavenward. "Poor dear."

They enjoyed a little weep together, and then Daisy walked homeward, calling at Mary Foley's house on the way.

Mary Foley was out. Great Aunt Devlin was too old to make such a long journey.

Daisy stood tapping a nervous foot on the pavement outside her own front door. Dare she go alone? Dare she not go?

Finally she decided that the dangers of penetrating the centre of Liverpool were less than the danger of losing the goodwill of the Welfare lady, who had so painstakingly collected sixpence a week from her for years to save up for new teeth.

Apart from five shillings put by for the redecorating of her late mother's room, Daisy still had three shillings left from the burial insurance money, so she decided to take a tram down to

Lime Street Station and another one out again to the Dental Hospital. She reckoned she would be safer on the tram.

Nellie had accompanied her when she went to have the impression taken for her teeth and they had walked, the appointment having been made for the day before Daisy drew her allotment from her husband's shipping company, a day on which she was always penniless. Michael's allotment was eighteen shillings a week and this, added to her mother's old age pension of ten shillings, had made the two women a shilling or two better off than if they had been dependent upon the Public Assistance Committee. Still, it was not very much.

Now as she sat demurely in the tram, hands folded neatly in her lap, as it trundled through the streets, bell pinging impatiently to make carters move their wagons off the lines, it dawned on her that her mother's pension would have ceased with her death; yet she would be faced with the same need to pay the rent, the same need for a coal fire and oil for the lamp; but she would have only eighteen shillings with which to do it all.

She was aghast. Under her warm shawl her body felt cold, and she trembled. All the small treats that made life bearable would be gone; no twopence for a beer at the Ragged Bear on a Saturday night or an occasional twopence for an afternoon cinema show with Nellie; even paying for a set of teeth at a painful sixpence a week for over three years would have been out of the question on a measly allotment of eighteen shillings.

Because her husband had, by sailing on a boat which never touched Liverpool, kept her off Parish Relief, Daisy had been able to hold her head high in a district where many of the English and Welsh inhabitants looked down upon her — they wore coats and she had only a shawl. But now she knew that though her income was still above the Public Assistance rate for one person, it was not going to be enough.

No more bacon ends from Mrs. Donnelly's! She would soon be as thin as Meg whose family was on relief. A fat lot of good teeth were going to be. For once, a tear of self-pity quivered in the corner of Daisy's deep-set blue eyes and rolled slowly down her plump face, which had been specially wiped with a wet cloth for the benefit of the dentist.

The earnest young dentist who had made her teeth for her awaited her arrival with something approaching agony. He had been unable to forget the interview with her two weeks earlier when he had examined her mouth and taken the impression for her teeth. The fearsome smell of her and of her clothing had been bad enough, the louse which he was sure he had collected from her had been worse. When she opened her mouth, however, he had recoiled like a young soldier going over the top and facing fire for the first time. He had hastily reached for a glass of mouthwash and made her gargle and spit her way through two complete glasses full before trying again.

This time he was prepared. The tall window nearest to him was wide open. In the cupboard rested another clean white coat, together with a large paper bag into which to thrust the one he was wearing immediately Daisy should have left. Neatly lined up by the tiny sink were two glasses of double strength mouthwash. He was ready.

Yet, when she entered not ungracefully with an old-fashioned, respectful half-bob, her plump face beaming in spite of her worries, he felt ashamed. To square his conscience he fussed around her a little, showed her the immaculately white teeth grinning on his side table, explained to her how to keep them clean, warned her that she might feel she was going to vomit when he put them in. He made her rinse her mouth till it stung with the disinfectant.

"Keep taking big breaths and you'll be all right," he advised. "In a few months you'll forget you've got them in your mouth and will be able to eat meat and anything else."

"Humph, meat!" grunted Daisy, her stomach already beginning to turn with fear of the apparatus surrounding her. The dentist, however, was treating her as a proper lady and she was enjoying that part of it, so she obediently opened her mouth.

In went the upper and lower teeth and Daisy's stomach began to heave.

"Guggle-guggle," she exclaimed, desperately looking round for the sink.

"Hold it, hold it!" urged the dentist frantically. "Remember, big breaths."

Daisy gasped in the cool autumn air from the open window, and gradually the nausea eased.

"Shlike havin' a golf ball in your mouth," she upbraided the dentist mournfully.

"Smile," he ordered her cheerfully, to take her mind off the nausea.

Blinking miserably she forced her mouth into a cheerful half moon.

The improvement in her looks was so great that the dentist was able to praise her appearance without stint. "Takes years off you," he assured her. "Now don't take them out except at night and to rinse them as necessary."

She nodded sad agreement. Four bloody pounds on teeth when what she was going to need was food to eat.

She heaved herself out of the dentist's chair, bobbed and simpered at him, said 'thank you' and clumped depressedly down the hollowed stone stairs and into the street.

She teetered nervously on the pavement outside the hospital and wished heartily that Nellie was with her to share the perils of the city. Every so often her new teeth would shift slightly and she would hastily breathe deeply to assuage the desire to vomit.

She watched the trams go by. They were packed with people going home and were not stopping except to let passengers down. She would have to walk down to Lime Street, she decided.

She trailed down Pembroke Place until she reached London Road. No one among the scurrying passers-by bothered her, and by the time she had reached the junction of the two thoroughfares she had gained a little confidence. She paused in

Monument Place. The brightly lit stores in London Road beckoned her; and when a small group of women shoppers started across the road she went with them, mesmerised by the lights and the cheery bustle of the crowd.

She wandered through two big stores, fingering sheets, caressing shiny furniture and looking open-mouthed at ladies' lingerie of such delicacy as to be shocking. She was pleased to see that they also stocked more sturdy garments, good fleecy cotton bloomers and woollen vests with high necks. She was so highly entertained that she forgot to be afraid; and even the discomfort of her mouth receded.

At closing time she left reluctantly with the other wanderers in the store, and continued her walk towards Lime Street.

"And it was there I went wrong," she told Moggie afterwards. "I shoulda come home. Only I felt comfortable, like, 'cos there was plenty of women like me in shawls, good Irish women, so I took me time."

She was waiting for the traffic to clear so that she could cross a side street, when a delicious aroma of fish and chips was wafted round her. She looked along the mean side street. The pungent smell was being blown towards her from across Islington, where people bearing large newspaper-wrapped packages were emerging from a fish and chip shop. One boy was actually running towards her, his hot parcel balanced carefully on one hand.

She lifted her nose and half closed her eyes. Her mouth was watering; her stomach felt as if it was flapping against her backbone, it was so empty. She forgot about going home and remembered only that she still had money in her apron pocket. She turned and almost ran the short distance to the shop.

The tiny window offered pie and chips, fish and chips, fishcakes and chips, tea and bread and butter, all laid out on thick white plates for passers-by to see. Behind the tiny display were two tables, at one of which a man and woman sat eating. Daisy swallowed and nearly choked on her teeth.

Could she eat with her new teeth? Could she bear to eat in public? It was, after all, not very nice having people watch you eat; eating was a private thing, like going to the privy.

I could carry the parcel home, she thought. She sighed with the effort of making up her mind. But then it would all be cold, she argued, as she paused uncertainly before the tempting display.

The door opened again, as a young woman with a baby wrapped in her shawl came out, bearing an aromatic bundle carefully wrapped in an old copy of the *Liverpool Echo*. Up the steps went Daisy, as if hypnotised, to join the throng of shabby people waiting for their orders to fry. When it was her turn to give her order she hesitated so long that the young man on the other side of the high, tiled counted said, "Hurry up, Ma. What do you want?"

She gulped, smiled nervously and said with difficulty because of her new teeth, "One fish and chips and tea and I'll take it here." She pointed to the vacant table in the bay window.

The young man shook up his huge net basket of chips so that the cauldron of fat spat and bubbled. "O.K. Sit down, Ma. Me Mam'll bring it to you."

Daisy turned and cautiously lowered herself into a chair at the greasy table. She chose a place that would show only her back to the other customers, so that they would not actually see her eat. In front of her the window was totally steamed up by the rapidly increasing damp heat of the shop. By now, the display of food congealed on plates which had tempted her from outside would be almost invisible to passers-by — and so would she be. She took out her teeth and put them in her apron pocket.

In a few seconds a big brown teapot, a chipped milk jug, a thick cup and saucer and an enormous plate of fish and chips joined the grubby sugar basin and the tomato sauce bottle on the table before her.

"Want some bread and butter?"

Afraid of how much it might cost, Daisy refused bread and

butter.

"That'll be sixpence," announced Mam, waiting with hand on hip while Daisy counted out the money.

For a moment Daisy contemplated the steaming fish, infinitely appetising in its crisp batter overcoat. Her mouth watered, and then slowly, sensuously she began to eat.

She used the last drop of tea to rinse around her mouth before putting her teeth back in, a task which was easier than she had expected.

Outside, she was surprised to find that it was dark. The lamplighter had already wobbled his way along the street on his bike and the gas lamps gave a friendly glow to the mean neighbourhood. She must have sat longer than she intended, she thought with a little laugh. It was, however, surprising how good food could cheer you up; even her new teeth felt more bearable.

She swung down the steps and without thinking turned left. She turned left again, fully expecting to find herself back in London Road. Instead she faced a narrow dark street. She looked irresolutely along it. There seemed to be no light other than the gleaming lamp above the door of a public house further down. There was a number of people about, however, and this reassured her. Feeling sure that it would lead her into Lime Street, she began to walk along it.

As she passed the public house, the buzz of conversation within made it sound like a beehive with the bees about to swarm. But when she plunged into the gloom beyond it an eerie silence faced her. Where were the surging crowds of Lime Street? The seamen, the prostitutes, the Welsh beggars?

SEVEN

The main door of the tavern was on the corner, and Daisy had hardly taken a step towards it when it swung open. Three young sailors in skin-tight naval uniforms rolled unsteadily out of it and came down the street towards her. Although it was early in the evening, they were very merry and, with arms slung round each other's shoulders, they were singing bawdily.

They took up the whole width of the pavement as they staggered towards Daisy, and she stepped back into the mouth of a narrow alleyway to await their passing. She was not particularly scared of them — they were only lads — and she chuckled as she watched them approach.

"Three German officers crossed the line to rape the woman and drink the wine," they roared in cheerful unison.

She knew the song well and began to hum the refrain in tune with them.

Arms over each other's shoulders, round navy blue hats perched precariously on the backs of their heads, they bellowed their way towards her; and, as she watched and waited, she hummed. They gradually became aware that there was a woman singing softly somewhere in the shadows before them, and they slowly staggered to a halt at the alley's entrance. Her white apron showed clearly, and behind it a generous, vaguely definable bulk loomed before them.

"'Ello, la," said the middle sailor. "Now what nice bit o' fluff have we got 'ere?" He let go of one of his friends, who promptly leaned against the warehouse wall for support.

Daisy took a nervous step backwards, but there was a sudden rustle as of a rat running behind her, so she hastily stepped forward again.

She gulped. "Aye, lads," she addressed them, her voice pitched uneasily high. "Can you tell me how to get to Lime Street?" She tried to edge her way out of the scant width of the alley but they were blocking it, so she beamed hopefully at their well-scrubbed faces.

"Well, now! Are you lost?" The boy's voice was slightly derisive.

Daisy's heavy-jawed, friendly face with its flashing smile gradually became visible, as the sailors' eyes adjusted to the darkness. They all swayed towards her and leered in true music-hall fashion, as she answered, "Yes, I am." She looked unhappily up and down the street, seeking a peaceful way to pass them.

"Wotcha want to go to Lime Street for?" two of them chortled together. "Isn't here good enough for business?" They winked at each other and dug their elbows into each other's ribs, as they laughed at her.

"Go on with you, you saucy buggers. I want to get a tram from Lime Street."

"Lime Street's got more'n trams in it," announced one of them suggestively. He moved closer to her, till his white vest nearly touched her. She could smell the comfortable beery breath of him. She eased away from him till she was brought up short by the wall of the alley. He put one hand on the dank brick wall behind her and leaned forward confidentially.

This is what happened to you when you went about alone, she reproached herself.

She gathered what courage she could muster and said as cheerfully as she could, "Come on, lad. Tell me which way to Lime Street." She pretended to laugh and tried to duck under his arm. One of the other sailors closed in and teasingly held out his arms, so that she would have sailed right into them. "Come on, luv," he shouted cheerfully.

"Shut up," said the third, who was leaning against the warehouse wall. "You'll bring the cops." He nodded his head towards the pub. "Come on, there's plenty more like her — let's go."

But the other two ignored him. The one who had held out his arms to Daisy whined ingratiatingly at her.

"Come on, Ma. Don't be shy. What about lifting your skirts for us?"

Daisy was flustered, her eyes darting up and down the dark road. "Eee, lads. I'm not that kind!" she protested, her heart pounding.

The boy who had first spoken to her and was closest to her let his hand drop from the supporting wall and, with a mischievous grin, curled his fingers round her neck. He pushed his lean body hard against her and rubbed himself against the comfortable rolls of flesh. One hand softly caressed her neck while the other fumbled under her well-formed bosom.

Daisy who had been staunchly faithful for twenty-nine years began to realise that the last eighteen months had been dreadfully bleak. Such a surge of passion ran through her that she found herself beginning to respond, and this shocked her.

"Not here," she panted. "I couldn't — I mustn't!"

Her breath was sweet from the dentist's disinfectant, as hard lips were pressed on hers and long arms were wrapped closely round her generous figure. She fought ineffectually, continuing her protests in ever-weakening whispers, as he eased her away from the wall and down the narrow alley into which she had originally stepped.

She tried to make herself cry out that he must not.

Holy Mother!

Fumbling hands found their way under long black skirt and petticoat, and Daisy was lost while still remonstrating faintly. He needed no caresses from her.

Afterwards, though her head was spinning and her body

smarting from making love after such long abstinence, she found herself leaning against the unfriendly wall still holding the boy to her and crooning inarticulately to him as if he had been her lover for years. He rested panting against her, his head on her breast, while in the back of her mind she told herself she should push him off and hit out at him for so misusing her. But when he looked up at her and grinned wickedly, she found herself smiling back.

"Hey, how long you going to be down there?" shouted one of his friends. Cigarette ends flashed brightly in the darkness, as the other sailors leaned against the corners of the alley and smoked.

Daisy's companion shouted back that he was coming. To Daisy he said with a grin, as he buttoned the flap of his trousers, "Ta, Ma."

He put his hand inside his navy blue blouse and brought out half-a-crown. It flashed in the dim light, as he pressed it into her hand. Scarlet and shaken, ashamed of her own feelings, she remained leaning against the wall as he made his way back down the alley to the street whistling cheerfully. He passed one of his friends rolling inwards.

"Any good?"

"Good as you'll get."

A startled Daisy roused herself from her lethargy to find another pair of exploring hands opening her shawl.

"Eee, lad!" she protested. "What is this?" She dropped the half-a-crown down her blouse neck and caught the hands which had descended impatiently to her skirts. "Come on, now, lad. I'm not one o' them."

The lad laughed tipsily and continued. "Tell me another, Ma," he sneered.

Though he looked thin, he was undoubtedly strong and he was by no means as gentle with her as the first boy had been. Daisy became suddenly deathly afraid of what he might do if she refused him — she knew about prostitutes who had been found murdered in just such an alleyway. So, without another word, she straddled herself across the narrow alley, one foot in the gutter, the other resting on the top step leading up to a door into a yard, so that she could accommodate him more easily. He whipped her skirts up over her raised knee, and she silently endured him.

"And there, in no time at all, at all, Mog, I found meself with another half dollar in me hand," she later told her stony-faced cat, "And another one coming up t' jigger at me."

As the third youth approached, it seemed to Daisy that her real self stood outside her body watching in scandalized horror a completely alien Daisy, filled with excited anticipation, await the boy coming towards her.

"Mog, it was as if the divil himself was in me. At first I thought I'd run away up to top of t' entry. But I could hear the rats rustling in the dust bins — and I'm more afraid of rats, as you know, Mog, than I am of any boy. So I waited for him."

As far as Daisy could judge in the gloom, the boy was younger than the other two, and he approached her shyly. Coming in from the lighted street he could hardly see her, though she being more accustomed to the darkness could see him. When his groping hand touched her, he paused.

After a moment's silence, he said, "It's O.K. if you don't want to, Ma."

Driven by forces she did not understand, she said softly, "Come here, luv."

Once more she steadied herself with one foot on the top doorstep beside her and then she opened her shawl and wrapped it round him as if he were a child she wanted to keep warm. To him she felt as cosy and warm as his own mother.

"It's my first time with a woman, Ma," he whispered.

She chuckled, feeling suddenly that she was at last in control of the situation.

"Come close," she ordered, with a surge of pleasure, her fears forgotten, "I'll show you." And she did.

She held him to her for a moment or two afterwards, until his friends, phlegmatically smoking as they waited, started to call him.

"Grinds like the bloody mills of God," one grumbled.

The boy dug around in the small pocket in the front of his sailor's trousers. "How much, Ma?"

Daisy smiled at him warmly and waved a hand negatively. "That's all right," she said.

"Oh, no, Ma! I have to pay." He sounded shocked.

He pressed a handful of small change into her palm and closed her hand over it. She leaned forward and kissed him on the cheek. "Ta," she said, and as he turned and swaggered back down the alley, she called, "Ta-ra, well," in farewell.

After they had gone on their merry way, a very thoughtful Daisy emerged slowly from the alleyway. She straightened her heavy skirts as she considered the deadly sin she had just committed. She could almost hear Father Patrick holding forth on the subject of lust; and a deep flush crept up her neck and over her cheeks. The two coins she had dropped down her chest fell to the pavement with a sharp clink and she bent down and picked them up. Her heart was still pattering unnaturally fast. In the light of the pub she counted the money in her hand. It totalled eight shillings and sixpence. Amongst the change given her by the last sailor were two threepenny bits.

She smiled at the two tiny silver coins. "Two joeys! I'll keep them for luck. He were a proper nice lad."

She sighed. She felt extremely shaky and decided she needed a drink. She went round the side of the pub to the parlour entrance. Over the door was a notice saying, "Ladies with Escorts only."

"Bugger them," she muttered forcefully.

A labourer with his beshawled wife pushed past her. She followed him in smartly and sat down on the same bench as they did. The place was blue with tobacco smoke and the conversation was lively but not noisy.

She sat primly down, hands folded in her lap, her worn wedding ring glinting softly on one swollen finger.

When the barman took her order for a hot rum toddy, he realised that she was without an escort, but she looked so primly respectable that he made no objection to serving her.

As she sat staring at her glass she felt that everybody must know what she had done, and she was thankful for the comforting glow that the rum engendered in her. Nobody spoke to her, however. St. Margaret, her patron saint, did not appear, to upbraid her, and God did not strike her down. Her heart returned to its normal beat and she began to feel clever that she could drink without taking her teeth out. She asked the barman who was easing his way among the crowded tables, a tray of empties poised on four fingers, how to get to Lime Street Station. He told her and she swept out with a great feeling of newfound confidence.

By the time she had boarded the tram for Dingle, her eyelids were drooping. The vehicle's steady swaying and its steamy heat made her doze.

At one stop the driver put his brake on rather abruptly and the shudder that went through the great vehicle awoke her.

Where was she?

She rubbed a spyhole in the steam on the window and peered anxiously through it.

There was the pub with the grocery store next door to it.

She hastily heaved herself off the wooden seat and proceeded unsteadily down the narrow centre aisle, while the driver tapped his foot impatiently. She clambered down the steep steps and wrapped her shawl round her tightly as the wind struck her.

Only when the tram had moved onward and had resumed its rhythmical clang-clang did she realise that she had descended at the Shamrock, instead of at the Ragged Bear.

She shivered in the chilly night wind, and cursed. Holy Mary, it was nearly a mile to her home and rain threatened from a lowering sky. Along the street the gas lamps seemed to march for dismal, frightening miles.

The door of the Shamrock opened and a gust of laughter came out with a patron. It would be at least half an hour before another tram came by, she thought; it would be quicker to walk. But first she would have another drink, to warm her.

The silver in her apron pocket made a happy jingle as she went up the steps, and she grinned ruefully, catching her lower lip with her new teeth.

"Ah'll have a gin, son," she ordered the barman. After all, gin was what you were supposed to drink if you didn't want to get pregnant. Then she remembered that she was past the age when she had to worry about pregnancy.

The gin tasted horrible, so she ordered a rum to follow. The world began to take on a kind of happy haze.

A heavily-built man on his way out paused in front of her. His close-clipped white hair did nothing to soften a wind-hardened red face. His greasy trousers and cap, his jacket ripped under the sweat-soiled armpits suggested a docker.

"Evenin', Mrs. Gallagher," he said. "Sorry to hear from George about your mother."

Daisy smiled dimly through the comfortable mist in which she was floating.

"Evenin', Mr. O'Hara. Thank you."

"Remember your Mam when she was a little girl. We both went to Mrs. Docherty's Sunday school to learn to read — afore the Board School was built."

"You did?" Daisy nodded her head.

"Oh, aye," He touched his forelock and with slow, clumping tread went towards the door. "Good night to yez."

Daisy wiped her nose with the back of her hand, finished her rum and, shortly after, followed Mr. O'Hara.

The wind had risen, and the smoke from the rows of chimney pots on the roofs seemed to rest on its side. All the shops were closed, though lights in the windows above them showed that their owners were not yet in bed. The whole street seemed to be relaxing from the clangour of the day. Daisy put her shawl up over her head and held it firmly under her chin, as she bent towards the wind. Her boots clattered noisily over the stone flags.

A woman in a red coat was standing under a lamp post. She was carrying a large handbag and was smoking a cigarette. Daisy recognized her, and pursed her lips.

A proper painted judy, that Violet, picking men up in the streets. Regular trade she did, according to Mrs. Hanlon at the Ragged Bear. Then a slow flush suffused Daisy's neck and crept up her face. What would Mrs. Hanlon say about Daisy's evening?

She'll never find out about it, Daisy argued with herself. Anyway, it was different. Why it was different from what Violet did, she was unable to say. But it was.

At last the brightly-lit doorway of the Ragged Bear came in sight.

"I'll have one more afore I go home," Daisy decided and plunged thankfully into the steaming warmth of the Snug, as the parlour was called.

The seat by the fire which she regarded as her own was occupied by Mrs. Donnelly, the grocer, sitting very correctly upright, black laced-up shoes exactly together, her large black hat straight on top of her piled up grey hair and her matching black coat neatly buttoned. She was delicately sipping a glass of port.

Daisy regarded her sourly as she plumped herself down near the door, a seat which was always draughty. She pushed her shawl back from her hair and smiled and nodded at those people she knew, pointedly ignoring Mrs. Donnelly.

"Half pint o' bitter?" inquired Joe Hanlon, as he pressed past her.

"No. I'll have a hot rum. It's proper cold outside. I'm clemmed." Her voice sounded slightly slurred.

Joe chuckled. "Doing yourself proud, aye?"

Daisy was immediately defensive. Her mind was not yet too

clouded to know that even a hot rum mid-week could cause local gossips to wonder where she got the money for it.

"I need it what with me Mam gone," she said, and then added haughtily, "I don't think she'd grudge it me out of her burial money."

"I'm sure she wouldn't," agreed Joe hastily. "I was sorry to hear about her. You gave her a lovely funeral, though. Me wife said she'd never seen a more respectful one."

Daisy's haughtiness vanished. She beamed at the publican as he took the measured glass of rum from his wife's hand and carried it over to the fireplace where the kettle bubbled gently on the hob. As the fragrance of the rum reached her nostrils, Mrs. Donnelly's expression became one of righteous disapproval.

Joe handed Daisy the steaming glass.

Daisy smirked, sipped her rum and gracefully accepted the condolences of two acquaintances sitting nearby. Mrs. Donnelly watched her drink in frigid silence. Daisy Gallagher owed her four shillings and tenpence, had owed it for a month, and there she was drinking rum — at mid-week! Mrs. Donnelly determined that the four and tenpence should be collected tomorrow at the latest, bereavement notwithstanding.

Greatly cheered by Joe's praise of the funeral, Daisy began to hum the song the sailors had been singing. She signalled to Joe Hanlon.

"I'll have another." She beamed beatifically round at her neighbours who, between polite gossiping, regarded her pityingly. Our Daisy was taking her sad loss very hard, they muttered.

"I think you'd better go home, Mrs. Gallagher," Joe said firmly. "Have you finished your drink?"

She stood swaying like a tall jelly pudding. "Yesh," she said. "But I want another. I don't want to go home. Nobody there. Why the hell should I go home?"

Joe put his arm confidentially round her shoulder. "Because I don't want you to become ill, Mrs. Gallagher. I would rather you came in again tomorrow and had another enjoyable evening." He eased her round till she faced the door. "Come on, luv." He pushed her firmly through the door, which his wife had opened, and she stumbled clumsily down the steps, staggered across the pavement and leaned against the gas lamp at the corner. She continued to sniff for a moment and lifted the corner of her apron to wipe her eyes. The clink of money in her apron pocket reminded her of the three sailors. She began to giggle a little ruefully, as she started unsteadily down the slope towards her home. She began to hum to herself, at first sadly and then a little more cheerfully.

Ahead, she could see the river glitter, as a brightly lit liner moved slowly downstream. She stumbled down towards it. Dear, friendly river — it was always there, sometimes scowling, sometimes smiling. Lovely river. She began to sing again.

"Three German officers crossed the line," she shrieked joyfully at the glittering water, as she leaned over the brick wall which separated her from the dock below in which lay a single ship, dark except for the watchman's lantern rising and dipping with the small movement of the water.

She waved drunkenly towards the river. "Hooray to yez, hooray to the bloody Mersey!"

EIGHT

Daisy stood for a long time leaning against the wall and looking out over the river, until she felt steady enough to cross the road again back to her own home. Moggie was complaining loudly on the doorstep and leaped ahead of her, as she stumbled into the dead dark front room.

The fire was out, and she felt around for the box of matches which she kept on the windowsill close to the entrance. The damp breeze from across the river was cold and she hastily closed the door behind her.

"Jaysus!" she exclaimed irritably. Then her fingers closed over the errant box and she fumbled to strike a match to light the lamp. She had not cleaned the lamp that morning and its wick was untrimmed. She took off its funnel awkwardly with one hand. The match sputtered out.

She put down the funnel on the table and got out another match. She paused as she was about to strike it and held her breath. She could distinctly hear heavy breathing behind her.

She had been cold. Now perspiration burst from her in sheer terror. Ghosts come back to haunt you, she knew that. Was her poor mother there? Unable to rest in her grave, unable to go to Purgatory because of what Daisy had done that evening?

She stood, match poised above the box, paralysed with fear. And the rhythmical breathing continued.

She screamed. Moggie brushed against her skirts. She shrieked again and crossed herself. "Holy Mother, help me!"

The breathing stopped with a snort.

"That you, Daisy?" asked a woman's voice from the direction of the old easy chair. "What's up?"

Daisy did not answer as the fright ebbed out of her and relief flooded in. But her heart was still pounding like a labourer's pickaxe against asphalt, when she answered cautiously, "That you, Nellie?"

"Course it's me. Where you been all this time?"

"My! Did you ever give me a fright." Daisy struck the match, shielded the wick while it caught, put back the funnel and turned, lamp in hand, to survey her visitor with drunken suspicion. "What you come for? You said you wasn't well."

"I wasn't. I was proper bad last night. But when I felt a bit better I come to see if you was all right. Did Mrs. Foley go with you to the Dental?"

"No. I went by myself."

Nellie got up stiffly from the chair and stretched herself slowly. She was a small woman with no flesh on her. Roughly curling grey hair haloed her hollow-cheeked, deeply lined face. Her mouth was tight, the lips hardly showing, partly from her lack of teeth and partly from being clenched when in pain. Daisy noticed that one steel-blue eye was still rimmed with yellow, where George had hit her a couple of weeks earlier.

George had always had the temper of Ould Nick, Daisy ruminated, as she gestured to her friend to be seated again and draw the chair closer to the fire. He and Meg were a right pair when it came to tempers.

She puttered over to the fireplace as steadily as she was able and picked up the poker. In response to vigorous poking the fireplace yielded a few hot cinders and she added a little coal by hand from a small pile on a piece of newspaper in the hearth — the coal scuttle was still in pawn.

She smiled at Nellie over her shoulder. "I'm glad you're feeling better," she said, as she fanned the reluctant coals with another piece of the *Liverpool Echo*. Soon a little warmth began to creep into the room.

Nellie nodded her head. "How do you feel with teeth in?" she asked.

"Not bad. It's hard to talk."

"Oh, aye. Let's see them."

Daisy obligingly put down the paper fan and took the teeth out. They were duly admired and then Daisy set them on the mantelshelf.

"Looks just like a skull grinning at you," remarked Nellie looking up at them.

Daisy shuddered. "Don't say that. Here, I'll put the kettle on and we'll have a cup of tea. I still got a bit of cake from the funeral."

She took the blackened kettle into the scullery to fill it from the house's single tap.

Nellie held her hands over the struggling fire and rubbed them to get the circulation going again. She pulled the chair even closer, so that her feet were inside the fender, and then wrapped her shawl round herself. "Tea'd be nice. God, it's cold tonight. It's the damp, I suppose?" She started to clear her throat at first slowly and then more rapidly.

"Aye, the damp's got into the house. I forgot to bank up the fire afore I went out." Daisy leaned over her friend, and plonked the kettle on to the hob and pushed it round over the fire. "You should've put some coal on."

"I didn't know if you could spare enough to keep the fire going when you wasn't cooking. And I thought you'd probably be back soon. Where *have* you been all this time?"

Daisy did not answer. She took up a pair of white, earthenware mugs from the table and, after a quick search, found the sticky tin of condensed milk on the chest of drawers, buried beneath an old copy of the *Liverpool Echo*.

"I'm out of sugar," she apologised as she opened a rusty tin box to display the remains of the funeral cake.

"Well, tell me. Did you go anywhere interesting all this time?" asked Nellie doggedly. She cleared her throat and spat accurately into the fire without hitting the kettle. The fire gave a sharp hiss.

"You *know* where I been. I went to the Dental to get me teeth. Then I had fish and chips." She reached up and took her new teeth from the shelf. With some difficulty she put them in again and grimaced at the discomfort.

Nellie looked up sharply from her contemplation of the fire, her own toothless mouth open in wonder. "Yes," she agreed. "But you was such a long time I thought something terrible had happened to yez. Anyway, lemme see them in."

Daisy obligingly grinned.

"My, you look nice! Like I remember you at my wedding!" Nellie's admiration was genuine. She sucked in her lips and then laughed as she teased, "Michael'll have to watch out now."

"What do you mean?" Daisy snapped out the question belligerently. The euphoria of the alcohol was wearing off.

"You know — you look so young, like. I was only joking." Nellie looked Daisy up and down. "You bin drinking?"

"Humph. Had a rum in the Snug on me way home," responded Daisy sulkily. A rum can take any amount of time to drink, so that should satisfy Nellie's nosiness. She poked the fire again, making it flare up, and Nellie nodded understandingly, her shadow on the wall bobbing in unison.

"Rum? Still got a bit of burial money, have yer?"

"I needed a rum after all I been through."

"To be sure," soothed Nellie. "You did so much for your Mam."

Daisy smiled, and swayed unsteadily. She reached down the tea caddy from the mantelpiece, took the lid off the teapot which was standing as always on the top of the oven, and discovered it still had the dregs of earlier brews in it. Muttering imprecations, she went out as steadily as she could to the scullery and opened the back door. The yard was absolutely dark but she emptied the tea leaves accurately on to what had once been a flower bed, which after generations of such treatment consisted largely of decaying tea leaves in which only weeds grew.

She measured out the tea, and, while she waited for the kettle to come to a rolling boil, she gazed reflectively down into the fire which was now burning quite cheerfully.

"If our Meg had been the new Nan, none of us would have got so much as a glass o' beer out of her," she remarked. "What's yours is hers and what's hers is her own."

"Don't be so hard, Daise. She's had a rough life."

"Oh, aye. I wouldn't want to be her. Going to a motherless home to look after a crabby old devil like Fogarty and two brothers-in-law as well as her husband." Daisy sucked at her new teeth. "And now she's got six kids — and might manage another afore the change strikes her."

"At least they're living," Nellie responded in reference to the children. She sighed sadly.

Daisy leaned down and put a compassionate hand on Nellie's wool-wrapped shoulders. "There, there, luv. The Lord giveth and the Lord taketh away, as Mrs. Temperance Thomas is always saying. And she's right."

Nellie's pinched-in lips trembled. "To take four of ours with the diphtheria — and then to take our Freddie when he fell into the hold of the *Fair Rita* on top of the coal she was unloading." She almost sobbed the last words. "It's no wonder our George gets into a rage at times, with only our iddy-diddy Joey left."

"I know, luv, I know." Daisy turned to rescue the kettle and pour the boiling water over the tea-leaves. Then she put the teapot on the hob to let the fire mash it to a formidable blackness. "Have a cuppa tea, luv. Make you feel better."

With the comforting heat of the mug of tea warming her hands and Daisy's gentleness, Nellie began to feel better. Daisy again filled the kettle with water and set it on the fire.

"What you boiling more water for? You made plenty of tea."

Daisy sat down on a wooden chair which creaked uneasily as it received her weight. She viewed her friend's face cautiously out of the corner of her eye. You couldn't breathe in without somebody noticing, she thought tartly. How could you tell a woman as clean-living and plain good as Nellie that you felt sore underneath because you'd had three sailors?

"Well, I thought as how I had the fire I'd maybe have a wash afore going to bed," she replied carefully. "Bring the bowl in here where it's warm."

Nellie stirred her tea with the single tin spoon which they had been sharing. "Mind you don't get chill," she warned. "Too much washing and you'll feel the cold like anything."

Daisy nodded agreement.

"You finished with blood a couple of years ago, didn't you?"

Daisy again nodded. She understood the import of her friend's inquiry. After a period one washed, but not much otherwise.

Nellie changed the subject.

"When's Bill Donohue coming to do out your Mam's room?"

"Tomorrow." The tea was helping Daisy back to normality. Eagerly she pursued the fresh subject of conversation. "Thought I'd get him to whitewash the ceiling as well."

"It'll cost you another shilling."

Daisy opened her mouth to say she had the money and then quickly clicked her teeth together again. Blast, she cursed silently. Aloud she said, "You're right. Maybe I can get him to throw it in, anyway. A bit of whitewash can't cost anything like a shilling."

The exchange reminded her forcibly that she must be extremely circumspect about the way in which she spent the eight shillings and sixpence which she had so unexpectedly acquired, or people would begin to surmise about her unaccountable prosperity. Still, it was good to feel the weight of the coins deep in her apron pocket. The money gave her an unexpected feeling of power as if she was now more in command of her life. It would help her over the first week without her mother's pension. She was going to miss that pension nearly as much as her mother. At the thought of her mother the dull pain of loss returned to her.

Nellie slurped comfortably at her mug of tea. "You must be missing Nan," she remarked as if she had read Daisy's thoughts. "What was the cause of her, er. . . ?"

"Doctor said it was the stroke again. Charged me two and sixpence just to say that and write out a certificate to say she'd passed on. I knew she was gone without him telling me!"

Nellie wagged her grizzled head knowingly. "Aye, but them bleeders down at the Prue wouldn't have believed you without a Death Certificate — and without their money how would you have buried her?"

They gossiped a little longer and then Nellie took her departure. The wind hit her as she went through the front door. She began to cough and leaned against the door jamb while she fought to control the spasm.

"Aye, Nellie, luv, you should ask Mr. Williamson up at the chemist's for summat for that cough." Daisy tried to keep the panic she felt out of her voice. "You must take care, Nell."

"Och, it's just me usual winter cough," responded her friend with a confidence which was far from genuine. "It's nothing — it'll pass," she added, as she hitched her heavy shawl over her head. She managed to hold back her cough long enough to kiss Daisy on the cheek. "Tara-well."

Daisy sighed. "Ta-ra, luv."

Holding her shawl across her mouth Nellie hurried up the street. Daisy shut the door and leaned against it, listening to the diminishing sound of her friend's steady coughing. Dear Virgin Mother, what a cough!

She moved uneasily towards the fire. Nellie really needed a doctor, she thought fearfully. But where would she ever get money for a doctor from?

The kettle was steaming merrily again, so Daisy went immediately into the icy scullery and took from the soapstone sink a battered tin basin and a sliver of coarse laundry soap. She picked up a grey rag of a towel from off an upturned oil drum

which served as a table and went back to the living room. She
set the basin on the rag rug in front of the fire and emptied the
kettle into it. Then she went back to the scullery, filled the kettle
with cold water and emptied this into the bowl.

Slowly she took off her serge skirt and black cotton petticoat
and then, after a moment's consideration, took off her blouse.
To take off her torn vest which was her only other undergar-
ment would be the height of indecency, so she left it on. Her
woollen stockings, held up below the knee by a button twisted
into each top, were reluctantly discarded. She had not had her
clothes off for several weeks, keeping even her serge skirt on at
night because the wind off the estuary had been so cold. Now
she shivered at the unaccustomed exposure.

It was against her beliefs to use soap on herself except after
her monthly periods, now long past; but this time she felt there
was a real need and she washed her fat thighs thoroughly and
then, after looking down at them cloudily, she washed her feet.
She dried herself hurriedly — the draught coming in under the
door was bringing her out in goose pimples. The sudden, hard
scrubbing made the louse and bug bites on her itch; normally
the bites did not swell — she was almost immune to irritation
from them — but now they bothered her and she scratched
furiously.

She had no other clothes so she put on again those she had
taken off. She remembered that, though her mother had had no
clothing other than a nightgown provided by the lady from the
Welfare, she had clung to her shawl and kept it round her
shoulders to ease the winter cold in the frigid room upstairs. The
shawl was still up there.

"Come morning I'll take it to the wash house and wash it,"
Daisy promised herself, "before that Meg wakes up to it being
there."

She rinsed out her stockings in the same water in which she
had washed and hung them over a piece of string stretched
across the front of the mantelpiece, to dry in the heat of the dy-

ing fire. She stood contemplating their woolly length steaming at the end nearest to the fire. There were holes in both heels and toes. She decided suddenly that since she did not have to feed her mother any more, sixpence out of her ill-gotten money might be expended on another pair of stockings.

"Nobody'll notice them," she comforted herself. "Black stockings is black stockings — they all look the same."

"And what about a new petticoat then — and a pair of winter bloomers?" inquired an extravagant devil within her.

At the thought of a pair of thick cotton bloomers, brushed to a warm fluff on the inside, she felt a craving for comfort that had never struck her before. She could not remember when she had last worn knickers of any kind. Her mouth watered as if the garment was something good to eat.

"I'll do it," she promised herself exultantly. "Nobody's going to see me bloomers, so they can't ask no questions."

"They'll ask questions if they see you buy them in Parkee Lanee or anywhere hereabouts. You'll have to go down town again to Hughes's in London Road."

This reminder brought her up short. She would have to venture again into the city; and do it alone. While she emptied the basin in which she had washed she thought about this.

Still nervously undecided, she lit a candle and trailed up to bed, but as she laid her head on the lumpy pillow she muttered, "I'll go. Nowt worse could happen to me than happened today."

NINE

Daisy woke with a start. A male voice was shouting "Mrs. Gallagher!" The front door was banged impatiently. "Are you there, Missus?"

"Oh," she groaned, as she swung herself off the bed. Though her head did not ache as it had done the day before, the floor had a curious tendency to come up to meet her. "Bloody so-and-so! Always coming early. Who the hell is it?"

Aloud she shouted, "Coming!"

When she opened the door, she found, fidgeting on the doorstep, Bill Donohue, a small, elderly man with a walrus moustache made ginger by tobacco smoke. He held several rolls of wallpaper tightly to his shabby suit jacket. From his little finger dangled a pail.

"Thought you'd never come," he said irritably as, uninvited, he walked into the living-room and looked around for a place to lay down the wallpaper. Every surface was cluttered from end to end, so he dropped it on to the floor.

"Didn't expect you so soon," replied Daisy sourly. "What colour you brought?"

Mr. Donohue looked affronted. "Same as always, of course — pink roses on a trellis with a white background." He sniffed. "All my customers like pink roses — they're proper pretty."

"I wanted blue for a change," said Daisy, not because she did, but because Bill Donohue was not going to get away with five shillings from her without suffering.

"They don't make it," replied Mr. Donohue loftily. "It's out

75

of fashion. Be back in a minute with me ladder and me paste. I'll need some hot water to mix the paste."

"I know that without being told," responded Daisy tartly. "And I don't believe you about the blue — you couldn't have looked."

Bill Donohue was making for the door in an effort to avoid an argument, but was stopped in his attempt to escape by Daisy barking, "And don't go so quick. Wait a minute. I want the ceiling done as well."

He turned slowly round, very surprised. He viewed her with distrustful, watery blue eyes. "It'll cost yer — let me see, it'll cost yer another shilling for plain whitewash."

It was Daisy's turn to be affronted. "Mr. Donohue," she said with huge dignity, "Have I ever failed to pay you?"

Bill teetered slowly back and forth on his heels while he considered this. "No," he agreed. "But it must be all of eight years since I done a room for you."

"You don't need to remind me," Daisy snapped. "I know when our Tommy died."

"Well, have you got enough for the ceiling?" inquired Bill bluntly.

Daisy went to the fireplace where her stockings still dangled like a pair of dried snakes. She reached up and produced two half-crowns from under the clock. She held them up for her visitor to see. Then she plunged her hand into her apron pocket and pulled out another shilling. " 'Ere ye are."

Bill touched his forelock respectfully, took off his cap, scratched his head and replaced the cap. "Have to go and buy some whitewash," he announced. "Back in half an hour." He stopped half way out of the door. "I'll do the ceiling first. Need hot water for the paste later on."

Daisy nodded proudly and put the six shillings back under the clock.

He was back before she had finished eating her breakfast of tea, bread and margarine, in front of the newly made fire. The fire was not burning very well because of the huge pile of cinders under it.

"Room empty?" inquired Bill.

"There's a bed and a chest in it."

"Better get them out afore I start with the whitewash."

Without asking permission, he took his pail and the packet of whitewash into the scullery. After a moment there was the sound of splashing water as he mixed the whitewash, combined with the faltering strains of "The Roses of Picardy". Bill Donohue prided himself on knowing the words of more songs than anybody else in the neighbourhood. He had a radio and he was fond of saying that he listened to it intelligently.

"Holy Mary!" exclaimed Daisy in exasperation as she hastily swallowed the last bit of crust, put her teeth back in and hauled herself out of her chair.

Half way up the stairs, she stopped to allow a spasm of headache to recede. While it slowly passed she remembered for a second the young sailor who did not know how with a woman, and her irritability vanished. She was chuckling to herself as she entered her mother's room.

The silence of the room struck her forcibly. Her chuckles ceased; the young sailor was forgotten. While she was downstairs she could have the illusion that her mother was quietly sleeping in the bedroom; now, faced with the empty bed and the need to clear it, she had to recognise again that she was alone. Slowly the tears came, accompanied by great hopeless sobs. Instead of having someone to lean on, to advise her, to bully her into staying on her feet when life seemed impossibly hard, she herself would have to be the adviser, the kind helper, the referee of family quarrels; hers would be the knee on to which grandchildren would climb to be comforted, hers would be the shoulder on which the women would weep out their bereavements and all the myriad sorrows of being mams.

"Aye, Mam," she whispered brokenly, "I don't know whether I can do it."

And it seemed to her, as she stood leaning against the door jamb, that she heard again her mother giving her what-for, as she called it, for standing around and not getting on with the job in hand. She almost felt the playful pat on her behind that her mother would give her, to send her back into the street fight she had lost, or to comfort her when there was no bread to assuage her hunger.

Obedient to that sharp, cheerful voice, she sniffed back her tears and surveyed the room to see what she should do first.

Bill Donohue clumped up the stairs with his bucket of whitewash and a brush. He viewed the floor and then the rest of the room with distaste.

"Need some new lino," he remarked.

"I know that," retorted Daisy. "You tell me how to get it out of an eighteen shilling allotment."

Mr. Donohue put down the bucket and rubbed his hands slowly down the sides of his paint-stained trousers. He scuffed a bare piece of board showing through the offending floor covering.

"You got a good oak floor, I reckon." He looked disparagingly at Daisy.

Daisy put her hands on her hips and leaned towards him. "And what good will that do me?"

Bill sniffed so that the dewdrop at the end of his nose wobbled. "If you tore up lino and scrubbed t' floor well — maybe scrape it where the lino's stuck . . . buy a tin of dark varnish and go over it — it wouldn't look bad at all. Dark varnish'll hide a lot o' marks."

Daisy looked again at the floor. Then she looked across at the window, over the misty river. As a child she had spent many a wet afternoon kneeling on a chair looking out of the window with Nellie, to see the ships go by. She knew the river in all its moods, she knew which company each ship belonged to because her father had taught her the funnel markings of each great company, Cunard, White Star, Ellerman's, and a dozen others, not to speak of strange boats from far away places like China and Russia. She could remember when sailing ships still floated in the Pool of Liverpool. She suddenly envisaged this little window on the world elegantly draped with a pair of Nottingham lace curtains, the sunlight gleaming through on to a shining floor, like an advertisement she had once seen in the *Liverpool Echo*.

She sighed rather hopelessly.

"Varnish is a good idea, Bill," she agreed. "I'll think about it." Then she ordered, "Do the inside of t'cupboard while you're at it."

"Cupboard not included — you know that," replied Bill stonily, as he spread out his step ladder. "Take candlestick off t' mantel. It'll get splashed."

Daisy snatched up the offending candle in its saucer and remembered also the chamber pot under the bed. She picked that up, too. "Come on, Bill," she wheedled, looking at him with eyes slanted under long, black lashes. "You could manage the cupboard with bits of left-over paper — it doesn't have to be perfect."

Bill's moustache bristled. "It's me time as well."

"How much now?" Daisy pouted.

"Cost you another — well, another tanner."

Daisy made a face at his indifferent back. "All right."

Bill dipped his brush into the bucket of whitewash and said placatorily, without looking round, "Room'll look proper nice." He raised a scrawny arm and carefully ran a line of whitewash back and forth across the ceiling.

Daisy hastily unhooked her mother's shawl from the cupboard and, dodging a rain of whitewash drops, took it with the candle and the chamber downstairs.

Moggie emerged from the oven, yawning and stretching first one long, skinny grey leg and then the other. Daisy let him out of the back door. She did not feed him; he hunted for himself and was adept at getting lids off dust bins to get at the contents.

Daisy collected her breakfast dishes and the glasses from the funeral wake, and washed them up in the same basin in which she had washed herself the previous night. One basin was a necessity in a house; two would have been luxurious.

She took a shovel and handleless bucket from under the sink and proceeded with the dusty job of clearing the ashes from the fireplace. She forgot to remove the stockings she had hung up to dry and some of the ash peppered them as well as the rag rug. Suddenly, there was a peremptory knock on the front door. Cursing under her breath, she got up from her knees, wiped her dusty hands on her apron and went and opened the door.

She jumped hastily back from the sill, as the wind from the river playfully blew Mrs. Donnelly's broad-brimmed hat off her head and into the room. It bowled across the floor and came to rest against the fender, its unsullied black collecting cinder dust all the way.

With the loose ends of her hair blown straight upwards by the wind and her red-brimmed blue eyes glaring at a non-plussed Daisy, the grocer looked like a witch who had just landed from her broomstick.

"I want me four and tenpence," announced Mrs. Donnelly frigidly.

"What four and tenpence?" The very sight of the grocer made Daisy's ire rise. Daisy had been wangling credit out of her since she was first sent on a message by her mother when she was five years old and Mrs. Donnelly had been a handsome, newly married woman. Mrs. Donnelly knew very well, argued Daisy to herself as she surveyed the unwelcome visitor, that she never needed to collect in person. She had only to mention the debt to Daisy three of four times while she was in the shop and hint that further credit would be cut off, and the next allotment day after that Daisy would pay.

"You know. You been owing it long enough."

"It's not so long that I've owed it!" Daisy put her hands on her hips and glowered at the grocer.

Undaunted by the scowl, Mrs. Donnelly pursed her lips primly. "Oh, yes, it is. If you can drink rum mid-week, then you can pay your grocery." She sniffed. "And I'd like me hat back, if you don't mind."

Daisy made no move to rescue the hat from the dusty hearth rug. Her eyes blinked and the tears began to rise as she remembered the exhausting days since her mother's death. "I needed a bit of something with me Mam only in her grave a few hours an' all."

Mrs. Donnelly could not have cared less about Daisy's bereavement — Mrs. O'Brien had been a trying customer in her time, too. "A blessed release to her, no doubt," she said icily.

Daisy's tears burst forth genuinely. "That's a cruel thing to say, Mrs. Donnelly," she sobbed, "and me nursing her all these years."

Mrs. Donnelly relented enough to say she was sorry Daisy felt so badly about it, and she would like her four and tenpence and her hat, if Daisy ever expected to get credit again from her.

Bill Donohue had heard the raised voices, and he came slowly down the stairs to see what was happening. He viewed the weeping Daisy with compassion as she turned back into the room. Everybody knew how good Daisy had been with her mother and how she shared what she had with her sisters' children when they came to visit her and were hungry. He watched her stumble round, feeling on the table for her little hoard of silver, then evidently remembering that it was in her apron pocket. She reluctantly came up with the two half crowns she had earned the previous night from the first two sailors.

"Here ye are," she said as, with brimming eyes, she thrust the coins into the scrawny outstretched hand.

Mrs. Donnelly produced twopence change from a small leather purse with innumerable pockets.

"Me hat," she demanded.

Still sobbing miserably before a silent Bill, Daisy went across to the fireplace to pick up the hat.

She wiped her eyes with a corner of her apron. "Now where is it," she sniffed. "Ah, there," and with a burst of savage rage she trod on it.

She picked up the shattered piece of headgear and carefully brushed the dust it had collected further into its black satin trimmings. The sight of the wreckage restored her aplomb a little, and Mrs. Donnelly's horrified shriek of "What have you done?" was particularly satisfying. Still snuffling, however, she handed the hat to its infuriated owner and slammed the door in her face.

"Bad cess to yez!" she snarled through her tears at the closed door, and still sniffing unhappily she went to the fireplace to warm herself.

Her ample breasts trembled under her thin cotton blouse, as she continued to cry softly, despite the joy of the ruined hat.

"Don't take it too hard." Bill Donohue's ginger moustache quivered in sympathy. "It's proper hard when your husband's away like Mike is." He had a strong desire to take her in his arms to comfort her. So much good womanhood going to waste. He stuck his thumbs in his braces so that his hands would not stray as he went closer to her. "She's a hard-nosed bitch," he said.

"Nearly cleaned me out, she did," confided Daisy between sniffs.

Bill looked alarmed, and the look was not lost on Daisy despite her grief.

"Don't worry. I still got your money. Though what I do till Tuesday when I get me allotment, I don't know."

Bill wagged his head in sad understanding of her predicament. He stood rubbing a bit of whitewash absently into one blue-veined arm, and then said, "I'll do the cupboard for you without extra. After all, I've known you and Michael a long time."

Daisy had put her teeth in immediately after having her breakfast, and now she favoured Bill with a watery smile which set his heart aflutter within his withered frame.

"That's proper kind of you, Mr. Donohue," she said warmly.

Bill bridled. "You're welcome, I'm sure," he said and went shyly back up the stairs.

TEN

While Bill toiled amid the rosy wallpaper. Daisy took her mother's shawl and a few slivers of soap wrapped in a piece of newspaper to the public wash house. Even the brick copper built into the corner of her kitchen was not large enough to hold such a heavy garment, and Daisy's skin rose in goose pimples at the idea of wearing a dead person's shawl without first washing it.

The tide was low and the weak October sun glanced and danced on the tiny waves whipped up by the boisterous wind. Far away, towards the coast of Wallasey, a solitary yacht ran fast before the wind. Daisy watched for a minute as its mast seemed to dip towards the water. She sighed. Michael knew how to sail a boat. As a young boy he had sailed on a clipper all the way to China to fetch tea, and he had always wanted to be rich enough to buy a bit of timber to build himself a rowing boat to take out on the river. Poor Mike. He was a bit feckless and hot-tempered, and once or twice he had given her a good hiding. They had always made up their quarrels, however, and she had usually been pregnant before his next voyage. And he left her an allotment. She told herself she couldn't really complain.

As she passed the Foley home, she said good morning to Mrs. Foley, who was seated on a chair outside her front door peeling potatoes into a piece of newspaper.

Lucky her, Daisy envied. Two married daughters and their husbands and kids to keep her company.

Daisy had for years been so busy trying to keep her children alive and then nursing her mother that she had, like Mrs. Foley, not had much time to miss her sea-going husband. But now as the wind blustered round her wide black skirt, she felt that being the wife of a ship's stoker was no life at all.

Now her mother was dead her loneliness appalled her. Relations she had in plenty, and Nellie was the dearest of friends. But the house was empty and so was her rough and noisome bed.

The wash house loomed before her, a dark and steamy cavern, a cavern equipped, however, with gas-heated boilers, lots of hot water and big sinks. Several women with sleeves rolled back from skinny arms were hard at work with scrubbing boards or were wringing out clothes through huge wooden wringers.

None of Daisy's friends or relations were there because few of them had anything to wash. The children were all stitched into their clothes for the winter, with warm pads of newspaper set between their vests and jerseys.

Daisy whipped up a good lather with her flakes of soap and a little hot water, then ran the thundering cold tap until she had a lukewarm mixture. She carefully lowered the shawl into the water and worked the soapsuds gently through it.

As she dabbled the heavy wool in the water, she felt as if she was slowly pushing her mother down into a watery grave, and she cried silently to herself.

Mrs. Thomas of Temperance fame was using the next sink. She would not normally have acknowledged the existence of the dirty Irish woman next to her. She noticed, however, her neighbour's tightly closed eyes and muffled snivels, and being by nature a kindly woman she touched Daisy's arm with a soap-frothed hand.

"Are you well, Mrs. Gallagher?"

Daisy swallowed a sob, and her eyes shot open at the sound of the inquiry delivered in a high-pitched Welsh sing-song. She hastily pushed her teeth into order with an impatient tongue. God, how sore her gums felt!

"Why, yes, Mrs. Thomas, thanks be. It's me Mam — I was washing her shawl — she passed on last Saturday — and, well . . . . "

"Yes, indeed, I saw the funeral pass by. You must be feeling very bad." Mrs. Thomas seized hold of the hot tap over her sink and set it roaring like a waterfall. Over the frenzied splashing, her voice rose, "I'm very sorry." She leaned over towards Daisy, her face earnest beneath her straight fringe of hair, and patted her wet arm. "Try not to grieve — the Lord giveth and the Lord taketh away," she added piously.

Daisy had often raised a laugh in the Ragged Bear by imitating Mrs. Thomas using her favourite quotation, and now she smiled bleakly.

The Lord could take away a hell of a lot, when he felt like it. He had in the shape of Mrs. Donnelly taken away four shillings and tenpence that morning — and, she admitted honestly, given her back sixpence via the kindly Bill Donohue.

She nodded acceptance of the well-meant consolation offered by Mrs. Thomas, rubbed the drip off the end of her nose with wet fingers, and continued to wash.

During the early afternoon, the lady from the Welfare called on Mrs. Thomas with regard to the provision of a wheelchair for her invalid daughter. Mrs. Thomas, feeling that Mrs. Gallagher must be very lonely and in need of consolation, kindly mentioned that old Mrs. O'Brien had died the previous Saturday and no doubt Mrs. Gallagher would be glad of a friendly call.

The Welfare lady understood perfectly the enormous gulf that lay between Welsh Mrs. Thomas, devout Presbyterian and Temperance worker, and Mrs. Gallagher, Irish Roman Catholic, which made it difficult for Mrs. Thomas herself to communicate with the bereaved woman, and she promised to call.

After finishing her business with the Welsh woman, she stood on the well-scrubbed pavement outside Mrs. Thomas's front door, and considered what she could say that would be helpful to Mrs. Gallagher.

She remembered suddenly that only the day before she had called at the Gallagher house to deliver a blanket for Mrs. O'Brien. Daisy had said that her mother was sleeping and had accepted a beautiful blanket squeezed out of precious funds specially for Mrs. O'Brien. She had not said that her mother was already dead.

Really the woman was intolerable. The Welfare lady climbed into her Austin Seven and slammed the door after her. She made a note in her notebook that Mrs. Daisy Gallagher was not to be helped again, except in the most pressing circumstances.

ELEVEN

Because she was feeling so depressed, Daisy did not go directly home from the wash house. She went to call on her younger sister, Agnes.

Agnes was not much help. She burst into a passion of tears within minutes of Daisy's arrival.

"Poor Mam," she whispered, as she took the teapot from in front of the fire and poured a boiling hot, black cup of tea for her sister. After setting the cup conveniently beside Daisy, she sat down herself, threw her apron over her head and wailed miserably into it.

Daisy had once remarked that there was more water in Aggie than in a whole wet week. She could turn on the tears like a tap.

Now Daisy did her best to turn off the tap. Instead of being comforted, she found herself doing the comforting, and this took some time. She spread her mother's shawl over the fireguard and let it steam while she held Agnes's shrouded head to her bosom. She felt like weeping herself, but now that she had taken her mother's place in the family hierarchy she felt she must do as her mother would have done, and lift Aggie's spirits somehow.

She patted Agnes's apron-covered head and held her close until the damp began to penetrate her blouse; then she began to divert her attention by mentioning that her son, Marty, aged five, would be home soon for his dinner and so would Winnie, her daughter. And would Joe, her husband, be home for dinner?

This reminder of her duties made Agnes emerge from her

apron and start fluttering about the room like Moggie playing with a screw of paper.

Despite her earlier cry of poverty to Bill, Daisy still had enough money left to buy a pair of bloomers and she was determined to make this purchase. She did not dare buy them at any local store — somebody would be sure to see her and make an awkward comment, so after a friendly cup of tea with Bill Donohue, she took the tram again to the city. She would buy the bloomers in one of the stores in London Road, where she had been the previous day. She felt very brave making this second expedition alone, and she comforted herself about the extravagance with the thought that the next day she would draw her allotment from the shipping office; and this would cover the rent and the cost of some coal and lamp oil. She could at worst pawn the fender again and the new blanket, if she could not manage until the following allotment day.

She spent a couple of happy hours roaming through the big stores and finally found what she wanted. She felt like a princess as she tucked the small parcel under her shawl, and she wondered how she could ever have been afraid of going to town by herself; around London Road there were plenty of Irish women like herself, long hair screwed up in a variety of Victorian styles, black shawls, black skirts, sometimes with aprons, sometimes without. It seemed quite homely.

As she strolled down the crowded pavement, she remembered her glorious repast of the previous day. Her mouth watered uncontrollably, and soon she was digging into a large plate of fish cakes, chips and peas. In the interests of economy, she ordered a cup of tea instead of a pot.

She again sat modestly with her back to the counter, so that she should not be seen eating, and this time she kept her teeth in. She ate slowly and with difficulty, and at times was sorely tempted to take the teeth out and set them by her plate. She was vain enough, however, to wish to keep her lovely new smile, and she finally shovelled in the last pea on the end of her knife with a great sense of achievement. Afterwards, she sat for some time watching the shadowy passers-by through the steamy window.

She was reluctant to go home. Bill Donohue would have finished his work and left, and there would be only Moggie to greet her. It was rather late to call on anybody, except her sisters. She had already seen Agnes and she doubted if Meg would have yet simmered down sufficiently to bury the hatchet. As she had once explained to a neighbour, "Our Meg is proper tempreementil. What you do you wait — maybe a week or two. Then you start up again as if nothing had happened."

It was after eight o'clock when she finally left the little fish and chip shop with a friendly "ta-ra" from the proprietress. Outside she paused, rubbing her arms under her shawl, as she gazed absently across the street.

The side road was quiet. A man in greasy mechanic's overalls whistled as he entered the pub at the corner, two shop girls, chattering in high-pitched voices, tottered by in high-heeled patent leather court shoes.

Daisy grinned to herself as she looked at the bright pub sign; and she hummed almost gleefully the tune the sailors had been singing the previous night. But enough was enough. She must behave herself. She folded her hands primly across her stomach; but still she did not move.

A constable on his beat passed her with only a casual glance. Her shawl and black skirt, her white apron and frowsy hair style were as common and respectable as his own uniform; prostitution was a rare phenomena amongst the Liverpool Irish. His indifference riled her.

"If I'd been decked out like a bloody pro," she fumed, "with furs and feathers and ear-rings an' all, he'd have noticed all right. He'd have stopped and told me to move on." She scowled at the constable's broad back as he turned the corner.

Perversely she began to sway her hips. With an irritable flip, she set her shawl further back on her shoulders in spite of the

cool weather, so that the curve of her breasts was better out-
lined. Slowly, humming the sailor's tune, she swung down the
street past the pub and turned round its garish opulence towards
the familiar alley. She walked well, and in better circumstances
would have been regarded as a fine-looking woman.

Still simmering at the pure indifference of the constable who
had passed her, she went down the street without incident. At
the end, where it ran into a cross street, she hesitated. The cross
street was very dark. She spun round fretfully so that her skirt
spread round her and drifted back up the slight rise again
towards the pub. When a middle-aged workman approached
her, she simpered at him, but he hardly noticed her and continued on his way. This provoked her even more and, as she
again approached the pub, she opened the two top buttons of
her blouse and tucked the ends in, something no respectable
woman would do. She gritted her teeth. She would show them.

She would not have been able to explain who "they" were, except that they were a vague, amorphous cloud of people to
whom the name Daisy Margaret Gallagher meant nothing.
They employed the police, they were relieving officers, they
owned boats that failed to dock in Liverpool, they paid out allotments across shiny mahogany counters, they ignored her when
she was sick and found her a nuisance when she was well and
wanted something. They surrounded her in ever-widening rip-
ples; there were a lot of theys and thems in courts who put one's
sons and daughters in prison. There were even more of them, as
Michael had often remarked, in places like London who cared
nothing about people who lived north of the River Trent, and
yet reckoned they owned the very land you stood on. In short,
they were ghostly menaces who threatened the existence of
Daisy Margaret Gallagher, who lived down on the waterfront in
a cold house where she had been often hungry.

Of course, if your son killed a man, reflected Daisy, as she
swaggered slowly up and down, they noticed quick enough.
Then you became a screaming biddie to be ejected from the

court room while they took your boy away from you. If you dressed in flowers and glittering earrings and walked up and down as she was doing, smiling at every man who passed, then you became a person important enough to be arrested. You might become important enough to have regular clients who knew you, men from outside the tight family world which was normally one's only hope in a wicked universe. You might even find yourself in bed with the beak instead of in the dock in front of him. At this last idea Daisy laughed out loud and forgot for a moment what she was doing.

"Hey, Judy," whispered a voice from the entrance of the alleyway.

She jumped with fright and flung one arm dramatically across her breast. "Holy Mother!" Then as she observed the shadowy figure of a man, her expression changed and she smiled cunningly. "'Ello, la," she greeted him.

The shadow materialized into a squat, heavily built man in a blue serge suit that was so crumpled it must have been rolled up in a kit bag for months. He grinned knowingly at her.

"What about it, Ma?" He nodded towards the comfortable darkness of the alley.

She looked him up and down, held back by a pang of fear.

"Give you three bob," he promised hopefully. He put out his hand and caressed her bare throat.

She smiled suddenly at him with her flashing white teeth and he almost dragged her into the black lair from which he had emerged, at the same time fumbling in his trouser pocket for the money. She held out her hand and he put three silver shillings into it.

He pressed her hard against the rough stone wall, prepared for only a moment or two's dalliance. Daisy, however, was not sure how much was expected of her. Now she was literally face to face with a client whom she had herself beguiled by flaunting herself in the street, she was nervous about her ability to please. She also feared that he might strike her if she tried to run away.

He was solidly built and stronger than she was.

As his hands ran down her back, however, her natural instinct to tease, to caress, took over; and she found herself acting in exactly the same way as she would have done if Michael had caught her in a dark corner. It did not take her long to have him gasping with desire. Afterwards, he did not hurry away, as she had expected, but leaned against the wall by her in a friendly fashion till his breathing returned to normal.

He took out a packet of Woodbines and offered her one. With eyes cast down she shyly refused the cigarette. She was trembling under her shawl and wondering what kind of devil lay within her that she could enjoy a strange man so much.

"What's your name?" he asked her, as he took a closer look at her through a cloud of cigarette smoke.

"Daisy."

"Been in this game long?"

"Well. . . ." She did not know how to reply. She had not considered that a man she picked up might carry on a conversation with her, and she turned her face uneasily away from him.

He saw her shyness, and he laughed softly. The laughter made a plain, hard face suddenly friendly. He flicked the ash off his cigarette. There was many a good woman nowadays who took a man occasionally to help out with the housekeeping, he thought shrewdly.

"Well, Daisy," he said. "See you again." He hitched his belt a notch tighter and rolled with typical seaman's gait back down the alley to the street.

She stood leaning against the wall for a while until she heard voices in a back yard further up the alley. It reminded her that people were closer to her than the deserted entry suggested. She moved slowly along to the street, where she paused uncertainly. Then an impish grin spread over her face and she resumed her promenade up and down the road. She felt young and excited and far from tired.

A negro in a blue suit and trilby hat approached her very diffidently, not certain whether she was a prostitute or just a woman waiting to catch a drunken husband coming out of the Ball and Chain. She stuck her nose in the air and snubbed him soundly. He slunk away.

"Can't stomach them blackies," she muttered. "Don't know how Mike can work with them. Proper scary — black like Old Nick himself."

A chill wind sprang up and she began to feel cold. She bit her lower lip and then tittered to herself as the three shillings in her apron pocket clinked against her. It was as easy as falling off a dock. These men's needs were no different from Michael's and, judging by his friendliness, she had really pleased the man in the rumpled suit.

The street seemed deserted, so she retrieved the parcel of bloomers from the top of the wall on one side of the alley and walked down to Lime Street, where she caught a tram home.

For the first time for years she felt bright and venturesome, as if she had discovered again something of the gaiety of her youth. There was also a feeling of wonderment that something she had done had been appreciated.

"He thought I was worth three bob," she marvelled.

TWELVE

Daisy never could decide what drove her yet again to the quiet street at the back of London Road. Perhaps it was the indifference of the clerk at the shipping office who slapped down Mike's eighteen shillings in front of her and made her sign for it — as if he were a bloody relieving officer and the money was public assistance instead of wages from Mike. Maybe it was the dead monotony of Father Patrick's voice granting absolution for the sin of anger against Meg, when Nellie dragged her to confession. The ghost-ridden empty house to which she returned did not help either. Moggie had left a half-devoured mouse on the rag rug. The house was so terrifyingly quiet and the mouse so bloody.

"Fair turns your stomach, it does," she muttered, as she cleaned up the unfortunate mouse and threw it into the fire.

Saturday brought little relief from the loneliness to which had been added a deep boredom. Nellie came for an hour in the afternoon. But her visit only increased Daisy's frightened intuitions about her.

They ate tea together, and after she had gone Daisy lit a candle and wandered up to look at her mother's room. In the uncanny stillness she held the candle high to see what Bill had done.

Frightened by the light, the bugs scattered off the new wallpaper. She grinned. She reckoned she would have to burn the house down to get rid of the vermin.

Bill had left the cupboard door open so that she could see the

97

inside of it. He had filled up an old rat hole with balls of paper and then put wallpaper over it, as he had explained to her, and it looked much neater. He had also cleared up the worst of the splashes of whitewash from the floor. She decided that if no one came to see her on Sunday, she would take up the old linoleum and scrub the floor.

She went to the undraped window and looked out over the dock. It was a fine evening with a thin rind of moon gleaming softly above the river. She pushed open the dormer window. It was stiff and gave reluctantly and she got a bit of damp paint on her hand. The candle flickered in the draught. She could hear men shouting to each other in a boat in the dock. Their voices in the night made her feel lonelier than ever.

She clumped down the stairs again and lit the lamp from the candle. Then she took down a bit of comb from the mantelpiece, pulled out her hair pins and put them in her aproned lap, while she combed and rebraided her hair, two braids to the front and two to the back; the two at the back were wound into a neat bun and the two at the front were draped back under each ear and pinned to the bun, leaving the bare ears neatly circled by plaits in a fashion the young Queen Victoria had once favoured. Her grandson, King George, was on the throne and women now had their hair cut and permanently waved, but such far-out fashions had not reached women of Daisy's ilk. She put on her shawl and went up to the Ragged Bear for her usual Saturday night half pint of bitter.

The pub was busy and a frail old man in a cloth cap occupied her usual seat by the fire.

"Evenin', Mrs. Gallagher. Glass of bitter?" asked Mrs. Hanlon, as Daisy, frowning petulantly, plonked herself down in another seat. The man she sat down by was a steward on a passenger liner when in work, and he fancied himself a bit too much, according to Daisy. She said a short "Evenin'" to him and he gave her a pained smile, while he edged away from her to avoid the smell emanating from her. She sensed his distaste, and this irritated her even more.

Two acquaintances in their best black shawls were hedged in by other patrons on the far side of the room. They waved and smiled at her but there was no room for her to join them, so she shrugged hopelessly, making a wry mouth at them. To make them laugh, she raised her eyebrows comically and pointed a derisive thumb surreptitiously at the steward beside her, who had turned away from her to talk to a youth on the other side of him. The women cackled with laughter and the steward looked up suspiciously. Daisy's nose was in her glass, however, and she looked the picture of respectable innocence.

She glanced round at the groups close to her. They were mostly men absorbed in their own arguments. It was going to be a hopeless evening. She finished her drink and left.

Half an hour later, she was again swaying up and down the street which had proved so fruitful on the two previous evenings. This evening, being Saturday, there were more people going and coming from the Ball and Chain, and Daisy was glad that her dress was so sober that most passers-by would not realise what she was about. She did not want them telling the scuffer about her.

She loitered for a good three-quarters of an hour, stepping hastily into the alley when the police constable on the beat ran up the steps of the pub, presumably to check that all was well, and then crossed over to continue his orderly preambulation along the side of a warehouse. At each door he stopped to try the lock; and each time he paused Daisy wondered nervously if he would suddenly turn around and come back. She could be accused of loitering, never mind anything else. He continued straight on, however, and was soon lost in the night. She emerged thankfully from the mouth of the alley and stood quietly with hands crossed over her stomach, feeling that she must be out of her mind to have come there at all.

Two young merchant sailors came laughing out of the pub. They saw her white apron gleaming in the poor light and rolled up to her. They winked at each other and then stared at her knowingly with hard, experienced eyes. Both of them smirked.

"What you doin' out so late, Ma? Without your old man?" one of them teased, while the other broke into a guffaw.

She fluttered her long black eyelashes at them and, with hands still clasped across her stomach, swayed a little towards them and tittered, "What do you think?"

"Hm, hm, that's the way the land lies, is it?" They leered at each other, clowning to make her laugh, which she did. She put her hands on her hips so that her shawl fell open, flung back her head and gurgled appreciatively. Her huge chest looked round and pillow cosy.

"What's you name, duck?"

"Daisy."

"Ha!" The seaman who had first spoken nudged his friend.

"See, we can't have Shanghai Lil — but we got Liverpool Daisy." He almost sang the last words.

The second man chortled and asked hopefully, "Like to make a trick, Daise?"

"Cost you half a crown and you got to put it in me hand first," she told him, looking very coy.

"Aw come on, Al, it's too early," the first man protested.

"It's never too early for me. Come on, Daise. See you in a few minutes, Joe," and he whisked Daisy up the alleyway as fast as anyone of her tonnage could be whisked.

She was leaning against the corner of the alleyway, breathless after the energetic attentions of Joe and Al, when an indignant female voice assailed her ears.

"What you doing on my beat? You get outter here!"

Daisy gulped, and turned to face a woman in a veiled hat, a pale blue coat and high-heeled shoes. A pair of malevolent eyes glared at her from behind the veiling.

Daisy slowly straightened herself and pulled her shawl around her. "What yer mean? Your beat?"

"You know what I mean," the voice was scornful. "I work

this bit. You get to hell outter here."

Daisy looked the woman up and down. Her breath had returned to her and she stuck out her chest like a courting frog and thrust her chin forward aggressively. "You mind what you're saying," she ordered in a growl. "You mind your own business and get away home!"

"I am minding my own business — and you'd better get home afore I tell Jim about you."

"Go on with yez," snarled Daisy. "I'm not doing you any harm — or your Jim, whoever he might be."

The other woman snorted. "I been here for months. This is my beat, do y'hear, and I'm not standing for anyone else." The voice rose. "If you don't beat it quick, I'll fetch Jim." She pushed her face close to Daisy's and her voice descended menacingly. "You don't want your face slashed, do you, luv?"

"Pah!" Daisy almost spat. "You get going afore I call t' scuffer."

"Cops!" the woman sneered and tossed her head. "Since when have cops been on our side, ducks? You make me laugh." And she screeched with high-pitched laughter.

"Having trouble, Maisie?" inquired a deceptively quiet male voice.

The laughter stopped abruptly. Maisie turned to the new arrival and said in ingratiating tones, sniffing as if close to tears, "Jim, I'm glad you come. This bloody biddie took a couple of men from under me very nose, she did."

The man was a foot shorter than Daisy and seemed curiously anonymous beneath a wide-brimmed trilby hat. He turned towards Daisy who would have bolted, had she not been hemmed in by the wall behind her and Maisie in front.

Jim's voice was low and even, though very threatening. "Get out!"

This order made Daisy angry enough to forget her fears.

"Nobody's going to tell me to get out, you little runt! This is a public street. *You* get out before I clout you into next week!"

She shook a hefty fist under the brim of his hat.

He hastily stepped back a pace and slipped his hand into his pocket. Daisy saw the movement.

"And you keep that knife in your pocket, you bleeder, or I'll start screaming right now. T' scuffer'll come. I saw him not more'n a minute back."

But Jim recovered his aplomb, though he did not take his hand out of his pocket. "And where will that get you? Up before the Old Man, I can tell you. I'll see to that, you dirty git."

Daisy's temper was up now. Slowly swinging her arms she advanced towards the pimp. He backed. "You shut your bleeding gob," she hissed at him. "I'll larn yer to interfere with a respectable woman, I will. I'll larn yer."

Maisie quickly got out of the way. She paid half her earnings to Jim. He had set her up. Let him take the punishment.

Jim felt as if he had taken on an elephant, an elephant which was slowly but firmly pushing him towards the revealing lights of the pub. The more he could see of Daisy the more he wished himself several streets away, where his other girl worked in comparative peace. He was going to have to really use his knife or lose his credibility with Maisie.

He whipped the knife out. Daisy heard the blade snick open. With all her strength she kicked out and with a howl of pain he doubled up and fell to the pavement. She brought her boot down heavily on his right wrist.

"Leggo," she roared. "Leggo o' that knife — or I'll jump on yer."

The weight on his wrist was agonising. He scrabbled frantically at her ankles with his left hand The stench from her was overwhelming. He brought his feet up suddenly and tried to kick her in her stomach. He was not too well balanced on his shoulders and she knocked him forcibly to one side. This wrenched the pinned-down wrist and made him moan. She ground harder on it with her foot and he screamed.

The door of the pub swung open, as a customer who had

heard the scream looked out.

"You bloody bastard!" yelled Daisy, stamping harder on the wrist. "I'm going to jump on you."

He saw her tense herself and with a violent effort he again rolled himself up on his shoulders and tried to kick her, but his feet got entangled with her skirt and he fought to free them, while she hit out at his legs with her hands.

A man came running down the steps of the pub.

"Wot you doing to our Daisy?" he shouted. Another man, laughing, followed him down the steps. They were both in a merry state of drunkenness, but still steady on their feet.

Poised to jump, Daisy was frozen into immobility at the sound of her name. She looked, to the approaching men, like a triumphant prize-fighter standing over his fallen opponent. Jim tried again to push her boot off his wrist with his left hand. She automatically renewed the pressure and he yelped and lay still, since the sound of pounding feet indicated some kind of help was coming.

Maisie fled.

"Wot's up, Daise?" asked one of the seamen who had enjoyed her favours only a short time earlier. "Yeah, Daisy, wot's to do?" inquired the other breathlessly. Several patrons from the pub crowded on to the steps to watch.

Daisy recognised her customers with great relief. "This bleeder tried to knife me," she told them, her voice shrill and suddenly shaky. "See, there's his knife."

Al picked up the switchblade.

"You dirty son of a dirty noseless mother!" He peered down at Jim, still pinned by Daisy's iron foot. "It'd serve you right if I carved her name on your face, you bloody git."

Jim whimpered. "I didn't mean nothing. She was upsetting my girl."

"Bloody pimp," added Bert. "What *shall* we do to him, Al?" He viewed Jim's ashen face with such joyful anticipation of the vengeance they could wreak that Jim nearly passed out.

Daisy was suddenly afraid that murder might ensue. She was
intensely grateful to Bert and Al and was, at the same time,
astonished at their coming to her aid. Maybe I'm better than I
know, she told herself. Aloud, she said, as she slowly removed
her foot from Jim's wrist. "Let him go, lads. If he knows you're
around he isn't going to bother me any more."

The pimp scrambled to his feet, holding the injured member
close to his chest to ease the pain. The two seamen were longing
for a good fight. They were enjoying themselves hugely in the
role of heroes, and they hunched their shoulders and swung
their arms as they crowded in on the man.

"Sure we're going to be around," Al grunted. His fist shot
forward and he nearly lifted Jim off his feet with the force of the
punch on the side of the jaw. Jim staggered, turned to run and
received a kick in the rear from the pointed toe of Al's best shoe.
He cried out, and ran zigzagging along the gutter into the
darkness at the bottom of the street.

Al brushed imaginary dust off the sleeves of his jacket. "He'll
not bother you again, Daise, will 'e, Bert?"

"Not he," Bert assured her. He looked at her face which had
blenched. "Come on and have a drink, luv."

Daise accepted the invitation in a wavery voice.

The customers returned to their seats, talking loudly about
how the streets were no longer safe for respectable folks, and
Daise and her two friends followed them in.

The waiter had watched the encounter from the pub window
and had told the landlord.

The landlord himself brought Bert's order. He looked Daisy
over and decided there was no accounting for taste. As he put a
tot of rum in front of her, he whispered, "If you solicit in here,
I'll call a cop straight off, d'yer understand? This is a respectable house."

Daisy folded her hands neatly across her stomach and looked
the landlord straight in the eye. "And what might you mean by
that?" she inquired and pursed her lips till she looked like a

model of injured virtue.

Though the landlord looked calmly back at her, as he put a clean ash tray in front of her and removed one overflowing with cigarette butts, he doubted suddenly the accuracy of his waiter's assumption about Daisy. However, he nodded his head up and down like a toy Buddha Daisy had once seen in Bunney's gift shop. "You know what I mean," he said firmly, and moved quietly away.

The two seamen had downed their shots of rum and were following them with glasses of stout as chasers, and they asked above their foaming glasses, "What did he say?"

Daisy scowled, but shrugged her shoulders. "It were nothin'".

She took a big sip of rum and grinned suddenly at her rescuers, her eyes dancing with malicious glee. "It was proper nice of you boys to come. You give him a proper doing over."

Bert dug her in the ribs with his elbow. "Go on, now. Got to look after our Liverpool Daisy. We'll need you again." He chortled as he looked knowingly at Al, and Al lifted his glass to Daisy.

The rum was warm, the company comforting and Daisy was filled with a surge of happiness. She shoved each man in turn with a plump shoulder.

"Go on with you, you impudent buggers," she said lovingly.

THIRTEEN

Bert and Al returned to their boat on Monday morning, back to the steady rhythm of greasing engines and trimming lamps. They sailed on the morning tide, and while they worked they told the story of their rescue of Liverpool Daisy. It lost nothing in the telling; and when they arrived at Lagos they met, apart from strangers, other Merseyside men; and in humid wharfside bars the tale was told all over again. The history of this female elephant, as they described her, made men laugh; and when they docked in Liverpool they remembered it and inquired for Liverpool Daisy. Soon everybody in the Legs o' Man and the other pubs near Lime Street knew where Liverpool Daisy was to be found.

Unaware of this free publicity, Daisy went one wet Sunday to Mass with Nellie, in the black neo-Gothic church they had both attended since childhood. Meg and Agnes were both there. Agnes spoke to Daisy, and Meg killed her with a look, as Daisy remarked to Nellie afterwards.

Daisy enjoyed a visit from Maureen Mary that Sunday afternoon; and little Bridie enjoyed the dried remains of the cake bought for her great-grandmother's funeral. She was a whey-faced little girl, with straggling blonde hair held off her face by a blue hair slide set with rhinestones, a birthday present from Daisy. While Daisy held her lovingly in her lap, she chewed the stone-hard currants in the cake very carefully, to avoid the caries with which her teeth already abounded.

Maureen watched her child's obvious pleasure at the fuss her

grandmother made of her, and worried that she would surely
pick up vermin from Daisy. She knew, however, that no amount
of nagging would make Daisy concerned about such minor
details as bugs and lice. Maureen Mary had been so impressed
by her late employer's rigid standards of cleanliness that her
own home was spotless; and yet, she felt as she looked around
it, the rumpled, smelly familiarity of her childhood home was far
more comforting to her than the carbolic sterility of her own
house. Anyway, cleanliness cost a lot of money, and she knew
that her father never left much of an allotment to his wife. He
liked to come home at the end of a voyage with his money in his
own pocket, to treat family and friends to drinks and extra food
before he vanished off again. A fat lot he had ever cared about
her mother's struggle to keep her children fed. Freddie might be
pernickety, but Bridie and she were well fed and clothed, she
thought. Her father had been away so long this time that she
wondered if he would ever get back to Liverpool — you never
knew with tramp steamers.

After tea they went to inspect the newly decorated bedroom.

"Eee, it's awful quiet now your Nan's gone," lamented Daisy.
"I wish they'd let our Lizzie or our Jamie out — real hard it is
for him. And me not able to afford to visit either of them and
all."

"What about having a boarder in here?" suggested
Maureen Mary. "It'd be company. Some young girl by herself,
like?"

Daisy looked down at the top of Bridie's shining head cradled
against her chest, and sighed. While she considered Maureen
Mary's suggestion, she got up and gently set the little girl down
in her place on the easy chair. The rain had stopped but the day
was overcast and the room was full of shadows. She lit the oil
lamp and the room immediately looked cosier. Then she took
down the two china dogs from the mantelpiece and gave them to
Bridie to play with. This was one of the treats of visiting
grandma, and Bridie slipped joyfully down on to the hearth rug

with them. Daisy smiled down at her; however hard-pressed, she had never pawned the china dogs since Bridie had taken a fancy to them.

"Aye, it's not a bad idea, that," she said heavily, in response to Maureen Mary's suggestion.

"You could put a notice in Mrs. Donnelly's shop window — it's twopence for a week, if I remember right — and you can have as many words as you like."

Daisy nodded, and bent forward to turn little Bridie's coat which had been hung over the oven door to dry. Maureen Mary's coat hung steaming from the back of a straight chair crowded with them near the fire. Winter was setting in, thought Daisy, and in the rain she would not be able to carry on her new-found lucrative trade. "I got a new blanket from the Welfare that I could put on the bed," she said finally. "If I could get a cheque from the club man I could buy some sheets and things. Last time I arst they wouldn't give me, 'cos I don't always have the money ready every week when the club man come to collect. Worse'n the rent collector, they are." She sniffed. "Got to pay it off every week, or you don't get another, he tells me."

The next day, the kettle was refilled and boiled most of the day, while Daisy scraped and cleaned the bedroom floor, after she had heaved out the rotten linoleum and stowed it in a corner of the yard.

Afterwards, she lay on her bed in the landing bedroom. Her mouth was sore, so she took her teeth out and laid them on the bed beside her, where they grinned at her in the half-light.

She thought wistfully how nice it would be to have a proper bed for herself, with blankets and sheets and a bedspread. Next time, maybe. This time she had to give the best bed to a lodger — at least for the winter.

FOURTEEN

The rain came down intermittently for most of the following week and put a temporary end to Daisy's street-walking. She managed to obtain a cheque from the finance company, and she bought a pair of sheets, two pillowcases, a small blanket and a cotton bedspread. Maureen Mary contributed a pair of curtains for the bedroom from her own house. She also helped her mother to stain and varnish the oak floor, while Bridie played with Moggie and the china dogs. There was a little varnish left over, so they did the chest of drawers as well.

Mrs. Donnelly put the advertisement, written on an envelope, in the window, amongst a dog-eared collection offering old furniture for sale, the services of Bill Donohue, painter, and Mary Devlin, sitter, kittens to give away and rooms for rent.

There was no response. Nobody came to see the room, except Nellie and Mary, Meg's daughter, who arrived together. Mary had retreated to the safety of her Aunty Daisy's house while a family row raged in her own home. Both visitors declared the room lovely, nicer than a hotel. Mary thought of the misery she suffered from sharing a bed with two younger brothers and a restless sister.

"I wish I could live with you, Antie Daise," she said wistfully.

"Yer Ma'd never let you," replied Daisy frankly, as she stroked her niece's lank brown hair. "There'll be a bit more room in your house when your Uncle Albert gets married — and maybe your Emily and her husband'll get a council house and move out soon."

111

"Yes," Mary agreed, and leaned lovingly against her aunt's comforting bulk.

"You're really lucky to have such a big house all to yourself," remarked Nellie, "A bedroom, a landing bedroom and all."

"Oh, aye, But this house's been crowded in its time. Remember when you and George was still here with your first two babies? God rest their little souls. There was me other older brother and Meg and Agnes and me — and me father and me Mam — and me father's sister what was single and had a flower basket outside of Central Station of a Saturday. Then Meg married and went to old Fogarty's house, and I married Mike and we had Maureen Mary here."

Nellie nodded her curly head over her tea mug. "Aye. It was fun sometimes. But your poor Mam thought she would go daft."

Daisy chuckled. "We had some good times and some good laughs, for all that." She leaned over, teapot in hand to fill up Nellie's mug, and then continued, "I'm going to get a lodger — to help me through the winter. Mike's allotment wouldn't keep a cat in fish — I'm hoping to find somebody who's workin'."

"Working?" inquired Nelly scornfully.

Daisy grinned. "There's still a few in work, though you might not think it. Those working on the big tunnel under the river is working."

Nellie shrugged. "Wish you luck."

In the evening the rain finally drifted out to sea and the moon rose clear and serene. Daisy thankfully flung her shawl over her shoulders and went up to the Ragged Bear for her Saturday half pint.

She got her usual seat on the bench by the fire, and spent a happy hour with two cronies from a few streets away, hearing all the latest tittle-tattle of births and deaths, all of which appeared to have been gruesome in the extreme.

She managed to make the half pint last until closing time at ten o'clock; then, after standing talking under the lamp post at the corner for a few more minutes, she made her way leisurely down to the river. There was a hint of frost in the air, and the nostrils of her strong straight nose dilated as she enjoyed the freshness of the breeze. She walked for a little while along silent Grafton Street, savouring the air. On her return, she paused to lean against the wall, to look out over the dock to the placid river, where the lights of Birkenhead and Rock Ferry twinkled back at her. Cigarette smoke had wafted round her for several minutes before she realised that a solitary man a few feet away was similarly engaged.

Normally, she would have quickly recrossed the road to avoid him — that's what a woman who kept herself to herself would have done, she told herself. But instead, she said cheerfully to him, "Nice night."

"It is," replied an Irish voice, with a brogue so thick that Daisy ventured to inquire if he was newly come from Dublin.

"Aye."

"Looking for work?"

"No. Me brother got me a job down there." He pointed to the dock below them. "Watchman."

Daisy clucked. If her brother, George, had had his wits about him he might have got that job. Then dear Nellie might have had the money for a doctor.

The stranger moved a little closer during her silence. She could see the friendly glow of his cigarette, as he flicked the ash over the wall.

"You're lucky," she said with a friendly grin.

He chuckled. "Luck of the Irish!"

A ship's bell rang the half-hour. The man heaved himself straight. He was a tall, thin man, with long, lanky arms. In the gloom, under a flat cap, she could just make out the handsome, though saturnine, face of a man in his early thirties.

"That must be ten-thirty," he remarked, in reference to the bell. "Don't have to be there till midnight."

A silence fell between them and they contemplated the river, until Daisy said cautiously, "That's a long wait."

"It is indeed."

Daisy sighed. "I must get home."

She moved from the wall, and the stranger turned with her towards the entry to the Herculaneum Dock. "You live round here?" he inquired.

"Aye, up past the Hercy."

They paced along together, Daisy with her arms folded under her shawl, he smoking his cigarette. She could feel herself beginning to shiver with a kind of joyful anticipation which by her standards no decent woman should feel.

"Your old man will be wonderin' where you got to?" ventured the watchman.

Daisy laughed. "Not he. He's been at sea for months." She looked slyly at her companion from out of the corners of her eyes. "I ain't got nobody at home at present." She sighed. "It's proper lonely o' nights."

The man agreed that it was proper lonely, and proceeded to make himself agreeable to the sufferer.

Daisy suddenly realised that she had a use for the newly decorated bedroom.

FIFTEEN

Daisy leaned over a faded collection of packets of biscuits, bottles of liniment and dusty imitation chocolate bars in order to retrieve her advertisement from Mrs. Donnelly's window. She screwed up the little envelope and threw it into the street.

"You got a lodger already?" inquired Mrs. Donnelly, as she put a side of bacon through the slicer. The slicer whirred with an ominous sibilance as if to warn of its sharpness.

"Yes," lied Daisy glibly. A lodger would explain away a man entering her house; and her new-found acquaintance had promised to come again. Three shillings from him was nestling comfortably in her apron pocket at that moment.

"Who yer got?"

You nosy so-and-so, thought Daisy. Aloud, she said, "He told me he's a night watchman at the Hercy. He's a quiet type — he'll be no trouble."

"Humph," grunted Mrs. Donnelly. "Will yer husband mind?"

"I haven't asked him," replied Daisy tartly. "I'll thank you for a pound of that bacon, Mrs. Donnelly."

Mrs. Donnelly slapped a handful of bacon on the scale. The indicator danced away below the pound sign. Daisy pointed accusingly at it. "Put it on slow," she ordered. "That's no pound."

With tight lips, Mrs. Donnelly put a finger on the scale to steady it, let it come to rest and then added another couple of rashers. "I can't be right all the time," she argued.

"You're always on the right side of right — your side," snarled Daisy.

115

Mrs. Donnelly rolled the bacon into a piece of paper and slammed it on the worn counter. Daisy scooped it up.

"That'll be tenpence." Mrs. Donnelly clenched her teeth together. She would not allow herself to be drawn into another fight with Daisy. She was still smarting over her ruined hat, and she shuddered when she considered what damage a rampaging Daisy might wreak in her store.

To her surprise, Daisy did not ask for the tenpence to be put on the slate at the back of the counter, where customers indebtedness was recorded for all to see. She produced the money.

Mrs. Donnelly took the coins and put them into the wooden till. She was still staring at the open till drawer when Daisy wheeled round and marched out.

"Nosy bugger," muttered Daisy.

Daisy fell into a routine which was comfortable to her. On fine nights she worked the small street behind London Road. When the weather threatened rain or frost, she would meander along Grafton Street and occasionally pick up a man there. Her house being the only one which faced the river gave her a high degree of privacy; and women rarely ventured along the dock road at night, not because it was dangerous but because there was nothing to attract them to it; so all she had to do was to be careful not to approach a local man. Sometimes she did well, sometimes she was out of luck, as she put it.

Money which she dared not spend locally began to accumulate in an old tobacco tin. She tucked the tin away at the back of the shelf in the cupboard in the front bedroom and covered it with two extra petticoats she had bought herself in the town. Nobody sees petticoats, she had told herself, as she bought them.

Christmas Eve was a fine night and London Road was thronged with eager last-minute shoppers, despite the amount of unemployment in the city. The pub near Daisy's beat was very busy with rubicund men and pale, shadowy women standing glass in hand even in the parlour.

Daisy had just come to the conclusion that everyone was too busy with family or friends to bother with a woman, when she was accosted by a small, shabby man in a bowler hat. They retired up the narrow alleyway.

Because Daisy was so plump and the man was so small in stature, matters did not proceed very satisfactorily and he demanded his money back.

"Go on with yez," retorted Daisy roundly. "You've had your bit of fun. Now piss off." She glowered at him as she buttoned her blouse.

"You give me that money back or I'll call the cops, you thieving bitch." He leaned towards her and seizing the neckline of her blouse ripped it open.

"Gerroff. What do you think you're doin'?" demanded Daisy furiously, hastily clasping her blouse together with one hand while she gave him a sharp push with the other.

He was surprisingly strong for his size and came back at her, one fist raised. "Give me me money," he snarled. He brought his fist heavily down on her half bare breast. She felt a sharp prick and looked down in sudden terror. Blood was welling up from a small wound.

She went white with fear and backed to the wall; the alley was so narrow that it offered her little room for manoeuvre.

"Want it in yer face?" He raised his hand again. There was a glint of steel in the faint light.

Her heart beat violently as she stared at him. Her panic was so great that she could not make herself either answer him or produce the money. If he wounded her, she had no one to turn to and if he murdered her, who would know or care?

"Well?" he asked, flourishing the weapon.

Her bleeding chest rose and fell with the big breaths she took as she continued to goggle at him.

She began to whine. "You had some fun. I didn't mean no harm. What you so fussy about?" With every show of reluctance, she felt around in the deep pocket she had made in her black skirt to hold her money.

The hand holding the razor seemed to relax a little, and, as a sense of outrage took over from panic, she took her time looking for his half-a-crown.

"Come on!" The blade moved closer despite the slight relaxation of his hand.

"I'm getting it! I'm getting it," she said testily. She sniffed, and drew out the coin.

Holding it up between forefinger and thumb, she gritted her teeth and sidled up close to him until the blade nearly touched her. She put her free arm round him and slid her hand suggestively down his back. The blouse released from her hold fell open. "Like to try again?"

"No, you filthy git." He snatched the coin from her fingers.

She backed away from him towards the further end of the alley, clutching her shawl over her nakedness. He laughed at her as he pocketed her money. "That'll teach you," he sneered.

"Ya, you gutter scum," she jeered back.

She whipped around and ran up the alley to where it joined a cross entry. In a few seconds she was panting along Lime Street, cursing under her breath.

She flung into her house as if the whole of the Liverpool Police Force was after her. She shot the bolt on the front door—it was stiff from infrequent use—and leaned against the inside, as if she had run all the way home instead of having sat on a tram for twenty minutes.

She felt her way to the table, found her matches and lit the lamp. Then, still holding her shawl round her she climbed the stairs to the bedroom, it being the most secret place she could think of. She put the lamp down on the brightly varnished chest of drawers and went over to the window and hastily flicked the curtains shut.

She sat down on the bed feeling overwhelmed with weakness. The bed creaked complainingly. Very slowly she let her shawl slip off her and looked down at the cut on her breast. Blood had trickled down to the waistband of her skirt and then dried, though the cut itself was still damp. She dabbed fearfully at the wound with her torn blouse, but it was no longer oozing and she let out a sigh of relief. Then she let drop from her other hand the wallet she had been clutching all the way home.

She was nearly as scared at the sight of the wallet as she had been of the cut on her chest. Pinching from Woollies or Lewis's was one thing; stealing from a man who might come back for revenge was another. And yet the bugger had asked for it, she told herself, and she had been smart enough to get it out of his hip pocket without his realising it had gone. With a bit of Irish luck he might not discover its loss for a little while, and then he could not be sure where he lost it.

It was an old, oil-stained pocket book, covered with a worn design of camels and pyramids. She opened it cautiously and with trembling fingers drew out its contents. She counted out seventeen pound notes and three ten shilling ones. She gazed in amazement at the pile of money. He must have just been paid off, she assumed. She looked through the papers it also contained. There was an identity card made out in the name of Thomas Ward by a shipping company in Liberia, a receipt or two, a snap of a group of negroes and another of a fat woman sitting in a deck chair on a beach.

The trembling of her hands spread to the rest of her body and she sat shivering helplessly for a few minutes. She had been bent on revenge and now she wondered fearfully what would happen to her if she were caught with the wallet.

Still shivering, she got up and went to the cupboard and took down the tobacco tin from under her petticoats. It was heavy with about five pounds' worth of silver in it. She added the notes to it.

"Serve the bastard right," she said savagely, though there was a tremor of misgiving in her voice.

She picked up the lamp to go downstairs to the kitchen to

bathe her wound. She wondered if she should go to a doctor; the scratch was deep and might be infected by the knife.

"And he'll want to know how you came by a knife wound," she warned herself, and then shrugged. "Och, it'll heal itself, it will."

The word 'doctor' reminded her of Nellie and how sick she was. Poor Nellie, she needed a doctor all right.

If you can afford a doctor for yourself, you dumb cluck, you can afford one for Nellie, her conscience reminded her.

She stood transfixed, lamp in hand. What a fool she had been. She would pay for Nellie to see a doctor, maybe even one of those in Rodney Street, specialists they were called. "Oh, Nellie, luv," she cried out joyously. "We'll have you better, we will."

She'll ask where you got the money from.

Daisy grinned. "I'll tell her Mike sent it."

There was a knock on the front door and she jumped in guilty fright.

"Are ye there, Daise?" her sister, Agnes, called. "Coom on, lemme in. It's bloody cold out here."

"Holy Mary!" Daisy swore. "Coming," she shouted.

She looked hastily round the room and then quickly put down the lamp and stuffed the wallet under the bed mattress.

SIXTEEN

"What you want to lock up for?" asked Agnes petulantly, as she pushed through the door the moment it was unbolted. "I'm fair clemmed." She shook out her shawl like a flapping raven and blinked in the lamp light. Then as her eyes became accustomed to its radiance and Daisy moved to one side to let her enter, she asked, "And what's up? Your blouse is torn and you're all bloody." Her protruding blue eyes popped wide, "And you're as white as a sheet."

"Eee, I-er-um," faltered Daisy, making a quick grab at her torn blouse to cover herself. She *must* give some explanation.

"I was just down the yard a few minutes back," she improvised hastily. "I caught me blouse on the latch of the privy and it tore." She gained a little confidence, and went on, "It caught me, too — it hurt proper sharp for a moment — that's what took me colour out. I was upstairs when you come, looking for something else to put on."

Agnes was shivering with cold and made impolite haste towards the fire, without commiserating with her sister. Cuts and bangs were nothing — they healed or they went septic and had to be poulticed with hot water till they were clean. She seized the poker and quickly broke up the damp slack with which Daisy had banked the fire before going out. "Are you short of coal that you bank up your fire so early?"

"Not specially," said Daisy. "I let it go out at night like always. But I went out a bit earlier to buy a Christmas present for your Marty, and I thought it could stay banked till morning." She sighed. What was one more lie on top of so many? "I've got an old blouse upstairs — I'll just put it on. Be back in a seccie."

Agnes rubbed her hands over the flames. "I'll put on the kettle," she offered hopefully.

"You do that," agreed Daisy, and escaped upstairs. She looked again at the cut but it seemed to be drying, so she put an aged blouse on over it.

She looked anxiously at the bed, and cursed that she had not been able to burn the wallet before Agnes came. It would have to wait now until she went.

When she came downstairs again the fire was blazing cheerfully and the kettle was singing on it.

"You oughtta write to Mike and make him send you some money," advised Agnes, as she viewed the washed-out, threadbare blouse Daisy was wearing. "He must have lots in his pocket by now." There was a hint of jealousy in her tone — other than Freddie, who did not count, Mike was the only man in the whole family who was in work. "Your allotment is proper mean, I think."

Daisy opened her mouth to retort that asking Mike for money was like asking one of Lewis's for it, but she hastily swallowed this reference to a dummy in Lewis's store window. Agnes, bless her, had confirmed her own idea of a perfect explanation for the presence of any small extras that she had bought with her ill-gotten gains. Mike had sent her some money — real generous, he was.

She beamed with the relief she felt. "I already done that. I'm hoping he'll reply soon."

"You don't have to spend money on our Marty," Agnes reproved her absently, in reference to the present Daisy said she had bought.

"Och, it's not much," Daisy replied, hoping that Agnes would not demand to see the present.

But Agnes's attention had wandered, as she looked round the

room over the rim of her tea mug. "You been doing some work here?"

Daisy had indeed been doing some work. With all the time in the world and no one to gossip to unless she walked at least as far as the Ragged Bear, she had slowly been cleaning up the long neglected house. To Mrs. Donnelly's surprise, she had purchased some Brasso.

"To clean t' fender," Daisy had explained sullenly.

Agnes looked down at the fender on which her feet rested, and remarked admiringly, "Whole room looks lovely."

Daisy heaved another of her long sighs. "Aye, I'd no time with our Mam in bed." She could not say that the saturnine watchman who had been her first customer in the house had remarked that it looked like a pig sty. They had joked about it but she had taken the remark to heart. She had no intention of bringing very many clients to the house — just a few to assuage that long, lonely hour before she went to bed — because, as she explained to Moggie, some interfering biddie will notice them if I do. She never considered that Mike might return home — that was something which might happen in the distant future — too far ahead to even be thought about.

"Are you going to Maureen Mary's for Christmas dinner — after Mass?" asked Agnes.

"Are you kidding? Only been to her house once and that was when I heard she was expecting Bridie, and I went and told her I didn't like her marrying a Prottie; but she should still come and see me. She never even asked me in — but I could see she had a proper nice home."

"She got real stuck up working in Lyon's."

Daisy grimaced. "Well, I know where I'm not welcome." She glowered resentfully, and then added, "They could be living with me, they could! It hurts, it really does."

"I'm sure," agreed Agnes. Then she giggled. "That Freddie! He makes me laugh."

"Aye, he's a proper panse. But he knows a lot — and he

treats me like a lady when he comes."

Agnes forebore from reminding her sister again that he never asked her to his home, even at Christmas. She told herself she was not a troublemaker like Meg.

"Is Lizzie Ann being let out for Christmas?"

Daisy's voice was despondent as she answered. "No. I posted a present to Jamie — don't know whether the bastards'll let him have it — and some scent to Lizzie Ann. I wish I could go and see them, but it's an awful long way and it costs a lot."

Agnes nodded her flaxen head.

"Maureen Mary'll come on Christmas afternoon. She allus brings a present."

"You come along and have dinner with us," ordered Agnes. "I raised a pair of hens along with our Joe's fighting cocks. Got some eggs out of them first and now they're hanging in the cellar. Feathered they are and all ready to go into the oven first thing tomorrow."

"Ta, ever so. I'll come. You was lucky not to have them stop you having them hens — and the cocks. Mary Ellen up the road — she tried it and her neighbours complained, bloody canting Presbyterians; they said they smelled."

Agnes laughed. "I got a couple of rabbits, too, ready for New Year's. Joe made a hutch for them out of a butter box."

For some weeks, Daisy had been collecting small gifts for her nephews and nieces, for her children and for dear little Bridie. They were all stacked together in a paper carrier bag in a corner of the living-room. She promised herself that, after dinner with Agnes she would walk round the various homes of the family and distribute her presents. She would even go to Meg's house, though Meg had continued to ignore her whenever they met.

She had a rewarding Christmas Day, putting little presents into small, grubby fists. All the parents except Meg, remarked upon her generosity and expressed the hope that she had not left herself short. She was home in time for tea with Maureen Mary and Bridie, and in the late evening she finished up at George and

Nellie's house. She presented Nellie with three boxes of the best snuff. Nellie put her arms round her friend and kissed her ecstatically. Her thin body felt hot to Daisy and her eyes glistened with fever.

"I don't know how you do it," Nellie half wept. "You manage your money so much better than I do."

George gruffly thanked Daisy for the tobacco she had brought him and gratefully lit up his blackened pipe which had perforce been empty for several days while his wife scrimped to give their last surviving child, Joey, "a bit o' Christmas". She had knitted the skimpy lad a pullover out of old wool retrieved from a garment she had picked up for a penny in a rummage sale, and he was wearing it with great delight. He showed it off with pride to his admiring Auntie Daisy. Nellie had also made a large toffee apple for him; the remains of it were plastered like a moustache along his upper lip. His father had over the previous month carved him a wooden horse and cart from a piece of driftwood and this also had to be shown to Daisy. The fine detail of the horse showed how well George knew the animals with which he had spent his life, until the firm for which he had worked had gone bankrupt.

When Daisy presented the boy with six tin soldiers wrapped in old tissue paper his day was complete.

"Thanks, Anty Daise," he breathed through a stuffed-up nose, and skipped off to show the present to his friends in the street. The adults sat silently listening for a minute to the clatter of his boots and his shouts to the other boys.

"I don't know how you managed to get them," said George with reference to the tin soldiers. He looked suspiciously at Daisy. "Our Nellie can't even feed us properly." He scowled at his wife.

Daisy did not want to point out that he spent too much of their Public Assistance allowance on beer and horses. It was not nice to start a fight at Christmas. Yet she saw the need to rescue Nellie from bitter recriminations breaking out the moment she left the house, so she lied gaily to help her friend.

"Nan and me were in old Donnelly's Christmas tontine before she died, so I had quite a bit to draw — and then I got a club cheque not long back for some bedding, and I used some of that for Christmas things."

"Humph," grunted George. "The tontine payments must have strapped yez?"

"Well, I written to Mike to ask for some money to help out," replied Daisy firmly. She stuck her chin up in the air as if defying him to ask any further questions. "Mike must have lots in his pocket by now."

George's response was acidulous.

"Money burns holes in Mike's pockets faster'n anybody I know."

Daisy's response was prompt. "Don't you criticise Mike. I know some others what wouldn't bear looking at." Then she realised that this would be the beginning of a quarrel; and Nellie was already looking alarmed. "Och, you're right," she said placatingly. "He does spend a lot at times. But there's no harm in asking him for some."

George cleared his throat and spat into the fire.

She glanced at her brother, and then went on cheerfully, "He'll send this time for sure."

SEVENTEEN

January brought another post card from Mike. It was pushed under the door by the postman, picture side up, and Daisy picked it up and looked at the highly coloured print of the port of Accra.

"He must have bought a dozen all the same," she thought as she stuck it up on the mantelpiece, along with two other identical cards received the previous year. She did not bother to turn it over to read it. Mike never said anything, except, "Doing fine."

She went out to collect her allotment from the shipping office.

On her return, she dropped off the tram outside the soot-blackened row house where Nellie and George rented the back room and a scullery. The front door led into a room occupied by a large family, so Daisy went down the back entry and came in through the tiny, walled back yard. She slammed the wooden door behind her and marched past a dustbin, out of which a cat scrambled hastily, and past the privy which was doorless and stank.

A dog within the house barked a warning.

She opened the door to the tiled scullery. It was empty except for an old terrier gnawing at a bone. He knew her and his tail flapped lazily in welcome, though he did not get up.

A dirty saucepan and the remains of a loaf of bread lay on a wooden table. Otherwise the room was as bleak as her own back kitchen.

"Hey, Nellie!" she shouted.

"I'm in here. Come in," responded a muffled voice from the other room.

Daisy opened the inner door into what had once been the kitchen of the house. Now it was home to Nellie.

The afternoon light filtered through a torn lace curtain which masked a tall, narrow window where cardboard inadequately covered a broken windowpane. In the large, iron fireplace a few cinders gleamed. On the far side another door led to the front part of the house. Daisy knew that the door was locked and that the key had been thrown away, to discourage a procession of people going through from the rest of the house to use the privy in the back yard; the tenants fumed and complained and walked down the street and up the alley to get to the lavatory. The atmosphere of the room was foetid despite the draught from the broken window. A double bed reached from the wall to the fireplace, and in the middle of the bed Daisy could see the small curled up figure of Nellie.

In the poor light Nellie seemed no bigger than a ten-year-old girl, and her black shawl covered her completely.

"That you, Daise?" she whispered, without bothering to lift her head.

Daisy laughed. "No, it's me ghost," she replied cheerily. She crossed to the bed and looked down at the tiny form on it. The laughter went out of her voice and she asked apprehensively, "What's up? You ill?"

Nellie slowly turned her head and opened her eyes. She made an effort to smile.

"'Allo, la. Sit down." A hand that was practically all bone patted the bed beside her.

Daisy sat down, and the sudden advent of her weight caused the bed to bounce. Nellie started to cough, and Daisy viewed her with alarm as the spasm continued.

"I got to spit," Nellie announced suddenly between spasms. Daisy got up hastily and assisted her friend off the bed. She spat into the fire but partially missed and, even in the poor light, a long streak of blood was clearly visible across the hearth. The spittle on Nellie's chin was also streaked.

"Mother of God!" Daisy exclaimed in horror.

Very gently she helped the suffering woman on to the bed, the coughing having eased for a moment. With tender hands she wrapped the shawl again round Nellie.

"Nellie, you're proper sick. You got to see a doctor. I got some money from Mike and I can pay." This latter remark was literally true since she had Mike's allotment in her pocket.

She leaned over Nellie and gently patted her shoulder. "But never you fret. I'm going to ask t' quack to come to you."

Nellie gasped for breath and made weak negative gestures with her hands. "No — oh, no, Daise! He'll put me into the infirmary and I'll die. And what would happen to iddy Joey — and our George." She clutched at her friend's arm as if to save herself from falling into a crevasse. "I couldn't bear it, Daise, I couldn't!"

Daisy's face was white, the mottles from fire burns on her cheeks standing out like a design for lace. "Aye, Nellie, luv, we got to do something. You can't go on like this." She knelt down by the bed and put her arm comfortingly over Nellie's shoulders. "You're spitting blood and you can't go on doing that."

Nellie took a labouring breath. "Been spitting for ages."

"Jaysus! Look, I'm going to get t' doctor. Lots of people with T.B. don't go into hospital. I know our Tommy did for a while — but I had him home most of the time."

A slow tear fell from Nellie's tightly clenched eyes on to the coverless pillow, which had several ominous dark stains on it. "Yes, he died at home."

The words were like an arrow shot into Daisy. The pain of the inference was so terrible she did not know how to bear it. She gasped for breath, while she tried to gather up her courage. Then she said, "Come on, now, Nell. You're not going to die — not if we get a doctor quick."

Nellie smiled but it was not a cheerful smile, rather it conveyed that she knew secrets hidden from Daisy, far away, unearthly secrets.

Daisy felt as cornered as she had done when she was threatened with a knife in the narrow alleyway she now knew so well. "Aye, Nell, come on," she rallied the other woman. "I'll get that doctor from Park Road to come down — he's proper nice, real kind, He'll know what to do."

"No, Daise!" The sick woman forced herself to raise herself on her elbow.

"Now, look here, Nell." Daisy's expression was grim. "I promise I won't let him put you in the infirmary or anywhere else, unless you change your mind. Hear me? We'll manage somehow. If you stay in bed you'll get better. Our Meg and our Agnes and me — we'll help you." She grasped her friend's hand. "You got to get better!" she cried in anguish.

EIGHTEEN

Daisy returned from the doctor's house feeling tired and thirsty. Nellie's tea caddy was empty, however, so she put some fresh water on the old leaves in the battered tin teapot and set it on the fire to heat. She had, before leaving, sifted the cinders from the accumulation under the grate and put them on the embers to burn. The result was not a very good fire but sufficient to warm the water.

"Got any conny-onny, luv?" she inquired of Nellie.

"On the kitchen shelf."

Daisy fetched the sticky tin of condensed milk, which was half glued to the shelf by its own drips.

Joey clattered in from school. He wore the pullover his mother had knitted for him for Christmas — it was already stained down the front — and a pair of shorts too small for him. His thin legs, grey with grime, were chapped in places. His boots were good, having come from the Public Assistance Committee; they were marked so that no pawnbroker would accept them. He had no socks.

He went straight to the fireplace and stood with his back to it.

" 'lo, Anty Daisy. How's yourself?"

He grinned up at her. The thinness of his face made his teeth look too big for his mouth and his nose was running like candle grease in a draught.

Daisy ruffled his hair. "Not bad, luv."

The boy turned to his mother. "I want a conny-onny sandwich, Mam," he whined. "I'm hungry."

His mother nodded and made as if to rise.

"I'll make you one," offered Daisy. "Your Mam's not feeling very well."

Joey was much more interested in the piece of bread spread with condensed milk than he was in his mother's indisposition. Mothers were always complaining about headaches or nerves. He snatched the sandwich out of his aunt's hand and ran off to play in the back entry, where the boys got up a game to see who could urinate highest up the wall.

"Doctor's missus said he'd come later on — afore he starts his surgery," Daisy reported to Nellie, after Joey had gone. She helped Nellie to sit up and drink a cup of the wishy-washy tea she had made. "Me side hurts," the invalid moaned as she tried to find an easy position.

"I got a brick heating in the oven," Daisy comforted her. "It'll take the pain out a bit."

Nellie sipped her tea.

"Where's George?" asked Daisy suddenly. Though she had been in the house some time she had not seen her brother, and she fully expected that he would be furious at her going to get the doctor without asking him first.

Nellie shrugged. "He won three bob on the 2.30 yesterday." Her mouth took on bitter lines. "He'll be bevvied when he comes in."

Daisy agreed. George got as drunk as he possibly could on his infrequent betting wins. That was the way men were. The coal hole was empty and so was the tea caddy; the only food in the house was the tin of condensed milk and half a loaf of bread; yet both women knew that to remonstrate with George would be a waste of time and might mean a beating for his wife.

She poked up the cinders to encourage them to burn. "I'll bring you some tea, after t' doctor's been," she promised, "and I'll ask t'coalman to drop by tomorrer."

"I won't have any money till afternoon," Nellie sighed. "George goes down to the Parish in the afternoon."

"I'll pay for it and you can pay me back later."

"Ta." Nellie's affection and gratitude burst out of her. "You're a proper friend, Daise."

"Known you a long time — it's a habit," chipped Daisy with a loving grin.

It was dark by the time the doctor finally arrived. He went to the front door, and was met by a surprised denial of need of him by the father of the family living there. Fortunately, Daisy heard the exchange rumbling through the locked door. She hammered on the door and put her mouth to the wood.

"Tell him to come round back," she yelled.

She could hear this message being relayed to the doctor, and she then whipped out of the back door and along the entry. She caught the doctor standing uncertainly on the doorstep, bag in hand, just as the front door was shut on him.

"Y' have to come up jigger, Doctor," she explained. "It's me sister-in-law. She lives in t'back. She's proper sick."

The doctor glanced nervously at his shabby Austin Seven parked in front of the house. Already a couple of urchins were looking it over.

Daisy appreciated the doctor's reluctance to leave his car out of his sight. She knew how her Jamie could strip a car within a few minutes. She shouted to Joey who was seated on the pavement playing a flicking game with cigarette cards.

"Aye, Joey, you and your mates watch doctor's car. Don't you let nobody near it or I'll clobber yez." She shook her fist playfully at him.

Joey grinned, and he and his two small friends moved over to the car to lean in a proprietary way against the doors.

Daisy jerked her head towards the alley. "He'll watch it all right."

The darkness made the alley look very menacing to the physician and he was not averse to having such a hefty person as Daisy precede him down it. He sighed as he glanced round the empty scullery and then entered Nellie's bare room.

Daisy had put a penny in the gas meter and had lit the gas lamp hanging from the centre of the ceiling. Though the mantle was damaged there was enough light to see in painful detail two wooden chairs and an older rocker with a battered copy of a racing paper on the seat, an orange crate set on end to act as shelves to hold a few dishes and cooking utensils, a candlestick with a nub of candle in it on the mantelpiece, a teapot and mugs in the hearth and over all the smelly grime of poverty.

Making a sharp clicking sound with it, Daisy put down on the top of the orange box the half-a-crown she had been holding in her hand, so that the doctor could see that she had his fee for the visit.

The doctor laid his bag on one of the wooden chairs. He smiled down at Nellie who was regarding him with the bright, scared eyes of a cornered animal.

"God evening, Mrs. er—"

"Nellie O'Brien, sir," whispered Nellie.

"Ah, yes. I don't think I've seen you before, have I?"

"No, sir."

"And this lady?" he turned gentle questioning eyes upon Daisy.

"She's me sister-in-law, Mrs. Gallagher."

"I see." He did not sit down for fear of picking up vermin in his clothes, but leaned over the patient to take a closer look at her. "What's the trouble?"

"It's me cough," said Nellie falteringly.

"She's bin spitting blood," interposed Daisy.

Gradually the story came out and Nellie's shrunken body was carefully examined as far as her sense of modesty permitted. The dried trail of blood in the hearth was pointed out by Daisy with a dramatic sweep of her arm.

The doctor slowly put his stethoscope back into his bag and straightened up. His face looked pinched and tired. He glanced around the pitiful room and then back at his patient who lay staring at him with unblinking, terrified eyes.

"Mrs. O'Brien," he addressed her, "I would like to have your chest X-rayed. You need hospital treatment, that is certain. I can try to get you a bed in the sanatorium, where they will probably be able to help you."

"I'm not going to no hospital!" Nellie's voice was surprisingly firm considering how ill she was. "It's T.B., isn't it, Doctor?"

The doctor did not answer. His brow wrinkled in a worried frown. Again and again he came upon patients with an almost superstitious horror of hospitals. Death and hospital seemed to be synonymous to them.

Nellie saw his hesitation. "You can tell me," she said baldly. "Am I going to die?"

Her piercing gaze allowed of no prevarication and he reluctantly replied. "It is tuberculosis, Mrs. O'Brien — but you are not necessarily going to die of it. The sanatorium has performed wonders of recent years."

The soft pink of Nellie's cheeks drained to an ivory white as her worst fears were confirmed. Daisy, too, blenched at the naming of the dread killer.

The women instinctively turned to each other and Daisy went down on her knees by the bed to put a protective arm around Nellie. Despite the doctor's words, they both felt it was a sentence of death.

Nellie put her hand into Daisy's strong grasp. Her breath was laboured, as she tried to conquer the panic which surged through her.

"I'll die for sure if I go to hospital," she murmured to Daisy through trembling lips. "Don't let them put me in hospital, Daise. You promised, remember!"

Daisy looked up at the doctor who had hastily stepped back from the bedside when Daisy had darted forward to comfort her friend. "Couldn't I nurse her at home?" she implored.

The doctor gestured helplessly with his hand at the poverty-stricken room. "She needs more than you can provide — warmth, fresh air, a good diet. Has she any children?"

"One lad."

"He should not sleep in the same room as her. She would have every care in the sanatorium. If she were at home I would have to visit frequently — and that would mean more expense — and drugs."

Daisy remembered again the big tobacco tin full of silver and stolen pound notes stowed away in the clean, airy room which had been her mother's. She squeezed her friend's hand. "Nellie!" she exclaimed passionately. "You could have Nan's room." She turned to the doctor. "I got a nice room with a fireplace. It looks straight out on to the river. She could have the windows open and a good fire." The words tumbled out of her. "I nursed our Tommy through T.B. I got a good new blanket and I could borrow some more." Her eyes pleaded with him.

"The expense would be quite high, Mrs. Gallagher. You could, of course, have the Parish doctor."

Nellie slowly withdrew her hand. She turned her head wearily from side to side on her pillow. Her whole expression was one of blank despair.

Daisy bent over her and wrapped her shawl close around her.

"Now, you rest, ducks," she ordered briskly. "I'm going to talk outside with doctor. You ain't going to have no Parish vet." She stroked the sick woman's white cheek with a tender hand. "You stop worrying. I'll fix it."

She turned swiftly, picked up the coin from the orange crate and put it on top of the doctor's bag.

"Can I talk to yez outside?"

"Of course." The doctor picked up his bag and the half-a-crown, which he slipped into the pocket of his shabby overcoat. He smiled down at Nellie. "Don't lose heart, Mrs. O'Brien. Stay in bed, keep warm. I want you to consider going into the sanatorium, and I will come to see you again tomorrow morning."

She nodded, her eyes closed. When she was alone, she took her rosary out from under her pillow and lay with it held to her chest for comfort.

In the scullery Daisy addressed the doctor urgently. "Me sisters will help me nurse her," she assured him, recklessly committing Meg and Agnes to the job. "She's proper ill, isn't she? I seen it so often."

"One should never give up hope, Mrs. Gallagher. The treatment of tuberculosis has improved greatly of latter years." In the almost empty scullery the pomposity of his voice was echoed from the walls, and he felt suddenly weak and inadequate before this forceful woman's shrewd gaze.

"They said that about our Tommy, but he died anyway, God rest his poor little soul." Daisy laid her hand on the doctor's thread-bare sleeve. "I'll take great care of her, I will. I can afford to buy her anything she needs. Maybe I can get her better."

The doctor looked down at the muddy floor. "I presume she is a widow?"

"No. Me brother is out . . ." she was going to say at the pub, "That is, getting his P.A.C. money," she corrected herself hastily.

"Well, talk it over with him. I shall be here again tomorrow. In the meantime, I will give you a prescription which will help her. Get it made up tonight." He took his prescription pad out of his breast pocket and scribbled on it. He handed the slip of paper to Daisy, and went on, rather hopelessly, "Feed her lightly. Eggs, milk, oranges."

"Whatever you say, Doctor," Daisy assured him. The fortune in the tobacco tin would provide it all.

NINETEEN

After the doctor had gone, Daisy went out to get the prescription made up at the chemist's, a magical shop filled with the delicate odours of lavender, naphtha balls and cought mixture and presided over by an elderly druggist, who often provided the only medical advice his neighbours received.

Daisy stood impatiently tapping her foot amid the mahogany and glass showcases. While inwardly she screamed, "Hurry, hurry!" she examined the clutter of soaps, perfumes, nailbrushes and patent medicines, and the chemist behind a frosted-glass screen carefully compounded the medicine. He soon presented her with a neat white parcel, sealed at either end with a drop of red sealing-wax. She paid him and, carrying it gingerly under her shawl, she ran to the dairy for milk and then to Mrs. Donnelly's for tea and sugar. The cows at the back of the dairy had not long been milked, and the milk was still warm when it was poured into Daisy's can.

By the time George stumbled through the darkness of the back yard to his home, Daisy had fed Nellie and Joey with bread and milk, dosed the invalid with the bright pink medicine, and had settled down by the dead fire to wait for George's return. Nellie was snoring gently; Daisy had tucked her up in her shawl and the old eiderdown which was the bed's only other covering.

Joey was rocking himself in the rocker. He had hauled Rex, the terrier, on to his lap to keep him warm.

Though George was not drunk he was not particularly sober

139

either. His heavily lined face was an unhealthy yellow and he
stood in the doorway of the room blinking stupidly in the gas-
light.

"What's up?" he asked, after silently taking in the scene.
Womenfolk did not usually visit each other so late.

"Shush," warned Daisy, turning to look up at him with a
scowl of disapproval. "Nellie's proper sick."

George ambled over to take a closer look at the invalid. He
swayed uncertainly over her.

Daisy caught his arm. "Come in t' scullery," she commanded, with a knowing look towards Joey. The boy had ignored his father's arrival and was busy investigating the inside
of the patient dog's left ear.

"Come on, now, I got something to tell yer."

George allowed himself to be guided into the icy scullery.

Daisy shut the door. This left them in darkness except for a
shaft of moonlight across the floor.

"Listen, George," Daisy whispered urgently. "I had the doctor to her this afternoon. He wanted to put her in a sanatorium,
but she won't go!"

"Sanatorium?"

"Yes. And you know what that means."

George considered the matter laboriously. Then his voice
came lugubriously out of the darkness. "Yes. I know. She's got
T.B. Always coughing, she is. Christ! What'll I do?"

Daisy explained her idea of nursing Nellie in her own home
by the river.

"Oh, Daise!" George began to weep drunkenly.

"Now, you shut up. You and Joey could come, too, except I
don't have time to look after everybody 'cos I'm working, see.
You could take care of Joey here — then he won't know too
much about the trouble with his Mam — and you could come
and help me in the daytime a bit — or maybe in the evening
when I'm working."

"I didn't know you was working. Where you working?"

Daisy was silent for a moment and then she flashed out, "That's none of your business."

George cleared his nose with a large sniff. "I only asked."

"Well — I'm working evening shift in t' bottle factory downtown. Mike's allotment isn't enough. And you listen to me, George." She shook a finger at him. "We're going to have to pay doctor and chemist and coalman and everything — so no more getting bevvied every time you get a few shillings. Hear me? You got to buckle to and help me."

All this was more than George's fogged brain could take in. Never bright at best, it seemed to him that his world had been in chaos ever since he had come home from the third Battle of Ypres in 1917 to spend a year in hospital while the quacks dug pieces of shell splinter out of him. Now Nellie was sick to the point of death — that much he understood. Beyond that he could only think about lying down before he fell down.

Finally, Daisy snapped at him, "Och, go and sleep it off — but don't you dare wake Nellie. I'll come over in the morning."

She opened the door and called softly to Joey. "I'm going home, Joey. Watch you don't wake your Ma when you get into bed. And mind you get off to school in the morning."

Joey grinned at her over Rex's rough back and nodded.

George pushed past Daisy and shambled into the room. "I'll take a strap to yez if you don't behave," he mouthed thickly.

Back in her own home, though the hour was late, Daisy built up her fire with extravagant hands, till it roared up the chimney and the room was bright with dancing flames and glowing coals. The room was more cheerful looking that it had been. Articles that had lain for months at the pawnbroker's were now returned to their proper place. A black enamel coal hod stood resplendently full of coal by the fireplace; a shabby red cloth with a fringe of pompons round its edge covered the table again. A pair of brass candlesticks, a wedding present from an aunt of Mike's, kept the china dogs company on the littered mantelpiece. From the oven came a fragrant odour of meat, potatoes and onions simmering in a casserole in the oven. Under a chair rested Daisy's best high-heeled, black patent shoes, which had been in pawn almost constantly ever since little Tommy's funeral.

The heat of the fire soothed Daisy as she sat down and baked in front of it. Her shins and her cheeks gathered new burn mottles. When some of her weariness and worry had seeped out of her, she took the casserole out of the oven and ate the contents with a battered tin spoon, while the heat of the basin in her lap added to her contentment. But when the casserole was empty and she had settled back in her chair, while the fire reduced to a rosy glow, a huge wave of fresh grief about Nellie rose in her. She remembered how they had skipped in the street together, wandered on the Cassy shore and gone to stare at the Chinese inhabitants of Parkee Lanee. They had shared every treat, taking turns, at times, to suck a single sweet.

Slowly she began to weep, at first quietly and then noisily. They had lain in bed together and talked about that mysterious thing called 'blood' and had giggled about boys, while an irate Meg and Agnes, who had also slept in the same bed and found a visitor added to their number too much of a crowd, had kicked them and told them to shut their gobs.

Nobody heard her lamentations and gradually they diminished to an occasional dry sob. She blew her nose through her fingers into the fire and then wiped her face slowly with her apron. Drained and exhausted, she stared into the embers.

Nellie! She must wake up and think what was best for the girl. She would have to break the icy silence which existed between Meg and her. Great Aunt Devlin might be persuaded to help, too, though she might have to be paid. Her mouth twisted wryly. She was going to need all the money she could make. She was going to have to work much harder. Like a judgement on her, it was. Served her right for going on the streets like a common tart.

It was after midnight when a knock came on the door.

Daisy jerked awake and tumbled Moggie off her lap.

She did not know the young man at the door. A merchant seaman, she judged, by the way he stood swaying on his heels as if to keep his balance on a heaving deck.

"Yes, lad?" she inquired, her hand still on the heavy door.

"You Daisy?" The voice was rich and deep.

"Yes."

"Pat — the watchman at the Hercy — sent me up. Said you were very obliging, like."

Daisy simpered. "Come in, lad," she said, her voice oily with friendliness.

After closing the door behind him, she sidled round-him and with a knowing smile, announced, "It's five bob for an hour."

She stood saucily in front of him, hands on hips, head thrown back, so that he could examine the goods, as she put it to herself.

He looked her up and down slyly, and then said, "O.K."

She held out her hand and he pressed two half-crowns into it.

She lit a candle and led him up to the bedroom, which was not quite as cold as usual, some of the heat having percolated from the living-room. She stood watching him leisurely take off his jacket.

"Well, what about taking your clothes off?" he asked, when she had made no move.

"Me! I never take all me clothes off!" The idea of exposing all of her body to anyone shocked her. She doubted if Mike had ever seen her naked. " 'Sides, it's too bloody cold."

"Aw, come on, Ma," he cajoled, as he continued to strip himself. "We'll warm each other soon enough."

She put down the candle and reluctantly began to unbutton her blouse.

"Come on. I'll help you."

His idea of how to undress her was so caressing that she found herself kicking off her boots and nearly leaping into bed.

Her satin skin and luxuriously long hair showed to advantage in the candlelight and they did warm each other. Daisy learned more in an hour than she had ever known before, and it was with a feeling of tired pleasure that she added the five shillings to the tobacco tin which was going to save Nellie's life.

After the stranger had gone, she stood with one of her long petticoats wrapped round her like a cloak, thinking that if she could get a bed under her every time, life could be a lot more pleasant — and she could earn more.

TWENTY

Daisy woke late and lay languidly looking out of the bedroom window at a pure blue sky, until remembrance of Nellie's terrible need forced her to move.

She tidied the bed ready for Nellie, made a cup of tea and drank it quickly and, thus fortified, walked round to see Agnes, who received her with pleasure and more cups of tea.

"Agnes is easy," ruminated Daisy. "You can sell her anything. When she gets in a panic, though, it's pure mairder."

There was no panic that morning, however. The news about Nellie only confirmed Agnes's own long held opinion. She was glad, she said, to hear about Daisy's job in the bottle factory and wondered if she could get a job there herself.

"Not a hope in hell," Daisy assured her hastily. "There's queues of them trying to get in every day."

It did not strike Agnes to ask Daisy how *she* got in; she accepted everything that Daisy said as gospel truth. Old Daise had always been straight with her — always traded under a lamp post, she did, never under a tree.

Daisy warned Agnes that sometimes she did an extra half shift, which meant that she would come home on the first tram in the morning, rather than on the last tram at night. Agnes assured her that she would never leave poor Nellie alone.

Meg was different, thought Daisy, as she hurried over to her other sister's home. Meg could argufy like a scuffer in front of the beak, and yet she was the best bet for real help with Nellie.

Meg's father-in-law, Mr. Fogarty, was the true head of Meg's household. The three-bedroom row house sheltered him, his son, John, who was Meg's husband, six of John and Meg's children, aged from thirteen to seven, his second son, Tom, and his wife, Emily, and their six-month old baby, and lastly his youngest son, Albert, when he was not in gaol. Meg remarked bitterly from time to time that she did not believe that Albert could be guilty of all the thefts for which he had at different times served sentences, because when he was at home he did nothing but eat and doze comfortably on the sofa in the living room.

As Daisy rolled into the scullery, her arms neatly crossed under her shawl, Meg looked up from the greasy dishes she was trying to wash clean without benefit of soap or hot water.

"Why, look what the cat's brought in!" she exclaimed acidly. "And what brings you here, Missus?"

"Oh, stow it, Meg," Daisy responded crossly, as she subsided, panting, on to the only chair in the scullery.

"Who's there?" inquired a cracked, male voice from the living room.

"It's only me, Daisy, Mr. Fogarty. How are you?" She rose and went to the door of the other room.

A very thin, old man, his white hair ruffled up like a cockscomb, was sitting in a straight, wooden armchair. His clean union shirt was open at the neck and the sleeves were rolled up as if ready for work. He regarded Daisy with bloodshot blue eyes.

"How do you think?" he replied disagreeably to her inquiry.

"Well, I was hoping the pain wasn't so bad," she said brightly.

He looked down at his cruelly twisted fingers. "With arthritis? Less pain? It's a bloody pain in the neck, I can tell you," he growled, and then cackled with laughter at his own joke. He raised his voice to shout to his daughter-in-law. "Meg, when you going to give me me aspirins?"

There was the sound of the tap running, and then Meg appeared with a nearly empty bottle of aspirin and a cup of water.

"You never remember on your own, do you?" he berated her. He opened his mouth and she set an aspirin on his tongue and then held the cup so that he could drink. "I'll have another," he said. "It's bad this morning."

"You won't have enough for the night if you do," replied Meg dully.

"I'll worry about the night when I get to it. I may be dead by then, and that would make you happy, wouldn't it now?" He gestured impatiently towards the bottle. "Well, shake a leg, girl, and give me another."

Meg obediently gave him another tablet.

"Cover me. I'm cold," he ordered.

Meg brought an old overcoat and tucked it round his knees. He looked cunningly at Daisy. "Our Albert'll get me another bottle out of Boots. Proper nimble fingers he's got. Nothing like having a croppy head in the family, eh, Daisy?"

Daisy had no doubt that Albert could lift a bottle of aspirins out of Boot's Cash Chemists in Lime Street, so she nodded agreement.

Meg silently returned to her saucepan washing in the scullery, and Daisy followed her. The house was quiet, except for a baby crying upstairs. "Meg's little nevvie letting everybody know," thought Daisy with a soft smile.

All Meg's own children were in school, and her husband John, had gone down to the docks to sign on as being available for work. He had to do this twice a day and stand around, rain or shine, in case he was needed. It was an empty charade. There was rarely any work for him, and he often returned at night sopping wet and frozen.

"Well, what do you want?" Meg pinched her mouth tight, as she rubbed away at a soot-blackened saucepan.

Daisy cast a stabbing look at Meg's thin back and then said in honeyed tones, "Listen, Meg. Nellie is terribly ill. The doctor come to her yesterday. Meg, she isn't going to live unless we do summat about it."

Meg paused in her work and let the saucepan slowly sink into the grey dish water. She watched the concentric rings of grease eddy out from it. "Going to die?"

Daisy fought back a desire to weep. She said, "It's T.B., Meg. She's spitting blood often now, and she can cough like you'd never believe."

Meg's narrow shoulders slumped even more as she slowly ran the dishrag round the pan. She liked Nellie — everybody did — but she did not like Daisy very much, so she asked sarcastically, "What am I supposed to do about it?"

"Well, I'm going to put her in our Mam's bed and nurse her. The quack wanted her to go into the sannie. But she won't go and I don't blame her — heartless bloody place."

Meg shrugged. "Well, she's *your* friend."

"I know. She's your sister-in-law, too, remember." Daisy sighed. "And it's going to cost a bit for medicine and things." Meg was smart and she must be careful what she said. "Maybe Agnes told you I got an evening job — and I don't want to give it up seeing as how I'll have to pay the doctor, 'cos George can't do it."

"Ho-ho, hum-hum!" exclaimed Meg in surprise, and half turned to look at her sister. "Working, are yez? Since when may I ask?"

"I been doing it off and on ever since our Mam died. Don't get her pension no more — and me allotment isn't enough."

"Where you workin'?"

"In t' bottle factory down town."

Meg stared at her fat sister doubtfully.

"What do you do there?"

Daisy floundered for a moment, then said, "Wash bottles and pack them in straw in cardboard boxes."

"And what do you expect me to do — on top of the ould fella an' all."

"Well, I was hoping you would come and sit with Nellie some nights. Keep the fire going and help her if she coughs up." Daisy rubbed her arms under her shawl, and added uneasily, "Sometimes I don't get home till early morning — doing overtime, like."

"What about George — can't he wake up long enough to do a bit?"

"You know our George. He allus was the dumb one and he ain't never been the same since he was in the hospital all that time. 'Sides he hits her sometimes."

Mr. Fogarty suddenly bawled from the next room, "Meg, come 'ere. I want to pee."

"Old bastard," muttered Meg. She turned on Daisy savagely. "I got enough to do. I can't do no more." She pointed an angry finger at the door to the other room. "He can't do nothing for himself now."

"Your Emily from upstairs could help you," Daisy suggested, a dark mantle rising up her neck. "Nell's your sister-in-law too, isn't she?" she added with asperity. "Make Emily do something."

"Ha," Meg sniffed. "She's expecting again and the baby only six months old," she flared. "Always whining. Wait till she's got six. I'll thank all the Saints if she gets a Council house and gets to hell out of here."

Daisy wagged an admonishing finger at her. "You got Mary to help you, anyways — and your husband — John is handy — and Tom and Albert is your brothers-in-law — they owe you something. You could find some time to help me with Nellie — I haven't got nobody."

Meg's thin nostrils expanded as she drew in a breath. She was tired beyond endurance, frantic that she would not be able to feed the brood which depended upon her, grief-stricken as she watched her husband's fine body deteriorate from lack of employment and poor food. She felt her sister to be grossly unfair.

"I can't do no more!" she cried with a half sob. "You got nobody to think about except yourself. Do you good to help our

Nellie."

"Meg!" came an urgent voice from the other room. "Bring the pot, quick!"

Daisy got up and flounced towards the door as Meg whipped a jam jar from under the kitchen sink and made for the other room.

"Albert could do that for his father," said Daisy furiously.

Meg paused. Her mouth twisted in a sneer. "You ask him!"

"Oh, go jump off the dock," shouted Daisy in return.

She threw open the back door and went grumbling down the back alley like a wood down a ninepins lane. Behind her anger the tears welled up. Where *was* she to get help? Nellie had no sisters or parents. She had lost one brother in the same Battle of Ypres that George had been wounded in, and her other brother had taken his wife and family and gone south to find work only a year before. "Holy Mother," prayed Daisy, "help me. Dear Holy Mary."

Meg bent again to her saucepan washing. For a while her wrath at her sister sustained her, and then she began to feel a qualm of conscience about Nellie. Such a good woman deserved help, she knew. But I'm so tired, she cried silently to herself. I'm so tired.

After the saucepans had been neatly arranged on their shelf, she took a bucket of rubbish and Mr. Fogarty's filled jam jar out to the rubbish bin and the lavatory respectively, to empty. When the repulsive jobs were done, she leaned against the door jamb to look up over the smoke-blackened brick walls of the yard to the sky, a pale, limpid winter blue through which two gulls sailed and swooped. She watched through half-closed eyes as their raucous cries came down to her. For a moment she shared their freedom of the upper air. Then from the house she heard the petulant cry, "Meg! Meg! What about a cup of tea? Where are you, Meg?"

She closed her eyes in exhaustion and lifted herself away from the door jamb. The latch of the door into the back entry clicked and her husband, John, come slowly in. He was a tall, lanky man and his long hatchet face was shaded by a flat cap. He had his hands clenched in the pockets of an old cloth jacket stained with oil and grease on the back and shoulders. He looked as exhausted as his wife felt, but his face softened when he saw Meg.

"'lo, luv. What you doin' out here? It's cold."

"Emptying the ould fella's pot." She put the jar down on the stone step and went to her husband.

He hastily took his hands out of his pockets and, with a quick glance round to see if anyone was looking, he enfolded her in his arms.

She laid her head on his chest and her arms crept up round his neck. He bent and kissed the top of her tidy braided head.

"No luck?"

"No. Maybe tomorrer."

TWENTY-ONE

Still smarting from Meg's rebuff, Daisy marched down the windy street to see George and Nellie. Her boots scuffed along the stone paving, as she muttered under her breath, "She's nothin' but a bloody bitch. No heart to her."

She found Nellie puttering slowly round her room, a coal shovel in her hand. A sober and obviously worried George was watching her from the rocking-chair. On his lap was a back copy of a pink racing paper.

"Jesus!" exclaimed Daisy. "Couldn't you make up the fire for her, George?"

She snatched the coal shovel from Nellie and added a few lumps of coal to the fire. She had gone round to the coal merchant the previous evening and paid him to deliver a hundredweight of the precious fuel to Nellie first thing in the morning.

George clamped his lips together sulkily.

Nellie intervened. "It's all right, Daise. I don't feel so bad today."

"Good. But you get back on that bed again," ordered Daisy. "Have you had any breakfast?"

"Just a cup a tea. That's all I ever take."

Daisy accepted this statement with a nod and plunked herself down on a chair, while Nellie obediently lay down on the bed.

Daisy then turned a malevolent blue eye upon the luckless George,

"Na, George. I don't know how much you remember about

153

last night," she commenced bitingly.

George glared at her. " 'Course I remember," he snapped indignantly.

Daisy grunted and looked round as if she had a large audience. "Humph, now that's remarkable, ain't it?"

"Don't be eggy, Daise. He knows," Nellie pleaded.

"Well, then, George, tell me. How are we going to get Nell to my house?"

Nellie half rose on her elbow and interposed hastily. "I don't need to go, Daise. I'll be all right here."

Daise swung round towards her. Her voice took on a cooing note, as she said, "Na, look, Nell. We got to get you well somehow. And I haven't time to come down here every day."

"George'll look after me."

"You haven't got the money to buy what's needed, eggs an' all. And he's got to sign on for work and go to the P.A.C."

"If she stays with you, the Relieving Officer will stop the allowance I get for her, t' bloody bastard." said George heavily.

"Not if you don't say nothing', you stupid bugger. You stay here and look after Joey, and if the P.A. visitor asks where Nellie is, tell him — well, tell him she's nursing me! So she's over at my place most days." Daisy chortled at this idea and Nellie giggled and began to cough. Even George grinned sheepishly.

"Our Aggie will come and sit with you of an evening some nights," said Daisy, turning to Nellie who was trying desperately to control her coughing, "But Meg has got too much to do with old Fogarty an' all, so George and Joey'll have to come some nights. Great Aunt Mary Devlin'll come, o' course, sometimes, but we got to pay her, 'cos she can't be sitting with other people if she's sitting with you — and she needs the money."

Nellie and George agreed about Great Aunt Devlin.

"Meg's got too much on her shoulders already," remarked Nellie, clearing her throat and managing to stop her coughing spasm.

"Pah!" snorted Daisy. "She should get that Emily off her ass and make her help. And John, too."

"Emily's bloody useless," said George with unexpected warmth. "And John's got to sign on twice a day, you know that."

"If Ellen hadn't gone to live in Southampton, she'd have helped," sighed Nellie, in reference to her brother's wife.

George ignored this remark, and continued, "Best way to move you, Nell, 'd be to borrow a handcart and lay you on it."

"Ha, using your brains at last," sneered his unloving sister. She turned to Nellie. "He's right, you know. Wrap you up warm. You'd be like Queen Mary in her carriage, you would." She cackled with laughter.

"Taffy might lend us his," said George, steadily pursuing a single line of thought.

Nellie raised her tousled head from her pillow. "Ah couldn't, Daise! What'd people think? Me sitting on a rag and bone man's handcart, like!"

"They won't see you," replied Daisy comfortingly. "We'll do it after it's dark, won't we, George?" She fixed George with a stony stare. "You get the handcart and ask John to help yer. And I'll get the fire going in our Mam's room and have it real warm by the time you come after tea."

George let the newspaper slip off his lap and nodded in a bewildered fashion at Daisy. Even if he had not agreed with her he would not have dared to argue. Arguing with Daisy was like arguing with a tank in Flanders. He wished suddenly that he was a seaman like Mike and could sail away from his troubles ashore for months at a time.

He got up slowly to go to see Taffy about the handcart.

Daisy got up, too. She took a half-crown piece out of her skirt pocket and stuck it on the mantelpiece. When she saw the movement, Nellie immediately protested.

"Daise! We can pay the doctor. George gets his dole today."

Daisy laughed down at her anxious friend. "Come on. I feel

rich today. Me American uncle been and left me a thousand pounds." She laughed again at her own joke. She felt like a monarch, as she bent to kiss Nellie gently on the forehead.

"Oh, Daise! You sure?"

" 'Course I'm sure. While I work I got money enough."

Nellie sighed, then smiled at her friend. She laid her head down on her lumpy, stained pillow and closed her eyes. For once, the room was warm. It felt good to rest, to drift for a while. She could be certain that Daisy would look after iddy Joey — and George. She put out her tiny hand towards Daisy. Daisy took it and squeezed it passionately, as if to pass some of her own strength to her.

When the room was empty, Nellie took her rosary from under her pillow, found the cross on it and, with her lips against its comforting presence, she fell asleep.

Daisy's first attempt at kindling a blaze in her late mother's bedroom went out, so she got a broomstick and poked around up the chimney. Clumps of soot tumbled down and covered her arms with fine black powder. She cursed, and shoved the broomstick up again. This time part of a bird's nest descended with a thud, as well as more soot.

She looked at the offending bundle of clay and fine twigs. "Must have built the bloody thing right in the chimney," she fumed.

She inserted her arm as high as it would go and felt around. She could find no more of the nest, so she swept up the soot and started a fresh fire. This time it burned well.

Clucking with irritation, she washed the soot off herself and changed her ruined blouse. Then she spread over the bed the new blanket intended for her mother and two others she had redeemed from pawn. Between the sheets she slipped two bricks which she had heated in the downstairs oven and wrapped up in newspaper. She emptied the chamber pot and replaced it under the bed.

The room smelled strongly of soot, so she opened the window

and leaned out and took a big breath. Though the night was damp, the air from the estuary smelled sweet and fresh. Daisy smiled. With clean, damp air like that Nellie would find her breathing much easier.

When she tidied up her living-room, she found a post card under the door mat. Mike, as usual, was doing fine, it said, so she tossed it on to the mantelpiece to join the other ones already there. She was tired of pictures of Accra.

The card reminded her of Elizabeth Ann's last letter, which had said that her sentence might be shortened because she had behaved so well. "Bless her iddy-biddy heart!" murmured her mother, as she leaned back in her chair and stared into the fire. A nice-looking girl who might bring a husband home to live with her mother, not like Maureen Mary. Let him be a man who smelled like a man, of sweat and dust or oil or coal, so as you knew he'd been working for you. She felt she could not endure another son-in-law who smelled of talcum powder.

With her stockinged feet on the fender, she began to doze. The young man of the previous night had tired her more than she cared to admit. As soon as Nellie had been put to bed, however, she would instruct George to sit with her, while she herself went out to turn an honest dollar. "You're a born tart, Daise," she told herself with a laugh.

Then her eyes sprang open with horror. With Nellie in the house, she could not bring a man home. Yet money in large sums would be needed. She would squeeze a bit of George's allowance out of him, of course. But it would not be nearly enough. An anxious frown creased her usually smooth forehead, as she tussled with the problem.

The rattle of the handcart over the stone sets of the street, made her leap out of her chair to answer the door.

Nellie was curled up on a pile of newspapers and her old eiderdown. She was covered by John's overcoat. The bumpy journey through the night chill had shaken her, and she lay exhausted with eyes closed.

"Maybe she's dead already," agonised Daisy, as she hurried out.

But Nellie opened her eyes and smiled weakly. "The boys were proper careful of me," she assured Daisy in response to anxious inquiries.

The two great clumsy men grinned sheepishly. They stood uncertainly, watching the women while Nellie slowly raised herself.

"Na, George. Don't just stand there. Lift Nellie out and carry her upstairs." She turned briskly back to Nellie. "Room's lovely and warm, luv, and waiting for yez."

Obediently George lifted his wife and carefully carried her in. She was so light that blind terror struck him that she might really die and he would be left with only iddy Joey. He paused on the doorstep, as memories of his ill-treatment of her rushed into his mind. If she died, the devil would take him for his wickedness, he was sure of that.

Nellie felt his chest heave under her and sensed the fear in him. She lifted one tired hand and stroked his face, just as she had had the habit of doing when they were first married. He looked down at her sharply and saw for a second the young, saucy Irish girl he had married, and not a dying woman.

"Nell!" he muttered, "Aye, Nell!"

Her hand closed gently round his neck under the band of his rough cotton shirt. She smiled at him very sweetly.

"Don't be afraid, Georgie, luv. Daise'll help us."

He nodded dumbly.

"Come on, George! She'll catch her death! Take her in," ordered Daisy, pushing impatiently from behind.

Like one of the cart horses he had tended in the past, George braced himself for the steep rise of the stairs, and then climbed them slowly and passed through to his late mother's room.

Daisy was right. It was beautifully warm, though it smelled strongly of soot. The fire glowed a welcome, and two candles flickered extravagantly on the little mantelpiece.

He laid his wife down on the bed, while John and Daisy crowded into the room. John looked around him with surprised interest at the new wallpaper and Maureen Mary's white curtains drawn over the window. The bed, too, looked lovely with two clean white pillows and a white sheet turned down over good blankets. He thought longingly how he would like to give Meg a room like this, with a fire in it and no children sharing it, so that they could relax in sensuous luxury like in a film.

His wistfulness was rudely broken by Daisy.

"You boys get outta here. I'm going to put Nellie to bed. Then I'm going to make her some bread and milk afore I go to work." She nodded at John. "You go down and put the kettle on the fire for some tea for her."

John clomped down the stairs with a "Ta-ra, Nell" as a goodbye to the invalid.

"Ta-ra, well," responded Nellie. "Thanks, John." She was still holding her husband's hand as if afraid to release it. Daisy went to her and slipped her boots off her feet and put them in the hearth.

"I can do for meself, after I've rested a bit," Nellie protested.

"Nay," said George suddenly. "You let Daisy help you."

Daisy nodded approvingly. "That's right. Now you get out of the way and I'll help her off with her skirt. She'd better keep 'er stockings on for warmth." She began to untie the tape which held up Nellie's gathered skirt. "I haven't got a nightie for you yet, luv. I thought I'd ask the Welfare lady for one — and a coat or something to go over you when you get out of bed. It'd be more comfy."

Nellie had never owned a nightgown and thought that Daisy was taking too much trouble on her behalf but, when she protested, Daisy pointed out practically that nighties were soon washed through and with the fevers she got she could become sweaty and then she would get cold.

Soon the little woman was laid in bed, the blankets tucked round her, a hot brick at her feet and another at her aching side.

"I'll get some new bags of sand, tomorrow," promised Daisy. "I threw out the ones I had for Nan 'cos they was leakin'. Sand does keep the heat better, there's no doubt."

George was again holding his wife's hand and Daisy grinned at him knowingly. "Three's a crowd. I'll go and make the bread and milk." And she bustled out with a speed and determination that surprised George, who had always regarded her as a lazy, gossiping bitch.

"Best get back to Joey, George."

He nodded. He felt bewildered and at a loss in this women's world of sickness, where the wings of death seemed literally to beat down at him from the shadowy ceiling.

"He's all right with Mrs. Higgins for now." The grip on Nellie's hand tightened. He wanted to get into bed with her and hold her closely as he had done in happier days, without fear that she would shrink from him because she did not want to carry another child.

"George," whispered Nellie. "Take care of iddy Joey. Bring him to see me tomorrow."

He roused himself with an effort. "Surely," he agreed. "He'll be over on his own in the morning."

"No." Nellie's voice was sharp. "See he goes to school. He can come after school."

George dropped her hand. "O.K.," he agreed irritably. An old wound in his back was aching and he moved towards the door sullenly. His wife watched him, her perception heightened by the fear of death.

"Aye, Georgie, come back here a mo'."

He paused, his hand on the doorknob.

"Come 'ere, now."

With a face as droopy as that of a basset hound, he came sulkily back to the bedside.

Nellie lifted her arms. "Come 'ere."

He bent over her, stark fear of her dying breaking through his churlishness. She wrapped her arms around his neck and pulled him to her. She patted his back as if he was a child and kissed his cheek. "And you take care of yourself, Georgie, lad." She held him to her tightly for a moment. "There's nothing to be afraid of, do you hear."

"Aye, Nell," he whispered brokenly, as he returned her embrace, "I'm so scared. What have we come to, you and me?"

TWENTY-TWO

The January night felt dank, and the wind coming through the dampness seemed more chilling than usual. The few people about hurried along with coat collars turned up or with shawls held tightly across their chests. Even the Ball and Chain, with all its lights gleaming through steamed-up windows, seemed to huddle miserably against the blackened walls of the boarded up warehouse next to it.

And Daisy could not find a client. She hummed her favourite obscene song hopefully in the shadows, every time a male figure hastened by. Then she moved closer to the lights of the pub and flashed her bright white smile. "Like to make a trick, dearie?" she whispered.

Most shook her off impatiently. One who knew her muttered querulously, "In this cold?" and made a rude gesture.

The general dampness turned to light rain, and Daisy cursed the weather roundly under her breath. She told herself despairingly that even a blackie would have been welcome on a night like this.

"You won't do much tonight, duck," remarked a feminine voice behind her, as she moved into a doorway of the warehouse to shelter. The voice was soft and carried a subdued giggle in it, as if the owner was permanently trying to suppress her laughter.

A figure nearly as plump as herself squeezed into the doorway of the warehouse at the same time as Daisy sought shelter there. She brought with her an overwhelming cloud of violet perfume; and Daisy felt her hackles slowly rise. She eased

163

herself round, to look at what she sensed was an intruding competitor.

Competition it certainly was.

Daisy's lips tightened as she viewed the cheerfully over-painted face surveying her from under a cheeky-looking veiled hat. A mangy fox fur encircled the woman's neck and she carried a large, light-coloured handbag in which she was now digging absently while she stared back at Daisy.

"Like a cigarette?" asked the intruder, bringing out a battered packet of Woodbines.

Daisy scowled.

"No." The single word came out as sharply as a pebble from iddy Joey's catapult. "And you get off my beat!"

"Aa, stow it!" responded the other woman, as she tore a match out of a folder and lit her cigarette. "I don't trade in t'streets. I got me own apartment, I have. Got me regulars." She blew out cigarette smoke which wreathed round Daisy's head, much to her discomfort. "Once you got some regulars, they tell the other boys and you don't have to go out that often."

Daisy blinked her eyes against the tobacco smoke. Then she inquired loftily, "And what may I ask, are you doin' here if you've got everything sewn up so bloody comfortable, like?"

The unwelcome intruder's voice was gleeful, as she replied. "Been to the pictures. Proper nice film at the Forum." She sighed blissfully. "Ronald Coleman is a bloody marvel. Have you seen it?" Without waiting for Daisy to reply, she went on, "Got pissed off with the whole bloody issue, so I took meself to the pictures." She laughed richly. "And I got a man when I come out — proper funny, it was." Her voice sobered suddenly. "But it isn't safe in Lime Street if you ain't got a pimp. You got a pimp?"

"None o' your business," snapped Daisy. She stuck out her hand to see if the rain had stopped. It had not.

"Well, I'm telling you, they got Lime Street so tightly laid out they're on you in a second. Bloody great switchblades, they got.

One girl got proper beat up only a couple of weeks ago. I was sweatin' they'd catch me tonight."

"I never go there," replied Daisy, shrugging her damp shawl more tightly round her shoulders.

It was quiet for a moment, while the smoke round Daisy increased rapidly, despite the encroaching rain. The uncrushable sharer of her shelter looked Daisy up and down, "How do yer ever make out in them clothes?" she asked.

"What's the matter with me clothes? You mind your own bloody business and I'll mind mine."

The other woman laughed. "We're both in the same business, luv. Seen you several times when I been going into the Ball for a quick one."

Daisy snorted. She was so incensed that she considered plunging out into the icy rain and going home. Then she realised that as far as Nellie and George were concerned, she was at work — and could not go home until a reasonable work period had elapsed.

"Bugger everything!" she growled.

The constable on the beat came slowly down the deserted street. The rain dripped unhappily off his helmet and his waterproof cape. Occasionally, he stopped and flashed his torch while he tried a door lock or checked a window.

When he reached the two sheltering women, he stopped and flashed a torch over both of them. The light rested only cursorily on Daisy, noting the unpainted face, the pursed up mouth and belligerent chin stuck up in the air as if daring him to ask her a question. The torchlight, however, ran thoroughly up and down her companion and came to rest on the heavily rouged face and the merry mascara-rimmed eyes.

"Na, ladies," he said, not unkindly, "Loiterin' ain't allowed. Move along, please."

"Come on, Officer," wheedled the painted female. "I'm only sheltering."

Daisy murmured agreement. This was the first time to her

knowledge that the constable on the beat had seen her and she was desperately anxious that he should not remember her in any way. Her well rounded throat quivered, as she tried to keep calm and look like a respectable Irish woman on her way home from St. John's Market.

The constable inclined his head towards the public house. "What about going to have a drink until it gives over?" he suggested.

The bright-faced female gurgled, "You going to stand us, Officer?"

The constable's voice hardened at this impudence. "Now you get moving, Missus Woman!" His eyes flashed in the shadow of his helmet. He gestured with his torch. "Out!" he ordered.

Daisy did not wait for any more. Like Moggie on the prowl, she slunk silently past the constable while his light was still on the other prostitute, and started up the street.

The other woman prepared to move also. She arranged her fox fur tighter round her chin.

"Bad cess to you," she muttered angrily at the irate constable.

"Want me to take you in?" he asked fiercely.

Her answer was lost, as she tottered out on very high heels, which were so worn down that she looked bow-legged as she wobbled up the street after Daisy.

The rain was hissing down now, penetrating Daisy's thick shawl and running down her back. What a night!

She paused at the corner, wondering what she should do. Nellie certainly made life complicated. Not for one moment did she regret taking in her dear friend — somehow Nellie was going to be fed and nursed back to health. But money had to be found to do it.

"Wait for me," shouted the gurgly voice again from further down the street. Daisy half turned and watched the woman totter up to her on her uncomfortable heels.

"Like to come and have a cuppa tea with me? You can't do

nothing in this weather." A wicked grin was flashed at her from behind the wilted veil. "Don't often have a woman to talk to now me sister's dead. It's all fellas around the place." The rich laugh came again and she cupped Daisy's elbow with her hand to guide her across the street.

"There's a couple of other women in our house, up on the second floor. Proper bitches, they are. Take the bread out of your mouth, they would."

Daisy glanced up and down the cross street. Cars swished behind them as they made their way over, and her skirt was splashed with mud from them. There was not a pedestrian in sight. And she could not go home yet.

"O.K.," she agreed — any port in a storm, she thought ruefully. "What's your name?"

"Ivy. What's yours?"

"Daisy."

"Daisy? I heard tell from a fella not long back about a woman called Liverpool Daisy." She scrutinized Daisy with new interest as she propelled her towards the side door of a small tobacconist's shop. "See, I wasn't far from home — Liverpool Daisy, now?"

"Some of the boys calls me that."

Ivy paused, her key extended towards the door lock, and glanced up again at Daisy. "You're bloody lucky. That young fella was proper nice about you. You're getting yourself a good reputation!" And again a surge of laughter rocked her, as she unlocked the door.

They entered a dingy hall lit by a single low watt bulb without a shade. A door, which Daisy assumed led into the tobacco shop, occupied one side wall, and straight ahead of her was a flight of stairs covered with shabby linoleum.

"Come on up," invited Ivy.

At the head of the stairs was a small landing with two doors facing them, while on Daisy's left the staircase continued upwards into darkness.

One of the doors had a grubby card pinned to it on which the name "Ivy Le Fleur" had been crudely printed in red pencil. Ivy unlocked this door and kicked her shoes off into the room which lay before her. She took off her hat and examined the sopping ruin regretfully.

She saw Daisy glance at the card on the door and her eyes twinkled, as she said, "Me real name's Ivy Brown — that's me name from when I was a dancer — it's Frenchy — good for me business."

Daisy was impressed by this display of business acumen and allowed herself to be led into the apartment which seemed to her to be very luxurious. It consisted of a single room stuffed with furniture. A large rumpled bed with numerous pillows and a bright green eiderdown dominated the room. On the other side of it a cage on a stand held a disconsolate looking canary. Behind the bird, the window was covered by shiny green curtains. An easy chair, faded to near grey, faced a large gas fire which Ivy immediately lit. The pop it made as the gas flamed, made Daisy jump, and Ivy chuckled.

"I got coal fires — more healthy 'n gas," said Daisy defensively.

"Too much work," replied Ivy, as she got up off her knees. "Make yourself at home while I fill up the kettle." She took off her coat, shook it out and hung it over the back of a chair, then laid the dripping fox fur over a line strung across the corner above an ancient gas cooker. She picked up a tin kettle from the stove and hurried out of the room. The gas stove had two shelves above it and these were crammed with a dusty assortment of dishes, small saucepans, packets of salt and sugar, all mixed up with a full ash tray, several boxes of matches, a tin of talcum powder and some greasy bottles.

Daisy strolled round the tiny space not committed to furniture. Behind an old hospital screen with faded cretonne curtains was a wash-hand stand, complete with jug and basin and a slop bucket underneath. The stand was also tightly packed, with odds and ends, tooth brushes, a soap dish, a sticky pot of vaseline, aspirins and liver pills.

A small dressing-table, with a mirror suffering from smallpox, was equally littered with powder boxes, a hair tidy, pin cushions, broken combs, hairpins, pots of cream, and a gadget which Daisy did not recognise. She picked it up and was examining it when Ivy came back into the room.

"That's me eyelash curler," she explained in answer to Daisy's query.

"Curl your eyelashes?" exclaimed Daisy in disbelief. She stared incredulously at the tiny contrivance and then burst into sudden laughter.

Ivy lit the gas jet under the kettle. "Aye," she said, looking up from her task, "That's better. You look real pretty when you laugh. Reminds me of me mother — she wore a shawl, too. Take your shawl off and put it on the fender in front of the gas fire. You're dripping." She bustled round, clearing a table and laying two cups and saucers on it. Then she quickly slipped off her damp dress, hung it on a hanger and put on a crumpled wrapper over her bright pink underslip. She snatched up a towel from behind the hospital screen and handed it to Daisy.

"Here. Here's a towel for your hair."

Daisy thankfully accepted this kind hospitality. The room was rapidly becoming deliciously warm and, as the chill went out of her, she began to relax.

She took off her shawl and laid it on the fender. Her thin cotton blouse was also sodden, as was the shift under it. The garments clung to her large breasts and Ivy eyed them enviously.

"You got a fine pair o' bristols," she remarked.

"Suckled all me kids," Daisy informed her. She sat down on the easy chair, and ran her hand round the neck of her blouse to loosen it from her skin.

Ivy sloshed hot water into a small brown teapot.

"Surprisin' how many men like fat women," she remarked, "Seein' as how the fashion is always for thin ones."

"Oh, aye," agreed Ivy.

Daisy took the pins out of her hair and began to rub it with the towel. She felt around for a piece of comb in the pocket of her wet apron and after she had found it she took the apron off and set it to steam beside the shawl.

Ivy sat down on a small straight bedroom chair and poured out the tea, ladling in spoonsful of sugar with a generous hand, while Daisy patted the front of her blouse with the towel.

Ivy handed her a cup of tea and she laid the towel across her knee while she took it gratefully.

"Ta," she said.

Ivy drew her chair closer to the fire.

"You don't wear no makeup?"

Daisy was shocked. "Never!" she spluttered into her teacup.

Ivy laughed at the strong denial. Her own makeup had run in the rain and she had grey rivulets of mascara down each cheek, giving her a clownlike appearance. Daisy eyed her resentfully over the steaming teacup. In her small world, only real whores like Ivy wore makeup. Of course, girls put lipstick on nowadays like their mothers would never have dared.

"Aaa, you should paint your face. It'd do a lot for you."

"Humph," grunted Daisy. She stirred uneasily in her chair. She wasn't a whore like this woman and she didn't want to look like one. She was unable to think why what she was doing for a living was different from what Ivy was engaged in; but to her it was not the same thing at all, at all, it wasn't. Further, she had realized instinctively that the normality of her dress was an advantage to her. If she was seen with a man he could pass her off as an acquaintance, a neighbour, a relation.

"You really should buy some makeup."

"I dunno. I dunno as it is a good idea. T' scuffer looked at you tonight — he hardly noticed me."

"A lot of men wouldn't notice you neither."

"To hell with her," thought Daisy. "I wish I hadn't come." Aloud, she said stiffly, "I do all right." She leaned over and helped herself to another spoonful of sugar. She whirled the spoon fretfully round her cup while she wondered if the rain had stopped.

Ivy picked up the sugar bowl and sat with it in her hand, as if to protect it from further raids by Daisy. She felt that Daisy was smarter than she was; yet, she suspected, Daisy did not know her own value.

"How much do you get?" she inquired.

"Half a dollar. If I don't like the look o' them, I try for five shillun." Daisy clapped her spoon into her saucer noisily. The woman was a proper Nosy Parker, she was.

"You could do better'n that if you had a room. Ever been to a hotel?"

"Me? In a shawl? Na." She reflected for a moment. Ivy's face expressed only honest interest, so she confided, "I got a house of me own. But I got someone living with me, so I can't take fellas there. Not now, anyway."

"Your ould fella there?"

"No. He's at sea."

"Don't he ever come home?"

"He's been away for ages this time. He don't touch Liverpool. He could be gone for years." She had not given any thought to the possibility of Mike's return, and Ivy's question introduced the disturbing idea that he might indeed come home.

Ivy took a tin of broken biscuits from the shelf under the table. She took off the lid and proffered the contents.

"Have a bickie," she invited and at the same time put the sugar basin back on the table.

Daisy took several pieces of biscuit and popped them into her mouth one after another. One piece got stuck in the top of her dentures and she had a bad moment getting it off her plate with her tongue. "Ta," she said.

"You married?" asked Daisy after she had downed the biscuits.

"Yes. Married to a comic. I used to be on the stage. He left me years ago with a couple of kids to feed. Me Mam looked after them while I was dancing — choruses — in panto mostly. Then it got hard to find jobs — they like you thin as a rake — so I began to take fellas home." The merry look went out of her face for a minute and she looked old and haggard. "Me boy's in the army — he sends me an allotment — a few shillings, bless 'im. Gloria, me girl, went to London. She writes at Christmas. Says she's workin'."

The conversation passed to Daisy's progeny; and Ivy was fascinated as a few sorrows over children were shared, including a tear shed for James doing time for dispatching a bloody Prottie, for little Michael, killed by a brewer's dray, and for Tommy who had coughed himself to death and even for John who had run away to sea so long ago that it was doubtful if his mother could have recognised him if he ever returned. The high drama of James's and Lizzie Ann's arrests was gone over to their mutual enjoyment.

Daisy was just beginning to feel that she had found a friend, and the tin alarm clock on the mantelpiece said ten past ten, when suddenly there was the sound of the outside door being opened and the clomp of heavy feet on the stairs. Raucous, drunken voices shouted bawdy jokes to each other, and one loud male voice bayed, "Hey, Ivy, hey Doris. Open up there. Your loved ones has come in from the rain."

TWENTY-THREE

In a matter of seconds, after opening the door and seeing the jocular crowd coming up the stairs, Daisy had been offered and had accepted Ivy's late sister's room next door, a noisome den still cluttered with the dead woman's belongings. She snatched up her shawl and apron from in front of Ivy's gas fire and followed her hostess into the dark room.

Ivy lit the gas jet and then the gas fire. "There you are," she said, as Daisy blinked in the doorway at the sudden light. "Landlord'll never know. Friend of mine has rented it as of next week." She gave Daisy a playful push in the stomach, as she turned back into the hall, where the first men were shaking the rain off their bare heads like collie dogs. One of them slapped a bewildered Daisy on the bottom, and this had the effect of propelling her into the room; the man followed so closely that she could feel his breath on her bare neck. Ivy slipped off her wrapper and wriggled her pink satin-covered bottom. "Come on, lads, It's five bob. Who's first?"

A bear of a man clasped her round the waist from the rear, and they danced a conga into her room. The door was left ajar.

A shaken Daisy took the first tram home in the morning. She was bruised, bitten and in pain. She felt filthy and degraded. All the buttons were off her blouse, which had been nearly torn off her back. Her first client, a man so big and so drunk that she had been afraid of him, had demanded that she strip and she had hastily abandoned even her shift.

For the first time she learned what her trade could really be

173

like.

" 'T was a judgement in the eyes of God," she thought bitterly.

Her mind had got muzzy as one drunk after another came slinking through the half shut door. Only one clear thought had stayed with her, that for Nellie's sake she must collect the money first. This she had done, shoving the precious shillings under the mattress as each man gave it to her. How many men could one take, she wondered? A goodly number judging by the happy shouts and yelps from Ivy's room. Must have been a bloody ship's crew, she told herself resentfully.

The two girls upstairs had opened their doors and screeched over the banisters, and this had led to a clatter of boots climbing to the upper floor amid cheerful whoops from the steaming mob packed into the tiny hall and staircase.

"How could men be such beasts?" Daisy asked herself as the tram trundled homeward. Now she had seen it all, for sure. She had been pushed around by men all her life, but never had she felt so helpless before them as she had done on this obscene night. Near to tears, she tried to console herself with the thought of the clinking contents of her skirt pocket. With that much money added to her present hoard she need not go out for several nights.

Sore discomfort had rapidly become sharp pain and she had begun to wonder wildly how she could shut out the still clamouring men, who leaned against the door jamb shouting encouragement to whoever was with her. She finally rebelled when a young stalwart demanded a service of her which she felt was unnatural. Horrified fury took possession of her, and the surprised youngster found himself propelled back through the door by a stark naked amazon mouthing language that surprised even him. He stumbled against the next man in the queue and for a second they were out of the doorway. Daisy slammed the door on them and shot the bolts at the top and bottom. Since she had already taken the money of her last would-be client, this led to a lot of bad language in return and much hammering on the old oak panels.

Terrified, Daisy glanced around her. She snatched up her skirt and petticoats and struggled into them, pushed her arms into her buttonless blouse, scooped up the money from between the mattresses and stuffed it, with her stockings, into her skirt pocket. With her shawl, apron and shoes tight under one arm, she ran to the window.

"Hi, open up," came a chorus from beyond the door.

"Holy Angels, preserve me," sobbed Daisy, as she flung back the tattered curtains to reveal a big sash window.

She turned the latch and with one hand tried to heave open the long unused bottom half. It would not budge. She put down her shoes and shawl and tried with two hands. There was a lot of laughter from the hallway and a heavy thud suggested that someone had put his shoulder to the door in an effort to break it.

"Holy Mary, pray for me now," implored Daisy as she tugged at the recalcitrant window. "Let there be a fire escape! Let there be one!"

The window gave suddenly and the rain blew cold on Daisy's flushed face. She leaned out.

There was an iron veranda running across both her window and that of Ivy's room. She could not see in the darkness whether it had a staircase at the end of it or whether it was enclosed. She crawled out and cautiously let her weight on to it. It shook uneasily but it held. She leaned back in and rescued her shoes, apron and shawl and then shut the window after her.

The wet iron hurt her feet and she put down her shoes and eased her feet into them. Then she flung her shawl over her hair which was tumbling down her back and wrapped it close across her naked chest. She put a shaky hand on the veranda railing and edged slowly along the complaining wrought iron beneath her feet.

She was numb with fear and sudden cold.

A shaft of light from between Ivy's curtains lay across her

path. Beyond that she could see nothing. She paused at the light to peer ahead and then turned to look through the chink in the curtains into Ivy's room. She caught a horrifying glimpse of Ivy standing stark naked astride a tin bowl. She was swaying like a dervish and flourishing an old towel round her head. Daisy could clearly hear her shout, "Come on, lads! Ivy's waiting!"

Daisy moaned under her breath and put out an exploratory toe past the line of light. The veranda appeared to continue, so she eased herself past Ivy's window. She put out her foot again and there was nothing under it. Daisy froze.

Afraid of what might be ahead and even more fearful of what lay behind her, she quivered with indecision.

"Perhaps I'm turned the wrong way," she managed to think. "Staircase could be from the other end."

Desperately she peered ahead of her. Below her she saw the sudden flash of a torch. The constable on the beat must be checking the back of the building, she decided. From the direction in which the torch moved it appeared that there was an open courtyard below instead of the usual tiny back yard. The light ran up the wall and illuminated for a second an iron staircase ahead of her. She nearly fainted with relief.

She waited until the torchlight had moved away and then edged herself carefully down the welcome stairs.

Careless of rats, she ran like an alley cat along the side of the building until she found an entry which led into a deserted side street. From there she found her way into Lime Street which was still quite busy, despite the rain. She huddled for a minute or two in the doorway of the Empire Theatre, until the sound of shunting in the nearby railway station penetrated her numbed brain. The familiar noise comforted her a little and reminded her that the station had a ladies' lavatory where she might tidy herself. She sneaked up the side of the station and darted quickly through the Victorian archway which led into the platform nearest the waiting rooms. She ran the last few yards, at the same time hunting through her pockets for a penny. For a dreadful second she thought that she had only silver, then her fingers closed over one at the bottom of her pocket. She thrust the coin into the slot on a lavatory door and nipped inside. Quickly she shot the bolt, despite the fact that both station and waiting room appeared deserted.

She leaned, panting and shivering, against the door for a long time. Then she combed her hair and rebraided it. She put on her blouse and tied the front of it together. Since nobody else seemed to be using the cloakroom, and she feared that she had missed the last tram to Dingle, she sat down on the edge of the lavatory until, through her dozing, she heard the first morning tram rumble by.

At home, she found an anxious Agnes, who had taken over the care of Nellie from George. It did not take much persuasion to get her to go home, and Daisy sank thankfully into her own armchair before the roaring fire which Agnes had kept up for her. Nellie was sleeping well, Agnes had assured her.

Daisy started to shake again from head to foot. She put her head down on her knees to stop herself fainting and let the tears come in floods.

TWENTY-FOUR

A lorry rumbling along the street warned Daisy that morning had come. She raised her head and shook it, as if to rid herself of some of her wretchedness.

"Smarten up, Daise," she told herself, "Nell will be awake soon — and what'll she think if she sees you lookin' like a wet week?"

She was painfully sore, and she ached from head to foot. But she forced herself to remake the fire, which had fallen low while she wept, and to put a kettle of water on to boil. When the water was hot she took it into the scullery and washed herself.

Never in her life had she had such a desire to scrub herself all over; the scullery was so intensely cold, however, that she compromised by washing her face and those parts of herself which were most uncomfortable. Afterwards she took out her teeth and rinsed her mouth again and again. She was covered with goose pimples by the time she returned to the living-room, to stand by the fire and dress herself in her two petticoats. With needle and thread garnered from the crowded mantelpiece and some buttons taken out of a spoutless teapot she managed to make her blouse useable again. From a dresser drawer she took out one of her precious pairs of bloomers — which she never wore during her trips down town. Their softness was comforting.

"When t' pedlar comes, I'll buy meself a couple of blouses," she muttered with a watery sniff.

A piece of broken mirror was propped up on the scullery window and she lifted it down in order to examine herself. She was marked quite badly round the neck and her eyes were red-rimmed from crying.

If Nellie or anybody sees them hickies the game's up, she decided. She mentally sorted through the little house for something to put round her neck. "Pretend I got a sore throat," she advised herself. "Ee, I know, now."

She went to the dresser and took out two old stockings and carefully wound these round her neck, pinning them in place with a safety pin.

She put the kettle on again for tea and spread her shawl and skirt over the oven door to dry. Though she was swaying with fatigue, tea and a bit of bread and margarine seemed urgent necessities before she slept. She hoped passionately that Nellie would sleep late.

After eating, she dragged her humiliated, weary body on to her bed in the landing room, heaved over herself the collection of old coats which formed her covering and fell into a deep sleep.

She was awakened by Nellie, who had pottered out of her room feeling stronger than she had done for some time. A warm bed and a warm supper had given her sounder sleep than she had known for weeks.

"You was sleeping the sleep o' the dead," chuckled Nellie. "What you doing with the stocking round your neck?"

Daisy heaved herself over to face the questioner and forced herself into consciousness. Every bone in her body cried out for more rest. Nellie, however, had to be cared for, so slowly she got herself up on to her feet. She was very cold.

"How are you, Nell, luv?" She rubbed her arms to restore their warmth. "Me throat seemed sore last night — that's why I put the stockings round it."

"Oh, I'm feelin' much better." Nellie looked concernedly at Daisy. "You must have got chilled. Your eyes is all red and your lips is swollen."

"Och, I'm not so bad," She grinned at her friend. "Now you get back into bed till I get the fire going again or you'll be the one with a chill. I'll bring you some breakfast. Did doctor say you should stay in bed all the time?"

"No. Said I could do what I fancied. To keep warm but have the window open. He's coming here today, he said, anyways."

"The devil he did. I'd better hurry up."

She got Nellie back into bed and crawled downstairs. The doctor would not be the only visitor, she was sure. The place would be like a bloody tram terminus, she told herself. "I'll need the patience of a martyred saint."

Daisy's forecast proved accurate. Visitors trickled in and out all day. Sickness held a morbid fascination for the community, and, when the doctor arrived, the bedroom was already overcrowded with three beshawled, high-smelling visitors sitting cawing round the bed like carrion crows. The invalid was looking exhausted, and the doctor instructed that there should be only one visitor at a time and only when Nellie felt like receiving them.

He had been shocked at the miserable state of the living-room through which he had passed, and sickened by the sight of the landing bedroom. Nellie's bedroom came as a welcome surprise; it was basically clean and comfortable, and the fire gave plenty of warmth to the tiny room.

Seeing that Daisy seemed quite intelligent, he spent some time teaching her how to manage Nellie's illness. It was apparent to him that she was herself, for some reason, exhausted, and he warned her to watch her own health.

"Och, I'm fine," Daisy assured him, "except for a bit of a sore throat."

Iddy Joey came to see his mother after school. He stood uneasily by her bed, shifting from one foot to another.

"When you comin' home, Mam?" he asked her.

Nellie smiled adoringly at him. "Soon," she assured him. "You missin' your old Mam?"

"Yep." He went to stand by the fire to warm his backside. "Yer Dad make your breakfast all right?"

Yes, the ould fella had made his breakfast O.K. and they had had chips for lunch and a boiled egg for tea. Dad would be over later. Yes, he had been to school, and the teacher had given him a pair of socks from the lost and found box. He exhibited these to his mother — they did not match but, yes, they were warm.

When his mother ran out of questions and leaned back on her pillow, he waited for a moment and then edged to the door.

"Ta-ra, Mam."

"Ta-ra, luv." Nellie longed to call him back and kiss him but dared not. To pass T.B. to Joey would be the end, she told herself sadly.

Relieved that his visiting duties were over, Joey bounced down the stairs. Moggie saw him coming, and retreated under the table, his back arched. Joey went down on his knees and crept towards him, growling menacingly as he advanced. The cat spat as it found itself cornered. Joey seized its swishing tail and dragged the animal out from its retreat. The maddened cat scratched him soundly, as he swung it exultantly into the air. Joey howled in sudden pain, and let go. The cat fled into the scullery.

Nellie called out in fright at Joey's sharp cry, and Daisy sped in from the back yard.

"What ails you?"

Wailing, Joey exhibited a thin wrist with a long scratch welling with blood.

"Och, you stupid git." Daisy bent down, picked the child up and carried him lovingly to the kitchen tap to have his wound washed. Then she gave him a penny and sent him up to Mrs. Donnelly's to buy a lollipop.

The postman brought another card from Mike. Daisy was so busy that she just stuck it up against the clock and forgot about it.

Maureen Mary, anxious about her gentle aunt, arrived in the

afternoon. When she let herself in, she found her mother boiling eggs. She greeted her daughter absently.

As Maureen Mary eased off her blue felt hat, she noticed the brightly coloured post card, and picked it up and read it.

"Our Dad's coming home! You never told me!"

Daisy was throwing the eggshells into the fire and raking them into the coals to drown the awful odour they made. For a moment, she stood transfixed as the blood ebbed from her face. Mike home? Saints in Heaven preserve us! She felt Mike's belt across her back as surely as if she had actually been struck; she felt his boot hit her bottom as he kicked her into the street.

Her hand shook as, with her back still turned to Maureen Mary, she dropped the shelled eggs into a cup and broke them up with a spoon. "Yes, isn't it grand?" she finally managed to gasp.

Maureen Mary stared at her mother's broad back. "You sound proper queer. Aren't you glad?"

" 'Course, I am. It's me throat being sore that makes me sound funny." She hastily put down her spoon and caressed her stocking-wrapped neck. Then she balanced a couple of slices of bread and margarine on top of the cup, picked up the salt packet and tucked it under her arm, took up a clean spoon and the cup, and thus laden, turned and said to her daughter, " I'll just take these up to your Anty Nell. I'll be back in a tick. You could go up and sit with her while she eats."

Maureen Mary nodded agreement, as she hung her coat on the back of the front door, and then watched her mother slowly climb the stairs. She seemed to find the climb hard, and Maureen Mary thought uneasily that her mother did not seem to be her usual brisk self. A twinge of fear went through her, as she realized that the elder woman might find the care of yet another invalid too much for her health. Even mothers were not indestructible.

Daisy herself was having the greatest difficulty in avoiding falling into hysterics.

" I'm demolished," she wheezed, as she stopped in the landing bedroom to catch her breath. " What in the Name of God am I going to do? "

TWENTY-FIVE

Scarified at the news of Mike's return, Daisy sought with flustered fingers through her collection of old newspapers for the latest copy she had of the *Liverpool Echo*. Did the dreaded words "home soon" mean a month hence or next week or tomorrow?

A Shipping List in a copy of the paper which was two days' old did not list the *Heart of Salford* under 'Vessels Due Soon.' With a sigh of relief, Daisy flung the paper on to the floor and sank down into her easy chair. Slowly the beat of her heart returned to normal. Jaysus Christ! What a predicament.

Mike would have money in his pocket when he returned. But most of it would end up in the Ragged Bear in payment for rounds of drinks for his friends. He would never give a thought to the cost of nursing an invalid, though certainly he would make no objection to Nellie's being cared for in his home.

"And you can tell him forever and he won't hear," grumbled Daisy sourly to herself, as she leaned forward to stir the contents of a large blackened saucepan on the back of the fire. She was making stew with plenty of meat in it for Nellie and herself. And meat cost money.

She wondered if Mike would swallow the story of the bottle factory and, after much vacillation and rubbing of her tired face with her hands, she decided that he might do so.

But she must have a room, like Ivy. She'd be safer from chance encounters with Mike's friends, if she had her regulars in a room.

When she thought about the room next to Ivy's she shuddered. Not even for Nellie could she again go through the nightmare of the previous evening. Men by ones and twos she could manage; a horde like last night's was a terrible thing to happen to a law-abiding woman. It had been like the tales that Agnes's husband, Joe, had told them about the Germans in Belgium during the war, awful tales of kitchen tables dragged into the streets and girls held down on them and raped until they died. Them bleeding Jerries had a lot to answer for. Her mind wandered back to the day during the war when she had helped to smash up a German's butcher shop in Parkee Lanee. Bloody Bosche. She and the kids had eaten meat every day for a week after that.

The sound of the chair scraping across the bedroom floor, as Maureen rose, brought her back to the present with a jolt. Where could she find a room? A place where the landlord would turn a blind eye? A place close to the Ball and Chain.

Hands clasped between her knees, she rocked herself backwards and forwards, while she endeavoured frantically to find an answer. Finally, as Maureen Mary, came slowly back down the stairs, she decided that she had no one to turn to for advice except Ivy.

With nothing on but a faded wrapper, a very bleary-eyed Ivy answered Daisy's knock. Her breath smelled strongly of spirits and her room stank, even to Daisy's tolerant nose.

Ivy groaned and swayed on her feet, as she let her new-found friend in. "Ugh, I feel like somethin' the cat brought in. How's yourself?"

"I'd hate to tell yez," responded Daisy. She sat down gingerly on a chair by the roaring gas fire.

"What happened to you last night? T'door was bolted when I come in atterwards, but you didn't answer."

"Couldn't stand any more," confessed Daisy, and she went on to explain her escape along the veranda.

Ivy took a tin teapot off the gas stove and poured out two

cups of the boiling liquid, and while they sipped tea together Daisy broached the subject of a room.

Ivy eyed her silently. It was bad enough having two younger girls upstairs and a dear friend moving in next door very shortly.

Daisy sensed Ivy's reluctance to have her nearby, and she said conciliatorily, "We take different kinds — most of mine is young boys — just occasionally an older man. You must get those as likes a more Frenchy type."

The flattering suggestion that she was more sophisticated made Ivy unbend slightly. She tucked her wrapper more modestly over her thighs. "Trouble is, I don't know anywhere. Not many houses round here — mostly businesses."

Daisy felt a qualm of anxiety that this last resort might fail her, while Ivy hummed and haaed and sipped her tea.

She finally remembered a tailor who had, until recently, lived over his shop. He had now moved out of this apartment, while retaining the shop beneath.

The tailor was still working in the back of his shop, sitting cross-legged on his table and sewing button holes. It was some time before he answered Daisy's persistent rattle at his door.

He opened the door a mere slit.

"I'm closed," he snapped. Then, when he saw that a shawl woman stood on his step, he snarled, "What do you want?"

"Ivy sent me — about the rooms over your shop."

A thin, lascivious grin split a cadaverous face. "Come in, Missus," he invited oilily.

At first he demanded a shilling for every man she brought in, but Daisy's language at this suggestion was so explicit that he paled. "What I want a room for is me own business and none o' yours," she roared. "What a way to talk to a plain, decent woman what keeps herself to herself." She looked around his workroom so fiercely that he feared for a moment that she might begin to ransack it.

Finally, a bargain was struck. Daisy could have the room at

the top of the side stairs and the use of the bathroom. The other two rooms he wanted as storage and workrooms.

A rent book was found. Old entries were torn out and Daisy's name and the first week's rent were entered in it.

After she had handed over the money, she realised she had not yet seen the room and demanded to do so.

Grumbling, the tailor led her out of his shop, locked the front door, and then unlocked the side door and took her up a narrow, dark staircase.

"T' room's got furniture in it," he said. "Stuff I didn't want to put in me new house." He unlocked the door, took a box of matches out of his pocket, struck a match and lit a single gas light near the fireplace. He then bent down and lit a gas fire.

Daisy looked around primly. To her, the place was princely. There was a double bed with a mattress, a dressing-table, a table with two chairs tucked under it, and a small easy chair in a corner. There were cheap chintz curtains over the window, and clean, flowered linoleum covered the floor. A door on the opposite wall indicated that there was a storage cupboard.

She sniffed. "I suppose it'll do," she said.

The bathroom was next door. It was a small Victorian washroom with a single cold water tap, a wash basin and a cracked lavatory.

"Lock up everything when you go out," the tailor instructed, "And any damage you got to put right, understand?"

"Och, you're getting enough rent to cover the whole army marchin' through," replied Daisy. "What you worrying about?"

"Friends of Ivy has lots o' visitors," responded the tailor grimly.

Daisy had a strong desire to lift a fist and clout him down the stairs. She restrained herself, however, with the thought that the place was ideally isolated once the little shops in the street closed; and if she allowed that the constable on the beat might try the door once in the night, she was likely to be undisturbed. She decided that she must at all costs remember to lock the outside door when a man was with her; otherwise the constable might enter to check for intruders.

"I'll move in tomorrer," she told her hunched, ungainly landlord, as he put his matches back into his waistcoat pocket.

He looked the big, comely woman up and down in the gleam of light from the hallway and decided he might have a go himself one day. He contented himself for the moment by saying, "I'm gonna get a gas meter put in."

Daisy had taken for granted that somewhere in the room there was already a meter into which she would have to feed pennies to obtain gas, so she just nodded, and turned away.

He watched her as, with black skirts swaying, she walked smartly up the street. With a bit of luck, he would set the gas meter in such a way that he would make as much out of that as out of the rent itself. That would teach her.

TWENTY-SIX

The wind was wailing through the streets, carrying an occasional flake of snow with it, so Daisy decided to go home. "I'll tell George and Nell there was no work for me tonight," she decided, as she clambered laboriously on to a tram. Mother of Christ, every bone in her body ached and her eyelids dropped with lack of sleep. She sighed heavily, as she rocked with the motion of the vehicle and watched the street lamps flick by.

At home, she found George asleep beside his wife, and little Joey was dozing in the easy chair by a fading living-room fire.

George looked like a stuck pig, with his mouth wide open. But Nellie admonished her, "Himself is proper tired. Let him sleep."

"There was no work for me tonight," Daisy yawned. "I'll make us all some supper and we'll get into bed."

As she trailed up and downstairs, distributing bread, cheese and tea to her guests, she worried about where she could hide her newly-acquired rent book and also her precious hoard of savings. George would be in most nights, and iddy Joey was as nosy as a hungry cur, not to mention the possibility that sharp, observant Meg might arrive.

"And there'll be all the old biddies from round about come a-visiting, every bloody cousin we've got, and Christ knows who," she muttered. "I got to get that money out of Nellie's room yet — it ain't safe there."

She thought fleetingly of opening a banking account. Then, despite her fatigue, she could not help laughing at the idea. Even if she was allowed by the commissionaire to walk in, she would face a supercilious probing of her business; someone dressed in a shawl and boots did not fit in with gilt, marble and mahogany. She decided she couldn't face it.

"I can put rent book under me mattress in me new room," she concluded. "Money's a different matter."

If Mike discovered what she was doing, he would go through the roof with the force of the self-righteous explosion that would ensue. But, far worse than that, he would almost certainly demand the money she had made.

The problem was still not resolved when, the next evening, she toiled up the narrow, dark staircase to her new room. She knew now what kind of a trade she wished to carry on and she was anxious that the room look pleasant for those who wanted to stay an hour or so. She was laden with a bedspread and bedding, a fringed cloth for the table and a flowered china candlestick and candles.

She arranged the bed, and afterwards pulled one of the chairs out and sat down. She looked round her domain with satisfaction. The night at Ivy's had at least paid for all that she had bought.

The sound of her own breathing seemed unnaturally loud in the still room. Gradually the unearthly quietness of the place became overwhelming, and she jumped when a piece of furniture gave a sudden creak. She found herself listening with abnormal intensity. But through the thick walls no sound of distant traffic penetrated, no human voice or footstep came from the deserted street below.

She looked slowly round the room as if she expected that someone or something would surely spring at her. But the sparse furniture remained in its place, the cupboard door remained shut.

She shuddered.

"Ee, I could be mairdered and lie here for a week before anybody found me — and they wouldn't know who I was when they did find me," she said out loud, and the sound of her own voice made her jump.

Then she laughed with a hint of hysteria. "Get out and find yerself somebody to bring in, you bloody fool. Only be a bit careful, like."

She got up and shook out her skirts, smoothed her hair in front of a small mirror on the wall, and smiled with artificial gaiety at her reflection. "Get moving, Liverpool Daisy!"

TWENTY-SEVEN

When next Daisy went down to the shipping office to collect Mike's allotment, she inquired about the arrival of the *Heart of Salford*.

She was assured that the ship was indeed coming home. She should watch the "Due Soon" column in the *Echo* for the exact date of arrival.

She forgot all about Mike immediately she lifted the latch of her front door. She could hear Nellie coughing frantically.

The invalid had crawled downstairs and the effort had set off a fit of coughing. She was sitting in the easy chair with her head on her knee, when Daisy entered.

"Holy Mary!" exclaimed Daisy. "What you been doing?" She ran to Nellie and eased her back till she rested against the cushion. "Nell, luv, ah thought you'd be all right in bed till I come. You should have stayed in yer bed, dear."

The coughing began to ease, and Nellie gasped, "I was fed up — thought I'd come down for a change." She sounded fretful, not her usual patient self.

"Well, never mind," said Daisy. "I'll get a cloth and wipe your face, and then we'll have a nice cuppa tea to clear your throat."

Never argue with them as has T.B., was one of Daisy's favourite adages. They're just plain bad-tempered. She soon had Nellie in a better frame of mind, when, after a dose of medicine, she was tucked up in the easy chair, her feet on the brass fender.

Over their tea, they reminisced about the funny things they had done when they were young together. Finally, the conversation turned to the man of the house.

"'E won't want me here," said Nellie apprehensively.

"Och, never give it a thought," replied Daisy. "He'll just be thankful it isn't me Mam that's up there."

Nellie chuckled at the memory of Mike's dislike of his sharp little mother-in-law, and then as if suddenly very tired she leaned back in the chair and closed her eyes.

Daisy viewed compassionately her friend's worn face. The firelight cast shadows in the hollow cheeks and darkened the eye sockets, till Daisy felt with a sense of panic that she was already looking at a dead skull. Her stomach muscles clenched. She could not endure the thought of losing Nellie and she wondered agonisedly what more she could do to help her. Food, medicine, warmth, all these had been provided with a lavish hand. What more?

Then with sudden inspiration, she asked, "Would you like to see Father Patrick, Nell? 'Cos you can't go to church at present, like."

Nellie's eyes shot open. Their expression was one of pure terror. When your relations started to think about sending for the priest, you were a sure gonner. It was one thing to feel that you were going to die, another to be brought face to face with other people's confirmation of it. She seemed to shrink into herself and become an even smaller lump beneath her enveloping shawl.

"Am I that sick, Daise?"

"Ee, na, Nellie, luv. You're not fit to go to Mass, so I thought you might like to see him."

Last time she and Nellie had gone to Confession, Daisy had, after prevaricating her way through a garbled admission of the sin of avarice, fully expected to be struck dead by lightning bolts. But nothing had happened, and she wondered now, as she waited for Nellie's reply, if perhaps God and His Holy Mother understood better than men what dire things could happen to a woman.

Nellie clasped and unclasped her hands, which looked like mis-shaped, blue-veined claws. She looked around the crowded, homely room where she had spent so many youthful, contented hours with Daisy and her brothers and sisters.

"Yes," she finally sighed unhappily. "Yes, I'd better see 'im. I want to ask him to help keep an eye on iddy Joey."

A couple of days later Father Patrick came to visit. Daisy left him with the invalid so that Nellie could, if she wished, make her confession.

The old priest conversed with Nellie for some time and promised to visit George and iddy Joey.

"Mrs. Gallagher seems to have made you very comfortable here," he remarked.

"Oh, aye," whispered Nellie. "She's proper kind. She's a wonder. She even works Saturdays and Sundays at her job, so as to get time and a half to help pay for everything. And then she comes home and takes care o' me. She's a true friend."

Father Patrick went slowly and thoughtfully down the stairs. Sometimes the manifestation of pure, self-sacrificing human love in his poverty-stricken parish was so humbling that it blotted out the remembrance of the drunkenness, the family quarrels, the street fights, the endless petty theft, of which he was painfully aware.

He blessed a flushed, embarrassed Daisy as he went out into the street.

Daisy began to use her new room each evening. She acquired a regular client, which pleased her. He was a young labourer working on the new tunnel under the River Mersey. He came in each Friday night, after the Ball and Chain closed.

She learned the timing of the police constable on his beat, and slipped her clients in and out circumspectly, so that his attention was never particularly drawn to the door beside the tailor's shop. She paid her rent promptly and maintained a stiff-lipped silence, when the tailor jeered at her with obscene remarks, though she sometimes longed to strike him.

She bought an old alarm clock to help her with the timing of the constable's beat and the length of her clients' visits. She nearly yielded to the temptation of paying for some additional bed sheets out of her earnings. But her earnings were for Nellie's needs, for bowls, soap, towels, nightgowns.

One morning, she went to see her old antagonist, the Welfare lady.

The moment the Welfare lady saw Daisy's file she remembered how Daisy had accepted a blanket for her invalid mother's use when that lady was already dead.

Daisy, seated suitably humbly on a wooden chair beside the desk, saw her stiffen with disapproval. Undaunted, she launched into a long description of Nellie's illness and the need for extra bedding in case she haemorrhaged unexpectedly.

"Why hasn't the doctor put her in the sanatorium?"

Daisy sighed. How to explain how frightening it was to be put in a hospital? That's where you went to die, if you had no one to care for you.

She shook her head negatively. "She didn't want to go. T' doctor didn't press her, 'cos she's got me to look after her."

"Humph. Terminal, I suppose?"

Daisy went white and there was a singing in her ears. You don't say things like that about a woman's best friend.

"No," she gasped out. "She's going to get better." She wiped a genuine tear from her eye.

The Welfare lady saw the tear and her manner softened. "I'll visit you tomorrow," she promised.

When the next morning her little car drew up outside Daisy's front door and a beaming Daisy let her in, she noticed immediately the improvement in the little home. She remembered it clearly as one of the more neglected and poverty-stricken in her district. In a thousand subtle ways it indicated to her experienced eyes either a great change of heart or a great improvement in circumstances. She began to wonder suspiciously if her help was truly needed.

She looked round doubtfully, at the glowing fire, the glittering fender, the new pat of margarine on the table. The comfortable smell of kippers outweighed the usual odour of vermin, and on the clothes line stretched along the mantelpiece some white, recently washed, underwear steamed in the fire's heat.

Mrs. Gallagher had declared her income as eighteen shillings a week allotment and Nellie's part of the allowance George drew from the Public Assistance Committee, out of which she paid seven shillings' rent. The woman must be a better manager than most were.

She asked to see Nellie and, again, was agreeably surprised. By her personal standards the house was still dirty and comfortless, but in comparison with others in the district Mrs. O'Brien's bedroom, where a good fire also blazed, was much superior.

If the Welfare Lady had expected to get any information out of Nellie as to how the transformation had been achieved, she was disappointed. Not even simple Nellie would discuss with a welfare worker what money one had — one discussed only what money was needed.

Downstairs, the Welfare worker asked Daisy, "Would you be prepared to pay, say, a shilling a week towards the cost?"

Daisy looked horror-stricken. "With less'n thirty bob a week coming in, and me with a sick woman to feed?" she asked, with a dramatic flourish of a hand across her heart. The thought of having to take a shilling each week to the woman's office or, alternatively, have a voluntary worker collect it, filled her with repugnance. More bloody nosy-parkers round the place.

A week later, Daisy received with real gratitude two pairs of sheets and a fine wool blanket. The blanket was made from small, brightly coloured hand-knitted squares stitched together, and she immediately spread it over Nellie's bed.

"Aye!" Nellie exclaimed, "It's proper pretty to look at when you feel low."

Daisy took the sheets down to her room in the city.

It seemed to Daisy that she was walking a narrow tightrope and that any moment she might, from sheer fatigue, lose her balance and go spinning to the floor. What little sleep she managed to get was frequently broken by a fretful cry from Nellie, who needed help now even to use the rose-wreathed chamber pot under the bed.

And the visitors trickled into the house steadily. Even Freddie came one evening, with Maureen Mary, just before Daisy departed for work.

Daisy had not seen her son-in-law since her mother's funeral, and she greeted him with rough good humour. Maureen Mary kissed her mother and then went upstairs to see her aunt, leaving Daisy alone with Freddie for a few minutes.

He stood with his back to the fire, giving no hint that the heavy stuffiness of the room made him feel nauseated. This was his wife's mother, and he knew that her influence on Maureen Mary was so strong that the slightest upset might culminate in Maureen Mary and little Bridie finishing up in Daisy's house.

He watched Daisy arrange her plaits carefully round her ears and add a couple of hairpins to the back of her head. She looked quite graceful, standing in front of the tiny wall mirror, and he realised suddenly where Maureen Mary had got her charm from.

She turned and picked up her shawl from the back of a chair and flung it over her shoulders. She smiled at him a little mischievously, and then said hesitatingly, "I got to go to work. You know I'm workin', Freddie?"

"Yes."

"Well, I'm trying to save a bit." Her smile faded and she looked suddenly terribly sad, the generous mouth drooping as if she might start to cry. "It's in case our Nell dies — she's hasn't got any insurance — no burial club. And I won't have her with a pauper's funeral." She bit her lower lip. "I don't know how to keep the money safe. I mean, banks aren't for the likes o' me — they'd laugh at me. And what with me husband coming home soon, and our George ... What could I do with it, Fred?"

The implied trust of the confidence made Freddie swell out his chest a little and rock himself confidently backwards and forwards on his heels. He put his hands in his trouser pockets while he considered the matter.

"Well," he replied judiciously. "The best thing would be to open a Post Office Savings account. Everybody goes to the post office." He grinned at her. "Just watch you don't lose the book."

"Aaah!" breathed Daisy. She relaxed, and some of the distress went out of her expression. "That's the gear! What would I do without you, Fred?"

She opened an account at the huge central post office, where it was practically certain that no one would recognise her. A deposit such as she made, if handed over in the local store which doubled as a post office, would have caused a sensation.

On the tram returning home, she smiled a little grimly to herself, as she felt the savings book through the thickness of her skirt. "I'll hide book in me room — with the rent book." Then she sighed heavily. All that money would have bought a lot of glasses of beer at the Ragged Bear, a lot of seats to see the pictures in the "Flea Pit", the local cinema. It was as well she could not spend much locally without drawing comment from her neighbours; otherwise, she might not have felt so strongly about saving for a funeral that she kept assuring herself would not take place. Nellie had to get better, not buried.

"Holy Angels from the Throne of Light, let her live," she muttered suddenly.

TWENTY-EIGHT

It was fluttery Agnes's turn to watch Nellie. She spent hour after hour of the dark winter evening sitting nervously by the sick woman's bed, gnawing her nails and muttering, "What'll I do if she dies while Daisy is out?" Every time Nellie, beset by fever, burst into incoherent speech, Agnes would half rise from her seat in panic and mutter, "Holy Mother, save us!" while she patted Nellie's shoulder to comfort her.

She was further unnerved when a strange man came to the door and asked for Daisy.

"Daisy's at work at the bottle factory," she said timidly, holding the door open only a crack.

The man sniggered unpleasantly. "Tell her Pat from the Hercy Dock came."

She nodded, and quickly shut the door.

When Daisy came home about three in the morning, she told her about the Irishman. Relief at Daisy's return overwhelmed her initial curiosity, and she failed to notice how white Daisy went at the news.

Good God and the angels! she thought frantically, I must tell those I know not to come to the house any more. She continued to worry as she and Agnes lay down together on one of the landing-room beds, since Agnes was much too scared to go home in the dark.

Both women awoke to the violent coughing of Nellie, from the front bedroom.

"Jaysus!" Daisy muttered as she stumbled out of bed and ran

to help her friend.

Agnes leaned out of bed and felt frantically for the candle and matches. Not even for Nellie could she persuade herself to get out of bed without a light.

In Nellie's room the candle had gutted and only a faint glimmer from the fire gave any light. It bathed the suffering woman in a dim, unearthly glow as, half raised on her elbow, she struggled for breath.

"Bring a basin, Aggie, and a towel," shouted Daisy, "and be quick about it." She put her arm around Nellie and eased her to a more upright position. "It's all right, luv, you'll be all right in a minute," she assured Nellie, as she stroked back the straggling hair from the woman's face.

Agnes fumbled with the matches and finally got a light. She tumbled out of bed and, shielding the precious candle flame with one hand, she fled to the kitchen for the towel and basin. The spasm of coughing seemed to get worse and she could hear Nellie's mourning sobs of pain in between the coughs. Tears burst from her eyes.

"Holy Mary, Mother of God," she prayed, as she ran into the bedroom, the candle flame lying flat and threatening to go out. "Dear St. Jude, hear me."

But Nellie did not die that night. The two women struggled to ease her as she haemorrhaged, then cleaned her tenderly and propped her up as comfortably as they could. The kitchen fire was stoked up, the hot water bottle was filled and salt bags heated to ease her pain.

As she emptied the basin, Agnes vomited uncontrollably into the kitchen sink. She turned on the tap, and, while she waited for the water to cleanse the sink, she cried bitterly, partly from fear of death and partly because her bare feet were icy on the stone floor.

She had left the candle with Daisy, but the faint light of early dawn gave some small illumination. Shakily she crept back upstairs in order to be close to Daisy.

She stood shivering by the fire in her petticoats while Daisy made soft crooning sounds to Nellie and stroked her forehead.

Daisy said irritably, "Go and get your clothes on and see if you can find a boy in t' street to go up to the doctor. Tell him to come soon."

A boy on his way to fetch milk from the dairy promised to get the doctor as soon as he had finished his message. Agnes pressed twopence in his hand and told him to hurry because somebody might die if he did not. Suitably impressed, he broke into a fast jog trot, his milk can jiggling madly on its handle.

The doctor again pressed Nellie to enter hospital.

Nellie clutched at Daisy's hand with what poor strength she had and kept nodding her head negatively throughout the discussion, and Daisy said flatly, "Our Nell's not going if she don't want to. I'll get our Meg to help me, too."

Resignedly, the doctor wrote another prescription and said he would come again the next morning.

Since neither woman wanted to be left alone with Nellie, they deferred taking the prescription to the chemist, in the hope that they could find a messenger to take it in the course of the morning. Agnes made some breakfast for them all. Nellie refused everything but tea. For the most part she lay quiet, but at times her mind seemed to wander and she would make some inconsequential remark as if she was talking to George during their courtship. This set Agnes fluttering like an autumn leaf in the wind and, with almost hysterical relief, she pounced on Joey when he arrived near lunch time.

"Take this to Mr. Williamson and wait while he makes it up," she said, thrusting the prescription into his hand. Then she shouted up to Daisy, "Can you give me some money for the medicine?"

"Aye," said Daisy and came down to get her purse, to which she had transferred her earnings of the previous night.

"Your Mam isn't too well, at all," she said to Joey. "Hurry."

Joey looked fearfully up at his aunt. Without a word he took the slip of paper and ran out of the house. He was back in five minutes. "He's makin' the stuff, but he wants another half-a-crown." He was white and panting.

Daisy looked at him with compassion. "You stay with your Anty Aggie and go up to see your Ma. I'll go for the meddie." She sighed. "Then maybe Antie Aggie'll make you summat to eat."

It took her a few minutes to walk up the sloping street to the chemist. Her boot heels dragged along the pavement and her shoulders slumped under her shawl. What a night! Still, street-walking was better than working in the laundry or the sack factory, she told herself. You can have a good laugh with t' men — and they're proper grateful when you give 'em a good time.

After leaving the chemist's, she went next door to the bakery and bought some fancy cakes in the hope of tempting Nellie to eat something.

Iddy Joey, looking a little less scared, was ensconced in her easy chair, a piece of bread and jam in his hand. "Cousin Winnie come to see if her Mam was still here. She says me Dad's just gone in to the Ragged Bear," he informed her. Over his hunk of bread, he glanced quickly round the room. "Where's Moggie?"

Nellie saw the gleam of the cat's eyes peeping down at the boy from the back of the mantelpiece. "Dunno," she said to him.

Blast George! She had forgotten that this was the day on which he drew his public assistance; he'd probably be too drunk to watch Nellie tonight. She pondered on the wisdom of asking Great Aunt Devlin to do a turn. But if, after her last spasm, Nellie saw her Great Aunt leaning over her, she might think she was near to death. "I'll have to ask Meg to help me tonight," she remarked dismally to Agnes, "George may be bevvied."

Agnes made a rude face. "You could send Joey up to ask her," she suggested.

Iddy Joey was surreptitiously opening the white paper bag of

cakes to see what was in it. Daisy leaned over and gave his wrist
a sharp slap. "Have you been up to see your Ma?"

"No," he said sulkily, as he rubbed his sore wrist.

"Well, I'll go and give her her medicine and you can come
with me."

Nellie was awake and staring silently into the fire. She smiled
weakly at her son, as he reluctantly sidled round the bed. "You
all right, luv?" she asked tenderly.

He nodded dumbly, while he stared wide-eyed at her and rubbed the back of his leg with one boot-shod foot.

"You should be in school," she reproved him.

"No — it's some old saint's day."

She nodded. When she put out a thin hand to touch him, he
retreated from her. The hurt look on her face, however, shamed
him, and he came up close again and put his arm clumsily round
her head, as it rested on the pillow.

Her smile was beatific. "That's my lad. Now you be a good
boy and do whatever your Auntie Daise tells you."

Back downstairs with Agnes, he crammed a mass of bacon
and potatoes into his mouth, prior to going up to ask his Auntie
Meg to come.

"You can have a cake, when you've finished your bacon, luv.
And another one after you been to Aunt Meg's."

Joey sighed blissfully at the thought of the cakes. Then said,
"I don't want to go. I'd rather stay with you."

"Nay, you go. She'll come if you ask. She'd not refuse you."

TWENTY-NINE

On the morning of desperate Daisy's capitulation to Meg, the m.v. *Heart of Salford* slid slowly over the bar. Salt-caked and rusted, it chugged up-river and docked at the north end. It was, however, late afternoon before Mike Gallagher was finally paid off and came sauntering down the gangplant, followed closely by his friend, Peter O'Shea, trimmer. Opposite the dock entrance, the lights of a pub shone out across the damp sets of the street, as a barman flicked them on, ready for the evening trade.

"Let's have a quick one," said Mike, reluctant to leave his friend and face the re-adjustment to his bleak home and formidable wife. The blast of warm air and the bright glitter of mirrors and well polished brass welcomed them, as they entered, and there they remained until closing time.

Meg was delighted to receive a token of surrender from Daisy, in the shape of iddy Joey begging for help. She patted the child's head and assured him she would come as soon as she had given her family their tea. She ran upstairs and ordered her whining, protesting, sister-in-law, Emily, to get the children and Mr. Fogarty to bed before ten o'clock. She moved through the house like light; and slow John had to hold her against the scullery wall, while he fondled her hopefully through her skirts.

"For the love of Christ, let me be, Johnnie boy," she cried fretfully. "I got enough to do, without you botherin' me."

But he would not let her go, and swung her out of the back door and into the absolute blackness of a corner of the tiny back yard, the only private place they had ever known.

She responded to him, despite her hurry, and clung to him, loving him dumbly, unable to communicate with him very well except sexually.

She entered her sister's house like a gust of wind, just as Daisy was wrapping a shawl round herself, preparatory to going to work.

Daisy had on a clean apron, which she had ironed with a huge flat iron now standing on the mantelpiece, next to one of the precious china dogs. The iron was a recent purchase from Hannigan's Second Hand Furniture Emporium. Her hair was neatly combed and plaited and her face scrubbed in cold water until it was rosy. Her gold keeper earrings which her grandfather had bought her, gleamed in her ears, having been rescued after a long sojourn in the pawnbroker's shop; Meg could not remember when she had last seen them. Her black stockings were for once neatly pulled up and secured by elastic garters below her knees; on her feet were her best patent leather shoes, bought originally for little Tommy's funeral. She wiggled her feet uncomfortably, because the shoes had become tight after the soaking they had received on the night that she had met Ivy.

"Well, isn't that the gear," remarked Meg, as she swept off her shawl and circled slowly round her sister.

Daisy flushed with embarrassment, and her teeth flashed as she muttered defensively, "Well, I got to look nice for work, somehow. Proper fussy, they are." By this time she had managed to build up in her mind a world in a bottle factory, for the benefit of Nellie who was naturally interested in her friend's occupation, so this statement came out without a moment's hesitation in response to Meg's sneer.

Meg shrugged and sniffed, then went to the fire to warm her hands. "How's our Nellie tonight?"

"She isn't well at all." There was a break in Daisy's voice. "Aye, I hate to leave her." She paused, and then went on heavily, "I need the money, though — her meddie this morning cost the earth — and the doctor an' all. And she gets pain, Meg — give her two spoonsful of meddie if it's real bad — and there's some salt bags in the oven to put by her side if she needs them."

Meg bit her lower lip and her voice was gentle as she replied, "Never you mind. I'll take care of her. It'll be a pleasure after old Fogarty. Is she eating?"

"A bit. Make her some tea."

"Where's Joey?"

"Upstairs, asleep."

Meg sat down in a straight chair and began to unlace her boots. "It wouldn't hurt your Maureen Mary to come down and give you a hand."

Daisy's face flushed. That was Meg all over. First, all kindness and light, and the next minute hitting you on a real sore spot. She controlled the retort that rose to her lips. She said carefully, "She hasn't anyone to leave Bridie with."

"Humph," grunted Meg, and dropped her boots into the hearth as if Maureen Mary was under them.

Daisy made haste to the door, lest she be provoked into saying something she would afterwards regret. "Be back about one, all being well."

"Christ!" exclaimed Meg, her round eyes wide, "That's late! How'll I get home?"

"Och, go in the morning when it's light. If they want overtime, I'll do it."

"You *are* after the money."

"And do you think as I would be going out in the middle of the night, if I didn't need it?" Daisy flipped the latch open impatiently.

"Is George up with Nellie?"

"No. He's bevvied. Joey says he's asleep in their old room." She clicked her tongue. "He gets his Public Assistance of a Thursday."

At least on the subject of George the two sisters were united in their disapproval, so Meg said, "What else would you be expecting him to do?" She wrinkled her nose in distaste.

Daisy sighed gustily. "Ta-ra," she said in farewell and slammed the door after her, remembering a fraction too late poor Nellie in the room above.

Meg ran lightly up the stairs in her stockinged feet.

The bed was rumpled by the sick woman's tossing and turning. She was muttering to herself as if she had fever.

When Meg laid her hand on her brow to check her temperature, Nellie opened her eyes and stared at her without recognition for a moment. Then she said with a faint smile, "It's our Meg. Aye, Meg, the pain is bad and I'm so hot." Her mind seemed to wander, and after a pause, she asked, "Has the baby come yet?"

The inconsequential question made Meg jump. Poor Nellie must be unhinged. She peered closely at her patient.

"Pain's real bad this time," Nellie whimpered. Her lips drew back over her gums, and she gasped. "How long do you think it'll be?" Her back arched suddenly as if she was indeed in childbirth. "Give me summat to hold."

Meg glanced quickly round the room in search of some object that Nellie might clutch to help her bear the pain. There was nothing suitable. She leaned over Nellie to straighten the bedclothes. "There, there, Nellie, luv. There's no baby; you're sick, that's all. But you lie still a mo' and I'll get the rolling-pin for yez."

Nellie seemed to understand, and Meg sped down to the scullery, where a candle burned in generous waste. Aided by its flickering light, Meg searched hastily along the cluttered shelves. Daise had more stuff on one long kitchen shelf than Meg had on half a dozen. For the love of Christ, where was the rollingpin?

She found it between a meat tin with a good inch of fat in it and a large Quaker Oats box, and snatched it up thankfully. Then she went to the kitchen oven, hauled Moggie out and found, behind the spitting cat's resting place, a fresh, hot salt bag.

Nellie had tossed the bedding off again.

"Here, Nellie, dear, you hold this," and she thrust the rolling-pin into Nellie's hands. Then she tucked the hot bag close to Nellie's side.

Nellie clasped the pin and seemed comforted by it. It was the same pin that Daisy had held through all the births and miscarriages she had endured. She lay still, while Meg straightened the bottom sheet and smoothed the edges under the mattress. When she tucked in the side furthest from where Nellie was lying, her fingers touched something between slats and mattress. She pulled it out. It was an old wallet, and she laid it on the floor while she finished her bedmaking.

When Nellie was well wrapped up again and had swallowed a dose of medicine, she seemed more herself, and Meg asked, "Shall I put your wallet under your pillow, luv? You might forget it under the mattress."

"Eh?"

"Your wallet. Where do you want to keep it?"

Nellie smiled dimly. "I don't have no wallet. I got a little purse at home. I didn't bring it 'cos there's nothin' in it." She gave a little laugh which hurt her, and she winced and closed her eyes.

"Must be one o' Mike's old ones or one o' Daisy's," Meg said. She took it close to the candle on the mantelpiece and idly opened it. She ran her fingers round its compartments. There was no money in it. There was, however, a card in it — a kind of identity card. She held it up to the candle flame so that she could read it. It was a seaman's card, made out in the name of a Liberian shipping company; and it carried the photograph of a middle-aged man. A signature identified him as Thomas Ward. She turned the card over in her hand. She was mystified.

Nellie's eyes were closed. The medicine and the warmth seemed to have soothed her, so Meg tiptoed from the room. In the landing bedroom Joey snuffled and turned over. Meg threw an old coat lying on the floor over his shoulders.

Downstairs, she pulled the easy chair up to the fireplace and sat down. Very thoughtfully, she opened the wallet again. Further exploration yielded three receipts, which she glanced at without much interest, and two photographs. One photo was of a fat woman sitting in a deck chair on a beach; the other was of a group of negroes in long, flapping costumes. She examined both pictures intently in the light of the paraffin lamp. She decided that she had never seen the woman in the picture; the picture of the negroes had palm trees in the background and she presumed that it had been taken in Liberia.

While the wind whined around the house, sometimes sending a gust down the chimney to blow puffs of smoke into the room, she toasted her toes in the hearth and thought about her find.

Had Mike or Daisy found it in the street, say? She pondered this idea and dismissed it. Who was going to push a found wallet under a mattress? It would be left lying around in the living-room.

Had Mike stolen it from another crew member? Meg nodded her head negatively at this idea. Mike would not risk a beating up from an enraged victim, who would almost certainly be bigger than Mike's miserable five foot two inches. Besides, he had not been home since Nan's death; and, as she had observed when she went to tend Nellie, the room had been done up since then, and the bed would have been stripped.

While the soot-encrusted kettle sang over the fire, she thoughtfully ran her fingers over the worn design of camels and palm trees on the outside of the wallet. She smiled grimly to herself.

Mike had been away a long time, far longer than he ever had before; and, though in Meg's opinion, he was a miserable runt of a man compared to her own John, Daisy probably missed him. She might have found herself a boy friend. Daisy had never been short of admirers when she was young, and why she had chosen to marry Mike was a mystery to Meg. Now, of course, she was old and as plump as a cottage loaf. Just that bit older than Meg that she did not have to worry about being pregnant, thought her sister savagely. Not too old to enjoy a bit of slap and tickle, though.

Meg caressed the wallet in her hand. She began to glow all over. "God give me a good vengeance," she said out loud.

THIRTY

Mike kicked his kitbag to one side of the room and dumped his tin suitcase down by it. He flung his cap on to the chest of drawers, where it landed with a rustle amid copies of the *Liverpool Echo*, which Daisy had forgotten to check over during the previous few days. He wiped his yellow-white face on his sleeve and advanced towards the fire, to rub his hands over it. He had travelled across the city on the swaying overhead railway and, on arrival at Dingle Station, his outraged stomach had rebelled and he had vomited.

"Where's Daise?" he inquired of Meg, who had hastily risen from her chair as he entered the front door. She was staring at him, as if he was a ghost, her round eyes barely able to assimilate the fact that the man she had been thinking about was suddenly standing before her.

"Workin'," she said, as she slipped the wallet hastily into her apron pocket.

"Her? What for?"

"Money, of course." Meg unexpectedly felt the need to defend her sister's absence, and she added with asperity, "She needed the money — the allotment wasn't enough after Nan died and took her pension with her."

Mike's mouth twisted sulkily. "She'd only herself to keep."

"Och, you men! She'd rent to pay and fire to keep just the same," retorted Meg. She took the teapot out of the oven, where she had been keeping it warm. "She's on night shift, according to Joey, so I don't know when she'll be home. Will you have a

217

cup of tea? Or would you like me to make you a bite to eat?"

Mike closed his eyes. He felt sick again. "Tea'll do," he said. He sat down suddenly on a kitchen chair.

She poured the tea for him and he took a slurpy gulp of the well-boiled liquid, and shuddered. "What's Daise workin' at?" he asked.

"In t' bottle factory downtown, so Agnes says."

"Why didn't she go to t' sack place? It's closer."

"Dunno. More money probably. Beggars can't be choosers. Now she's got Nell to look atter, she needs money."

Nellie's illness was explained to him, and her presence and that of iddy Joey upstairs. He accepted this as a natural happening, after which silence fell.

While Mike drew out a cigarette and lit it, Meg surreptitiously slipped her feet into her boots. It was not seemly, she felt, to be observed without footwear by one's brother-in-law.

She tried to think of something to say to him. But women did not gossip much with men in her small world and nothing suggested itself, except a desire to ask him if he knew a man called Thomas Ward. She cleared her throat nervously, and this roused Mike from the warm stupor into which he had fallen.

"I'll not wait for Daisy," he announced. "I was workin' all night and we was docking today — it was a long day."

Meg jumped up, and said with relief. "I'll tell Daise you're here. Nellie is in the front room and Joey is on one of the beds in the back."

"Humph. I'll find a place."

He was soon snoring irregularly beside Joey. His booted feet, sticking out at the bottom, twitched occasionally as he dreamed.

Joey, half-wakened, assumed his father had arrived and cuddled down again, to add his modest snuffles to his uncle's stentorian performance.

Meg came up, slipping past the sleepers like a mouse, and made up the fire in Nellie's room. Daisy must be going through coal like an ocean liner, she decided.

She poked up the fire in the living-room. She was so accustomed to having too much to do that to sit for long was difficult to her. Once again she took out the wallet and fingered its worn surface. What *had* Daisy been up to? There wasn't much opportunity to be unfaithful in a place where everybody knew everybody else. Gossip went round too fast.

She was still musing over the mystery when a footsore, worn out Daisy arrived home soon after three.

She entered slowly, dragging one foot after another, and Meg yawned and jumped up. She glanced at the clock. "My God, you're late!" she exclaimed. She sounded almost compassionate, when, after viewing Daisy's bedraggled appearance, she added, "You look real tired."

"I am, b' Jaysus. Missed the bloody tram. Had to walk." She slumped down on to the straight chair on which, earlier, Mike had sat.

"I'll make some fresh tea."

"Ta, Meg."

A spark of real gratitude went through Daisy. Thank goodness, Meg seemed willing to bury the hatchet at last. She heaved herself close to the fire, put her feet on the fender and pulled her skirts back over her knees.

This evening she had not had to walk the streets at all and she had over a pound in her skirt pocket. But sharp-eyed Meg was here. She must be careful. She pulled her black shawl up round her neck. Lord, how cold she was. If it had not been for Nellie, she would have put a shilling in the gas meter and stayed the night in her secret room.

"Mike come home," Meg informed her cheerfully, as she put a fresh kettle on the fire.

Daisy swivelled round on her wooden chair as if she had been struck.

Meg looked up from ladling more tea into the pot. Her sister's face had drained to an unearthly white, except for the burn mottles on either cheek. She stared at Meg, her mouth agape.

Meg stood with a teaspoonful of tea poised over the pot and stared back at Daisy's horrified expression.

"What's up?" she asked. "Wasn't you expectin' him?"

Daisy's bosom heaved as she sought for breath to enable her to answer Meg. Her terror was so great that the words would not come.

The tea spilled from the overfilled spoon. Meg looked down at the fallen leaves and swore. She hastily dropped the remaining leaves into the pot.

The diversion gave Daisy a moment in which to control her panting.

Meg kneeled down to brush up the dry leaves from the hearth with a piece of newspaper. "Didn't you know?" she inquired.

"No. Well, yes. He said he'd be home soon," Daisy floundered. "I didn't expect him yet, though. I forgot to watch the shipping list in the *Echo* — and them bloody shipping clerks down at the office, they never tell you nothin'. Ee, what'll I do?"

Meg sat back on her heels. "Well, I'd have thought you would have been glad after all this time." She tittered as she got up off the rag rug. "What you so upset about? He'll keep you warm at night. He's been away a long time." Her voice was heavy with innuendo.

Daisy rubbed her face wearily with her hands. "Mike?" she gasped derisively, as colour began to come back into her cheeks. "Him?" She clapped her hands down on to her knees and looked up at Meg. "Naught left by the time he comes home. Where is he?"

"Gone to bed. He's bevvied." Meg made a face. "Smelled as if he'd coughed up."

"Humph."

"I must get home meself."

Daisy was recovering from her first panic; Mike's coming home drunk put him in the wrong immediately — which was very convenient if you looked like being in trouble yourself. She said kindly to Meg, "You might as well stay till daylight. You can kip down with me. How's our Nell?"

Meg sighed, then stretched herself and yawned. She swung her arms hopelessly down to her sides.

"She's sinking, Daise, to my way of thinking."

"No, she isn't," snapped Daisy. She sniffed, and wriggled her shoulders unhappily under her shawl. "She's going to get better. I'm giving her everything so as she can, poor dear." Daisy's voice rose in protest, "She's got to get better."

"Well, I don't like the look of her at all, I don't."

"You're welcome to your opinion." Daisy leaned forward and spread her cold hands to the fire for a moment; then she took her teeth out of her mouth and slipped them into her apron pocket.

"Tush," said Meg irritably. Daisy was the most provoking bitch she had ever had to deal with. She could never agree with you for more than two minutes together. And she'd taken over their mother's home without so much as a by your leave. Meg's nostrils distended and her mouth compressed. She stuffed her hands into her apron pockets and touched the wallet.

Her eyes gleamed with sudden malice. She pulled out the wallet and sidled towards her unsuspecting sister, who was trying to fight down a fear that Meg was right about Nellie being close to dying.

"I found this, Missus, while I was making Nellie's bed — and I'm wondering who is Tom Ward."

Daisy turned from contemplation of the fire to look at Meg's face, and did not at first notice what she had drawn out of her pocket. Her own expression showed genuine bewilderment.

"Tom Ward?" she queried, as she considered the name. "I don't know no Tom Ward."

Meg thrust the wallet under her nose. "This!"

Slowly Daisy's deep-set eyes widened until Meg thought they would pop out of their sockets. For the second time, her face drained of blood. She flung one hand dramatically across her heart. "Saints in Heaven, save us!" she cried hysterically, and fainted.

The sudden slackening of her buxom body made her roll off her wooden chair and on to the rag hearth rug. She struck her head against the brass fender as she slipped. She lay still, her shawl flung back from her slack flesh.

Meg dropped the wallet and flung herself on her knees beside Daisy.

"Daise!" she cried. "Daise, I didn't mean nothing. Daise!"

Meg tried to lift her sister but the weight was too great for her. She slipped her skinny arm round Daisy's neck and held her lolling head close to her chest. She looked down appalled at the white face with the sharp red mark on the forehead where Daisy had hit herself on the fender.

Frantically Meg patted the icy cheeks. There was no response. Daisy, already exhausted, had been terrified out of her wits and was also partially stunned by the blow she had received.

"Holy angels, help me," pleaded Meg desperately.

She laid her sister's head carefully down on the rug again. She leaned over and undid the buttons of her blouse, with the idea of loosening her brassière or any other tight garment she might be wearing underneath; it would help her to breath, she reasoned.

But Daisy had only a shift on underneath. It had been partially ripped down the front and the marks on the heavy, creamy white breasts made Meg lean back on her heels with a soft whistle. So Tom Ward did exist — and he was the mauling kind, she thought grimly, judging by the savage marks. Heaven help Daisy if Mike saw those. Though Mike was small and easygoing, Meg had seen him wield a belt with surprising viciousness; he might find consolation among his shipmates or with women ashore, but he would not tolerate his wife straying, that was certain. Very carefully Meg turned her sister's head so that she could look at her neck. Even in the poor light of the paraffin lamp she could see that she had been marked there, too, though the scars were only faint and were nearly healed.

Very thoughtfully, Meg began to chafe Daisy's hands and call her back to consciousness.

"What's up, Meg?" The whispering voice from the top of the stairs nearly caused Meg to faint, too.

Meg whipped Daisy's shawl over her bare chest.

"Aye, Nell," she protested, looking upwards at the dark staircase. "You didn't ought to be out of bed. It's naught. Daisy's fainted, that's all. She'll come round in a minute, don't worry. You get back into bed. I'll be up in a minute to see yez."

The faint shadow of her sister-in-law's nightgown fluttered; and, as if she had not heard Meg, Nellie sat down on the top stair and slowly and carefully began to ease herself down the stairs. One thin hand moved slowly down from one baluster to the next, as she progressed; the other hand she kept pressed to her side as if to ease her pain.

"Blast!" muttered Meg. She hastily began to pat Daisy's cheeks again, while she continued to urge Nellie to return to her bed.

Nellie took no notice of her. "Poor Daisy," the invalid gasped, as she rested for a moment near the bottom of the staircase. She looked like a wispy ghost, her grey curls roughed out like a halo, one hand on the newel post, the other clutching the front of the flannel nightgown which Daisy had bought her.

Nellie closed her eyes as a spasm of pain rolled over her. Then she asked, "Is it George upstairs? You could get him to lift Daisy up."

"It's Mike up there — he's drunk."

Meg jumped to her feet. She felt for a moment like the heroine of a Hollywood film, the centre of a great drama. "I'll get some water. You go back to bed, dear."

Nellie ignored Meg's order. Balancing herself by holding on to the table and then the easy chair, she advanced shakily to the hearth rug.

Daisy stirred.

"Poor Daisy. Why did she faint? Did Mike hit her?"

"No, he come in drunk," Meg's voice floated in from the scullery where she was filling a mug with water, "He went to bed afore she come in."

"Daisy, luv." Nellie's trembling voice reached Daisy through folds of darkness which she felt too tired and too exhausted to part.

Very carefully, with the aid of a hand on the wooden chair, Nellie went down on her knees beside her friend. The world whirled around her for a moment and the pain in her side was excruciating. Tears of weakness sprang to her eyes. "Daisy, luv. Say something."

Keeping one hand on the seat of the chair, to steady herself, Nellie reached forward and ran her hand round Daisy's waxen face. There was no response. Nellie began to shake with pain and fever.

Meg hastened in with the mug of water. She, too, knelt down on the rug. She dipped her fingers in the mug and began to flick the water over Daisy's face.

Daisy felt the cold droplets trickling over her cheeks and stirred again. Faintly she could hear Nellie's heavy, laboured breathing near her.

"That's better, duck," cooed Nellie.

Meg lifted Daisy's head and forced a little water between her lips. Most of it trickled down her neck, and Meg put down the mug and mopped the wetness with the end of Daisy's shawl.

Daisy tried to raise herself on her elbow and then fell back. The weak movement was, however, enough for the shawl to fall away from her chest.

Bared for Nellie to see where the fine white breasts, now marred by a series of cruel bites and red blotches. Between the breasts was a fresh bruise, and other scars in various stages of healing were scattered on both chest and throat.

Meg held her breath, expecting an immediate outcry from Nellie. But Nellie was too heavy with drugs and too anxious about her friend's fainting to realise at that point the import of the marks; and the crisis passed.

Mechanically Nellie reached over to Daisy's shawl end and folded it over her nakedness. Then she closed her eyes as she herself felt faintness stealing over her.

"Go back to bed, Nellie," implored Meg, afraid she might have a second woman collapse on the overcrowded hearth rug. "I'll get Daise round. She had to walk from town and it was too much for her."

Nellie opened her eyes and looked blearily at Meg. A tear welled from one eye. She said clearly, "Aye, she's doin' too much — an' all for me, poor dear." Then her mind seemed to wander again. She began to rock herself slowly backwards and forwards and to keen softly to herself as if Daisy were dead.

"Now, Nell, don't upset yourself. She's got a bit of colour in her cheeks now — she's coming round." Meg laid Daisy's head carefully down on the dusty rug. She got to her feet and gently lifted Nellie up. She was shocked as she felt how wasted Nellie's frame was.

With many backward glances, the invalid allowed herself to be half carried upstairs again.

Meg hastily flipped the bedclothes over Nellie and rushed back downstairs.

As Meg approached her, Daisy opened her eyes. "Where am I?" she asked, and then, as her strength returned, "What happened?"

Meg stood over Daisy, arms akimbo. "You fainted," she said shortly, fuming irritation replacing her earlier fears.

Daisy raised herself on her elbow and put her hand to her bumped head.

She remembered the wallet, and again she felt as if she would faint. She flopped back on to the rug and instinctively pulled her shawl over herself. She closed her eyes again and, while her senses swam, she tried frantically to find a likely sounding explanation for the presence of the wallet.

Meg picked up the wallet. Her eyes were hard now, as she

observed a return of more natural colour to Daisy's face. She's faking, she thought, as she lovingly rubbed her fingers over the old wallet. And now I've got you, she addressed her thoughts to Daisy, and I can make you crawl like a dog that's been kicked. I'll shut your gob for you for ever.

THIRTY-ONE

Daisy had no illusions about Meg's ability to use the finding of the wallet as a tool to discredit her, both with family and neighbours. Meg would enjoy succeeding her as the Nan.

Slowly, as her senses returned, and she felt the warmth from the fire penetrating her cold body, inspiration came to her. She wanted to laugh. She glanced at Meg through the shadow of her lashes. Meg had sat down on the easy chair and her face was creased in a thin, satisfied smile. She held the wallet in her hand.

I'll wipe that grin off your bloody face, Daisy promised herself.

"Help me up, Meg," she ordered with deceptive quietness.

Meg was startled out of her daydreams. She put the wallet down on the floor, sprang up from the chair and, making every movement very warily, she helped to raise Daisy to her feet.

Daisy flopped into the chair that Meg had vacated. Meg righted the wooden chair which had fallen over when Daisy slipped off it; she did not sit down on it, however, but watched Daisy with narrow, distrustful eyes, one hand clenching the chair back.

Daisy took her time. She rested for a moment with her head leaning against the aged upholstery. Then she bent slowly down and retrieved the wallet from the floor.

"You was showing me me wallet," she remarked in dulcet tones. "I'm sorry I fainted on yez. It was the long walk home what did it."

At the sweetness of the voice, Meg felt like taking off like a

227

coursing greyhound. She stood poised half on her toes, unsure from which direction the attack would come. "*Your* wallet!" she exclaimed, her voice pitched high with nervous strain. "It's got papers belonging to a man called Tom Ward in it."

"I know. Iddy Joey found it a long time ago and gave it to me. I kept the photos and such to show to Mike. There was no money in it, so I thought I might as well keep it and put me own savings in it." With elaborate nonchalance she opened the wallet, looked surprised and ran her fingers round the various pockets.

"Where's me money? Me savings?"

"What money? There wasn't any money in it."

"Yes, there was, Missus." Daisy raised an accusing finger and stabbed at Meg with it. "What you done with it?"

A frightened cry of inquiry from Nellie above stairs was ignored by both sisters.

It was the turn of Meg's face to drain of colour.

"There wasn't any money," she declared stoutly. "You're just saying there was to make trouble." She put her hands on her hips and stuck her nose in the air defiantly.

Daisy was feeling stronger now. She got up slowly and threateningly from the chair. "Oh, yes, there was," she declared. "I got over five pound in there — in ten shilling notes," she added, to give an air of veracity to her accusation.

Meg leaned forward, so that her face was within a foot of Daisy's.

"Well, there wasn't when I found it," she retorted hotly. "You're just trying to get out of telling me how you come by that wallet." She snatched up her shawl from the back of a chair and began a retreat to the door. "Maybe iddy Joey or George knows where it is," she insinuated cunningly.

"Not they. How would they know it was under the mattress?"

As Meg retreated, Daisy advanced towards her, chin thrust out, arms swinging, until Meg was pinned against the closed front door.

"I want me money back," hissed Daisy, feeling strength surge back into her.

Upstairs, Nellie began to cough, but neither sister heeded it. They were engaged in a test which went beyond the matter of the wallet; the real dispute between them was about who would rule the family, who would be the Nan in place of their late mother.

Frightened though she was, Meg had no intention of giving up the fight. With her back against the door, she endeavoured to push her stout sister away from her.

"I haven't got your bloody money. I don't believe you had any. Lemme go."

"You calling me a liar?" Daisy raised her clenched fist to strike.

"No!" She struggled with her hands on her sister's shoulders to push her away. "Yes, I mean. . . ."

Daisy's fist caught her on her cheek, and Meg's head swung to one side with the force of the blow. She clapped one hand to her face. "You stinking bitch!" she screamed, and kicked her sister's shins with two fast movements.

Though muffled by her thick skirt, the kicks from such heavy boots hurt; and Daisy, mouthing curses, seized Meg's bun of hair and twisted it painfully, meanwhile taking a battering on her chest from Meg's fists.

Shawls fell off and blouses burst at the armpits.

Joey woke suddenly to the sound of female combat and with a sob of dismay hid his head under the filthy bolster. Long experience had taught him not to intervene in adult disputes; you could end up being beaten yourself.

In her room, Nellie wept silently.

Daisy hauled hard on Meg's hair. It came loose from its few hairpins, and Meg clawed at her sister's face to make her lose her hold. Struggling and screaming obscenities, they staggered round the tiny room, as Meg fought to get free. With a quick lunge she gave Daisy a wicked scratch on the face.

Daisy let go, and instinctively put her hands to her face to protect herself from another quick rip. She jumped back and seized a chipped enamel plate from the crowded table. She flung it like a boomerang at Meg. It missed and crashed against the fireplace.

Meg whipped round to look for a suitable missile. Another plate zoomed over her head. She ducked towards the hearth, picked up the poker and sent it flying murderously in Daisy's direction. A tin mug flew back at her and caught her on the shoulder.

In a paroxysm of rage, Meg lifted one of the china dogs from the mantelpiece and raised it to take careful aim at Daisy.

Daisy, a chair lifted above her head, stopped dead.

"You throw that, y' divil, and I'll kill yez!" The snarl was so intense, the threat so forceful, that it penetrated through the fog of Meg's hysterical rage.

"And why not, you great fat turd?"

"It's our Bridie's and she loves it."

"No, it isn't. It was Nan's."

Meg began slowly to skirt round the easy chair, swinging the china dog maddeningly between two fingers.

"I won't stand for it!" screamed Daisy, and lunged towards her. She tripped over Mike's kitbag, stumbled and fell. Sprawled on her stomach, she pounded the ancient flagstones with her fists. "I won't stand for it! I won't! I'll tell your John, I will."

The original reason for the fight was forgotten in this new threat to her grandchild's plaything. In total hysteria she flung herself over on to her back. Then pounding her heels on the floor like an outraged child and her fists flaying in a similar tattoo, she screamed again and again.

Joey whimpered in terror, and Mike snored on.

Meg ran forward, picking up her shawl as she ran.

With great care she held the dog over Daisy's face, as, with eyes close shut, Daisy yelled on. Then she dropped the prized possession on the gaping mouth. It was sufficiently heavy to bring a trickle of blood from Daisy's nose and to bruise her already sore mouth. It bounced off her and smashed on to the stone floor.

Daisy stopped in mid-stream at the sound of breakage. She rolled on to her side, saw the scattered pieces of china, and nearly blind with rage, she shot out a hand to catch Meg by the ankle as she made for the door. Meg was quicker. She grasped the latch, kicked out at her sister, opened the door and fled into the silent night.

THIRTY-TWO

Nellie lay helpless upon her bed, slow tears welling from half closed eyes. Daisy and Meg had been fighting all their lives and Nellie had regarded the spates of rage and jealousy with humorous exasperation, something to be borne patiently till they wore themselves out, like the sudden rainstorms that sometimes swept up the river to soak a pile of washing newly pegged out in the back yard. Tonight, however, the turmoil seemed almost unbearable. Her fever seemed to have left her temporarily and her senses seemed unnaturally acute; even the sound of a bug falling off the wall came to her with irritating clarity. She sobbed silently to herself.

Meg's sudden exit silenced Daisy. There is no pleasure in enacting a great drama without an audience. And with the loss of the treasured china dog, real tragedy had suddenly entered the scene. She lay still on the stone floor, her nose running with blood. Then she wiped the gory trickle with the back of her hand. The blood thus revealed to her would have caused her to faint again, if she had not still been boiling with a terrible, cold fury.

"I'd like to feed her powdered glass, I would," she hissed.

It was anger which gave her the strength to get up in response to a nervous cry from Nellie.

She staggered to the foot of the stairs.

"I'll be up in a minute, ducks," she called softly. Her breath came in gasps, and she was still raging inwardly while she ran the kitchen tap and splashed water on her face to clean the blood off it and ease the pain of her swollen lip. Every bone in her body ached, every muscle seemed to have its own peculiar pain; yet the excitement of her fury gave her the energy to move swiftly.

She lit a candle and, with bodice still unbuttoned, she climbed the stairs, and passed through to Nellie's room, without so much as a glance at her inebriated spouse or iddy Joey, who was cowering under his bolster.

Nellie was lying on her bed, with the blankets flung off her, as if she had tried to get up again and had failed. She sighed with relief at the sight of Daisy.

"Daise, whatever happened between you and Meg?" Her voice, though weak, was clearer than it had been for several days.

Daisy made herself laugh. "Me and Meg got into a fight — as usual. She's got a filthy temper, as you well know." She put the candlestick down on a large paint drum which George had brought in for use as a bedside table. "It's proper late — you should be asleep, luv."

"Aye, I know. Sit down with me a bit, Daise. I got fair shook up by the noise — and I couldn't come down again. We can sleep a bit in the morning." She shivered. "And I've gone and got meself cold, like a mug, pushin' off the blankets."

Daisy nodded soberly. Her anger left her as she lifted the bedclothes and covered Nellie. She glanced hastily at the fire grate — the fire was still quite good.

"Sit with me, Daise." Nellie struggled to get one hand free; and Daisy loosened the covers so that she could do this, and then sat down on the side of the bed. Her weight was sufficient to make the bed dip; and Nellie rolled half on her side towards her.

The glow of the fire lit up Nellie's tiny hand, mis-shapen by rheumatism and work, as she lifted it to stroke Daisy's ruffled hair. The candle on the oil drum flickered and flared in the **breeze** from the window.

Nellie let her swollen forefinger travel down the line of Daisy's neck till it pointed to the marks on her breasts. She tried to lift her head to peer closely.

"Daise," she cried incredulously. "What you been doing? You're marked all over." Her eyes twinkled suddenly. "Mike been busy with you?"

The twinkle faded. Nellie's eyes widened as if with shock. "Mike only come home a little while back. I heard him. You won't have seen him yet — he's never stirred from his bed since he come up." She stopped to cough and then swallowed hard. Her head fell back on the pillow. "Daise, what *have* you been up to?"

"Oh, nothin'." Daisy yawned heavily and hastily closed the blouse with its hooks and eyes. "You get all kinds of bruises when you're workin'. Movin' a lot of bloody bottle around, you get clumsy by the end of the shift."

Nellie was not convinced. She slipped her hand into Daisy's, while with apprehensive, honest eyes, she appraised Daisy's weary, scratched face and swollen lips. Daisy's hand was remarkably soft, considering she was supposed to have been washing bottles for nights on end.

"You should get to sleep," repeated Daisy. Her own fatigue was so great that she could hardly mouth the words coherently. Her muddled mind could hold only the idea that she would never forgive Meg as long as she lived for breaking the china dog; she'd learn her who was boss, if it took her till the end of time.

Nellie's feeble voice forced her to attend. Nellie was saying, "Them's love bites on you. I seen 'em when I was downstairs, but I was proper confused and I didn't think I was seeing right." She touched one deep red imprint gently with a finger. "And not one man did all that, Daise."

The shock of this deduction made Daisy jump, and Nellie felt the tremor through her friend's hand. No! O Holy Virgin say it's not true, Nellie silently implored. But with the clarity of vision sometimes granted to the dying, she looked into Daisy's deep-set eyes, as Daisy sought frantically for a feasible explanation to give to Nellie; and she saw that it was true.

"You're on the streets? It's true, isn't it, Daise? There ain't no bottle factory." The whispering voice gathered horror, "Daise! You done it for me."

"Nah. Me? What chance would I have on the streets? I'm too fat. You don't have to worry about me. You just go to sleep and sleep yourself better. I'm O.K." She turned her face away from Nellie's intent gaze and sought to release her hand, but Nellie's grasp tightened.

"Stay a bit, Daise. I got to know. I'm not long for this world, Daise, and I got a lot to say as well as a lot to know." The long sentence took her strength and she closed her eyes and winced in pain. Then she said gently, "We never had secrets from each other from the time we was little kids playing on the Cassie and watching the tide come in, now did we?"

At this recollection of their shared childhood, Daisy's eyes began to fill with tears. She said firmly, despite her desire to cry, "You ain't going to die yet. Doctor says so."

"Don't try to kid me, Daise. I know. Sometimes I think I see the Holy Angels from the Throne of Light waiting for me." She gestured towards the open window, and Daisy instinctively turned round to look out. She almost expected to see a Heavenly Host fluttering in the darkness outside.

Nellie sighed, and said, "It's just a little while now."

Daisy's lips trembled. "No," she muttered vehemently, "No!"

She flung her arms round the invalid and laid her head on her shoulder, but there was not enough room on the bed for her to lie beside Nellie and she slid to her knees on the floor. She clasped her friend to her and tears poured down her scratched face. "Don't say that, Nell."

Her face was close to Nellie's and Nellie gently touched the wet cheeks with her free hand. "Don't cry, Daise. You done so much for me . . . and I'm afraid what else you done."

Daisy sobbed softly, her face half hidden by her loosened hair in which a few white hairs glinted in the candle light. The room was silent, except for Daisy's lament, and Nellie could clearly hear Mike's steady snores from the other room. In Nellie's mind, the snores boded ill for Daisy. If Mike saw those marks he would beat the daylights out of her; not, thought Nellie cynically, because he really cared much, but he would feel that he was supposed to do something. It would express his continuing authority over his wife without much permanent damage being done; he could then forgive her magnanimously. But he would never fail to bring the matter up whenever they quarrelled again — and this would drive Daisy mad with rage.

"Daisy, lovie," she said weakly. "Listen to me, Daise. Why did you go on the streets?"

Daisy half lifted her head from Nellie's shoulder. Her voice was muffled by the folds of her friend's flannel nightgown. "I never."

"You must have done 'cos of the hickies and that."

"No, I never."

But Nellie pressed, and finally Daisy sniffed, "Well, what if I did?"

"Oh, Daise — and for my sake?"

Daisy turned her wet face towards Nellie, and wagged her head negatively. "No, not just for you."

"Well, how come?"

Daisy hung her head. She was so tired and she longed to sleep. But again Nellie asked.

"It were an accident," she said dully, and she went on to tell the story of her new teeth and how she had met the three young sailors and how lonely she had been. "I needed the money as well," she said sulkily, "'Cos our Mam took her pension with her when she died."

"God save us," breathed Nellie, "And Meg atop of that."

"Aye, Meg. She was set on being the Nan, though she's younger'n me."

Poor Daisy, with her own children scattered or dead. It was against nature, reflected Nellie. And Maureen Mary never lifting a finger to help her mother. It was too hard.

Tenderly she stroked Daisy's hair.

"You might have caught the pox," she said suddenly.

Daisy jumped. She had not seriously considered this danger, except to heed Ivy's warning to avoid Americans. She shrugged her aching shoulders, however, while weary sobs ran through her plump body. Then she whispered sadly. "Lots o' people got it, anyway. Wouldn't be so many blind kids if it wasn't so." She paused, and then said heavily, "Suppose I could get it from Mike, anyway. He's got an eye for the girls, he has."

Nellie ignored this last remark; there was no point in adding to matrimonial strife. "The scuffer might have caught you and then in gaol you'd be for sure."

"Och, no. Just one night and the next day the beak fines you. I got enough money to pay, if I ever have to."

"That's bad enough, on top of everything else. Listen, Daise, I got to ask you something."

Nellie sighed, and a spasm of coughing which she did her best to suppress bothered her painfully for a minute or two. Daisy bestirred herself. Still on her knees, she measured out a dose of medicine into a sticky spoon and gave it to Nellie. It seemed to relieve the coughing, and Nellie continued, "Daisy, when I die will you take iddy Joey and be a mother to him."

"Well, you're not going to die." The response was mechanical and did not carry conviction.

"Well, if I do?"

"Of course, I will. You know that."

"Would Mike mind if George came back here, too?"

"Not if I say so."

"Well, take care of him, too, Daise. He's a good carter — he knows horses — and he'll get work again one of these days and maybe stop drinking — he never drank, as you well know, until he'd been out of work so long that he lost hope. And the pain from his old wound in his back hurts real bad sometimes. Nobody'd take care of him like you would, Daise — putting hot poultices on, like."

Daisy gave a weak, affirmative nod.

"And he'll bring a bit of money into the house even if it's only a bit of relief — you must say he's a lodger, not your brother — so the Relieving Officer don't cut it down 'cos you've got money coming in from Mike. What with him and Mike together, you might be able to manage for all of you and not have to go on the streets — oh, Daise, that was proper awful." She made a clucking sound of disapproval, and then said, "And one of these days Elizabeth Ann and Jamie will finish their time and come 'ome — and they'll bring money in — and a husband or wife, maybe, to help out."

Daisy had ceased to sob. She lay almost in a coma while Nellie slowly built her a family over which to rule. Nellie was right. Even if she did not die and Daisy did not inherit her family, Elizabeth Ann would undoubtedly come home to her mother one day. And maybe Maureen Mary, too, for all her swanky husband and fancy house, if Daisy played her cards right. And little Bridie — there was still one china dog for her to play with. At the memory of the broken ornament, some of her lethargy left her and she nearly choked as her ire rose in her.

"You're a dear, Nell," she burst out passionately. "You've got to get better."

But Nellie only smiled enigmatically and continued to stroke her friend's hair. Then the immense effort she had made to soothe Daisy became too much for her. Her hand fell to her stomach and she closed her eyes. Daisy started uneasily to get to her feet.

Nellie's eyes shot open; they were twinkling faintly.

"And there's one thing, Daise. You know that high necked blouse you got?"

"Yes?"

"You wear it for the next few weeks. Mike never makes love

with a light on, does he?"

"Oh, no." Daisy was shocked at the idea, though many of her clients had demanded that the candle be left lit. But they were not her husband.

"Then if you're careful, he don't need to know about anything, and you'll be all right, won't you now?"

Slowly Daisy nodded agreement, and the friends smiled at each other.

THIRTY-THREE

Mike staggered out of bed the next morning. The house was still enough for him to hear Moggie scratching his flea bites, while he waited by the front door to be let out. A bit bewildered because there was not a heaving deck under his feet, he teetered downstairs as quietly as possible so that he did not wake Joey. The boy was asleep on his back, mouth wide open, a bolster clasped to him as if it were a teddy bear.

The living-room fire was out, and on the floor near the front door were scattered pieces of broken china. He unbuttoned his shirt and scratched his chest while he contemplated the scene. Moggie continued to scratch, too, as if he knew that no male of the house was going to be bothered opening a door for a cat.

Where is Daisy? Mike fretted.

Thinking that she might have gone to the privy, he went to the back door, peered into the brick-lined yard, and called, "Daise! Are you there?"

There was no reply. Moggie shot between his feet and through the door, and he cursed the impatient animal. From over the high yard wall came the sounds of the city waking up, a rumble of lorries, a clanging of trams, screeches of children on their way to school, the slow squeal of a bridge being swung across a dock.

"Bugger everything," he snarled.

He stumped back into the living-room. It felt cold and dank, and he shivered. Where was the bloody woman? What a welcome home! He was clemmed and needed his breakfast. He reckoned she must have gone out to borrow something from a neighbour or to Mrs. Donnelly's shop.

He inspected the grate. It was choked with cinders, so he sought in the hearth for the poker in order to rake it out.

There was no poker.

Bloody Jaysus! He turned to go into the kitchen to look for something else to poke out the dead fire with; and suddenly spotted the missing tool lying on the table across an opened packet of sliced bread, its point buried in a lump of margarine.

"Well, I'll be buggered," he muttered, as he went over to get it. He stood looking at its greasy point for a moment before he started to clean out the grate; but the poker offered no clue as to how it had managed to arrive in such a peculiar place. He shrugged, and then raked out the cinders. He found a bundle of wood chips lying above the oven, and the coal hod was full. He soon had a fire going and then filled the kettle and put it on to heat.

While the kettle sang, he stripped off his shirt in the scullery and washed himself under the running tap, the icy water splashing out at him from the old, soapstone sink. This cleared his head and removed the smell of vomit from him. He took a piece of towel from a nail on the back of the door, and, rubbing himself vigorously, he went back into the living-room to warm himself by the newly made blaze. He put on his shirt and slicked his thin, black hair with a pocket comb he took from his jacket pocket.

Where was Daise? He opened the front door. The street was empty. A weak sun was making the river's heaving, grey waters almost silver, and a morning mist was dissipating rapidly. He stood outside and stretched himself, thankful for the moment to be away from a boat's cramped quarters and a weary, quarrelsome crew. It would be good to have a wife to sleep with; Daisy had always been obliging in bed — bed was the only place in which he was king, he thought irritably, in a home which had always been his mother-in-law's. But where, in the

Name of God, was the girl?

He turned back in, his eyes dazzled by the daylight. It seemed uncanny that Daisy should be in the room, standing over the fire warming her hands. It was as if she had materialised out of nothing, like a bloody ghost.

She looked like a ghost, too, when she glanced up at him. Her face was like paper, the eyes two black rings drawn with ink.

" 'lo, Daise. Where you bin? I bin lookin' for yez." He advanced towards her. She shivered and held her shawl closer. I bet you've been looking, she thought; you'll have but one idea now you're home.

"I was with Nell. Did Meg tell you about her?"

"She did. It was so quiet I didn't think of you being in there." He went, with a hopeful smile, to put his arms round Daisy, but she pushed him off mechanically, her thoughts elsewhere.

She shivered again and looked at him with such despair that he felt for the first time in his married life a real concern for her.

"What's to do?" he asked.

"It's Nell, Mike. You'll have to go up for the doctor." She glanced up at the clock. "Before his surgery — that's at half-past nine." Her voice had a sob in it. "She's terrible ill this morning."

He drew in his breath exasperatedly. To be sent for the bloody doctor, when you haven't been with your old woman for months, even before you've had your breakfast.

He scowled.

Daisy looked at him imploringly. "I can't help it, Mike. She's dying, I think. I'd go myself, only I don't want to leave her." A great sob wracked her.

Without another word, he reached for his jacket, his face suddenly blenched at the idea of a death in his own age group.

"Where's George?"

"At their house, I think."

"Right. I won't be long. Put some tea on — I'll get George at the same time."

"Ta, Mike." Her gratitude was so apparent that he immediately forgot his impatience and felt like a hero.

While he was out, Daisy ran upstairs again, took the high-
necked blouse out of the chest of drawers in Nellie's room and
hastily hooked herself into it. Nellie seemed to be in a coma and
was breathing with slow, shallow inhalations as if to avoid
further pain.

Daisy took the dirty bowl into which Nellie had spat her life
blood down to the scullery and washed it out. A reluctant iddy
Joey was hauled out of bed and hurried off to school. He paused
on his way out of the front door to kick a piece of the china dog
cautiously with his toe. He took a bite out of the jam sandwich
he was carrying, and asked, "How did you break your china
dog, Anty Daise?"

Daisy had done her best not to show any distress while she
hastened him off to school, but now she snapped, "It got dropped last night. Now away with you. Go on, now, duck, or you'll
be late." Her pain at the breakage of the ornament for a second
obliterated her grief over Nellie. I'll kill that Meg; I'll kill her, she
promised herself savagely. By God I will.

Joey grinned at her wickedly, took a bite from his sandwich
again, slammed the door after him and ran happily up the street.

During that terrible day, Daisy held Nellie in her arms practically the whole time. The doctor, Father Patrick and a truly
concerned Mike seemed to Daisy to float on the periphery of a
world which held only Nellie and herself, a world which Nellie
was preparing to quit. In the late afternoon, under pressure from
Great Aunt Devlin, she yielded Nellie's wasted body to a distraught George. But she would not go further away than the top
of the stairs, where she sat with her head on her knees in an
agony of misery. Mike brought her a strong, hot cup of tea, but
she would not raise her head and he set it down by her on the
stairs, where it went cold. When, with rough concern, he put an
arm round her shoulders, she shook it off, and he slunk away.

Around four o'clock, while iddy Joey played in the side street under the kindly eye of Mrs. Foley, his mother slipped quietly out of a life which had held little but sorrow; and Great Aunt Devlin led a weeping George out of the room.

When she saw them emerge, Daisy leapt to her feet, her hand to her mouth as if to hold back a scream.

"She's gone," announced Great Aunt Devlin.

"Oh, Mother of God, no," mourned Daisy, and she pushed past them and rushed into the bedroom.

Great Aunt Devlin had lifted the sheet up over Nellie's face, and when Daisy saw this she began to scream. She flung herself passionately on her knees beside the corpse and rocked herself backwards and forwards before it, her forehead touching the bed with the forward movement. Scream after scream came from her in hopeless hysteria.

Mrs. Foley heard the first shriek, borne by the wind, and with considerable presence of mind called iddy Joey in to share her children's tea.

Mike sat George down by the fire and let Daisy shriek on, while he poured a glass of gin out for him from a bottle proffered by Great Aunt Devlin. Then, whistling under his breath, he ran upstairs with the quick short steps of a sailor, head tucked down between shoulders as if traversing a narrow companionway.

"Daise," he called her firmly.

She ignored him and shrieked again.

He strode round the bed. Though smaller than her, he shovelled coal for a living and was a bundle of muscle. He seized her by one shoulder, half swung her round and administered the hardest slap he could on her face. It stung so sharply that she stopped immediately, gazing up at him with appalled, black-ringed eyes, her toothless mouth another black shadow on a white face where the mark of his hand was already apparent in bright scarlet.

"Come on, Daisy. There's nothing you can do for her. Come on, now. She's at peace."

She allowed herself to be helped to her feet and Mike put his arm round her ample waist and led her downstairs. He persuaded her to sit with George to comfort him.

While Great Aunt Devlin laid out the body, Mike, feeling the need for more female support, called Mrs. Foley from her seat on the front step of her house. She dispatched her eldest boy to call the rest of Daisy's family.

Agnes arrived, streaming with tears, accompanied by her lugubrious-looking husband, Joe. Mike immediately sent Joe up to the Ragged Bear for a large bottle of whisky.

John came soon afterwards. Instead of Meg, he brought with him his eldest daughter, Mary, who was whimpering quietly to herself.

George sat, elbows on knees, his face buried in his huge hands; his great shoulders heaved with his stifled sobs. From time to time, Daisy would give a little sob and lean forward to pat his knee. He did not look up at the arrival of his relations.

John did not tell him of the fight he had just had with his sister, Meg. She had said, "There's nowt I can do for our Nell. God rest her soul, poor dear. And George deserves to lose her. And as for our Daise, she can rot in hell for all I care."

Nothing would persuade her to enter Daisy's house again, she had announced in final defiance.

Nobody wanted to tell iddy Joey, still playing with Mrs. Foley's children in their kitchen, that he was now motherless. Finally, Daisy said, between little, quivering sobs, "I'll tell 'im. I promised Nell I'd be a Mam to 'im," She mopped her face with her apron and sobbed more loudly into it, while the menfolk stood round uneasily. "I'll come up to your house, if you don't mind, Mrs. Foley?"

"To be sure, Mrs. Gallagher." She put her arm round Daisy's shoulders and, thus supported, Daisy went round the corner and up the street to fulfil her promise to Nellie.

Holy Mother, she wondered as she went, how long can you go without sleep? How long can you bear a pain like this?

A terrified iddy Joey, howling like a dog left out in the rain, came back to Daisy's house, clinging close to her, his head on her hip under her shawl. He was rocked on Daisy's knee by the fire until the howls became sobs, the sobs became sniffs, and he began to doze.

In response to a command from Daisy, Mike carried the little boy up to the landing bedroom and laid him on one of the beds. The child began to whimper again, so Daisy said soothingly, "I'll stay with you a bit, luv." The candle light shone on her own tear-stained face, and Joey began to cry again in real earnest.

Daisy turned to Mike. "You go down and do what you can for George, you and John together." She heaved herself on to the bed beside Joey and covered him tenderly with an old coat. "Now, luv, you're safe with your Anty Daise." She took no more notice of Mike, but put her arm protectively over the child and in a second was asleep herself.

Mike glanced sardonically at George. A fat lot of good he had ever been to Nellie. Maybe he was weeping because his conscience was hurting him at last.

But George's grief was genuine. It seemed to him that Nellie's death was the final culmination of all the terrible things that had happened to him since the first piercing agony of the shrapnel wounds he had acquired in Flanders; he had lived, but in that moment his youth, his hope, had died. Now he felt that nothing much more could happen to him. He had no work, his strength was gone from lack of exercise, all his children, except iddy Joey, were dead from the diphtheria; and Nellie, on whom he had vented his frustration, had slipped away; and he realised that with her had gone all that he knew of love and faithfulness.

THIRTY-FOUR

Exhausted in mind and body, Daisy slept until noon the next day. When she woke, the house was very quiet, and she lay for a little while, staring up at the water-stained ceiling. A spider was swinging from one of the beams, and a weak ray of sunshine turned its thread to silver. At first she felt completely emptied of feeling; and then, with painful clarity, memory of the happenings of the previous day swept back into her mind.

She turned her face into her pillow and bit at the material with toothless gums, to stem the anguish within her.

"Oh, Nell!" she mourned.

Great Aunt Devlin heard her turn over and the little cry. She floated out of Nellie's room and over to Daisy's bedside, like a black wraith.

"Ye awake, Daise?" she whispered. "Our Agnes come just now and took iddy Joey over to her house. We thought we'd let you sleep."

"Ta, Anty," Daisy said into the pillow. Holy Angels at the feet of God, care for our Nell.

"T' undertaker come," Aunt Devlin said; and to Daisy the words seemed like a kick in the side from a steel-toed boot.

"George and me fixed the funeral for tomorrer," the old sitter went on. "T' undertaker asked if there was any burial money. George didn't know. Do you know? Proper upset George was. He thinks she might have to be buried by the Parish."

Daisy turned her tear-sodden face towards her aunt. Suddenly her street-walking seemed worthwhile in every respect. She turned over and swung herself into a sitting position, as she said pridefully. "She ain't going to be buried by no Parish. I got enough money to give her a real funeral — with black plumes and flowers an' all."

Followed by Aunt Devlin's murmurs of approbation, she walked with new-found dignity down the stairs, her bootlaces making small tapping sounds on each step as she descended.

George was seated by the fire, exactly as she had left him the night before. He had, however, shared with Mike the second bed in the landing bedroom and had had enough whisky poured into him to make him sleep heavily.

He lifted his face from his hands, in response to Daisy's kindly, "'allo, la."

"'lo, Daise," he responded glumly, his eyes vacant. Then, as if to avoid further conversation, he picked up a racing paper brought in by Joe and began to read it.

As Daisy went to the scullery for bacon, a frying-pan and some plates, in order to prepare a meal for him and for Great Aunt Devlin, she asked, "Where's Mike?"

"He went down to see the Second on his boat — see if there was any news about her, like. Wants to sail on her again when she's ready."

Daisy nodded, and began to fry bacon on the open fire. Presumably, iddy Joey would have his dinner with Agnes. Already her brow was acquiring the two anxious furrows across it, which seem to mark all harassed Mams with their calling.

George broke into her reverie by unexpectedly remarking, "I'll put a bob each way on Hairpin Bend in t' two-thirty tomorrow."

Daisy turned a rasher of bacon, and sniffed. She opened her mouth to tick him off about wasting money. Then she thought sadly that today she should not add to his misery. She said instead, with artificial brightness, "Do you allus bet both ways?"

"Aye, You're proper daft if you don't. Win or place is always best."

That afternoon a very quiet Daisy walked round to see the undertaker, to choose a coffin and pay a deposit. She wore with pride her patent leather shoes and her keeper earrings. Her fresh white apron and neatly plaited hair gave her an air of elegance, and the wind whipped a little colour into her face. She had washed her teeth and put them in, so that all together the undertaker would be able to deduce that he was dealing with a woman of substance, a woman with money in the Savings Bank.

She wept copiously as she chose the coffin — one with a proper polish, she insisted, and good brass handles. Afterwards, she walked slowly back along Park Road. Her mind was beginning to work again now, and she pondered on how best to organise her new family — and cope with Mike, who was sure to be put out by the arrival of George to join his household.

She paused to look at the chocolate boxes in a newsvendor's shop window. "I'll get a box for Nell," she murmured, and then remembered that Nellie was not there any more. She stood very still, while she allowed a surge of grief in her to subside. You've just ordered the last box she'll ever need, she upbraided herself bitterly.

When a small boy pushed past her to enter the shop, she went in with him, anyway, and bought a small box of chocolates for iddy Joey and the latest racing paper for George. She blinked back her tears, as she came back into the bustling street again. George and his racing. Always bet both ways, he had said.

She continued to make her way homeward. Then suddenly she remembered her secret room. The rent was due today. What should she do about it?

She stopped in the middle of the pavement, as if transfixed. Women in shawls, old men in cloth caps, girls carrying grubby babies, pushed past her like grey waves down either side of a battleship, a tattered battered crew carrying with them the stench of poverty.

Mike was home. Could she get away with what she was doing, with him around?

He might sail again in a week, or he might be under her feet for months, unemployed like George. Two unemployed men and iddy Joey to feed, not to speak of herself, on unemployment pay or public assistance; hunger would be laying desolation between them all.

Forced to make way for a woman wheeling a pram load of coal, she moved slowly along the edge of the pavement. Good St. Margaret, help me.

Cyclists zipping along in the gutter tinged their bells. The rumble of drays and the steady clump of horses' hooves belaboured her ears. She hardly heard the noise, as she fought with her fear of Mike and struggled to come to a decision.

If a scuffer caught me, I suppose I could say I was a poor widow woman. There must be thousands of Margaret Gallaghers in Liverpool. Who would care which one I was? And the ould fella on the bench ought to have pity on a widow. That way they wouldn't find Mike, to charge him with living off the avails of prostitution.

The open window of a butcher's shop caught her eye and mechanically she moved across the pavement, to look at the chops and liver, roasts and kidneys, all neatly laid out with bits of parsley between them. Behind the display huge links of pale pink sausages hung from a bar, like delicate flower wreaths. She leaned over the meat to take a close look at them. Mike loved a bit of sausage with a black pudding, and she really fancied some herself.

Unworried by the cost, she went in and demanded two pounds of the best beef sausages and four black puddings. She watched with a satisfied smile, as the butcher dexterously whipped them into a neat, brown paper parcel. Afterwards, she teetered uncertainly on the sawdust-strewn step.

Keeping that room meant having sausages for tea, like the old song said. It meant having twopence left for a glass of beer at the Ragged Bear on a Saturday evening — or for a matinee at the cinema; when she thought of the latter, she realised that there was no Nellie to accompany her any more, and a great lump rose in her throat. She rubbed her hand across her eyes. She mustn't think of Nellie for a while — it hurt too much.

But if she worked, iddy Joey could have socks to wear and a blazing fire to come home to, and something better to eat than conney-onney butties. She could be a real mother to the poor little lad.

And what if Mike finds out? First thing is, she argued, he's not likely to find out. Nobody we know ever goes past Park Road — I would never have gone meself, if it hadn't have been for me teeth. And if he *did* by a fluke find out, he'd say everything but his prayers, till I was fed up with him. And he'd use his belt till me back was sore. And then he'd ask what I'd done with the money. And I'd tell him he'd eaten it! She laughed at the thought.

There's no reason for him to connect me with Liverpool Daisy, even if other men talk. If he ever came in search of her himself, I'd have him nailed better'n on the cross. But I'll take care of him. I've learned a lot while he's been away in that bloody boat. I'll keep him in such a state he won't have the strength to so much as look at anybody else. She stepped out into the street, laughing so hard, that a passing chimney sweep, pushing his barrow of brushes, laughed back at her.

She ran out into the street, almost under the nose of the leader of a team pulling a wagon loaded with bales of raw cotton. Nimbly she jumped on to a tram temporarily halted by a police constable on point duty. The conductor caught her arm and heaved her up the second step.

She grinned at him. "Ta, lad." As she sat down on the bench by the back entrance, she produced two pennies from her placket pocket, and handed them to him. "Lime Street, lad. Nearest stop to the Legs o' Man."

The conductor laughed, and punched a ticket for her. "Goin' down to Lime Street to find yourself a boy friend, Ma?" he teased.

She looked up at him quite cheerfully. "Go on with yez, you cheeky bugger. I'm goin' down to pay me rent."

The Liverpool Basque

This novel is dedicated to my friend,
Doroteo Vicente Elordieta, a Basque from Liverpool,
whose wonderful stories about the city
inspired me to write it

This is a novel and its characters are products of my imagination, its situations likewise. Whatever similarity there may be of name, no reference is intended to any person living or dead. The loss of the ship, the *Esperanza Larrinaga*, in 1920, is part of the history of Liverpool, and I have allowed one of the characters I have created to die in it.

Just as the twig is bent the tree's inclined

Epistle i, line 149
Moral Essays
Alexander Pope, 1688–1744

Chapter One

Ignoring the pouring rain, he came out of the house, and then turned to check that the front door had closed properly behind him. Satisfied, he walked slowly down the path between the flowerbeds, empty except for a few winter aconites cautiously beginning to open.

When he reached the two steps which led down to the pavement, he paused before carefully descending them. As the wind off the Strait caught him, his shiny black oilskin flapped against his lean frame. A fringe of white hair fluttered round the edge of the black beret set firmly on his head; the beret had been arranged so that it had a small peak to protect his forehead and encourage the rain to fall down his cheeks instead of veiling his sight.

Safely on the narrow pavement, he lingered for a moment to look across the Juan de Fuca Strait. The Olympic Mountains were obliterated by the downpour, but nearer to hand a freighter was stubbornly butting its way through the sheeting rain towards Victoria Harbour. With a seaman's eye for weather, he looked up at the louring clouds, pursed his lips and muttered, 'Cold enough for snow.'

Water was trickling down his neck, so he heaved his collar up higher and then proceeded along The Esplanade towards the cemetery. He walked with his head bent, his shoulders slightly hunched, as if expecting to hit his skull on a door frame if he straightened up. Though his gait was light and steady, his old Wellington boots made an intermittent squishing sound as he slopped through muddy puddles.

In the large inside pocket of his oilskin was a single pink rose wrapped in damp tissue paper. He had bought it yesterday from the florist in Cook Street; throughout the winter he had a standing order with her, to purchase the flowers four at a time. He kept them fresh in a cut-glass vase on the dining-room table, and, regardless of the weather, he took one each day to the cemetery to lay on the grave of his wife, Kathleen.

Sometimes the florist was not able to obtain the pink or white blooms which he requested, and he would have to make do with red ones, which Kathleen had not loved quite so much. In summer, he cut roses in shades of pink or cream from the bushes which she herself had planted in their garden when first they had retired to Vancouver Island. While she had the strength, she had tenderly pruned and fertilized them herself. Then, when she had begun to fail, he had pushed her wheelchair on to the lawn, and had learned to look after them for her, doing his best to hide from her the agony of mind he had felt, as he watched her suffer the multiple infections to which leukaemia laid her open.

Seamen don't get much chance to garden, he ruminated, as he gazed down at yesterday's offering, which lay, tattered and sodden, on the grave in front of the memorial stone. But Kathleen had loved her garden, and every day he made this small pilgrimage to tell her that he was caring for it and for her household icons, and that he loved her still. Mostly, however, he came to ask her forgiveness for having failed, when she was so ill, to keep her out of pain. Mixed with the rain, tears ran down his face; no matter how the years since her death rolled along, they failed to obliterate from his mind the torture he had watched her endure. There were, of course, days when he took the walk to the cemetery from force of habit; but all too often he went in the hope of easing his own haunting memories. Today, his nightmare was very close.

He bent down carefully to avoid the dizziness which, nowadays, sometimes bothered him, and picked up yesterday's battered bloom. Regardless of its wet condition, he stuffed it into his outside pocket. His chest felt tight, and he paused to take a few short breaths of the cold, damp air, before slowly opening his oilskin to retrieve the slightly flattened fresh rose from his inner pocket. He unrolled the tissue paper from it and laid the flower in front of the headstone. The wind was strong and capricious, so he picked up a small rock and laid it on the stalk to hold it down. Most people had a vase into which they put their flower offerings, but he laid them on the ground; in his mind's eye he always saw the roses as lying between his wife's perfect white breasts.

Then he addressed the marble headstone. He did not see the words cut into it, *In loving memory of Kathleen Echaniz, beloved wife of Manuel Echaniz, born 3rd June, 1914, died 20th January, 1984. At peace.* His first words were, as always, 'Forgive me, my darling, forgive me.' He paused, as if waiting for a reply. Then he swallowed hard, and lifted his head a little, to look out towards the heaving waters of the Strait. He saw his wife's smiling face, her eyes unclouded by illness; he felt her fullness beneath him, before suffering reduced her to a skeleton; and, as he had always done, either by letter from distant ports or when they lay comfortably in bed together, he told her all that had happened to him in the previous twenty-four hours, all the funny things, all the small disasters. Today, he said that he had washed her Royal Doulton figurines in the cabinet in the sitting-room and had set them back exactly as she had left them, that last night he had cooked himself some fish for supper, and that Veronica Harris, her friend from next door, had brought him in some homemade cookies, as she did each week.

The soft words came out like a litany, not in Kathleen's native English, but in a strange evocative language known only to a few, a language which Kathleen had never been able to master.

He spoke in Basque, a unique language of farmers and shepherds in the enclaves of the Pyrenees, of fishermen in the Bay of Biscay, of iron workers and factory hands in big cities like Bilbao and smaller ones like Guernica and Pamplona; it was also spoken by lonely, elderly shepherds and their descendants in Nevada, Utah and Arizona, and by small groups of emigrants in Eastern Canada. It was a language so old that it was unrelated to any other language in the modern world, preserved by people shielded by nature's walls, the Pyrenees, between France and Spain. It had the advantage that anyone in the cemetery who heard his words to his wife would not understand them.

Manuel Echaniz was a Basque. Though he also spoke Spanish quite fluently, he seethed with anger when he was frequently mistaken for a Spaniard. He would occasionally flare up and say that though General Franco had, in the Spanish Civil War, bombed into submission his grand-parents' native city of Bilbao, he had never succeeded in making its Basque inhabitants into Spaniards, any more than Roman and Moorish invaders of Spain had been able to do so in much earlier times.

He himself had been born in England, in the port of Liverpool, and he spoke English with a pronounced Liverpool accent. Nevertheless, he would affirm indignantly that, like his father and grandfather before him, he was a Basque and very proud of it. For the benefit of Canadians, he would add, also, that he was proud to be a Canadian citizen – but he was still pure Basque!

He had married Kathleen Weston, a Vancouver Island girl, whom he had met, during the war, in Halifax, Nova Scotia. She had tried several times to learn his native tongue, but had finally given up, arguing that his command of English was so good that they could communicate perfectly in that language. Because he had spoken to her con-

4

sistently since babyhood only in Basque, his daughter Faith understood the language – but she would always answer him in English. As for Lorilyn, his only grandchild, now aged nineteen and doing her first year at the University of British Columbia, she would laugh and tell him to stop 'talking funny' and speak English.

Sometimes, without his Canadian Kathleen to support him, he wondered why he stayed in Victoria. He frequently longed for the familiar dockside streets of Liverpool, for the warmth and friendliness of the Baltic Fleet or the Flags of all Nations, both pubs that he remembered as being packed with an international gathering of seamen, all talking exuberantly at once. And he wanted to hear again St Peter's church bell calling him to Mass, a Mass celebrated in Latin. He could go to Mass in Victoria; he could even ease his soul by going to Confession; but it would all be in English, as lately ordained by the Vatican, and would have little of the comforting magic of a Mass chanted in Latin, as it had been when he was young. The Latin Mass, untouched by war or pestilence, unchanging like God himself, had been a dear familiar ceremony, no matter how strange a port his ship had been tied up in. If he had to listen to Mass in the vernacular, he wanted to hear it in Basque – and for that he would have to return to Vizcaya, the province of his forefathers.

He sighed as he turned from Kathleen's grave and began slowly to make his way homeward under the dripping pine trees. Both Liverpool and Vizcaya were a long way off; journeys to either of them were not to be undertaken lightly by an eighty-four-year-old. Then there was Faith who lived with her Canadian husband, George McLaren, in Vancouver; she was his living link with Kathleen. She did come occasionally, with her family, to visit him, but never frequently enough. He would smile when he thought of her and try to shake off his depression. Yet, sometimes when he could not sleep, a fearful inner loneliness would overwhelm him to the point of terror, and older voices called him, voices of others whom he had loved, Basque voices, Liverpool voices, people who were part of his very nature, people he had not been able to tell Kathleen much about.

He knew that he dreaded dying in this pretty city on the west coast of Canada, even if they laid him beside Kathleen. It was too lonely – a single Basque name in a cemetery full of British pioneers. Kathleen was amid her own, but he would not be.

He wanted, at least, to lie in a Liverpool churchyard or cemetery, surrounded by headstones with Basque names on them, to be laid to rest by Basques speaking either the thick colloquial English of his childhood friends or the language of his roots, Basque.

As he pushed to one side a rain-dropped branch of Scottish pine, he considered soberly how strange it was that, when he thought about his own death, all that had happened to him in Canada was wiped out of his mind, even the long, contented years with Kathleen. What was left – the essence of himself – was Liverpool Basque; and he wanted to lie with his parents and grandparents and friends in a corner of Liverpool they had made their own. Afterwards, he wanted toasts to his memory drunk in wines familiar to him and funny stories told about him in pithy Basque phrases.

Back on the pavement that led to his home, he shivered. It was not easy to have a conscience formed by Jesuits in the back streets of Liverpool. They taught perfection – but an ordinary man could do only his best – and he had done his best for Kathleen.

Chapter Two

Although the morning's winter storm had been so intense and Victoria's Scenic Drive had been, for once, deserted, Manuel's expedition had not gone unnoticed.

Seated in the bay window of the bungalow next door, Sharon Herman, daughter of an old friend of Veronica Harris, had noted with mild interest the very old man going for a walk despite the inclement weather.

She was a nurse who specialized in the care of the terminally ill, and she had just arrived to take up a position in a local hospital about to open a palliative care ward. Her interest in the elderly pedestrian was kindly and caring – she felt he should not be getting soaking wet at his age.

She turned towards Veronica, who was seated at her computer across the room, trying to unravel the complexities of Townsman's Tailors' accounts outstanding. An elderly widow, who lived alone, she earned her living by keeping the accounts of small businesses in the neighbourhood. Today, she was finding it difficult to work with someone else in the room, though she did not grudge, in the least, offering her friend's daughter temporary accommodation until she found herself a flat conveniently close to the hospital.

'Veronica, who's the old man next door? He's just gone out – in this weather! He'll get soaked – hasn't he got a car?'

Veronica turned impatiently towards Sharon. Then she glimpsed through the bay window the bent figure plodding up the road. Her expression changed, and she smiled. 'Oh, that's Manuel Echaniz – Old Spanish, Kathleen's husband.

7

She was the friend I told you about – died of cancer.'

'Is he Spanish?'

'No. Kathleen told me he was born in the UK. She said he's a Basque, whatever that might be. He speaks English and Spanish – and his own language, which only Faith seems to understand – that's his daughter, you know.' She paused to rub her eyes, tired from concentration on the computer screen. Then she said, 'He'll be going up to the cemetery.'

'Does he work there?'

'No. He goes up every day to put a flower on Kathleen's grave. I've never known him miss a day since she passed away – must be eight years now.'

Sharon laughed. 'You're kidding?'

'No, I'm not. You should've seen them together. They were great!'

Sharon moved uneasily in her chair by the window, and her book slid off her lap. She bent to pick it up. 'He could take some flowers up every week – it would save him time. Or he could drive up on a day like this.'

'Well, he does have a car – he doesn't use it much, though.' She smiled indulgently. 'Weather never bothered him – I guess because he went to sea for years. And as for going every day, he told me once he wanted her to know that he thought of her each day.' Her smile faded, and she sighed a little despondently; she had often wished that Manuel would think of her every day. He still seemed to her an attractive man, with his wide smile and twinkling black eyes. His finely lined face was still healthily tanned, and the long, narrow shape of it, with its flat cheekbones, still had the firmness of a much younger man.

'Sounds like an old movie,' Sharon was saying, as she put her book on a side table. 'Do you think he's got a screw loose?'

'Not him! He's in his eighties now, but there's nothing wrong with his brains – and I've never known him be sick.'

8

She hesitated, and then added, 'He's a great old guy.'

Sharon made a wry mouth. 'Veronica, you're too senti-mental,' she teased. 'Men aren't like that. Do you think he feels guilty about her in some way?'

The question irritated Veronica. Sharon, still smarting from a recent divorce, might be bitter about men – but she was, Veronica felt, being very unfair to Manuel.

'You've read too much pop psychology,' she responded huffily, and swung her chair round to face the computer screen again. 'I would have thought that you, with your special training, would know how long a person can grieve.'

The rebuke, from a woman who was usually very mild-mannered, jolted Sharon. She realized that the question had arisen from the resentment she still felt as a divorcee. Veronica was right; each individual needed his own time in which to recover from bereavement.

Ashamed, she inquired in a conciliatory tone if Veronica would like her to make a cup of coffee. Privately, she thought how glad she would be to begin her new job on the following Monday; it would take her mind off her own troubles.

Thankful to get her guest out of the room for the moment, Veronica said politely that she would like a cup very much, and the coffee was on the bottom shelf of the cupboard next to the sink. She wished heartily that the rain would ease, so that Sharon could resume her hunt for an apartment.

In the cluttered kitchen, Sharon put a clean filter in the coffee maker, followed by spoonfuls of coffee. She swore softly as the old kitchen tap spattered water over her when she turned it on. After filling the pot, she stared with some despair through the kitchen window at the sweeping rain. The weather was as cold and dismal as she felt herself; her only consolation was that Winnipeg, from which she had come a couple of days before, would be suffering infinitely

9

worse temperatures. In her pocket lay a well-thumbed last letter from her lawyer, enclosing his final bill for negotiating a parsimonious settlement with her husband. The letter wrote *Finis* to a whole segment of her life.

Divorce had been much more painful than she had expected. After seven difficult years of a childless marriage, she had anticipated a sense of joyous freedom; instead, she felt a numbing sense of loss. Was this how one felt after a bereavement? Was this how Old Spanish felt? God help her, if she still felt like this at the end of eight years. One thing was certain, *her* husband would never waste time putting flowers on her grave.

She had worked all her married life. Now, she was going to start anew, away from the people who had known her when she was married. It was the kind of work which would demand a great deal from her, as she dealt with the dying and with their grief-stricken families; yet, she knew from experience that the close relationship between patient and nurse was not a one-way situation; at no time did one come so close to a person as when that person was on his or her deathbed. Beside that experience, she considered as the coffee percolated, what was a divorce? Particularly when there were no children involved.

She carefully poured the coffee into two mugs, and told herself sharply to cheer up. After the coffee, she would go out to look at the apartments she had marked in the newspaper rentals column. Blow the rain. She took Veronica's mug to her, and drank her own coffee despondently in the kitchen. Then, she quickly put on a raincoat, and took Veronica's umbrella off a hook in the hall cupboard. Opening the door into the living-room a crack, she called to Veronica that she was going to look at an apartment and that she was not to bother about lunch for her. Then, map in pocket, she went firmly out into the rain.

The rain was lessening and the umbrella hardly necessary. She remembered suddenly her parents still living together in their Florida condominium and managing to keep extraordinarily well for their age, under the Florida sun. Married for thirty-five years, she considered with some wonderment, as she crossed the road at a traffic light. How did they do it? Old Spanish must have been married at least as long. Some people had all the luck.

But was it luck? Or was it some secret formula that the older generation used to build a happy marriage? Cynics said they stuck together because women had no means of earning a living, but it could not be that alone, because even slaves in the States who had no hope at all used to run away.

She looked up to check the street number of an apartment block and then absently pressed a bell marked *Building Manager*. No matter what the secret is, this is where you begin all over again, she told herself as she waited for a response.

Chapter Three

Unaware of the interest he had sparked in Sharon Herman, Old Manuel stood in his narrow back hall and shook the rain off his beret and oilskin before hanging them to drip in a small washroom by the kitchen door. Without them, dressed in a white shirt and sleeveless pullover, he seemed extremely frail and thin. As he paused for a second to watch the water running down the oilskin, he smiled to himself; his daughter, Faith, was always warning him to keep himself warm and dry. At his age, she told him, he must take care not to get wet.

He would always tease her by replying that Basques had been pounded by rain in their native mountains for at least five thousand years, and they were immune to it.

He slowly heaved off his Wellington boots and laid them neatly in a boot tray. Like many men who had been to sea, he was extraordinarily neat, because he was used to making the most of the tiny space of a ship's cabin.

In his thick white socks, he padded into the kitchen to find something to eat for lunch. He slapped a cheese sandwich together and then plugged in the kettle to make some instant coffee, and looked forward to the nap he always took after the midday meal.

As he put his plate and coffee mug down on the kitchen table and pulled out a chair, he asked himself ruefully, 'Manuel, my lad, what have you come to, when all you look forward to is having a nap?'

The answer was a resigned shrug of one thin shoulder; he had sensed lately that his time was running out.

He decided that after he had slept a little, he would ring

up his friend, Jack Audley, and suggest that he should come over for a game of pool on the billiard table in the basement family room. Jack was twelve years younger than he was, but they shared a common interest in fishing and ships — Jack had been a merchant seaman, too.

To help him get through his days without Kathleen, Manuel structured them as meticulously as he could, so that all the necessary domestic tasks and the garden were attended to. Sometimes, however, a thoroughly wet day upset the schedule.

If Jack was not at home, he thought, he would write to his young Liverpool cousin, Ramon Barinêta. He had already, on the first of the month, written to his oldest and dearest friend, Arnador Ganivet, another Liverpool Basque, who had been a Professor at the University of Liverpool, and he smiled gently at the recollection. Between himself and Arnador there was a frankness and concern for each other which probably exceeded that which might have been built up had they both spent their lives in Liverpool; the older they grew, the richer became the correspondence.

After supper each day, he added a page or two to the memoirs of his early life, which he was writing for the benefit of his granddaughter Lorilyn. He had a vague hope that, when she was older, she would read them and become interested in her Basque forebears. At times, her youthful scorn at his pride in his ancestry had hurt him so much that he longed to slap her; her ignorance of the world and its people, despite thirteen years of education, was absolutely abysmal, he fulminated. In frustration, he took to buying her, for her birthdays, books on European and Asian history. As far as he could tell, she never read them; the books were put on the bookshelf in the McLaren family room, their dust-jackets unbesmirched by handling, their pages stiff from never having been turned.

13

He never quite gave up on her immutability, though he had long since done so in the case of her mother.

He had remarked to Faith's Grade Six schoolteacher that the child seemed to have no interest in her family's past or their customs. The schoolteacher, who was an immigrant from Scotland, had tried to comfort him by saying that first-generation Canadian children were often so busy trying to be like the other children that they tended to discard, as much as possible, any trace of their immigrant origin. 'It's your grandchildren who will be passionately interested in where they sprang from; they'll feel more secure,' she had assured him.

But now, in Lorilyn, he had a grandchild, and she never read any book that she did not have to for her university courses. And what was she proposing to study? Engineering, God save her! Not a decent womanly occupation, like nursing or teaching.

While strolling along the cliffs with Jack, one fine summer day, when the gorse was in riotous yellow bloom and the bees were humming like tiny dynamos, he had broached the subject of human roots.

He said, 'You know, Jack, people move around too much. A lot of 'em never see another relation, even their grandparents. Come to that, they don't see much of their mum and dad either, in some cases.'

'You're right.'

'All they've got is kids the same age as themselves or television to set the pace. They've no idea that we've learned ways to endure bad times – cope with difficulties – take disappointments in our stride. And the first time things don't go just right – well, they're sunk.'

He paused to watch a small yacht trying to tack against the wind, and muttered irritably, 'He'll drown if he don't watch out.' Then, picking up the original subject again, he went on, 'There's nothing much to make kids feel safe, no standards, no customs. They get no religion even – our

14

Lorilyn's never seen the inside of a church since she were christened — and I wouldn't like to offend her father by askin' what she's doing with that young man always hanging around her.' He gave a barking laugh. Then he added, 'There's no family discipline — I wouldn't like *my* grandfather to see her; he'd have made her toe the line a bit, and he'd have had the backing of everybody else. Sometimes I feel like a voice in the wilderness. Do you?'

Jack's round red face wrinkled up in a wry grin. Before he answered, he stopped to strike a match and light his pipe, shielding it from the wind with his curved palms. Then, as the pipe glowed and they continued to walk, he nodded agreement. 'I used to slam my kids when they needed it. It didn't do much good, because I wasn't around that much — the wife had to manage while I was at sea.' He drew slowly on his pipe. Then he continued, 'And things seemed to be changed almost every time I came home. Nobody else's kids were going to church any more — so ours wouldn't. Discipline in school went out, and drugs came in. Like you say, the kids went around in herds all the same age — and there were no cow hands to keep them in line. And God help a cop who boxed their ears for them. I knew what I wanted for my kids, but I didn't have much luck putting it over.'

Manuel dropped his cigarette butt and ground it out with his heel. 'Seems to me that when we were having Faith, nobody dared touch a child — even to bath the poor little bugger — unless they had read at least three books by experts! Kathleen had a row of books.'

Jack laughed. 'Same with us. It was like learning to dance from books — as if we'd no ideas of our own. My mother never needed a book to tell her what to do, and we all grew up knowing what was right and what was wrong — even if we weren't perfect. I wish my mother had been around when our lads were growing up.' His red face under his straw hat was filled with pain.

15

Manuel could have kicked himself for bringing up the subject of children. He had, for the moment, forgotten what a bitter disappointment both Jack's boys had been to him. They seemed to lack motivation and found it difficult to keep jobs – like homing pigeons, they came back from Vancouver every few months, to live on their father.

Jack was saying bitterly, 'I wish I'd taken a shore job, so I could've been home more.'

'It's not your fault, Jack. I'm sure of it. It's the way things are. They're treated as kids for far too long. In the old days, by thirteen or fourteen, they would've been learning a trade under a weight of older men, who'd have kept them in line; and they'd have learned there's a limit to what you can get away with.'

'Jobs are different now. How many of them ever go to sea?'

Manuel snorted. 'Maybe we should send the whole pack of them to sea for a bit,' he suggested, trying to lift Jack's spirits. 'They'd either drown – or learn their responsibilities mighty fast.'

Unexpectedly, Jack chuckled. 'They'd soon learn who's boss.'

Manuel began to laugh. 'Oh, aye, they would. It would be great to see some of the little bastards in a force ten gale, telling the Old Man they were as good as him – or arguing they had rights, while waves as high as the mast were coming at them!'

'Mannie, they don't know nothing about natural things, like waves.'

'I wouldn't put it past our Lorilyn to explain the physics of a breaking wave to me!' responded Manuel.

This made Jack really laugh, as they plunked themselves down on a bench, two old men silhouetted against the rippling sea, which had taught them most of their skills with an iron discipline.

'Are you glad you went to sea?' asked Jack from behind a cloud of tobacco smoke.

'Never dreamed of doing anything else. Not till I met Kathleen, that is; she'd got her eyes on a shore job for me. After we was married, she kept on her nursing and she put me through college, and I come out a marine architect. We had a good life – but I missed the sea.'

'Humph. My dad was a fisherman, and he took me out to sea when I was nine or ten. I was wet and cold and seasick, but I felt I was a real man. At fourteen, I was a deck boy.' He made the statement with pride, and then a grin flashed across his face, as he added, 'I'd never heard of being a teenager; I was a lad learning to be a man under real men. Had some good laughs, though.'

'Oh, aye. I were happy when I were a little kid, too, with me dad and me Uncle Leo coming and going from sea – and being took down to visit their ships, and listen to them grumble and laugh. And getting a bit of pie from the ship's cook.' He paused to light another cigarette, and then went on. 'And in the house, there was me granny and grandpa to tell me stories. After me mam slapped me for being naughty, me gran would wipe me face – and explain why I got the slap!' Both men were silent, as they smoked and contemplated the sea and the mountains before them. Then Manuel said in a puzzled way, 'Our Lorilyn never seems to need a grandpa at all.'

While he recalled this rambling conversation with Jack, he took the handmade patchwork quilt off the bed and folded it carefully and laid it on a chair, and sighed. Though he had tried, he did not feel that he had been a very good grandfather – unlike his own grandfather, Juan Barinèta.

He sat down on the side of his bed, pulled a faded crocheted shawl out of the drawer of the bedside table, and slowly eased himself down on to the bed until he lay on his back. He paused for a moment, while every bone and

17

muscle in his body flashed with sudden aches, then he laid the shawl over himself, clasped his hands over his chest and thankfully closed his eyes. In the moment between waking and sleeping, he remembered Kathleen upbraiding him for resting on top of the patchwork quilt. Although he was tired from a very scary wartime voyage, he had pulled her down on top of him. They had forgotten about keeping the bedspread pristine, while they spent until nightfall making love so satisfactorily that even now, nearly fifty years later, he remembered it with awe. Had he really been that strong? And she so responsive?

After her death, he had come across the old quilt folded away at the back of the linen closet. Still beautiful, its colours muted by many drycleanings, it had been like meeting an old friend again. In a way, it had comforted him for the emptiness of the other side of the bed.

He had returned to his ship on the day following his happy afternoon with Kathleen, and her letter telling him the news about her pregnancy with Faith caught up with him in Galveston, Texas.

He remembered how excited he had been about the child, overwhelmed by the divine mystery of its existence and the sense of responsibility that it had laid upon him.

He had shouted the news to the few members of the engine room crew who had not gone ashore, and they had congratulated him on his sexual prowess with explicit pithiness. His news broke the astonished silence which had seemed to grip them at other news they had received that morning. The Yanks had dropped an amazing bomb on the port of Hiroshima and blown the whole city and its inhabitants to bits. The city was known to most of the crew and they had found it hard to accept its death – even if it was supposed to shorten the war. It was a port – like Liverpool!

He had immediately scribbled a few lines to Kathleen, expressing his pure joy at her news. After she was dead, he had found the letter in her jewellery box; she had kept it all her life.

He had also written to his mother, Rosita Echaniz, in Liverpool, urging her to come on a visit as soon as the war was over, to see the babe as yet unborn.

He had hoped for more children, but Kathleen had been adamant about limiting their family. 'How will we ever afford to send them to university?' she had asked. 'And if you go back to college after the war . . . ?'

Manuel was still uncertain that he himself wanted to return to college, and had never considered that a real university might be within the reach of any child of his, so he had reluctantly said he did not know.

The family remained at one.

The rainstorm which had swept the Juan de Fuca Strait came to an end. The sudden quiet woke the old man from his nap. He rose stiffly and put the shawl which had been keeping him warm back into the bedside drawer. With an amused awareness of his own finickiness, he carefully replaced the bedspread on the bed.

When he phoned Jack Audley, Mrs Audley said he had gone to Vancouver for the day.

Before going to his old-fashioned roll-top desk to write to Ramon in Liverpool, he went into the kitchen and took down from a cupboard a bottle of wine, already opened. He poured a glass of it carefully, so as not to disturb the sediment at the bottom of the bottle. Then picking it up, he went to the window and stood idly twirling it in the light of the first rays of the sun to pierce the rain clouds.

Instead of his own long, gnarled fingers holding the stem of the glass, he saw, with unexpected clarity, his grandfather's huge paw holding a wine glass under his nose, to savour a bottle of a new year's crop smuggled into Liverpool from Bilbao.

Those early years in the safety of his grandfather's great shadow had been good years, he thought wistfully. He remembered how the old man's beard waggled when he laughed, and when his grandfather picked him up it was like being hugged by a friendly bear.

He took his glass of wine into his den, where he had a small desk piled with notes and exercise books. Above the desk hung a ship's chronometer, put there, he had told Jack with a laugh, to remind him that his time was short.

He put his glass down on the desk, drew up a chair and sat down. With slightly trembling fingers, he sought for and found a well-thumbed school exercise book. In it lay the life of a Basque; in fact, the lives of many of them, set down in the hope that Lorilyn would, one day, be interested in some of the men and women who were the cause of her existence. Like many Canadians, she shared a Scottish origin, too; but not everybody in the world is Scottish, considered Manuel tartly. He wanted her to know that she had roots in the oldest culture in Europe, going far back beyond written history. He wanted her to preserve something of it within her own being.

So that she would understand, he wrote in English, in an old-fashioned, neatly sloping, cursive hand. He poured out to her, as best he could, the story of his childhood and what little wisdom he felt he had acquired in the long years of his life, especially during the time that he had been part of a Basque community; he did not feel that he had to include much of his life with Kathleen – Lorilyn understood Canadian life – and the finale of Kathleen's existence was, in any case, too painful for him to write about.

It was dark by the time he had to stop because of fatigue and he had forgotten, for the moment, his intention of writing to Ramon. He leaned back in his chair to stretch himself. His eyes were watering and his shoulders ached from the concentrated effort he had been making.

When he looked again at what he had written, he wondered suddenly what lay behind his own boyhood memories. What was going on amongst the grown-ups, who surged in and out of his grandparents' kitchen-living-room? Were they happy?

It took a minute or two for him to bring himself back from Wapping Dock in Liverpool, and when his mind was clear of it, he was left with an aching longing to go home to it, to shake Arnador's hand once more and see Cousin Ramon, and speak Basque with both of them.

Although Faith will have a fit, if you suggest that you want to do such a long air journey, you *could* do it, he told himself. And perhaps you should, before it's too late!

He grinned wickedly. This summer, he promised himself. And don't tell Faith until it's too late to cancel the flight.

Chapter Four

Ports from which men go to sea are matriarchal societies; it is women who are in charge. They have to have their babies without any support from their husbands; and they have to teach their sons, as well as their daughters, to behave and mind their manners. Father is not at home frequently enough to take a strap to a delinquent lad.

Manuel, aged eighty-four, was trying hard to explain to Lorilyn, aged nineteen, that, even before feminism was invented, some women ruled their families.

In our house, he scribbled, it was Grandma Micaela Barinèta who was the undisputed boss. She was my mother's mother, a shrunken ball of energy, always clothed in black, a piece of knitting, with a cork on the end of the needles, usually tucked into the pocket of her black apron. Even to me, when I was only three or four years old and all grown-ups seemed very tall, she appeared too little to possibly be the mother of my two uncles, one of whom, Leo Barinèta, lived with us. Whenever they had done something of which she did not approve, she lashed out at them with her tongue and scared them into line. She would not tolerate any nonsense from me, either, though I was only a toddler; and I soon learned to sit quietly, while the priest droned through the Mass, or to run away and play if she was gossiping with a neighbour.

Of course, Grandpa Juan Barinèta, who no longer went to sea, believed that he ruled the three generations in the house. He certainly received first consideration from Grandma — and from my mother, Rosita Echaniz, who always seemed to be in league with Grandma. Nevertheless, it was the two women who collected the men's earnings from them and the rents from the emigrant lodgers, and laid out the family income to the best of their joint abilities. They bargained in the market for food, decided when new clothes would be bought, purchased coal for the fires, and paid the rent each week; they put every penny they could into three old biscuit tins under Grandma's bed, until a few shillings had been accumulated to put into Post Office savings accounts.

If I had been good on the day that Grandma decided to go to the post office, she let me accompany her, and I had the honour of licking the savings stamps, which she purchased from the postmistress to put into her savings books; I must have licked pages and pages of sixpenny stamps, as Grandma laid away money, first for a rainy day, then for clothes, especially boots for all the menfolk, and finally for education.

The Basque community, nestled by the dock road, was united in its belief in education for their children; and the whole family was determined that the second child, which Mother was expecting, and I, should both go to a good private day school, rather than to the local Catholic school. In this emphasis on their children's future, they differed somewhat from their polyglot neighbours, who tended, simply, to be thankful if their children managed to grow to adulthood in noisy, polluted Liverpool, knowing enough reading and writing to get a job in the docks or as deckhands.

I grew accustomed to hearing my future discussed, over many a glass of cheap, smuggled wine, by Grandpa, Uncle Leo, and my father, Pedro Echaniz, when he was home. Words like 'university' . . . 'doctor' . . . 'solicitor' whizzed over my head, strange words rarely used in our street.

At the beginning of each voyage, Father arranged with his employers for Mother to receive part of his wages each week. This was called an allotment, and, together with

Grandpa's and Uncle Leo's earnings, was used for living expenses.

Grandma gave back to the men a little pocket money for wine and tobacco, both discreetly brought into the country by Basque seamen lucky enough to be sailing to and from their homeland, Vizcaya, in Spain.

A meal isn't complete without wine, my grandfather would often say. Smuggled wines were cheap, and, on the whole, the customs officers did not worry too much about collecting duty on a few bottles of our native wines, as long as its illicit importation was on a very small scale.

Though ours was a very united household, it was not a placid one. Argument, debate were the salt of life, and, in addition, there were all kinds of small vendettas within the Basque community. The community became a solid block, however, whenever it felt it had, as a group, been insulted. The supreme calumny was to be referred to as *Spaniards*! Such a blunder was frequently made by our cheerful, easy-going fellow Liverpudlians, especially the Irish, who seemed sorely lacking in a knowledge of Iberian history, and by English clerks behind official counters, who didn't really care what we were.

Amongst the men gathered round our kitchen table for a smoke and a gossip, such an allegation produced a glowering animosity; they sputtered like half-lit sparklers, and muttered about the improbable origins of all the accursed Spaniards they had ever met. Many of them spoke Spanish as well as they did Basque, and they could be equally rude in both languages; even in English, the English of the back streets, they could be quite lurid. My knowledge of lively curses in all three languages began at an early age.

So, from the time I was big enough to be carried around on Grandpa's or Uncle Leo's shoulder, I learned that I was a Basque and to be proud of it. I learned to speak Basque first; it was the language which flowed around my small world of kitchen-living-room and bricklined backyard; I learned good Castilian from the Spanish priests of St Peter's Church – they were frequently in and out of our homes, to counsel or console, their lean, dark figures the epitome of God's authority over little boys. And I learned English from my playmates in the street.

Grandpa had a beard heavily streaked with grey. His head was bald, except for a thin ring of neatly clipped black hair. Most of his teeth were deep-stained by tobacco, but a missing one had been replaced by a gold tooth which flashed as he talked; I was fascinated by it and my first ambition was to have a flashing gold tooth for myself. He had gone to sea in the days of sailing ships, and was proud to say that he had several times breasted the storms of Cape Horn, a place of terror at the most southerly point of Chile, where many a ship was lost before the advent of the Panama Canal gave a safer entry to the Pacific Ocean. 'They don't know what seamanship is, nowadays,' he would grumble testily to my father, when he told of *his* adventures in a steamer.

For many years now, Grandpa Barinèta had held the agency for Basque emigrants passing through Liverpool on their way to Nevada, Arizona, California and Washington. An Agent was essential to protect such travellers from exploitation in a strange port, where their language was not spoken. He saw that they were housed and fed, while they waited for their ship; he kept their luggage safe, and delivered them to the correct ship at the right time. It was his pride that, to his knowledge, he had never lost even a piece of luggage, never mind an emigrant.

Many of these people were lodged in our own house, which was a large eighteenth-century dwelling, and I was quite used to our home being suddenly filled with strangers, who equally suddenly vanished a few days later. Even as a little child, I sensed how touchingly thankful they were to be in the hands of a fellow Basque, who took care that they were not robbed or cheated by local rascals who made a living by preying on confused travellers trying to get to the New World; and I will never forget Grandpa's slow smile of satisfaction when he could close his ledger after a boat sailed, and sink into his carving chair at the kitchen table to enjoy a quiet glass of wine with Grandma and Mother.

These transitory invasions made our house a very lively one, and a centre for resident Basques, who often drifted in to hear recent news of Vizcaya from the emigrants. The house was opposite the Wapping Dock, except that across a narrow street, the tall flat-iron building of the Baltic Fleet intervened. This public house was a popular meeting place, almost a club, to the Basque community, and emigrants often took their ease there, too. My mother told me that she sometimes went for a drink there with my father, and that she used to park me, sound asleep in my pram, by its ample walls, while she went inside. No wonder it was one of my favourite pubs when I grew up!

As I grew a little bigger, my greatest ambition became to climb into the toast-rack horse-bus, with its little canopy over the rear seats, and have a ride with the emigrants down to the big ship which took them over the ocean to the New World. On the bus's side was the name of a steamship company, and on a grubby white board at the front was the name of the ship on which the emigrants were booked. The bus was drawn by two patient, blinkered work horses, heads hanging and untidy short manes blowing in the sea wind, as they waited for the harassed, worried emigrants to be loaded.

'Grandpa! Let me go down to the dock – please, Grandpa. I'm five now. I'm big enough,' I pleaded, one sunny September day in 1913.

He stood on the pavement, between our front door and the horse-bus, in his hand a piece of board with innumerable sheets of paper pinned to it, his peaked cap pushed to the back of his head, while he supervised the people climbing on to the bus. I clutched at his long, serge-covered legs, and peered up at him to catch his eye.

He looked down at me impatiently. He was fond of me, I knew, but at that moment I was a nuisance, as round him swirled an anxious group of heavily laden men, women and children, all of them desperately dependent upon him. 'Manuel Echaniz! The bus is too full,' he responded with exasperation. 'Go and see your mother in the kitchen.' As I reluctantly let go of his leg, his voice rose to a shriek. 'Mind out! You're too close to the wheels. Get out of the way, boy.'

My face fell. I wanted to cry. At five, I felt I was grown-up enough to be able to keep out of the way of wheels and horses' feet. But when Grandpa spoke like that, everyone obeyed, even Mother and Father. Sullenly and with difficulty, I turned away and pushed myself between long, trousered legs and flowing black skirts issuing from the house, an incredible stream of people. A white-faced little girl, with whom I had played for the past week, said shyly, 'Goodbye, Manuel,' as I shoved by her. I did not reply, as I fought my way kitchenwards. Through my ill humour, I smelled the emigrants' underlying fear, and it made me uneasy, as baskets, bundles tied in old shawls, and the bare feet of small children carried in their parents' arms brushed or bumped my head.

When I was a little older, I was able to visualize more accurately the discomforts of the long voyage in steerage still faced by our visitors, and could understand their dread. Meanwhile, infected by their fear, I almost ran down the deserted back part of the passageway leading to the kitchen and safety, while Grandpa, his pencil tucked behind his ear, continued to cope with the travellers.

Grandpa had a habit of rubbing his short beard when hard-pressed by nervous questions from his charges.

Already tired from the journey from Bilbao, and distressed at leaving home, however poverty-stricken, the emigrants seemed to find great comfort and reassurance from the self-confident old man. Now, at the time of parting from us, some of the women were invariably near to tears; not only did they have yet to face the long voyage to New York, but also a long train journey to the West, with children and husbands to keep fed and happy. In some cases, they had to sustain a pregnancy and, at the end, a confinement amid strangers.

On the other hand, there was always a group of young, single men, excited, strung-up and sometimes drunk, for Grandpa to control; on each he pinned a numbered identity disc, while they laughed and joked, and talked of making a fortune in their new land. Not for ever would they tend other people's sheep in Nevada, they assured each other.

In the big, stone-floored kitchen-living-room, with its high ceiling covered with a century of soot, my comfortable, plump mother took no notice of my entry; she was holding her youngest brother, Uncle Leo Barinèta, tightly to her and was weeping bitterly.

Frightened, and not a little jealous, I paused in the doorway.

Uncle Leo was saying, 'It's not for ever, Rosita. I'll come back.' His voice rose with false cheerfulness. 'Come on. At worst, a seaman can work his way home again – even from Nevada! Don't cry, Rosita.'

Mother leaned back in his arms, to look up at his face. 'You've got a home with us,' she wailed. 'You can go on sailing out of Liverpool. Why move? Nevada sounds a godforsaken place.'

'Tush, Rosita. I want to better myself. There's land there, almost for the asking.' He dropped his arms to his sides in a hopeless gesture, realizing that land meant nothing to her.

She drew away from him, and wiped her tears on the

28

corner of her white apron. 'Mother's broken-hearted,' she reproached him.

I watched wide-eyed. Uncle Leo was an essential part of my small world; it was frightening that he should be about to vanish like all the other emigrants. People poured in and out of our house, but the family members always came home; as seamen, Uncle Leo and Father, even Uncle Agustin, reappeared regularly, armed with presents for small boys. But Mother's tears told me that this departure was very different.

'Mam!' I cried in a strangled, scared voice, and ran to her.

Mechanically, she picked me up and held me against her shoulder. I felt her slump slightly, and turned my face towards hers. Her pretty, little mouth was drooping, her whole expression woebegone. She was gazing at Uncle Leo as if she could never take her eyes off him. 'I'll miss you so much,' she whimpered. 'And Mother's nearly out of her mind, up there on the bed.'

Uncle Leo swallowed, and I thought he was going to cry; it was a new and scary idea to me that a young man could cry. He controlled himself, however, and, instead, he put his arms round both of us together. He kissed my mother's cheek and then I felt his lips on the back of my own head. He loosed his hold on us, and said, 'I know. Mam's been upset about it for weeks. Comfort her, Rosita — I feel bad about it. But I'll be back, never fear.'

He turned abruptly and went out through the hallway to say farewell to his father and to join the embarking throng.

It was over nine years before I saw Uncle Leo again.

Mother stood silent for a moment or two; then she seemed to gather herself together and become aware of my own trembling. Through her tears, she smiled at me. She said brightly, 'Pudding's got a great surprise for you. Come and see.'

*

I missed Uncle Leo for his own sake. But, as I grew up, I learned that the loss of a man from a family weakens that family immeasurably. No one knew it better than Basque mountain farmers and their descendants, who dwelt in the rocky, inhospitable Pyrenees, between the French and the Spanish. For century upon century, they had to watch their younger sons leave their stony fortress, because the land could not feed them; they became famous mercenaries in foreign armies, or fishermen in the Bay of Biscay or iron workers in the foundries of Bilbao. When the New World opened up, they took their skills as shepherds and as seamen to it, and Uncle Leo, full of hope, went with them.

Mother slowly slid me to the floor. As she tried to control her grief, I saw her fine, round breasts rise and fall quickly under her black blouse, and I knew that Uncle Leo's departure must be something very disturbing to her.

My childhood fears soon gave way to curiosity, as she led me to a small cupboard beside the big kitchen range on which she and Grandma cooked. The door was open, and she squatted down beside me. 'Have a look,' she urged me.

I approached the small, dark cavern of the cupboard with caution. Pudding was a very large, black cat with expressionless pale-green eyes; she was quite capable of giving a small boy a sharp clawing, if she felt her dignity was at stake.

She was curled up on a piece of grubby blanket in the darkest corner. Her green eyes flashed as she looked up quickly at her visitors, while round her crawled four tiny black bundles. Surprised, I put out my hand to touch one of them. Pudding peremptorily nuzzled my hand away.

In some astonishment, I turned to Mother. 'Kittens! Where did she find them?'

'She had them inside her. They came out in the night.'

The reply was so unexpected that I knew my mother

30

was teasing me. I looked at her knowingly, and laughed. 'They couldn't. How would they get out?'

Mother hesitated, before she replied. Then she said, 'Pudding won't let me touch her at the moment; she's tired. Tomorrow, I'll lift her up and show you.'

Though she had been born in Bilbao, my mother had close relations who lived in the countryside, where, as a matter of course, children saw animals born and die. It had apparently not struck her that her little son was ignorant of birth – and, possibly, also of death.

Chapter Five

Laden with greyish sheets to be washed, Grandma Micaela came slowly and heavily down the stairs, and, as she entered the kitchen, I looked up from watching the kittens. A shaft of sunlight from the tall, narrow kitchen window lit up her paper-pale cheeks, wet with tears.

I was shocked. Grandma never cried. The worst she ever did was scold; and she was my rock, my safe refuge, when both Mother and Father were cross with me. Now, as Mother scrambled hastily to her feet, Grandma looked imploringly at her and quavered, 'I can't make myself go out to see him leave. I can't bear it. I'll never see him again!' She dropped the sheets on to the stone floor; her hands, heavily veined, and scarlet from too much immersion in hot soda water, dangled helplessly at her sides.

Mother ran to her and took her in her arms. She patted her back and rocked her, just as she did me when I had hurt myself. 'I know, Mam. I know,' she crooned. 'I can't go out, either.'

'He's my baby,' cried Grandma, with a further explosion of tears.

I stopped stroking Pudding, and interjected, with some derision, 'Uncle Leo isn't a baby – he's a big man.'

Obviously startled, both women turned to look down at me, as I knelt by the open cupboard.

Grandma was the first to recover. She swallowed a sob, and then laughed through her tears. She slowly nodded her white head, and responded tenderly, 'You're right, my precious dumpling.' She let out a long sigh, and lifted a finger to touch Mother's round, pink cheek, a tiny, loving gesture of affection. She said, 'He's right. I mustn't forget it. He *is* a real man – and I have to let him go.' Then her tired voice rose, as she added, 'But it hurts, Rosita. It hurts.' Tears again trickled down her cheeks.

Mother hugged her, and said determinedly, 'We'll pretend he's simply gone to sea again – on a long voyage. It'll help. And he'll write to you.'

Did grown-ups have to pretend things? I wondered uneasily. Like small boys do?

'And, next month, Agustin should put into Liverpool. That'll be nice for you – for all of us.' She was referring to my elder uncle, who was an able seaman in a freighter which docked periodically in Liverpool with cargoes of iron ore. Between voyages he lived with Grandpa Barinèta's brother and his two motherless daughters in Bilbao, because he himself was still a bachelor.

'Yes,' agreed Grandma heavily. Uncle Agustin was a dark, silent man, not nearly so exuberant or lovable as his younger brother, Leo. But Grandma smiled, and I felt better when I saw it.

My mother began to pick up the sheets that Grandma had dropped on the floor. 'Let's put these to soak – we can boil them later on this afternoon. Let's do the bedrooms now. Would you like a glass of wine or a cup of camomile tea to carry round with you?'

Grandma sniffed. 'No, thanks,' she replied with a sigh. 'I'll have something at teatime.'

Uncle Leo was the first person to pass out of my childhood. For months, Grandma watched for his letters, but he wrote only two from Nevada, to which she replied immediately. Since she had no other address except the one he had given her in Nevada, she continued to write to him there, and she was always the first to reach the front door when a letter slid through the letter box and across the cracked tiled floor. But no more letters arrived, and she mentioned her son less and less and ceased to hope.

Unaware of the despondency the lack of news from Uncle Leo caused her, I regarded her as my own special property, always there to dispense comfort, wipe my nose and wash painfully grazed knees when I had fallen down.

Unlike Uncle Agustin, Uncle Leo and I had been born in Liverpool, and we spoke the thick catarrhal English, with a strong tinge of mixed Irish accents in it, that was current in the streets around the docks. Uncle Agustin spoke only Basque and Spanish.

It had been Uncle Leo's custom during times of un-employment to go to Spain, to his maternal grandfather's small farm in the Pyrenees, to work there in return for his food. It was there that he learned to care for sheep; and it was this skill that he hoped to build on in the United States. I had heard him discuss this with his father on a number of occasions, and I knew that he hoped eventually to have his own sheep farm.

Though he did not say much in the two letters Grandma received, I learned later that he had set his expectations of Nevada too high. Ashamed to tell his parents that he had not done too well, he put off writing to them, and moved to Arizona and, later on, wandered through Utah and Colorado. Grandma's replies to his letters never reached him. He always told himself that he would write when he was settled, but as the years went by and memories of Liverpool dimmed, he had nothing very hopeful to tell his parents so he did not write.

I forgot him.

With a steady, though small family income from Grandpa's activities amongst the emigrants and from my father, we were able to visit Spain occasionally. Carrying our own food in a big market basket, we sailed for Bilbao in Basque-owned fishing boats or small freighters. In part-return for our passage, Grandpa worked as a member of the crew. In Bilbao we stayed with Grandpa's brother and his daughters, and, occasionally, our visit coincided with the homecoming of Uncle Agustin. A more rapid form of transport was sometimes used by both families, if they felt the need to see each other on some urgent matter; they went by rail. They caught the train from Liverpool and went to Dover, crossed on the Channel ferry to Calais, and took the train from there to Bilbao. This, however, was considered very extravagant because eight pounds had to be expended on the fare – and why part with hard cash, when you could go all the way by sea for almost nothing? Grandma's sense of economy was almost as well developed as that of Mr and Mrs Wing, who owned the Chinese laundry and were the parents of one of my best-loved playmates, Brian Wing.

My childhood memories of Spain are faint, evoked mainly by the smell of baking bread and of farm animals, or the heavy odour of newly harvested hay, and a sense of having been particularly happy there, blissfully unaware of the hardship and oppression endured by the grown-ups. I took for granted callused hands and bent backs, chilblained fingers and toes, rooms where one moved like a small snake amid people, because homes were so crowded. In fact, the closeness in which everybody I knew lived was very comforting to a small boy.

As I grew bigger, I would, after a few weeks in Bilbao or up in the mountains with my father's family, the Echanizes, and another bumper crop of Barinèta second cousins, suddenly feel homesick for Liverpool. Healthy from the mountain air and the coarse fresh food stuffed into me by endless loving relations, I longed to return to the lively world centred on the Wapping Dock. I wanted to play with a shoal of small friends, Malayans, Chinese, Irish, Filipinos, and black people both from Africa and the Caribbean, as well as one or two Basque boys who were a little older than me and sometimes condescended to let me join in their games. We darted like minnows in and out of dark, familiar narrow lanes and alleys, Brian Wing and I at the end of the line because we were the smallest. The black and bleak city, rich with the smell of horse manure, vanilla pods, fish and raw hides, was to us a wonderful playground. We barely took note of the racket of horses' hooves and steel-bound wheels on the streets' stone setts or the constant roar of machinery in the workshops round us; it was simply part of everyday life.

Despite our diversity of race and religion, all my small friends had two things in common: as the children of dockers, shipyard workers or seamen, our lives were inextricably bound to the sea; and we all shared a true Liverpool sense of humour – life was intrinsically so hard that one learned early to make a joke of it. How we laughed, Lorilyn! Deep belly laughs that I rarely hear nowadays.

After seeing off the emigrants on the day of Uncle Leo's departure for Nevada, Grandpa Juan Barinèta came slowly into the kitchen and dropped his papers and house ledger on to the well-scrubbed deal table. His wooden chair, which he had made himself, scraped on the stone floor as he pulled it away from the table and wearily flopped into it. He said heavily, to nobody in particular, 'Well, that's that lot.'

Mother and Grandma Micaela had just come up from the cellar, after putting the sheets to soak in the copper before scrubbing and boiling them.

Seeing his wife's red-rimmed eyes, Grandpa said kindly to her in Basque, 'The boy's going to be all right, never fear, my dear.' He turned to my mother, and asked her, 'Rosita, get out a bottle of wine – if there's anything left after last night's party. Let's all sit down and have a drink.'

The reference to the previous night's send-off party for Leo made even Grandma smile, though rather wanly.

Already packed with emigrants, the house had been

further jammed as Basque neighbours dropped in to say farewell.

Uncle Leo and Jean Baptiste Saitua, who lived up the road, both had excellent singing voices, and they had sung all the old Basque songs they could remember, vying with each other in a good-humoured way.

Sitting on Mother's lap, leaning on her swollen stomach and clinging to her so that I did not accidentally slip off, I had watched the oil lamp light up her bright red curls. Then, as I had listened, I had turned slightly to watch the spell-bound faces crowding round us; loving faces, cunning faces, fair faces, mahogany faces, bearded, sad old faces, young bright faces; not a dull or stupid face amongst them.

In this magic circle of friends, I must have fallen asleep, because I have no memory of being put to bed, only of being surrounded by warmth and lovely sounds of singing.

Chapter Six

Manuel put down his pen and took off his spectacles, to rub his eyes. He stretched and yawned. He had better make some supper. Mechanically, he felt in his shirt pocket for his cigarettes, took one out and put it between his lips. He was just feeling in his trouser pocket for his matches when he heard the front door bell ring. Patting his empty pockets, he rose stiffly from his chair and looked up at his chronometer. 'Five o'clock,' he muttered irritably. 'Must be Veronica.' Veronica Harris was a creature of habit.

Outside, on his doorstep, Veronica, with a plate poised on one hand, turned to Sharon and said cheerfully, 'He never answers on the first ring – I don't think he hears all that well.'

'Maybe we shouldn't disturb him now.' Sharon felt a little embarrassed at being coerced into calling on someone without first telephoning.

'Oh, he's used to me running in and out. He won't mind.' She pressed the bell again.

Manuel stood in the middle of his den and wondered if she would go away, if he stayed perfectly still. Veronica was kind, but he had never liked her very much; he was uneasily suspicious that she would have enjoyed taking Kathleen's place, an idea which made him shudder. Since Kathleen's death, he had been distantly polite to her, and reluctantly accepted her baked offerings because she insistently pressed them upon him to the point of rudeness.

He never went to her home; in fact, since Kathleen's death he had rarely visited any of their friends. Their abounding energy made him feel tired. In nursing Kathleen for months, his strength had been sapped, and all he wanted was to be left alone with his grief.

He stood perfectly still in the back of the hall, but the bell was rung for the third time.

'Why not leave the plate on the doorstep?' suggested Sharon, who had already done an eight-hour shift in the Palliative Care Unit and found her feet to be aching abominably.

'The dogs might get it,' Veronica replied shortly.

Resigned, Manuel put down his unlit cigarette on the hall table and answered the door. As he opened it, he did his best to show pleasant surprise. He wondered who the other woman was – not a bad-looking judy.

Without hesitation, Veronica stepped into his hall, and he backed hastily. 'Ah!' she cooed. 'I thought you'd never hear me. How are you doing?' She half-turned towards Sharon, who was still teetering on the step. 'I want to introduce you to Elaine's daughter – you remember Elaine? She's staying with me until she finds an apartment. Come in, Sharon.'

Old Manuel gave up.

He retreated further into the little hallway, while Sharon, loath to intrude, stepped into the doorway.

Who, in the name of God, was Elaine? Old Manuel could not remember.

Blithely oblivious to the lack of welcome, Veronica moved firmly through the archway that led to the sitting-room. 'I've brought you some cold roast beef,' she announced. 'I got a roast when I knew Sharon was coming – and it's too much for us, isn't it, Sharon?'

Sharon smiled, and fidgeted uncertainly. What was she supposed to say?

Veronica was asking Manuel if she should put the meat in the refrigerator for him. He hastily took the plate from her. He had no desire to have her poking through the entrails of his refrigerator.

'No. That's OK. I'll take it. I'll put it on the table here.' He darted through the opposite arch, which led into the dining-room, with an alacrity surprising for a man in his eighties. If he were quick enough, he thought, he could shoo her out of the door again quite rapidly.

He was too late. Veronica was already seated on the flower-covered settee in the sitting-room, and was patting the cushion beside her to indicate to Sharon that she, too, should sit down.

From the archway, Manuel viewed them both with trepidation, while Veronica chirruped on about Sharon coming to nurse in the Palliative Care Unit, and wasn't it great that they would have such a unit in their closest hospital? Such a shame that there had not been one when Kathleen was so ill.

Manuel stiffened. He was not too clear what exactly a Palliative Care Unit was meant for; but he certainly did not feel like discussing Kathleen in front of a stranger.

The lack of welcome was all too obvious to Sharon, and her colour rose as her embarrassment increased. She glanced directly up at him, wondering how to retreat with grace. What she saw in his face was the closed-off look of suffering, all too familiar to her in her work.

She got up immediately and filled the gap in the conversation which Manuel's silence had caused. 'It's suppertime, Veronica,' she said firmly. 'We should leave Mr Echaniz to enjoy the beef, and perhaps we could meet again another day.' She held out her hand to Manuel, and, since Veronica had not introduced her properly, she added, 'I'm Sharon Herman. It's nice to meet you.'

The relief which flooded Manuel's face was so blatant that she wanted to laugh. Her eyes must have twinkled, because there was the hint of an answering grin suddenly flickering round his wide, thin mouth.

She let go of his hand, and bent to help a disconcerted Veronica up from the low settee.

God's blessings on the girl, the old man thought, as he assured her that he was pleased to meet her.

With her hand under Veronica's elbow, she steered her towards the front door, which was still open, and guided Veronica down the steps. Not too sure what was happening to her, Veronica did her best, and said to Manuel, 'I hope you'll like the meat. You can bring the plate back another time.'

In her heart, she knew that he would never bring the plate back – the next time she called it would be sitting on the hall table, in a paperbag, waiting for her to pick it up.

He nodded agreeably to both of them. Then he shut the front door after them. He stood leaning against it for a moment, as if to make sure that they would not come back in. Veronica had been Kathleen's devoted friend, he reminded himself for the umpteenth time. 'And for her sake, I must be pleasant to her – even if she's a real cross!'

As he retrieved his unlit cigarette and started back to his den to find some matches, he looked down at the plate of meat. He had a great urge to empty it straight into the rubbish bin – but she did mean kindly, and the young woman with her had understood well enough to take her away. Furthermore, it would save him cooking for himself.

He laughed at himself as he put the plate in the refrigerator, and then went to get his long-delayed smoke.

Nice young woman, he considered, as he thankfully drew on his cigarette. Just what does she do in palliative care?

Outside, as the women went down the steps to the pavement, to walk round to Veronica's house, Sharon said soothingly, 'He looked so exhausted and so upset when you mentioned Kathleen, I thought we'd better not stay.'

'Oh? I didn't notice.' Veronica's expression was puzzled. Then, accepting Sharon's explanation, she said, 'Well, I suppose at his age . . .' And left it at that.

*

41

As he smoked, Manuel stood staring out of the window, rocking slightly on his heels, as if he were in a boat and must keep his balance. He did not notice the two ladies pass beyond his budding lilac tree. His mind had reverted to the memoirs he had been writing for Lorilyn, before the visit.

He smiled slowly at a sudden remembrance of a ship's master saying to his Grandfather Barinèta that his crew were a lot of 'hard cases'.

'Oh, aye,' he muttered to himself. 'So were me granddad and me dad – tough as old boots. They could fight anybody if they had to – even other "hard cases" out on a spree of a Saturday night.'

Very thoughtfully, he stubbed out his cigarette in an overcrowded ash tray, and then stood absently rubbing his nicotine-stained thumb and forefinger together, as if to erase the yellow stain on them.

Was he remembering correctly? Had his life in Liverpool really been as golden as he had described? Had the other boys with whom he had played been as good mates as he remembered? While he played or went to school, safe in the shelter of his ferocious old grandfather, what was going on between the adult members of the family?

Chapter Seven

Manuel would soon be six years old, a thin streak of a child, tall for his age. Filled with resentment, he was clutching his bag of marbles to his chest for fear that Andrew would snatch them from him.

Seven-year-old Andrew had just won his best blue-streaked ollie from him, and Manuel felt sure that Andrew had cheated him, but he was not certain how. Tears of rage sprang to his eyes at the smug look on Andrew's face as he stowed the disputed marble in the pocket of his ragged shorts.

'You don't play fair,' he yelled. 'I'll tell my dad of you!'

Andrew's lips curled. 'Who's afraid of your dad? He's not home.'

'Me dad's a Master Mariner, and he'll get you when he does come home,' cried Manuel furiously. 'So there!'

The youngest of five unruly boys, Andrew was the off-spring of a Filipino and an Irish girl, who lived in a nearby street. Nearly a year older than the young Basque, he enjoyed lording it over the smaller lads in the vicinity. Now he made a lewd gesture. 'My dad's a stoker, and he's stronger 'n yours. He's stronger than anybody in the world!'

Too angry to care that he was probably stirring up a hornet's nest, Manuel went a step closer. He thrust his chin towards Andrew and ground his teeth menacingly. He snarled, 'No, he isn't! And you cheated! I want me bluey back.'

Andrew pushed his face close to Manuel's. Blue eyes,

bloodshot with conjunctivitis, glared into clear brown ones, as Andrew made the worst grimace he could conjure up. 'You're not getting it back, see. You shut up, or I'll put me brothers on to you!' He stepped back, and grinned. 'Me dad showed us how to break a man's arm real quick last night.' To demonstrate, he did a vicious twist with his right hand.

Apprehension cooled Manuel's rage; he was scared suddenly of being beaten up by five known bullies. He glanced quickly around in search of adult help. None was visible.

Brian Wing, even younger than Manuel, had been watching Manuel's defiance of Andrew in silent astonishment. Now, he squatted quickly down on his heels and began to pick up those of his marbles still on the pavement. Deftly, he shovelled them into a cotton drawstring bag. Manuel knew that he was preparing to run back home to the laundry, if a fight should start; Brian did not worry about being called a cowardy custard. When trouble threatened, he was the first to vanish. At this moment, as he rose to his feet, he was beaming amiably at both prospective combatants, his eyes thin slits above pudgy cheeks.

Manuel glanced again at Andrew. With a satisfied smirk, the bigger boy had taken the blue out of his pocket, and was holding it up to the sunlight. Manuel snatched unsuccessfully at it, and Andrew laughed.

Brian fled.

From round the curve of the street suddenly floated Grandma Micaela's strident voice. 'Manuel! Manuel Echaniz! Where are you?'

With total relief, Manuel edged back from Andrew, and shrieked, 'Coming, Grandma!' Then he turned and ran for home. It left Andrew in command of the field – but, Manuel solaced himself as he tore back to the safety of Grandma, he now had nobody to play with.

Thanks to Grandma's calling him, his retreat was an honourable one; even Andrew would admit that. When

44

mothers called, you responded fairly promptly. If you did not, you got soundly slapped the minute you showed your face at home — and there was always the overwhelming threat from the females of the family, 'When your dad gets in, I'll tell him about you!' Fathers whacked much harder than mothers did; they sometimes took their belt to you.

Grandma bent to catch him in the curve of her arm. 'Come along, dumpling,' she said in Basque. 'We're going up to the market. Your dad's docking tomorrow; and your mam wants to have chicken ready for him when he gets home.'

'Do I have to come?' asked Manuel in a whining voice. He had been to school, had his tea, and had then gone out into the street to play, only to find himself up against Andrew. He was tired, and the thought of the long, boring walk up to St John's Market made his legs ache.

'Yes, dear. With Auntie Maria only just out of hospital, she can't watch you. Who'll take care of you while we're out? Your grandpa's gone over to the Baltic for a game of chequers and a drink.'

With the threat of Andrew and his brothers still in his mind, Manuel saw the point of this, and made no further demur.

On her return from the hospital the previous day, Manuel had watched his spinster Aunt Maria being laid carefully on the old sofa in the big kitchen-living-room, so that Grandma and Mother would not have to run up and downstairs to and from her bedroom while nursing her.

She was his mother's elder sister, and she and Manuel were great friends. She had taught him to play snap and snakes and ladders, and she usually took care of him whenever the others were out.

Now, back home, she was exceedingly quiet, her face white and haggard, except for a single hectic pink spot on either cheek.

45

It was called convalescence, which Manuel understood was another word for getting better. But he had noticed that all the ladies who had crowded in to see her during the last twenty-four hours looked sad, and sighed. 'TB's a terrible thing, God save us,' they had murmured to each other. Then they had spoken to Auntie Maria in bright, artificial voices.

Even seventy-eight years later, as he wrote about them in his Canadian home, for Lorilyn, he could still remember clearly the black-clad women, their arms wrapped in their woollen shawls, despite the summer heat, while they smiled determinedly and chirruped like birds, as they bent over the stricken invalid.

Grandma took his hand and led him up the worn sandstone steps into the soot-blackened house, to see if his mother and two of her Basque friends were ready to set out.

Rosita was just wrapping Manuel's new baby sister, Francesca, into the folds of the black shawl she wore. He felt a sting of jealousy at the baby's privileged position in his mother's arms; she had usurped his place. Admittedly, Grandma had been particularly kind since Francesca's birth – but Grandma was kind to the baby as well.

As he waited in the crowded kitchen-living-room for the women to marshal themselves, Aunt Maria put out a bone-thin hand and held his fingertips, as she smiled up at him. Manuel looked down at her. Neither said anything, but Manuel found it consoling that he still appeared to be his aunt's favourite; *she* had never even held Francesca in her arms, as far as he was aware.

It was always a matter of earnest debate between Grandma Micaela, Rosita and Aunt Maria whether it was better to go to the market early in the morning, when there was lots of choice; or to go at the end of the day, when it was possible to beat down the prices of wares which vendors did not want to have to take back home. Since a live chicken was as fresh in the late afternoon as it would have been in the early morning, they had decided to go at the last possible moment.

Aunt Maria felt well enough to be disappointed that she would miss the excitement of the market, and she said wistfully that she wished she had an invalid chair to go out in.

Grandma grunted. Invalid chairs were beyond the dreams of avarice, so she said comfortingly, 'Never mind, dear, save your strength for tomorrow. We'll get you up and dressed in time to greet Pedro when he arrives. He'd be so happy to see you up and about – so you mustn't tire yourself today.'

Mollified, she allowed Grandma·to prop her up with another cushion and put an extra shawl around her, though the day was warm. With a glass of water, her spectacles and her rosary on a stool by her couch, she settled down resignedly to await their return.

By the time the four chattering ladies reached the beginning of the narrow lane at the back of the market, where poultry was sold, Manuel's feet were dragging through the straw which littered the cobblestones. Fine beads of perspiration lay on his forehead, and he clutched Rosita's black skirt, in order to keep up with her. The smell of poultry droppings and other manure lay like a blanket over the crowded lane, and was not improved by the intense odour of dozens of unbathed women, who sat amid their goods for sale. He felt stifled and began to grizzle.

Amid the din and the thick black skirts flapping round him, his wails went unremarked. Men and women shouted, puppies yapped, ducks quacked; fouled in their own excrement, kittens mewed pitifully and scratched at the bars of their cages; next to a cage of clucking hens, a lone goose hissed at passersby. Only rabbits crouched quietly, their quivering noses a tiny indication that they were still alive, despite the heat.

47

The approach of a small group of Basque women, chattering loudly in their own peculiar language, did not raise the hopes of the purveyors of poultry. They, too, were hot and weary. An impending Basque invasion made their spirits wilt: if the women bought anything, it would only be after strenuous bargaining; it would surely make any stallholder they fastened upon late home for his tea.

After strolling the length of the still busy lane, the target of the Basque attack became a small cage holding three hens, which appeared not to have sold because they were rather scrawny. Before showing any direct interest in the birds, Grandma Micaela led a distracting minor scrimmage by examining carefully a pair of rabbits. She poked at them through the bars of their cage, and they stared back at her without hope. She drew Rosita's attention to them, and she also poked disparagingly at them. Rosita's two friends, who had accompanied them, pursed their lips and agreed loudly with one another that they weren't worth sixpence each. The man in charge of them said something inaudible under his breath.

Sighing, they looked desultorily at a pair of slaughtered hens, not yet cleaned or feathered, hanging heads down in front of the next small stall.

'Here ye are, ladies,' called the stallholder, beaming at them. 'A real nice dinner. Good fat birds. One and sixpence each. Feather 'em yerself.' He unhooked the hens and held them against his forearm for inspection. Four ladies pinched the hens' breasts and declared in chorus that they had no fat on them.

The man lost his amiability as quickly as it had been assumed; the price he had asked was fair for two good birds. 'Pack of bloody Israelites!' he muttered, and turned angrily away to accost another shopper.

Though Grandma's eyes were weak and she could not see any of the products very well, prompted by Rosita, she opened negotiations with the man who had three live hens. They were, apparently, the last of his offerings for that day; several empty cages had already been piled on a hand-cart behind him.

'What do you think, Mother?' Rosita asked.

Grandma bent down to squint carefully at the hens. One of them tried to peck her, and she hastily drew back. She nodded her head negatively, and said dolefully, 'They might make good soup. Nothing on them for anything else.' She glanced up at the vendor. 'How much do you want for them?' she inquired, her English difficult to understand.

'How much?' interjected Rosita. Her two friends stood behind her, politely silent, ready to murmur approbation or denigration, as required.

'A bob each,' he told her, hoping to get rid of three birds in one sale, so that he could wander off for a much-needed pint of bitter, before going home.

Rosita translated the price, and Grandma's heavy eyebrows rose, as if in shock. 'For those?' She turned to their silent friends for confirmation of her horror at such an outrageous price. Like a Greek chorus, they nodded agreement and stared coldly at the stallholder. Still holding his mother's skirt, Manuel scrubbed one small boot against another, and sighed; he had seen this pantomime so often. He watched a woodlouse, surprised by his shuffling feet from under a few wisps of straw, hasten into hiding beneath a couple of feathers.

Meanwhile, the face of the chicken vendor went as dark as an angry cockerel's comb. 'Wass the matter with 'em?' he asked indignantly. 'Best roastin' chicken you could buy. Why, one of 'em would feed six, easy.'

Manuel saw his mother's generous chest expand, as she readied herself to dive into the fray. It was going to be a long and boring battle. He let go of her skirt and wandered down the sloping lane for a few yards, to look at ugly white dishes laid out on straw; they were tended by three Irish women from the north end of the city.

'Mind your clumsy feet!' one of them shouted at him, as he stumbled over a cobblestone. He backed hastily away; to a small boy, they seemed very big and threatening.

Further down, towards Elliott Street, there were still a few puppies for sale, and he paused to watch them, as they stumbled over each other in the dirty cage. In the background, he could hear his mother arguing volubly, as she sought to bring down the price of the hens; she was demanding that they be taken out of the cage, so that she could feel how much flesh there was on the unfortunate creatures.

He was wondering if he could persuade his father, when he came home, to get him a puppy, when there was a chorus of female shrieks accompanied by a roar of male anger. He jumped, and whipped around to see if his mother was all right.

His view was blocked by a large woman with a shopping basket on her arm. He tried to edge around her. She looked down kindly at him, and said, 'Careful, sonny, mind the pile of saucepans behind me.' Then, at a slight noise, she glanced back. 'Holy Mary!' she cried shrilly, and jumped to one side, sending the pile of iron saucepans in all directions, so that cursing market women leapt to their feet to avoid them.

Flapping awkwardly on clipped wings, a terrified, squawking hen sailed over their heads. The poor bird was unable to gain any height and came down to earth, momentarily, in front of Manuel. He laughed, and instinctively grabbed at it. It managed to scuttle a few feet away from him towards Elliott Street. Then, seeing a break in the highly amused crowd, it took off again in a series of desperate hops and flaps.

Manuel forgot his mother. Hens lived in cages, so this one must have escaped. In high glee, he scampered after it, dodging in and out between piles of kitchenware and ironmongery. He bumped into two young men entering the lane. 'Watch it, kiddo!' one shouted after him, irritably.

Driven by panic and despair, the hen managed to soar upward a little. Absorbed in the chase, Manuel ran faster.

As the bird descended, to perch for a moment on top of a fire hydrant in busy Elliott Street, the boy plunged across the pavement towards it, tripping up and confusing the crowd of office workers hurrying homeward. A young clerk made a playful grab at the bird, to the amusement of the girl accompanying him. The frantic hen immediately hopped off its perch on the edge of the pavement, and staggered into the heavy traffic, as if to cross the road. Intent on catching it, Manuel shot after it.

The hen ran directly under a work horse pulling a small cart. The horse reared in fright. The cart skidded past Manuel. It missed him by a hand's breadth, as the carter swore and fought to rein in the animal. A few yards behind came three errand boys on their bicycles, hurrying to finish the last deliveries of the day. They swerved to avoid the child. Two of them collided and tumbled off, the packages in their front baskets scattering amid both lines of traffic; the third boy managed to reach the gutter, and dismounted; he yelled imprecations at a heedless Manuel, while more cyclists wobbled and dodged around the two bikes tangled in the middle of the lane. Two chauffeur-driven private cars came to a screeching halt, and the drivers impatiently blew their klaxon horns.

All traffic was coming quickly to a halt; and harsh words were exchanged between drivers and carters in the near lane, as horses, set to breast the upward slope of the street, were hauled to a clattering stop, their shoes striking sparks from the setts, and foam from their mouths splattering passersby.

Nobody attempted to rescue Manuel – or the hen.

At the sight of the traffic coming the other way, he had,

in the middle of the street, suddenly ceased his headlong chase; he could see that, on the other side, the hen had found a safe perch on the high windowsill of a bank.

With disorganized traffic still edging past him, both before and behind, he was suddenly very frightened. As he stood frozen, at the back of him the driver of a carriage with two ladies in it, leaned down, whip in hand, and shouted at him, 'Gerroff the street!' He glanced up over his shoulder, and the high wheels, far higher than him, rolled past him dangerously closely. He turned back towards the opposite pavement. A tram, unable to stop quickly, rolled slowly past him on its rails. It was followed by a brewer's dray which had been successfully slowed by the drayman; it was pulled by two huge horses and the dray itself was piled high with barrels of beer. Though the upward slope meant it would be hard to start the horses again, the driver drew to a careful stop, thus blocking any further traffic in that lane. He stood up and called to the frightened child, 'Get on pavement, luv. Quick, now.'

Though all Manuel could see was the slavering mouth and huge, bronze-coloured legs of the lead horse, he heard the voice, and he obediently trotted, almost under the great animal's nose, to the safety of the pavement.

As the traffic began to move again, he stood, bewildered, on the kerb, and looked up at the hen. From the safety of the bank's windowsill, the hen opened its eyes and looked down at him with grave suspicion; then, the lids closed again.

Distraught, the child began to cry.

Standing against the bank wall, an elderly newspaper-man was calling to the homegoing crowd of pedestrians, 'Echo! Liverpool Echo! Read all about it!' Perspiration was running down his bulbous red nose, as he shoved a neatly folded newspaper into any hand proffering the necessary coppers for it. On a blackboard beside him was scrawled the day's headline, *Countess of Derby Opens Crippled Children's Hospital.*

He glanced down at the weeping child, while saying to a customer, 'Fourpence change, Sir. What's to do, lad?'

'I want me mam,' howled Manuel, hastily taking refuge beside the news-vendor's second blackboard, which proclaimed in white chalk, *Big Fire at Huskisson Dock.* 'And I can't reach me hen!' He pointed upwards to the refuge on the windowsill.

The newspaperman squinted quickly upwards, and grinned. The hen had squatted down, eyes still closed, and looked like a bundle of feathers. 'That's yours? Not to worry, lad. Soon as this little rush is over, I'll get it for yez. It don't look like it's goin' to fly away.'

Manuel nodded, wiped his nose on the sleeve of his jersey, and continued to weep, though at a lower pitch. He had no idea where he was, and he didn't really care what happened to the hen; all he wanted was his mother.

Meanwhile, Rosita and Grandma had assumed that Manuel was still in the market lane, looking at the pets for sale, and had contentedly bought the two remaining live hens. The stallholder, still fuming over the loss of the third hen, sullenly wrung the birds' necks, while Grandma went to the nearest greengrocery stall by the door of the main market, and bought onions and garlic.

The crowd in the lane was thinning rapidly; the Irish women were packing up their remaining plates; some of the disconsolate, unsold pets had already been whisked away. Manuel was not visible, and Rosita became anxious.

To save her carrying the baby around unnecessarily, her two friends ran the length of the lane, but there was no place in which he could have hidden. They came back panting and gesticulating.

'Who you lookin' for?' asked a young woman, hooking a cage of kittens on to the handlebars of a bicycle, near the Elliott Street entrance.

Rosita told her.

'Oh, aye,' she replied readily. 'He were nearly run over, he was. You'll mebbe find 'im across the road. I'll bet you'll find 'im in the station there – kids love trains.' She smiled, and mounted her bike and wobbled over the cobblestones in the general direction to which she had pointed.

'Oh, goodness!' Rosita exclaimed, her face paling, as, united, the four women pushed their way to the edge of the Elliott Street pavement. A break in the traffic revealed Manuel, with his mouth as wide as a choir boy's singing a Te Deum, shrieking, 'I want me mam.'

Rosita's expression changed immediately to one of parental outrage. With baby Francesca bouncing on her chest and followed by the other three, shawls flapping like the wings of angry magpies, she surged through a break in the traffic, to face her tear-stained son. Before the child could do more than turn his face to her and reduce his sobs, she scolded him, 'What do you mean by running off like this? We bin scared stiff for you. I'll tell your dad about you, when he gets home!' With her free hand, she grabbed him by the shoulder and shook him.

Far from being more upset by this, Manuel recognized the typical reaction of a mam who had indeed been scared. His sobs became sniffs, as she alternately cajoled and scolded again.

Meanwhile, Grandma Micaela, who was feeling extremely tired, looked on silently, and the news-vendor asked her, 'Do you want the 'en, Queen?' He pointed up to the bank windowsill, on which the hen lay inert.

Grandma blinked, and her eyes followed the line of the man's finger. She peered at the bank wall. Halfway up, she saw a vague, copper-coloured lump. 'On the windowsill,' the man said impatiently.

Grandma was under five feet tall; the sill was impossibly high up for her. 'Could you possibly reach it?' she asked shyly.

54

The man grinned. 'Anything to oblige a lady,' he responded with sudden gallantry. He reached up and managed to gather the bird into his hand. After inspecting it dubiously, he said, 'It looks like dead, Missus.'

'It's fresh enough to cook,' she told him, with a little laugh. Her faded blue eyes, though partially clouded by cataracts, still had a twinkle in them, and the news-vendor returned to his pitch feeling pleased with himself.

Grandma laid the hen on top of the other two in her calico bag. Rosita had finished her scolding and was wiping Manuel's face with the corner of her apron. Her friends stopped gossiping about the high price of rabbits – and the party straggled down Hanover Street towards home.

At home, the oil lamp had been lit. Grandpa was seated at the kitchen table, writing in his ledger. Behind him, on the wall, the huge map on which Pedro recorded his voyages, glimmered softly, the net of inky lines linking the ports of call looking like a tangled mass of black cotton thread.

As the shoppers entered, he closed the book wearily. He nodded to his wife and to Rosita, as they entered and thankfully plonked the shopping bags on the draining board by the kitchen sink. The baby was beginning to whimper from hunger, and Grandma said she would make a pot of tea before starting the evening meal. Rosita nodded agreement, and sat down in a rocking chair. She unbuttoned her black blouse and modestly arranged her shawl round the baby's head and her breast, while she fed her new daughter.

Manuel slunk to the other side of the fireplace, where Aunt Maria had, in their absence, established herself in an easy chair. He leaned against his aunt, who put down the knitting she had been struggling to do and put her arm round him. He was grateful for her presence; he had missed her during her stay in hospital.

He could not have articulated his sense of desertion as

he watched his mother feed the baby. He only knew he longed to be cuddled by her and to lay his head on her milky breast. Not even when she called him her *big* boy, and sent him off to school with a loving pat on his behind, was he comforted.

Auntie Maria suddenly began to cough. She withdrew her arm, and fumbled for her handkerchief in her dressing-gown pocket. She put it to her mouth, and tried to smile at Manuel over its folds.

As she had taught him, he stepped back from her while the spasm lasted. 'I don't want to splutter all over you,' she had once explained to him. 'It's not very nice.'

Aunt Maria's cough was part and parcel of Manuel's childhood; he slept in the same room as she did, and the sound of it comforted him when he woke in the night after a bad dream; it meant that she was awake, and if he were very scared, he could scramble out of bed and run to her. It puzzled him, however, that, unlike his mother, she would never let him into her bed, however much he was shivering with fright; and she was the only one of his doting relations who did not kiss him; even Grandpa kissed him sometimes. He occasionally thought that he would never understand the idiosyncrasies of grown-ups.

After feeding Francesca, Rosita laid the dozing child in Manuel's old cradle, near the fireplace, but far enough from it not to be spattered by the fat in which Grandma was frying fish for tea. She then unpacked the three hens and took them out into the brick-lined backyard, to feather and singe them. Though the stallholder had obligingly wrung the necks of the two hens, he had complained sourly that he would not have lost the third one if Grandma had not insisted on the cage being opened. He could not run after the flying bird himself, he said bitterly, because it would have meant leaving his stall untended in an area where petty theft was a fine art.

After the meal, the hens were brought in and drawn

on the draining board, giving Manuel an early lesson in anatomy, as he watched the operation.

The naked birds were then washed and hung up in the larder overnight. Manuel stared up at them, and decided they did not look much different from Francesca, after she had been bathed in front of the kitchen fire.

That night he dreamed that he had been hung up in the larder, by his feet. He was too terrified even to run across to Auntie Maria's bed, and he lay quivering under his cotton sheet until sleep overtook him again.

Chapter Eight

In the golden summer days of 1914 his view of his world was that of a child, considered Manuel. His was a permanent world which Grandpa Barinèta would rule for ever. Ample food arrived on the table at least three times a day, and boys did their best not to offend Grandma Micaela or Mother, who ruled the kitchen-living-room like royal queens.

Close by his home was the world of school, where nuns in white wimples and long black dresses talked of eternity and the need to be a good Catholic boy; so that when one died – an event which would take place so far ahead that one could not envision it – one could, in a state of grace, enjoy eternity sitting on the right hand of God, where, hoped Little Manuel fervently, there would be no nuns with sharp voices and spanking rulers to tell you that you had been naughty again. He had secretly wondered if God liked nuns. Old Manuel reflected that the latter thought had seemed so wicked that he had hastily stifled it and had hoped that St Peter would not make a note of it.

At the edge of his world, not counting St John's Market, lay St Peter's Church in Seel Street, where, every Sunday morning, he went to Mass with either Grandma or his mother. Though the conversation of the congregation was split between Spanish, Basque and English, the Mass was said in Latin; his father said that it did not matter which port he was in, the Mass was always there, always the same – in Latin. Little Manuel began to think that there was something magical about Latin.

Some of the priests were Jesuits and good scholars. Scholarliness was not something particularly appreciated in the dockside parish, but the Jesuits' awesome reputation as missionaries, many of whom had come to untimely ends in foreign parts, gained them a grudging respect. They always made Little Manuel feel nervous. They seemed so disciplined; and he could not imagine them sneaking off to see a music hall show or having a drink in the local, like any normal human being.

At home, he took for granted the constant work which engaged Grandma and his mother, how they washed and scrubbed and cooked, knitted and sewed, in a house with one cold-water tap and no electricity or gas. In addition to their usual chores, they endured the house being periodically filled with emigrants, all wanting to prepare food, wash clothes and cope with husbands and babies.

He never considered that his grandfather might be very tired and long to retire, but could not because he had never been able to save much; or that he might be homesick for his native country. It never occurred to him that his father had any feelings beyond affection for his son – and a curious desire to lie on her bed with his mother, with the big iron key turned in the doorlock.

It seemed a very safe world, though Mother sometimes announced herself worried. Exactly what she meant by that, Little Manuel was not very sure, except that it manifested itself in the form of a sharp slap if he did not come straight home from school, and an irate warning never to go with a strange man or accept a sweet from one; the vague warnings of dire results, if he ever took a sweetie from a stranger, remained with him long after he understood what lay behind them, so that even as an adult he always refused a proffered sweet.

The fear of unemployment must have haunted his father, considered Old Manuel. Some of his friends' fathers were out of work from time to time; and their mams grew short-tempered, and hoped they would not have another baby that year.

Mr Connolly, who lived next door with his wife, Bridget, and little Mary and Baby Joey, was periodically without employment. But he was more cheerful than his neighbours, and he would sit on his front doorstep and play simple hand games with Manuel and Mary. It was he who taught the little boy how to catch and throw an old tennis ball. He was so good at lip-reading that it was a long time before Manuel understood that he was deaf, the usual fate of ships' scalers, who spent their working lives inside ships' boilers chipping away at accumulated scale, a job which created tremendous noise.

Pedro was fortunate in being steadily employed by a small freighting company sailing out of Liverpool, though he always hoped that when times improved he would get a better ship. When he was at home for a few days, he would take Manuel swimming, or up to the park to play ball. Sometimes, they walked down to the Pier Head, and, looking out across the river, he taught his small son how to identify the ownership of the vessels plying the river, by the colours of their funnels. Manuel also learned that each country had its own flag fluttering from ships belonging to it; when he and his father got home, they found the countries on the big map pinned to the wall of the kitchen-living-room.

Pedro had a shrewd eye for what might interest a boy and told him stories about the ports he had visited, including small details which Old Manuel still remembered, like the kind of sweets on sale in the streets of Bombay or the kind of clothing that ladies in Yokahama wore.

'You'll see them all yourself, one day,' his father assured him, certain that his boy would follow in his footsteps, though with better qualifications.

*

As he wrote for Lorilyn, Old Manuel wondered if Faith would remember him with the same uncritical love with which he remembered his father. He doubted it; his Canadian wife and child seemed to live lives crammed with commitments. They were far too busy to spend much time listening to what had happened to him in his last absence from them; they appeared to exist deep in a women's world of school, voluntary work, dancing classes, music lessons, skating classes, teas and ladies' bridge parties. Sometimes, Kathleen did a spell of nursing which gave her a whole new collection of women with whom to become involved. Men seemed to be expected to keep to their world and not intrude — even to their half of a room, if they were at a party, Manuel remembered with a rueful smile.

Perhaps it was his own fault, he thought. Even when he had become a marine architect, he had sometimes been away for weeks. As a seaman from a family of seamen, this had not appeared unusual to him; but it had probably made Kathleen and Faith cling more closely to each other for support.

He sighed, and paused in his writing to light another cigarette. He had got to know Kathleen in her final illness better than he had ever known her before, and, in his current loneliness, he regretted that he had not tried harder to be closer to her in their earlier married life. They had not been unhappy, he considered, just not quite as happy as they might have been.

In marrying a Canadian and settling in Canada, Manuel had achieved a much higher standard of living than he could have reasonably hoped for if he had stayed in Liverpool. After qualifying as a marine architect, he had worked in Montreal, and he had had to acquire a working knowledge of yet another language, French; it had added to the difficulties of adjusting himself to North American life.

After enjoying the close support of an extended Basque community in Liverpool and Bilbao, he had been, for a

61

time, intensely lonely. It was some time before he met anyone who knew what a Basque was, and he remembered his intense thankfulness when he met a sprinkling of fellow Basques and could speak his own language to them. His neighbours were supremely indifferent that he could switch in and out of four languages – being multilingual was something that born Canadians were not supposed to worry about; English-speaking Canadians seemed to take it for granted that even their French compatriots would be able to speak English – just as the Spaniards expected the Basques to be competent in Spanish, thought Manuel tartly.

Though sometimes he tripped up, for Kathleen's sake he made a great effort to sink into her world. He had, however, done his best to teach Faith to speak Basque, and as a little child she had always spoken to him in that language – until she went to school, when, under the tight conforming pressure of her school life, she had soon discovered that it was convenient to forget that her father was an immigrant.

As he worked on his notes for his granddaughter, Old Manuel wondered if his quiet, capable father felt like a stranger in his own home, when he carried a kitbag full of grubby clothes up the steps of Grandpa Barinèta's house, at the end of long boring weeks at sea in a tramp steamer.

Was it difficult for Pedro Echaniz to re-establish a rapport with his wife and mother-in-law and his rather forbidding father-in-law, all of whom seemed to talk to him at once?

Mulling over his memories of his father sitting in the crowded kitchen-living-room, smoking his pipe and listening to the chatter, Old Manuel realized that, sometimes, it may have been quite hard; only when he was alone with Little Manuel had the dam burst, and Pedro himself had talked and talked, creating a fabulous world of distant places and homespun philosophy for his small son. God keep him, prayed Old Manuel, with a surge of love.

The day after the three chickens had been carefully prepared for cooking, Pedro had run up the steps of his father-in-law's house. The front door was hospitably ajar, and through it wafted an excellent smell of cooking — olive oil, garlic, onions, herbs and chicken. How good it would be to eat some decent food!

In the narrow hall, he slung his kitbag to the floor and threw down his heavy jacket and peaked cap.

'Rosita!' he shouted, over the clamour of the riveters in the workshop immediately to the rear of the house. Dear God! How could she stand that kind of noise all day long? 'Rosita!'

She heard him and came running, plump face beaming and blue eyes flashing, her mass of wavy red hair bouncing round her shoulders. She flew into his arms, and, over the odours of cooking and babies, he smelled the freshness of her. He always swore to himself that every time he returned home he fell in love with her again.

Before the family caught up with them, he hugged and kissed her, cupping one breast in an eager hand, feeling the dampness of her milk soaking through her starched flowered pinafore.

She giggled happily; seconds of privacy were precious in a house full of relations — and often with emigrants as well.

He dropped his hand, as his tiny mother-in-law came pattering after her daughter, followed closely by Grandpa Juan Barinèta. Behind them, Manuel stood shyly by the kitchen door, waiting to be noticed.

Over his wife's head, Pedro greeted his parents-in-law; he was struck by how old they seemed suddenly to have become. He was fond of both of them, and was thankful that Rosita had their company while he was at sea.

With a twinge of anxiety for the old people, he loosened

himself from Rosita, to bend and kiss Micaela's cheek. He then embraced Juan.

'It's been a long time,' Grandpa said, keeping his arm round the younger man's shoulder. 'Come in, boy. Come in.'

Pedro moved down the passage, and then saw Manuel. He stopped and squatted down close to him. 'How's my big lad?' he asked, and opened his arms to him, and the boy went joyfully into them. There was the feel of his father's beard on his cheek, the smell of sweat and tobacco and wine, the total comfort of his being.

Manuel chuckled in his father's ear, and said shyly that he was all right.

In the steamy kitchen, Pedro stretched himself and looked around the familiar domain. Auntie Maria shyly and carefully rose from her chair to greet him; she was dressed in her best black skirt and black silk blouse. Jet earrings hung against her cheeks.

'Maria! You're up and about!' exclaimed Pedro, as if he had already been primed by Grandma what to say to the stricken woman. Without hesitation, he went to her and put his arm protectively round her shoulders, as she subsided again into her chair, and kissed her on both cheeks. 'I thought you would still be in hospital.'

She glowed, as she looked up at him with frank yearning. Why tell him that she was at home because the doctors could do no more for her?

'I'm doing quite well,' she affirmed. 'I can sit in the yard – or on the steps, and I'm hoping to walk out soon.'

He looked into the big blue eyes turned up towards him, so like his wife's but without her beauty; and he knew that she was lying. He played up to her, however, and joked about all the young Basques who would ask her out when she could get about again. Manuel came to lean against her, so as to be included in his father's attention. He realized that nobody but his father ever kissed Auntie Maria, and he sensed his aunt's pleasure at being so closely touched by another human being, though he did not yet fully understand her inner loneliness, caused by other people's fear of catching her dread disease.

Grandma Micaela turned quickly away from the little group, and went to fetch some wine glasses from the dresser. There was a lump in her throat and she wanted to cry. With Leo gone and Agustin rarely in Liverpool, her daughters were doubly precious to her, and yet she had to accept that Maria was preparing for a much longer journey.

She took a big breath, and, with her hands full of glasses, she turned back to the family. 'Let's have a drink,' she suggested gaily. 'Juan, dear. Get a bottle out for us.'

As Grandpa produced a bottle of good Basque wine, Rosita said cheerfully to Pedro, 'You haven't met your daughter yet!'

She bent down and scooped the child out of her wooden cradle, and thrust her into her father's arms. Francesca stared up at him with some perplexity. She opened her tiny mouth to cry. Pedro suddenly laughed, and said to Rosita, 'She's the dead spit of you. Look at her! Blue eyes and all that red fluff on her head.'

His wife playfully shook her red mane over the baby's face. 'She's goin' to be just like her mam, aren't you, luv,' she said to the child, and Pedro's loins ached, as the creamy skin of his wife's neck came close to him.

The baby whimpered uncertainly, and Rosita snatched her back. Manuel promptly eased himself on to his father's knee. Over his head, Pedro asked her, 'Did you have a bad time with her?'

'Not too bad,' she told him.

He took a sip of his wine, and looked wickedly over his glass at her. She flounced provocatively away from him to return the child to her cradle, and stood, hand on hip, watching him, as she rocked the cradle with her foot to soothe the baby.

The kitchen fell silent after this as everyone sipped their wine, and listened to the tolling of the bell of the dock railway train, as it passed along the street under the overhead railway, and to the usual turmoil of the machinery in the buildings at the back of the house.

While the train clattered rhythmically on its way, Pedro stared at his half-empty glass and wondered what to say. Once greetings had been exchanged, he had to pick up the threads of his life ashore; it was like trying to understand the gist of a novel after commencing to read it in the middle of the volume.

Rosita wrote to him regularly during his absences, though, occasionally, he received the letters only when he returned to Liverpool; in any case, they did not really convey to him the daily ups and downs of the family. It took time to understand all the references made in the course of the family's conversations.

There were times when Pedro felt that his shipmates were closer to him than his family was; they certainly knew more about each other than their families did. He had sailed with some of them for years. Yet he loved Rosita; and Manuel was someone to boast about through many a monotonous day at sea. He felt guilty that his first inner reaction to the new baby had been that it would be something to tell his mates about when he returned to sea – another beautiful redhead. He ran his fingers through his roughly cut hair; it was sticky with salt. He could use a good scrub down in the old tin bath; but he could have it only when all the family had gone to bed, and he could have the privacy of the empty kitchen-living-room. He sighed, and puffed at his pipe.

The awkward silence was broken by Manuel. With his head against his father's shoulder, he asked shyly, in Basque, 'What've you brought me, Daddy?'

Pedro immediately snapped out of his reverie and put down his pipe. 'Aha!' he exclaimed mysteriously.

'Wouldn't you like to know?' He clutched the boy tighter, enjoying the child's warm trust.

Manuel giggled and pushed himself off Pedro's knee. 'Let's see,' he urged, and trotted towards the kitbag, still lying in the hall.

Underneath all the impedimenta of a seaman's life, just when it seemed to Manuel that his father must have lost the gifts he had purchased, they unearthed a cream jug in the shape of a cow, for Grandma to add to her collection of little jugs, and a big tin of good Virginia tobacco for Grandpa.

A parcel, wrapped in tissue paper, was handed to Rosita, who cautiously peeped into it, and then blushed and giggled when she discovered a lace-trimmed petticoat. She hastily wrapped it up again, while Manuel's mouth drooped and his eyes grew wide with disappointment. A further burrowing in the bag produced a pretty pair of hair combs for Auntie Maria.

Pedro glanced up at Manuel, as he felt down to the bottom of the bag. 'I hope I haven't lost it,' he said, with mock anxiety. He pulled out an old sweater, and then another one. But the second sweater was wrapped around something.

Very carefully, Pedro loosened the bundle and lifted out a model yacht, its mast and sails folded flat. He handed it to his son. 'Guaranteed to sail – and not to sink,' he told his son.

Manuel took it gingerly from him. Nobody amongst his school friends had anything to equal it – he was sure of that. 'Will it really sail?' he asked, as he twisted it round to have a better look at it.

'Given a decent breeze it will – like a real one. Tomorrow, we'll go up to the park and try it on the pond. You'll soon get the hang of it.'

The pond? That was where grown-up men took their model yachts, yachts carefully pushed through the town in old perambulators, because they were too big to carry.

The child's face was beatific. He determined that he would never let Andrew get even a glimpse of the little boat; he was not going to chance its being taken from him.

Grandpa leaned forward. 'Let me see it, Mannie.'

Manuel used both hands to pass it to his grandfather, and the old man took a closer look at it: the brass rails, the finely polished wood, and the correct rigging. 'Nice piece of work,' he said. 'Must've taken a while to do that.'

'Aye, it did. It's to scale.'

Juan handed the boat back to his grandson. 'You don't take that up to the park by yourself,' he instructed. 'When your dad's away, I'll come with you.' He, too, was aware of the predatory children, some of them homeless, who ran wild in the streets.

Manuel promised.

Rosita bent over them, to admire the little vessel, and Pedro slyly pinched her bottom.

She shot a shocked glance of reproof at him. 'Not in public!' she hissed, trying to look suitably outraged.

A further diversion, which relieved Pedro's feeling of strangeness in his own home, was created by the sound of hob-nailed boots in the hall, as Jean Baptiste Saitua and two of his sons stepped tentatively through the open front door; it did not take long for the Basque community to learn through the grapevine any bit of news, like a return from sea, and these old friends of the entire family felt free to step in and inquire how Pedro was.

Grandpa leaned back in his chair to look down the hall. 'Come in,' he shouted. 'How are you, Jean – Domingo – Vicente?'

They tramped in and shook Pedro's hand and slapped him on the back, while Rosita quietly slid over to the fire-place, to remove the chicken casserole from the oven and place it on the warming shelf above the fire; she winked at Aunt Maria, sitting quietly watching the scene. 'Heaven only knows when we'll get our tea,' she muttered to her sister. 'Would you like another glass of wine?'

Maria smiled gently and nodded. 'Yes.'

Grandma, equally resigned to a long session of male reminiscences, was already getting more glasses and another bottle of wine. Jean Baptiste was a bosun with a small Basque shipping company sailing out of Liverpool; he had a couple of nights' leave. Domingo was a ferryman, and Vicente was in his last year at school. After much joking, Vicente was allowed a glass of wine, though Jean Baptiste said his mother would probably be after him, if she smelled it on his breath.

The cakes intended for dessert were brought out and handed round, and the party became quite merry. Pedro abandoned hope of a bath that evening, and Rosita was beginning to wonder if she could stretch her chicken casserole to feed three extra men, when Maria began to cough violently. The hilarity ceased immediately, and Grandma said, 'Don't worry. I'll take her upstairs – it's just the smoke.'

Fat, jolly Jean Baptiste quickly rose from the table, however, his heavy jowls suddenly drooping. 'Ah! I forgot!' He looked round the room, thick with blue tobacco smoke. 'I'm sorry, Maria.' He turned to Grandpa, and said, 'We can meet in the Baltic later on; some of the other lads'll be sure to be there.'

With grave dignity, he eased himself and his sons out of the crowded room, calling his thanks to Grandma for the wine and cake.

His sons clattered down the steps to the pavement, while he paused at the top, to speak to Juan and Pedro. 'The wife told me Maria was back home. I thought she must be well again. How is she?'

Grandpa's shoulders went up in a hopeless shrug. 'They can't do anything for her – but you mustn't worry about the tobacco smoke; she loves to be part of what's going on.

If we put her upstairs all the time, she'd die of loneliness.'

'Of course, poor girl. It must be a terrible worry to you.'

He turned to Pedro. 'See you later, lad.'

And Pedro, who simply wanted to go to bed with his wife, nodded agreement.

Chapter Nine

While Micaela unbolted the back door to open it, to let out the tobacco smoke, Rosita quickly filled a glass of water and handed it to Manuel. 'Give this to Auntie; it'll help her stop coughing.'

The little boy obediently took the glass over to his struggling aunt. Rosita leaned over the sink to heave up the sash window; it had been partially open during the Saituas' visit; now she struggled to push it up further, but after a couple of inches, it stuck in its rotting wooden frame. 'Blast,' she muttered, 'I'll have to tell the rent collector when he comes.'

Micaela pushed her slightly aside, so that she could damp a towel under the tap. As she turned and wiggled her way between the scattered kitchen chairs to get to Maria, she said grimly, 'You can tell him – but don't expect him to do anything. Better to get your father to have a look at it.'

Maria had been coughing so violently that she had not been able to take the glass of water from Manuel; he was standing by her, wide-eyed, not knowing what to do.

The sick woman held a big man's handkerchief over her mouth to catch the blood-streaked phlegm which she was coughing up.

'It's all right, Mannie, dear. Put the glass on the little table, and go and help your mam.' Micaela gently wiped her daughter's face with the damp cloth, and, as fresh air entered the room, the coughing lessened enough for Maria to be eased on to the oil-cloth-covered sofa and be propped up with a myriad of patchwork cushions. Her mother covered her with a knitted shawl, and persuaded her to take a sip or two of water.

After chatting for a minute or two with Jean Baptiste Saitua, Juan and Pedro sat down on the front doorstep to continue their smoke. They remained there, in companionable silence, until Rosita called them in to eat.

While Rosita took a bellowing Francesca out of her cradle and put her to the breast under the cover of her shawl, Micaela served the family. She put a plate of food in front of Rosita, so that she, too, could eat, while nursing the baby.

Before sitting down, Pedro looked across at his sister-in-law, lying limply on the sofa. 'Sorry the smoke made you cough, Maria. Cigarette smoke's the worst. I'll smoke outside in future.'

The kindly meant words spoken softly in Basque brought tears of weakness to Maria's eye. She made a small gesture with her hand, as if to say it did not matter.

Micaela took a little bowl, put a spoonful of rice in it, and covered it with a ladle of gravy from the casserole. Very slowly, teaspoonful by teaspoonful, she got the food into the invalid. Only then did she sit down to eat herself.

Pedro had been praising the dinner to Rosita, and she smiled happily, while she shifted the baby to the other breast. She remembered suddenly what had happened when she had bought the hens in the market, and she told him the story of the third hen, retrieved from the bank windowsill.

Juan was silent during this recital. He carefully masticated his last piece of chicken and swallowed it, and, with his fingernail, released a bit of meat that had lodged between his front teeth. He did not laugh at the story; he sounded grumpy, as he said, 'I hope you paid for that chicken?'

Rosita laughed. 'We paid for the two we bought.'

'The third one was dead when we found it,' Micaela told

him. She obviously expected Juan to shrug and say no more. But the old man stiffened up. He rubbed his beard, as he always did when thinking something over. 'So you didn't pay for it?'

'Well, of course not. We just found it dead.' She put down her fork.

'But it was still good enough to eat?'

'You've just eaten it! Rosita wouldn't cook anything that had gone bad.'

Grandpa looked at her frigidly. 'In that case, shouldn't you have gone back and paid for it?'

Micaela was annoyed at this. She replied huffily. 'It was lost – and we found it. Anybody else who'd found it would have taken it.'

'But you asked for the cage to be opened. If you hadn't, it would not have been lost.'

Manuel realized that a sharp family tiff was in the offing, and he wondered if he could get down from the table, without first asking Grandpa. His grandfather was looking extremely grim, however, and he decided he had better sit very quietly and not draw attention to himself.

Micaela tossed her head. 'Tush!' she exclaimed. 'The poultry man must've believed it had got crushed underfoot in the crowd – or in the traffic. He'll never know we found it.'

Juan's long, dark face darkened further, his beard tilted up as if in pride. Pedro discreetly kept his mouth shut.

'My dear, it should be paid for; it was our fault it was lost.' Though the words were not unkind, it was an order.

'Juan! You're being unreasonable. You really are.' Impatiently, Grandma made to rise from the table. 'He'll have forgotten about it by now.'

'I want it paid for. He won't've forgotten that the whole hassle was caused by a bunch of Basque women, and he'll talk about it. We've got to *live* here; and we Basques have a good reputation – and it's small things that keep that reputation up.' He slapped his hand crossly on the tabletop. 'And what will your grandchild think? That if he can get away with something, it's automatically all right?' His gold tooth flashed between his beard and his moustache. 'Not on your sweet life! What a Basque takes, he pays for.'

'Really, Juan!' Grandma was trembling now, her face flushed, her fingertips on the table to steady herself. Rosita opened her mouth to join in, but was quelled by a look from Juan.

'Listen to me. You and Manuel – I want him to go, too – go back to the market tomorrow and pay for that bird.'

'But, Papa . . .'

'Tomorrow!'

Grandma took a big breath, and then said, 'Well, if you feel that strongly about it, Manuel and I can walk up and do it.' Then she spat out, 'But I think you're being terribly fussy!'

Grandpa got up from the table. 'I know what I'm about,' he growled. 'Come on, Pedro, let's get down to the Baltic; Jean Baptiste'll be waiting.'

Chapter Ten

Calmly clipping the hedge in the early-morning peace of his Victoria garden, Old Manuel smiled over this episode, which he had included in his notes for Lorilyn as an example of the stiff honesty of Basques; and wondered if he should also include what extraordinarily able smugglers they were.

'What are you laughing at?' asked a cheery voice from behind the hedge.

Surprised at his peace being intruded upon, he told Sharon Herman that it was a memory of his childhood; and continued clipping along the hedge, while he asked politely how she was.

Sharon had a plate of buttered toast in her hand, and as she followed him down the hedge, she continued to eat. 'I'm just fine,' she told him. 'Got myself an apartment, but the possession date isn't for a month. So Veronica says to stay with her till it's ready.'

'She's very kind,' Old Manuel replied dryly, and put his shears down, while he pulled at an old bird's nest tangled in the hedge.

'She is, isn't she?'

I wish Veronica wasn't so persistent, thought Old Manuel. High above his neighbour's roof a gull soared effortlessly and he speculated idly that in another few seconds it would dive to snatch a piece of Sharon's toast. But she turned suddenly towards him, and the gull flew swiftly seaward.

'Tell me what you were laughing at,' she demanded playfully.

He told her the story of the lost hen. 'My grandfather knew that it isn't enough to be honest – if you were foreign immigrants, like we were, you've got to be seen to be honest.'

As he slowly clipped his way down the length of the hedge, he told her of his Basque origins and the tiny community near the Wapping Dock. Then he paused, to hold his shears in his left hand, while he carefully stretched the fingers of his right hand. He saw her glance at his hand, and said, with a rueful smile, 'It's a touch of arthritis. Hurts sometimes.'

She nodded sympathetically, and he went on, 'I never thought of being foreign – I were born in Liverpool and christened in St Peter's. All the little kids I played with were born there – though their dads came from all over the world – as near as Ireland or as far as the Philippines.'

'Like Canada.' Sharon bit into another piece of toast with strong, even teeth.

He agreed. She looked much healthier than she had done when Veronica had brought her to his house, and he was glad. Her fair skin had acquired a slight tan, and her blonde hair was blowing in a wild tangle in the wind. She wasn't exactly pretty, but she had a pleasant open look about her and her figure had a cuddly roundness which reminded him of his mother. She was very likeable, he decided. Easy to talk to.

'I've got to get to work,' she told him briskly, and his wise eyes nearly vanished amid the wrinkles, as he smiled goodbye to her.

The next time he saw her she was seated on a huge log on the beach, staring disconsolately out on to a placid pale-blue sea. She was obviously crying, her shoulders heaving under her sweater.

He hesitated in embarrassment. They were the only

people on the shore that morning. She must have felt sure of her solitude to cry so openly, he debated uncertainly with himself. Should he go to her or not?

Aware of a sense of inadequacy at the idea of dealing with a young woman's tears, he decided to avoid invading her privacy, so he curved up the beach to pass well behind her. He was sure that she had not noticed him, but the crunch of pebbles under his feet drew her attention, and she turned a woebegone face towards him. She lifted a hand in slow salute and, embarrassed, he waved back, continuing to plod slowly on his chosen route.

She quickly took a paper handkerchief out of her pocket and wiped her face and blew her nose. He had only just passed her when she shouted, 'Are you walking home?'

He stopped, and nodded his head a little guiltily.

'Wait a minute, and I'll walk with you.'

'I'm rather slow,' he called back. Though her distress troubled him, he hoped she would change her mind and allow him to go on walking alone. She ran lightly over the pebbles, however, until she reached him.

He looked her up and down in a bemused way. She had cried enough to make her face swollen and her eyes mournful; yet she did not seem to want to hide it. 'I guess you didn't hurt yourself, if you can run like that,' he remarked tentatively, to give her an opening if she wished to explain her distress.

As she fell into step alongside him, she asked with a tight, wry grimace, 'You mean you thought I was crying because I'd fallen or something?'

He considered her query, and then said, 'Well, I didn't know. I didn't want to intrude. I thought I should let you be.'

She sighed. 'I'm OK. I was feeling a bit down, that's all – a bit lonely in a new place, I guess.'

Walking on pebbles was tiring him, and he wished he had taken the path at the top of the cliff. 'You're working in the new ward at the hospital, I think Veronica mentioned?'

'The Palliative Care Unit? Yes.'

'Patients who are going to die are put in there? Must be hard on you.'

'Not really.' She went on to tell him how worthwhile she thought her work was. Her enthusiasm surprised him.

Though he was interested in what she was saying, he began to feel that he must sit down to rest; there was an unpleasant tightness in his chest. He stopped, and said, 'At the top of the cliff staircase here, there's a little park kiosk that sells coffee. Would you like a cup?' He was panting slightly and his speech came slowly. 'We have to get up the cliff, somewhere, to get home.'

She looked at him with concern. 'Could you climb the steps all right?'

'If I do a few at a time.'

She was immediately practical. 'Let's sit on the bottom steps for a few minutes – until you get your breath.'

Manuel thankfully sat down suddenly on the steps, and they listened to the waves lapping on the beach for about ten minutes. Then she asked, 'Have you seen your doctor lately?'

Manuel's mouth turned up in a quick grin; he was feeling better. 'Saw him in the winter. He always says the same thing – you're in great shape – for your age! He's a nice kid.'

She laughed. A wonderful old dear, gentle to the point of passivity.

She judged him wrongly. Manuel was feeling a little exhausted – but he was cussing inwardly at his weakness. He got slowly to his feet, and looked down at her quite blankly. What was the girl's name? For the life of him, he could not recall it.

Unaware of his dilemma, she took his hand to help him up the wooden staircase.

'I'm all right,' he told her a trifle peevishly, and she quickly withdrew her hand. Old people could be quite tetchy about being helped, she knew.

Over coffee and muffins, which he insisted on paying for, he sat quietly for a few minutes, thinking that Jack Audley would be highly amused when he told him that he had, that morning, taken a bright young thing out to coffee!

'Why were you crying?' he finally asked her baldly, and then felt that he was being inquisitive and should not have said anything. She answered him without hesitation, however, and told him, 'We lost a patient last night, not unexpectedly. It was her widowed daughter's reaction that got me. She had lived with her mother for years. She's got no children; and she was beside herself.' She paused, her expression desolate. 'I guess I could relate to her feeling of being bereft.'

'How do you mean?'

'The feeling that nobody is left to care what happens to you.'

'Tush. A bright young woman like you must have lots of friends — and even parents still alive!' He tried to sound cheering.

Sharon bit her lower lip. 'Well, you see I'm divorced, and I don't have any kids — and Mum and Pop live in Florida; I'm their only child.' She sighed. 'When I was married, I went to live in Toronto. My husband wasn't the social type, so we didn't make any friends to speak of. I was a fool to marry him. We weren't really suited to each other from day one.'

He nodded understandingly. 'So what brought you here?'

'Well, I need to work — and I'm a qualified nurse. I saw the ad for this job at the hospital, and applied. When I was a very little girl, I lived here — and it's such a truly beautiful place. I'm glad I came — but I've got to start again, making friends.' She smiled suddenly, and said, 'At least I've made one, haven't I?'

Manuel gave a little chuckle. 'Of course,' he assured her. Loneliness makes strange bedfellows, he thought with amusement; then decided hastily that 'bedfellows' was not quite the word – not at your age, old boy, he told himself.

She caught the smile that flicked across his face. 'Now, what are you laughing at?' she demanded, smiling herself.

'I don't think I can explain it to you,' he replied with a chuckle. Then he laughed.

Laughter is infectious and soon they were giggling like a couple of children, about nothing.

Nevertheless, when he got home, he was thankful to crawl on to his bed. But he was still smiling to himself.

Chapter Eleven

In June 1914, Rosita announced that she wanted Pedro's
family to see Francesca, who was their first granddaughter;
Pedro himself was at sea, but to Juan and Micaela it seemed
a good opportunity to take a holiday, so a visit to Spain
was arranged. Little Manuel was thrilled.

Juan tried to persuade Maria to accompany them. 'You
could go up into the mountains with Rosita to visit the
Echaniz family, while your grandmother and I are in
Bilbao. It would do you good to breathe mountain air,' he
told her.

Maria was feeling a little better and, at first, had been
tempted to make the journey. Then, when she discovered
that the family would be travelling by sea, she said she
could not face being seasick.

Though horribly disappointed, Micaela said she would
remain at home to care of her.

Rosita looked at her mother's bent, tired figure and, at
first, said nothing; instead, she went to see Bridget Connolly next door. Rosita often looked after Mary and Joey,
when their mother was helping to nurse a sick neighbour
or delivering a baby. Now, she asked a favour on Micaela's
behalf.

Would Bridget keep an eye on Maria, if Micaela went
to Spain for three weeks in July? If Bridget could watch
her during the day and cook for her, she thought that Mrs
Saitua's daughter, Panchika, could be persuaded to sleep
overnight in the Barinèta home and give Maria a bit of
breakfast.

'Panchika doesn't have to be at work till eight o'clock,'

she explained to Bridget. 'She's got a daily job as a cook-general in a fine house in Princes Road, with very nice people.

'Maria can get herself to the can in the yard, now,' she added. 'And she can keep a fire going, if someone'll bring in the coal for her and start it each morning. And she can wash her hands and face at the kitchen sink. But she's not strong enough to stand and cook – or go to the shops, or anything like that.'

Bridget was seated by her own fire, sipping a mug of vintage tea – it had been simmering on the hob for hours. At Rosita's suggestion, she nodded her head; her black hair was done up in untidy, coiled plaits, from which the hairpins constantly threatened to fall out; before answering Rosita, she absently pushed one back into her hair.

Plump, patient and very knowledgeable about the needs of the sick, she looked up at her neighbour, and said, 'Oh, aye, I could do that, if you could manage to pay for the food I'd give her. It'd only be the price of a potato or two and what we're havin' ourselves – me housekeeping won't stretch to feed another.' At the latter statement, her voice was full of apology.

'I'd get the coal up from the cellar for her, Mam,' her daughter Mary volunteered; she had been listening avidly to what Rosita had had to say. 'And I could chop some wood chips for her every day – and put it all in the hearth. It wouldn't take a minute, then, for Panchika to make her fire for her.'

Panchika Saitua, a grumbling, middle-aged spinster, was ordered by her mother to sleep in her neighbour's bedroom and to get up half an hour earlier, so that she could build Maria's fire for her and give her tea and bread and margarine for breakfast.

Although she had not seen so much of her since she had been in service, Panchika knew Maria quite well; her working day was long and exacting and the idea of making the effort to visit someone, except, perhaps, on her Sunday off once a month, filled her with added gloom.

In the event, however, she thoroughly enjoyed her time with Maria, away from under her mother's thumb. They spent an hour or two each evening before bedtime contentedly commiserating with each other; so much so, that, even after the family returned from Spain, Panchika discovered that she could endure to walk down the road in her carpet slippers, in the late evening, for an hour's visit to Maria.

Maria was very appreciative of her visits, and missed her sorely when she failed to let herself in and come through to Rosita's busy kitchen, to sink on to the chair by the old sofa, and gasp, 'Ee! Me pore feet!'

Once the trip to Bilbao had been arranged, the family looked forward to it very much. The summer of 1914 was a gorgeous one and they could hope for a pleasantly calm passage. Grandma included in the food basket a gift of fresh eatables for the crew, whose diet was very monotonous. The present was much appreciated.

It was clear that Juan enjoyed such temporary returns to sea. It gave him a fresh audience of younger Basques, to whom he could relate stories of his early days sailing before the mast, when they had none of these new-fangled steam engines. 'Seamanship was seamanship, in those days,' he told them. 'Rounded the Horn four times, I did, in storms like you'd never believe – and the cold!' He shuddered.

This time, one young man told him, with equal pride, that he'd gone through the Panama Canal on an experimental voyage the previous year. 'We were scared stiff,' he said, 'because we were afraid landslides would block us in, and we'd die of fever if we had to come out overland.'

'Oh, aye. You're right about the fever. That canal's a waste of good money. Whole crews'll get fever going through it – like the navvies building it get sick and die.'

When they arrived in Bilbao, they were met by Juan Barinèta's brother, who looked even tougher and older than Juan himself. Little Manuel viewed him with awe. Rosita said he worked in an iron foundry, and that that accounted for the mass of white scars that crisscrossed his hairy arms, his hands and his face. 'They're from burns,' she explained.

Great-uncle was a widower. His two single daughters looked after him; they also took care of Uncle Agustin, Rosita's brother, when he was in port or out of work. Both young women did piecework at home, and their eyes were black-rimmed and bloodshot from long hours spent peering at the silk shawls they embroidered. They were gentle creatures, who, much to Manuel's annoyance, adored baby Francesca and presented her with an exquisitely embroidered bonnet which they had made for her. They patted him on his head and exclaimed at how much he had grown; then they encouraged him to go out into the street to play with another small boy, who had wandered in from next door, to stare at the new arrivals.

In the narrow, medieval street sloping down to the river Nervión, he felt, at first, closed in, and unnerved at facing a number of strange urchins, who looked him over as if he were a peculiar animal of some kind. When the boys discovered, however, that he had never tried to play pelota vasca, they produced a rock-hard ball and showed him how to hit it against a wall with his bare hands. They approved of him when he bore stoically the pain of it, and he was almost overwhelmed by their friendly advice and instruction; he went back to his great-uncle's house with several self-appointed coaches in tow, and badly bruised hands.

Before the evening meal, his hands were washed and regretfully cooed over by his two second cousins. Grandpa laughed, and said they would soon toughen up; he showed

Manuel two of his fingers which had been disjointed when he had played as a young man.

At the end of a week, he was leaping about in front of the wall with the same abandonment – and lack of finesse – as the other youngsters. Then he was told that he and his mother and Francesca would be going up into the mountains to see Grandpa and Grandma Echaniz, while Juan and Micaela remained in Bilbao.

As a baby and a toddler, he had already made three journeys to Spain, but he had few clear recollections of them. Going first by train and then in a rickety donkey cart up narrow roads into the foothills was a new adventure. He tucked his small aching hands underneath his jersey, and was relieved not to have to play pelota that day.

Grandpa and Grandma Echaniz were younger than Micaela and Juan Barinèta, and Little Manuel noted that they did not talk so much. They greeted the little family, however, with bear hugs and kind kisses; small in stature, sun-burned and stolid, they were not otherwise particularly demonstrative, but it was obvious that they were fond of their beautiful daughter-in-law and very taken by Francesca's blue eyes and red hair.

Rosita explained to Manuel that, once upon a time, his father had had two brothers to play with up here in the mountains, but they were now with God. Later, Manuel felt that perhaps the loss of her two middle sons accounted for Grandma Echaniz's affection for himself. She took him into the big living-room of their wooden house and made him her special companion. He had a great time, helping to punch down bread dough and learning how to milk a cow – he had stood, astonished, watching a pail slowly fill with milk. His grandmother let him try to milk a particularly patient cow; and he was wild with excitement when he managed to spray himself with milk. She gave him a small basket and showed him where to find eggs from the hens and ducks. He was warned not to go too close to a nanny-goat tethered to a tree in case she butted him. He discovered with amazement that she also produced milk.

The donkey lived under the house, in a small stable, next to a series of storerooms, though, since it was summertime, it was left to graze in a little field near the house; his grandfather amused him by giving him a ride on it occasionally.

While Rosita sat on the high front steps in the sun and nursed Francesca, Grandpa Echaniz took him, one morning, further up the mountain to see his father's surviving elder brother, Uncle Vicente, who was shepherding the family's flock of sheep. The climb made all the aches he had acquired playing pelota ache a lot more.

At first, he was nervous of the sheep, which looked quite large to him, despite the fact that they had been sheared of their winter coats. The bellwether ram lifted its nose out of a weed patch and looked him up and down with cold brown eyes. Then, satisfied, it returned to its grazing. When Manuel moved, the other sheep bounced away from him, towards the bellwether, whose bell tinkled as he led the flock a little away from the strangers.

They approached a series of rough shelters, fronted by a stone hut, but could not find Vicente. While his grandfather looked for him further up the mountain, Manuel turned to look back along the path they had just traversed.

Far below him lay the valley dark with trees, interspersed with tiny fields nearly ready for harvesting. From the chimneys of toy houses curled the smoke from kitchens like Grandma's. He could see a whole village, with a church spire, and a road winding through it. It was very quiet, except for the occasional jingle of the bellwether's bell and the shush-shush of the sheep as they followed him. To a child brought up amid the constant racket of machinery and traffic, it felt unearthly, and he was relieved when Uncle Vicente shouted that he was coming down; he had been sitting on a promontory further up, from which he could see the whole flock at a glance. When Manuel looked up, he saw a tall, lanky man coming slowly down towards his grandfather, who had climbed a little way to meet him. From under the man's black beret fell the same golden hair as his father had, and the sun glinted on his beard, stained with tobacco smoke just as his father's was.

Vicente greeted his father, and then came running down the slope towards Manuel. He flung down his staff and picked the boy up to toss him in the air with a friendly shout. Then he put him down on his feet again, and, while he held the child's hand, he looked into his face. 'You look exactly like my mother,' he announced. 'Her dark hair and eyes. Doesn't he, Dad?'

Grandpa Echaniz chuckled and agreed.

'When's your dad going to come up and see us?' Vicente asked Manuel, as they turned towards the stone hut.

Manuel smiled shyly. He did not know what answer to give and looked towards his grandfather for a reply.

Grandpa said, 'He'll try to get up here next time he docks in Bilbao. Last time he only had an hour or two ashore, Rosita says, so he went to see the Barinètas.'

The shepherd nodded. 'Come on in,' he said, as he led the way into the stone hut. He pulled off his beret and threw it on to a wooden bench against the wall. Then he mopped his face with a red cotton handkerchief from his trouser pocket.

After staring round the little hut, Manuel found his voice, 'What about the sheep, Uncle Vicente? Won't they get lost?'

His uncle looked down at him and laughed. 'No,' he assured him. 'Come and see.' He took him to the door, and pointed with a stubby, brown finger. 'Look past the sheep, right over there.'

Manuel looked and saw nothing but sheep, sparse grass and rock. Then he saw a slight movement a little above the sheep's sheared bodies. 'Is that a dog?' he asked.

'Yes. It's my sheep dog. He won't let any of the sheep wander very far.'

'He can't talk to them,' responded Manuel rather scornfully.

'He barks at them – and runs round and round until he gets a stray back with the flock.'

Manuel felt a little sceptical at this; it was his experience that grown-ups sometimes told tall tales. He was too polite to say anything, however, and allowed himself to be sat up on the table, while Uncle Vicente got three grubby mugs down from a shelf, and Grandpa slung a bag he had been carrying on his back on to the table beside him. 'Brought you some bread,' he announced to Vicente. He took a bottle of wine out of his pocket and placed it by the bag.

While Uncle Vicente rifled the bag of food his mother had sent up, and took out a knife to cut the bread, Manuel looked round him.

Grandpa Echaniz had picked up Vicente's staff and brought it into the hut. It was now propped in a corner beside a heavy cudgel. From wooden pegs driven between the stones making up the wall hung the shepherd's leggings and dark-coloured cape. A narrow wooden bed, with a couple of coarse blankets on it, lay against another wall. A stool and a bench made up the furnishings. A chipped enamel bowl flanked by a large tin of tobacco stood on a shelf, with a bar of soap in a saucer, a candlestick and a lantern. To Manuel it did not seem much more bleak than one or two of the rooms he had seen round Wapping Dock, when he visited some of his playmates, except that it had no fireplace – and no stout mam presiding over it.

Vicente handed him a slice of fresh bread with a piece of hard cheese on top. He poured wine into two of the mugs. Then he put a little into the child's mug and added a ladle of water to it from a jar covered by a cotton cloth, which Manuel had not noticed before. 'Mustn't send you home drunk,' he remarked, as he handed the mug to his nephew.

Manuel smiled up at his new uncle, and Vicente chucked him under the chin. 'You're a great lad,' he told him. Then he took his own drink and sat down on the bench by Grandpa. 'Pedro's lucky,' he said, and lifted his mug towards his father before taking a sip.

The old man lifted his own in return, and said, 'You'll do as well yourself one of these days. You'll have this farm.'

'I suppose,' replied Vicente. 'But I'd like a girl who wants to marry me, not the farm!'

His father laughed, and bit into his bread and cheese.

With his scratched and aching legs dangling from the table top, Manuel copied his uncle's movements exactly, lifting his mug to drink from time to time and eating his bread. He listened, while the two men discussed a modest increase in the price which they had got for their fleeces. They speculated that the increase might be due to a sudden demand in Europe for woollen cloth for army uniforms, as a result of war threatening to break out. Far from the political turmoil of Madrid, they scented profit, if the Spanish government had enough sense to remain neutral.

'God give them enough sense to stay out of it,' said Grandpa Echaniz fervently.

Grandpa's prayer proved most effective. The Spanish did remain neutral throughout the conflict, and Bilbao and its hinterland profited exceedingly well.

After making the acquaintance of Uncle Vicente's dog, who wagged his tail at them absently, but never took his eyes off his sheep, Grandpa and Manuel walked companionably back home. Manuel wondered if Uncle Leo, far away in America, had a stone hut with lots of sheep nearby, and a lovely black dog.

All through his life Manuel remembered the quiet of the mountain shepherd's surroundings and their beauty. Not even a whole range of Rocky Mountains could take the belief from him that his father came from the most beautiful place on earth.

When he was grown-up, the Second World War provided him with greatly increased wages, but it cut him off from visits to Spain; meeting Kathleen in Canada and marrying her had added to the separation. He rarely saw *his* mountains again.

When adding to his memoirs in a fit of deep nostalgia, he described for Lorilyn the perfection of this moment of his life when he fell in love with a place, not a person. Then he closed his exercise book. His Echaniz grandparents died of influenza after the First World War, and Uncle Vicente took over the farm. When Uncle Vicente's grandson finally inherited, Manuel lost touch with the family. But he never quite forgot them.

It was the declaration of the *First* World War, however, which cut short his childhood stay with Grandma and Grandpa Echaniz.

When he and his grandfather walked into the farmhouse, after visiting Vicente and his sheep, the carrier had brought a message to Rosita telling her to return to Bilbao as soon as she could, because Grandpa Juan Barinèta wished to sail home to Liverpool, before hostilities cut them off.

Manuel's narrow, sallow face had grown brown in the mountain air, and his flat cheekbones had a healthy pink in them. To Rosita, looking at him as she passed on Grandpa Barinèta's urgent message it seemed as if he had suddenly grown from being a toddler into a boy, so much so that she unhesitatingly plonked a fretful Francesca into his arms, while she resumed packing their valise, and then bundled up napkins, still warm from drying in the sunshine, into an old shawl. She tied the shawl up with sharp hasty tugs.

'Why can't we stay up in the mountains?' he asked,

wanting to cry and to put down Francesca, who was heavier to hold than he had imagined.

'And who will look after your Auntie Maria, if we get marooned here – or your Papa, hm? And him in a British-registered ship!'

Manuel could not see the significance of his father's being in a British ship – what was so wonderful about that? He always sailed in the same boat. He put the question to Rosita, as he staggered to a footstool, to sit down and lay Francesca across his lap.

'Because the Germans might sink it!' his mother replied testily. She was not feeling well. She was pregnant again and it was not improving her temper.

Manuel felt sick; he knew that when ships went down men sometimes drowned. He was not too sure what drowning entailed, but he knew men went to be with God after it. He shivered and clutched the baby tighter. Francesca gurgled at him and the tiny mouth formed a smile; at that moment she became a person to him, and he began to lose some of his jealousy of her. It was comforting to hold her, while he tried to come to terms with the sense of panic that swept him, at the idea that his father could be in real danger.

They said farewell to Grandma in her big kitchen and asked her to give their love to Vicente, since there was no time to go back up the mountain to give it personally. Grandma clung to the little boy. She had already lost two sons, and she had seen immediately the threat to Pedro's life now that the British had declared war, and she was inwardly terrified of losing him.

She watched the little donkey cart wind its way down the narrow mountain road, waving until it vanished round a bend. Then she went silently back to her washboard to scrub her husband's shirts.

Grandfather Echaniz delivered them safely to the house in Bilbao. He stayed only long enough to have a glass of wine with the Barinèta brothers, before starting back to his farm. 'Got to get the hay in,' he said.

The Liverpool family was to sail early the following morning, and the sun was barely up when Rosita called Manuel to get ready to leave. There was a second flurry of hasty packing of baby clothes in a shawl, and to help his mother, Manuel bumped a valise down from stair to stair and then ran up again to get the shawl bundle. 'When will we have breakfast, Mam?'

'In the ship,' she responded morosely, as she buttoned up her blouse after feeding Francesca. She was feeling a little sick and dreaded the discomfort of the voyage home.

When he came downstairs for the second time, he found Grandma Micaela in the hall. She was wrapped in her shawl and was sitting on a suitcase. When he had put down the bundle, she handed him a mug of milk. 'Your auntie brought this for you, luv.'

He thankfully took the milk from her and drank it, while she observed his forlorn expression.

'What's the matter, dumpling?'

He laid the empty mug in the corner of one of the stairs, and went to her, his bottom lip trembling. He put his arm round her neck and laid his head on her shoulder. 'It's Daddy. I'm so scared.'

'Oh, dear. What are you frightened of?'

'Mam said the Germans might drown him.'

How could Rosita be such a fool! She embraced the child, and assured him that Pedro was fine. The Germans were not going to waste ammunition on a little old freighter.

'Mam's frightened. I'm sure she is.'

'Well, a war is a shock to us all,' his grandmother admitted. 'But when you get as old as me you know you can get through them all right.' She pushed him away from her a little, so that she could look at him. She laughed, and then added, 'Your dad's a great swimmer!' She continued to hold him close to her, while the family slowly gathered by the front door, waiting for a friend of his great-uncle's to bring his horse and cart to take them down to the dock, where lay the small freighter on which Grandpa Barinèta had secured a passage for them.

It was his great-uncle who lifted him on to the cart and told him to hold the side tightly. He helped Rosita up, so that she could sit beside the driver, and handed Francesca up to her.

'Take good care of yourself,' the second cousins cried to her in chorus. 'You mustn't lose it.' They giggled together, as they stood back from the horse.

While Manuel watched the street of fine old houses roll past and waved farewell to new friends, the old people walked behind the cart. They did not say much to each other; they did not need to.

At the wharf, Juan's brother clung to Juan's and Micaela's hands, as if loath to let them go. In their earlier life in Spain, they had had plenty of experience of turmoil and strife; and it was as if they all sensed that this newly declared war would be extremely bitter. 'You could be better staying here,' he suggested to Juan. 'There'll be plenty of work, if Spain stays neutral.'

Juan sighed. 'We don't know yet. Let's see what happens.' He held his brother's hand closely and put his other arm round him in an embrace. 'If it were only Micaela and me – we'd stay here. But I have to think of Pedro and Rosita – and Maria, not to speak of the kids. I'll wait till Pedro comes home, and talk to him.'

The voyage was fairly placid, until near the Isles of Scilly where they hit choppy waters. Though a queasy Manuel and an equally uncertain Grandma Micaela, carrying Francesca, managed to go on deck, to sit in a protected corner, Rosita lay on a bunk and heaved helplessly into a rusted enamel basin. Not only was she sick, but she was also short-tempered – her current pregnancy was sapping her strength. It had come too soon; she still felt tired from having Francesca. Micaela, who had every sympathy for her, did her best to keep Manuel and Francesca away from her.

She assured Manuel that his mam was not seriously ill; she would be better the moment she was on land again. He was relieved to hear Micaela say this; mams could die, too.

Grandpa Barinèta sat cross-legged by him on the deck and told him seamen were rarely sick, which was far from true, and taught him how to tie several complicated knots. 'When you go to sea, when you're a big man,' he said to the boy, 'you'll need to know knots.' With a couple of pieces of string in his hand, Manuel sat by Micaela and practised them assiduously. She praised his efforts and hoped he would do better in life than go to sea.

When they reached the beginning of Liverpool Bay, the sea was calmer, and a shaky Rosita was able to crawl up on deck, to sit cross-legged with them. Manuel thankfully curled up by her, grateful that she seemed more herself.

As they waited for the pilot to come aboard, Micaela began to worry aloud about Aunt Maria.

'I hope she's all right. It's a pity she couldn't come with us.'

Rosita pushed her red, windswept curls back from her face. 'She didn't want to come. She hates boats – even going on the ferryboat. And, you know, neither she nor I really belong in Vizcaya. Maria's always saying that she belongs to Liverpool – and I feel like that, too.'

'You were glad enough to come to Vizcaya!' Her mother's voice was unusually sharp.

'Well, of course I was. It's lovely to go for a holiday, and Pedro's family was very good to us. And they loved seeing Francesca. But I mean, not to go for ever.'

Grandma felt too old and tired to argue. She would have

liked to have gone to see some of her own relations, in Santiago de Compostela, while they were in Spain. But they had had to keep the cost of the visit to a minimum, so she had not mentioned this desire to Juan. Now, she wondered if she would ever see them again. She was painfully homesick, and was upset at her daughter's lack of attachment to her homeland. She pursed her lips in disapproval.

Beside her, Manuel lay flat on his back and watched the seagulls swoop and climb above the boat. The sun shone warmly on him. The chatter of the crew, standing at the rail while they watched the approaching pilot boat, came to him as a comfortable male buzz. He had not been listening to his womenfolk's conversation; reassured about his father, glad to see his mother on deck, his mind was a contented blank.

Far away in Canada, Manuel remembered those golden moments, lying contentedly on the deck. They were his last truly happy moments of childhood before his sense of total security was shattered.

Chapter Twelve

On his return to Liverpool, Manuel quickly discovered that his playmates were not interested in his adventures in Spain; most of them had exotic grandparents on the male side, anyway. Andy Pilar was bursting with the news that he had had the measles. 'Me ma had to get the doctor, 'cos me temperature was a hundred and ten! You should of seen me spots – all over me stummick, they was!'

More temperately, Brian Wing told him that he had had the measles, too, and that Mrs Connolly had remarked that, as a result of the disease, he might have to wear spectacles – as soon as his father could afford them, that was.

'I feel I'm in a bit of a fog,' he explained to Manuel, as they amiably swopped cigarette cards. He had to peer closely at each card, which Manuel found most peculiar.

At the tea-table that evening, Manuel mentioned Brian's need of spectacles. Grandma Micaela immediately suggested that he tell Mrs Wing that the pawnbroker sometimes had second-hand glasses for sale; so, after the meal, he ran along Mersey Street to the tiny laundry to inform her of this.

He found her surrounded by piles of dry washing, busy damping and rolling each shirt or sheet, preparatory to ironing them. Several irons were hooked into the bars of the fire-grate to heat; and in a corner the copper heaved and bubbled with further washing. The tiny room was stiflingly hot.

On a bench against a wall sat Mr Wing, his older son, Fred, and Brian, each with a coarse pottery bowl in his hand. With a dexterity which mesmerized Manuel, they shovelled rice from the bowls to their mouths with a pair of sticks.

Manuel blinked, and turned to Mrs Wing to give the message about the glasses. She smiled and bowed over her ironing table, though it was doubtful if she understood what he was saying. Mr Wing understood, however; and the kindly thought behind the message.

'Please to thank respected grandmother,' he said to Manuel; his English came slowly and was pronounced with difficulty.

Manuel nodded. 'Can Brian come out to play?' he asked.

Brian must finish his tea, first; then he could go out for a little while, Mr Wing said gravely. He would come to Manuel's house.

Grandma Micaela was seated on the front step, when Manuel returned. He sat down by her, to wait for Brian, and repeated Mr Wing's thanks to her.

She gave a slow, sweet smile; it was nice to be called 'respected', even if it was only by a Chinese.

'Why doesn't Fred come out to play, Granny? He never plays with anyone. Is he too old, do you think?'

'I don't think he's too old,' responded Grandma. She spoke, as usual, in Basque. 'I've seen the lad carrying huge bundles of laundry on his back, along South John Street, and, once, pushing an old pram full of it, in Princes Road. It's my guess he delivers and collects washing from little hotels and cafés, for his dad. He won't have time to play.'

Nor energy, she thought with a sigh. When she considered the abject poverty of the Wing family, she knew she was rich. She hugged her grandson to her and thanked God that he was well fed and clothed.

The hot weather concluded with a heavy thunderstorm, and the drainpipe at the back of the Barinètas' house collapsed. Micaela asked Juan if he could repair it.

'If we wait for the landlord to do it, we'll wait for ever,' she told him. 'The water's trickling from the gutters all down the walls – there's a real puddle, even in the cellar. The coal's getting damp.'

Juan had not been very busy with emigrants during the summer: the threat of war had made people hesitant to travel overseas; its outbreak, and the subsequent sinking of three British cruisers by a single German U-boat, had, apparently, confirmed the nervous fears of many who had intended to emigrate; they deferred their crossing of the Atlantic in a British ship.

Juan was, therefore, thankful to be given something to do. He got up from his chair, opposite Maria's couch, and, on the top bar of the fireplace, knocked the dottle out of his clay pipe. Maria was thankful to see him go. The smoke from his pipe had been bothering her; but nobody dared to tell Juan that he could not smoke in his own kitchen-living-room; he had a fixed idea that only cigarette smoke was bad for Maria. Maria sometimes wished fretfully that he would go back to sea and take his pipe with him.

In the rain-soaked, brick-lined back yard, Grandpa viewed the damage, while Grandma stood behind him, her arms crossed over her stomach. The rain had stopped, but both could clearly see the water dripping from the hole left in the gutter after the collapse of the drainpipe. Below it the rainwater barrel was brimming, a length of drainpipe protruding from the water. At a point level with Grandpa's eyes, a further piece of pipe was still fairly firmly affixed to the wall by a clasp. A third piece, rotten from rust, had fallen into the yard, and Manuel joyfully picked it up and staggered round the yard, blowing into it as if it were a trumpet.

The old man peered up at the sodden wall. 'Tush,' he exclaimed irritably. 'The whole pipe must be absolutely rusted out – and that wall needs repointing. You'd best tell Fleet, when he comes for the rent – show him it.'

Though his words were firm, he knew and Micaela knew that the landlord's agent would never do anything about it. He and Leo had done innumerable repairs themselves; now he wished the younger man was still at home, to get out the heavy ladder, mix the cement, try to find a reasonable piece of piping in some builder's yard and fix it up. He was acutely aware of his own ageing, his lack of physical strength, as he turned towards the back door.

Micaela looked up at the louring sky. Though she was resigned to the house being persistently damp, she knew that the loss of the drainpipe would rapidly worsen it.

'It looks as if it's going to rain a lot more,' she said doubtfully to her husband's back. 'Couldn't you somehow knock the pieces together – use an old tin to join them and some rags for binding them – just to hold it for a few days? I'll ask Roy Fleet when he comes next Friday.' Her husband had stopped and turned to face her, a hand on the doorjamb. She urged him again. 'More water in the cellar's going to soak the coal – not to speak of the kindling I've got down there.'

He did not reply, and she realized suddenly how he had aged recently, but she continued, 'With the wall so wet, the plaster'll fall off the big back bedroom – it's got holes in it already.'

Manuel had paused in his trumpeting, to listen to his grandparents. Now he said generously, 'I've got an old pineapple tin – my spare marbles're in it. You can have it.' He looked eagerly up at Juan; helping Grandpa mend a drainpipe could be fun.

Juan glanced down at the boy, and grinned. Then he shrugged, and said to his wife, 'All right. Get me some rags – and plenty of string. Manuel, you get the tin – I'll need more than one – and I'll see what glue or paint I've got to hold it all together. Have you got any more tins, Micaela?'

Grandma and Rosita hoarded everything; very little was ever thrown away. It did not take them long to produce a large ball of string, made up of short pieces knotted together into one strand, a remarkable pile of rags, neatly torn into squares for patching or for dusters, and three largish, round tins, in which they had been storing bits of candle grease for starting the kitchen fire, a button collection and Grandma's hairpins. While they scraped out the grease and found another home in old jam jars for the buttons and the hairpins, Juan fetched an extendable wooden ladder from under the lean-to next to the lavatory in the yard. He extended it to its fullest length, and, in the narrow space between the house and the brick-walled lavatory, he managed to lean it against the wet wall.

'I'll take a look at the gutter itself, first – before I put a lot of work into mending the pipe – it's probably rusted, too – it mayn't take the weight of the tins and the rags, as well as the drainpipe.'

He climbed slowly up, while Micaela held the bottom of the ladder, and Manuel watched, fascinated. Rosita, busy peeling potatoes, tried to look upwards through the kitchen window.

Through the open back door, she and Maria heard her father call down fretfully, 'It looks too far gone to do anything about.' A small hail of rusty bits of metal descended past the window, as he felt along the gutter. Micaela looked up and stepped back hastily to avoid getting flying bits into her eyes. Her husband leaned over and gave a sharp tug to the gutter a bit further along. It held.

'Humph,' he grunted, and shifted his weight on the ladder.

'Watch out, luv,' shrieked Grandma suddenly, and Manuel, alarmed, ran back towards the kitchen door.

There was a cracking sound. Not a big sound, recollected Old Manuel, but a deadly one, as the three top rungs of the ladder came out of their sockets.

Grandpa's wet boots slipped, and the ladder swayed badly. He grabbed at the gutter. It came away in his hand.

Wrongly pitched in the narrow space, the ladder swayed outwards from the wall. Grandma leapt away, as Grandpa came crashing down. As he fell his head hit the edge of the slate-tiled lavatory roof, cutting off his scream. He slid down the sloping roof and landed on the ground with a heavy thud and a splash of water from the puddles. His head lay at an impossible angle.

Micaela did not cry out. A paralysed Manuel watched her sink slowly to her knees by the stricken man. Very gently she lifted his head. As she touched him, his life went out of him and his body relaxed. As a horrified Rosita squeezed her way past a clutter of chairs in the crowded kitchen and Maria cried out in alarm, she curled her arms tenderly round his face. 'My dear,' she whispered. 'My dearest dear.'

Manuel awoke from his shock. 'Mam,' he yelled to his mother. 'Mam!'

A frantic Rosita had caught the bow of her apron on the knob of the dresser drawer. She tore at the apron string, freed herself, and pushed Manuel to one side, as she flew into the yard, to stand, appalled, looking down at her parents. Micaela lifted a face to her so empty of expression that she might have been dead herself. 'The ladder gave way,' she said simply. 'He's gone.'

Rosita wanted to scream. She swallowed hard, trying to control her panic, and fell on her knees by Micaela. 'Are you sure?' she asked her mother desperately.

'Yes.'

Manuel began to whimper. His mother turned her head towards him, and said as calmly as she could, 'Auntie Connolly's out, I know. Run up to Mrs Saitua's and tell her Grandpa's had an accident. Ask her to come quick – and to bring any of her boys who are home. Understand? Don't cry, luv.'

Manuel nodded, and began to move towards the door. 'Wait a minute,' Rosita called. 'Then I want you to go across to the vicarage, and ask Father Felipe to come – or any of the priests. Run, sweetheart.'

As if he had not heard her properly, he paused to stand and stare at her, not understanding why Grandpa lay so still. His mother's face, however, was a ghastly white, and she was trembling. He himself began to shake.

'Run, dear. Run, quick. It's urgent!'

He dragged himself uncertainly through the kitchen door. Then, ignoring his aunt's cries of, 'What's up?' he made himself run, through the house, down the steps, round the curve, pushing past three girls bouncing a ball against a wall. He ignored their furious cries as they retrieved the ball from the flooded gutter, and panted his way up Corn Hill.

He paused for a second in front of the Saituas' open front door, to get his breath, and then took the two front steps at a bound.

Mrs Saitua was scrubbing the living-room floor, her black skirt hitched up and tucked into its waistband. Her fat bottom was draped by her grubby white petticoat and from under it protruded the dirty, callused soles of her bare feet.

At Manuel's precipitous arrival, she sat back on her heels, and quickly turned a scarlet face dripping with perspiration.

At the sight of the gasping small ghost of a child, she dropped her scrubbing brush and stumbled to her feet. 'What's up, duck?' she asked.

'It's Grandpa. And me mam says will you come quick.' He paused to gulp a breath. 'And bring Domingo and Vicente with you.'

Madeleine Saitua had already shoved her feet into a pair of down-trodden carpet slippers, and, before he had actually finished speaking, she was shouting up the narrow staircase for her boys to get up quick. 'Something's happened at the Barinètas',' she yelled.

Manuel was already on his way out of the front door, when she turned back to him to say, 'Tell your mam I'm coming.' She was hastily straightening her bundled-up skirt.

'I've got to get Father Felipe,' Manuel panted.

'Jesus Mary! What happened?'

'He fell off a ladder,' replied Manuel, and flew down the steps, to race up the slope to the vicarage.

As he stood on tiptoe to bang the knocker on the priests' door, he was sick with fright. He leaned against the wooden door, and nearly fell in when it was opened by the housekeeper.

'Be careful, lad!' she snapped, as the child caught at her black, serge skirt to steady himself. She spoke in Spanish.

He looked up at hard brown eyes in an equally brown face, and burst into tears.

In Basque, he howled, 'I've got to get Father Felipe.'

'Be quiet. Father's busy. What's the matter?'

Manuel's Spanish was, as yet, limited. He did his best to control his sobs and to gather the words he needed, but they would not come. He continued to howl and the housekeeper continued to scold in Spanish.

The ruckus brought a priest from a back room. Manuel did not know him, but the long cassock and sandalled feet were comforting. 'It's Grandpa,' he wept to the young man. 'And me mam says to get Father Felipe quick.'

The housekeeper grudgingly gave way to the priest, who squatted down on his heels until his face was level with the child's. 'Don't cry,' he said in stiff English. 'Tell me what happened.'

'He fell off the ladder – and he's lying in the yard – and Mam says to get Father Felipe.'

The young priest's face immediately became very grave. 'Wait here a minute,' he said. 'I'll get Father Felipe. What's your name?'

Manuel told him.

Father Felipe was commendably quick. He gathered what he needed in order to administer Extreme Unction, took Manuel by the hand, and together they hurried down the narrow, black streets. 'Did your mother send you for the doctor?'

'No,' panted Manuel. He was a little surprised at the question; when you fell down Mam bandaged you up – or, maybe, Mrs Connolly, who was very good at it.

The priest's dark face looked suddenly more lined than usual; he glanced compassionately down at the child who held his hand so confidently; the death of the man of the house in this desperately poor neighbourhood was a particularly terrible loss. He hoped he was in time to administer the Last Rites.

Chapter Thirteen

As she knelt beside her mother, Rosita's stomach heaved and she feared she would vomit. Her breath came in short gasps, as she made herself cautiously slip her hand under her father's pullover to feel for a heartbeat. She could not find one, so she took his limp wrist to feel his pulse.

Nothing.

She put her arm round her mother's bent back. 'I'm sorry, Mam,' she said brokenly.

Her mother did not answer her; it was as if she had forgotten her daughter's presence. Even when Maria, clutching her flannel nightgown modestly round her, crept into the yard in bare feet and knelt down on the other side of her, Micaela seemed unaware of her daughters. Her whole being was focused upon her husband, as if she believed that if she kept on crooning to him, he would come round from being stunned; yet it was clear from what she had said that, somewhere in her shocked mind, she understood that he was dead.

'What happened?' whispered Maria. She was shivering with cold and fear. 'Is he dead?'

Rosita nodded. She laid her cheek on her mother's back, and hoped she would not vomit; her current pregnancy was not proceeding as comfortably as the earlier ones had and, most mornings, she felt nauseated.

'Please, Madeleine, come quick!' she prayed, as she waited for Madeleine Saitua to arrive.

Maria began to cry, the slow, helpless crying of the very weak. Through all her painful, hopeless illness, her father had been the pillar of her life; her mother nursed her, but her father had ungrudgingly provided a home for her. 'Even extra milk,' she moaned aloud.

A little startled, Rosita lifted her head. Maria saw the movement, and rubbed the tears out of her eyes, as she explained. 'He thought of everything for me – even more milk.'

'He did,' replied Rosita in a low voice. 'He looked after us all.' She hugged her shocked mother more tightly, while beyond the brick wall of the yard, the riveters continued their merciless clangour, and beneath her the puddle in which she was kneeling slowly soaked through her heavy, serge skirt. Would Madeleine never come?

Her agitated thoughts leapt fearfully to the future, as the import of Maria's words sank in. Pedro would now be the sole breadwinner; he would have seven people to maintain, if she included the baby now on its way.

Still in her carpet slippers, Madeleine Saitua laboured up the front steps and ran through the open front door and through the kitchen-living-room to the back door. She was a heavy woman, unused to moving fast, and she had to pause for a moment to catch her breath, as through the back door she observed the three women kneeling round Juan.

'Looked like something out of a church window, they did – and him so peaceful,' she said that night to an acquaintance in the Baltic, while she enjoyed a sustaining glass of port and considerable attention from other customers, always interested in a tragedy.

Now, however, she was forced into action.

At the sound of the scurrying flip-flap of her carpet slippers as she descended the back steps, Maria shuffled round on her knees to see who was coming; through her flannel nightgown the rough bricks hurt her knees, and her whimpering became a loud wail.

Very shaken, Madeleine peered down at Juan and at her old friend, Micaela. There was no doubt in her mind that she was looking at a dead man; the angle of his head indicated that quite clearly.

Rosita scrambled to her feet. She was so white that Madeleine was immediately alarmed that she would miscarry.

She did not want another catastrophe on her hands, so she said sharply to her, 'Take Maria in and wrap her up by the fire. And get yourself a glass of water – and sit down. I'll take care of your mother – the boys'll be here in a minute – they're just putting their kecks on – lucky they're both home – Domingo's on the evening shift this week – and there's no hurry for Vicente on a Saturday.'

She bent over Micaela who had ignored her arrival. She said soothingly, 'We're getting help, luv. It won't be a minute.'

Taking Rosita's place, she squatted down on her heels and put her arm round the mourning woman. Then she leaned forward and firmly closed the dead man's eyes. She looked up at Rosita, who had taken her shivering sister's arm and lifted her to her feet. 'You'd better call the doctor,' she advised.

'It's too late,' responded Rosita dully. She tugged Maria's arm. 'Come on, now. Be brave. Come on – indoors.'

Still wailing, Maria turned towards the house. Rosita bent down to stroke her mother's white hair, trying frantically to think how to comfort her. 'Manuel's gone to fetch Father Felipe, Mama,' she told her, her voice choking on the words.

Her mother made no response. She continued to sit with her husband's head in her lap and to stroke his cheek, while she muttered brokenly, 'My dear, my dear.'

Mrs Saitua sighed. She did not argue about the need for a doctor, though she knew someone would have to tell the coroner of the accident; Juan was, indeed, beyond medical aid. In a minute or two reality would strike Micaela; she would be wild with grief; and there was the chance, also, that Rosita might begin to miscarry. She hoped there was some whisky or brandy in the house. Maybe Father Felipe would insist on the doctor's being called, she thought anxiously, as she muttered to Micaela, 'There, there, luv. There, there.'

She was thankful when, almost immediately, there was a distant knock on the front door, followed by the tramp of hob-nailed boots. Her sons burst into the yard, one of them still struggling into a navy-blue pullover.

'Christ!' Domingo exclaimed. 'What's to do, Mam?'

Their mother looked up at them fiercely. 'Hush!' she admonished. 'Juan's had an awful accident. Lift him into the house – put him on the couch in the sitting-room. Gently, now!'

She turned back to Micaela. 'The boys are going to carry Juan into the house, dear. They'll be very careful of him. Now, you come along of me.' She put her hand under her friend's chin and made her turn to look at her. 'Come on, luv. The rain's starting again.'

The shaken young men edged round the two women. Domingo very cautiously lifted the dead man's head away from Micaela's lap. Micaela glanced at him in bewilderment.

Madeleine stood up and put her hands under the armpits of the tiny kneeling woman; then, bracing herself, she eased her to her feet. It was like lifting a sagging sack of potatoes. Micaela's eyes were on the boys, who were used to shifting heavy weights. As they picked up her husband she saw the pity in their eyes. The agony of her loss struck her and she opened her mouth and screamed.

The terrible shrieks roused her neighbours. They whipped their shawls over their shoulders and shot out into the street. Bridget Connolly was standing on her step, about to open her front door. She froze at the sound of the scream.

'Holy Mother!' exclaimed young Peggy O'Brien from

two doors down the street. 'What on earth was that?' She and two other women rushed towards Bridget. 'Which house was it?'

'Micaela – Rosita, I think!'

She ran down her steps and up the Barinètas' steps. Followed by the other women, she burst into the narrow hallway, to find her way blocked by Domingo and Vicente turning into the parlour with their heavy burden. Behind her, women crowded up the steps, their speculations cut short by a glimpse of the young men's grim faces.

The little crowd fell back, to allow Father Felipe, with Manuel clutching his hand, to enter a house close to pandemonium. Already terrified, Manuel clung to the priest.

As the cleric's presence was realized, people began to quieten. Space was made for him to squeeze into the small parlour, leading the child with him.

They were both faced with the dead man clumsily propped up on the horsehair sofa; Micaela was on her knees, her face buried in his lap as she loudly lamented something about a drainpipe and that it was all her fault.

While Manuel hid his face in the priest's coarse robe and clung to him, Father Felipe resolutely took command. He recognized most of those present, including Maria still in her nightgown, though someone had thrown a shawl over her shoulders. The other daughter, Rosita, looked as if she would collapse at any moment, as she turned magnificent, sorrowful blue eyes upon him. In the distance, he could hear a baby shrieking, untended. At the back of the tiny room, two young men – the Saitua boys – and their mother stood uneasily watching the scene. Three other women had crowded in; and, when entering, he had pushed past three more, whispering at the foot of the front steps.

His first thought was for the terrified child clinging to him. He recognized Bridget Connolly standing to his left; Bridget, he knew, had a lot of experience of children and nursing. He bent and picked up Manuel, as he spoke to her. 'Could you take Manuel and look after him for a little while?' he asked in stilted English.

She automatically opened her arms to the white-faced little boy, who showed no signs of wanting to go to his mother. 'Of course. Now, you come with Auntie Bridget, me dove. Father Felipe's going to do what he can to help your granddad and grandma – and your mam.' She hugged the boy to her, and wrapped her shawl round him. 'You come and have some dinner with our Mary and Joey.' Space was made for her, as she eased through the parlour door. 'And then you can have a little play together in our yard, till your mam comes for you.' Her soft Irish voice and familiar red face were comforting and normal, so he went with her without demur; Grandpa looked so peculiar and everybody had obviously been making such a fuss before the arrival of Father Felipe that the instinct was to escape. He knew from experience that Auntie Bridget always gave you a straight answer – she never said 'perhaps' or 'maybe' – so if she said that Mother would come for him, Mother undoubtedly would.

As they squeezed past him, the priest patted the child's back and smiled at him, 'Well done, Manuel,' he said. 'You were a clever lad to bring the message so quickly.'

Manuel smiled wanly back; only later did he appreciate that he had been praised by a priest; it was like being praised by God himself, he decided; it was something good shining through an awful day.

Father Felipe turned to Mrs Saitua, who seemed calmer than the other women. 'Has a doctor been sent for?' he inquired.

She looked across at Rosita. 'No,' she said.

Rosita said, 'He's dead.'

'You should get a doctor immediately, Mrs Echaniz.'

Rosita nodded helplessly, her strength nearly gone.

'I'll go,' Domingo told her, and thankfully left the room.

*

Puzzling over his notebook seventy-eight years later, Old Manuel wondered how to explain to Lorilyn the trauma of that week, how his childhood home had been invaded by an unknown something called Death. Grandpa had simply fallen off a ladder, and had in a second or two gone to God. It was called dying. Nobody had tried to hide it from him; in fact, he had been called upon to help – he had run to get Mrs Saitua and Father Felipe.

In the sanitary world of North America, at the age of nineteen what would Lorilyn have seen of death, other than through the monstrosity of television? Would she have any idea that the victim's pain and death would be an agony to those who loved him?

Nowadays, on the whole, people lived long lives. Pain and death were dealt with by hospitals and batteries of doctors and health-care workers; even the carnage of the streets was quickly shovelled into ambulances and the streets washed down, so that no one would be offended by the sight of blood. At the end you lay in a mortuary until you had been tidied up and made fit for public inspection.

Would she even know how to lay out a loved one, as he knew his mother and grandmother had done for his grandfather? Would she sit a whole night by her dead father as Maria had done, saying her rosary over and over again? Doing all of it as a final outpouring of affection?

He knew that she would not.

It was a sore point with him that he himself had not been allowed to lay Kathleen out. Faith had been on her way to visit her mother, that morning, and had used her own key to enter the house. She found him sitting by the bed in the sitting-room, holding her dead mother's hand, and she had immediately taken charge. Her face stony, she had consulted the yellow pages of the telephone book, called a funeral director, called her husband, asked if he had had any breakfast, insisted on his moving into the dining-room and having some coffee. He was so exhausted that he obeyed her. The only thing he had said to her was, 'Call the doctor.'

He had not finished the coffee Faith had thrust into his hand, when the doctor arrived, followed closely by the funeral director. They held a committee over poor Kathleen's body, and then, while the young general practitioner came to sit with him for a few minutes, Kathleen was removed.

He half rose from the table in shock, when he saw what the funeral director and his men were doing. He looked in bewilderment at the doctor, but words would not come to him – he was so tired. He wanted time with Kathleen, but the doctor grasped his arm firmly, and said kindly, 'Everything's been taken care of – you must rest now. Faith will deal with everything.'

His rage at his daughter's quiet efficiency had simmered in him throughout the funeral and for long afterwards. He never considered that she was holding in her own grief, while she tried to make things easier for him.

Since there was no reason to stay in his own house, he went home with her for a few days and slept most of the time, until the coroner released the body and they went back to Victoria for the funeral.

People swarmed through his bungalow, drinking coffee and wine and eating cocktail-type nibbles. But when the ladies, including Veronica, had washed up the last cup and saucer and put them back into the china cabinet, he saw them all to the door. Faith had protested that he should come back to her home in Vancouver. Her big kindly husband had assured him he would be most welcome.

But he wanted to be alone with Kathleen's ghost, even if everybody else considered that a funeral finished everything. As far as he was concerned it did not.

He sat alone on the bed, which had been heaved back upstairs and into his bedroom by three male neighbours, and stared out of the window, while he mentally beat himself for allowing her to suffer so much — and at the end be so tired that he had not protested at her hasty removal.

Bearing in mind his own pent-up wrath, perhaps it was as well that Lorilyn had been in Europe, at the time. She was doing a special, high-powered course in French. Faith told him that she had written to her daughter telling her that, since she could do nothing for Grandma, she should not return for the funeral, but, instead, should take her impending exam.

And yet?

Not do anything for Kathleen? Weren't prayers and paying one's respects something? At the time, he hated his phlegmatic daughter — and his granddaughter for not disobeying her mother. Furious, he had shut himself up for weeks, frequently refusing to answer the doorbell or the telephone. He had never gone back into the social circle to which Kathleen and he — well, mostly Kathleen, he admitted — had belonged; and it had taken the best part of a year before he could do more than simply endure his daughter's and granddaughter's visits, when they inspected the food cupboard and the freezer to make sure he had enough to eat.

Then, slowly, sanity returned. He realized, shamefacedly, that both women — and his son-in-law — had done their best for him according to the society in which they lived, and that it was grossly unfair of him to expect anything different.

The more he thought about that time, the more he realized that Faith had shown the same calm, stolid endurance of grief that his own mountain grandparents would have shown. She had, indeed, done her utmost.

As for himself, it slowly dawned upon him that he was far too like Grandpa Barinèta, who, when he was angry, had always had a real tantrum, stalking round the kitchen.

like an enraged cockerel until he had extracted apologies from everybody in sight.

However did Kathleen put up with me? he wondered.

Chapter Fourteen

Although Manuel had allowed himself to be taken by
Bridget Connolly to her house, while Father Felipe dealt
with his stricken family — when a priest gave an order, you
obeyed — he was very scared at being removed from the
scene of the action; he could not put his fears into words
and he wished suddenly that his father was there; he longed
for his quiet orderliness; he would be able to explain what
was truly happening.

But his father was at sea on the other side of the Atlantic
and had no inkling of the disaster in his home.

When, in addition to midday dinner, Bridget kept him
for tea, he protested strongly, crying that he wanted his
mam. He quarrelled with Mary and Joey, who were very
possessive of their territory and few toys; he was not a big
child for his age, and they tended to treat him with the
condescension usually reserved for a much younger play-
mate; it confused him even more.

With a sigh, Bridget picked him up as if he were, indeed,
still a toddler. With him straddled on her hip, she struggled
to make ready her husband's tea. Manuel found her closeness and warmth comforting, and his loud crying became
soundless sobs, which made Bridget want to weep herself.

When Pat Connolly arrived home from work, his wife
shouted into his ear the reason for Manuel being unexpectedly in their care.

'Juan had a bad accident,' she told him briefly, since she
did not want to emphasize in front of her children exactly
how deadly the accident had been.

Her loud voice frightened Manuel even more, though

he knew Mr Connolly could not hear properly. He cried helplessly, making no attempt to rub his eyes clear of tears.

She turned back to the child. 'There, there, Mannie, luv. Your mam'll come soon,' she soothed, wondering at the same time how his bereaved family was getting on.

Pat Connolly made no response to Bridget's explanation. He swept one of Pudding's granddaughters off a battered easy chair, and sat down suddenly and closed his eyes. The dislodged cat eyed him malevolently from under the deal table. Mary brought him his slippers, but he made no attempt to take them from her. She set them down by his feet and crept away.

As he watched him from the safety of Bridget's broad hip, Manuel's tears tailed off. Mary and Joey's dad looked so different from his own father. He smelled different, not only of old sweat. He had a curious metallic odour as well. He was practically bald, with a grey fringe round the sides of his head. A day's beard glinted whitely on his chin. The lids of his closed eyes were bright red, as was his nose, and the rest of his skin was an unhealthy yellowish-white, whereas Manuel's father had skin the colour of a ripe hazelnut and a thick thatch of fair hair – *and*, Manuel thought, *his* dad did not come home to sit silently in a chair; he first hugged and kissed his mother and himself.

Only when he was a little older, did Manuel understand from the conversation of adults the appalling conditions under which men like Pat worked and their absolute exhaustion by the end of the day. As Mr Saitua once remarked, 'You have to be a bloody contortionist to do that job. Never mind the racket!'

Bridget swung the boy round towards the table, while she poured a mug of tea, which had been simmering on the hob for some time. She picked up a tin of condensed milk from the draining board by the sink, and let a generous amount trickle into the black brew. Then she spooned some sugar out of a small blue bag on the table. She stirred everything up vigorously, then picked the mug up and said to her weary spouse, ''Ere you are, luv. Lovely and hot, it is.'

The scaler opened his eyes and there was a hint of a smile in them, as he accepted the tea. As he drank it, he began to relax and become his usual amiable self.

'How was your back today?' she inquired.

He sighed, and then said, 'It weren't so bad as yesterday.'

'I'll rub it again tonight for yez. Nothing like a bit of Sloane's liniment for backs.' She noticed that Manuel had been diverted by the cat leaping quietly over the fender, to curl up close to the fire, so she slid him down by it. He knelt down and put his hand over the steel bar, to stroke its black satin back. The warmth of the blaze was comforting, and the cat stretched itself under his careful hand. He laid his cheek on the warm fender just above the animal. His stroking became slower and, despite the hardness of his pillow, he fell asleep.

Bridget paused in her bread-cutting to look down at him compassionately. 'Poor little bugger,' she mouthed at her husband, careful not to wake the child. 'He were proper upset. Terrible for him to see his grandpa killed.'

Pat understood what his wife was trying to convey. 'Oh, aye,' he agreed softly, some of his exhaustion receding as he rested his legs. 'It isn't going to be easy for them, without the Ould Fella; he did well, he did, with his emigrants and all.' There was no hint of shock in his voice; his fatigue was too great. Juan was an old man; his time had come.

'This is where they could use Leo.'

'The lad what went to America? Oh, aye. Young Pedro will have his hands full, feedin' a houseful of women and kids.'

When Manuel woke up, he was startled to find himself in his own bed, Pat Connolly having kindly carried the sleeping child in for Rosita. Across the room, Auntie Maria was seated on the edge of her narrow, iron bed, telling her beads by the light of the moon filtering between the window curtains. She wore a black shawl over her heavy, flannel nightgown, and her old carpet slippers on her feet. She was crying.

Manuel struggled to sit up; he was still in his jersey and shorts, but his boots and socks had been removed. 'Where's Mam?' he asked immediately, and yawned.

Aunt Maria gave a big sob. 'She's downstairs with your granddad and grandma – and Peggy O'Brien is with them; she'll watch all night with them.'

'Why? It's dark – it's bedtime.' He pushed off his blankets, as if to get out of bed.

Auntie Maria immediately put down her rosary, got up clumsily and shuffled over to him. 'No, no, dear. You can see your mam in the morning.'

Manuel remembered suddenly his grandfather hurtling through the air, and the sickening crash as he hit his head on the tiled lavatory roof; and then Father Felipe and Mrs Connolly.

He shivered. 'Is Grandpa very hurt?' he asked, knowing in his heart that something much worse than being hurt had happened, though he could not put a name to it.

Aunt Maria loomed over him like a dark ghost, as, for once, she bent to kiss him on the forehead. Her face against his felt wet, as she quickly pulled herself back.

'Yes,' she said softly. 'He's gone to God.' She pushed him gently back on to the bed and lifted his bedclothes over his shoulders.

'Does that mean he's dead?' Manuel asked tentatively, afraid of the reply.

'Yes.' The single word came out slowly, like the beginning of a long lamentation.

'So Mam and Granny have to stay with him?'

'Yes. Tomorrow, Grandma and I'll sit with him, so your mam can get a little sleep – and Peggy O'Brien will go home. Maybe Mrs Saitua will come to sit for a little while to be company for Grandma and me.'

'Doesn't Granny want to go to bed?'

'I don't think so, luv. She'll want to be with Grandpa.'

'Is he lonely because he's dead?'

The question was almost too much for Maria. She clapped the back of her hand to her mouth, to stop herself from crying out. She did not answer, while she sought to control herself, and then she said softly, 'We don't really know, dear. But we think he might be.'

'While he's waiting for his Guardian Angel?'

She smiled faintly through her grief. 'Yes, dear.'

To his knowledge, Auntie Maria, like Bridget Connolly, rarely lied, so he was satisfied that Grandpa would soon be taken wonderful care of by his own private golden guardian, complete with wings, to bear him to Heaven. Still very weary, he turned over and was soon asleep again.

His aunt went back to her bed and her rosary. Her belief was almost as literal as the child's, and she was comforted by the reminder of a heavenly being standing close to each one of us. She would miss her father dreadfully, but it was nice to feel that he would be looked after, and that, despite dying unshriven, he could hope for a seat in Heaven, because he had been such a good parent.

Chapter Fifteen

The day after Juan Barinèta's unexpected death, Manuel was sent back to school. He wore his Wellington boots and a macintosh, because the rain was sheeting down; it was as if winter had suddenly set in. His mother had silently given him his porridge and milk and, equally subdued, he had eaten it. Grandma and Aunt Maria did not appear at all; he guessed that they were both in the parlour, the door of which was firmly closed.

Rosita sat by him at the table, a cup of tea in front of her, and suckled Francesca. Her magnificent red hair had not been combed and, in the light of the kitchen fire, it shone like a halo. Her expression was such that Manuel had a scared feeling that the last thing she was thinking about was a jittery small boy.

When he was ready to leave, however, she handed him two biscuits for his elevenses, wrapped in a piece of paper saved from a cereal box. Then she squatted down in front of him, kissed him and told him he was being a very good, helpful boy.

He felt better and grinned shyly at her. She patted his bottom, and sent him on his way. She did not want him at home when the undertaker, alerted by Vicente Saitua, came to measure her father's body for a coffin later that morning.

On the previous day, the doctor had come immediately in response to Father Felipe's request. The accident was explained to him and the broken ladder shown to him. He wrote an appropriate certificate, and told Rosita gently, 'I have to inform the Coroner's Office, and they will probably send someone to look at your father. If the coffin arrives before they do, please do not put Mr Barinèta into it until they have made their examination; they will want to see the body – and the ladder.'

At this intimation of an invasion of their privacy, Rosita had looked so defeated that the doctor had to reassure her that the official would probably be both compassionate and brief. 'And you should lie down for a little while,' he advised. 'Mrs Saitua said you were expecting – and you don't want to lose the child.'

She merely shrugged; there would be other pregnancies.

'Would you like to ask Mr Biggs to look after the body for you?'

'You mean now? Give Father to the undertaker?'

'Yes. You might feel a little better to be relieved of it.'

'Good Heavens! No! Mother's broken-hearted enough already.'

Watched by Maria, Micaela, Rosita and young Peggy O'Brien had tenderly washed and shaved Juan and laid him out as soon as the doctor and Father Felipe had departed. They had wrapped him in a clean sheet and bound his jaw closed with a strip torn from another one. Two copper pennies were laid over his closed eyelids to keep them shut.

To keep him flat and straight, before rigor mortis set in, Domingo and Vicente had opened up the folding flaps of the parlour table and had laid him flat on his back on it. The women did not attempt to straighten his neck, in case the Coroner demanded further medical examination.

'When they hear about a man being suddenly dead, they always think he's been in a fight – especially when it's down in the docks,' Peggy remarked sagely. 'That's why they want to take a look –'cos then it would be murder. Lucky we are, nobody called the police, or we'd have had them on our backs as well.' She had been practical and calm, and, before she hurried home to her out-of-work husband and her babies to give them their tea, Rosita had hugged her and thanked her.

'You're so young to face all this,' she told her. 'But I couldn't ask Bridget, because she's minding Manuel.'

'It's not so bad for me. Me mam was like Bridget, and she taught me. As a young girl, I often helped her bring a kid or lay somebody out.' She wrapped her shawl round herself, and added, 'When I've got the kids to bed, I'll come back and sit with you for a spell.'

After Peggy had departed, Rosita felt suddenly very alone. There was much to do. She must first persuade her mother and Maria to eat something – and she had better have a bite to eat herself – what with Francesca not yet weaned and the demands of the child inside her. The nappies hadn't been washed, the fire needed remaking – it was nearly out; and she must do Juan's job of bringing some buckets of coal up the cellar step, not something she *wanted* to do while pregnant. And Manuel would be back soon, she supposed. She hoped Bridget had given him some tea.

In the event, it was Peggy who carried up the coal. She returned more quickly than Rosita had hoped. And it was she who took Manuel's boots and socks off before Pat slipped him into his bed still sound asleep. She stayed until early the next morning when she had to go to attend to her own children.

Not only Peggy and the other women had proved their worth on that awful day. Father Felipe remained for a while with Micaela. Though Spanish, he knew enough Basque to speak comfortingly to the distraught woman in her own language. Firmly, gently, he helped her to regain control of herself. He had remained with the family until after the doctor's call and the removal of the body from the sofa to the table, where it was temporarily covered with a sheet. Rosita brought them both wine, and the priest and the broken old woman sipped it together. It was he who suggested to Rosita that, to give themselves strength, they should eat before formally laying poor Juan out.

Micaela smiled dimly at this, but as soon as Father Felipe left, she insisted that the laying out be done right away. Wearily, Rosita agreed, but said she must feed a screaming Francesca first.

Working neatly and carefully, as she always did, Micaela had seemed better as she gave the last service she could to a well-loved husband of forty years. Within, she was beating herself because she had asked him to do a job, at his age, which involved climbing a ladder; it did not help her to remind herself that he had spent his youth climbing the rigging of sailing ships and had always had excellent balance.

Afterwards, she had eaten a little, as did a tear-sodden Maria. Then she had gone into the parlour, rosary in hand. Maria had determinedly blown her nose and had followed her in, to sit with her until Peggy returned to join them. Dry-eyed and drained, Rosita had settled Francesca for the night and washed a couple of nappies, ready for the morning. She was thankful when, later, Manuel was brought in sound asleep.

She was worried about the strain on Maria, already so weak and frail, and, as soon as she could, she had gone to take her place in the parlour. 'Bed, Maria,' she had ordered briefly, as she took out her rosary. 'You must keep your strength up.' So, protesting feebly, Maria had gone upstairs to the bedroom she shared with Manuel and had wept very quietly so that she did not wake the child.

Only a few minutes after Manuel had been sent to school the following morning, Ould Biggs, the undertaker, presented himself. He was brief, obsequious and politely sympathetic. He delicately inquired if they had Burial Insurance.

As Rosita led him into the parlour, she assured him that they had and that it was paid up to date. He nodded his head in acknowledgement of this welcome news, as he approached Micaela and took her hand and silently held it for a moment.

Then he briskly whipped out his tape measure and measured Juan. He was respectful of a man who had given him a lot of work for his horse buses when dispatching Basque emigrants and he did not touch the body.

He then turned back to Micaela and, taking her hand again, he asked her very kindly if she would like to step round in the afternoon to choose the kind of coffin she wanted. 'You and your daughters, like. And a memorial stone – I've got a nice line in them – and I've several beautiful coffins in stock.'

The candle on the table at the head of the corpse flickered from the weight of the sigh that Micaela let go, before she whispered her agreement to the visit. Tears rolled slowly down her cheeks to drop on her black apron. Maria, seated on the horsehair sofa, put her head down on her knees and wept, her silver and ebony rosary dripping from her fingers in the candlelight, as if its tiny glitter were tears and that it wept for her as well. The doctor had left a sedative for her to take, but she had not swallowed it. It lay forgotten on the mantelpiece.

Rosita had hardly ushered him out of the front door, when a grand gentleman caused a stir in the street by arriving in a motor car, a contraption rarely seen by the local inhabitants. He announced that he was from the Coroner's Office, and Micaela, wearied from mourning and lack of sleep, managed to rouse herself sufficiently to give him a fairly coherent description of the accident. He inspected the offending ladder and the broken drainpipe, while rain poured down on his bald head; he had, of course, removed his bowler hat on entering the house. He assured Micaela that she had nothing to worry about and that she could go ahead with arrangements for the funeral. The Coroner's Office would see that Mr Biggs was informed that all was in order for him to proceed.

Just before Manuel was due back from school for his midday meal, Madeleine Saitua dropped by to deliver a piping hot rabbit pie, which she put into the kitchen oven to keep warm. Rosita seized the opportunity to ask her if her boys would help her to rearrange the parlour furniture, after Juan had been coffined, so that the coffin could be supported by a chair at either end, and the neighbours could move round it when they came to pay their respects.

Madeleine gazed compassionately at the white-faced younger woman, and said, 'Of course, luv. Just send Mannie up with a message when you're ready. And you try to get some rest, luv.'

Rosita agreed that she would and saw her out with an expression of thanks for the pie. She was still watching her plod up the street, when Peggy came by on her way to the corner grocery. She asked if Ould Biggs had been yet, and when Rosita said he had, Peggy remarked, 'Manuel'll be able to see his granddad when he's all peaceful in his coffin – with flowers round him. Frannie'll be too young to remember him, more's the pity.'

Rosita had not yet had time to weep herself and, at this remark, she felt suddenly choked with grief. She managed, however, to answer her kindly, blundering neighbour, by saying cautiously, 'If the boy would like to.'

After doing his best to describe the loss of his grandfather to Lorilyn, Old Manuel leaned back in his chair and gazed abstractedly out of his study window at the distant mountains of the United States on the other side of the Strait of Juan de Fuca. He could only guess at the sorrow and despair of his grandmother, his mother and his delicate aunt; they had done their best to swallow their own grief and reassure their frightened little boy.

Chapter Sixteen

This was the second year during which Manuel had attended St Peter's Catholic School, and he was accustomed to its highly disciplined system. He knew that when he was bigger and more able to travel safely by himself, he would be sent to St Francis Xavier's, a Catholic Grammar School, and, there, his real education would begin.

On the morning after his grandfather's death, when he pushed open the wrought-iron gate and entered the asphalted school yard, the atmosphere of the school seemed, unexpectedly, very peculiar; the children were too quiet. Instead of rushing about to make the most of their last moments of play before they were sent indoors, they were hanging about uneasily.

Andrew Pilar, usually belligerent, came with a crony to stare at him; Manuel tried not to cringe, as he prepared to slap away hands which often pinched him cruelly in his private parts.

To his surprise, Andrew simply snorted and turned away, followed closely by his slouching friend. Then Miss Carr, usually so brisk and acid-tongued, took him by the hand and put him quietly in the line being formed by the youngsters in his class, preparatory to being marched into their classroom. As if he did not know that he was supposed to line up, he thought bewilderedly. Behind him, Andrew in the next higher class, was given short shrift and pushed into his proper place. No child spoke to Manuel, though many stared at him.

Miss Carr stood in front of the ragged lines. In response to a sharp command, the children shuffled to align themselves by stretching out their left arm to put their hand on the right shoulder of the person next to them.

Four lines behind him, there was a small sob and a girl began to cry. Miss Carr blinked behind her pince-nez. She said kindly, 'Rosemary, come and stand by me, child.'

Manuel did not dare to turn his head, as the children behind him made way for Rosemary, who was one of the *big* girls, aged ten. This morning, her straggling flaxen hair was even more untidy than usual, and her white pinafore, worn over a navy-blue serge dress, was crumpled from being used to mop up floods of tears.

'Come to me, dear,' Miss Carr said softly, her own mouth quivering. She put a protective arm round the girl's shoulders and held her close to her, as she quickly glanced up ferociously at her other charges. 'Stop shuffling,' she ordered. Then Manuel was aware of her worried frown, as her gaze rested on him for a moment.

She gave a deep sigh, and ordered, 'Standard One! Attention!'

She successfully marshalled her charges into the hall of the school for the morning Assembly. On a small platform stood the Headmaster, flanked by some of his teachers. Behind them hung portraits of George V and Queen Mary.

In addition to the usual hymn, announcements, prayers and short homily, the pupils were ordered to pray for the soul of Rosemary's father and for all The Fallen; Manuel was far from sure who or what The Fallen were. Could you lose your soul without being dead, perhaps? If, however, praying for Rosemary's father would cheer her up a bit, he was willing to do it.

He felt that if one was supposed to pray for The Fallen, it was very disappointing that the Headmaster did not order prayers for Grandpa. With a sigh, he assumed that it was because he had only fallen off a ladder and that that did not count.

On their way home for their midday meal, he discussed

this a little anxiously with Joey and Brian Wing, and they agreed that since Grandpa did, indeed, fall, he must be one of The Fallen. Manuel began to cry helplessly, and Joey and Brian became scared, because they barely understood what had happened to his grandfather; they were relieved when they reached the Echaniz doorstep and could leave him.

When he entered the kitchen-living-room it was so quiet that he could hear Pudding energetically washing her face. His mother sat at the table, writing a letter. Two addressed envelopes were propped against the milk jug. Though the fire had been lit before he left for school, there was none of the usual smell of dinner cooking.

At his entry, Rosita looked up. 'Hello, darling,' she greeted him absently, and then continued to write. He heaved off his Wellingtons and flung them into the boot cupboard by the fireplace, where Pudding usually gave birth to her kittens. He took off his macintosh and hung it on the back door – he had to stand on tiptoe to reach the wooden peg.

'Where's Granny?' he asked. 'And Auntie?'

His mother signed her name at the foot of her letter, and folded it carefully. As she slipped it into an envelope, she replied, 'Grandma's resting on her bed for a bit, and Auntie Maria is sitting in the parlour by Grandpa – Madeleine Saitua's there, too.'

As she licked the envelope to seal it, Manuel watched her, trying not to grizzle; he was disconcerted at the lack of the usual bustle surrounding the production of the midday dinner.

'Hasn't his angel come yet?' he inquired cautiously.

Taken aback by the question, Rosita paused in her sealing of the letter. She looked down at her son, and saw the traces of tears. He had put his hand on her lap, as if to concentrate her attention on him. When she did not answer him immediately, he explained, 'Auntie Maria told me that

Grandpa's Guardian Angel would come to take care of him.'

Rosita put down her letter, and lifted the child on to her knee. She felt guilty that she had paid little attention to him since her father's accident; Francesca had, of a necessity, to be fed and her napkins changed, or she would have screamed steadily; but her quiet elder child had been fobbed off on to Bridget next door.

As he curled up thankfully in her lap, she struggled to keep her voice normal, as she replied, 'The angel bore his soul away when he fell, dear. We've only to take care of his body. Grandma's having a beautiful box made for him to rest in, and we'll put lots of flowers round him, and Father Felipe will help us to say prayers for him. Then he will be laid in the cemetery under the trees, where it's quiet and peaceful. We think he'll like that.'

With his head against his mother's shoulder, Manuel considered this explanation, and then looked round the kitchen-living-room. 'I'm awfully hungry,' he said heavily.

Rosita gave a broken laugh. 'I haven't forgotten your dinner, luv. I've a nice piece of rabbit pie waiting for you in the oven. Mrs Saitua brought it just now – wasn't it kind of her?' Manuel slipped off her lap, as she rose, and she went on, 'Grandma says she's going to cook something hot for us for tea.'

It was suddenly infinitely comforting to hear that Grandma would be undertaking some of her usual tasks. He ate his rabbit pie, and went back to school feeling better.

His mother, who had not shared the meal with him, walked part of the way with him; she had to post the letters she had written to Pedro, to Great-Uncle in Bilbao and to Leo. She had addressed the latter to Nevada, in the hope that it would be redirected to Leo wherever he might be. She sighed, when she thought about her brother; he was barely twenty, completely alone in an area of the States noted for its lawlessness. He was hardly literate, but she wondered if he realized how thankful his mother would be to have even a couple of lines from him regardless of whether the news was good or bad.

She promised herself that that evening she would tackle letters to her elder brother, Agustin, and to the Echaniz family on their farm in the Pyrenees.

Leo never received his letter, and Pedro was given his only when his boat docked at Liverpool two months later.

That same day following his grandfather's death, Bridget invited Manuel over to play with Mary and Joey after tea. 'It will keep the kid occupied – keep his mind off things,' she told Rosita.

The two little boys were swopping cigarette cards on the mat in front of the Connollys' blazing fire, when Manuel's mystification about The Fallen was clarified a little.

Bridget was washing the dishes and Pat was reading the back page of the newspaper, where the sporting news was usually featured. 'Proper awful about Frank Abbott,' she shouted.

'Eh?'

'You know, Frank Abbott. He's a stoker in the Royal Navy – on the *Abouki*.'

'Oh, aye. Something happened to him?'

'The Jerries sunk his ship. She got the telegram yesterday evening, poor soul. And her with three kids.'

Pat put down his newspaper, and nodded. 'There's going to be a lot of them,' he prophesied.

Joey interrupted. 'Is that Rosemary's dad?'

'Yes, luv. She'll have to go into service or summat. No more school for her – or the two boys either – they'll have to work.'

'Why, Auntie Bridget?' This from Manuel.

She looked kindly down at the boys, while the sooty water from her saucepans ran slowly down her fat arms. 'Well, when you haven't a dad there's no money coming in. Even if their mam can find work, it won't be enough.'

Pat had caught the gist of her remarks, and he said, 'Ethel Abbott'll get a bit of a pension.'

'Ta, ever so,' replied his wife with heavy sarcasm. 'With a bit of luck it may feed the cat. And him serving his country, and all.'

Pat made a wry face. 'It's true. They don't care a tinker's cuss about folk like us. Dying for your country! That's a joke.' He returned to his sporting news.

So if you were drowned at sea, you had died for your country and joined The Fallen. He swallowed. The idea frightened him – Papa was at sea. And Grandpa, who had been king in his own home, would not be there any more; the thought gave him a dreadful, empty feeling in the pit of his stomach. The news that, because Rosemary's father had been killed in the war she would have to go into domestic service, did not help. All Basques knew that to be a servant in a private house was humiliating in the extreme; Panchika Saitua was the only person with whom he was acquainted who served in a private home – and Grandpa had always said that Saitua's daughter was the stupidest woman he had ever met – which probably accounted for her situation.

Dying for your country did not help your family, ruminated Old Manuel. He had certainly learned that from Rosemary's tragedy, and, in adulthood he had borne it in mind – not that it had done him much good; his legs ached every day of his life from the effects of another war, another time.

He remembered Miss Carr again – and the other anxious teachers. For years afterwards, as men were lost at sea or killed in their thousands in the trenches of France, those women must have tried to comfort their pupils, while their own brothers and sweethearts were constantly at risk. He still recollected them with respect.

Chapter Seventeen

The cost of Grandpa's funeral was paid from his Burial Insurance with the Prudential. Their representative, a small, neatly dressed man in a bowler hat, brought the money and delivered it to the widow with some ceremony. He had been coming to the house for years to collect sixpences as premiums. His appearance in the street always caused the same worry and, occasionally, consternation to housewives that the rent man did; nobody missed paying him if they could help it; the thought of being condemned to burial in a pauper's grave was too terrible to contemplate. He was a kindly soul, however, and had been known to help out a harassed family by putting their contribution in himself, hoping that they would pay him later, in a week when there was more work in the docks.

It was with genuine sympathy that he sat with Grandma for a few minutes, conveying his condolences and that of his company, as he passed the cash to her. 'Mr Barinèta was a grand man, Missus. We shall all miss him,' he told her, as he took out a handkerchief, grey with much washing, and blew his nose hard.

She smiled dimly at him, and Rosita pressed a glass of wine on him. When he rose to leave all three women thanked him effusively for coming so promptly.

He insisted that Manuel should see him out, which the boy did, while the pound notes slipped from Micaela's lap on to the rag hearth mat, as she turned to cling silently to Rosita, and Maria wept.

Carried by his mother, Manuel was taken into the parlour to say goodbye to Grandpa, before the coffin was finally closed. He had been nervous about this, because a girl at school had told him that she had been made to kiss her dead aunt in her coffin, and her cheek felt cold like a frog and she smelled horrid.

No such gesture was expected of him.

Grandpa looked strangely young, not really like the volatile old man he had known; he had a bandage round his jaw, which made him look odd. He said, 'Goodbye, Grandpa,' and slipped down from Rosita's arms, to run back to the warm familiarity of the kitchen.

He remembered the funeral itself quite clearly. His mother, Grandma and Auntie Maria wore black headscarves, and their blouses, skirts, shoes and stockings were the same dead colour. He himself wore his best black Sunday suit, which was rather short for him at the cuffs and ankles. The elaborate, horse-drawn hearse was followed by numerous women, their flowered pinafores doffed for the occasion, so that they, too, were in black. Those few men who were not at sea, or who were not working that day, followed the women; they, too, wore their black Sunday suits with black berets on their heads; some were very old and limped along with the aid of walking sticks; Manuel did not know many of the latter – they were the men with whom Grandpa had played dominoes in quiet corners of the Baltic Fleet. At the end of the procession, two Irish neighbours, both of whom worked a night shift, followed respectfully; they were distinguished from the Basque community by their flat caps and grubby grey raincoats. Both of them had a band of black ribbon sewn around their left sleeve, to indicate that they were in mourning.

Next to the hearse in the procession was a carriage for the immediate family. Auntie Maria had insisted on being dressed and accompanying her mother, so Mrs Saitua came in the carriage with them, to help Maria in and out and generally sustain everybody. Nobody spoke. As they passed up the street, any men who saw the procession, whether acquaintances or strangers, took off their hats as a mark of respect to the dead. A sprinkle of newly uniformed soldiers saluted the hearse, rather than doffing their caps.

After the funeral, everybody crowded into the Barinèta home for cakes and sandwiches made by Rosita and her neighbours, washed down by all the wine in the house and by strong black tea for those who liked it.

It was not as grim as Manuel had expected. The kitchen-living-room was filled with men, smoking like fireplaces on days when there was an east wind. They talked quietly in a mixture of Basque and English. They sometimes laughed as they recalled amusing stories of the dead man.

Grandma Micaela's rocking chair had been moved into the parlour, the two chairs which had supported the coffin having been hastily moved back to the kitchen-living-room.

Surrounded by a phalanx of women, she sat with Francesca sleeping soundly on her lap, and received, with bent head, the commiserations of her friends and neighbours. To Manuel, she seemed to have become suddenly very old, with none of her usual sprightliness and quick movements. Beside her sat Auntie Maria, coughing, and weeping steadily into a black handkerchief.

Rosita, aided by Bridget Connolly and Madeleine Saitua, patiently filled cups and glasses, put out a number of saucers to act as extra ash trays, and accepted, with gratitude, small gifts of food or wine brought by kindly neighbours.

Old Manuel put down his ballpoint pen, and stretched himself stiffly in his swivel chair. Having been bereaved of Kathleen, he now understood something of his Grandmother's despair. For a while, after the funeral, she had been almost completely closed into herself – terribly lost to the world continuing to struggle round her – as if her mind had ceased to function. She would do slowly and mechanically anything Rosita asked her to do, and, when it was finished, would sit in her rocking chair, her hands in her lap.

It was Rosita, who, with a worried frown, took on the difficult task of making Pedro's allotment stretch to cover all the needs of three women and two children. She tended to be short with her son, and he was glad to go to school, he remembered.

Rosita herself felt far from well. As the weeks of her pregnancy progressed, she ceased feeding Francesca herself, and gave her bottles of diluted cow's milk and bits of mashed up vegetable from her dinner plate.

In those early weeks, without the weekly sum handed out by Juan Barinèta from his cash box, they had had to augment the housekeeping by taking money out of the boxes under Micaela's bed, money saved for clothes, for extra coal for bitter winters and other small emergencies. This worried Rosita desperately.

She had hoped that her father had something still in his cash box, kept at the back of the wardrobe. Sometimes, after a group of emigrants had passed through, it could be expected to hold quite a sum. When she and Micaela opened it, however, it proved to have very little in it. It dawned on them that they had not had any lodgers for some months before Juan's death. He had mentioned that the threat of war must have made would-be emigrants nervous about taking a long sea journey. He had joked about it, but, as they surveyed the small pile of silver and a few pound notes, they realized that he must have been very worried about his financial situation; yet, he had not bothered them with it. 'Perhaps he was thinking of going to sea again,' suggested Micaela. 'That's what he would have likely done in time.'

Rosita nodded. It made no difference now. With the money they managed to buy a new jersey and boots for Manuel at the beginning of the school term – the child had grown out of his current garments. They also bought three months' supply of coal, before the price went up for the winter months.

They did their best not to touch the Post Office savings account in Micaela's name – because that was intended, in the long term, for school fees. They were driven eventually to draw enough for two weeks' rent, rather than get behind with such an essential payment.

Rosita wrote to Pedro again, care of the company, asking if he could increase his allotment. She hoped that the owners of the tramp steamer, of which he was first mate, would be aware of at least one of the ports which the boat would touch, and would forward her letter to their agent there.

'That's the worst of tramps,' Rosita remarked to Bridget Connolly, who met her on the way to post the letter. 'Even the owners often don't know, for sure, where a ship is – wandering from port to port, picking up and putting down – and not getting back to Liverpool until God knows when.'

Bridget hugged her shawl round her. There had been a bit of a frost that morning, and she had been thinking how nice it would be to have a real overcoat – with a lining to it. She said doubtfully, 'Pat mentioned that your Pedro was trying for a berth with Larrinaga's. It would be proper nice if he could get one – at least you'd know when he was likely to be home.'

Rosita shrugged. 'I wish he could. I haven't heard from him yet in reply to my letter about my dad. And I wrote to him earlier that I'm expecting again. He writes to me, but he isn't getting my letters.'

'Aye, luv. Try not to worry. At least he's in work. Have you heard from Leo?'

'Not for a long while. I can't imagine what's happened to him. I worry myself sick sometimes. And my other brother, Agustin – he's in a tramp steamer, like Pedro – and my uncle in Bilbao – Agustin lives with him – doesn't know where the lad is going, half the time.' She paused, and then added grimly, 'Agustin's lucky, though — his ship is Spanish-registered — nothing to fear from the Germans.'

'So he still lives in Bilbao?'

'Oh, aye. He's been courting a Bilbao girl for years. They're waiting on a house in the same street as Uncle, so the girl will have plenty of company, while he's at sea.'

'So you can't expect much help from him — or your uncle?'

'No. They have a struggle.'

'Well, let's hope Leo comes home.'

Rosita's lips trembled. 'I wish he would, Bridget. I wish he would.'

Unaware of Rosita's financial worries, Manuel played with Brian Wing and Joey Connolly, whipping in and out of the alleyways in wild games of tag or cops and robbers, or plodding up to Princes Park to collect conkers from the horse chestnut trees. The chestnuts were put in corners of the kitchen fireplace to dry out. A hole was then carefully bored through the centre and a piece of string inserted. After that, a boy was fully equipped to play conkers for months, until all his chestnuts had succumbed to hits from those of the other boys, after which everybody had to wait for next year's crop of nuts.

When he felt the need for male support, Manuel gradually turned to Pat Connolly. He learned that if he faced the deaf man squarely, Pat could read what he was saying from the way his lips moved, a discovery which made Manuel feel very clever. Pat himself got pleasure from playing with him and with Joey.

One winter afternoon, when Grandma had been invited to a glass of wine with another Basque lady, equally wizened, Manuel unwillingly accompanied his mother down to the shipping office to collect his father's allotment, which was paid out to her each week.

'Auntie Maria isn't feeling too good, but she's going to watch Francesca for me, and I don't want her to be bothered with you, too.'

Manuel had not the slightest desire to visit the shipping office, and he whined fretfully that he was fine with Joey.

'Joey's mam's delivering a baby,' Rosita told him shortly. 'Peggy O'Brien is watching Joey. She doesn't need anyone else cluttering up her kitchen.'

Manuel resigned himself to a boring walk down to Water Street.

Instead of the usual acne-covered clerk, Rosita was dealt with by a bald, older man, who was obviously unaccustomed to the task of coping with the wives of ships' crews crowding round his beautifully polished counter; the wives were interspersed with noisy toddlers, who tried to see what was going on by scrambling up the ornamentation of the counter; they left dirty fingermarks all along the top of it and scratches on the customer's side. Enough to drive a decent man out of his wits.

As he carefully checked his account book, one woman called teasingly, 'What's happened to our Charley? Why isn't he here?'

The clerk looked up and answered sourly, 'He's volunteered – and about time.'

The woman grunted, and made a face at the wife standing next to her. 'There's a lot as has done that.'

'This country has to be defended, Madam. It is the duty of all men – of the right age – to join the colours.' The remarks sounded like a reproach to the menfolk of the waiting women, and a whispering grumble went through them. Didn't he know that they all had menfolk at sea, who were in constant danger from German attack? However, none of them dared to respond to his remark; you never knew how word might get back to the managers, and a job be lost in consequence.

Rosita had intended to ask Charley which would be the best port to write to and what the agent's address was, in order to get a letter to Pedro; but she was unnerved by the portly man she faced. She picked up the money he threw down in front of her, signed for it, and then counted it carefully in front of the clerk. He sucked through his teeth in irritation at the delay.

Flustered by his aggressive stance, Rosita counted it again. 'I'm short a joey,' she said finally, a tremor in her voice.

'You telling me I made a mistake?'

'Yes,' she whispered.

'I don't make mistakes.'

Faced with such male intransigence, Rosita prepared to sacrifice a threepenny piece she could ill afford, when the woman behind her, braver than the rest, addressed the cashier. 'There's a joey underneath your cuff, you stupid bugger. I seen it roll. Slap money down like that and it'll fall all over the place.'

Rosita glanced round. A heavily built, middle-aged woman, her black shawl decently draped over her head and shoulders, was glaring at the discomfited clerk. She had a face like a bulldog, and at the moment it was flushed red with indignation barely suppressed. 'You don't have to put up with the likes of him,' she assured Rosita roundly. 'Youse right. And there's the joey.' A fat forefinger shot over Rosita's shoulder to point at the tiny silver coin, which lay where a second before the clerk's arm had rested.

As if it were something dirty, the clerk flicked the coin across to Rosita with his thumbnail.

At this further display of discourtesy, a murmur went through the crowd of women.

Rosita picked up the coin and put it carefully into her change purse. She turned to smile at the woman who had been so helpful. The woman gave a wide grin, displaying a mouth empty of teeth, except for one incisor. 'We're going to miss our Charley, aren't we, duck?' she remarked loudly.

Rosita agreed, and small titters at the clerk's discomfiture were audible amongst the onlookers.

'What's volunteered, Mam?' Manuel asked, as they went slowly down the stone steps of the shipping office.

'It means Charley's gone to be a soldier.'

'What for?'

'To fight the Boche in France.'

Manuel considered this information for a minute or two. Then he asked, 'But why, Mam?' There was general puzzlement in the small boy's tone.

The brush with the cashier had upset Rosita, and she answered him impatiently. 'For goodness' sake, stop asking silly questions. I don't know.'

And when, later on, she considered his question, she really did not understand *why* Britain had gone to war. Let the damned Frogs look after themselves, she thought bitterly, as long as Pedro comes home safely.

As she turned the handle of her front door, she paused, her head against the woodwork. She felt exhausted, and the immense courage she had shown since her father's death suddenly deserted her. The bullying in the shipping office, the sense that Charley would probably get himself killed, the fear that Pedro was in danger, her unwanted pregnancy, and the loss of a good and well-loved father all came together. Her underlying grief finally exploded. She burst into wild tears.

'Mam,' cried Manuel in alarm. 'Ma, what's up?'

'It's all right. I'll be all right in a minute,' she gasped.

Chapter Eighteen

Micaela had returned from her visit to her Basque friend. Now, seated in her rocking chair with her sewing box beside her, she was stitching a button on to the neck opening of one of Francesca's vests. She whipped round when she heard the hysterical crying.

Both Manuel and she were filled with consternation, as Rosita threw herself on to her knees and buried her face in her mother's lap to weep broken-heartedly.

Micaela dropped the little vest on to the floor. 'My dear! Whatever happened?' She lifted her daughter up to embrace her.

The boy was appalled. He had never seen his mother cry before. In dismay, he bawled, 'Grandma!' and crowded close to her as if to displace his mother and crawl on to her lap. Grandma was *his* lap, *his* rock, not his mother's or Francesca's. He, too, began to cry, as Micaela put out an arm to him.

'It's Father!' Rosita sobbed. 'What shall we do without him?'

Their joint grief came out in a flood of tears, and it washed away some of both women's misery.

As their weeping began to subside, Micaela slowly let go of both Rosita and Manuel. She lifted the corner of her flowered overall and wiped Rosita's swollen eyes, and then did the same for her scared, woebegone grandson. As she wiped her own face, she smiled slightly at Manuel, and said, 'My goodness! We're worse than a wet week, aren't we?'

She sounded a little more like the Grandma he had

known before his grandfather was killed, and he smiled weakly back.

Rosita stumbled slowly to her feet. 'I'm sorry, Mam,' she said to her mother. 'The clerk in the shipping office was as rude as hell – he wasn't the usual one – and it was the last straw.'

Micaela pulled her handkerchief out of her sleeve, and handed it to her. 'Never mind, my love,' she comforted. 'A good cry can set you up again.' She tightened her arm round Manuel, and planted a firm kiss on his cheek. She then got up, her rocking chair swinging behind her with the suddenness of her movement. 'Now, what we need is a good, strong cup of tea, and we'll all feel better.' As a faint wail came from upstairs, she added practically, 'You'd better get Frannie up from her nap.'

'Can I have a cup of tea?' asked Manuel, with a sudden desire to be promoted to more grown-up customs. 'I'm six, now.'

'Yes,' agreed Grandma, as she filled the kettle from the single kitchen tap. 'You're a big boy – you can have tea.'

With Francesca on Rosita's lap, contentedly sucking at an old ink bottle filled with milk and with a rubber teat on it, and Manuel sitting with them at the table, manfully sipping tea out of a mug, the women began to discuss what they could do to improve their financial position.

As the house was quite big, they agreed that a couple of rooms could be sublet. 'It would help to pay the rent,' admitted Rosita, with a dry sob left over from the intensity of her weeping.

Content that life seemed suddenly to be a little more normal, Manuel left half his tea and slipped down from the table to go out to play.

Still anxious about Rosita's storm of tears, Micaela tried to focus her eyes upon her daughter's face, but it was difficult to see quite straight these days; everything looked slightly misty. She wished heartily that Pedro or one of her sons would dock. Why hadn't Juan insisted that Leo stay in Liverpool? A home needed as many men as possible.

Since Leo had left for Nevada, she had had only two letters from him, both of them not long after his departure. In neither of them had he seemed very happy about what he had found in his new country; he had said sarcastically that if he were to be a shepherd all his life – which seemed to have been the fate of other Basques he had met – he might just as well keep sheep in Vizcaya.

After Juan's death, Micaela watched eagerly for a letter; surely he would reply to their letters to him about the accident, however bad he normally was at correspondence. But there had not been a single word from him. Had something awful happened to him as well? And no one in Nevada to write to tell her about it?

She forced herself to turn her attention to her immediate worries.

'There might be a decent Basque boy who'd be glad of a clean place to lodge,' she suggested to her daughter.

Rosita responded glumly. 'I haven't seen a new face round here for months – the lads are probably getting ships out of Bilbao – they'd be safer in neutral ships. And some of them'll be working ashore – places like Uncle's foundry in Bilbao must be that busy with armaments, they'd take on anybody who came through the gates.'

Micaela chewed her lower lip. She nodded agreement.

The hinges of the front door squeaked, as the door was pushed wide, and they both turned as they heard the slow dragging steps of Maria coming down the passage. After Micaela had returned from her visit, Maria had slipped out for a gossip with an old acquaintance, who lived just round the curve of the street. Now, as she returned, she threw back her shawl from her greying, sandy head to survey them with sombre, watery blue eyes. She was swaying with fatigue from her tiny walk. As she noted the two women bunched closely together at the table, she inquired nervously, 'Anything wrong?'

Both women smiled, and Rosita said calmly, 'No, we were talking, that's all. Like a cup of tea?'

When Maria had slowly seated herself on the sofa, and, with a thankful sigh, put her feet up, Rosita set a cup of tea on the small table beside her, and Micaela said, 'We were thinking we could rent a couple of rooms – to help out. What do you think?'

'Oh, aye,' Maria responded, as she stirred her tea and eyed them suspiciously.

Because she was sick, they did not habitually discuss family problems with her – as if, from her place on the sofa, she did not see most of what went on, she considered sardonically – and she resented this; she wanted to be part of the living world as long as she could. Though, at the moment, she was very tired, Micaela's remark gave her a chance to be included, so she continued aloud. 'Well, now, I've been up with Mrs Halloran, to see how her Eileen is – I don't think her Eileen's long for this world – and she mentioned that they're going to extend the blacksmith's workshop behind her house – and they're going to pull down some houses at the back to do it.' She put her cup down in her saucer with a loud clink, as if to express anger, and added, 'No thought of the families living in the houses, of course!' She paused, to ruminate.

'Mother of God!' exclaimed Micaela. 'As if there isn't enough racket already! Yesterday, the steam hammers started up and shook the table so much that the sugar basin was nearly jiggled off it – I caught it just in time.'

'Oh, aye. It's bad,' agreed Maria. 'And it'll be worse. Just listen to the horses' hooves at this minute. There must be half a dozen drays in the road – and every horse'll have left us a little present, I'll be bound.' They all listened as, through the open front door, came the shouts of the dray-men and the clack-clack of their clogs or hob-nailed boots.

'Phew!' exclaimed Rosita, and went to shut the door as the strong odour of new manure swept into the house, mixed with the permanent fishy smell from the sardine-packing plant nearby. 'Those that go to sea don't know what they're missing!' she said with a laugh, as she sat down again.

Aunt Maria finally picked up again the original thread of her discourse. 'Because of the new workshop, Mr Halloran's brother, George, and his wife, Effie – you know Effie – have got to look for a place. Works for a brewery, he does – drayman on deliveries. They'd pay their rent, they would.' She put down her teacup and coughed politely into her hanky.

'Well, that's an idea,' Micaela replied diffidently. Having a woman in the house would mean her cooking on Micaela's own kitchen range – which would cause problems.

Maria was, however, secretly filled with glee, when Micaela reluctantly took her advice and arranged to rent the large first-floor room to Effie Halloran. Both the Halloran sons had volunteered for the Navy, so the couple felt that they would have plenty of space in such a big room.

Once they had moved in, there were the usual complaints between the women about the sink in the kitchen-living-room being full of each other's sooty saucepans after cooking, and arguments about who was responsible for this or that bit of cleaning.

Regularly, Effie would announce loftily and tearfully, 'I'll look for something else, I will. I'll get out of here.' But Mr Halloran would point out to his wife that cheap housing was almost impossible to find.

'You can talk,' Effie would spit back at him, her dark, careworn face wrinkled up in disgust. 'Youse at work all day. It's me as has to put up with Them.'

Them, in the shape of Grandma, trying hard to get a

grip on life again, insisted on a cleaned-up sandstone sink and fixed hours for each of them to use the kitchen oven. A disgruntled Effie held her tongue, as far as she could, and acceded.

Though the women got on each other's nerves, there were days when they would sit comfortably on the front step in the autumn sunlight, to discuss the latest hurried marriage in the neighbourhood, or the tragedies of local men killed – or worse, missing, presumed killed – in France or at sea.

Effie Halloran could not read and Micaela read English only with difficulty, so Rosita would often read the *Evening Express* to them, after George Halloran had finished poring over the sporting pages to see if the horses he had backed had won.

The reading, added to the gossip which George picked up, as he drove his cartloads of barrels of beer from public house to public house, meant that the women probably knew as much about the war as most local people did.

As he hauled the empty barrels out of the pubs' cellars, and then carefully rolled the full ones down to the pot boy waiting in each cellar, George heard, at second hand from the pot boy, numerous seamen's stories of what was happening at sea; and he sometimes regaled Effie with them, as he ate his tea. Occasionally, an innkeeper would stand him half a pint of beer to replace the perspiration he had lost in heaving heavy barrels about, and they, too, would pause to discuss the latest news.

'We don't know half of what They're up to,' George would often say sagely to his wife. 'They don't tell us nothing.'

Though George Halloran was much surlier and less knowledgeable than Grandpa, he was stout and reliable-looking, and Manuel adopted him as part of the family. He also enjoyed being petted by Effie.

Effie missed her boys. 'It's as if something's been cut off

me,' she would explain wistfully to anyone who would listen to such an insignificant shawlie.

Micaela and Rosita regarded her as much beneath them; they had considerable pride in being Basques, and in being literate. Poor Effie's pride consisted in keeping her room well scoured and being able to boast that both her boys were in the Royal Navy. She kept her head bowed and hoped only that her lads would survive the war.

Rosita admitted to Maria that she had been correct in saying that the Hallorans would pay their rent. Effie knocked at the kitchen-living-room door every Friday night, and silently proffered the opened rent book, with five shillings in silver balanced precariously on it.

In late October that year, when Manuel was beginning to look forward to Guy Fawkes Day, a weary and dirty Pedro walked into his home. Hastily stuffed into his back pocket were Rosita's letters; they had been brought on board by the Mersey pilot, who had come to take his boat up the river to Liverpool. Already exhausted by a long, difficult voyage, he was greatly upset by the letters' contents.

As he entered the kitchen-living-room, he was greeted and fussed over by his womenfolk — even Maria broke her iron rule and clung to him and kissed him again and again on the cheek. He sat down thankfully close to the fire to rub his icy hands by the blaze, and accepted a mug of tea, heavy with sugar, as yet unrationed.

He was surprised when tiny hands grabbed his serge trousers, as Francesca crawled towards him and tried to pull herself up to stare at the new arrival.

His mind cluttered with weariness and bad news, Pedro stared back. Then a delighted grin creased his face, as he looked down at a tiny replica of his Rosita with the same wide blue eyes and tiny tendrils of bright-red hair.

He forgot his fatigue, put down his mug and grabbed her up to hug her with joy, despite a sopping wet nappy.

He looked over the child's head at his wife, and both of them laughed.

'She's the spitting image of you,' he told her. And then he asked, 'Where's Mannie?'

'He's playing next door. He'll be in for his tea in a minute.'

Micaela laughed when Pedro ruefully realized how wet his daughter was. She said to the child, 'Come to Grandma, and I'll change you. You're making your daddy all wet.'

Rosita came over to stand by him; she felt shaky with the relief of his safe return after such a long voyage. She gently caressed the back of his neck. 'Where've you been?' she asked. 'Did you get our letters?'

'The pilot brought them aboard today,' he replied heavily. He looked at Micaela. 'I'm so sad for you,' he said to her, and stretched across the fireplace to catch her hand in his. 'It must have been awful for you. I nearly had a fit when I read your letter. What happened exactly?'

Micaela did her best to control a fresh bout of tears, while behind her, Maria, humped up on the sofa with two shawls round her, bent her head over her teacup and shook with suppressed sobs.

Pedro looked anxiously at them. Both women looked as if a good gale would blow the pair of them to Kingdom Come. Even Rosita didn't appear too well. What a bowl of trouble it all was. He wanted to weep himself; but men can't cry. He badly needed a good meal and his bed, and some clean clothes to put on – he had not had his clothes off for days.

'It was a true accident,' Micaela told him dully, her veined eyelids drooping to hide her agony of mind. She was still haunted by the fact that it was she who had urged Juan to do a job which, she felt, should have been done by a younger man.

After Micaela's cracked voice had faltered through the story, Rosita took Francesca from her, and herself changed the child on the table. She glanced back at her husband and said, 'You look as if you've been in the wars. Where've you been, luv?'

Pedro picked up his mug of tea again, and drained it. 'All over the bloody Atlantic,' he told her exasperatedly. 'Afraid of subs – and miles off course. They shouldn't have sent us to New York in the first place.'

'New York? I thought they always did the west coast of Africa, and that way?'

'Oh, aye. Most times that's what we do. Not this time! We went from New York up to Halifax and Montreal. Then back south again to Charleston and then to New Orleans. I've been down as far as Argentina. The fellas were getting desperate that we'd never get home again, with one thing and another.' He rubbed his tired eyes. 'The war's changed everything.' He felt in his pocket for his cigarettes, took one out and lit it, while the women watched in silence. Then he said, 'Finally, we got a cargo for Liverpool, and were we thankful! But we had such foul weather and were blown so far south that the Ould Man was worried about coal being enough, never mind whether we'd be spotted by German subs.'

Rosita was worrying about what she was going to give the unexpected arrival to eat, but she said, 'You poor dear. Was the ship damaged at all?'

'She's got one or two nasty cracks in the deck. She needs a good overhaul. The Ould Man and the Chief are talking in the office now – and they'll not be mincing their words. She's that old, she's near falling apart, she is. They want a refit.'

Rosita was still holding Francesca. She put her free arm round his shoulders, and he leaned against her. He wanted her.

'The company'll fire them for speaking up like that,' Micaela said nervously. 'Even a ship's master must mind what he says.'

'Not nowadays,' he said with a sudden grin. 'They're getting short of men. Too many gone into the Navy – called up from the Reserve.'

Rosita put Francesca down on the floor again and the child crawled away on her own small voyage of exploration. Her mother was anxious. It was unlike Pedro to complain seriously about anything. He carped occasionally, like all seamen did but it did not mean much; like his mates, he had a doglike patience and endurance, an acceptance of the dangers of his calling and of company parsimony. Now she felt sick at the thought of enemy submarines meeting a boat that probably could not travel at more than ten knots; it would be a sitting duck. As if in agreement with her apprehensions, the baby within her kicked quite energetically.

She pulled herself together, and said firmly, 'I bet you're hungry. I haven't got a lot in the house, but I've got bacon and eggs – and fried bread?'

He nodded. 'That sounds good,' he assured her.

Manuel came wandering in in search of tea, and greeted his father exuberantly. Now Daddy was home everything would be all right, and Aunt Maria would stop bursting into tears every time you looked at her.

Micaela made herself get up briskly. 'What about a wash and a shave,' she suggested, 'while Rosita gets the tea?'

'Oh, aye,' Pedro responded, with feeling. He put his young son down from his knee. 'Go and get the bucket from the outhouse,' he told him. 'We'll fill it from the oven tap, and I'll go up and have a good wash.'

Obediently, Manuel went to collect the enamel bucket always used for this purpose and set it in the hearth under the shiny brass tap of the hot water tank. He squatted down and turned on the tap; it belched a thin stream of nearly boiling water. While he watched it trickle into the bucket, he wondered what his father had brought him this time.

Later, Micaela refilled the tank with cold water from the tap over the sink because Pedro forgot to do it.

'How long will you be home, Pedro?' Micaela asked, as she stretched upwards to lift some dinner-sized plates from the dresser shelf.

'Depends on what the Ould Fella fixes with the bosses,' he responded morosely. 'Maybe a few weeks.'

A few weeks!

Even the threat of temporary unemployment if the ship were laid up made Rosita pause, frying-pan in hand. Despite Effie's rent, the best she had been able to do with her housekeeping was to avoid drawing further from the Post Office account and keep herself out of debt. Saving was impossible. A spurt of deep anxiety broke through her general relief at having her husband safely home, and a shiver went up her spine.

She laid the pan on the draining board while she went to the pantry to get bread, bacon and eggs and lard. They had never been short of food, she considered anxiously, though Grandma and she had contributed to this by keeping house with the greatest care, as if every farthing was the last one they had. Now, she worried. In the past if Pedro was laid off, there had always been Juan or Leo who were working. Now there was only Pedro.

It became a difficult evening, because Pedro was himself worn out. It was made worse because there was no wine in the house to alleviate the strain – one of Rosita's economies had been to do without it; and, then in the early morning, Francesca woke and howled miserably, aware, perhaps, of an extra person in the bedroom. Rosita made a mental note to move her the next day to a tiny bedroom over the hall; it was time she learned to sleep alone.

A sleepy Pedro was kind about the expected child; Rosita had been afraid that he would have been annoyed at such an early addition to his family. 'Kids are sent by God,' he told her; but it did not make him any happier.

Chapter Nineteen

The next morning, while Rosita was still urging little Manuel to hurry up or he would be late for school, Pedro quickly shaved himself and washed his face at the kitchen sink. At Micaela's insistence, he gobbled a bowl of porridge, while standing with his back to the fire to warm himself. Then he grabbed his cap and jacket from the peg on the back door, gave Rosita a quick peck on her cheek, and said, 'I hope to get back tonight.' He hurried out of the house, to look at his damaged ship.

The previous night, as he turned over in bed before finally settling to sleep, he had told her that they would talk about their finances tomorrow; and he asked who the woman was he had met on the stairs, as he came up.

'Effie Halloran,' Rosita had replied cryptically. Further explanation could wait until morning.

Now he had fled back to his ship, Rosita felt vexed. She knew that he had responsibilities there, but she needed to *talk* to him, quietly and sensibly. Then she realized that if the ship were laid up for some time, there would be too much time for discussion – and no income to discuss. She shrugged, as she turned to deal with Francesca, who was whining because she was hungry.

Under the bleary eyes of the third mate, the ship was being unloaded. They had taken a mixed cargo from New York to Charleston; there, they had picked up armour plate destined for Liverpool. The boat was teeming with men, from company clerks to stevedores, though the job was nearing completion.

The crew members who lived nearby were returning glumly to work; others would get shore leave later on.

Pedro went to look for the bosun; he had to arrange with him for innumerable small repair jobs to be done, and a lot of general maintenance which had been neglected during the voyage because of bad weather.

Perhaps it was the bad weather which had kept the U-boats fully occupied, too. It was a miracle that they had not encountered one. Off course, overloaded, too slow to be part of a convoy and obviously battered by the storm, any U-boat commandant who had spotted them would have licked his chops over them, thought Pedro grimly.

'The Ould Man's fit to be tied this morning,' the bosun told him in reference to the ship's master. 'And the Chief's down in the pit, giving hell to everybody in sight. The office told the pair of them to quit crying into their milk; this is no time for refits, they said; there's a war on!'

In fluent Basque, Pedro cursed all owners, and stuffed his chapped hands in his trouser pockets. The bosun grinned. He did not understand Basque, but the tone conveyed the meaning. He said to Pedro, 'They got some fellas down below looking at it; it mayn't be as bad as we think.'

Pedro did not reply. He had sailed for three years in this old tub, because nothing better had offered. He had, however, been trying for a berth with de Larrinaga, a Basque family firm trading with the West Indies, out of Liverpool. Now that he had more experience under his belt, he felt that he should try again; before the war began, he had been thankful for a job; but, now, merchant seamen were in a little shorter supply and he might stand a better chance. The ship's turnaround was, however, much quicker than he had expected, so he had to defer his job-hunting.

Against the better judgement of the ship repairers who had been called in, minor repairs only were made and some rigging which had been lost in the storm was replaced.

Intent on a speedy turnaround, the owners gave short shrift to the complaints of the chief engineer about the needs of his engine room. A few days later, the ship sailed for New York, largely under ballast.

Painfully aware of the war being waged in the Atlantic and that he was serving in a ship which, as his second had remarked, was not much better than a bloody sieve, Pedro was careful not to communicate the crew's unease to his family. Rotten owners who ran rotten ships were one of the hazards of a seaman's life.

Nevertheless, he and Rosita were heavy-hearted on the day he sailed. Though she was pregnant, he would have loved to take her to bed that evening; but it was not possible with the eyes of his mother-on-law and Maria on him all the time. Sometimes, Rosita, too, wondered savagely if the two women really understood anything about human longings for the comfort of a regular sex life; how difficult it was to be faithful when your man was on a long voyage and other men looked hopefully at you. Did Maria understand the tension between Pedro and herself, as they sat gravely by the fire together, unsatisfied? The pain of loving a man so much was pain indeed.

That last evening, they had sat around discussing their money problems. Anxious that there should be no dissension between Pedro and Rosita, Micaela took the initiative in explaining to Pedro where his allotment went. As she spoke, her knitting needles flashed steadily; she was knitting her son-in-law a new navy-blue sweater.

Pedro listened without comment, while he cleaned out the bowl of his pipe with his penknife.

When she had finished, he said uneasily, 'The minute I got your letters, when the pilot came aboard, I knew what you were up against. And I know you do your best – I've never seen either of you waste anything.' He was grim-faced, as he drew on his cigarette. 'I've been thinking that I can increase the allotment to Rosita to the maximum the company will let me. And I'll hope to give you a bit more when I dock. I have to keep some money by me, you understand. Ciggies don't cost much, because I don't buy them in England; I sometimes have to stand the lads a drink – they're my mates, and I have to live with them.'

Rosita was patching the seat of a pair of Manuel's trousers; she was an excellent needlewoman, and the stitches barely showed. She looked up at her husband, letting her work fall into her lap, as he stopped speaking. He looked so tired and melancholy, as he slumped in his chair, that it hurt her. She said cheerfully, 'Not to worry, luv. We'll manage somehow – with the bit extra you'll leave us. I've still got Francesca's baby clothes, so we won't have to buy anything new for the baby when it comes.'

His face softened. She was a sweetheart, and he longed to cuddle her. His face lightened slightly, as he said in a rueful tone, 'I won't be able to bring much in the way of presents for you.'

'Tush, don't worry about that.'

In the golden glow of a Canadian summer evening, Old Manuel slowly dug over a small flowerbed in his Victoria garden and thought about Pedro. He remembered his bringing him a small blue lorry that he wound up with a key. He had run into Pedro's open arms to hug him in his excitement at the present, loving the comfort of those strong arms round him and the stubbled chin against his face. That was how he had always remembered him – and always would, thought Manuel, as he stopped digging to let his aching back recover.

Chapter Twenty

After Pedro's return to sea, Manuel actively missed him. Until then, his father had been a friendly person who came and went, whom he only vaguely remembered between times. It had been Grandpa who had been the stalwart backbone of his life, and, like most backbones, had been taken for granted.

Occasionally, Manuel had nightmares, when he seemed to be flying through the air and then falling to hit the tiles of the lavatory roof. He was grateful when Auntie Maria heard him cry out and lit her candle, and, like a friendly ghost, crept across to his bed to comfort him.

One day, after noting his mother's swollen figure, he asked, 'Are we going to have another baby, Mam?'

Rosita smiled. 'If God wills,' she said.

'Will it be a boy or a girl?'

She laughed softly. 'We don't know. It doesn't matter.'

But it does matter, thought Old Manuel, as he remembered this tender moment with his mother. I love Faith, but I would have loved a son, as well. I'd have taught him how to fish – and build and sail a boat – and I could've talked politics with him. He would've been a real Basque in his ways.

He could not find any irrefutable argument to confirm his idea that a son of his would have embraced his Basque traditions with enthusiasm; he simply sensed that it would have been so.

He wondered if he would have a great-grandson by Lori-lyn, a boy who might have pride in his Basque forebears, who would be as handsome as Pedro and have the wisdom of Juan Barinèta.

He realized suddenly that this dim hope was why he was writing down what he remembered of his early life; he wanted his notes to be passed down to this phantom descendant. Basques were becoming fewer and were scattered, like the Jews, all over the world. He wanted with all his heart to leave on earth a child with the tough independent outlook and the physical and mental strength of his Basque forebears.

Heavy with her pregnancy, Rosita once lamented to Effie Halloran that it was great to be a man. 'Away at sea — away from all the troubles at home. It's the life of Riley.'

'We all has our troubles,' comforted Effie. 'It's no joke having a man under your feet all the time. And your Pedro's good to you.'

The winter mists of 1914 engulfed the city. Around the Wapping Dock, there were no trees to lose their leaves and announce the approach of winter. It was the increasing sound of fog horns bellowing across the water which told small boys that Guy Fawkes Day was imminent.

Manuel, Brian and Joey, with a horde of other small children, began to collect bits of wood, abandoned scraps of furniture, old newspapers and wooden crates, anything that would burn, ready for the bonfire they would make on the fifth of November.

Manuel negotiated with Rosita for the loan of Francesca's push-chair in which to push the guy around.

'And what happens if you break it? I'm not having it run all over the place — for a guy!'

On her way to the outside lavatory, Effie heard Rosita's refusal, and paused to say, 'Himself'd knock a handcart together for yez. All he'd need is a soap box and a couple of wheels.'

George Halloran was very agreeable to being drawn into

preparations for the anniversary of the Gunpowder Plot, and soon put together a most satisfactory vehicle for them.

The guy itself was made a monstrous object. The lower part of the body was made out of a pair of old overalls once worn by Grandpa. They were stuffed with newspaper. Mrs Connolly provided a hopelessly torn pullover of Pat's which was also stuffed, to make the upper part of the body; and, to Manuel's delight, Auntie Maria made a wonderful head by stuffing one of her old black woollen stockings and embroidering a gruesome set of features on it with a length of red knitting wool. A long-since-abandoned beret, which had for years been used as a hot-water bottle cover, gave the guy an unexpectedly Basque appearance.

The effigy was arranged in the soap box, and a whole string of small boys took turns in pushing it all the way up to Paradise Street, where they collected a number of pennies for it from the seamen around the Sailors' Home. They then pushed onward into Church Street and up to Bold Street, shouting to the well-dressed shoppers, 'Penny for the guy, Missus,' or, more belligerently, 'Remember, remember, the fifth of November, Gunpowder, Treason and Plot!' The shoppers seemed to feel that grubby urchins with an improvised wheelbarrow had no right to be there, so they only got a few farthings out of them.

Stolid little Brian Wing was trusted by everyone, so he was the group's treasurer. He carefully put all the coins they collected into his marble bag, since it was not the marble season. Afterwards, they crowded into Mr Wing's steamy back room, while he obligingly counted the proceeds for them.

While Mrs Wing smiled through the steam as she ironed shirt after shirt, they decided shrilly on their fireworks shopping list. Catherine wheels and rockets were the prime favourites, closely followed by a banger for each boy, and two volcanoes.

Though Mrs Wing would have been thankful for the amount they collected, to add a little pork to their evening rice, nothing was said. Boys usually gave their mothers most of the odd pennies they earned for going messages for other housewives, or minding horses, or catching a line for an incoming boat. Money collected for Guy Fawkes Day seemed sacrosanct; it was the children's great day.

Because of the war and creeping shortages of many peacetime products, it proved difficult to find fireworks. A very small shop in Park Lane finally yielded a gratifying number, left over, perhaps, from the previous year.

The joyful little boys streamed back to Wapping, to ask Joey's father, Pat Connolly, to keep them safe from being accidentally blown up. He also undertook to build their bonfire, having acquired a reputation, from previous years, for being very good at bonfires.

'For sure,' he said, 'and I'll find a bottle or two to set the rockets in.' Then he asked, 'Have you got any spuds to roast?'

Crestfallen, they admitted that they had not; and what was the good of a bonfire without potatoes to roast?

Then Manuel announced grandly, 'Me mam'll find us some,' and he fled next door to make good his promise of at least twelve spuds.

'How many do you want?' asked Rosita, a little anxiously. She had a sack of potatoes in the cellar, but they had to last for months – and prices were going up at a frightening speed.

'There's five of us – and Mr Connolly – and there'll be some more on the day. Could I have twelve, to be sure?'

About four pounds of potatoes, at least. Rosita bit her lower lip.

At her hesitation, Grandma Micaela ordered firmly, 'Give them him. Compared to the lot out there, we're not poor – Pedro's in work.'

It was a matter of pride.

'All right,' Rosita agreed reluctantly.

George Halloran's willingness to help on occasions was not the only kindness received by the three women.

Domingo Saitua, who worked on the Birkenhead ferry, came in one night, and said shyly, holding his beret between his great red hands, 'Mam said you wanted a wheel put on.'

Thankfully Rosita produced the push-chair and the loose wheel, and he squatted down by the back door and neatly put it on for her. It was a labour of love – he considered Rosita the most beautiful woman in Liverpool.

Another time, a pane of glass fell out of the kitchen window and shattered in the yard outside. The following day, a wizened old man, who must have been in his seventies and said his name was Pablo, came with a piece of glass, cut it to size and puttied it into the frame. 'Used to have a drink with Juan often enough,' he told Grandma, grinning toothlessly.

Afterwards, Rosita laughed. 'I swear I never told anybody the pane was broken – I haven't left the house since it fell out!'

'Grapevine,' replied Grandma, as she neatly turned the heel of a sock and Pudding tried to bat at the swiftly moving knitting wool.

'Well, I'm very grateful. Otherwise, I'd have had to fill it with cardboard.'

Numerous small acts of kindness like these helped Micaela in another way; the short visits of other Basques were a comfort to her in her loneliness. She was the oldest woman in the community and this set her slightly apart. Because of her rapidly increasing blindness, which was accepted as a natural result of ageing, she tended to sit more at home, doing jobs that did not require her to move about so much. So she was more easily approached by the

Basque wives of the kind helpers; tired, harassed women, they came to ask her advice.

Aunt Maria also enjoyed the visits. The old couch in the kitchen-living-room had become her permanent bed, so that she did not have to climb the stairs. Manuel missed her and her candle in the bedroom. Lots of old people slept in living-rooms, so he did not see the significance of the new arrangement. He did notice, however, that Father Felipe visited her rather more often than he had done before Grandpa died, and that, though he encouraged Grandma to walk up to the church to attend Mass, he apparently did not expect Auntie Maria to accompany her.

'Why do we have to go to Mass, and Auntie's let off?' he asked his mother crossly, when he had been called in from a great game of Boches and Allies to be made clean for church.

'Because she's frail, dear,' his mother had replied, as she scrubbed his face, hands and knees with Sunlight soap and a piece of flannel.

As he dried his face with the thin kitchen towel, he stared at the patient figure propped up on the couch, her rosary held in her listless hand. She had taken no notice of the exchange between his mother and himself.

Manuel had forgotten the tiny incident, until soon after Faith had been married.

Kathleen had always accompanied him to church, though, being a Protestant, she did not take the Sacrament. One Sunday, she said she felt too tired to walk the short distance to Mass, but that she would like to attend.

She had never complained before of fatigue without an obvious reason for it, and it was with some anxiety that he got the car out. Because parking was difficult to find and the distance not very great, it was the first time that he had ever driven to church.

It had been the beginning of the end, he thought

163

helplessly, as had been the increasing number of visits to Maria by Father Felipe.

Kathleen had not had the consolation of priestly visits; the church had so few men that pastoral visits had, largely, become a folk memory. Instead, she had had innumerable hospital visits for blood infusions, to counteract the leukaemia which had struck her down. She had been admitted at other times for all kinds of infections, to which she had been laid open by the underlying disease. He shuddered when he remembered the lingering misery of the last years of her life, and cursed modern medicine with good old-fashioned Basque curses for extending a life not worth living. Then he reminded himself not to be ungrateful; nowadays, modern medicine could have cured Aunt Maria.

So that she, too, could die of cancer? he asked himself furiously in his distress over his suffering wife.

Distraught at the memory of Kathleen, he pushed his notes to the back of his desk, and went to the kitchen to get a glass of wine. He felt shut in, dreadfully alone. No one to talk to. None of the close neighbourliness of his youth to sustain him. He thought of Sharon, one of the very few who seemed to invite confidences; she always spoke to him if she saw him in the garden. Of course, Veronica also stopped to speak; the trouble was that she never stopped speaking! And she had her own axe to grind, he considered grimly.

He slowly put on a jacket and zipped it up. Then, slapping his beret on his head, he went out to walk by the sea.

Chapter Twenty-one

Guy Fawkes Night did not turn out at all as Manuel had expected.

Pat Connolly built one of his perfect bonfires and lit it. To the pleasure of the small crowd which had gathered to watch, the fireworks all went off with appropriate bangs and whooshes. The potatoes had been roasted to blackness on the outside and steamy perfection inside. But a thoroughly frightened Manuel had clutched Jean Baptiste Saitua's hand, and had, at first, even refused to put a match to his own bangers.

He was obsessed by the nightmare scene he had witnessed at home, immediately before Jean Baptiste had whipped him away to join Pat Connolly.

Aunt Maria had begun to moan, saying that she had a terrible pain in her side. She started to thresh about on the couch; her crochet, her rosary, her smelling salts, her medicines were scattered suddenly from the tiny sidetable; her hot-water bottle and her shawls fell off the couch.

With unusual agility, Grandma had leapt up from her own chair; and his mother, after glancing quickly round, hastily deserted the washing-up, and, as she squeezed round the table, dried her hands on her apron.

'Give me a towel, quick!' Grandma shouted to her.

Rosita grabbed the kitchen towel and threw it across the room to her. A paralysed Manuel saw it turn scarlet, as his aunt doubled up and spat blood.

At that moment, Jean Baptiste Saitua and Domingo came through the unlocked front entrance to collect Manuel.

Jean Baptiste gave one horrified glance at Maria, and

said immediately to the boy, 'Ready to go? Let's go down to the bonfire.'

Easing her way round the furniture towards Maria, Rosita said quickly, 'Yes, luv. Away you go. We'll look after Auntie.' She added softly to Jean, 'Ask Bridget to come quick and Madeleine.'

Though filled with dread, Manuel allowed himself to be led away. While he and Jean Baptiste knocked on Bridget's door, Domingo ran fleetly back to his home to get his mother.

'What's to do?' asked Bridget apprehensively, seeing the child's white face in the light of the street lamp.

'It's Maria. Go quick.'

'Jesus Mary!' It was a call she had been dreading, and she fled back to the kitchen to get a clean apron.

Manuel silently walked down to the corner of Corn Hill. He was afraid to ask the big Basque what was happening to Auntie Maria, because he dreaded an honest answer. He had expected that his grandmother and mother would come to join in the fun; but he realized now that they must look to his aunt's needs. He hoped that her Guardian Angel was on the watch and doing better than Grandpa's had.

Persuaded by Pat Connolly, he obediently carried bits of wood and rubbish from a niche, in which it had been hidden by the boys, to the bonfire to keep it blazing.

Pat had stored the fireworks on top of a wall, well back from the fire, and young Vicente Saitua had been stationed near them to guard them from thieves.

Even the excitement of the rockets sparkling in the cold November sky failed to divert Manuel completely. He kept glancing over his shoulder and wondering if he dare run back home.

Jean Baptiste was well aware of what was probably going on in the Barinètas' home; his wife had sent back a message with his son that on no account must Manuel be allowed to go home.

Instructed by his mother, Domingo asked Manuel casually, 'Where's little Frannie?' and was much relieved to hear that she went to bed early.

'Me mam said she was too small and would be afraid of the noise,' Manuel explained.

'Oh, aye,' agreed Domingo. 'This is fun for big lads, like us, int it?' and this had coaxed a faint smile out of the frightened child.

Though they did all they could to make a happy evening for the children, both Pat and Jean Baptiste were heavy-hearted. Consumption was a wicked disease, and you never knew who would be struck by it next. The Basque families, better fed and slightly better housed than most people in the dock area, had no other case that he was aware of. But even the rich feared it, particularly amongst their women and children.

'It's rough on old Mrs Barinèta,' said Pat, under his breath to Jean Baptiste, as he heaved some stringed bundles of newspaper into the flames. 'The wife says she hasn't got over losing her hubbie yet.'

'Will they call the doctor?'

'I doubt it,' replied Pat. 'He can't do nothing for her. It'd be more expense for the family, and wouldn't do no good. He might put her in hospital. They wouldn't want her to die there.'

'They'll have to get him for the Death Certificate, won't they?'

'They'll worry about that later. Bridget'll help them as much as she can.'

'Oh, aye. And our Madeleine, too. Better to die in your mother's arms, with friends round you.' Jean Baptiste stepped back from the bonfire, to join Domingo and Manuel.

'Come on, Mannie,' he said kindly. 'I'm going to send a rocket up specially for you.' He took the long-stemmed firework from the top of the wall, and squatted down, to put it into the long neck of a beer bottle as straight as he could make it stand. 'Now,' he said, 'if you set it like that and put a match to it carefully, it'll go straight up into the air — and not into somebody's bedroom window!' He struck a match and handed it to Manuel. 'Now, you light the fuse, here.'

They were surrounded by a small squad of slightly older boys, who said they remembered other Guy Fawkes Nights, when rockets fizzled and then seemed to go out, only to suddenly take flight dangerously close to the faces of all of them. As Manuel put the match to the fuse, they all seemed to yelp together, 'Nearly took me ear, it did.'

Manuel wanted to back quickly away, but he was hemmed in by the boys' big boots round him. The rocket, however, after a preliminary spit, soared upwards, leaving a stream of red and green stars after it. It did a splendid arc, and the onlookers let out a collective exclamation.

Manuel was impressed. He watched the firework until the last green star died in Liverpool's overwhelming smog, and Jean Baptiste smiled down at him, and said cheerily, 'That was the best rocket I've seen in a long time. You must've lit it exactly right.'

He was relieved when the lad looked up and grinned at him.

Pat Connolly had been watching the potatoes bake in the ashes, turning them occasionally with a spade. They were now giving out a delicious smell, so he pushed them out of the fire and lifted them to the edge of the pavement to cool.

Manuel was suddenly very hungry, and Pat Connolly chose a particularly big one and split it open with his pen-knife. 'Got a hanky?' he asked.

Manuel quickly produced a grubby piece of rag from his pocket, and the potato was carefully laid on it; a welcome heat from it permeated to his hand. Everybody wanted a potato, but Pat was careful to give them only to his own little party.

With shrieks and squeaks at the heat, the potatoes were slowly eaten with the fingers. Manuel ate all the soft inside of his potato and threw the blackened crust into the fire; but Brian Wing ate every scrap, his chubby face getting liberally blackened by the potato's well-burned skin.

Then the Catherine wheels were, one by one, nailed to a warehouse door. When lit, they whirled out a huge circle of sparks, and the children danced back from them to avoid being burned. An older boy set off a couple of bangers amid the long-skirted women who had come to see the bonfire. The jokes became raucous, as the women lifted their skirts and petticoats, for fear of their catching fire. Some of them ran up nearby steps, exhibiting black woollen stockings and bare thighs. In the light of the glowing ashes, with their long shadows dancing on the brick walls of a factory, they looked to Manuel like real witches.

The party was being taken over by grown-ups. Brian's big brother was the first to realize it, and politely and discreetly began to withdraw with Brian. Brian protested loudly and tried to kick his patient brother. Pat and Jean Baptiste nodded to each other, and Pat took the hand of a sleepy Joey. He turned to his young daughter, Mary, now a skinny eight-year-old, and ordered, 'Our Mary, you take Manuel's hand. He's coming to our house tonight. His auntie isn't feeling too clever, and we don't want to wake her up with him coming home, and all.'

Mary nodded. 'Give me your hand, Mannie,' she said; she was used to being the big sister in charge of a small brother.

He backed away from her. His face was covered with smuts and he looked as if he were about to cry. 'No! I want to go home,' he whined. Then, more hysterically, he wailed, 'I want me mam.'

Jean Baptiste swept him up into his arms, and told him

peremptorily, 'Your mam wants you to stay with Mary tonight. Now stop crying – you're a big boy now.'

Jean Baptiste's red face looked like carved granite under his black beret. He had spoken crisply in Basque, exactly like Grandpa used to when he was cross.

Manuel's wails became a subdued snuffle.

Trotting along slightly behind Mr Saitua, Mary looked up at the unhappy face peering down at her over the big Basque's shoulder. 'Mam's making hot cocoa for us when we come in,' she promised.

She did not know what was happening in the Barinèta household, except that it had been obvious to her at the bonfire that something was wrong, because Rosita had not joined them. She had, however, already learned from her mother to protect Joey from some of the hard facts of the raw life around him; and now she was doing her small best for Manuel, despite her own nervousness that her mother might not be at home.

She smiled up at him and wrinkled up her nose. He smiled wanly back and stuck his finger in his mouth. He liked Mary.

Chapter Twenty-two

Auntie Bridget was not at home, so Mary carefully made cocoa for them all, and they drank it while sitting on the rag hearth rug before the dying fire. Then Mary took them upstairs, ordered them to take off their outer clothes, while she took off her own dress and stockings. She then put Joey and Manuel into a double bed and climbed in after them. After a few minutes of pushing and shoving, they settled down to sleep, and the next thing that Manuel knew was Auntie Bridget's smiling face, as she shook each of them and told them to hurry up or they'd be late for school.

Downstairs, a bowl of porridge with a little sugar and milk awaited them. Pat Connolly had already gone to work; his empty porridge plate still lay on the table.

Though Bridget Connolly had been up all night and was so tired she felt fit to drop, she sent the children off with a pat on each small behind, and the injunction to Manuel that she was sending them off a bit early, so that he could pop in and see his mam.

A tide of relief went through Manuel. He had a wild hope that everything at home would be all right. Auntie Maria would smile at him from the old horsehair sofa; Grandma would be washing the breakfast plates in the chipped enamel basin in the sink, and his mother would probably be making the beds, or perhaps sweeping the staircase with a dustpan and brush.

He pushed open the front door and walked in. The house was deadly quiet. The parlour door was shut.

He peeped into the kitchen. There was no one there,

and the horsehair sofa held neither Auntie Maria nor the rumpled pile of bedding which usually surrounded her. The sight of the exposed black oilcloth of the sofa made him turn white.

'Ma!' he shouted shrilly. 'Mam, I'm home!'

His mother came slowly down the stairs. Her hair was a wild tangle of copper, her face white and haggard, her big blue eyes suddenly sunken and bloodshot. She winced, as she slowly descended.

Manuel stared up at her, and then whispered, 'Where's everybody gone, Mam?'

Rosita reached the bottom of the stairs and sat down heavily on the second stair. She ignored Manuel's question, and pulled him to her. 'Did you have a good Bonfire Night, darling?' she inquired, with a forced smile.

His eyes wandered round the gloomy stairwell, as he answered absently, 'Yes.'

'Good. Had breakfast?'

His eyes came back to her face. 'Yes.'

'It's chilly this morning. You'd better put your woolly scarf on.'

She felt him tremble in her arms. 'Ma, where *is* Auntie Maria – and Grandma – and Frannie?'

'Well, Auntie Peggy O'Brien invited Frannie to play with her little Theresa, so Effie took her round the corner earlier on. And now Grandma and Effie –' She paused to sigh heavily. 'Well, they're in the parlour.'

Manuel glanced fearfully over his shoulder at the closed parlour door, and then looked back at his dishevelled mother. 'Is Auntie Maria there, as well?'

He had never seen his mother look so ill, and, as tears welled out of her bloodshot eyes, he was appalled.

'Mam,' he whispered. 'Oh, Mam!'

They had been speaking in Basque, and their close communion was made more intense by their own language.

'She's gone to Heaven, lovey.' Rosita wept uncontrollably into her son's serge jacket, the horrors of the night still too close.

Manuel was engulfed by such primeval fear as he was not to know again for many years; the understanding of the remorseless inevitability of death was lodged in his mind for ever. It appeared to him to be an awful monster waiting to gobble up anyone whom one loved. Creepy-crawlies seemed to be climbing up his back, and his hair rose, like Pudding's did when an alien cat intruded.

If Auntie Maria was lying dead in the parlour, how long would it be before his mother lay there – and Grandma? His mother looked as ill as Auntie Maria had done. If they both went, Frannie and he would be alone; in his consternation, he forgot his patient father, at that moment still chugging slowly across the Atlantic.

He clutched his mother tightly round her neck and felt her curls damp against his wrist.

Rosita raised her head and pushed her hair away from her eyes. 'I'm sorry, dearest. Auntie Maria was mother's big sister – and I'll miss her.' She again put her arms round her clinging son – she was so heavy with child that he could not sit on her lap, though he wanted to.

'I love you, Mam – and I love Auntie Maria,' he said softly.

She made a valiant effort to pull herself together, despite her enormous fatigue. She pushed him a little away from her, and said quite briskly, 'I love you, too – my big boy. Now, I don't want you to be too sad about Auntie Maria. You know she had a dreadful cough – and it hurt her a lot. Sometimes she would ask God to take her to Him, so that she wouldn't have any more pain.' She gave another shivering sigh. 'And now he's done it. And Father Felipe told her that everything would be all right – he was here last night – and he said that she was such a good woman that she would be happy with God.' She tried to smile. 'But we'll miss her, won't we?'

Her last words became part of an involuntary whimper, and she suddenly clutched Manuel very tightly.

'Mam! Are you hurting?'

His mother was biting her lower lip, as a long, slow roll of aching pain ran round her waist. Manuel was near to fainting with fright.

She saw his expression, and, as the pain softened, she laughed ruefully. 'It's nothing really, pet. But I wouldn't be surprised if you got a new brother or sister today. Now then, you're not to worry – it's perfectly normal. When you go out, just run back to Auntie Bridget, and ask her to step in. You may have to go to Mrs O'Brien's for your midday dinner – but don't worry.'

Reluctantly he let go of her and pulled his woolly scarf from the peg in the hall, and wound it round his neck. As he opened the front door, he looked back at her, and saw that she was rubbing her back and her eyes were closed, her jaw set grimly. He wondered how he was going to make himself walk to school.

His mother was silently saying a Hail Mary, as she rubbed her back, and worrying about how to pay Bridget for two calls in less than twenty-four hours. She didn't charge much, but, in addition, Rosita felt she should send a decently big casserole over to Peggy O'Brien in thanks for her help. Normally, she considered frantically, Micaela and she herself could have managed a birth together. But Micaela was weeping her heart out on her bed. And to send for the only alternatives, a professional midwife or the doctor, was too expensive to consider.

Whether she was paid or not, Bridget would come, she was sure; they had been friends for years. But Bridget had to augment Pat's wages somehow.

Rosita held her head in her hands, as she crouched on the stairs, and cried for Micaela, for Maria – and for herself. Then she suddenly lifted her head, arched her back and moaned. Effie heard her and came running down the stairs, and Rosita accepted her help to get up to her bedroom. She feared to ask Effie to help with the birth, in case the tiny woman lost her nerve in the middle of the delivery – and Effie probably did not know about how clean a midwife must keep her hands – childbed fever, Rosita knew from her reading, travelled from mother to mother via the midwife – and it was deadly.

Perplexed and frightened, Manuel nearly fell over Mary, as he took the two hollowed-out steps in one careless bound on his way to school after leaving his mother.

He paused in surprise, and said, 'I thought you'd gone with Joey.' She looked pinched and cold, though she had a tam o'shanter on her head and was encased in a shabby black coat too big for her.

She scuffed one small boot against the other, and said, 'Mam said to walk with yez.'

'I've got to ask her to go in to me mam for a minute.' He ran up Bridget's steps, pushed open the door, and shouted down the passage, 'Auntie Bridget, me mam wants you.'

Bridget Connolly had just gone upstairs to lie down for half an hour, before starting her housework. She swung her stockinged feet to the floor, and went to the top of the stairs, 'What's up, Mannie?'

'Mam says it's the baby.'

'Mother of God! At seven months?' Bridget muttered, and then shouted back, 'I'll be there in a minute or two. Now you get to school. Hurry – you're late.'

Little Maria, as she was called all her life, not only because she was small of stature but also to differentiate her from her Auntie Maria who was with God, was born that evening. Peggy O'Brien resignedly fed Mary, Joey and Manuel with thick slices of bread and margarine and bowls of vegetable soup at lunchtime, and more bread and margarine, with tea to drink, at teatime. She hoped that Bridget would share with her a bit of the fee she would get for the delivery; otherwise, so tight was her housekeeping, she would not be able to feed her own three children and hungry husband the following day. Yet, it never occurred to her not to help Rosita and Bridget; she knew they would be among the first to come to her when her next baby was on the way.

Late in the evening, when Peggy was beginning to feel harassed to death with so many children in her kitchen, and a very tired husband grumbling amid them, Pat Connolly came to take them home.

In answer to a question from Manuel, he told him that the baby had arrived safely; and, to the boy's relief, he was delivered to his own doorstep. He was met by a grave wraith of a grandma, who silently hugged both him and his sister tightly, before leading them upstairs to see their mother.

She was lying quietly in her own bed, looking very tired and white. Though her eyes had large black rings round them, he was thankful to see that she was not crying. A big woman in black was putting more coal on the bedroom fire. She half-turned to smile at the children. Francesca ignored her and toddled straight over to the bed. Manuel paused to stare back at her. He knew where she lived, but he did not know that she was a more experienced midwife, whom Bridget had sent for, because the baby had presented herself upside down.

As the boy moved towards Rosita, Francesca demanded to be lifted on to the bed. Laughing, Bridget laid her carefully beside her mother, where, from under the quilt, she eyed Manuel triumphantly at being allowed to be there, while he was not.

Though so young, Francesca had been acutely aware that something was terribly wrong in her small world, and she had objected strongly when she had been taken straight from her bed into Effie's room, to be hastily dressed and fed with bread and milk before being taken to Peggy's house. She had howled like a banshee as Effie pushed her doggedly in her pushchair, though she had recovered somewhat after she had been with Peggy to the corner shop to spend a halfpenny, provided by Effie, on an ounce of dolly mixtures. Now, with her mother's arm curved protectively around her, she felt safe once more.

To Manuel, the bedroom smelled peculiar – faintly like a meat stall in the market. As he bumped against the bed, his mother smiled sleepily at him, and asked if everything had gone well at school and whether Peggy had given Francesca and him some tea.

'Yes,' he replied, and she stroked his head and smiled again. Then she said, 'Go and look in the drawer over there. You and Frannie have a baby sister.'

Obediently, he went towards the fire, which the midwife was now poking into a blaze. In front of it, set on two straight chairs was a drawer taken from the big dresser in the upper hallway. Exactly like Grandpa's coffin, he thought with a burst of fear. In the drawer, however, was a bundle no bigger than Mary Connolly's doll. A shawl that Auntie Maria had crocheted was wrapped round it, so that only a wizened red face was visible. A tiny tongue licked perfectly formed lips, and the closed eyelids looked like the small pink shells he had once picked up on New Brighton beach.

He turned to Rosita. 'What's its name?'

It was Grandma who interjected immediately: 'Maria, of course, after your auntie.' Her shrivelled brown hands were clenched in front of her, and Manuel sensed, nervously, how distressed she was beneath her calm exterior.

'Of course,' agreed Rosita immediately. 'Little Maria. Now you go downstairs with your granny, and then you must go to bed.'

He was astonished when his grandmother picked him

up, to hold him to her and to give him an unexpected kiss. Micaela had, for some time, been telling him that he was too big a lad to be picked up or sat on her knee. Her red-rimmed eyes suddenly twinkled close to his. 'Now you've got another person to add to your prayers,' she said, as she put him down. 'You run downstairs, while I put Frannie into her own bed. I'll be down in a moment.'

Because the damp winds of winter were making the old house cold, Grandma collected his nightshirt from Auntie Maria's bedroom. She brought it downstairs to the kitchen-living-room and put it on the oven door to warm, together with the kitchen towel. Then she brought the enamel basin from the sink and filled it with warm water from the oven tap. She set the bowl on a wooden chair beside the fire. In the warm glow, he stripped and washed himself, while she made cups of cocoa for both of them. Afterwards, they sat knee to knee, he with her shawl over his shoulders to keep him warm, while they drank their cocoa together.

Looking back, Old Manuel, snug in his Victoria bungalow which boasted a fine warm bathroom, as well as a cloak-room, could not imagine sitting in its glossy pinkness to drink cocoa, in close communion with a loving grand-mother, his cotton nightshirt so hot on his back that he could hardly bear the first touch of it. He had never seen Lorilyn being bathed when she was a child – or Faith, for that matter. Perhaps it was because he had been away so much – or, perhaps, an innate prissiness of Kathleen's.

Vaguely puzzled, he returned to his notes.

Without Auntie Maria presiding from the sofa, the kitchen-living-room seemed empty, though his grandmother was being wonderfully comforting. He wondered if she missed Auntie Maria as he was doing; yet, she was still in the house – in the parlour – and Grandma was, he realized with relief, still strong and well, even if she did have to feel her way round the house.

What a frightful twenty-four hours it must have been for the women concerned, mused Old Manuel, feeling very tired himself. A painful death with a subsequent laying-out with all its grief, to be followed almost immediately by a premature birth.

His grandmother must have summoned all her courage to make that evening seem cosy and normal to him; inside, she must have been storming with grief at the loss of her elder daughter. She had heard his prayers there, by the fire, ordering him to include Auntie Maria, as well as Little Maria. As if I would forget Auntie Maria, the little boy had thought indignantly, as he got up off his knees.

Because she had a chronic disease, Burial Insurance for Maria was unobtainable, so she had a pauper's funeral. No men followed the coffin, except for Father Felipe and the undertaker and his employees. It was a sombre, black-clad procession of women, carrying small bunches of flowers, who piled into the tram that would take them to the cemetery. Only Grandma, Rosita, with Little Maria in her arms, Manuel, Francesca and Father Felipe rode in a carriage kindly provided free by Ould Biggs. It was a bitter, frosty day and all the mourners were thankful when it was over, and they could crowd into the Barinèta home for tea and cakes and a good warm.

Unlike Francesca, who had been a placid, contented baby, Little Maria filled the house with steady yelling for some months after she was born. Even a neglected Manuel was sometimes pressed into service to sit in a chair and rock her. All the women visitors, who came in to admire her, laughed knowingly and said she was colicky, whatever that was, and that she would grow out of it. Manuel wished intensely that she would simply shut up. He would wake in the night to hear her screaming; and his mother looked daily more tired and sounded ever more irritable with young boys.

Chapter Twenty-three

The frazzled mood of the family was lifted somewhat by an unexpected visit from Uncle Agustin. His ship had docked in Birkenhead, across the River Mersey, and he had begged shore leave to see his family, because of the loss of his father and sister.

When Manuel came home from school and found his uncle sitting at the kitchen table, he had not, at first, recognized him; Agustin had been at sea during their last visit to Bilbao, and he had not docked in Liverpool for some time before that. Then, when the thin, saturnine man had greeted him by name and grinned at him, the boy said delightedly, 'Uncle Agustin!' His relief at having a male relative sitting in his home was so great that he laughed aloud.

Though Agustin had not lived with his parents for years, he had felt keenly the loss of his father and his sister, and when he entered Rosita's house, he was very downcast. His arrival caused a fresh burst of grief to well up in his mother and Rosita, which he tried hard to alleviate by delivering affectionate messages to them both, from aunts and uncles, cousins and friends, of whom Manuel had little recollection. He told them, also, that he had just married his sweetheart – very quietly because of Juan's death. The news about Maria had reached them two days later.

He spoke in Basque, and Manuel immediately felt a close fellowship with him and with his relations in Vizcaya.

After Agustin had returned to his ship, Grandma sat wrapped in thought for some time. Manuel had heard her beg Agustin to write to her from time to time, and he had said he would.

'But he never will,' Grandma said later to Rosita. 'He never was any good at learning his letters.' Then, perhaps feeling that she was being unfair to her eldest child, she added, 'But your father always said he was a born seaman.'

As Agustin left the house, he dropped some silver coins into his mother's apron pocket. It was the first money that she had received, which she felt she could call her own, since the Prudential man had brought her husband's burial money. She knew Agustin could not spare it; but she carried it for several days, jingling it comfortably in her pocket, until Rosita suggested that she buy a new, much-needed pair of winter boots with it. After some persuasion, she did this, and Manuel remembered her smiling down at their shiny, laced-up newness.

Rosita wrote to both Leo and Pedro about Maria's death and the premature birth of the new baby. Without much hope, she addressed Leo's letter to Nevada, but again there was no response. Her letter to Pedro, however, did catch up with him, and some weeks later both Micaela and Rosita received kindly letters of real sympathy. He also said how he himself would miss Maria, who had, he wrote, always been so easy to talk to – and to please. He was glad the new baby had been called after her. Although Rosita had not told him how difficult the birth had been and how weak she still felt, he must have sensed something was wrong, because he inquired anxiously after her own health, which he rarely did.

By late January 1915 Little Maria's shrieks had been reduced to occasional spasms, and her mother began to think that, after all, she would not go out of her mind for lack of sleep.

'There's nothin' more exhausting than a colicky baby,'

agreed Micaela. 'Now she's napping a bit in the afternoon, you must rest, too.'

So Rosita retired to bed for an hour with a battered novel from the second-hand shop whenever Little Maria closed her eyes in the afternoon. As her mother said, 'The front steps won't hurt, if you scrub them only every other day, instead of every day.'

In the middle of a blizzard carrying heavy sleet, Pedro thankfully docked in Liverpool, to unload a cargo of raw cotton. Though they had not been attacked by German submarines, the whole crew had once again been drained by the tension of crossing the Atlantic in a slow tramp, unable to keep up with a convoy. The men were irritable and on edge, longing to get ashore as soon as they could: to get thoroughly warm in dry clothes, and eat a well-cooked meal.

Rosita met him with her usual hugs, and yet there was a restraint about her. She was not her former bubbling self.

He dropped his suitcase and kitbag in the narrow hall, and held her pallid face between his wind-chapped hands. His own weariness was forgotten. A spasm of fear hit him. In nursing Maria, had she caught the same dread disease?

She smiled weakly at him.

'You look ill,' he said gently. 'Are you OK?'

She sighed, and enclosed one of his hands against her cheek. 'I'm not sick,' she assured him. 'I'm tired, that's all, what with Maria being so ill, and Little Maria screaming her head off, night and day.'

He dropped his hands from her face and put one round her waist, as they went into the back room, where Micaela had discreetly waited, sitting in her rocker, to give the young couple a chance to greet each other.

Pedro went straight to his mother-in-law, and put his arms round her as if she were his own mother. 'I'm so sorry about Maria, Mother,' he said. He was shaken to see how Micaela had, in a few short months, aged so much; and he realized from the slightly fumbling way in which she sought to clasp his hand that her sight was nearly gone.

Both the women were quick enough, however, to prepare a fish meal for him, which, with the bottle of wine he had brought in his suitcase, cheered them all up considerably.

When Manuel came home from school, he was ecstatic to see his father. Pedro had Francesca on his knee, and the boy stood in front of him, grinning from ear to ear, scrubbing one boot against the back of the other. He longed to dislodge his sister but had learned from experience not to try to – if she were thwarted, she had a scream which would outdo Little Maria's best efforts.

Pedro laughed and caught the boy in his free arm, and Rosita said suddenly, 'You're the spitting image of each other, except for Manuel's dark hair.'

It was true, considered Pedro. As the boy lost his baby nose, he was acquiring a slightly flattened one with wide nostrils, exactly like his own, and the child's face was already longer and narrower, with flatter cheekbones than most children round the neighbourhood. He *looked* Basque, and Pedro swelled with pride in him.

Once Little Maria had been persuaded to go to sleep in her cot in the corner of their bedroom, and Micaela had retired to her own room, Pedro lay naked beside his wife, and grinned wickedly at her. Her hair on the pillow was a flaming background to her pale face. The blue eyes were shadowed, however, as if she did not want to look at him. He began to caress her and tried to kiss her mouth, but she turned her face away.

'What's up?' he asked surlily. She had never behaved like this before. Then, in the candlelight, he saw tears glisten on her long golden lashes. 'Is something wrong, love?'

She opened her eyes and really looked at him. She said

hoarsely, as if forcing herself, 'I'm scared. I don't want another kid.'

He stared at her bewilderedly, and she hastened to say, 'I love you. I want to make love. But I'm afraid of what happened with Little Maria happening again – and killing me. You'd never believe the pain I had.'

He stirred uncomfortably, some of the desire going out of him, with the unexpected disappointment. Then he shrugged. 'Kids come from God,' he said.

There was a sudden twinkle in her fine eyes, as her sense of humour began to surface. 'They come from men, you old rogue.'

He nodded. 'I suppose.'

She turned towards him, and her long generous curves so close to him roused him again. He wanted to take her by the shoulders and shake some sense into her; he was her husband, wasn't he? He wanted what was his God-given right. But she was speaking again. 'I'm tired to death, what with being so torn with the baby, and nursing Maria – and no sleep – and Mother not able to help so much now. And then Mannie and Frannie. I couldn't face another baby.'

He kept a hold on himself, torn between his own needs and her obvious distress. He closed his eyes, while she spoke again.

'I want to ask you something. You know Mary Challoner – lives in Park Lane – she's a Prottie, but she's a decent woman for all that. She was sitting next to me the last time I took Maria to the doctor. She thought she was pregnant, she told me. Then she said, "But I've had a good run for my money – four years since the last one."'

It took all his patience to make himself listen, but he did.

'When Maria had gone into the surgery,' Rosita continued, 'and there was no one else in the waiting room, I asked her what she meant – and she said her hubbie did his best to see she wasn't left with a kid.

'He covers his you-know-what with a rubber cover – buys 'em in London and in France, when he goes there. She says they still have a good time – but no baby.' She propped herself up on her elbow, and added earnestly, 'It's not like aborting a kid – I know women who'll do that for me – but it's terribly dangerous – and it's wrong.'

Her husband responded bitterly, 'Priests think any kind of birth control is wrong. Fat lot of practice they get – they'd change their minds if they had a horde of kids – I know what you're getting at.'

'Couldn't we do like Mary's hubbie?' Her eyes were imploring now. She badly wanted to please Pedro, to enjoy herself.

He whistled to himself, and the candle danced in the small movement of the air, as he silently considered wife versus church. What did he really believe himself, amid the welter of teachings handed down by a celibate church hierarchy? He knew he had never, until this moment, questioned their teachings. But one thing he knew from the society around him – it was deadly easy to lose a wife in childbirth. He would, he knew, sell his immortal soul rather than lose his lovely wife, if it could be avoided.

He nodded, and ran his hand down her thigh. 'I'll go shopping,' he promised. 'But not a word to anyone, remember. Promise?'

She smiled her old, seductive smile. 'I promise,' she said. Then, after a moment's hesitation, she asked, 'What do we do now?'

'Don't worry,' he said, as he pulled her close. 'I won't go in. And I'll try to make it good for you.'

Before he sailed again, there was a lot of earnest conversation between him and his wife and mother about giving Manuel a better education. They spoke volubly in Basque.

'Jean Baptiste wanted his youngest to go to St Francis Xavier's, but he had a good spell unemployed, and they couldn't do it. Manuel could be a doctor or a solicitor, if he went on into university,' Rosita told him.

'University?' Pedro looked at her incredulously. 'A kid from Wapping Dock?' He had had in mind keeping the child in school until he was sixteen.

'Why not?' demanded Rosita. 'By the time he gets his Matric, there might be some way he could get there. Madeleine says there are a few scholarships, even now.'

Pedro was not too sure what a Matric was. While he considered this lofty ambition, he sipped his mug of tea. If you went to university, he knew you could become a doctor or a lawyer and have a good house in West Derby. It seemed like a pipe dream to him. His own father had scraped money to keep him in school until he was fourteen, and had helped him to take time out from going to sea while he studied until he had got his Master's Certificate; and it had made a world of difference to his life.

But an economic downturn meant he could be out of work very easily – any seaman would tell you that – and, since his father-in-law's death, Pedro had done what he could to quietly put away a little in his own private Post Office savings book, to help tide him over such bad times.

'He could go into the Navy – that's regular. Twenty-one years, you can do.'

'Humph,' responded Rosita doubtfully. 'If ever he's going to be an officer, he must go to grammar school, and he must learn to speak good English. Tell me, where will he learn to do that except in a better school?'

Pedro was not sure that he wanted a son who was an officer and spoke like one. Wasn't his own English good enough?

'We speak English,' he said defensively. 'And the lad was born in Liverpool – not like me – so he's eligible to serve in the Navy. He could work his way up a bit – they'd train him.'

She replied stubbornly, 'He's got to speak English – like Father Felipe talks.'

'That bloody Spaniard?'

'Tush!' interjected Micaela. 'How can you speak like that? He's a priest!'

After the last few nights with his wife, Pedro was feeling resentful of the Church and all its works, and Father Felipe's exquisite, carefully learned English seemed patronizing to him; even his poor attempts at Basque were annoying, as if he were trying to descend from his lofty position as a Castilian to hob-nob with nobodies. What did a priest know about real life? Pedro wondered, with all the antagonism of a Basque for a Spaniard.

Poor, overextended Father Felipe would have been sorely hurt, if he had been aware of his parishioner's lack of esteem. He would, however, have earnestly encouraged young Manuel's further education. He had already suggested to Micaela that the boy should be given to the Church; and Micaela knew that a child in the Church brought his family instant prestige.

Micaela now spoke up. 'He's the eldest boy – the only boy, up to now. We should try our best for him.'

Manuel, sitting at the table carefully boring holes in the last of his conkers, preparatory to drying them out on top of the oven, was dreaming of being able to smash Andrew Pilar's best one, and only half took in the conversation of his elders. He assumed that if he were sent to St Francis Xavier's, all the other children he knew, like Joey and Brian, would be going, too.

His elders decided that if they all practised the most rigorous economy, they would manage to send him.

'As well as fees, there'll be tram fares – and uniform,' Rosita fretted, suddenly afraid that she was being too ambitious.

Micaela looked up from her knitting. 'We'll manage,' she assured her daughter serenely. She already saw a purple biretta covering her grandson's tousled dark hair. God would provide, she was sure.

Chapter Twenty-four

In 1916, when, at the age of eight, Manuel entered St Francis Xavier School, he felt very lonely; Joey and Brian showed no signs of being able to follow him. On his first day he feared that he might be the only Basque boy attending because he was the only one in his class. He soon discovered that there was a sprinkling of them in the upper classes, though they were drawn from all over the city. They ignored him because they did not know that he was a Basque – he was just another new pupil, younger than they were.

Occasionally he heard them speaking to each other in Basque, frequently making derogatory remarks about English boys who had been too rough with them, because they were slightly sallower in complexion than British boys.

Real fights were rare in the school yard, but one day proud Manuel was called a dago by a nine-year-old Scot. Furious, Manuel struck out with all his force at the scornful, freckled red face of the bigger lad. He became immediately embroiled in a fight with a known bully that he could not win. The other boys formed a circle to egg on the Scot. With his nose already bleeding, it was clear to anyone passing that, despite his best efforts, Manuel was getting the worst of the encounter.

Held down on the asphalt playground, Manuel took a punch in the eye which made him cry out.

His cry was followed by a sharp yelp from his antagonist, who received a quick series of kicks in his ribs from a tall, thin youth standing over the pair of them.

The newcomer scowled at the ring of boys. Then he bent down, got a good grip on the back of the braces of the enraged Scot and hauled him off Manuel. He shook the boy, as he hissed into his badly scratched face, 'Pick on someone of your own size, you little twerp!' He shoved the boy away into the crowd.

Lying on the asphalt, trying to get his breath, a surprised Manuel viewed his rescuer through his unhurt eye. He was even more surprised when the boy said curtly in Basque, 'Get up.'

The back of Manuel's head was throbbing badly where he had hit it when falling backwards. His nose was still dripping and his eye seemed to be swelling. He staggered slowly to his feet, while his rescuer snarled at the retreating boys, 'Get going you stinking pack of cowards, before I tell on you.' They reluctantly dispersed, taking the young Scot with them, muttering to each other as they went.

The Basque boy was several inches taller than Manuel, blond, blue-eyed and pallid-skinned. He looked Manuel up and down, and said again in Basque, 'Gosh, you do look a mess. Better get cleaned up before a teacher sees you.' He picked up a blazer lying on the ground. 'Is this yours?'

Manuel nodded dumbly, as he steadied himself on his feet. He felt his nose running and wiped it along his shirt sleeve. He was shaken to see a long streak of blood on the white cotton. His mouth began to tremble, and he had a strong desire to cry.

'We'll go to the cloakroom,' said the older boy more kindly. 'And get you cleaned up. You should have more sense to keep out of fights you can't win — he's much heavier than you.'

Manuel humbly agreed. Then, as they trailed round the edge of the playground, so as not to disturb the various games of football being played with tennis balls, Manuel said furiously, 'He called me a dago!'

Pale-blue eyes were turned reflectively upon him, to examine a face which already showed something of the long flat planes of cheek and jaw, an upward curving mouth with full lower lip, which would be his as a man. 'Well, you're dark, but you don't look like a Spaniard,' the older boy said at length. 'Did you tell him you were Basque?'

'Na. He probably wouldn't know what a Basque is,' responded Manuel scornfully. The blood was beginning to coagulate in his nose, and he badly wanted to blow it. The eye still stung painfully.

The other boy was grinning. He said, 'Dad says nobody really knows who we are or where we came from.'

They reached the cloakroom with its scuffed floor and long lines of black, iron clothes hooks. A tiny washbasin, cracked and grubby, was affixed to the far wall, and next to it hung a roller towel.

Manuel managed to pull the roller towel far enough to damp it under the solitary tap and then wipe his face with it. Streaks of blood were left on the towel. He damped it again and pressed it against the hurt eye. His nose still oozed slightly so he wiped it again.

'Don't touch it any more,' advised the strange boy. 'It'll dry up in a minute. Wash the muck off your hands and put on your blazer.'

Manuel obediently soaped his hands and left a fair amount of greyish foam on the soap tablet and in the sink.

'You'll pass now. There goes the bell. You'd better hurry!'

Manuel gulped. He did not want to return to his classroom, but he knew he must. 'Thanks,' he said heavily. 'Thanks for hauling Stewart off me.'

'It's nothing,' the boy replied, and turned to wander off to his own classroom, as if to belie his own instruction to hurry. When he had gone, Manuel gave his nose a further good wipe on the towel, put on his blazer and fled before he could be chastised for the mess he had made. He slid quickly into his desk, and was, for once, thankful for the fat boy who sat in front of him and partially masked him from the teacher's icy stare.

After his mother had washed his face for him and bathed the black eye, clucking her tongue at the damage, and he had had his tea, his grandmother was surprised at the question suddenly fired at her. 'Granny, what *is* a Basque?'

Before answering him, she knitted the two stitches remaining on her left-hand needle. Then she replied with puzzlement, 'Well, *we* are Basques, dumpling.' Although she could barely see him, she sensed that the answer had not sufficed, that he was still in some kind of quandary, so she added, 'From Bilbao.'

'I know that. But a boy at school – a Basque – said that nobody really knows what a Basque is.'

Micaela rested her knitting in her lap, while she considered this assertion. Then she said, 'People have always moved about in the world, so they say that they come from the place their parents settled in. After a while, they become part of that place and its history. Your great-grandfather told me, though, that Basques had *always* lived in the Pyrenees and had married each other – for thousands and thousands of years, long before people wrote down their history. And nobody was able to shift us from the mountains – not Arabs, not French, not Romans nor Spaniards. We've been there since time began, so that even the stories of our beginnings have been lost.' She was suddenly interested about the boy he had mentioned, and inquired, 'He was a real Basque?'

'Yes – not from round here, though.' Manuel had been leaning against the side of her chair, and now he made to get on her lap. She quickly swept her four sharp needles and ball of grey wool on to the floor. The chair wobbled furiously as Manuel settled himself comfortably in the curve of her arm, and she laughed. 'It's a long time since you've done that,' she told him. 'You're too big to be nursed. What was the boy's name?'

He grinned up at her and laid his head on her shoulder. 'I don't know,' he replied. Though he was proud to go to St Francis Xavier's, he had felt very lonely today, with no Joey or Brian to help him in a fight. He needed the comforting warmth of Grandma, who always had time for him. She was always there and always would be. Or would she?

Micaela felt a faint shudder go through the child's thin body. 'What is it, dumpling?' she asked as she carefully stroked his hair back from the black eye.

Manuel hesitated, and then answered, 'I was thinking of Auntie Maria.'

His grandmother sighed. 'Yes, dear?'

'I miss her — and Grandpa.'

'We all do, dear.' Micaela hugged him closer, as the fearsome pain of loss went through her once more. They sat in silent communion together, the chair rocking slightly under them.

There was the patter of his mother's carpet slippers, as she came downstairs. She called back up to Mrs Halloran, 'Don't let the girls bother you — send them down if you're tired of them.' As she hurried into the living-room-kitchen, she said in a quieter tone to Micaela, 'I don't want them to spend too much time with Effie — the girls'll learn bad manners.'

'Tut! Effie was a parlourmaid once — she knows her manners,' Micaela immediately admonished.

Rosita shrugged, and then began to discuss the strange Basque boy.

She leaned against the sink and folded her arms, which were aching from hours of washing clothes and bedding on a scrubbing board. 'There are a few other Basques scattered round the town — you do hear about them occasionally. Mostly, they've been here a long, long time.'

'I was glad he came along,' Manuel said with feeling; his eye was aching badly.

His mother nodded. 'You know, dear, you must learn not to get into fights.'

Manuel sat up straight in Micaela's lap, and the rocking chair rocked rather violently. 'Stewart called me a dago,' he said indignantly.

Rosita sighed. 'When you're foreign, you have to ignore petty insults, my pet.'

'I'm not foreign. I live here.'

'Yes, dear. But you're Basque, same as Brian is Chinese and Joey's Irish.'

'Are we all foreign?'

'Down here, we are.'

Manuel slumped back into his grandmother's arms and gave up.

Chapter Twenty-five

About a week later, they met at the tram stop, two nonde-
script schoolboys in grey woollen shorts, their bare knees
chapped by cold, damp winds. They both wore navy-blue
gabardine macintoshes, and caps with the St Francis Xavier
badge on them. Each carried on his back a satchel of books
required for that evening's homework. Neither boy looked
particularly healthy, their complexions pale and eyes
ringed.

Manuel ventured a shy grin, and the older boy nodded
lordly acknowledgement of it.

A horsedrawn delivery van splashed through the puddles
in the gutter. They both stepped back to avoid their shoes
and socks being soaked, and the bigger boy asked, 'What's
your name?'

'Manuel Echaniz. What's yours?'

'Arnador – Arnador Ganivet. Where do you live?'

Manuel told him, and Arnador looked at him speculat-
ively. Wapping Dock was where a lot of first-generation
Basques lived. According to his father, they were poor and
illiterate seamen working for de Larrinaga. It definitely was
not what his mother would call a good address. *His* parents
and his grandparents had all been born in Liverpool; they
did not mix with common seamen's families, though they
were quite proud of their Basque origins. He wondered, if
he brought a Basque boy home, which attitude would
weigh heaviest with them, that he could speak good Basque
or that he was lower class.

He decided that he did not care; he admired Manuel for
having taken a bad licking from a bully while defending

his Basqueness. He grinned at Manuel, and asked, 'How does your eye feel?'

Manuel grinned back. 'It feels OK. It's a bit yellow still. Where do you live – which tram do you take?'

'I usually bike to school, but I couldn't today – I've got a couple of broken spokes – my uncle's going to put new ones in tonight. Anyway, I'm going across the water – I'm going out to tea with my cousin.' He frowned, and added, 'She's a girl. Awful bore.'

As a cumbersome tram rolled down towards them, sparks flying from its pole when it touched a crossline, they stepped out into the street to get on it, and he added, 'I live in Catherine Street. We've a flat – two floors.' They swung up the winding stairs to the upper deck, and sat down together on a wooden, slatted seat at the front. As they took off their satchels and laid them at their feet, he went on, 'A dentist has the ground floor. It's handy for Dad – he's a ship chandler, down on Chaloner Street. He likes to walk down the hill to work every day.'

Manuel was impressed; he had never before heard of a Basque who owned his own business – he discounted the Basque shipowners in the city – to him, they were as far removed from normal life as earls or lords were. In his own small, sea-going world, everyone worked for somebody else.

'Have you got any brothers or sisters?' Manuel asked.

'One sister – Josefa. She's a nurse at the Ear, Eye and Throat on Myrtle Street – she walks to work as well. She's nearly nineteen. Have you got any?'

'Two little sisters.'

'What does your dad do?'

'He goes to sea.'

They spent the rest of the journey down to the Pier Head exploring their interests in cricket and who they liked and disliked amongst the teaching staff at school.

As they descended from the tram, Arnador to catch the

ferry across the river, Manuel to cross the roads back to the Goree Piazzas and Strand Street to walk along to Wapping, they called cheerfully to each other, ''Bye. See you tomorrow.'

He was exhilarated by the new contact, and his mother was pleased when he told her about it; a slightly older Basque friend might smooth the path through school for Manuel.

A week, two games of football in the school yard, and a number of amiable conversations later, Arnador invited his new friend to Saturday tea.

Rosita was delighted. Scrubbed until his skin was red, and dressed in his Sunday shorts and best jersey, he walked up the hill to Catherine Street and nervously pressed the lower bell of two big brass ones by the Ganivets' white enamelled front door.

He was received with mild approval by Mrs Ganivet, and, later on, by portly, bald Mr Ganivet, whose late arrival upon the scene was explained in English by his wife, who said, 'He were doin' his books in the front room. Always goes over his books of a Saturday, don't you?'

Mr Ganivet gave a dignified nod.

'Now, as you're here, luv, we might as well have tea. It's ready.'

Indeed, it was. While he played a game of lotto with Arnador on the gaily patterned hearth rug, he had surreptitiously watched a young maidservant lay the table and then bring out plate after plate of food. He had already formed the mistaken opinion that the Ganivets must be very rich, much richer than even the Saituas, who now had three men in the family, all working; and, when he saw the groaning table, he was certain of it. There was sliced ham with sliced tomatoes, bread and butter, scones accompanied by a huge glass dish of jam, and a big fruit cake on a fancy glass stand. There was a large silver cruet stand, in which were set a pot of mustard, a bottle of vinegar and dishes of salt and pepper with a tiny spoon in each. There were table napkins rolled into confining silver rings, and a mystifying array of knives and forks, plates and glasses in front of each chair. Finally, the maid staggered in with a tray resplendent with two linen-covered teacosies, which Manuel presumed was the tea arriving.

Despite Manuel's feeling rather overwhelmed, Mr and Mrs Ganivet were very kind to him; it was the beginning of a lifelong friendship between the two boys. At school, Arnador, one year older than Manuel, was the closest Basque in age to him. Living in the upper half of a Victorian house in Catherine Street, where there were few other children, the older boy had been extremely lonely. He was a deeply intelligent child and a born leader; he found great solace in Manuel's increasing admiration of him.

Like a Highland Scot, Manuel had imbibed from his father and grandfather a natural grace of manner and a certain pride in being what he was. To Mr and Mrs Ganivet, stout in figure and their belief that being a Basque was a gift from God, Arnador's new friend was welcome.

'His granddad was the Basque emigrant agent for years, he says,' Mrs Ganivet whispered to her spouse, 'and his dad's got his Master's. And his Basque is better than Arnador's; Arnie'll learn from him – it would be awful if he lost the language.'

An expression of irritation passed over Mr Ganivet's round, pink face. His daughter, Josefa, refused to speak her mother tongue, and she insisted upon being called Josie by her English friends. She had said tartly to her parents that she was a third-generation Liverpudlian – she had never been to Vizcaya – so why couldn't she be like other people?

Mrs Ganivet had earnestly hoped that her daughter would meet some nice Basque boy and would give up her nursing, to settle down and breed some more little Basques.

It appeared, however, that strong-minded Josefa would end up as a formidable nursing sister, a spinster like her heroine, Florence Nightingale. Her mother had been appalled when, at home, Josefa had dared to criticize the work of some of the doctors at the hospital, and said that if she were a doctor she would do things very differently. It was wicked, stormed Mrs Ganivet, like criticizing the Pope; a woman's place was to serve, not pick holes in physicians' diagnoses or want to be a doctor herself.

Manuel was an answer to her prayers that Arnador might grow up to be proud of his linguistic group, and marry his cousin from Wallasey, who spoke perfect Basque.

Not for nothing were Arnador and Manuel descendants of mountain people and of whalers and other seamen; they were born explorers. They ranged around Liverpool as far as they could walk; they had so little pocket money that neither would waste a penny on an unnecessary tram fare. Once or twice, Arnador and he cycled out of the south end of the city, Manuel sitting uncomfortably on the luggage carrier of Arnador's bicycle. When he heard about it, Mr Ganivet put a stop to it – it was dangerous, he said.

'He's more afraid that I'll park it somewhere, and wander off and it'll be stolen,' confided Arnador, with a wry grin.

'But you've got a chain and lock – you lock it at school.'

'It's fairly safe at school, after they've locked the front gates. Anywhere else, someone with a pair of tin snips or a wire cutter could snap the chain.' He laughed, and added, 'Or pick the lock in seconds.'

Arnador was not at all put off by the humbleness of Manuel's home. He fell hopelessly in love with Rosita, and was delighted to eat with the family. He tolerated the two little girls, and was quite willing to put together a street cricket team with Joey and Brian, using beer bottles as wickets. He had a happy knack of adapting himself to his surroundings; when they were grown men, he once said to Manuel that he learned as much about how people functioned, while sloping round Wapping Dock and up through the tough north end of the city, as he ever did in university.

While men died in scores in French battlefields, the boys swam naked in Wapping Dock, until chased out by the watchman, and on wet days lounged through bicycle shops and Lewis's Department Store, until they were shown the door by the shopkeeper – or, in the case of the larger shops, by the shop-walker. They warmed themselves by the coke fires of nightwatchmen on construction sites, and Arnador would get into conversation with the garrulous old men who took these cold, thankless jobs. They heard wild tales from them of the days of sail or of being navvies building railways or canals, of being gloriously drunk on paydays and very hungry the day before.

Arnador taught Manuel how to avoid direct confrontations with other youngsters, how to make friendly jokes to avoid unnecessary scrapping. As they wandered into unknown territory, he also warned him against men who hung around public lavatories, or in the narrow back alleys. He was surprised that Manuel was well aware of child prostitution and the sickening diseases, deadly at that time, that he could pick up, if he allowed himself to be touched by an older man.

'Auntie Bridget told Joey and me to watch out for ourselves – and the locals to stay clear of. If you want to know anything, you can always ask Auntie Bridget, and she'll tell you flat – she doesn't hide things like some grown-ups do. She told me how babies come.'

'How do they?' asked Arnador. 'I've never been sure.'

Manuel was surprised to find there was something he knew that Arnador did not; and he gave him a short lecture on human mating and reproduction that did real credit to

Auntie Bridget's clear teachings. 'She says that to father a baby outside marriage is mortal sin.'

Arnador was impressed. Unlike Francesca and Little Maria, Josefa was much older than him, so he had not had the advantage of seeing a girl naked in her tin bath. He had observed from paintings of nudes in the Art Gallery that women apparently did not have penises; but Manuel had confirmed that what some of the boys said at school was true – they really did not.

When Manuel forgot to draw his bedroom curtains one night and the light of his candle shone out across the yard, he got a different kind of lecture from his mother. She told him crossly, 'I've told you before about the Zeppelins, for Heaven's sake. Remember to draw the curtains before you light your candle. They're waiting up there to see a light. A single one could bring bombs straight down on us. And that would be goodbye to all of us.'

Suddenly afraid, Manuel dutifully blew out his candle and then drew the curtains. He had heard of the Germans' cigar-shaped airships that could float silently over a city and bomb it. His mother had mentioned them before. But he had recently seen a picture of one in Pat Connolly's newspaper, which proved to him that they did indeed exist – he had rather suspected before that they were figments of his mother's imagination, like Jack the Giant Killer and a number of other story-book characters. The war seemed suddenly to close in on him from a direction other than the sea.

Though no adult ever discussed the matter with either lad, they knew about the terrible losses of ships and men at sea. Wherever women congregated, in tiny corner shops, outside the church after Mass, in little groups gossiping in the streets or back kitchens, women talked in quavering voices of dead husbands, sons or sweethearts; of allotments cancelled because ships simply and inexplicably went missing; of children going hungry. They wept into their aprons or on the shawl-draped shoulders of other women, ignoring the children who stood uneasily round them or played at their feet.

Many of the women in the dock area normally wore black. To a casual observer, their state of mourning did not stand out so much as it did amongst the upper classes, whom the boys passed in the centre of the city and around Arnador's home. In fashionable shops in Church Street, Bold Street and Lord Street, however, young girls worked long hours stitching black mourning dresses and mantles. Another group trimmed black hats and, for older women, black bonnets, both with long veils to cover the faces of the bereaved. It was to become a thriving industry before the war ended.

When the headmaster rose, one morning, to report, not without pride, that most of the boys who had left the school in 1915 had given their lives for their country, the war began to breathe down the backs of the necks of the younger pupils. Though they listened quietly to the rhetoric about the nobility of giving one's life for one's country and never doubted whether it was necessary or not, the fear of death was there. In the school playground, boys boasted about which regiment they would join, as soon as they were old enough, and what they would do to the bloody Boche as soon as they could get to France. But Arnador said nothing, as his quiet orderly mind examined the whole idea of war. Manuel said flatly he would be going to sea, and felt sick at the reminder that his father was actually out there, facing submarines and battleships alike.

Chapter Twenty-six

Every time his father docked during the First World War Manuel's tight-clenched stomach would relax, and he looked forward to their doing things together. As he grew bigger, he understood clearly that it was Pedro who maintained the household. His mother worked very hard; when she was not scrubbing floors, she was cooking, washing or driving bargains in the market. In her spare time, she knitted and mended, as she gossiped to neighbours, who wandered freely in and out of the house.

But women had only the money their husbands or fathers gave them. And without money everything collapsed. Manuel looked forward to when he could go to sea, and, when he returned, drop money and chocolates into his mother's lap. He ignored his grandma's hints about the Church and university; having to go to school until one was sixteen was a long enough stretch.

Arnador did not agree with Manuel about his future; he had his own eyes fixed on university, though he was unclear what he would study.

On his return, Pedro was invariably greeted with almost hysterical relief by Rosita and Micaela. Not for them were the grumbles of other local women about the meanness of their menfolk, or the groans at the likelihood of another pregnancy. There was an abiding love and general agreement between Rosita and Pedro, and quiet, patient Micaela had a place both in their hearts and in the home.

Manuel had little idea how lucky he was to have such a peaceful home; he took it for granted. If, when visiting his young friends, he stumbled upon a family row with dishes flying, or a wife or son being beaten, he was always alarmed and nonplussed. Rosita might shout at him for entering the house with dirty boots or slap her little daughters for being rude, but it had nothing of the ferocity he observed elsewhere.

Street fights were rare in his small corner of the dockside. Arnador said, however, that they were common in the north end of the city, particularly when the pubs closed on Saturday night. 'Sometimes the police get beaten up,' he told Manuel.

By silent consent they kept out of that area. Arnador was careful, and had a disarming way of dealing with people, considered Old Manuel, with some amusement. He could not recall his ever getting into a physical fight, though he could be a formidable debater, the old fox.

While Pedro was at home, Rosita's face would look a little less drawn, and Micaela would lose some of the gravity which had become habitual to her. The house would be cheered up by the friendly rumbling of Basque voices, as friends of Pedro's dropped in to see him, on their way to the Baltic Fleet.

Like most seamen during the war, Pedro had an uneasy feeling that his time might be short. Whenever he was at home, he made a habit of taking Manuel to the park to sail his boat on the pond, or they played pelota against a warehouse wall. To the amusement of the dock watchman, who knew Pedro quite well, they sometimes swam together in Wapping Dock; it was common to see boys diving off the steps there, but it was rare to see a man. The watchman, who was supposed to keep people out of the water, sometimes turned a blind eye.

They also went across the river in the ferryboat, to explore the Wirral countryside beyond Birkenhead, or, when the tide was in, to swim in the sea at Hoylake.

One evening, Pedro found Arnador doing his arithmetic homework with Manuel at the kitchen table. He found

Arnador's slightly pompous character amusing, and, when he heard from the boy that he hoped to go to the university, he was keen to foster the friendship with Manuel. If Mannie was destined for higher education, he had better have friends who also studied; he realized that Wapping Dock boys were unlikely to comprehend the necessity of hard work at school.

Manuel forgot about little Brian Wing, the last hope of the Chinese laundry, who, most evenings, sat by his mother's ironing board, while she heard him spell in English, a decrepit dictionary at hand to confirm the correctness of his efforts. His eldest brother now worked full-time in the laundry, and the next one had just gone to sea, but, with the elder boys now adding to the family income, Mr Wing wanted better things for his smallest son; the child never moved out of the steamy laundry until his homework was done.

Pedro was the first seaman with whom Arnador became friends. His father dealt with them every day in his chandlery business, as they came to buy all the requirements of a ship from rope to teapots; but Arnador was not encouraged to visit the warehouse. He was much more fascinated by Pedro's stories of his life at sea than Manuel was. Manuel had listened to his father and his grandfather talking about their lives ever since he could remember; he regarded their adventures as a man's normal life. He believed that everybody understood seagoing and docks and foreign ports – they were all part of the life you hoped to escape to the minute you could finish school and be a man, preferably not later than aged thirteen. It was as well that he did not take seriously his family's determination that he should have further education; if he had, there would probably have been an instant rebellion; he accepted the discipline of St Francis Xavier's, but he assumed it would not last for that long.

*

It was through a horse that Pedro made the acquaintance of Arnador's mother. Once, on shore leave, he took both boys to see the Annual Horse Parade in Lime Street. Liverpudlians flocked there to see working horses groomed to perfection, their tails and manes plaited with coloured ribbons. Their polished harnesses glittered with brightly shining horse brasses and had flowers attached to them.

Though Francesca had little idea of the reason for the outing, she howled to be taken along. As usual, she was bought off by Rosita's promise of a halfpennyworth of dolly mixtures from the corner shop. Rosita would have enjoyed going to see the Parade, too, but she earnestly wanted Manuel to have his father's company; amongst seagoing families, too many boys barely knew their fathers, except when they sat, downcast, by their empty fireplaces, unemployed.

In Lime Street, Pedro and the boys stood behind a temporary barrier to watch the heaving, shining mass of animals. While Pedro, a cigarette drooping from the corner of his mouth, gossiped with another man in the crowd, Arnador and Manuel sucked boiled sweets produced from the depths of Pedro's tobacco-dusty pocket. A few police kept the crowd orderly, so that no one was kicked by an irate horse or run over by a backing wagon.

Living at a distance from the docks, Arnador did not see as many horses as Manuel did, nor had he had the regular warnings from his mother to keep out of reach of them. He was enthralled by the sheer beauty of the animals, which were not ordinarily so well groomed. The nearest to him was a neat little carriage horse with a coat like polished coal; it was in the shafts of a light trap. The driver held the reins loosely in his lap, and tipped his straw hat to someone on the other side of the carriage. A lively exchange of jokes ensued, and the horse stirred uneasily.

Cautiously, Arnador slipped under the barricade, and approached the dark beauty.

Pedro called, 'Hey! Come on back, lad.'

Arnador ignored him, and patted the horse's neck.

'Arnador!' Pedro was not used to being disobeyed.

The youngster half turned, grinned at Pedro, and said, as he stretched out his hand to stroke the animal's nose, 'He's OK, Mr Echaniz. He likes it.'

Pedro saw the animal's lips curl back from its yellowed teeth, as it moved its head from the caressing hand. He swiftly ducked under the barrier to pull the boy back. Arnador saw the movement and reluctantly turned to obey Pedro. The irritated animal leaned forward and bit into his shoulder. The heavy teeth did not manage to bite through his jacket, but had a firm enough grip to give the boy a sharp shake.

Arnador screamed with pain. It gave another vicious shake, and then let go, as the alerted driver hastily reined it in.

As the horse tried to rear, Pedro snatched the boy away.

'You stupid bugger!' he shouted, and shoved the crying boy back under the barrier.

Nearby horses shuffled uneasily, and the crowd round Manuel pushed backwards, away from the restive animals.

In the space left, a furious, scared Pedro shook Arnador like a terrier shaking a rat. The boy cried out in pain and fright.

A constable pushed his way along the front of the onlookers. 'What's this? What's this?' he shouted. 'Keep back there.'

Pedro cursed under his breath; the last thing he wanted was an over-zealous constable making a fuss. He let go of Arnador, and growled at the boy, 'Shut up! You're not dead yet.' He urged both boys towards the shops behind the crowd, muttering, 'Excuse us, please.'

A passage was made for them, and for the constable who followed. Arnador was doing his best not to cry, but his face was as white as Rosita's front doorstep.

Manuel whispered uneasily to his father, 'Should we take Arnie home?'

As they took refuge from the crowd in a shop doorway, the constable said, 'Now then. What's up?'

'The boy went under the barrier to pet a horse – and it nipped him. He's all right,' responded Pedro.

Scared that the constable would demand his name and address, because he had crossed a police barrier, Arnador snuffled agreement with Pedro. 'It gave me a fright,' he said. 'That's all.'

'Lucky you weren't kicked,' the constable told him, and turned away.

Arnador still looked very white, so Pedro said, 'We'll take you home – make sure your shoulder's all right.'

'I can see myself home,' Arnador protested. He was afraid Pedro would tell his father that he had been disobedient.

'Nonsense!' Pedro eased the boys away from the Parade, and they went over to Renshaw Street, to get a tram up to Catherine Street.

When Arnador put out his hand to grasp the upright rod in order to swing himself up the tram steps, he cried out, despite his earlier protestations of being able to manage alone.

Pedro helped him on, and they sat in the downstairs part of the vehicle; young men usually went upstairs so that they could smoke.

Arnador's eyes were clenched tightly shut; the shoulder was hurting badly. Pedro regretted his burst of temper, as he saw the boy struggling to be brave. Manuel watched both of them with apprehension.

Arnador was too young to have a key to his home, so when they rang the doorbell, Betty, the maid, answered it. She viewed Pedro's handsome face with insolent interest. What was their Arnie doing with a common seaman?

'Something wrong?' she asked, making no move to let them enter.

Pedro asked to see Mr or Mrs Ganivet.

'She's restin',' replied Betty, opening the door just sufficiently to let Arnador in.

Pedro's eyes narrowed. 'Tell her that Mr Echaniz wants to see her.'

It was an order, and she reluctantly let them into the hall. He removed his peaked cap as he entered, and she viewed with scorn his navy woollen sweater. What would the mistress think? Then she turned sulkily and flounced up the stairs. Arnador held one arm against his chest, to ease the pain, and led them into the red velvet opulence of the Ganivet sitting-room.

The boys hung uneasily round the doorway, while Pedro stood in the middle of the room, and was made suddenly aware of the bareness and shabbiness of his own home. Arnador struggled out of his jacket, and winced as Manuel helped him loosen it from his left shoulder.

Mrs Ganivet nearly ran into the room, tucking loose strands of her hair into her bun as she came. 'What's wrong?' she asked, as Arnador turned his blenched face towards her.

She turned to Pedro, and he made himself known to her. He explained briefly what had happened, and finished up, 'He's probably got a nasty bruise. I thought I'd better bring him home.'

'Stupid boy,' Mrs Ganivet exclaimed tenderly. 'Take off your jersey, luv. Let's have a look.'

Arnador cried out when she heaved the garment off him, and pulled down the shoulder of his undervest. There was a clear line of bruises on both sides of the snow-white shoulder where the horse's teeth had gripped him.

'Dear me!' she exclaimed. 'Mr Echaniz, do sit down a mo', while I get the arnica bottle and a towel. You must have a cuppa afore you go.' She turned to Manuel, 'And you sit down, luv.'

She pushed her son to the red plush sofa, and told him, 'Arnie, dear, you rest here.' She tucked a matching red cushion behind his back. 'There, that'll be more comfy. Back in a mo'.'

As she ran upstairs, they could hear her shouting to Betty to make some tea and put out the cup cakes.

'How does it feel?' asked Pedro of the sufferer.

Anxious not to be thought a coward, Arnador replied that it was easing. 'Mother always makes such a fuss,' he added in apology.

Aware of the fussiness of mothers, Manuel made a face at him.

When his mother dabbed arnica liberally over the bruises and then padded the shoulder with one of his father's big cotton handkerchiefs, so that the arnica would not get on to his jersey, Arnador drew in his breath sharply.

'There you are, dearie. Now you lean back on the cushion. You'll feel fine when you've had a cuppa cha,' she told him.

She turned to Pedro, who had been watching her ministrations without comment. 'It was proper kind of you to bring him home,' she said. 'He'd have probably been all right by himself, but it must've been scary for him — you don't expect to get bitten by a horse, do you?'

As Pedro agreed, she sat down by a little mahogany table. He half rose to go, but she saw the movement. 'Stay a bit,' she urged. 'Betty's making the tea. It's nice to meet Manuel's father.' Within her, she was acutely aware of the handsome man before her and was slightly ashamed of herself. How could a decent Catholic woman feel like that?

To cover her embarrassment, she plied Pedro with quick questions about where in the Pyrenees his family lived and confided that her husband's and her own grandparents had come from Pamplona. As she spoke of Pamplona, she shyly changed from English into Basque, and Pedro smiled and spoke Basque in return.

While the adult conversation flowed back and forth, Manuel watched Arnador. Though his colour was better, he reclined awkwardly on the sofa. His eyes were closed and he was, for once, silent. 'Is it still hurting?' Manuel whispered.

Arnador opened his eyes, and nodded.

'Sorry,' Manuel muttered.

Chapter Twenty-seven

The day after Old Manuel had written for Lorilyn how Arnador had been bitten by a horse, he awoke to a flawless summer morning. When he looked across the drive at the Strait dappled with sunshine, he decided that he would take the *Rosita* out in the afternoon; if the wind were right, he would sail her up the coast. First, however, he had to take the rose up to Kathleen's grave and then go to buy some much-needed groceries.

Because of the need to carry the groceries home, he took the car out and carefully drove it up to the cemetery. He did not linger there very long; just stood looking at her memorial stone, which was brightly lit by a shaft of sunlight, and then, with a sigh, went back to the car, and drove downtown to Safeway's.

In the car park, he parked carefully between a couple of trucks, and went into the shop. As he entered, a blast of air-conditioning made him wish he had put on a pullover; sudden changes of temperature bothered him sometimes.

He looked very frail as, with slow care, he moved down the aisles, picking out the things he needed. Sharon Herman noticed his entry, as she contemplated the offerings of the meat department. His frailty and the resigned droop of his shoulders moved her in a way she could not explain to herself. She quickly dropped two lamb chops into her basket, and walked towards the aisle down which he had vanished. She soon caught up with him, as he stopped to pick up a tin of coffee.

Manuel was startled by a plump, soft hand being laid

over his thin brown one pushing the shopping trolley. 'How are you?' asked the feminine voice.

He jumped, and looked up.

Not Veronica, thanks be to Holy Mary, but her house guest. His brown eyes twinkled amid a myriad of wrinkles, and his wide mouth curved up into his usual quirky smile, as, with some relief, he assured her that he was very well. He could not think of anything more to say, so, on the spur of the moment, she asked him if he would like to have a cup of coffee with her. She joked that the store had a small corner with a coffee machine, which was meant for the use of senior citizens – she was tired and needed to sit down – but she was really too young to sit there without embarrassment – it would be so much easier if he could spare the time to sit with her!

He laughed, and wheeled his trolley over to the corner she indicated. They filled paper cups with coffee, and sat down at a small table. Manuel put two packets of sugar into his coffee and stirred it with a plastic stick. 'Bridget! That's it,' he said, as he looked earnestly into her face.

She looked so startled that he had to smile again. 'You remind me of someone I knew when I was a small boy. She delivered babies and often she nursed people who were sick. She actually brought me into the world. She wasn't a qualified nurse, like you, of course.' He was too shy to tell her that everybody loved and trusted Bridget.

She was interested, and, because it had been in the fore-front of his mind the previous evening, he told her how his friend Arnador's shoulder had been treated at home with arnica; and its partial dislocation discovered over twenty years later when he volunteered for the Royal Air Force.

'I used to carry his school satchel for him, because his shoulder hurt him – and he never played cricket again – or pelota. But I'm grateful for it,' he assured her. 'If he had gone into the Air Force, he would probably have been

killed in the Battle of Britain – so many of them died. As
it is, he's still pretty spry. Best friend I could ever hope
for.'

'Really?'

Manuel's face was suddenly a little wistful. 'He's a great
lad. I get a letter from him most months. I wish he were
nearer.'

'Has he ever come over here?'

'Oh, yes. He came a couple of times when Kathleen was
alive. And he's been twice since – since she passed away.
It's my turn to go to Liverpool.'

'Are you going?'

'I hadn't thought of it – not seriously, that is.'

'Perhaps you should.' She did not want to point out that,
at their age, one or the other of them might die quite soon.

He caught the implication of her remark, however, and
considered it for a moment. Then he replied, 'Perhaps I
should. I won't tell Faith, though. At least not until the
last moment.'

'Who won't you tell?'

'My daughter Faith. She always worries when I travel.
Says I'm too old.'

'Live dangerously!' she advised. 'Do what you want to
do.'

He laughed, as he turned to look at her. 'You're dead
right,' he told her. 'I will.'

Chapter Twenty-eight

At the eleventh hour of the eleventh day of the eleventh month, 1918, the great war to end all wars came to a finish. Throughout the war, my daily life had gone on much the same, wrote Old Manuel to Lorilyn; yet, behind everything I did, it lay like a threatening black shadow; your Auntie Francesca and I used to dread that Father would be killed, and we were so relieved every time he docked, especially when he came home a few days after the war ended. We knew then that he was safe.

On 11 November, Rosita stood on her doorstep, leaning against the doorjamb, one arm round ten-year-old Manuel, and thanked God that the child had been too young to serve in the conflict.

At her feet, on the step, sat Francesca, aged five, and Little Maria, just four. Between them sat Grandma Micaela. They were watching fireworks rocket into the sky, and riotously drunk neighbours dancing round a bonfire. Micaela could actually see nothing, but she could hear the crackle of the fire, the reports of the fireworks and the shouts and shrieks of the dancers; earlier, she had heard all the church bells of Liverpool ring out the victory. In her mind, however, she heard the frantic weeping for those who would not return home – and she saw the shocked faces of wives whose husbands had returned so badly mauled that they would have to be nursed for the rest of their lives – on minuscule pensions, if they were lucky enough to get one.

While the little girls chattered excitedly and drew her

attention to scenes she was too blind to see, she fingered the rosary in her pocket. Her faith had been tried to the limit by the senseless slaughter of the war; and yet, she ruminated sadly, what hope had she to cling to, other than the belief that God knew what he was doing.

Francesca snuggled down closer to her. 'I'm cold, Granny,' she said in Basque.

The old woman opened her shawl and wrapped it round her little granddaughter.

The huge bonfire fell in with a crash and a rain of sparks, and some of the more noisy dancers went in a mob to the Baltic Fleet. Joey Connolly asked his father to take him closer to watch a few Catherine wheels whizzing bravely on warehouse doors. Pat agreed, and asked Manuel if he would like to come, too.

Rosita had expected Manuel to leap at the offer. But he scuffed his feet, and said he did not want to go. Though he and Arnador often played with Mary and Joey, he was beginning to feel oddly uncomfortable in his own neigh- bourhood. A better education and a growing awareness of a bigger and more interesting world than that of Wapping Dock or being a seaman was beginning to make him feel cut off. At times, when playing in the street with the inter- national collection of children from nearby, he found him- self carefully silent; they had once or twice given him a hard time when he had made some ill-considered remark, which, in St Francis Xavier's, would have passed for humour.

On Armistice Night, he sensed the terrible sadness beneath the jollity of the singing, dancing people, and he felt sick.

Arnador, bespectacled and earnest, had never shared his schoolfellows' jingoistic acceptance of the nobility of dying in muddy trenches; there had to be better ways of stopping the Germans, in his opinion. He read the papers far more thoroughly than Manuel did, and observed the increasing number of discharged, wounded men on the streets, many of them dressed in hospital blue. He told his father flatly that he would never be so stupid as to volunteer and probably would not answer a call-up.

Mr Ganivet lectured him angrily that, though he was a Basque, England was his country and he should be prepared to lay down his life for it.

Afterwards, Arnador told Manuel about the ensuing family row, and said angrily, 'It doesn't make sense. Who wants to be blown to bits? I bet the Germans don't.'

Manuel was quite shaken by Arnador's passionate outburst. He responded promptly, by saying, 'Well, they can stop fighting.'

Yet, twenty years later, when the German Nazis threatened Britain, Arnador had tried to get into the Royal Air Force. Perhaps he had felt that a fundamental principle was at stake that time, Manuel decided.

One of Manuel's saddest memories of the First World War was that of Effie Halloran sobbing bitterly in his mother's kitchen-living-room, because both her boys had been killed. He had wanted to run away from grief so close to home. But he had sat at the kitchen table trying to do his homework, and chewed the end of his wooden penholder. Awful things happened to women, as well as to men, he had thought. Men went to sea and faced danger daily – that, in his head, was the essence of being a man – but he felt uneasily that the women at home had to be pretty brave, as well.

Men poured home, ships were laid up, war factories closed. Women who had worked hard and well during the war years were impatiently shoved aside and told to go back home and raise a family.

Women resented this, not only because their modest wages had given them a modicum of independence, but because for many of them earning was a necessity; they had lost husbands, sweethearts, brothers and fathers, and had, therefore, to maintain themselves. It was some time before such women were absorbed by light industry as welcome cheap labour.

The land fit for heroes was slow in arriving. Pedro's ship returned to its old routes down the west coast of Africa, and he took good care not to give a hint of his desire for a move to another company, until he was sure of a 'hit'. Meanwhile, cargoes were not so easy to come by and, to cut costs, the quality of food supplied by the owners deteriorated from poor to worse. Seamen and engine room crew were increasingly recruited from Lagos at wages much lower than those asked for by Liverpool men. The officers made little complaint; they were worried enough about retaining their own jobs, and, as repairs were deferred, how long the old tub would stay afloat.

When ashore, Pedro looked up all the men he knew who worked for de Larrinaga, most of whose crews were Basque. His friends all said mournfully that the competition was wicked; every company had its own group of men who had served it before and who were competing anxiously for any vacancies.

Pedro understood the pressure only too well. Some of the Negroes in his current ship felt themselves to be so vulnerable to unemployment that they hastened to sign on for the next voyage immediately the previous one was completed, to make sure of retaining their job; in effect, they never stepped off the ship for months at a time.

In the event, another enemy swept through the population. Spanish flu, incurable, unstoppable, took thousands upon thousands of lives, particularly amongst young adults, already thinned out in Europe by the slaughter of the war. It left those who survived the attack weakened and deeply depressed. Ships' crews were far from immune, and that was, perhaps, why a jubilant Pedro suddenly hit on a berth with de Larrinaga in the *Esperanza Larrinaga*. It had a Liverpool crew, mostly Basque.

'The wages aren't a lot better,' he told Rosita. 'But the conditions are. Jean Baptiste knows the cook and says he's great.'

He suggested that with the small increase in pay they might manage to send Francesca and Little Maria to a good school run by nuns; the fees were not very great. Rosita was overwhelmed that he should give such consideration to his small daughters. 'I can't think of anybody else who would try that hard for their girls,' she told him, as she hugged him hard.

He kissed her and said, 'I want them to have decent jobs – not to have to sew till their eyes drop out, like you had to when you were little.'

Remembering her long apprenticeship as a seamstress, Rosita was in hearty agreement with him.

A delighted Micaela expressed the hope that one of them would become a nun.

'If she has a calling to it,' replied Rosita cautiously. She had observed that her own small world of the dockside and the city centre was not returning to its pre-war pattern. The brighter girls were trying for clean factory jobs, or, better still, office work, which paid more.

Even the Church felt subtly different. A lot of her neighbours had never been particularly devout – but there was a wavering in the ready acceptance of priestly pronouncements, a sly shift in the way people addressed their hard-working Jesuit mentors – they were still polite, but not so respectful. Even her own belief had been shaken. How could one worship a God who had taken away Effie's boys, her only joy in a bitterly hard life? It was all very well to tell the poor demented soul that it was God's will – but what kind of God was he to allow men to murder each other?

As Manuel grew bigger, she worried constantly that he might fall into bad company. The church still offered a certain discipline in this regard, and she insisted that he say his prayers and attend Mass.

She was glad that he had a nice, steady friend in Arnador; only yesterday, he had brought his books to her house to do his homework with Manuel; and he had helped Francesca with the more difficult words she had to learn to spell. Two decent lads together could sustain each other.

She smiled as she went to get water and a big stick with which to clean the outside drains; she was so lucky to have Pedro and Manuel – and the girls. Best of all, Pedro had, at last, got a decent berth with a good company.

Chapter Twenty-nine

In 1919 the Liverpool City Police went on strike. As a result, there was so much violence in the city that both Mrs Ganivet and Rosita warned the boys not to go near the north end of the town. They scolded almost identically. 'With no police, you don't know what may happen to you – they've got *soldiers* on guard – with rifles, and they shot somebody last night. And see how it's raining; you'll be soaked!'

Determined not to miss the excitement, each boy told his mother cheerfully that he would be visiting the home of the other one.

In macintoshes and boots, their identifying St Francis Xavier caps stuffed into their pockets, they trudged along Lime Street to look at the London Road shopping area, which it was said had been hard hit by looting rioters. They found themselves in a fairly large crowd all going in the same direction.

They were struck dumb by what they saw; other appalled sightseers whispered to each other, as if they were at a funeral. Even Arnador seemed awed by the destruction. Though the pavements appeared to have been swept, bits of glass from shattered shop windows crunched under their feet or lay in neat heaps along the base of the gaping display windows, empty except for fluttering price tickets and knocked down shelves and stands. Behind them, the boys caught a glimpse of interiors reduced to a shambles. Some windows had already been boarded up, and, in front of others, men were at work with sheets of plywood closing off the rest from the wrath of further rioters.

They were relieved that the army did not appear to be on guard.

A solitary constable stood rigidly at a corner, truncheon drawn.

Arnador viewed him with interest. 'The strike isn't one hundred per cent,' he remarked thoughtfully.

Manuel whispered back. 'I thought they were all out.' He gazed at the unmoving constable; there was something touching in the way he stood alone, waiting for further mobs to descend on the cruelly smashed tiny businesses.

Arnador's eyes dropped, as the constable became aware of his stare. He said uneasily, 'Perhaps he doesn't believe it's right to let ordinary people suffer, when it's not their fault. It could be our house – or his – next.'

Manuel's eyes widened in horror. 'Do you think so?'

'It's possible.' He waved a hand towards a corner shop, particularly devastated. 'The mob that did this probably got upstairs and cleaned out the owner's home, as well.'

Manuel felt slightly sick. 'Mam says that they're so poor up Scotland Road, it's pitiful. They'd take anything.'

'They're very poor round Wapping Dock.'

'Well, nothing happened round us.'

'In the war, they sacked a German butcher's shop on Park Road.' The older boy paused to watch a man hammering boards over a side window, which, somehow, still had its glass intact. Then he added, 'Because he was foreign – and the enemy. We're foreign, and people would turn on us, if they didn't like what Spain was doing.'

Manuel responded stoutly, 'I'm not foreign; I was born here – and we're not Spanish.'

Arnador smiled. 'They don't know the difference. And you look foreign.'

'You don't!'

'I'm fair. I blend in better – it's very convenient!'

As they climbed the hill and, with others, viewed the endless damage, a small fear entered Manuel's heart.

Would people hurt you simply because you looked different? In the polyglot area in which he lived, he had never been made to feel different, except when, at school, Stewart had called him a dago. Could the brutes who had caused such chaos in friendly London Road turn on other people? If there were no police?

Sickened by his own thoughts, he was suddenly dimly aware that it was the police, taken for granted like letter boxes or lamp standards, who normally stopped people from wreaking havoc. At this moment, except for the defiant, almost heroic figure they had passed on the corner, there were no police.

'Let's go home,' he urged Arnador.

They were dripping wet and they moved towards a shop entrance, to shelter for a minute, while they decided what to do. A deep voice said sharply, 'Move along there, please.'

They jumped, and turned. A soldier not much older than themselves, his rifle on his shoulder, stood deeper in the entrance-way. He looked very grim.

Without a word, the youngsters moved away, and then, suddenly frightened, clattered as fast as they could through the thickening crowd, back down to Lime Street.

Actually being given an order by a soldier in khaki uniform, with a gun, confirmed their mothers' scoldings. This was as serious as the paper said it was. Soldiers were normally men on leave; they did not order civilians around; they were meant to fight wars.

Though the strike was not undertaken without cause, none of the striking men got their jobs back. New recruits, many of them Irish, were taken into the Force; this was deeply resented by many people on Merseyside, and remained a rankling grievance for half a century.

Even seventy-three years later, Old Manuel recalled how terrified he had been at Arnador's idle remark about mobs turning on people. Until then, he had always believed that a man belonged where he was born, though he could also be proud of his racial origins. Perhaps, he considered, as he carefully shaved himself one morning, it was that incident which had made him more stubbornly Basque than he would have otherwise been.

He grinned, as he peered into the bathroom mirror to dab a small nick in his chin – despite Kathleen's best efforts to convert him to an electric razor, he still shaved with an old-fashioned cutthroat. We always were an obstinate lot, he told his mirror image with blatant pride.

That same year, Brian Wing electrified the neighbourhood round Wapping by winning one of the very few scholarships then available, to the highly respected Liverpool Institute.

Struggling to keep their little laundry going, his father and mother were considered poor even by the hard-up residents around them. How could Brian have ever learned enough to do it? Manuel and Arnador wondered.

Auntie Bridget Connolly, who was credited with knowing everything about the area, soon told them that the family had given a home to a poor university student of Chinese descent, on a promise that he would tutor Brian in maths and English. The young man and the nervous little boy had liked each other; and the pair of them were so proud of their success that, according to Bridget, 'When I saw 'em this mornin', they were grinnin' at each other like two Buddhas out of Bunney's gift shop.' She smiled softly at Manuel and Arnador, and went on, 'He looked proper nice in his uniform, he did. He's a lovely little lad.'

'He'll probably be the only Chinese kid in the school,' Pat Connolly remarked, as he checked the racing news at the back of his newspaper. 'Poor little tyke.'

'He won't have no trouble,' Bridget assured him. 'He's smart at avoiding it – watched him many a time I have.'

Manuel and Arnador agreed. They were both intrigued at having another friend in Wapping who, like themselves, would be better educated.

The next time Manuel went up to the laundry to see Brian, Rosita instructed him to tell his small friend how happy the Echaniz family was at his success.

Brian's eyes became slits behind his Woolworth's glasses, as he grinned. He was dressed in his usual slightly large woollen shorts, handed down from his older brother. 'Got any ciggie cards to swop?' he asked.

Still the same old Brian, Manuel decided with an odd sense of relief.

Pedro missed the fun of preparing for Christmas.

Manuel did all kinds of small jobs round the Pier Head and the dock, to earn pennies to buy presents for Grandma Micaela, Rosita, Francesca and Little Maria, and for his father. He caught ropes thrown by boatmen approaching the dockside; he held horses occasionally for delivery van men – horses that pulled drays were too big for him to cope with; for a halfpenny, he watched a telegraph boy's bicycle at the kerbside; and, once, he actually watched that a motor car remained untouched, when a very well-dressed man wanted to walk down to the Pier Head to take a photograph of a ferry coming in. He shared the latter job with Brian, and they stood one on each side of this most unusual vehicle and scowled ferociously at any street kid who came to stare at it. The man gave them twopence each, when he returned and found it safe and unblemished. Both boys were ecstatic. Manuel also got a whole series of pennies from Mrs Saitua, for running her messages for her. She had caught the Spanish flu and, though she had survived it, she still had not recovered her strength, so she was very glad of his help.

Pedro docked a few days after Christmas. Since he had missed the traditional Christmas Eve feast, though he had

had a Christmas dinner aboard ship, Rosita and Micaela again made some of the customary Basque Christmas Eve dishes for him, and the family enjoyed roasted bream, fried potatoes and new bread, followed by a big plate of choux pastries filled with cream and covered with chocolate. The Saituas, two sturdy Basque friends of Pedro's, the Connollys and the Hallorans were invited to visit and share the cakes.

Bottles of wine and a box of cigars were opened, and, in the ensuing merriment, even Rosita's tired, pale face began to show some colour.

Mysterious parcels were unearthed from Pedro's kitbag and hidden until 6 January, Epiphany, when they would be placed in a basket in the front window as gifts from the Three Wise Men on their feast day.

In English fashion, Manuel, Francesca and Little Maria had all hung their stockings up in front of the fireplace at Christmas, into which both grandmother and mother had contrived to put small presents. None of them seemed to remember that 6 January was still to come.

While Francesca was cuddled on her father's lap, Manuel leaned on the back of his father's chair until he reeked of smoke from Pedro's cigar. He longed to have his father to himself for a little while; but, meanwhile, he listened to a heated discussion of British and Spanish politics, interspersed with joking references to the hazards of shipboard life. Sometimes, the words poured out so fast that the Basques present broke into their own language, and everything had to be quickly translated by Rosita for the benefit of the Connollys and Hallorans, as she refilled glasses and handed round the cakes.

When Pedro asked Rosita to pour half a glass of wine for the boy, Manuel felt he had suddenly become an adult. Francesca and Little Maria promptly demanded a glass, too. Drops of wine were put into two glasses and then surreptitiously topped up with water. Everybody laughed when Little Maria carefully held her glass by the stem, exactly as Micaela did.

Even though the war was over, Bilbao was doing quite well, Pedro told them; he had gleaned this news from other Basques in his new ship, and now he floated the idea of, perhaps, going back there.

Mr Saitua made a face over the rim of his glass. 'It won't last,' he said. 'The blasted Spanish'll drain it dry.'

'There's a lot of talk of fighting for a country of our own. What do you think?'

Jean Baptiste Saitua pulled another face. 'There's always been talk – but have you ever heard of a Spaniard letting go of anything he thinks he owns?'

Rosita intervened to ask her husband, 'Do you think the children would have a better chance there than they do here?'

Pedro again looked to Jean Baptiste for comment on this.

The older man scratched his sunburned bald head with huge, swollen fingers. 'I doubt it. My boys are in steady jobs. And Manuel could do better, if he stays in school long enough.'

Pedro felt that now he was with the de Larrinaga Line he was doing fairly well himself, though one never knew with certainty when a ship might be laid up. If Manuel got into a profession, however, he would never be out of work – and the possibility of that was much greater for him in Liverpool. He nodded his head, and said to Rosita, 'I believe he's right.'

A day or two later, Pedro sailed again. Manuel was playing football with Brian Wing further up the street, and the two little girls had gone together to the corner shop to buy a penny block of salt for their mother. In the dark hall, Pedro held his wife in his arms, while Micaela busied herself making beds upstairs. She laid her head on his shoulder and said, with a sigh, 'I wish you didn't have to go.'

'It'd be much worse if I didn't have a ship to go to!' he replied. 'There've been a few that have been laid up recently.'

He felt her shrug slightly as she said, 'I wish you could've had Dad's Basque agency. You could have had it, if you'd asked.'

'There aren't that many emigrants going through, nowadays.'

'Humph.' She giggled suddenly, as he fondled her. 'Get away with you,' she told him. 'Start that little game and you'll never get down to the ship before she sails. Come on, now. Let go!'

He laughed, loosed her, and gave her a quick kiss, before picking up his kitbag and tin suitcase. 'See you soon, luv. Ta-ra.'

She opened the door to let him out, and stood on the step to watch him swing down the road towards Queens No. 2. Then she shivered, wrapped her woollen cardigan closer round herself and went slowly indoors.

Seated in his neat Canadian kitchen, Old Manuel read a letter from his cousin, Ramon Barinèta, in Liverpool, sipped coffee, and, with half his mind, considered the steady rhythm of Rosita's work during her husband's absences.

She was always busy in the stone-floored, eighteenth-century house. He himself had loved the old lodging house and had, as a boy, never noticed its total lack of convenience; or that his grandmother was steadily becoming more frail and dependent upon her daughter.

As he grew older, Rosita had prevailed upon him to do some of the jobs his grandfather had done for her. Grumbling, he had chopped up kindling wood, and carried buckets of coal up from the cellar each day. Once or twice, he had hung out the family wash for her in the tiny back yard. His undeveloped muscles had ached, as he sought to avoid the wet sheets dragging on the ground as the freezing wind from the river caught them. He was embarrassed at pegging out his mother's bloomers and his sister's small undergarments, and he prayed, as he hung up a row of female stockings, that none of his friends would come through the door from the back alley, while he was doing it.

Now, as a very old man, he remembered with a pang his mother's scarlet hands, so swollen from scrubbing clothes on a wash board and scrubbing floors with hot soda water that her wedding ring cut painfully into her finger.

He remembered, too, with some amusement, that in a burst of compassion at her fatigue he had undertaken the fortnightly cleaning of the flues of the big kitchen range on which she cooked and which gave warmth to their living-room-kitchen. He remembered inserting the long wire brush into the main flue and pulling it out too quickly, so that the whole room had been doused in soot. His mother kept finding the thick black powder in odd corners for months afterwards.

He decided to include in the notes he was writing for Lorilyn a list of domestic tasks that he hoped that she would never have to face.

He carefully made the list. Then he wondered if a female electrical engineer would deign to do any housekeeping at all. Once he himself had qualified in a similar field and had gone to sea, he had never done any domestic work – until Kathleen died.

He chewed his thumbnail and wondered if Lorilyn might serve at sea, once she had her degree. In the middle of describing his mother's hard work, he suddenly wrote something that was a denial of his family's traditions. 'I hope you will neither have to serve at sea or marry a seaman, my dear. It causes too much heartache.'

She wouldn't go to sea, would she? Well, some women were nowadays doing men's jobs. He pursed his lips. She couldn't say he hadn't warned her.

He would leave the sentences in.

Chapter Thirty

One miserable, overcast January afternoon in 1920, when
the gas lamps in the street had already been lit, Madeleine
Saitua flung open the Echanizes' back door and rushed in
like a flustered hen. With her came a blast of cold air and
noise from the workshops. A surprised Rosita mechanically
closed the door after her and the clangour of panel beaters
was sharply reduced. 'Madeleine! You shouldn't come out
in felt slippers in the rain; you'll catch your death!' she
scolded.

Madeleine pulled out a kitchen chair from under the
table, and sat down suddenly, realizing that she was still
weak from the flu. She patted her big breast, as she panted
to get her breath back.

Manuel had just returned from school and was
unpacking his satchel, to return to his mother the piece
of greaseproof paper in which his sandwiches had been
wrapped; the paper would be used again and again. Now
he stared at Madeleine apprehensively; it was not like Mrs
Saitua to hurry about anything.

'Rosita, is it true that Pedro's ship's overdue?'

Rosita gaped at her friend. 'No. I haven't heard anything.' Her blue eyes were wide with shock. 'They would've
let us know if it was – wouldn't they?'

Manuel's heart gave a painful thud, and he turned
quickly to look at his mother. She was slowly blenching.
Madeleine had not said 'late'; she had said 'overdue', with
all that the word portended.

At Madeleine's precipitous entry, Micaela had stopped
knitting, and lifted her head towards the sudden rush of

cold air; she sensed trouble. Now, from her rocking chair close to the fire, she cackled suddenly, 'They wouldn't let us know until they were sure she was lost, they wouldn't.'

The women's silence after Micaela's remark scared Manuel; it was clear that none of them wanted to face the import of Madeleine's anxious inquiry.

The kettle on the fire boiled, and spat angrily. Without taking her eyes off Madeleine, Rosita told Manuel to take it off and put it on the hob. Then she asked, 'Where did you hear about it, Madeleine?' She pulled out a chair for herself and sat down carefully, afraid she would fall in a faint.

Madeleine had recovered her breath, and she responded promptly, 'Well, Jean Baptiste was visiting friends living in Scottie Road, and the landlord of the Throstles Nest tells him – knowing he's Basque, like. Said a couple of lads from Harrison was talking about it. He told me just now, when he come in. So I gave him his tea, and I run down to see if you was all right – if it were true, like.' She leaned forward to lay her hand on top of Rosita's which was clutching the table edge. 'Have you been down to the office lately?'

'No,' Rosita answered her dazedly. 'Allotment's not due yet.' She took a big breath, and said, 'The Harrison Line men could be wrong.'

Manuel interjected. 'I can run down to the office and ask them for you.'

Rosita glanced up at the old alarm clock on the mantelpiece. 'They'd be closed, luv, before you got there.' She grimaced, as she added, 'And you being young, they'd fob you off with some official nonsense.'

'Oh, aye, they would,' agreed Micaela, and again picked up the sock she was knitting for Manuel, as if to impart some sense of normality to the frightened little group.

The kitchen-living-room was so still, while Madeleine waited for Rosita to say something more, that the click of the knitting needles and the tick of the clock could be clearly heard, despite the roar of machinery and the clatter of metal sheets. Madeleine shivered.

Rosita did not know what to say. Her mind wavered between a frantic need to know the truth and the fact that the only place which could give her accurate news was shut until nine o'clock the following morning.

Watching her livid face and unable to bear the women's unnatural quietness, Manuel suggested, 'First, we don't know if they really are overdue, do we? Dad could simply be late because they've had to stop for a repair or bad weather – a gale could have set them off course.'

His mother's expression did not change; it was as if she were staring down a long, dark tunnel, which she did not wish to enter. She did switch her gaze towards her son, however, and it came to him vividly that she knew his father was dead.

But she couldn't know, could she? It wasn't logical. Passionately, he went on, 'Maybe there's something in the evening paper. I'll go up to Park Lane and get one.'

Seeing the boy's obvious anxiety, and worried about Rosita – she was far too quiet – Madeleine seized upon Manuel's idea. She leaned closer to Rosita. 'Let him go up and buy one,' she advised.

Rosita nodded. 'There's some coppers in my purse over there, on the sideboard. Run and get one, dear.'

Rosita could hear her daughters chattering, as they opened the front door on their return from school. She frowned; she must teach them not to dawdle on the way home, now that the nights had drawn in. Manuel shot past them, twopence clutched in his hand, as they called to their mother and hung up their coats and hats in the hall.

She made herself call a cheery, 'Hullo,' as Madeleine tried to comfort her by saying, 'Even if it is late, they'll probably turn up. Pedro said a number of times what good mates he had – real experienced.'

'Yes, you're right. He was very happy with them.' As she forced herself to her feet, to greet Francesca and Little Maria, she realized that she had expressed herself in the past tense, and it took all her courage to suppress her panic. She turned to the little girls and hugged them both, while she listened to the stories of their afternoon, and gave them a biscuit each to nibble on until tea was ready.

Over their heads, she looked warningly at Madeleine, and nothing more was said about the ship. Micaela needed no prompting; she knitted briskly, as she looked up to greet her burbling granddaughters.

Manuel stood in the tiny newsagent's shop and frantically turned the pages to find the shipping news, while the newsagent stood patiently behind his magazine-laden counter. 'I'm looking to see when Dad's ship's due.'

The newsagent took a puff from his cigarette. 'In trouble, are you?' he joked.

'No. Mam wants to know.'

He hastily folded the paper, tucked it under his arm and ran home as hard as he could.

The *Esperanza Larrinaga* was not mentioned in the shipping news.

Chapter Thirty-one

The rumour had spread. When, the next morning, after the children had been sent to school, Rosita put on her shawl and went down to the shipping office, there was a number of flustered women besieging the clerk at the counter. The frail-looking young clerk, only recently discharged from army hospital himself, said that the vessel was, as yet, listed only as being late. Inquiries were being made.

Whey-faced wives and mothers bowed their heads and went home to wait.

A few days later, in the newspaper, the ship was reported missing. The first half-pay allotments were withheld.

Rosita and Micaela were thrown back upon the diminished savings in the boxes under Micaela's bed. 'Keep the bit you've got in the Post Office,' advised Micaela. 'You may not need to use it.' She came from a family of fishermen, and she comforted Rosita by saying insistently, 'I've seen it happen more than once. Fishing boats, and all; and you're fit to die yourself. Then the whole crew turns up weeks later in some outlandish spot. Been picked up by another small vessel – and had to go with them to whatever was their destination. And that may be what the company's thinking – they haven't written to you yet.'

Manuel was refilling the coal hod by the kitchen range from a bucket he had brought up from the coal cellar.

'But, Grandma, if they'd been found, we'd know by radio, wouldn't we?'

Grandma pulled a face. 'Not many ships have got such new-fangled things. For sure, if your dad's ship had it and they were in trouble, they would have sent a message, I would think. I doubt they've got a radio.'

Manuel agreed. 'I think Dad would've mentioned it if they'd had one.'

Rosita tried to smile. 'You could be right, Mam. They're safe in a boat without a radio,' she said, but her mind was in a turmoil of sheer terror.

Manuel talked about it with Arnador when, as usual, he came to the Echaniz house to do his homework with him and with Francesca. Arnador had never been able to express his intense loneliness to his friend; he simply arrived with his school books most evenings, and thankfully sat down to work in Rosita's busy kitchen-living-room with the family around him. Mrs Ganivet could never understand this, and always pointed out shrilly that he had a bedroom with a gas fire of his own. He told her dully that he and Manuel worked well together, which was true.

That night, as they sat at the table together, they whispered about Pedro's ship, while, by the fire, Grandma and Rosita entertained two Basque ladies; the adults tried to keep their conversation free of reference to the feared disaster, so as not to frighten the children.

Struggling with an essay — at least a paragraph, Sister Winifred had insisted — on 'What I Did in My Christmas Holidays', Francesca caught the boys' whispers. She looked up at Manuel and Arnador aghast. 'Daddy's ship's lost?' she hissed.

Manuel was jolted. He had forgotten that Rosita had not told his sisters. He quickly said comfortingly, 'It's a bit late — and everybody worries about men at sea when the winter storms are here.'

'Are you sure?' Her pinched little face lacked a trace of colour, as she spoke.

'My dad hasn't mentioned it,' interjected Arnador. 'He would know about it, and would have told us at home —

because it's a Basque ship.' He was sliding swiftly round the truth, trying to protect his friend's little sister.

Francesca half-turned to ask her mother what had happened, but Manuel caught her and said, 'Not now. It's not fair to worry Mam.'

'I want to,' hissed Francesca.

'Mam's friends may have men in Dad's ship. You'll scare them!'

She stared resentfully at her brother through red-gold lashes, and said sulkily, 'All right. How do you spell "plentiful"?'

Arnador told her.

When he returned to Catherine Street, his father was sitting in a red velveteen-covered chair in their sitting-room, with the newspaper spread out on the tea table in front of him. Mr Ganivet did not like being disturbed when he was perusing the newspaper; but Arnador was sufficiently shaken by Manuel's news to ask, after he had divested himself of his outdoor clothes and hung his satchel up beside them, if he knew anything about the missing *Esperanza Larrinaga*.

'Indeed, yes. We were talking in the office about it. A terrible loss to us, if it has foundered.'

His ponderous, often insensitive father seemed genuinely upset. Arnador inquired, 'Do you mean to the business – or to us personally?'

Mr Ganivet looked nonplussed at the question, and then said almost indignantly, 'A loss to the Basque community, of course. The crew is almost all Basque – it will be very hard on the families.' He began to fold up the paper. 'What made you ask about it?'

'Manuel's father's on it.'

'Oh, my goodness! That's terrible! There are three children, I believe you said?'

'Yes, and Grandma – she's blind.'

Mrs Ganivet came bustling in to say that her husband's

evening supper and Arnador's bedtime cocoa awaited them in the dining-room, and she would be with them in a minute. She trotted out again, and Arnador said to his father, 'Manuel loves his father — there's nobody like him.'

The stout little man nodded absently, his thoughts already on the Cheddar cheese and crackers awaiting him.

Arnador followed him to the dining-room; he thought resentfully that he never seemed to be able to get close to his father; he could talk to Pedro more easily. As he sipped his hot cocoa, he wondered idly what his mother would do if *his* father was suddenly missing. Would he himself then be responsible for her? At fourteen? It was a shattering thought, and he wondered if it had occurred to Manuel, who was not yet thirteen.

A few days later, Micaela heard the flap of the letter-box rattle, as a letter was pushed through it. She went into the hall and ran her foot gently round the floor near the front door, until she heard the soft swish when her foot moved a letter. She picked it up and felt the ominous length of a business envelope.

'Rosita!' she called down the cellar steps. 'There's a letter come.'

Rosita had been checking how much coal she had in the cellar; Manuel often neglected to tell her when he brought up the last bucket of slack. Now, wild with hope that it would be a letter from Pedro, she flew up the stone steps.

When she saw the long narrow envelope in her mother's hand, she paused, too scared to take it from her.

'Here, luv,' prompted Micaela, and held it out to her, while she waited for the sound of its being torn open. She tensed herself to cope with a wild explosion of grief.

She heard, instead, Rosita walk slowly into the kitchen-living-room, pull out a chair from the table and sit down. Only then did she hear the letter being slowly torn open.

Micaela felt her way to the table and also sat down.

From the alley at the back of the house, clearly over the racket of workshops, came the singsong shout, 'Any old iron, ra-ags, jars or bones?'

As the sound receded down the passageway, Rosita said wonderingly, 'How could such a big ship go down with all hands — without a trace?'

'Dear God! Is that what they say?'

'Yes.' It was only a whisper. 'They say they've searched and searched.' She looked beseechingly at her mother, begging for a denial of the news. But her mother's blind eyes were closed, the toothless mouth pinched, a thin line in a bloodless face, as if she were overwhelmed.

'Mam! Mam!' Rosita screamed at her in sudden agony, and hammered the table with her fists. 'Help me, Mam! Help me, Mam.'

Micaela dragged herself back to her daughter's desperate pain. 'My lovey,' she crooned, as she made herself get up from her chair, to hold her well-loved, stricken daughter.

The awful shrieks penetrated the thin wall which separated them from Bridget's house. At the first scream, Bridget paused, her paring knife suspended over a potato. When the second one assailed her ears, she dropped vegetable and knife, whipped off her grubby apron, shoved her bare aching feet into her husband's carpet slippers, and fled next door. She had been waiting for this dread day, having heard the rumour about the *Esperanza Larrinaga*. Only yesterday, she had begun a special novena to the Virgin Mother to protect Pedro — but she knew from the frantic cries coming from next door that she had been too late. On her way out, she snatched up half a small bottle of gin, which Pat had bought cheap from a docker the day before; it was the only sedative she had in the house.

When Manuel came home from school, the house was deadly quiet. He almost tiptoed into the kitchen-living-room, past the parlour door, which was open.

By the fireplace, his grandmother sat in her rocking chair,

eyes closed; she was so still that, for a second, Manuel thought she had been taken ill. By her side, in a straight chair sat tiny, shrunken Effie Halloran. Both had their rosaries wound round their fingers.

At his entry, Effie turned a lugubrious face towards him. Tears oozed down the deep lines in her wizened face. 'Hush,' she said. 'I think she's dropped off.'

Manuel carefully laid two text books on the table. He was scared. 'Dad?' he asked.

Effie nodded. 'I'm proper sorry, duck.'

'Where's Mam?' The question came urgently from white lips.

'Upstairs with Mrs Connolly. She's havin' a little lie-down.'

He turned and took the narrow staircase two at a time. He burst into his mother's bedroom. On the bed lay Rosita in the arms of Bridget. The younger woman was wailing into her friend's shoulder, and Bridget was saying, 'There, there, me darling, there, there.'

As the boy came up short by the bed, Bridget said softly to him, 'I'm so sorry, luv.'

'Oh, Bridget!' he exclaimed frantically. 'What shall we do?' He began to cry hopelessly.

'You poor lad!' she replied softly. The boy needed comfort, and the little girls would be in soon. Yet, she did not want to let go of the stricken woman in her arms.

Desperately, she asked him, 'Could you be a brave lad and run up to Madeleine's and ask her to come. If she's not in, get Peggy O'Brien from across the road — she's got little kids, and I don't want to ask her unless I have to.'

Manuel wiped his tears on the sleeves of his blazer, as he tried to control himself. He sniffed hard. He was grateful to be asked to do something positive.

Bridget said, 'Before you go, give your mam a hug and a kiss.' She loosened her hold on Rosita, and with her face still buried in Bridget's shoulder, his mother lifted an arm vaguely to encompass him. He bent to kiss her and she held him for a second. She smelled of gin. Fighting back his own grief, he said, 'I'll get Mrs Saitua for you.'

The faded red-gold head nodded slightly.

Within five minutes, Madeleine and her daughter, Panchika, who had been enjoying an afternoon off, came running through the front door, followed by a panting Manuel. They brought with them a bottle of wine and a big loaf of bread, fresh out of the oven.

Micaela awoke from her doze of exhaustion. She felt tired enough to die herself. 'Is that you, Madeleine?' she asked.

'Yes, dear – and Panchika.' She went to Micaela, ignoring poor Effie, and kissed her. 'We'll soon have the kettle on – and I'm going to ask Manuel to get Father Felipe.'

Effie heaved a sigh of relief. It had not occurred to her to go and get a priest; she was not an ardent Catholic.

While Madeleine spoke, Manuel had stood, white and trembling, by the door of the room, with no idea what to do. During the previous few days, he had done his best to prepare himself for this situation; but all his good intentions had gone out of his head and all he wanted to do was find a quiet place in which to cry. Now he said, 'I'll go now, Mrs Saitua.'

'They're all out,' the priest's housekeeper told him, not unkindly. 'Except Father Clement. It's your dad, you say? In the *Esperanza Larrinaga*? You're the fifth one today.' She nodded her wimpled head sadly. 'It's a bad day for the parish. Come in, lad, and I'll ask Father Clement if he thinks he could walk down to your house – he's very frail now and it's hard for him to walk.'

Manuel, cap in hand, stepped into the linoleumed hall which shone with polish.

Wrapped in a cloak pressed upon him by the housekeeper, together with his walking stick, the old priest slowly accompanied the young boy down to the dock road. He asked Manuel to steady him by holding his arm, and Manuel respectfully did so; he had rarely touched a priest before. Priests were holy — you did not go too close to them. As they walked, the priest spoke very gently to him about the wisdom of God in all He did, and suggested that he could express his love for his father by a series of prayers for his soul. Brokenly, Manuel said he would.

The crowd in the Echanizes' kitchen-living-room had been augmented by Francesca, who, like Manuel had tried hard to prepare herself for this day, and Little Maria, who did not exactly understand what had happened to Daddy, but that something awful had, and was howling steadily in Grandma's arms.

At the entry of the priest, all the to-do ceased, and Manuel hastily put a chair under the old man. In a way, thought Old Manuel, tears springing to his eyes at the memory of the loss of his father, though he himself was an old man now — in a way, Father Clement had been better than Father Felipe would have been; his age and frailty commanded added respect, and his mother had knelt before him to be comforted with charm and delicacy. Her rosary had been found for her; prayer suggested; the smell of gin ignored.

'He was so good to me, Father,' she told him brokenly, as she wept. And the old priest thought that he had not heard that kind of praise very frequently from bereaved wives in a parish which was both poor and harsh.

When finally he left to confer with his fellow priests about a Mass for the souls of all the men lost, the family was still weeping, but he had exorcized the hysteria. It was as if he had taken away with him some of the agony of mind and now carried it himself.

Old Manuel remembered sadly that, on that day, he would have sworn that he could eat nothing; but he had been a healthy growing lad, and he ate everything Madeleine prepared for tea, and this encouraged a tear-stained Frannie and Little Maria to eat, too. Micaela sipped tea, but refused anything to eat. His mother had been taken back up to her bed, and, with Bridget on one side of the bed and silent Effie on the other, had drunk a cup of tea as black as shoe polish with a good dash of rum in it. Mr Halloran had come in in the middle of the uproar, had gone upstairs to fetch his small hoard of spirits, and handed it to his wife. He then sat down in his room to wait, with what patience he could muster, for his wife to come up and make his tea. He was not alone in the parish; quite a number of husbands had similar waits, while their wives went to help their friends.

Chapter Thirty-two

A couple of nights later, after the girls had been put to bed and the dishes washed up, Rosita sat down at the kitchen table to write to Pedro's mother and father on their far-away farm in the Pyrenees, while Manuel tried manfully to concentrate on his homework at the other end of the table; Arnador had not come down to their home since the bad news; he said to Manuel that he would not intrude at such a time.

Manuel wished that Francesca was still up and doing her homework, but Francesca, terribly distressed and frantic that her mother would also be lost if she left her, had not been to school, nor had her bewildered little sister. Finally, tonight, Bridget had popped in with a pill which she carefully split into two. She made each child swallow half, and had then taken them both up to bed, telling them that they would be fine in the morning and looking forward to going to school. The exhausted girls dropped off to sleep almost immediately, and, when she came downstairs, she kissed Rosita and said the sedative was a mild one, and to send them to school in the morning.

Now, Rosita sat staring at a piece of lined notepaper. How do you tell parents that they have lost their son? She chewed her wooden penholder till its tip began to disintegrate.

Manuel's own misery and his mother's fidgeting troubled him so much that he finally suggested softly to her, 'You could simply say that you are sorry to have to tell them that . . .'

Thankful to be given an opening, Rosita wrote as he

directed. Micaela, lying on the sofa with her eyes closed, listened to the scratching pen, and, when the sound was replaced by that of Rosita folding up the letter, she said, 'Have you given them my love and say how I grieve for them, too? Poor souls, they have only one son left, now.'

'No.' Rosita unfolded the letter and put the message in at the bottom of the page, and added 'With love' before her own signature, crossed it out and put, 'With all our love.' The old couple had always been very kind to her.

'Now write to my brother-in-law in Bilbao. He should hear it from us – that his niece is a widow.'

At this reminder of her solitary state, Rosita broke down and cried again. Both Manuel and Micaela immediately got up to comfort her.

It was a while before her sobbing ceased and she could write to her uncle and his two elderly daughters, all of them trying to scrape a living and with worries of their own.

As she finally licked the envelopes closed, Manuel said, 'I think you should write to Uncle Leo.'

Back on the horsehair sofa, Micaela sighed. She said despondently, 'I wrote several times in the war, and when I wrote for Christmas, 1918, the letter came back marked *Gone away*. I'd hoped that, perhaps, another clerk might make an effort to forward it – seeing that it was Christmas.' She had felt intensely her lack of letters from her emigrant son; though he had difficulty, he knew how to read and write, she thought with resentment. Unless, of course, he had been killed in the war, which was a fear which haunted her.

Now, she said to Rosita, 'You must be tired, dear. You could write to Agustin tomorrow.'

Rosita was finding it almost impossible to concentrate, so she agreed. 'One more day is not going to make any difference,' she said with a sigh.

Before she could put the pad of paper and the pen and

ink back on the dresser, Manuel interjected. 'Mam, couldn't I write to Uncle Leo – to save you a bit? Suppose I wrote him a letter to the only definite address we've ever had for him – the one in Nevada, and put it in an envelope addressed to the postmaster there, with a little note asking if he would help us to trace him, because the matter is urgent. If the postmaster knew it was urgent he might take the trouble to inquire for us. For instance, he could ask other shepherds coming in to collect their letters if they knew him and knew where he was.'

Rosita shrugged rather hopelessly. Let the boy try. She pushed the pen, ink and paper towards him. 'All right. Thank you, luv.'

As Manuel let the letters slip into the bright red pillar box with its royal insignia of George V, on his way to school the next morning, he prayed that Uncle Leo would reply. He was a grown man and would know what the family should do.

As he trudged through the morning rush to work, he grizzled miserably, his chin tucked down into the school scarf round his neck, so that passersby would not notice that he was crying. He presumed that he would now have to leave school and go to sea, though he had, as yet, not discussed it with his mother. He thought of the wide expanse of nothing which was the ocean – and of his father drowning in it because there was no one to rescue him – and he did not feel very brave. He was thankful to see Arnador waiting for him at the school gate.

At home, there were numerous visitors. Not only Rosita's Basque friends and other neighbours called upon her; one or two other wives of missing crew members came simply to share their common sense of despair. Among the latter was the downtrodden, woebegone slip of an Irish woman, Bridie Pilar, wife of a Filipino stoker and mother of Andrew

Pilar, who still tried, sometimes, to bully Manuel, especially when he was in his school uniform.

When Rosita opened the door to her, Bridie burst into tears and flung herself upon Rosita, her black shawl flapping round her like the wings of a bat.

It took Rosita a second or two to realize who she was, but when she did, she urged her to come in and sit by the fire.

Seated in Micaela's rocking chair, Bridie rocked herself back and forth in desperate agitation, her face in her hands, greasy black hair falling forward in rat tails.

Micaela, who had been dozing on the sofa, woke up and asked anxiously who was there.

Rosita, standing by the weeping woman, told her. She herself was not certain of the import of the visit. Bridie was not a close neighbour – she lived in Park Lane. Micaela was also a little mystified, but she heaved herself off the sofa, and said, in a resigned voice, 'I'll make some tea.' Unerringly, she reached into the hearth for the poker. With it she located the hob on which the kettle stood, and lifted the kettle to weigh whether there was any water in it. Satisfied, she pushed the hob round with the poker till it stood over the fire. The kettle began to sing.

Rosita, with her hand comfortingly on Bridie's shoulder, watched her mother anxiously; she did not want to interfere unnecessarily, but she was always afraid that blind Micaela would get too close to the blaze and burn herself, though she had never done so.

Bridie began to shriek. 'What am I going to do? And me with five boys to feed? It'll be the workie for us, it will, for sure.'

At the mention of the dreaded workhouse, Rosita shivered. It was a threat of which she had been agonizingly aware ever since she had received the news of the ship's foundering.

She said, 'Don't take on so, Bridie. There'll be a compensation award; it'll give us a bit of time to find work.'

Micaela put the old beret which was the teacosy over the pot. 'Have you got a dad who'd help out?' she inquired. She was upset herself and her hands trembled, as she got down the mugs from the dresser.

'Me dad? He's drunk most of the time – if he's got any money. And me mam half-starved, and afraid of being beaten if she opens her mouth. And me brothers are in a state, 'cos two of 'em died, one with the flu and one in France – and that means two widows pestering them already.' She gave a mighty sniff and accepted a mug of tea from Micaela. 'What am I to do?'

Rosita let her arms fall to her sides and turned to sit down herself. Through long nights she had wept herself to exhaustion; now she had to give thought to the same question. The compensation would be a small lump sum, which would not last long, and she had nearly as many mouths to feed as Bridie had. And she badly wanted to keep Manuel in school, if she could.

'There'll be the Burial Insurance, too.'

Micaela opened her mouth as if to say something, and then thought better of it, when Bridie said, 'I haven't got none.'

'Have your lads got any work?' Rosita asked.

'Andy's muckin' out the milkman's cowshed and washing his cans for him. The others sometimes bring in a few pence, runnin' messages, like. But I got rent to pay, and I'm owin' more than a week already.'

Rosita thankfully sipped at her mug of tea. She began to resent having to comfort someone who was not a friend and whose boys were known pests. 'Well, I'm going to let every room in this house, to start with.'

'You're lucky. I've only got two rooms, and I'll lose them if I don't pay up.'

When Micaela heard her daughter say that she would let rooms, she foresaw a lot of trouble. Life was difficult enough, sharing the kitchen-living-room sink and the kitchen range with Effie Halloran; to have others also using the same facilities would be almost intolerable. The thought of the noise, the inevitable arguments, and the total lack of privacy for her family left her daunted. And yet, what else could Rosita do?

As if in answer to Micaela's unspoken query, Rosita continued speaking to Bridie. 'I'm going to look for work I can do at home,' she said determinedly.

'What work? You nor I don't know nothing.' Bridie leaned back in the rocking chair, small sobs intermittently escaping her. 'He were a proper nice fella,' she wailed.

'Before I was married I was a seamstress. I served my time at Cripps'. I'm going to ask them.'

'Lucky for you,' responded Bridie tartly. 'And you're pretty – you could marry again. Many a man wouldn't mind taking on a couple of little girls – and a boy ready for working.'

Rosita dismissed the suggestion with an impatient shrug. How could she face anyone but Pedro in her bed? The insensitive bitch!

Micaela swallowed. It was clear that neither woman understood exactly what her legal position was. Bridie had brought up a point which Micaela felt she should clarify. There were not too many marriageable women in the Basque community and Rosita was still young enough to have more children. She might, indeed, get an offer of marriage. It would be her best chance of a new life – when she was free to accept it.

She swung her feet to the floor and leaned towards the two widows. In her distress, she unthinkingly spoke in Basque. 'There's something I have to tell you about,' she began, 'because it seems as if you don't know about it. Neither of you can get married again – at least, not for a long time.'

Rosita turned a startled face to her mother. She did not

want to remarry, but the remark was very unexpected. Bridie had not understood what Micaela had said, but she understood from Rosita's reaction that it was something extraordinary.

'What do you mean, Mam?'

'What did she say?' asked Bridie suspiciously.

Rosita quickly translated. 'Why, Mam?'

'My love, your hubbie isn't yet dead – not in law.'

A wild irrational hope shot through Rosita, and died.

Micaela heard her quick intake of breath, and her voice broke, as she added, 'The ship is *presumed* lost with all hands. Nobody knows for sure that it has foundered. So, unless you can produce his body, you have to wait seven years, in case Pedro or Mr Pilar turn up again. After seven years, you can apply for them to be declared dead. Now – well, you're not a widow, you are still a wife. Which means you are in limbo.'

Bridie said anxiously, 'Tell me what she's saying. You look like a ghost.'

Micaela repeated her warning in English. Since she had lived in the seagoing community for over forty years, neither woman doubted what she told them.

Bridie burst into wild laughter, swinging the rocking chair madly backwards and forwards. 'Does that mean we won't even get the compensation? Be treated like whores living in sin? And me without even bread in the house?'

Micaela felt suddenly very old; the world was too cruel. Unwilling to leave either woman without hope, she said, 'I think they'll pay – because they are a good company. But they could hold off – you never know. The Prudential won't pay the burial money either, without a body with a death certificate.'

At this added burden, Rosita closed her eyes. She wanted to go upstairs and crawl into bed and never get up. Grief overwhelmed her again, as Bridie continued to yell. She did not see Micaela hoist herself to her feet and cross the fireplace, to administer, quite accurately, a very sharp slap across Bridie's face.

'Hysterics won't do you any good,' she told her firmly. 'You've got to keep your wits about you.'

Bridie's laughter ceased abruptly. 'You didn't have to do that!' she retorted, as she rubbed her tingling cheek. 'I've got a right to be upset, I have.' Ordinary tears began to trickle forth again. 'And no bread – not a crust in the house.' She looked up appealingly to Micaela. 'Could you lend me a shilling, luv? I haven't got nothing.'

Chapter Thirty-three

When Pedro's ship went down, Mr Ganivet was genuinely sorry that Manuel's father was lost. It was the talk of the waterfront, as everyone surmised what must have happened to the ship. He liked young Manuel, and he asked the boy, one day, when he was having tea with his son, what his mother was going to do.

Mrs Ganivet leaned over the tea tray with its huge tea-cosy and pot, and said, 'Now don't you worry the boy, luv.'

'Of course not,' her husband responded irritably, and continued to Manuel, 'I'm naturally concerned about you and your mother.'

'We've got a big house – she's letting rooms,' Manuel answered stiffly; he thought that letting rooms was probably beneath the Ganivets. 'It used to be an emigrants' hotel.'

'Of course. I remember. I met your grandfather once or twice – a fine old man.'

Nothing more was said, but a few days later, in the early afternoon when he could safely assume Manuel to be in school, Mr Ganivet walked along the dock road from his warehouse, to call on Rosita.

Rosita did not know who he was, when she answered the door, and was completely flustered when he made himself known. She invited him into the parlour, as yet unlet. The room was both cold and damp, so she hastened to bring him a glass of wine to warm him a little. Slowly and shyly, he explained the reason for his visit.

Though Rosita had not taken off her flowered pinafore,

or had time to comb her hair, Mr Ganivet was impressed by the woman's dignity and touched by her air of sadness; she must have been a real beauty, was his first thought. His wife had told him what a fine man her husband had been, and the sight of Rosita increased Mr Ganivet's determination to do what he could to help Manuel.

Very carefully and courteously, as if he were wooing the business of a shipowner, he suggested to her that he would be happy to undertake Manuel's school expenses until he was fourteen.

'I imagine,' he said, 'that the boy will want to go to work to help you, but I understand he is not yet twelve and that is too young. When I was talking to Arnador's schoolmaster, the other day, I mentioned Manuel to him, and he said he taught the boy maths – and that he was good at it – worked hard. It seems to me that he should, at least, continue at St Francis Xavier's until the usual school-leaving age. He will be bigger and stronger by then.'

Rosita was stunned at such an offer of help. Tears sprang up in her eyes, and her lips quivered. And he was a real Basque, speaking Basque!

She had been worried to death about Manuel. He had said he would try for a job as a ship's boy, and lie about his age. But she had told him tartly that his fees were paid until Easter – and he had not yet grown out of his latest set of trousers and blazer – so he should continue at school. Despite her deep anxiety about money, she added with artificial cheerfulness, that she and Granny would probably find his future fees from somewhere, at least until he was fourteen.

Now, by the Grace of God and a small ship's chandler, her forecast could come true.

Mr Ganivet, enchanted by her, was continuing. He said, 'Boys grow so fast – I would help with his uniform, as well, of course. As long as you can manage to feed him . . .'

She felt she could take this offer of help from a fellow

Basque — it would be different, she told herself, if he had been of another nationality — so she thanked him gratefully.

He rubbed his hands and smiled jovially, and she wondered suddenly if there was going to be a price to pay for the help. But he did not touch her. He finished his wine, got up and said, 'I will write to you in a few days.' He felt it would not be the best of manners to open his wallet then and there, and give her the money; he would post it to her.

He did not tell his wife what he had done. Mrs Ganivet was extremely good to Manuel when, increasingly, he and Arnador did their homework in Arnador's room because of the growing turmoil in the Echaniz home. She did not, however, feel it necessary to call on his widowed mother; nor did it strike her as odd that he was able to continue school. Wapping Dock was a faraway place, like China, as far as she was concerned.

To Rosita, Mr Ganivet's offer of help seemed like a miracle, and the memory of it helped to sustain her through the bitter early days of her widowhood. Behind her mourning had lurked the worrying thought that Manuel would not be thirteen until September 1921, and was, consequently, physically immature to be sent to sea, where the work was usually very demanding. At fourteen, he would have some muscle on him. He would also benefit, in the long term, from having completed the minimum schooling required by the Education Committee.

She quietly wept into her pillow, however, as her dreams of letting him matriculate and, perhaps, go to university faded and died.

Chapter Thirty-four

On his way to his wife's grave with a pink rose in a plastic grocery bag, to protect it from a buffeting summer breeze, Old Manuel thought about his mother in her years of limbo. With his own Kathleen in her grave, he could understand her anguish and despair. She and his father had been so close, despite his being much at sea. Much closer than Kathleen and he had been, he thought with regret. But then Rosita had not had to contend with such a formal society as Kathleen had; Rosita's life *was* her family which flowed gently alongside that of other families close by, where most of the little neighbourhood saw each other every day; they did not have to make appointments with each other, or give formal invitations in order to mix. There were no organized charities to be run – you simply helped the neighbours when they were in crisis – and, then, men understood that need as well – they themselves often helped, if they were ashore and muscle-power was required.

The few real rows he had had with Kathleen had been about her not being home when he returned from his travels; or, if she were at home, she went off to some meeting or other, rather than sit with him over supper to hear his adventures. He had done his best to accept Kathleen's world, because she was still the woman with whom he had fallen in love and, in bed, he could still express that love. She was trustworthy with money, too, a very important facet of married life. He grinned to himself, as he walked along; Basques at least shared the Canadians' belief in saving. She had many virtues.

As, for the hundredth time, he went over in his mind

what had been missing in his married life, he felt again a sense of mental confusion, doubts as to how he had dealt with his life in Canada, with Kathleen. After he had become aware of the enormous gap in understanding of each other's background, he had stopped complaining, accepted whatever was happening as best he could, though within him had grown a terrible sense of isolation. The isolation had been mitigated while he was at sea, in company, as usual, with mates that he knew. To a lesser degree, he had been glad of the male world of designing ships, too. Only when he had retired and was at home all the time had it hit him full in the face, that men and women in the affluent society in which he found himself lived very separate lives.

'There didn't seem to be any time to do nothing very much together,' he told himself. While, between voyages, Pedro sloped around in his father-in-law's kitchen, doing a few odd jobs for Rosita and Micaela, there had been a good deal of communication in an unthreatening, non-confrontational way. It had been the same with his grand-father, Manuel remembered. The old man had been very dogmatic and acted as if he were the cock of the walk, but he was aware of how the others felt, and tacit adjustments were made to accommodate the needs of his family.

Maybe it was because they were used to living on top of each other; if there were a verbal quarrel or a physical fight, it was difficult in a tiny living-room to carry on for long. He laughed to himself – there wasn't enough room! And there would always be family onlookers, who would separate the combatants and take them away to be soothed in different corners, and point out the good reasons for not fighting.

Manuel paused in his walk to take out a cigarette from his shirt pocket and light it. As he drew hard on it, he thought with satisfaction that his had been a wonderful tribe, Barinètas and Echanizes alike. He had been lucky, except for the loss of his father, and Kathleen had never faced the kind of problems that had ensued for Rosita.

At the time of Pedro's being lost at sea, there was no Widow's Pension for Rosita, though the shipping company did pay a lump sum in compensation. With five of them to feed, however, it had not lasted very long. Similarly, there had been no government pension for his grandmother, when his grandfather had been killed; Pedro had, as a matter of course, maintained his mother-in-law, though he must have hoped, at times, that Leo would return to help them.

Only in the last few months, since Old Manuel had begun to write his memoirs, had he truly appreciated the dogged courage of the two women, as they brought up his sisters and himself. Neither was ever idle – except Micaela in the last month of life – and what physical and mental stress Micaela must have endured as a blind widow, crippled by arthritis, in a foreign country – with nothing of her own!

And his mother? As she faced the devastation of her life, she had still been handsome, though with hands roughened by years of scrubbing, and a waistline expanded by pregnancies and the need to make do with a starchy diet. Though the passion she had shared with Pedro must have eaten into her very being, she had never, to Manuel's knowledge, taken a lover after her husband's death; nor did she marry again, when after seven years, she had been free to do so.

At the latter thought, Old Manuel made a face. Those were the days when, at the age of forty, a woman was considered hopelessly old; and, in fact, he could remember a swath of neighbouring men and women who had died around that age – or were invalids, living on the kitchen sofa.

As each room was let, the old house by Wapping Dock rapidly became a nightmare to live in. The women vied with each other for the use of the kitchen oven; for other cooking, they tramped back and forth through Rosita's kitchen-living-room with buckets of coal from deliveries dumped in the back yard, to build fires in the small bedroom fireplaces. From time to time, there would be bitter quarrels, as tenants accused each other of stealing their coal. At other times, they would make a tremendous dust in the tiny back yard, as they sieved cinders from the ashes to burn them on subsequent fires.

The single lavatory in the back yard frequently became choked, as tenants, unused to modern plumbing, failed to flush it. They all had chamber pots in their rooms, so that they did not have to come downstairs every time nature called. The pots were not always carried through Rosita's room to be emptied when they should have been; and the stench became all-pervading in the house.

Periodically, Manuel was faced with having to clear the lavatory. To drown the disgusting smell and to control his desire to vomit, he began to smoke, and smoking became a lifetime habit.

Rosita did not dare to ask the help of the landlord's agent to improve the plumbing, because the agent would probably have insisted on turning out most of the sub-tenants – or have demanded an increase in rent to reap some of the financial benefit.

The only water tap in the house was in the kitchen-living-room, so pails of water were filled and slopped across the room, to be taken upstairs – or to the parlour, where an elderly hospital cleaner existed as best she could.

In the days when emigrants had filled the house, it had been for very short periods; as soon as a group embarked for New York, Micaela and Rosita had been able to give the house a thorough cleaning. Many of the emigrant women had been good housewives, who left the room they had occupied immaculate. This was not so amongst the type of tenants who had to live permanently in such primitive circumstances.

Though two of Pudding's great-grandchildren hunted industriously and grew fat on their efforts, the whole dock area was cursed with rats and mice; and in a house where food was kept in every room, rodents and cockroaches began to flourish.

Rosita's greatest dread was dealing with tenants who failed to pay their rent. She had no man to threaten them, and, in any case, as the years crept on, unemployment with its consequent hardships became a city-wide, chronic disease.

She would sit by her own, often empty, fireplace, and weep to Micaela. 'How can I turn Iris Mary out, with her expecting, and her hubbie with no work – they hardly eat!'

Bundled up in a blanket on the sofa, in increasing pain from her arthritis and with little heat to assuage it, Micaela would not reply, because there was nothing to say that would comfort.

Rosita continued to try for finishing work from the big dress houses in the city; but the elaborate dresses of pre-war days, with their infinite amounts of embroidery to be done and flounces to be hemmed, had given way to very short, comparatively plain fashions; and she was turned away.

Chapter Thirty-five

Fifteen months after Pedro's ship foundered, when softer winds blowing up the Mersey heralded the spring of 1921, and the corner shop had a pile of small Easter eggs on its counter, George Halloran had a stroke and died on his bed, upstairs. Once again, the house resounded to the cries of bereavement; and the women gathered to comfort hysterical, penniless Effie, who wept not only for her husband but for her dead boys.

After the added sorrow of a pauper's funeral because Effie was behind with her burial insurance, Effie wiped her reddened eyes and said she would find a job. Micaela was thankful, because the woman was a week behind in her rent as a result of George's unexpected demise.

Even in the worst of economic times, there are jobs that no one wants to do, and, for a while, Effie toiled in a stapler's workshop in St Anne Street, where all day long she teased wool for stuffing mattresses.

She would return home, worn-out, her black shawl a mass of fluff. The same fluff clung to her hair; and Micaela said that if you touched her you could feel the fine hairs stuck to her face and arms; she began to cough, as the hair accumulated in her lungs.

By the time Effie had obtained her job, she had missed another week's rent, which was a serious problem for Rosita.

'I can't make myself turn her out,' she said anxiously to Manuel, and the boy instantly agreed with her; Effie had become almost part of the family.

'If only I could get some sewing work,' Rosita fretted.

'It would really help. I could do it at home and watch the tenants don't pilfer food or coal – now your grandma can't see, she can't really watch.'

Since her search for sewing work was fruitless, she borrowed the *Evening Express* from Pat Connolly, and finally found an advertisement put in by a firm which offered a small fortune to those who would affix green baize linings into cutlery baskets – at home. Upon inquiry, she discovered that the company, in the shape of a small, sharp-faced man called Mr Holley, would pay ten copper pennies per basket for this fiddling piecework.

The family became accustomed to her sitting at the table, snipping at the green baize, and cursing quietly when the glue made the pieces stick to her fingers. Manuel did his best to help by contributing the two shillings and sixpence a week which he earned by doing an early-morning paper round; and both he and Francesca handed over any pennies they earned by going messages for the neighbours.

Though Manuel would not be fourteen until September 1922, he could legally leave school at the end of the previous summer term. He was counting the days until he would be free to look for a job. His mother had been so forceful about the importance of his continuing in school until he was fourteen that he had obeyed her. When he had asked impatiently, how she could pay the fees, she had snapped, 'I'll manage, somehow. Don't worry.'

She did not want to tell him of Mr Ganivet's help, because she felt it might spoil the easy friendship between Manuel and his son. 'Arnador's a good friend to him,' she said to Micaela. 'And I want to keep it that way.'

Micaela agreed.

Deep in his heart, Manuel's desire to go to sea to help his mother was tempered by the memory of Pedro's fate; yet, he told himself crossly, most of the men in the neighbourhood faced the very real threat of injury or death, wherever they worked. But you never heard them complain about it.

He wished he could discuss this cowardice with Arnador. Arnador was very practical, however, and he knew he would say immediately that Manuel should stay ashore and try for a fairly safe job, like clerical work. And if I do that, thought Manuel fretfully, not only would I be a coward, but Mother would have to spend my wages on food for me; if I go to sea, I get food thrown in – and she can have all my wages.

One warm Friday evening in June, near the end of his last term at school, Rosita put her head down on the kitchen table and unexpectedly burst into tears.

Micaela got up from her sofa and hobbled towards the sound of weeping, while the children asked in alarm, 'What's up, Mam?'

'It's the rent,' she wailed. 'First the collector ticked me off this morning because I couldn't pay the arrears. And this afternoon, the agent himself – Roy Fleet – came, and said if we don't pay up he'll put us out – on Monday morning.'

'But we've been in this house for thirty-five years,' protested Micaela, as she bent over her daughter.

'I told him that. But I've got behind since Pedro went – because the tenants don't pay me regularly.'

Micaela sighed – she still could not believe the threat. 'To think that Juan or Pedro did all the repairs!' she exclaimed. 'Isn't that worth something?'

A very shaken Manuel bent to pick up a scared Little Maria, who was not sure what the threat was, but had begun to whimper. He held her close and whispered to her not to be afraid, while Francesca, who had been laboriously knitting by the empty fireplace, put down her pins, and sat like a small white statue, staring at him, aghast.

'Mr Fleet's not a bad man,' Rosita said dully, 'but he's

got an owner pushing him. He's knows I'm a widow – and he'll be thinking that I can't afford such a big house any more – but it's only because I let rooms that I can get by.'

'What happened finally?' Manuel asked, as he mechanically patted Little Maria's back to comfort her.

'Well, he said if we could pay a pound by Sunday night, and the rest of the arrears at a shilling a week, he'd rescind the eviction order. He's given me his home address, so that I can pay it any time up to eleven o'clock Sunday night. I suppose he's trying to be kind.' Elbows on table, her head between her sticky hands, she wept again. 'I haven't got a pound – and neither your grandma nor I know what to do.'

Her arm still round her daughter's shoulder, Micaela felt defeated. Though blind, she could feel the dampness of the house from leaking gutters and drainpipes, and she could smell the extra smokiness from downdraughts caused by a crumbling collection of chimneys. Rosita had remarked recently that, after one hundred and fifty-odd years of use, not a door handle or a lock worked properly, and every door and window rattled in the wind.

'Conor and Lily and Effie – they've all missed paying this week. They can't help it sometimes when there's no work – and Effie changed her job this week, so she's short.'

'Have you got any money at all?' asked Manuel. He jumped as Francesca sidled up close to him. He looked down and winked at her, and said to her, 'Don't you be afraid. We'll fix it somehow.' His deep-timbred voice sounded manly and comforting.

His mother sobbed. 'I've two and sixpence – your newspaper money. I have to keep that for a bit of food for us.'

'Phew!'

'Lily Rawlings says her hubbie's got work for Monday and Tuesday – she'll pay me Tuesday night. They owe two weeks now, because he didn't have any work last week – and she's got morning sickness so bad that she can't go charring for a bit – till it settles down.' She wiped her eyes with the back of her hands.

A small voice piped up. 'What about going to the post office to get some money?' Going to the post office with Granny had recently been one of Little Maria's delights – because she sometimes was allowed to buy a halfpenny lollipop on the way back.

Her grandmother replied honestly, 'The post office doesn't have any more money, dumpling.'

'Could we pawn something?' Manuel asked.

'We haven't got anything that would raise a pound. I had to pawn even Granny's and my wedding rings a few weeks back, to pay for Frannie and Maria going to school.'

Shocked, Manuel looked down at his mother's left hand. It was bare – and he had never noticed, he thought ashamedly. 'Dear God!'

He glanced wildly round the room. 'Could we at least hide the furniture, so that the bailiffs don't get it?'

'I'm going to ask Pat to help us put it in his yard – I hope it doesn't rain.'

'What about the tenants' stuff?'

'They won't take that. They'll be mad, though, when they can't find ours. Not that they'll get more than a few pence for each piece – *if* they manage to find it and auction it.'

Rosita was slowly collecting herself. She looked up at Little Maria watching her fearfully from the safety of Manuel's arms, and said, 'Don't be afraid, pet. Mummy's going to finish a lot of cutlery boxes by tomorrow noon, and Mr Holley'll pay me for them.' She added, for the benefit of Manuel and Francesca, 'He closes on Saturday afternoon.'

A frightened Francesca leaned against Manuel, frozen by a gnawing dread of that vague monster, the workhouse, which everybody seemed to hold up as the ultimate punishment for being poor. Her mother's decision to work on her boxes gave her a ray of hope, and she said, 'You go on with the boxes, Mam. I'll do the dishes and see Little Maria into bed.'

Manuel put Little Maria down, and, after a doubtful glance up at him, she wandered back to the hearth rug, to collect her rag doll. Francesca briskly made her way to the kitchen sink and the dishes, while the youth said to his mother, 'The newsagent's will still be open – I'll ask him if he'll advance next week's half-a-crown to me.' He walked quickly round the table, to take down an old jacket of his father's hanging on the back door, and put it on. 'When I come back, I'll go round all the tenants and try to squeeze a bit out of each of them.'

His mother nodded; she had no hope of his success; but he was back within a few minutes with a shilling in his hand. 'One,' he said triumphantly. 'All we need is nineteen more!'

The shilling was carefully deposited on the mantelpiece, while he determinedly plodded up the stairs. As he went up, he heard Little Maria gabbling her prayers at her grandmother's knee. The child finished, 'Amen. Can I have a piece of bread and jam before I go to bed, Granny?'

He paused halfway up the staircase. His mother snapped, 'No, you can't. Get up to bed.' He turned and ran down again. Never before had he heard his mother refuse any of them food, except immediately before a meal.

'Mam!' he cried reproachfully. 'She didn't have much tea.'

His mother paused in her application of glue, and with brush poised, said sulkily, 'I must keep what I have for breakfast.'

Little Maria, halfway into her nightgown, began to cry, and Micaela shifted herself to embrace the child.

Standing in the doorway, Manuel snorted indignantly. 'Mam! She's only little! You can give me a slice less at breakfast!'

He thought his mother was going to weep again, but, instead, she said resignedly, 'All right. Get her a piece.'

While he got the loaf out of the bread box and carefully cut a slice, Francesca stacked the washed dishes on the dresser. She was hungry and the bread smelled so good; but she felt that she was nearly grown up, like Manuel, so she did not ask for a slice herself. She watched while Little Maria climbed on to Micaela's knee, and, with a bright smile, accepted the bread. Then she went to stand by her mother, as Manuel put the rest of the loaf back into its box, and slowly turned to go heavily up the stairs again.

She said to her mother, 'Mam, I could cut the pieces of baize for you, especially if you made me a paper pattern.'

Rosita doubted the steadiness of the child's hand, when it was necessary to be precise. She replied doubtfully, 'The divisions of the baskets are not identical, dearest; that's why it's such a slow job.'

Francesca picked up the next box and looked attentively at it. 'Let me try, Mam. I'll measure very careful over the box itself.'

'Well, try one. Cut the baize fractionally bigger than the section – not much bigger, or we'll run out of baize. Then try the piece in the particular box, and trim it very carefully. When you've cut out a set, I'll glue it in – and we'll see how well you've done.'

As Manuel climbed the narrow staircase, to knock first on the Rawlingses' room, he quaked inwardly. The young couple lived on the edge of penury; and he knew that Lily Rawlings was expecting – most mornings, when he got up, he heard her vomiting.

Rawlings was, however, much more worldly-wise than the stripling facing him. If the bailiffs came when he was out, they could easily haul out what bits of furniture *he* owned; and he knew that he would never find a more kindly landlady than Rosita. Further, Lily would need helpful women around her if the baby were to survive. Manuel's request for money – any money – had to be taken seriously.

He turned to his anxious wife standing behind him, her cotton dress tight across her stomach. 'Lil, have you got any cash at all?'

She replied unwillingly, 'A couple of bob – for food till Tuesday. Have you?'

He made a rueful face at her. 'A tanner for ciggies,' he owned up. He dug the sixpence out of his trouser pocket, and stared at it in the palm of his hand.

'Go and get your two bob – I got work for Monday and Tuesday, for sure.'

'You've got to eat!'

'Ask Mrs Betts at the corner to put it on the slate till Tuesday night.'

'I don't know that she will,' protested the girl weepily, but she obeyed, and brought the silver two-shilling piece from under their alarm clock on the mantelpiece.

Rawlings plunked his cigarette money into Manuel's hand, and Lily reluctantly proffered her florin on the palm of her hand, hoping that he would not actually pick it up. But Manuel took it; it was her roof as well as his own that he was trying to save.

Auntie Effie greeted him with affection and asked him in. Her face fell when, seated by her minute fire, he asked her if she could pay a bit towards her rent.

'I did tell your mam I'd pay next week. I started a new job in the bottle factory – washing bottles and jam jars. Me chest is bothering me something awful, and I lost three days' before I got this job.' She nervously chewed her overlong thumbnail, and Manuel noticed that a thick grime lay under all her nails, despite having her hands in water much of the last two days.

Manuel waited. Effie's mind worked like a clock about to run down.

She heaved a great sigh, and felt in her skirt pocket. 'Bailiffs?' she asked.

'Monday morning,' Manuel assured her. 'Mam's got till Sunday night to find a pound.'

He felt dreadful when she slowly counted out half a week's rent into his hand. 'I were paid two and a half days yesterday,' she muttered, 'and I don't know what I'm going to do. Maybe, if I work Monday, the boss would let me have the money for that day.'

'They will do that sometimes,' Manuel said. 'Pat told me once.'

Conor said flatly he hadn't a cent. Not till next week. Iris simply wept, and her youngsters behind her looked like death's heads. The hospital cleaner in the parlour said crossly that she had never missed paying her rent; it was unreasonable to ask her to pay in advance.

Manuel gave up.

That Friday night, Rosita, Francesca and Manuel worked on the silver boxes until after eleven o'clock. Francesca's eyes drooped with fatigue; her back muscles and arms ached from working at a table too high for her. Nevertheless, when she heard the alarm clock go off in her mother's room the next morning, she crawled out of bed, and joined her mother at the kitchen table, to slowly snip the pieces of baize for her. As soon as Manuel had finished his paper round, he joined them, to paint the insides of the boxes with glue.

Micaela made tea without milk or sugar; the two little girls were each given a slice of bread to eat. Francesca sat looking at her slice for a moment and then slowly tore it into two, to share it with Manuel.

'You eat it up,' he ordered firmly, and, when she hesitated, he told her, 'The newsagent's missus gave me a cup of tea and some biscuits.'

As the morning progressed, hunger bit into all of them, and they became slower.

Rosita's voice was dull and hopeless, as she said, 'We have to do eighteen boxes to make up the rent – and to pay the ferry across the river to deliver the money.' She laughed suddenly and wildly. 'I don't know how I am going to manage next week, even if we manage to pay to-morrow.'

As if to deliberately add to their torment, the noise from outside the house seemed to be even more trying than usual; the riveters, the horses and carts and the clatter of clogs and boots on the pavement seemed particularly active. Sometimes the kitchen table shuddered as the great presses in the factory behind the house worked through the Saturday shift, so that Rosita had to pause, a strip of baize in her hand, until the upward swing of the biggest press allowed the table to be steady for a moment and she could quickly and accurately place the piece of baize in the box.

By eleven o'clock in the morning, they had completed sixteen boxes. Their time was short. Manuel quickly washed the worst of the glue off his hands, and began to pack the cutlery boxes into two cardboard containers. Though not terribly heavy, the two cardboard boxes were clumsy to carry, and Manuel said to his mother, 'Wash your hands, Mam. I'll carry these up to Mr Holley's for you.' His mother had not eaten since yesterday's teatime, a meal of bread and margarine, and he feared that she might faint on her way to her employer's warehouse. 'Hurry, Mam. We can't risk missing Mr Holley!'

Rosita wearily dragged herself to her feet, and did as he had bidden her. 'All that work – three of us doing it – for thirteen shillings and fourpence!' she said to Micaela. 'And we still haven't got a pound.'

Micaela nodded. Manuel said, 'Well, it's better than nothing,' and he carefully tied twine round the two cardboard boxes to make them easier to carry.

They caught Mr Holley, just as he was tidying up before

going home. He amiably checked the boxes, however, and paid the stony-faced woman.

Outside, on the pavement, Rosita looked up at her son. She was swaying on her feet. 'I'll have to use the two and sixpence you gave me for food,' she said brokenly. 'I'd hoped to put it towards the rent – but I can't. We must eat.'

Manuel put his arm in hers to steady her, and asked uneasily, 'Do you think Mr Fleet would accept a bit less?'

'Not a hope. He meant what he said.' A tear trickled slowly down Rosita's cheek. 'And I can't get any more on tick at the corner shop.'

That tear and the hopelessly disillusioned look in his mother's tired blue eyes were something Manuel never forgot.

As they walked slowly towards a corner shop, Manuel said, 'If Jean Baptiste was in work, he'd help us.'

'Certainly – but he isn't. They're only saved because their boys are older and are working.'

'I could ask Mr Ganivet,' suggested Manuel.

'We can't.'

'He's very kind, Mam.'

'He is,' responded Rosita with feeling. Then she told him how his school expenses had been paid for over two years by the kindly chandler.

Manuel was stunned. 'Does Arnador know?'

'I don't think so.'

They paused at the entrance to the little shop. 'You should have told me,' he reproached her.

'I thought that if I did you would feel awkward with Arnador.'

He did not answer her, because he did not know whether that would have been the case.

She said gently, 'It's only a week, now, to the end of term. And you'll always be able to say that you went to

St Francis Xavier's until you were fourteen. It's a good recommendation for work.'

Manuel nodded bewildered agreement. It would have been even better, if he could have stayed until he was sixteen or seventeen and got his Matric. While his mother entered the shop and he waited for her outside, he stared unseeingly at the tiny window space of the shop, packed with dusty cards advertising everything from tobacco to paraffin and Sunlight soap, and tried to think of someone who could help them.

He realized for the first time how the number of Basque families in the neighbourhood had been sharply reduced by the war, when the menfolk found it safer to sail in Spanish ships out of Bilbao. Others had been able to move to more salubrious neighbourhoods, as their children grew up and began to earn. Of the remaining little community, Mr Saitua was not the only man out of work; and there were one or two families with whom they had never been friends, because Grandpa Juan had not approved of them – his polite term, Manuel suspected, for small vendettas; like anyone else, Basques could carry grudges for a long time.

He wished suddenly that Arnador was his brother, so that he could confide to him the details of the nightmare they were facing. Arnador was so sensible.

But Arnador was not a blood brother, and, moreover, Arnador's father had already helped them very generously.

Manuel felt sick with hunger and fear.

Chapter Thirty-six

On Saturday night, the family rejoiced in a meal of potatoes boiled with chopped cabbage. They cooked it on a shovelful of coal borrowed from the widowed hospital cleaner who lived in the parlour, an Irish woman who kept to herself. In fact, the family hardly ever saw her except on Friday, which was rent day, because she worked such long hours and tended to stay in bed on her days off.

Nobody went to Mass on Sunday morning. Instead, Rosita and Francesca began work on a new pile of boxes, given to Rosita by Mr Holley in return for the completed ones. Manuel did his heavy Sunday newspaper round first, and then sat down to help. Whether they saved their home or not, the family knew they must try to obtain a little money on Monday, in the hope of keeping themselves out of the workhouse; Mr Holley was their only hope.

The spectre of the workhouse haunted Manuel particularly. In a week's time, he would be looking for work, and being dressed in workhouse uniform would not recommend him to an employer; in their eyes, it would label him a shiftless ne'er-do-well. He would be wiser simply to take to the streets, he thought passionately.

Little Maria played in the street with one of Peggy O'Brien's little girls; and Micaela, wrapped in a blanket, silently nursed her arthritis. They had each had a piece of bread for breakfast. They had been unable to boil water to make tea, and this had made the women feel very low.

They had worked for a couple of hours, when their boredom was broken by an exclamation from Micaela, who was fighting her way out of the encompassing blanket.

'Claire Carrandi — she would. It's not much to ask, is it?'

Rosita paused in her careful smoothing of a piece of baize. 'Who?'

'The undertaker's wife. You must remember her! She's a Basque — married to Carrandi, who died of a fever in the West Indies. We were quite friendly for years. Then, when she was widowed, she married Ould Biggs, the undertaker — and that seemed to take her away, somehow.'

'I do remember — when I was a young girl.'

'She's nearer my age than yours. I haven't seen her in a long time. Juan gave her hubbie plenty of carting work — transporting the emigrants and their luggage down to the dock. Ould Biggs owes us plenty. Now, Sunday afternoon is a good time to go to see an old friend. Little Maria can take me up this afternoon, while you get on with the boxes. Claire will lend it.'

Rosita looked a little anxiously at her mother. 'Could you manage the walk up to Park Road, Mam?'

'I'm the only one who can ask her, so I'll do it — somehow.'

It was true that probably only Micaela could negotiate a loan from Claire; but it was with reluctance that Rosita watched her set out, with her arm around the shoulder of Little Maria. The journey was not a long one, except for the pain that Micaela would probably experience, and the fact that she could not see.

As Rosita came back into the kitchen-living-room, Manuel sensed her worry. 'Granny'll be all right,' he assured her, as he dabbed glue into a corner of a box. 'Little Maria's good with her granny — she warns of all the steps up and down — and the traffic.'

Though it did take a long, painful time to crawl up Sparling Street and along Park Lane to the undertaker's premises, Micaela's visit to Claire was not a protracted one.

The Biggses' front door was shut, and the whole place

seemed locked in the calm of Sunday afternoon. Micaela told Maria to lead her down the side of the building and into a cobbled yard, where lay a couple of carts and a toast-rack horse bus, together with a dust-laden black carriage, all with their shafts up. At the back of the yard were stables in which the horses could be heard shuffling and snorting. Beside the stables were two wide doors, held shut by a large padlock, behind which rested the pride of Ould Biggs's collection, his beautifully carved black hearse with its etched glass panels.

'There's a door up some steps at the left,' Micaela told Maria. 'Run up the steps and bang the knocker.'

Maria had to stand on tiptoe to reach the lion's head which was the door knocker. It gave a reverberating thud, when she let go of it. She ran back down the steps, to stand by Micaela. While they waited for someone to answer, she eased her round to face the door.

An elderly maid, with long black streamers falling from her white, goffered cap, responded to the knock; Ould Biggs never knew when a bereaved client might hammer on his door, and he insisted that the maid give the right impression of solemnity.

Micaela asked to see Mrs Biggs, and was politely asked into the big sombre hall. To Maria, it was rather frightening; she wondered where Mr Biggs kept the bodies.

Claire came out of a back room immediately, and sashayed down the hall towards them. She was wearing a black, knee-length frock with a small, white frilled collar, her plump legs encased in flesh-coloured silk stockings. Her very high-heeled, black patent shoes were held in place by three cross-straps, each with a glittering black button.

Maria stared at her in fascination. She had never seen an older woman in such short skirts. Her grandmother was garbed from chin to ankle; she had not changed her style in fifty years. Even her mother still wore gathered black skirts that reached her ankles.

'Micaela!'

'Claire!' exclaimed Micaela, as Maria helped her up the steps, and led her into Claire's open arms. They kissed each other on both cheeks, both genuinely glad to meet again. The visitors were led into the dining-room at the back of the house, because, Claire explained, Mr Biggs always had his Sunday nap in the sitting-room.

Claire's last visit to Micaela had been after Juan's death; she had sent a note of sympathy at Aunt Maria's death, not sure how to cope with the fact that Maria had been buried by the City because, owing to her severe illness, she had been uninsurable. She now felt guilty that she had not visited her for a very long time. She felt worse when Micaela stumbled when seating herself, and Claire perceived that there must be something wrong with her sight; maybe that was why Micaela had not visited *her* lately.

As she rang the bell for the maid, she inquired in Basque, 'Is everyone in the family all right?'

Micaela's face crinkled up in a smile. 'Nobody's dead,' she assured her jokingly in the same language, and Little Maria squirmed, and laughed up at their hostess.

Claire smiled back at the child. 'God be thanked,' she said virtuously, and then exclaimed, 'She's so like you, Micaela!'

Little Maria was hurt. Surely she didn't look so wizened and untidy as Grandma did?

She was consoled by a large piece of fruit cake from a tray brought in by the maid. She sat quietly eating it, currant by currant, while the two ladies caught up with accounts of their lives since Aunt Maria had died.

Maria became anxious that her grandmother seemed to have forgotten the family's dire need of a small loan; and that she made a joke about their running a boarding-house again. 'It's different from having emigrants go through – but it brings life into the house,' Micaela finished up.

Maria noticed that her grandmother was cautiously feeling round for her cup of tea; she had managed to set it on the table, originally; but now, apparently, she could not judge where it was.

'Allow me,' said Claire quickly, and put the cup and saucer carefully into Micaela's hand. 'Are you having trouble with your sight?'

Grandma took a sip of tea and then laughed deprecatingly. 'I can't see at all, except light and shadow,' she admitted baldly. 'I can still knit, though.' She turned towards Maria, who had stolidly returned to eating her cake. 'Little Maria – and Frannie have to be my eyes.'

'It must be very difficult for you,' Claire sympathized.

'Rosita's good to me.'

Micaela's cake on its flowered plate still lay on the table. Maria slipped down from her chair, and said, 'Give me your empty cup, Granny, and I'll give you your cake.'

'Thank you, dumpling.'

When it was handed to her, Micaela felt across the plate to locate the cake and then broke it into two. She took one half and stuffed it into her mouth. Saliva gathered at the corners of her lips, as she swallowed it almost whole.

Claire watched her in dismay. Then she jumped up and pulled the bell for the maid. 'How stupid of Mary Ellen,' she exclaimed. 'She forgot to put the scones on the tray.'

When the maid appeared, Claire instructed her to bring in a plate of buttered scones. She said to Micaela, 'Mary Ellen makes the best scones you've ever tasted – you simply have to try them.'

Little Maria gave a small sigh of anticipation. Scones as well as cake?

Micaela felt that she should have told Claire not to go to so much trouble for her – but her hunger was intolerable – and Basques were very hospitable, anyway.

Three scones and another piece of cake later, Micaela remained seated for another ten minutes or so and then said that she should go home. 'Come and visit me soon,' she urged. 'I would enjoy it so much.'

Totally dismayed, Little Maria thought that her grandmother had forgotten the money they so badly needed. She did not dare to mention it herself, and felt quite frantic when Micaela told her to go ahead into the hall and put on her coat like a good girl.

The two friends embraced again, both happy to have been reunited by the visit. Micaela drew back a little in Claire's arms, and asked diffidently, 'Claire, could you lend me two shillings, until I can get up to the post office to draw some money tomorrow afternoon?'

Claire replied without hesitation, thankful to assuage her sense that she had neglected Micaela. 'Of course,' she agreed. She loosed her hold on the old woman, and went to the sideboard, opened a drawer and took out a change purse. She pressed a florin into Micaela's hand.

Later, her husband came sleepily out of the sitting-room, trailing sheets of newspaper after him. 'Who came?' he inquired.

'Micaela Barinèta – Juan's wife. You remember them?'

'Oh, aye.'

'She's blind now. They seem in a pretty bad way – do you know, she was wearing a shawl – not a coat – she never did that when Juan was alive – at least, not on Sundays. Poor Rosita's husband was lost in the *Esperanza Larrinaga*, you may remember – it was in the paper, the time when I had Spanish flu. It took me such a long time to get better that I never went to see her.'

Henry Biggs took his pipe and tobacco pouch out of his jacket pocket and sat down on a dining-chair, while his wife stood by him, staring into the blue flames of the gas fire and remembering Rosita's handsome husband. She roused herself to say, 'Young Manuel's finishing school next week. He was in St Francis Xavier's. Must've been a struggle to keep him there — because they haven't got a wage-earner now. Nobody.'

'The lad can go to sea. That'll help them.' Henry lit his pipe. He then let his hand run up the backs of his wife's silk-clad legs, and tickled her gently.

'Oh, Henry!' she exclaimed. 'You really are naughty!'

'It's Sunday afternoon,' he reminded her, as she gave a delighted, though muffled shriek at his further advances.

Chapter Thirty-seven

That Sunday evening, Manuel saw his mother on to the Seacombe ferry, which would take her across the river to Roy Fleet's house. In her clutch purse she carried a pound in small change, and, separately in her pocket, fourpence to cover her fares, which she would pay on the other side of the river.

As the ferry backed away from the landing stage with much splashing and shuddering, he waved to her, and then stood idly for a few minutes looking at the ships anchored in the river. They ranged from small, grubby tramp steamers, with the crew's washing flapping merrily over the forecastle, to a huge Chinese freighter, so rusty that Manuel wondered how it had made the voyage from Shanghai, which, in chipped, white paint, was indicated as its port of registration. Tugs were moving a stately White Star transatlantic liner up river, perhaps to the Gladstone Graving Dock. In the distance was a single, tiny yacht, also going up river.

He was hailed by Domingo Saitua, who worked for the ferries and was waiting for the next New Brighton boat to come in. He wandered over to him, and, as the landing stage began to heave up and down under the pressure of the incoming tide, he asked Domingo what chance there was of a job on the ferries.

Stocky, beer-bellied Domingo looked him over. 'How old are you, now?'

'Fourteen,' lied Manuel. 'I'm leaving school next week.'

Domingo straightened his navy jersey, emblazoned in white with the words *Wallasey Ferries*. He made a glum face, and said briskly in Basque, 'Not a hope, lad. They like men who've been to sea. For instance, I went to sea with my uncle for a while – he was a fisherman.'

Manuel replied stoutly, 'My dad and my granddad went to sea.'

Anxious to comfort a boy who was his neighbour, Domingo said, 'Oh, aye, they did. You're a likely-looking youngster. Try getting in with a ship's steward, who'd look out for a job for you – find you a job as pantry boy, like. Better than being a deck boy.'

Manuel agreed. He could not, however, recall anyone in the Basque community who was a steward; if there had been one, he would not have hesitated to ask for help.

Domingo saw that the New Brighton ferry was coming in, so he prepared to catch a rope from it. 'Good luck, Mannie,' he said.

Manuel went home to do some prep for school. When ten o'clock came, he was worried that his mother had not returned, so he told Micaela that he would go down to the Pier Head again, to meet her.

The landing stage was deserted, except for Domingo, and he said that he had not seen Mrs Echaniz land. Manuel began to wonder if, possibly, she had lost the twopence for her return journey. His aching lack of food and his increasing apprehension made him feel dizzy. He wondered what he should do if she were not on the last ferry.

As the night took over, the silence on the landing stage became oppressive. Domingo went off to attend to his work, and only the slow rhythmic plop of a tug tied up at the end of the dock or the distant sounds of voices from ships anchored in the river broke the quietness.

To his intense relief, Rosita dragged herself off the eleven o'clock ferry. He hastened forward to take her arm and ask, 'Whatever happened?'

Under the brim of her out-of-date black straw hat, her

eyes glittered in the rays of a lamp. 'I had to walk much further than I expected to their house. They were nice to me – Roy and his missus, though. Kept me talking a bit.'

As they ambled slowly up the gangway which led to the Pier Head itself, she described her visit.

'Roy was still at church, when I got there, but he had told his missus that I might come, so she stayed home. She's a nice lady, like you don't see very often, and she's got a lovely sitting-room, all in green. We had a nice cup of tea together.'

Rosita paused, as they crossed the street. On the other side, a few prostitutes loitered in the shadows, their faces occasionally dimly lit up, as they struck matches to light their cigarettes. When they had passed them, she continued, 'I told her what happened to your dad – she was horrified, especially when I explained how I'm a widow but not a widow. She asked if I had a job, and I told her about the cutlery boxes, and how I had applied to Cripps' and was hoping they'd find me some sewing, because I used to work for them. And I told her I'd one or two lodgers living with me – but I didn't tell her how many! I said how they'd steal from me if I didn't work at home. She was so sympathetic, I felt like crying.'

They reached Wapping, where even the lights of the Baltic Fleet had been turned off. Manuel squeezed his mother's arm comfortingly, and asked what Mr Fleet had said about the rent.

'He said he thinks it'll be all right, if I don't get further behind – and pay a shilling a week off the arrears. He's going to talk to the landlord himself.'

As they stood on their own doorstep, Rosita lifted her eyes to her hungry son, put her hands on his shoulders and laid her head against his chest. She burst into tears.

'Oh, Mam! Don't cry. Everything's going to be all right. You'll see.'

She looked up and smiled through her tears. 'Yes, lovey,

we'll manage, I expect. I'm crying with relief, and because she was so kind. It was such a relief to tell somebody. I couldn't even bring myself to tell Bridget – she's got enough worries of her own at present, what with her hubbie being out of work – though she must have guessed how hard things are with us.'

Though Mrs Fleet knew that her husband had to be tough with some of the tenants for whom he was responsible, she was genuinely moved by Rosita's story of her woes, and she did not forget her.

Every Thursday afternoon, she went to Liverpool to shop and meet some of her friends over a cup of tea in Lyons' tea shop. On the Monday following Rosita's visit, she scribbled a short note to a friend she had not seen for a number of weeks; Muriel was a cutter, who had worked for Sloan, Dressmaker, ever since Mrs Ada Sloan, dressmaker, had set herself up in 82 Bold Street, in 1915. Dorothy Fleet invited her to lunch at Fuller's on the following Thursday, and when they met, she asked her elegant friend for outwork for Rosita.

As Muriel nibbled a sandwich and considered this, Dorothy said anxiously, 'I wouldn't ask anyone else but you – we've known each other so long. And you did tell me, once, that you have been awfully busy for the last few seasons altering the dresses your clients bought in previous years.'

Muriel's neatly pencilled eyebrows rose a little. 'Yes, we still are.'

'Mrs Echaniz was trained by Cripps'. By the sound of it, she's done every kind of sewing in her time . . .' Dorothy urged. 'They don't have any work for her at the moment.'

'Cripps' don't do as many alterations as we do – they take up a lot of time. But the client returns to us when she wants something new! So it's worth it.' Muriel laughed delicately, and her jet earrings swung. She tucked a curl absently back under her small cloche hat, and then looked pensively down at her coffee. Finally, she asked, 'What's the woman like to look at?'

'Clean and very neat. Shabby, though. She's still quite pretty.'

'You're really quite taken with her, aren't you?'

Dorothy smiled faintly. 'I suppose I am. I hate to see a bright, intelligent woman ground down. She needs work very badly, Muriel,' she pleaded.

Muriel sighed. 'Well, I'll try – though I'm not sure what I can do. We've more than enough outworkers, as it is. What's her house like – is it clean?'

'I asked Roy that – because of the fine materials she might be sewing. He said it always was when he was actually collecting their rent – before he got promoted to run the whole agency.'

'I'd need a reference from Cripps'. Could *you* give her a personal reference?'

'Certainly.' Dorothy pushed a glass dish of dainty sandwiches towards her guest.

Muriel refused another sandwich. 'With these new short dresses, I have to watch my figure – flatness is the fashion now!' She slipped on her gloves, smoothing the soft leather over her long fingers, and picked up her clutch handbag. 'Get me the references. Perhaps I can get her a little finishing, to see how good she is.'

The following day, an astonished Rosita received a letter from Dorothy Fleet, telling her to get a reference from Cripps' and, on any weekday morning, to take it, with the enclosed reference from Dorothy herself, to the back door of Sloan's, Bold Street, so that she could be interviewed by Miss Muriel Hamilton, with a view to being given some outwork to do.

Wildly excited, she read the missive to Micaela.

'Jesus Mary!' exclaimed Micaela, pushing herself upright

on the sofa. Then she said in Basque, 'Make yourself as smart as you can; Sloan's are fine dressmakers, as you well know.'

Manuel heard the news immediately he came home from school. He threw down his satchel, and hugged her. 'It's a new beginning, Mam.'

Over the weekend, Rosita's grey-streaked red curls, which normally hung untidily over her shoulders, were shampooed with Sunlight soap and combed up into a neat chignon. Then she cut a black skirt into a narrower, shorter fashion to give her a more modern appearance, and, for the sake of speed, machined it on Bridget's treadle sewing machine. Bridget lent her a plain black coat to go over it, both for her visit to Cripps' and to Sloan's.

'Aye, luv, I hope it leads to something decent for yez,' she said to Rosita, as she kissed her and wished her well.

At first the work given to her was routine hemming or unpicking, but soon she began to receive more complicated work. She sat long hours at her kitchen table, which was covered with a white sheet to protect the delicate materials she stitched so carefully. At the beginning, she earned little more than she would have done lining cutlery boxes; but it was clean work for which she had been very well trained.

When he was not looking for work or writing letters of application, Manuel lined cutlery boxes for her. He was helped by Francesca. Both girls were free, now that the summer holidays had begun, and, to give their mother time for her sewing, they did many of the household tasks.

The tenants, as they passed through the kitchen-living-room, were very interested in the pretty materials of Rosita's new work; she had to reprove them sharply when they wanted to touch the delicate georgettes and fine wools.

If I can get enough work, I'll stop renting the front room,

Rosita promised herself savagely, and make it into a workroom.

Dorothy Fleet and Muriel Hamilton often went on a Saturday afternoon to a matinée at the Empire Theatre; and, occasionally during these outings, Dorothy would inquire if Rosita continued to do satisfactory work. Her gentle reminder of Rosita's existence at the bottom of the dressmaking world eventually bore fruit. When a cuff hand was required, Rosita was asked to work two full days a week in the workrooms.

For the first time since she had lost Pedro, Rosita had a glimmering of hope that life would improve. She jumped at the offer, and hoped that a noisy bolt which Manuel managed to put on the cellar door would prove sufficient deterrent to light-fingered tenants – Micaela would certainly hear if the squeaky bolt was drawn.

Chapter Thirty-eight

On the Monday morning after Rosita's trip across the Mersey to pay the rent, Manuel left home ostensibly to go to school. He had eaten a breakfast of a slice of bread with milkless tea, Effie having boiled a kettle for them on her fire. He had no lunch in his satchel.

If his mother had not already been hard at work on her cutlery boxes, she might have noticed that he turned left along the street, instead of right; if she had seen him, she would have come flying after him to inquire where he thought he was going, since school lay in the opposite direction.

Manuel had no intention of going to school that morning. To make him less obviously a truant schoolboy to any passing police constable, he had put his St Francis Xavier cap into his plain brown satchel.

Bearing in mind Domingo Saitua's suggestion that he should find a ship's steward who might look out for a job as pantry boy for him, he was now marching determinedly along Chaloner Street to see Mr Ganivet in his chandlery warehouse. It was just possible that Mr Ganivet himself might give him a job; but, in any case, he had recalled from a conversation at Arnador's house, that the chandler sometimes did business with stewards; Mr Ganivet had been telling his wife about a steward who had returned fifty teapots, because the spouts dripped so badly on the white linen tablecloths of his First Class dining-room.

Considering that everybody the boy knew was complaining how bad times were, the Ganivet warehouse was very busy. At the loading bays, horses and carts vied with two snorting lorries trying to back in; and men in thick cotton aprons shouted to each other, while a closed pantechnicon eased out of the double gates.

He stopped one hurrying youth to ask where the office was – Mr Ganivet always referred to working in his office. He was directed to a narrow stone, corkscrew staircase which wound up through the centre of the eighteenth-century building.

At the door of his office, Mr Ganivet, his face nearly purple, was shouting at a bald-headed wisp of a man in a beige cotton jacket, who during brief gaps in the shouting said humbly, 'Yes, Sir,' or 'No, Sir.'

Manuel loitered at a discreet distance in the wooden-floored passage until the exchange petered out and the reprimanded man had zipped past him, looking very chastened. Mr Ganivet continued to stand at the door of his office, trying to regain his breath. As the high colour in his face subsided, he noticed the boy in the passage.

'Good gracious, Manuel! What are you doing here? Shouldn't you be in school?'

Seventy-odd years later, Old Manuel remembered vividly his sense of panic at the question fired at him. Of course, he should have been in school. Mr Ganivet began to roll down his shirt sleeves over his hairy arms, as Manuel gaped at him, unable to speak.

The older man turned into the littered, dusty office, glancing back over his shoulder at the white-faced boy. 'Come in, come in, lad,' he ordered not unkindly. 'What's up? Shut the door and have a seat.'

The chandler plonked down into a wooden, swivel chair beside a roll-top desk.

All the way up Chaloner Street, Manuel had rehearsed what he was going to say. Now the words tumbled out breathlessly. 'I've got to leave school at the end of term, Sir, because Mam can't afford to keep me any more – I'll be fourteen in September – and I was wanting your advice,

Sir, about going to sea. A friend of mine suggested I should get in with a steward, who might give me a chance. And I thought that, one day, maybe, I could be a steward myself.' He paused to take breath and to glance up at Mr Ganivet.

With a pencil Mr Ganivet was tracing circles round the edge of an invoice, so Manuel continued. He had been speaking in Basque, feeling that this made a connection between himself and the man at the desk. He now said, 'I remembered that you did business with stewards and cooks and people, and I wondered if you could recommend me to someone?'

He had hung his head as he spoke, fearing a quick dismissal, and all Mr Ganivet could see was the smooth dark crown of his head. 'As a pantry boy,' he finished hopefully.

'Humph.' Mr Ganivet fiddled with his pencil. Then he heaved a big sigh, which made his waistcoat, with its gold watch chain hung with seals, rise and fall like a slow wave on the Mersey. 'Well,' he said, 'I had hoped to see you go to university with Arnador. I believe that's what your dad hoped for you?'

'He never said anything to me, Sir, except that he wanted me in school until I was sixteen, but it's impossible; he's not here any more – and neither is my granddad.' The boy raised his head, and Mr Ganivet surveyed the long gaunt face with its flat cheekbones, the wide quirky mouth and rather deep-set brown eyes. A fine face, the chandler thought, almost that of a grown man; but no sign of a beard yet. He felt uneasy about what might happen to such a fine-looking boy on a long sea voyage, if he were not under the close supervision of a more senior crew member. It would not do for him to sign on without a family man to keep an eye on him, he decided.

The silence between them deepened. It was finally broken by Manuel, who said shyly, 'I want to thank you, Sir, for helping to keep me at school since Dad died –

Mother told me about it yesterday. It was very kind of you, Sir, and I really don't have any right to ask you for more help – but I don't know which way to turn.'

Mr Ganivet responded to the boy's thanks with a little smile, and then asked, 'Do you want to go to sea?'

Manuel was surprised by the question. 'Never thought of doing anything else, Sir. All our family went to sea.'

Mr Ganivet nodded. The boy had obviously never had the advantages of advanced education pointed out to him; perhaps, in the circumstances, it was as well.

He put down his pencil, and said, 'You were welcome to the small help with your schooling; I would've liked to continue it – but I have to prepare for Arnador's going to university – and I can't do both.'

'It's not expected, Sir.'

Mr Gavinet ignored the interruption, and went on, 'I can imagine the difficulties of your mother, and the need for you to earn. And, of course, at sea you would be fed, which would ease her burden. Of course, you'd have to pay for your kit.'

There was a knock on the office door, and the bald man in the beige jacket entered. 'The cordage has just come in, Sir,' he told Mr Ganivet nervously.

'Well, fill Ellerman's order. Send it in the big lorry – they're waiting on it. And hurry, man. Hurry!'

'Yes, Sir. Of course, Sir.'

The door clicked shut, and the chandler turned back to Manuel. 'Get me a written recommendation from your headmaster and bring it to me. Meanwhile, I'll see what I can do. I can't make any promises, and it may not be in catering.' He got up from his chair, to indicate the end of the interview. 'I'm not sure what I can do for you, so be thinking what else you might do.'

Manuel got up. He smiled, and said with enthusiasm, 'Thank you, Sir. I'm very grateful.'

As they walked together to the door, Mr Ganivet smiled

back, and ruffled the boy's hair. He wished that Arnador had something of his friend's warmth of character.

A week after Micaela's visit to her to borrow two shillings, Claire walked down to Wapping to see Micaela. The streets she traversed seemed smaller and meaner than they used to be when she had lived there with her first husband. The pavements were more littered, and the noise and foul odours from the factories and workshops were more intense.

As she knocked on the open door and a flustered Micaela called to her to enter, her heart sank. The house stank as it never had done in earlier years, the hallway blackened with soot from coal fires and tobacco smoke. She walked determinedly in, however, to find Micaela lying on a sofa in a muddled kitchen by an empty fireplace.

She laughed at Micaela's distress at not being able to offer her even a cup of tea, and said she had just dropped by for a moment to offer Manuel a part-time job.

She had squeezed out of Ould Biggs a Saturday morning's employment cleaning out the stables – their present man was getting old – and occasional help with putting the horse to and other odd jobs in connection with the bigger funerals, like polishing the hearse and the carriages.

Micaela jumped at it, with the thought that the boy's first wages – sixpence an hour – must go to paying back the two shillings she owed Claire.

So after Manuel had done his early-morning paper round and had had his breakfast, he went once a week to help Ould Biggs, who found him very useful, and sent for him several times during the weeks that Manuel was looking for regular work, to help with funeral processions.

Claire always gave him a huge mug of cocoa and a thick slice of bread and butter; and he would stand in the yard and gratefully consume these delicacies.

Sometimes, he would dream of a time when he would be able to keep some of the money he earned – and take Mary Connolly to a music hall matinée – and buy his mother and Bridget Connolly pretty quarter-pound boxes of chocolates.

If it had not been for the Second World War, when she joined the Forces and met a Polish soldier who married her, I might have married Mary myself, considered Old Manuel. She'd have made a good wife for a seaman. As he considered whether he should mention, in his notes for Lorilyn, the upheavals of the civilian population during the war, he was very slowly digging over his vegetable patch; the soil was waterlogged and heavy.

He paused to lean on his spade and catch his breath; digging was difficult. Next year he would get a man to do it for him. He smiled grimly to himself – perhaps he should say, if he were here next year, he would do so. He felt that time was running out, like water dripping from a leaky tank, drop by drop. Maybe he should visit Ramon and Arnador in Liverpool this year – and after a rest there, go on to Vizcaya; it would be wonderful to see the Pyrenees again.

In the midst of his meditations, he was surprised when Sharon Herman came quickly round the side of his bungalow.

'Hi!' she greeted him cheerfully. 'I came to collect some stuff from Veronica's house, but she isn't home – so I thought I'd pop in to see how you are.'

Old Manuel grinned at her. 'Fine,' he assured her. He pushed his spade into the loam, so that it would stand upright, and said, 'Come in. It's getting chilly out here.'

Over a glass of wine, she thanked him for a piece of fish he had left for her with one of her new neighbours in the apartment block. He smiled and shrugged. 'It's nothin',' he said.

Sharon's eyes wandered round the sitting-room, while she considered what she should say next, and came to rest on a beautifully cased sewing machine, and she wondered about the woman who had sat at it, or had sat in the bay window to hand sew in a good light.

'Do you have any kids?' she asked him suddenly. 'Besides Faith – you mentioned her once, I think.'

The question was a personal one, and he sipped his wine, while he thought how to answer her. Then he grinned. 'Only Faith – and I don't suppose she wants to be regarded as a kid. She's forty-six. I've got a granddaughter, though – she's going to be an electrical engineer, she tells me. She's at the University of British Columbia.' Pride in Lorilyn made him more talkative, and he took a cigarette out of his pocket and lit it. Then, remembering that Sharon might smoke, he proffered her the packet. 'Seems as if girls has gone off nursing or teaching.'

Sharon refused the cigarette, and endured, with amusement, the smoke that slowly surrounded them.

He told her that he had decided to go home this summer, and she asked lightly where home was. England or Spain?

He hesitated, and then said, 'Both, I guess.'

They began to talk about a trip he and Kathleen had done the year before she was taken ill, and as he described it he grew slower.

He's tired, thought Sharon guiltily. I should not have come; and yet she did not want to stop his talking. As far as she knew, he had nobody to talk to.

He rubbed his eyes, and she was distressed to see that they were filled with tears. His chin trembled, and he hastily pulled a Kleenex from a decorated box on the table beside him. 'I'm sorry,' he muttered. 'It takes me back a bit, talkin', like.'

She crossed over to sit by him on the settee, and put her arm round the bent, thin shoulders. He did not brush her off, but wept quietly into a bunch of paper handkerchiefs.

She felt a great, unreasonable anger that his daughter was not by him – or even his clever granddaughter. Such grief should have been allowed to express itself long ago. She tightened her hold on him, and he tried to control the explosion. But he could not.

'Just cry,' she said very gently. 'I do understand about these things.'

Families don't have the experience of dealing with bereavement, she thought, trying to drown her sense that his family should have helped him more. Death isn't all round them like it used to be – or like it is with me. They have no experience to draw on.

She held him quietly, gently rubbing his back with her arm, as if he were a sick animal, until finally he drew a big sobbing breath, and said, 'I'm proper sorry. I don't know what came over me.'

As he leaned forward to pull some more handkerchiefs from the box, she let him go, and he added, 'When I were a little kid, people died all round you; you accepted it. I should have got used to it.' He shoved the damp handkerchiefs into his shirt pocket, and then went on, 'Doctors was different, though, in them days. They knew you – they came to your house; and I'm dead sure they helped those in pain go more quickly. And then they stayed a while, to comfort the family like, and the neighbours came in and out to see you was all right. And the priests were there . . .' He cleared his throat, and said in a less wistful voice, 'If you had to manage without a doctor, there was always neighbours to help – like Bridget – I think I once told you about her.'

She smiled softly. 'Yes, you did,' she said. 'And don't worry about crying. Even men should cry good and hard sometimes. And we're friends, aren't we?'

'For sure,' he said, as he slowly stood up in front of her. He had a desperate need, suddenly, to go to the bathroom, but he was too shy to admit it. After her last remark, she had playfully held out her hand to him, and now he slowly shook it to cement the friendship. When she rose, feeling that she was dismissed, he held on to her hand and then leaned forward and gently kissed her cheek.

'Thank you, my dear.'

She smiled again, and asked, 'If you go to Liverpool, have you any family there to take care of you?'

'I've got Ramon, me cousin. I'll stay with him. And I've got me old friend, Arnador Ganivet — better'n a brother, he's bin to me, all me life.'

'Go soon,' she advised, and kissed his withered dark cheek, and left him.

Chapter Thirty-nine

Manuel's hopes of help from Mr Ganivet began to fade, and there seemed to be hordes of boys vying for jobs as errand boys or office boys in the city. He haunted the Sailors' Home in hope of picking up a berth as deck boy or pantry boy, without success.

He discussed with his mother the idea of applying to de Larrinaga on the grounds that his father had served them. He was surprised when she did not immediately agree. When she did answer him, she said heavily, 'His discharge book went down with him.'

When he protested that they would have a record in their offices, she told him uneasily that it did not seem to be a good idea. She was, in fact, superstitiously afraid of history repeating itself, and that he would go down like his father; the idea was ridiculous, and she knew it, but she could not shake it off. She said, 'Well, you know, he wasn't with them very long.'

He could not shift her.

Mr Ganivet had not been idle, however. He had spoken on the boy's behalf to two regular customers, and the result was that, in September, a few days before his fourteenth birthday, he sailed in a large freighter, as galley boy. The ship was carrying a mixed cargo for Havana and the southern United States. He was under the tutelage of the chief steward, the cook, two galley men and a cabin steward, none of them very patient.

Old Manuel often laughed when he remembered the first time he went to sea, proudly armed with his own discharge book and a straw-stuffed palliasse for his bunk. He had considered himself the most overworked, bullied youngster ever to sail in a ship, though he might have had a different opinion had he had a father to tell him what to expect. As a little boy he had been taken down to the docks to see his father's ship and he had sailed to and from Bilbao; but being a member of the crew, he found, was different; he had forgotten that, though it might be considered romantic to go to sea, it was a rough and dangerous occupation, where men had to be able to depend on each other a great deal. Further, he had spent the last few years mainly amongst women and gentle priests which did not help his adjustment to the harsh reality of seafaring.

In truth, though the freighter was an old, coal-burning ship, it was well run; and Mr Figgin, the steward, despite being an accomplished nagger, took good care to see that he was not sexually abused or knocked about on the long, slow voyage.

The cook, an ageing black man with a strong Glasgow accent, was good-natured, and supplemented the indifferent food supplied to the crew with bits left over from the officers' mess. Manuel soon learned to call these small treats 'ovies'. It seemed to Manuel, however, that everyone was quick to cuff him if he lingered too long in his journeys up and down companionways and along the heaving passages, often armed with slopping mugs of tea for officers on duty.

If, when sweeping or scrubbing, he missed a corner, the galley man would upbraid him in the richest of Liverpool language. Anxious to keep in with the cook, he learned to peel his way through sacks of potatoes at a commendable speed, and to wash dishes without chipping them as the water in the sink sloshed about with the movement of the ship. He also learned to watch carefully, during bad weather, that he was not hit by a boiling saucepan skidding off the stove; a ship's galley could be a very dangerous place. He hated every job he was given.

The dark, silent, morose cabin steward called Jimmy was of uncertain racial origins. He came from Swansea, and, when he did find reason to speak, he had the sing-song accent of South Wales. When the boy was sent to help him, he would be ordered to fetch this or carry that – as if I were a Labrador dog, Manuel thought indignantly. Helping Jimmy, however, took him into the officers' quarters, and, when he saw them, he decided that compared with being crew, an officer's life must be pure paradise.

He confided this observation to Jimmy, one day, when he was helping to strip bunks and sort washing. 'One day, I'm going to be an officer,' he told him.

Jimmy managed a faint smile. 'That don't come to folks like us,' he said.

'My dad had his Master's,' responded Manuel, as he watched Jimmy deftly tuck in the corners of clean sheets.

'Humph. You got to have schooling for that – and be white.'

Manuel was startled. Schooling, yes – but white? All his life he had played with boys of every race, and he knew that below decks crews were often coloured. He had assumed that there were no officers amongst them because they lacked education. 'But why?' he asked, his arms full of sheets that Jimmy had thrown over to him.

'Don't ask me. I've sailed in this old tub for years. When we dock, to make sure I keep *this* berth, I always sign on again right away for the next trip. And I don't even go ashore that often. I might never get another "sight". And why, Sir? Because I'm as black as the coal in the hold. Pass me them pillowcases.'

'That's not fair!'

'First thing you learn at sea, lad, is to keep your place and be a good mate to the other fellas. And keep your head down – and don't say too much.'

Once having broken the barriers of his self-imposed silence, Jimmy had many friendly conversations with Manuel. He taught the boy how to fish — fish was a welcome addition to a crew's austere diet. The man was a walking book on fish, Old Manuel once ruminated, and had given him a life-long interest in them.

He was not allowed ashore at Havana. The chief steward demanded a special clean-up of the galley. As he scrubbed and scraped caked-on grease, Manuel seethed with frustration. He had found the confinement hard to bear and had been looking forward to going ashore for a walk and to post letters to Arnador and his mother.

He formed the idea of jumping ship at the next port, which was Houston, Texas; but the chief steward, wise in the ways of youngsters, put him in the charge of the ship's carpenter who was going ashore to stretch his legs. Fuming, the boy trudged along to Woolworth's with the easy, amiable carpenter, to buy a pair of socks. Rousing himself, Manuel purchased three bead necklaces at five cents each and a small brooch, the latter for Grandma Micaela who did not wear necklaces.

Since Houston was a Prohibition area and the carpenter was no great drinker, he took Manuel to a soda fountain, where he was introduced to the glories of an American sundae.

He had never seen such a wondrous concoction, a halfpenny ice cream being the limit of his experience. He waded through layers of cream and nuts, ice cream, chocolate sauce — and a cherry on top; and wondered what other delights the United States could offer — once he got away from the carpenter, of course.

The soda fountain, however, was well known, and two other members of the crew wandered in to drink coffee and eat ice cream. Flanked by three adults, Manuel knew he would not be able to slip away. Hooked for ever on American ice cream, he went regretfully back to the ship.

A letter from his mother awaited him, full of love and instructions to remember that he was a good Catholic boy – and a Basque – Basques were always honourable and upright. Brian Wing had dropped by to inquire about him, and Arnador had written to him.

He received Arnador's letter when he docked again at Liverpool.

Chapter Forty

Afraid that Manuel might spend his wages, or be robbed of them before he arrived home, Mr Figgin insisted on accompanying the boy to his own doorstep and handing him over to Rosita, who answered his knock.

He told her that the boy had done well, and that he would see that he was taken on again in a few days' time. He refused a cup of tea, and went off to catch the overhead railway train to Dingle, where he lived.

Delighted to see that Manuel had gained weight, his mother hugged him; and Francesca and Little Maria came running down the stairs to bounce around him, as he slung his kitbag on to the floor – exactly as his father used to do, Rosita thought with a pang.

He hugged them all – and wondered why they seemed to be blocking the entrance to the kitchen-living-room.

As he unbuttoned his jacket, Rosita looked up at him, and said in faltering tones, 'I've bad news for you, dear. And some good news, too.'

At her words, the girls suddenly stood still, and looked as if they might cry.

Manuel stared apprehensively at the three of them, and then asked, 'Grandma?'

'Yes, dear. The funeral was last Friday. It was a heart attack, the doctor said. She went quite suddenly.'

'Oh, Mam!' He took her into his arms again and she clung to him for a moment, and then she said firmly, 'We're not going to cry too much, are we, girls? Granny was very, very old – and she wished to go to God.'

Manuel hastily picked up his cue. He squatted down in

front of the girls and put an arm round each, as he said, 'You're right. We'll remember Granny when she was all cheery and energetic – and we'll be thankful that she won't be blind any more.' He grinned at their solemn white faces and pulled them close to him. 'She'll be able to see the angels now!'

Bless his heart, thought Rosita thankfully.

The idea that Grandma could now see was a new one to the girls, and Francesca said in wonderment, 'Of course, she will,' and their faces lightened.

Their mother said, with false brightness, 'And now we've got a tremendous surprise for him, haven't we?'

Their solemnity gave way immediately to excitement. 'Yeth,' breathed Little Maria, whose front teeth were not yet quite full-grown and gave her a lisp. She pulled Manuel towards the kitchen-living-room. 'Come and thee!'

Laughing, he allowed himself to be tugged down the passage, rather expecting to find that Pudding now had half a dozen new great-great-great-grandchildren by the current cat.

Then he was in the tiny old room, and was stunned by what he saw in the light of the oil lamp on the table.

In Grandma's old rocking chair sprawled a thin, long-legged man with close-cropped greying hair. The poor light of the lamp made his face look darker than it was and showed the deep lines which only a hard life could carve.

For a second, he thought his mother had taken a lover, and he was stung by jealousy. Then his eyes widened in disbelief as the man rose shyly from his chair.

'Uncle Leo!' he shouted, and flung himself into the stranger's arms. 'Jesus! I'm glad to see you.'

While they hugged again, Manuel was aware of a faded check shirt covering an iron-hard body, of tired but dancing brown eyes, and hair prematurely grey. This was not a man who had made a fortune in America. But, God, how good it was to see him.

'Where've you been? What happened?' Manuel asked as they laughingly surveyed each other. 'It's amazing – you're here! I can hardly believe it.'

'Well – it's a long story. I've told your mam all about it.' He let go of Manuel, and sat down again, to pick up his smouldering cigarette which had been poised on the edge of Aunt Maria's little table. Francesca came to lean against him; she had been badly shaken by the loss of her grandmother, and it felt comforting to have this big, slow uncle here, a man whom Rosita and Manuel obviously loved. Little Maria must have been of the same opinion, because she shoved past Francesca so that she could clamber on to Leo's knee.

'When did you arrive?' Manuel's voice was muffled by his navy-blue sweater which he was hauling off. A good fire was making the room too warm.

'Last week.' He was quiet for a moment, and then said, 'I missed Mother by a day. We always leave things too late!'

Manuel said a little accusingly, 'She always hoped you'd come home.'

'I should've written – I know that now. With Agustin in Bilbao, it wasn't right not to.' He cleared his throat, as if it were hard to get the words out. 'I always assumed Pedro and Father were here, though.' His thoughts reverted to Agustin, and he added, 'Rosita's written to tell him about Mother.'

Manuel stood near him, his back to the fire, while Rosita filled the kettle at the kitchen tap. 'Why *didn't* you write?' But when there was no reply and he glanced at his uncle's face he was surprised to see his eyes closed and his jaw clenched. Rosita made a small negative signal to him with one hand, so he remained quiet. She said, 'Come to the table, luv, and you, too, Leo. The meal's all ready – I read in the paper when the ship would dock – so I was able to cook for you.'

He whistled when he looked at the spread table. Only money from Leo could have provided this. 'You've been busy,' he said, and grinned at her.

As Manuel sat down in his father's old chair at the table, he felt that he was re-enacting his father's return from a voyage. After three and a half months' absence, he felt a strangeness, a sense of being distanced from his family. It seemed as if he had been away from them for half his life – like Uncle Leo had. In his head were jumbled a myriad of impressions, about which he longed to talk; and yet, beside the absence of Grandma and the arrival of Uncle Leo, it all seemed too petty to talk about.

Rosita was saying, 'I got your letter from Houston – and Arnador dropped in to say he had had one from you. He thought that, if I hadn't heard, I would like to share his letter. Kind of him, wasn't it? He stayed quite a while.' She filled the teapot and came to sit at the table with them. 'Tell us how you got on?' she asked, and turned to scold Little Maria for taking two slices of bread at a time.

He muttered that, yes, Mr Figgin, the chief steward, had looked after him – too well. He was very bossy, he added, with memories of being escorted ashore by the carpenter.

He caught a twinkle in his quiet uncle's eye, and knew that he understood – he must have come home from sea when he was a boy feeling much the same. But where had he been more recently? Doing what? With whom?

Rosita refilled his tea mug and said, 'Arnie'll be down tomorrow night to see you – he had to go across the water this evening – to his cousin's.'

'Good.' For once, he would have something of interest to tell Arnie; usually, it was his infinitely curious, infinitely observant friend who introduced the subjects of their discussions. He said to Leo, 'I think I'll have about a week home. I've got to see Mr Figgin tomorrow.'

Uncle Leo said unexpectedly, 'We'll talk about that tonight.'

Manuel was a little surprised by the remark. He'd got a ship, hadn't he? The chief steward had been positively benign on the last day, and had said that he could hope to be taken on again. He had four pounds twelve shillings and sixpence in his pocket for his mother, and would be going back to earn some more for her. It was peculiar that he had been home only an hour; and yet he was ready to return to his much-hated shipboard life, to tell Jimmy, in their tiny mess, about Old Figgin seeing him all the way home, and have a good laugh over it.

Buoyed up by this sudden sense of independence, he pushed back his chair and went into the hall to open up his kitbag.

He took out a small Woolworth's bag, and said to Francesca, who had followed him down the hall, 'Blue's for you, and red for Little Maria.'

She snatched the bag from him and danced joyfully back to the kitchen-living-room to explore the contents with Maria.

He took out two more little bags, and stood in the dark hall for a moment, wondering what to do with Grandma's present. Then he went slowly back to the family, and handed one of the paper bags to Rosita. 'I hope you like it,' he said shyly.

Rosita took out a long, pale-blue necklace of china beads. Her eyes brimmed at the memory it evoked of her husband. She got up and came round the table to give the boy a kiss. 'It's beautiful,' she said, as she wound it round her neck. Manuel recollected that that was exactly what she had always said to his father, and he grinned with pride.

'What's in the other bag?' asked Little Maria, and the grin was wiped off his face. He slid a pretty little brooch with a silver finish into his hand. 'It was for Granny,' he told his small sister. He leaned forward to show it to his mother. 'Would you like it, Mam?'

Rosita's lips quivered, and she hesitated before answering. Then she said, 'You know who I think would love to have it? Auntie Bridget. She was so good with your gran, and she laid her out. I think she'd love to have it in memory of Grandma.'

Bridget thought it was wonderful.

Chapter Forty-one

He would never forget the walk with Uncle Leo that he took that night through the deserted streets of Liverpool, ruminated Old Manuel, as he fried bacon to go with a tin of beans for his supper.

He had remembered dimly the young man who had kissed him on the back of his head, before going out to climb into the horsebus waiting to take him down to the dock, to a ship and to a new life. He remembered him as particularly tall and thin, even at a time in his young life when adults appeared to be all legs. As he walked, that momentous night, he was surprised to discover that he was nearly as tall as Leo.

They had sat for a while in the old churchyard of St Nick's – the seamen's church – and had then wandered down St Nicholas Place to take a look at a Cunarder at the Princes Landing Stage; and all that time, Leo talked.

He talked as if he had had no one to confide in for a very long time – and he probably had not, considered Old Manuel, chewing on a bacon rasher as he waited for his beans to heat. Uncle Leo had spoken in Basque, sometimes pausing to hunt for a half-forgotten word, sometimes pouring out an idea in a quick, rumbling flow.

At first, they had walked in silence, until Manuel asked shyly, 'Did you get any of Granny's letters – or the one I wrote to the postmaster in Nevada?'

'Other than two when I first went out, and I answered those – no, I didn't get any – that is, not exactly.' He grinned at the youth beside him. 'But I *heard* about your letter – so I came home.' He relapsed into silence while he stopped, hands in pockets, to watch a Furness Withy boat being moved downstream, its lights winking at them like distant stars.

'I'm thankful you've come, anyway,' Manuel ventured. 'Will you be able to stay with us?'

Leo rocked gently on his heels. 'I want to.' He spoke absently, as if his thoughts were elsewhere. 'Provided I can get a berth.' The December wind was chilly, and he pulled up the collar of his jacket.

Manuel nodded, and then asked, 'What did you mean when you said you had heard about my letter?'

'Well, it was strange. I heard through a Basque AB we took on at Corpus Christi – I was working in Argie boats. He'd come down from Colorado, in hope of shipping out on a British boat – he was a Liverpool man like us – though I didn't remember him at all. While he was hunting for a ship in Corpus Christi, he met two other Basque lads from Nevada, who'd got just as fed up with the place as I had. They'd tried all kinds of jobs and finally quit; and, like me, had decided to go back to sea.' He paused to light another cigarette, and then went on, 'One night in a bar they were talking about how Basques were scattered all over the world; and they told him about going into a post office in some goddamn awful place in Nevada, where they had spent a night, and reading a letter pinned up on a notice board. It was from a kid in Liverpool telling the postmaster about his uncle, Leo Barinèta – how things were bad in Liverpool, and he was trying to trace him. They remembered it, because they had sailed out of Liverpool, en route from Bilbao to Nevada; and they remembered that the Basque agent there was called Barinèta.

'When this lad shipped with us and heard my name, he came and told me. Simple as that.'

'Jesus Mary! Had they stayed in our house?'

'I don't know. Heaps of youngsters went through our house.'

'So you came home?'

Leo stopped to ponder, while he watched a laundry van inch through the gate to the Princes Landing Stage. Then he said, 'It wasn't that simple. I couldn't come right off. Reckoned I'd sign off next time I got to Corpus Christi – which was a regular port for us. I was fed up with Argies anyway. I knew that if I then went to Galveston or Houston, there was a good chance I'd find a British ship short of crew – if anybody's going to desert a British ship, they'll do it there – or in New York.'

Manuel's conscience gave a small jolt, as he remembered his own intentions at Houston.

'But why didn't you look for a British ship when you gave up in Nevada? Then you could've come straight home.'

'Well, you know how it is. I didn't want to come home and tell the Old Man that I'd made a wrong decision; he thought Nevada was paradise on earth – but he'd never been there! I only stuck it for six weeks – there was almost a war going on between cattle ranchers and sheep-herders – and we were being harassed by gangs of cowhands. I couldn't stand the bloody sheep either – stupid buggers.'

'Mam wrote to you when Grandpa was killed.'

'So she said. I never got it, though – I'd moved over to try Colorado by then, I think.'

'Grandma was never the same after he died.'

'I can well believe it.'

'You know, you could've written to us,' Manuel upbraided him, his expression resentful below the black beret he was wearing.

Leo made a wry mouth. 'I'm hopeless at writing. I kept thinking I'd do it when I was settled. It took years, though. Kept trying different jobs – but an immigrant is dirt – even if he can speak three languages – and all you get is labouring jobs. I was out of work, so I came down to the coast, and shipped on the first freighter that looked anything like

– and it wasn't a bad ship; I've been sailing out of Bahia Blanca for over six years now. And I suppose I was settled. To be honest, it was as if I'd never lived in England. Like a lot of emigrants, I was looking forward all the time – not back.'

Listening to his uncle, Manuel had been leaning against a fence, watching basket after basket of laundry being shoved into the side of the liner. Now he transferred his gaze to his uncle. Leo's face was set, with the same closed-off expression that Manuel had noticed when he had first arrived home. He looked like Uncle Agustin – who never wrote either. 'Are you all right, Uncle Leo?' he inquired.

Leo shook his head, and then said slowly, 'Yes. I'm all right. I lost the wife about a year ago, and sometimes it hits me again – especially because of finding Mother gone, as well.'

'Wife?' Manuel looked at him with complete astonishment. He had always imagined his uncle to be a footloose bachelor. 'What happened? Was she a Liverpool girl?'

They turned to walk along the Princes Landing Stage, past the empty, folded-up gangways which served the ferryboats. In the lamplight, Manuel anxiously watched the play of expressions on his uncle's face, while the man got a hold on his feelings.

'I'm sorry,' he said to Leo. 'You must feel like Mam did when Dad was lost.' He was tremendously curious about this new-found romance, and he ventured, 'Tell me about her.'

Leo was, in truth, glad to tell someone about his loss – he had not bothered Rosita with it, as she unburdened to him her stories of years of struggle and grief written all too clearly on her lined face. Sometime he would tell her, but not for the present.

He found it difficult to express to an untried stripling the unexpected happiness he had found when he had met Consuelo, and the appalling emptiness when she had died.

He threw down his cigarette butt and ground it under his heel. Then he said, 'I met an Argie girl, first time I docked in Bahia Bianca; she and her mam were selling fruit in a little street market. I was just a deckie then, an AB, and I'd been signed off. I was alone and I'd a bit of money to spend, and wondering what to do next, though I expected to rejoin the ship in about three days' time. She said she knew by my clothes that I was no Argie; she thought I was American, so she tried her bits of English on me. She was a pretty little thing, all curves, if you know what I mean?' Manuel nodded; he knew because his interest in girls was growing daily.

'Well, she and her mam were surprised when they got an answer in Spanish, and we joked quite a bit. Then, when I went down to the ship, they had a cargo and were going to sail again in two days' time. So I signed on, and away I went. But I didn't forget her. Next time we docked, I walked up to see if they were still in the market. And they were.'

He looked at Manuel, and the boy was glad to see his eyes suddenly twinkle. 'Now you should know you don't play around with Spanish girls; they often have strong-minded dads and brothers! Anyway, her mam settled it, by asking if I'd a place to stay when I was in Bahia Blanca – seeing as how I seemed to be sailing out of the port regularly – I'd told them I was a Basque, originally from Liverpool. Now, I told her, I was in a sailors' lodging house and wasn't too happy about it, so she said she had a spare room where I could safely leave my gear – and stay when I was in port. I didn't know then that she had *three* daughters with no dowry money to marry off!' He suddenly laughed at the recollection, and his whole character seemed to change; he lost his quiet withdrawn look, and was suddenly very much like his father, Juan Barinèta, who had always appreciated a joke.

Manuel chuckled. He said, 'She was trusting, wasn't she?'

'She'd got me weighed up. She was a wise old owl. And Consuelo and I got along fine, no doubt about that. So I married her,' he finished simply, 'and we lived in with her family – and it worked quite well, because I wasn't under their feet that much; and when I was there, the girls spoiled me rotten!'

'I bet they did,' agreed Manuel. 'No father around?'

'No. Nor brothers. The father took off when they were young, and their ma had managed to bring the girls up herself – and nice girls, they were.' His face went dark again, as he said, 'Then we were hoping for a baby and we began to watch out for a place of our own near her mam, so she wouldn't be too lonely while I was at sea. I wasn't worried about her, because her mam was there.' He sighed. 'I was away, and she was about four months – and, one day, so her mam told me, she suddenly went down with fever – fevers are common there, because the land is swampy and they don't have much in the way of drains or clean water. Anyway, I came home to a grave and three demented women.'

'That must've been awful.'

'Oh, aye. There were a few other deaths in the neighbourhood, and my guess is that it was cholera – it kills that quick, you'd never believe it. The others were lucky they didn't get it.'

Manuel put his arm round his uncle's shoulder. He shuddered. Cholera had visited Liverpool in times past.

Leo felt the shudder, and said, 'It's the way life is, lad.' Though the remark indicated resignation, the tone did not. Then, making an effort, he said firmly, 'But I didn't bring you out to talk about me. I want to think about your mam and the girls – and you. Let's sit down here a minute – I wanted to speak to you first, before I talk to your mother.' He indicated a seat at the end of the landing stage, and they sat down. 'Now, what I had in mind is . . .'

It was obvious that Leo had been thinking hard during

the week he had been with Rosita, and that he had been distressed by the obvious discomfort of having lodgers intruding on her all the time. He suggested that he should live with them in a cheaper, smaller house – if they could find one with three bedrooms, and he would make Rosita a regular allotment. 'Somewhere up in Toxteth, maybe – where she wouldn't be too far from her dressmaking or her friends. How does that sound to you?'

It seemed wonderful to Manuel, as the sickening sense of responsibility which had haunted him for years seemed to ease at the thought of having another man to share it. He said, almost boastfully, 'I'll be able to make her an allotment as well.'

'Oh, aye. But that's what I really want to talk to you about. The way you are, you aren't going to get anywhere much. I want you to do as well as Pedro did, and go to technical school in January, if they'll take you. Take some kind of engineering, so you can work ashore when you get older. A lot of fellas do that, if they get the chance.' It was cold sitting on the bench, so he shoved his hands into his pockets. 'I got a bit saved for when Consuelo and I got a place – and a bit for the baby that was coming. I can use this to start you off – and Rosita and I could feed you, I expect.'

'Don't you want to get married again?' Manuel asked baldly.

'I thought about that. But it's unlikely I'll meet another Consuelo.' He smiled at the boy beside him. 'If, by chance, I do, we'll worry about it then.' He took his hands out of his pockets and rested them on his knee. They looked big, callused and capable. He muttered, 'I doubt I will.

'Saitua was saying the other night, when he came in, that you're the brightest lad here amongst the Basques. I want you to go to technical college, and then do courses between going to sea – and we'll have a qualified engineer in the house before we know it.'

He stood up, and clapped the shoulder of the astonished boy, whose life had been changed in five minutes.

'Come on, now,' Leo urged. 'It's very late – and Rosita's going to scold us for being out in the cold for so long.' He struck a match on the heel of his shoe; and in the tiny flame, Manuel saw his eyes twinkle, as he said dolefully, 'Have to behave ourselves now, because Rosita's going to boss the pair of us.'

Chapter Forty-two

Manuel's new home was in a decent, tree-lined street of working-class homes in Toxteth. The front room had a small bay window which jutted straight on to the pavement, and, when Rosita managed to buy a second-hand treadle sewing machine, she put it in the window, so that she had a good light for her sewing. Increasingly, however, as Sloan's realized her skills, they tended to employ her for full weeks in their workrooms, which meant that, between her wages and Leo's allotment the little family felt quite prosperous. While in college, Manuel worked in his spare time at various odd jobs, and was able to bring home a little additional money to Rosita.

The house was much closer to Arnador's apartment than their previous home had been; so, while he was still at school and Manuel was attending technical college, they often worked together on the living-room table in the evenings, and were of help to each other.

Anxious to be thought grown-up, Francesca and Maria sometimes claimed the other end of the table to do their modest assignments. As they all grew older, they would, at the weekends, frequently play cards together or go for walks in the parks. When Manuel finished college and went to sea, as a very junior electrical engineer, and Arnador was doing his first degree at Liverpool University, the boys spent a lot of time together during the periods Manual was ashore.

At first sight, it seemed as if their lives would diverge, as Arnador was drawn into the university world, and the young men pursued their vastly separate careers. It was not so. They had the easy association of brothers who liked each other, without the natural jealousies of blood brothers. Manuel was aware of how easy it could be for a man at sea to get cut off from friends ashore, and he made a particular effort to keep in close touch with his friend. To Arnador, Manuel was as much part of his life as his family was, and he automatically included his friend in his social life, if Manuel were in port. Because of the tight Basque connection, with its ties of language and culture, Rosita, Leo and Mr and Mrs Ganivet frequently asked the boys to meals; and birthdays, Christmas and Epiphany were days when a special effort was made to see each other.

When she was sixteen, bright, intelligent Francesca, with her delicate red curls and flawless skin, obtained a post with Boot's Cash Chemists, to work behind their cosmetics counter. Boot's had an exceptional staff and a job with them gave a girl a certain prestige. Once she had some experience, Francesca was encouraged by modest promotions. Rosita saw to it that her black dresses were always perfectly cut, her white collars starched and neat. She loved her work, which led to a career in cosmetics lasting a lifetime.

A year later, her more prosaic sister went into a bakery as an apprentice. She enjoyed what she was doing and became a skilled confectioner, much in demand to decorate elaborate wedding and birthday cakes. She had a merry, teasing way with her, and had lots of admirers.

Manuel and Arnador explored the world of women together. They were careful not to commit themselves to any particular one, mainly because they both knew that it would be some years before either of them could afford to keep a wife and family.

For fear of finding himself permanently entangled with a girl, Arnador refused to go out with female fellow students. He would say scornfully to Manuel, 'They're husband-hunting – and I suspect that their mothers watch them like cats.' Then he would add unkindly, 'And what's more they're boring!'

So they laughed, and picked up girls at dances or in cafés. They played cricket with scratch teams, attended football matches, got drunk, and, altogether, did not allow their studies to weigh them down too much. With other male students, they sat around in pubs and cafés, eyeing the girls, and argued politics hotly over pints of beer or cups of coffee.

It was during one of these rather shallow debates, at the time when, in Germany, Adolph Hitler was rising to power, that Arnador soberly forecast another war. In fact, neither he nor Manuel was the least surprised when the Spanish Civil War broke out, though it was Arnador who said sadly, 'This is only the prelude.'

A number of Liverpudlians, including some Basques, went to Spain to fight General Franco. Neither of the friends was keen to go, Arnador because he felt Franco would win and Manuel because he knew he must help to maintain his mother and Uncle Leo when they grew too old to work.

Those were good times, thought Old Manuel wistfully, despite the thundering of European dictators and the shadows cast by the war in Spain, not to speak of the worry about his relations caught in the conflict. His and Arnie's lives seemed to be set on hopeful courses, and they had all the optimism of youth.

As he remembered, he was looking down at the huge fountain in Butchart Gardens, a few miles out of Victoria. Jack Audley and his wife had persuaded him to join them for dinner in the restaurant in the Gardens. Though crowded with tourists, he had enjoyed the riot of colour that the Gardens presented. Now, however, he was very weary, his legs ached and he needed to take a pill to assuage the pain. His mind was tending to wander, and he wished suddenly that Arnie was beside him.

Arnie was now eighty-five! Manuel found it astonishing, regardless of the fact that he was eighty-four himself. Arnie's sister, Josefa, was even older — a formidable harridan in her nineties, with whom Arnie now made his home. When he was young, Manuel had, on the few occasions when he met her, been afraid of her as she swept into the Ganivet house, so sure of herself with her starched uniform rustling round her. During the war, she had suddenly become more human to him, when, as a result of a passionate encounter with a Royal Air Force Pathfinder much younger than herself, she had shocked everybody by becoming pregnant, something which had not become obvious to her family until after her Pathfinder had been shot down over Hamburg. Pathfinders' lives, during the war, had been nearly as short as those of merchant seamen, Old Manuel reckoned.

She was forty-one years old and well advanced in her nursing career. She was totally distraught because she could not bring herself to seek an abortion. Her parents were shocked beyond measure. They had rallied round her, however, as had her nursing colleagues; and Josefa subsequently picked up her career again after six months' quietly given leave — surgical nurses were worth their weight in gold at a time when wards were filled with casualties. Her mother tenderly babysat her solitary grandchild, a girl who was christened Josephine.

Josephine was now an accomplished concert pianist. She was unmarried, and, when she was not on tour, she enlivened Josefa's and Arnador's retirement by making her home with them, and contributing a share to the upkeep of the household.

She had been good for her Uncle Arnador, who was now a Professor Emeritus at the University of Liverpool, considered Old Manuel. She encouraged him to take a bus down to his department twice a week, to read the journals connected with his subject, and continue his interest in the vagaries of human population.

As the fountain sprayed him lightly with water, Old Manuel chuckled. He still felt that it was lucky that Arnador had been a demographer; it meant he could understand and take an interest in his friend's discipline. If, for example, he had become a physicist, Manuel admitted that he would have been sunk.

'What are you laughing at?' Jack Audley asked. He was bored with watching the fountain; but his wife had involved herself in a long conversation with a Japanese visitor, who had come specially from Osaka to see the Gardens. The Japanese spoke English well, and Mrs Audley was encouraging him to take a look at the Japanese garden which formed part of Butchart Gardens.

Manuel turned to him. 'I was thinking about old Arnie. Remember him? He's been to stay with me a few times.'

'Sure.'

'He had a funny career. He counted heads all his life – like, whole populations. From his figures, he can often forecast what's likely to happen to a country – or even an individual, like whether you'll get work or not. He makes me laugh because he's better than a gypsy coming to your back door to tell your fortune.'

'Humph.' Jack Audley did not believe him; he was also feeling grumpy. He said deflatingly, 'Don't get any gypsies out here.'

Manuel was irritated. Sometimes, he got from Jack an annoying reminder that, though he had been in Canada for years, he had alien roots and different formative experiences. It made him feel at a loss, when his interests were summarily dismissed – even a tiny one, like a knowledge of gypsies.

It's time I went home to visit Arnie, he decided, feeling quite as grumpy as Jack. Jesus! How his legs ached!

Chapter Forty-three

It was only when she went to live in Toxteth that Rosita understood how much the small community in Wapping had supported each other. Apart from the crises that they faced together, the daily casual contacts in the narrow streets and the freedom to walk in and out of each other's houses had, over many years, knitted them inexorably together. Now, even to go to the cinema with Madeleine Saitua entailed sending a note by post to arrange a date, where once Rosita would have run up the street to ask her and to enjoy a cup of tea with her. Even worse, Bridget and Pat Connolly's house had been condemned by the city authorities as being unfit for human habitation, and they had been moved out to a soulless new housing estate, called Norris Green, on the edge of the city.

'I have to take two trams to come and see you. I might as well live in China,' Bridget had remarked bitterly, on one of her rare visits to Toxteth. 'Our Mary and Joey are that miserable out there, you'd never believe it.'

Though her new neighbours were civil enough, Rosita was never able to establish a closeness with them. As she said sadly to Bridget, 'I expect it's because my kids are grown-up. You get to know people through the children playing with each other.'

Bridget agreed. 'Perhaps that's why I can't take to Norris Green,' she said.

When Old Manuel looked back on the nineteen-thirties, he marvelled that he had managed to get through college; and then, like Uncle Leo, go to sea steadily through the worst Depression of the twentieth century. Neither man had been paid very well nor were their living conditions aboard ship particularly good, as shipping companies struggled to survive. Nevertheless, by pooling their resources with Rosita, they came home at the end of each voyage to a house that was warm and comfortable by the standard of the times.

Sometimes Old Manuel laughed quietly to himself, as he remembered those times. Not all seamen spent their earnings riotously when they were ashore. Rosita and Uncle Leo had been absolute Tartars about his saving money. Just like Grandma Micaela, Rosita drew their allotments and collected the residue of their pay for them when they arrived home, gave them each back some pocket money, took out an agreed amount of housekeeping and banked as much as she could, against the day that one of them failed to get a ship. She dealt similarly with Francesca and Maria, when they began to earn.

Uncle Leo never married again, though, for many years, he had a widowed lady friend whom he solemnly took out for a drink every Saturday night that he was in port.

It was too comfortable to last, Old Manuel thought, with hindsight. Life never remains static; it's almost impossible to forecast anything – unless you are a demographer, of course!

In 1937, with the family bank account in a healthy state, Rosita and Leo had persuaded him to stay ashore for a time, and add to his qualifications by taking another course or two at the College of Marine Engineering.

He had agreed, and, thanks to a lot of reading while he had been at sea, he was not finding the work too difficult. Walking home from college, one June afternoon, whistling 'Happy Days Are Here Again', he was feeling very content. He was looking forward to going to the Playhouse with Arnador; since they both had to be careful about money, they always sat in the sixpenny seats at the back of the balcony.

As he turned into his own tree-lined street, basking quietly in the late afternoon sunshine, he stopped dead.

In front of his home stood a black car, a very rare sight in Toxteth.

His heart jumped. Was it a doctor's car? Had something happened to Maria? As a baker who worked nights, she was the only one at home in the daytime.

Galvanized by sudden fear, he sprinted down the street.

The front door was open. He shot inside, and was met by a flood of voices speaking Basque and the sound of a howling child. To his astonishment, his way to the living-room, whence the noise came, was blocked by a customs officer, fidgeting uneasily, cap in hand.

He looked round, as Manuel halted behind him.

'Whatever's up?' Manuel demanded, a little breathlessly.

At the sight of the new arrival, the customs officer's face showed considerable relief. 'It's some of your family from Bilbao – we're on our way to the hospital . . .' Without a word, Manuel pushed impatiently past him, and was dumbfounded by the scene before him, though everything seemed rather dark after being in sunlight.

A woman was lying on Grandma Micaela's old sofa, and by her knelt a man. On the hearth rug stood a tiny, filthy toddler with black curly hair, screaming hard. As Manuel entered, the child lost his unsteady balance and flopped to the ground, looked around him, and heightened his screams. By the table, stood Maria in her dressing-gown, her hair tumbled from sleep, tearing up a white pillowslip, as if her life depended upon it.

Thoroughly scared, Manuel exclaimed, 'Christ! What's happening?'

The kneeling man looked up. Out of a face blackened with dirt, a pair of tortured, blood-shot eyes stared at him.

Manuel did not know him and turned, in bewilderment, to his sister.

She was quickly folding the white cloth into a pad, and she said in a frantic tone, 'Thank God you've come, Mannie!' She gestured towards the sofa. 'Quanito and Carmela have escaped from Bilbao. They've brought little Ramon to us, while they take Carmela up to the Royal. She's in such pain that I'm just making a quick bandage to put over her face before they go.'

Manuel turned to the settee. His eyes had adjusted to the shadows of the room, and he could hardly believe what he saw. One side of the woman's face did not look like a face at all.

All the flesh seemed to have been ripped away, to expose a glimpse of bone or teeth. Though blood had clotted in some places, in others there was a soggy, yellow mass. The forehead, the chin and the neck were red and very swollen. Whether the eye was there or not, he was not sure; the swelling was too great. She seemed hardly conscious, though she was moaning.

He looked again at the man. 'Quanito?'

The man nodded. He seemed ready to collapse, too.

Maria impatiently pushed the men back. 'Give me space,' she ordered. She leaned over Carmela and said softly, 'I'm going to sponge the good side of your face. Then I'm going to put a pad over the wound; it's wetted with salted water. I'll put my summer scarf round it to hold it, until you get to the hospital.' She spoke in Basque.

The woman fought her weakly, but Quanito held her hands and whispered comfortingly to her.

Not knowing what to do, Manuel turned to the toddler, who had ceased to scream and was now sobbing hopelessly. He picked the child up and was promptly kicked for his pains. He persisted, however, and held the child close to his shoulder while he tried to hush him.

The patient young customs officer, who had edged into

the crowded room, said to Manuel, 'We could not get the lady to relinquish the child. She insisted on coming into the house with it, though I doubt she really knows what she's doing. Otherwise, I would have had her in hospital by now. I had a real shock, when I saw her, poor thing.'

Manuel nodded. While Maria murmured to Carmela and Quanito, he inquired of the officer, 'How did they come?'

The man replied, 'In a fishing smack – we've had a few like that. There were seven of them in the boat. They landed not more'n an hour ago.' He glanced across at the tableau by the sofa, and said softly, 'The medical officer took one look at the lady, and asked for a car to take her to hospital immediately. I was just going off duty, so I got the job.'

'It's very good of you,' Manuel responded, as he patted the back of the sobbing child.

Her face a mask of anxiety, Maria stepped back, and Quanito asked Manuel brusquely, 'Help me lift her back into the car.' He did not know who Manuel was, but supposed him to be family.

'Of course.' Manuel turned and bundled the little boy into Maria's arms. He told her that he would go up to the hospital with Quanito, and once Carmela had been seen by the doctors, he would find a public telephone and phone Rosita at Sloan's, and ask her to come home.

Maria clasped the child to her and commenced to rock him gently, though she looked very distraught. Manuel could see that she was trembling.

'Mam'll come quick, I'm sure,' he said.

He and Quanito eased Carmela into Grandfather Juan's old carving chair, which had arms to it. By this means, they carried the wounded woman to the edge of the pavement with a minimum of handling her. The customs officer held the car door open while they eased her inside. She felt very hot and she moaned as they moved her. Quanito crawled in with her, to hold her upright, and Manuel got in beside the driver.

The worried young customs officer took off like a racing speedboat, his hand on the horn. He used the horn every time he approached a white-coated policeman at a corner, directing traffic, and the constable, seeing the uniform and sensing a crisis, stopped the traffic so that they could pass over the intersection. Much to the ire of a porter, who seemed to think they should have parked elsewhere and walked into the hospital, they followed an ambulance and drew in behind it.

The man was more civil, however, when the customs officer climbed quickly out. Here was Authority. A stretcher was sent for, while the officer ran inside, to capture a nurse and explain that the Port Medical Authority had sent them an emergency case.

Thanks to the customs officer's efforts, Carmela was carried straight in, to be seen by a doctor and then admitted.

Quanito was not allowed to accompany her. Nearly beside himself, he was sent with Manuel to wait in a crowded waiting room. The customs officer inquired if they would be able to get home again all right, and when Manuel said they could go by tram, he said goodbye. Both Quanito and Manuel thanked him profusely for his help.

The numbers in the waiting room slowly declined as the evening approached. Finally, when they were the only two left, a passing nursing sister stopped to ask what they were doing there.

Manuel stood up and explained that they were waiting for news of Quanito's wife. A perplexed Quanito glowered beside him; he spoke no English, but he sensed that the sister did not approve of them. It was not surprising; Quanito was still wearing the clothes in which he had tried to rescue his family from under the ruins of their home.

Covered with dust, he had then got wetted down with spray while in the fishing boat. With little water in Bilbao, he had not had a wash for a week and smelled very badly.

'You'd better return in the morning,' the nurse said coldly.

Manuel's lips tightened. He drew himself up to his full height, and said belligerently, 'My cousin has just come from Spain – Bilbao. He has lost almost his entire family in the air raids, and his wife is terribly wounded. They have been through hell. Hell, do you understand! Please tell me where I can inquire.'

A nursing sister was not used to such speech from the lower classes, and she flushed with anger. Then she asked suddenly, 'Bilbao? Spain? How extraordinary! What's her name?'

'Mrs Carmela Barinèta – from Bilbao.'

She looked again at Quanito, and then said, 'Wait here. I'll inquire.'

She swept away in a rustle of starch, and they sat down to wait again. Quanito leaned back against the wall behind the wooden bench on which they were sitting. 'I wish I'd thought to ask Maria for a glass of water. After so many days of little to drink, I'm dried out.'

'I'll ask for you,' Manuel said, and he got up and went to a desk at the other end of the big room, where a young woman was writing busily.

'Could I have a glass of water?' he asked.

She glanced up impatiently, and then across the room at Quanito. 'I'm not here to run around getting glasses of water,' she told him. 'You should think of these things before you come.'

Furious, Manuel made an obscene gesture at her, which, mercifully, she did not appear to notice. He walked all round the edge of the room, in the hope of finding a lavatory, where he could get water. If there was one, it was well hidden.

He returned angrily to Quanito. 'No luck,' he said. 'Blast them.'

'It doesn't matter,' Quanito replied, and closed his eyes.

Until that moment, Manuel had forgotten to telephone his mother. He looked at his watch, and realized that Rosita would now have arrived home. He had been so anxious to support Quanito and Carmela that he had forgotten Maria and the baby. To help the time of their waiting pass, he had inquired what exactly had happened in Bilbao, and was horrified by the reply.

'All the family in Bilbao is dead, except us,' Quanito had hoarsely whispered to him. 'It's sheer luck that we're still here. You see, everybody thought that Bilbao could hold out indefinitely against Franco's armies – we'd wear him down and break out and take the countryside back again. But we hadn't counted on the Germans helping him.'

'Germans?'

'Sure. It was the German Luftwaffe that bombed the hell out of us, not to speak of being shelled by German guns. Other towns had fallen. But they weren't fortified like Bilbao is. We couldn't shoot planes down with the guns we had, though. So they swept down on us and dropped bombs wherever they fancied – and machine-gunned the streets.' He stopped for a moment, as if hit by acute pain. Then he went on with an effort. 'We've held out for nearly six weeks – but, I tell you, the city can't take much more.'

He again stopped, and Manuel thought he was going to cry. But instead he sighed and turned to face Manuel. He said brokenly, 'Father and mother – your aunt and Uncle Agustin – and my younger brother; Great-uncle Barinèta and our two cousins – three old people – all of them died in the ruins made by one bomb. I couldn't believe the wreckage when I saw it. We lived in the next street, and when I heard the crash, I ran through the raid to see if they were all right. The neighbours came, and we all worked like demons trying to get them out. Then the broken wall of a warehouse at the back of them teetered. We ran for it – and down it came. And that was that.' He looked down at his torn, filthy clothing. 'I've never had a chance to change my clothes since it happened.'

Manuel shivered. 'My God!' he muttered.

Quanito cleared his throat. 'That's not all of it. You know I had two other boys older than Ramon?'

Manuel did not know. He said apprehensively, 'Did you?'

'Yes. When the raid seemed over, they wanted to play in our street – they were tired of hours of being in the cellar. So the wife let them out to play by the door-step.'

'Not them, too?' Manuel whispered in horror.

'Yes. Out of nowhere, a plane suddenly dived, and machine-gunned the street. Took my boys and two of a neighbour's. We buried them together in an old churchyard nearby – it was the only place we could dig in. My lads were only three – twins. Then, on the way back to our house, they began to shell us.'

'Was that how Carmela got hurt?'

He nodded. 'We started to run for home, and a piece of shrapnel hit her. Took that whole chunk out of the side of her face. I got her home – but she was in agony. So we laid her in the cellar, and the other couple stayed with her and Ramon. I ran like mad for the nearest doctor – and his house was flat! I was nearly out of my mind. I thought, I'll never be able to get her to a hospital, with all hell let loose – and she so badly hurt.'

'What did you do?'

'I went back home. And then the idea came to me, to try to get down the river and over to England – to you people – because we lived right by the river – in the Old Town.

'As soon as it was quiet again, my friend and I put what food and water we had into my boat. We brought two lodgers living with my neighbours with us. Between us, we bandaged Carmela and carried her down. And we came out by night – without lights, though a lot of fires tended to light up the water. I began to think we'd never make it.'

'It must have been terrifying.'

'It was – especially for Carmela, particularly when her mouth swelled up. She couldn't even bear to cry.'

Manuel shivered. These things didn't happen to you or your family, did they? The newspapers didn't tell you about people like Quanito; so you imagined that they must be managing through the reported battles. He said nervously, 'Mother wrote to Uncle Agustin – your father – a couple of months ago suggesting he should bring the family to Liverpool.'

'I know – but we didn't seriously think that Bilbao would fall. It's a fortress of a place – but we didn't count on German bombers and long-range cannon.'

In the bleak hospital waiting room, the two men had almost given up hope of hearing anything about Carmela. Even the supercilious woman at the desk on the far side of the room had departed, turning out most of the lights. Then the door opened and the nursing sister hurried across the empty room. She was wearing her cloak, as if ready to go home.

She said quickly to them, 'Mrs er – Barin – what is it? Your wife has been put under sedation and is comfortable. You may come in tomorrow to see how she is.'

Quanito watched the faces of the other two, and saw from Manuel's expression that all was not well. His face darkened under its coat of dirt, and he asked anxiously for a translation, as the nurse began to move away. Afraid Quanito might make a fuss, Manuel hastily thanked the sister and told Quanito that the nurse had done her best. As they moved out of the hospital after her, he gave a fuller translation, and Quanito shook his clenched fist at the black stone frontage of the hospital. 'She's my *wife*,' he hissed at Manuel. 'Surely I can see her?'

Manuel did his best to comfort the man. He said, 'She'll be sound asleep under sedation, and the doctor will probably have her in surgery, as soon as she's a bit rested.'

Quanito bowed his head and accepted what he did not seem to have the power to change, and Manuel took him home by tram. The few passengers stared at such a wreck of a man accompanied by a young man decently clad in a tweed jacket and grey trousers.

At home, a startled Rosita had been faced with Maria standing in the doorway, looking for her, while she rocked a grubby, dozing child in her arms.

'Good gracious, luv! Who've you got there?' Rosita exclaimed, as Maria turned back into the hall so that she could enter.

Maria babbled out the story of the day, while a work-weary Rosita took off her hat and coat and hung them up. Then she peeped at the tear-stained little face against Maria's breast, and exclaimed, 'Poor little lamb. Maybe he'd sleep for a while, if we put him on the sofa and wrap a shawl round him. Which one of theirs is this? Ramon?'

'Yes. The baby.'

'Where are the other two?'

'They're gone, too, Mam.'

'Oh, God!' Rosita pulled out a chair and sat down suddenly, as Maria carefully laid Ramon on the sofa, and shook out a shawl which normally lay folded on the back of it. As she tucked the shawl round the child, he stirred, put his thumb in his mouth and then seemed to drop off to sleep.

'Agustin?' inquired Rosita shakily, as Maria turned to face her.

'Dead. He was home from sea, and one bomb took him and his family, and Great-Uncle and his family next door but one.'

Maria had held up very well until then. But now she began to cry, while her mother reeled visibly under the blow of her news. 'Don't cry, luv,' she said to her daughter in a pitifully small voice. 'We've got to be the brave ones, and help them.' Inside, she wished frantically for Bridget, to help her bear the grief.

'Holy Mary. Give me strength!' she prayed. She made herself get up and put the kettle on the gas stove, which she lit with a match. Then she went to her daughter, and held her and crooned to her, just as Micaela had done for her in years past. 'Frannie'll be home soon, and she'll help us,' she comforted the younger daughter. 'We're going to have a good strong cup of tea, and then you go back to bed for a while. I'm going to make a big supper. I bet Quanito hasn't had much to eat these past few days – and he's got to keep his strength up. Thank goodness, I've plenty of fish in.' Then she added brokenly, 'Poor Carmela! Poor woman!'

Maria continued to cry for a little while and to hold on to her mother. 'Come on, my dove. You have to go to work at midnight,' Rosita said. She mopped the girl's eyes with her hanky, and then inquired, 'Has little Ramon had anything to eat?'

'I got a cup of hot milk into him – but that's all.'

As her mother made tea and then poured it, Maria sat down and, speaking softly so as not to wake Ramon, she expanded on the tragedy which had struck their extended family. She said, 'Quanito was so thankful for the kindness which they received, once they came over the bar and were spotted. There've been other small boats coming in and the pilots were watching for them, when they went out to other ships. They brought mostly kids with one or two priests looking after them. They've been sending them to

Basque camps. I suppose that's what they'll do with the neighbours who came with Quanito.'

Rosita took a big gulp of tea. She gestured towards the sofa, and replied firmly, 'Well, that little chap's never going to a camp. He stays right here in this house – and so do Quanito and Carmela, until they want to go home.'

Maria smiled faintly at the intensity of feeling in her mother's voice. She could guess that Rosita was already working out how to squeeze three more people into the little house. Comforted that her mother was now in command and that Francesca would be home soon, she finished her tea and agreed to go back to bed.

When Francesca returned from work, Rosita told her of the tragedy, and she immediately set to to help her mother make the evening meal. In the middle of this, Arnador arrived on his bike, which he parked in their back yard. He knocked at the back door and entered without waiting for a response.

Expecting to pick up Manuel and walk down to the Playhouse, he was very shaken to hear their dreadful news.

He sat for a few minutes with Rosita, while Francesca continued to peel a pile of potatoes, and expressed his sympathy at such a tragedy. Then he said he thought he should get out of their way. 'I think I'll go back home to tell Mum and Dad and Josefa – I know they will feel a deep sorrow for you. I'll drop by tomorrow evening to inquire how Carmela is.'

Very soberly, he let himself out of the back door and wheeled his bike through the yard entrance.

Rosita returned to cutting up fish and breading it. 'He's such a nice lad,' she said. Francesca nodded. Within herself, she was sick with horror, and she would have been glad if sensible, reliable Arnador had stayed a little longer.

When Manuel and Quanito returned about eight o'clock, Francesca was whipping mashed potatoes, and Rosita had a pot of hot fat on the back of the stove waiting to receive the fish. Bread, cheese and a bowl of Australian apples graced the table; a bowl of tinned peas was keeping hot in the oven.

Rosita did not know what to say, as the apparition which was Quanito entered her living-room. Was that dried blood on his jersey? She opened her arms, and he went into them like a child who had been lost. He said, 'I'm so tired.'

She held him, while dry sobs shook him. Then she said gently, as she led him to a chair, 'Sit down here a minute. I'm going to give you a big glass of decent Basque wine, to set you up a bit. Then Manuel'll take a bowl of hot water upstairs for you, and you can wash yourself, and take those clothes off.' She turned to Manuel. 'Mannie, you go and get out a pair of your pyjamas for him and your dressing-gown.'

Without bothering Quanito with a single question, she soon had the family round the table. She herself held a whimpering Ramon. She made a joke of feeding him with well-mashed spoonfuls from her plate, and, after a moment's hesitation, he seemed to accept her soft, Basque voice, and ate. When she saw that he had a fair number of teeth, she gave him a piece of fried fish in his fist to feed himself. She pressed more wine on his father, and Manuel, remembering his thirst in the hospital, brought a jug of water to him.

After Manuel had taken Quanito upstairs, to sleep in Uncle Leo's bed, Rosita asked Frannie to get a bowl of water and put it on the table, and she tackled the job of cleaning up Ramon, who was in a disgusting state. She washed the little boy while holding him on her lap. She had no children's clothes to put on him, so a towel was torn in half to make two clean nappies and then she wrapped him in the shawl from the sofa. As she worked, she played with the child, and finally made him gurgle and smile.

Together her daughters stripped her bed, to put an old oilcloth tablecloth under the bottom sheet, to preserve the mattress from Ramon, who was, as yet, far from water-tight. For several nights, he shared Rosita's bed, until the second-hand shop in nearby Granby Street was able to provide a small truckle bed for him.

When Ramon had been topped up with as much hot milk as he would accept, he was laid in the bed, still in the shawl, and Rosita lay by him until he slept. Then she went downstairs again. She was immensely tired herself, but she had, somehow, to plan for the next day. She had no time to grieve.

Downstairs, she found Manuel describing the details of the family in Bilbao to the two young women huddled on the sofa together. The only relation whom the girls had seen before was Uncle Agustin. They knew he had a wife and sons, and that one of his sons was married and had children. But, except for Francesca's visit as an infant, neither girl had been to Bilbao, so they were not well acquainted with their cousins. Manuel told them, 'Quanito knew our names, though when he first saw me he did not know, for certain, who I was!'

'What are we going to do, Mam?' Francesca asked. 'I can't believe what happened to them – it's too awful to face.'

'It happened,' Rosita assured her. 'And Carmela is obviously very sick.' She examined her needlepricked left hand, and heaved a great sigh. 'Well, as I said, they'll stay with us for now. Just how I cope with tomorrow, I'm not sure.'

Her children stared at her. They understood the complication of having a small boy to care for, when all of them went to work – or, in Manuel's case, to college; and Quanito would, tomorrow, want to go immediately to the hospital to see his wife.

After an uneasy silent pause, Manuel said, 'I could miss my morning lectures – I could get a pal to give me his notes to copy – so I could take Quanito up to the hospital. He doesn't know the city – and it's two trams.'

Rosita flexed her aching fingers, and said to Manuel, 'If you and Quanito could watch Ramon first thing tomorrow, I'll run down to the phone box and phone Sloan's. Thank goodness, Miss Hamilton doesn't retire until next year. I can tell her what's happened, and say I'll be in on Monday. It's Friday tomorrow, so I'll only lose a day and a half. It'll give me a chance to talk to Quanito and, maybe, get up to the hospital to see Carmela.'

Maria spoke up. 'If I can get a few hours' sleep when I come off shift tomorrow morning, I can watch Ramon, so you could get up to the hospital in the afternoon. Then Mannie can get to his afternoon lectures.'

The coming of Ramon had already begun to alter their lives. In her heart, Rosita feared the little lad would soon be motherless, and she knew that, at a stage in her life when she needed the most peace because her menopause was upon her, she was going to have to bring him up. She had no idea how she was going to do it.

Chapter Forty-four

There were no sulpha drugs in those days to save Carmela
from a dreadful death, thought Old Manuel sadly. By the
time she had medical attention, she was in a shocking state.
Twenty-four hours after her arrival in Liverpool, she died
of septicaemia.

Because Quanito was penniless, her funeral expenses
were paid from Rosita's and Leo's bank account. Later,
proud Quanito's fishing smack was auctioned to pay the
dues incurred by its presence in the Mersey river. He
insisted upon giving Rosita the balance of the money raised
by the auction, in part payment of the funeral costs.

Immediately after his wife's death, he nearly went mad.
For hour after hour he raved of vengeance, vengeance on
Franco and his Spaniards and on his German allies. He
swore by Almighty God that he would make them pay for
the death of Carmela and their beautiful sons and for his
entire family. Again and again, he swore it aloud.

On that awful evening, Manuel and Arnador finally made
him so drunk that he did not come round for thirty-six
hours. When he did regain his senses, he was deadly quiet.
He sat with a fretful Ramon on his knee, frozen with grief.

Rosita, almost constantly in tears herself, fluttered round
him, trying to comfort him with food and with tender
promises to be a mother to his small boy – though God
only knows how, she thought to herself. There was room
in her small home to house both father and child, if the
British would allow them to stay in Liverpool, she assured
him.

*

As refugees, Quanito and Ramon were reluctantly allowed to stay temporarily in Liverpool; and, when Manuel, Leo and Quanito happened to be in port at the same time, the back bedroom was rather crowded. Ramon was comforted by his truckle bed being pushed close to Rosita's, and he was spoiled to death by Francesca and Maria, as well as Rosita. He thrived on it.

Until the Spanish War was over, Quanito found a berth with a small Basque shipping company sailing out of Liverpool to the West Indies. After the vicious conflict was ended early in 1939, Quanito applied for British citizenship; but he had not been in the country sufficiently long to be considered for it. He was, however, given permission to reside with his son in Liverpool. He thankfully accepted this.

When travel was possible, he went back to Bilbao to see if his home still stood. He left Ramon with Rosita, and crossed the English Channel by ferry and went by train to his home city.

Rosita received a postcard to say that he had been to see his old home, but it had been pulled down as unsafe and was now a heap of rubble surrounded by a temporary fence.

After that, he vanished and Rosita never heard directly from him again.

From time to time, a shy Basque seaman, carrying a verbal message, would arrive on the Echaniz doorstep. He was always invited in, fed and plied with wine. Then the news was whispered to them.

Quanito was up in the mountains with the Basque Separatists, who were fighting for a country of their own. They had blown up the car of a Spanish general – with the general inside it. They constantly harried Spanish businessmen until, in fear of their lives, they left Basque cities. They picked off informers and any Spaniard unlucky enough to come within the sights of their guns. They had

had to bury some of their own men and some were in prison – but not Quanito, who, though very daring, was also very smart, the seamen said.

Rosita wrung her hands. 'When are they going to stop?' she asked an older man, who was one of the messengers.

'When we have a country of our own,' he replied with a shrug. 'When we've seen their cities burn, as ours did. Who's going to accept Spanish rule, after all we've been through? We'll never give up.'

Each night visitor brought a small sum of money for the maintenance of Ramon. Rosita accepted it and banked it for the child; none of the family inquired from what source Quanito had acquired it. Rosita asked Manuel or Leo to change the foreign currency, since seamen often had such money to change, and the transaction would not cause so much comment as it might have done if a woman undertook it.

Even after the commencement of the Second World War, Quanito did not forget them, and money continued to arrive. Rosita took to writing anonymous small notes to her nephew, saying that Ramon was thriving. She asked the messengers to pass them on, if they had the opportunity. She never knew whether Quanito received them.

Encouraged and cosseted by three women and two men, the boy knew little about his parentage until he was about ten. In the meantime, he was simply told that they had died in the Spanish War. As far as he was concerned, Rosita was his mother and Uncle Leo was cast as father. Manuel was the big brother who played endlessly with him, when he was home, and brought him presents from foreign places.

Ramon's lack of a birth certificate worried both Leo and Rosita. They tried to adopt him, since he was their grand-nephew; his mother was dead and his father, they told the authorities, had deserted him.

They were immediately caught in floundering red tape. First, the Spanish Government and the Spanish Roman Catholic Church were anxious for all refugees to return to Spain, and Ramon and his father were refugees; the fascists felt it was insulting that many Basques did not wish to return to live under their oppressive regime. Second, the would-be parents were brother and sister, not husband and wife – it was, therefore, an unstable home declared the British, and, even if the child was an orphan, it was not wise to place him in it.

Patient Leo said angrily to Manuel, one day, that he wanted to scream at the woman dealing with the case. When he heard this, Arnador gave them the name of a good solicitor. Quite a lot of their precious savings were expended on his fees.

It took time, but the solicitor proved his worth. Ramon got official permission to reside permanently in the country and to apply for citizenship when he was aged twenty-one. Meanwhile, Rosita and Leo were declared his official guardians. It was not what his elders had wanted – but it worked.

Perhaps it was as well that Ramon's situation had been formalized, because eighteen months after the Second World War broke out his wrathful father became internationally famous. Still an ardent Separatist, he travelled secretly to Madrid, and neatly shot dead two German diplomats visiting their fascist allies. It was the first of a number of German assassinations carried out by an unidentified crack shot, believed to be a Basque, until, in Argentina, he missed his target and, unintentionally, killed an eminent Argentinian. Cornered on a roof top by the Buenos Aires police, he must have decided that this was the end, because, rather than be captured, he shot himself.

Long in their graves, his father and mother, his extended

family, and his beloved Carmela and their sons had been methodically revenged. Few Basques grudged him such a reprisal.

Chapter Forty-five

It was obvious to Rosita that she could no longer work full-time at Sloan's, now that she had Ramon to care for, so she begged an interview with her old mentor, Miss Muriel Hamilton, and explained the situation to her.

'I need to work,' she explained, 'and I love working for Sloan's. But now I've got young Ramon . . .'

Rosita's exquisite work with a needle was more precious to her employer than she imagined. Younger women coming into the trade were not nearly as well versed as their mothers had been. Miss Hamilton hummed and hawed, and agreed to provide work for her at home. Rosita would not earn nearly as much, but, added to what the rest of the family was bringing in, she knew she could manage.

Neither Miss Hamilton nor Rosita foresaw the havoc that would be wrought in the women's clothing industry by the war, hovering on the horizon, and the consequent rationing.

Because she was at home more, Rosita began to notice that Maria was being courted by Madeleine Saitua's younger son, Vicente, and she was very upset about it.

'You're too young for him,' she stormed at her daughter, one night after Ramon had been put to bed. 'He must be at least fourteen years older than you are. Do you want to be a widow for half your life?'

'Don't be silly, Mam. I'm nearly twenty-three. I know what I want.' Maria fought back stubbornly. 'He's always been in work – being a carpenter, he can work ashore or in a ship. What's the matter with him?'

There was nothing the matter with him, except that he was thirty-seven years old; and Rosita knew it. She had known him for most of his life, and Madeleine Saitua, now a widow, would be a kindly mother-in-law. Sulkily, she returned to a collar she had been embroidering for Sloan's.

Boiling with rage – and yet made fearful by her mother's remarks about widowhood – Maria went out to meet her beloved and go to the cinema, before going on nightshift.

Later on, when Francesca returned from a meeting of an amateur dramatic club to which she belonged, she found her mother sitting dejectedly in Grandma Micaela's rocking chair, the *Liverpool Echo* unopened in her lap.

Aware of how tiring Rosita was finding the care of Ramon, she inquired a little anxiously, 'Are you feeling poorly, Mam?' She sat down on a straight chair facing her mother. Rosita thought she had never seen her look more beautiful.

The older woman sighed, and told her about Maria and Vicente.

Francesca laughed. 'They've been going together for over a year now. Didn't you know?'

Rosita made a face. 'I suppose I didn't notice him amongst all her other hangers-on!' She sounded tart.

'Come on, Mam. Vicente's as nice a fellow as you can imagine. He'll treat her like a princess. Isn't that better than being misused by a younger, more thoughtless chap?'

'She says she wants to be engaged. He's asked her.'

'Tush, Mam. Let them be. We don't know what lies ahead of us. It's better for her to be happy now.' She took the hat pins out of her hat and laid them on the table, while she removed her hat carefully from her head. 'Be agreeable to their getting engaged – and see what happens. It may not last.'

'But, Frannie, when she's forty-five, he'll be fifty-nine and close to the end of his life.'

'That could leave them over twenty years of contented married life!'

Rosita frowned, and then laughed suddenly. 'You're wicked girls – you always defend each other! And what about you, young lady? When are you going to get yourself married?'

'When a nice Basque asks me,' replied her daughter cheerfully. 'Maria and I are agreed – we both want Basques for husbands – Grandpa and Daddy were such golden examples, that neither of us can consider anybody less!'

At the mention of Pedro and Juan, her mother smiled at her. Her smile was sweet, and she said, 'If you do as well as I did, it'll be good.'

So no more was said to Maria about her choice of Vicente, and within the month she had a modest diamond ring on her finger.

It seemed to Rosita that the family had hardly got its collective life adjusted to their joint sorrows as a result of the Spanish Civil War, when the Second World War was upon them. As Basques, they had a better knowledge of what it might entail than most of the population of Liverpool; and all of them worried about Ramon, who, by the age of approximately two years, had had enough of conflict to last a lifetime.

When war broke out on 3 September 1939 Manuel was nearly thirty-one years of age. Though he was now a refrigeration engineer in ships carrying fruit, and usually had a neat small cabin of his own – which he had promised himself on his very first voyage, he remembered with amusement – he was not paid very well. Like many during the Depression years, he had not thought seriously of marriage, because he, like Leo, had a commitment to help maintain the existing family home; to take a wife and start a new family could cause endless problems. Besides,

Arnador was still single, and free to range with him as a fellow bachelor.

A year older than Manuel, Arnador had at last established himself as a lecturer at the University of Liverpool, after doing post-doctoral work in Manchester. But even university staff were not paid that well, he confided to Manuel.

Manuel was at sea when war was declared, but he docked a couple of weeks later, and came up to Toxteth to see his mother in a brief shore leave. Perhaps because the fright of the declaration of war tended to make some people look around them more and re-evaluate their lives, he noticed how greatly Rosita seemed to have aged; her red mane of hair had grown sandy-looking with the white in it; she was stouter and her movements slower. She greeted him cheerfully, however, with her usual ebullience, and Ramon toddled round after her, chattering all the time – speech which had to be translated for Manuel by his amused great-aunt. 'He's trying that hard to talk, bless him,' she told Manuel.

Manuel's and Leo's homecomings did not often coincide, though Leo had been home once since Ramon's arrival. At that time, he had not seemed to have changed much. He was a bosun and enjoyed his job – he never seemed to change ships. He had gone bald and put on some weight under his navy jersey, and, sometimes by a turn of his head or a hand gesture, he reminded Manuel of Grandfather Juan. He had been badly shaken by the news of the loss of his brother and the Bilbao family, and he had been completely in agreement that Ramon and Quanito should stay with them as long as they wished.

It had been expected that immediately upon the declaration of war, the city would be heavily bombed, and Rosita had received instructions from the newly appointed air raid warden about her being evacuated to the country with

Ramon. If the boy had been at school, he would have gone with his teachers; the schools would be closed.

'As if I'd leave you to be bombed!' Rosita said to Francesca and Maria. 'I'll make a bed for the little lad under the cellar steps – that's the safest place in the house, according to the air raid warden. The poor little lamb isn't going anywhere.'

So Ramon spent most nights, during the years of the war, sleeping soundly under the cellar steps, amid the smell and dust of the coal ration.

The evacuated children drifted back from the country in such numbers that the schools had to be re-opened. In the meantime, Ramon learned how to put on a gas mask.

Men were called up, further disorganizing businesses, which were trying to adjust to producing articles required for war, rather than for peace, amid stiff rationing of resources. Women in factories began to earn very good wages and to find that there was little to spend them on.

Rosita suddenly found she was getting dozens of requests from young women in the immediate vicinity to make dresses for them. Most of the material presented to her was undoubtedly obtained on the black market, but she was also asked to recut dresses bought in second-hand shops or to make blouses out of men's shirts, skirts out of men's trousers – as brothers were called up and trustingly left their civilian clothes hanging in the wardrobe at home.

At first she refused, but the young women were prepared to pay so much more than she had ever earned before, that she decided to leave Sloan's, who were having their own problems, and concentrate on this new, very lucrative business.

In 1940, Ramon was sent to school in nearby Granby Street, and she had more time. Her sewing machine in the front room whirred throughout the war, as she put money away for a better education for Ramon.

The boy grew up to be a typical Liverpool lad, unusual

only in his ability to speak two languages. He played football, and, as he grew bigger, was always importuning for money to go to football matches. He became a sturdy boy with wavy black hair and a fair skin; and he blended into the amorphous mass of the population of the great port. Few would have guessed that his father had been a famous guerrilla, fighting a murderous battle of revenge against the fascists.

On the outbreak of war, Vicente obtained a special licence, and he and Maria were quietly married in St Peter's Church by an aged and sad Father Felipe. Francesca was the bridesmaid and Domingo Saitua was the best man. White-haired Madeleine Saitua put on a pretty wedding breakfast for them in her house, at which Domingo's wife and daughter, Rosita and Ramon were the only guests. Manuel and Leo were both at sea. The newly married couple went to live with Madeleine, who said rightly that she had more than enough room in her house.

Three months later, Boot's regretfully told Francesca that their cosmetic trade would be almost wiped out by the lack of stock; they hoped she could find another post more closely connected with the war effort and would return to them when the conflict was over.

Disconcerted, she discussed with Rosita the idea of volunteering for the Forces. 'I don't have any particular skills, Mam. I don't know what else to do.'

Her mother took off her spectacles and rubbed her eyes. She glanced doubtfully at her beautiful daughter; she did not want the girl in uniform – uniforms were for men. 'You can speak and write three languages,' she reminded her.

'I've never found them a commercial asset,' replied Francesca, with a wry grin.

Rosita picked up a reel of cotton and carefully rewound

a piece of thread on to it – appropriately coloured cottons were beginning to be in short supply. 'Look, Boot's have given you two weeks to find another job. Mannie'll be docking in a few days, and I would like you to discuss it with him before you do anything drastic.'

In the event, it was Arnador who settled the matter with one word. He said, 'Censorship!' He and Manuel were of one mind; neither of them wanted Francesca in the Forces, a very common state of mind amongst the male population, when their own sisters were involved!

Encouraged by the young men, she applied to the Censorship Office and was sent to Glasgow. When, on 18 December 1941, the call-up of women was announced, she found, like many others, that she could not change her job without Government permission. She found the work so interesting, however, that she was happy to stay there. 'And it is vital to the war, Mam,' she told Rosita.

Similarly, Arnador himself was co-opted by the Government to do highly secret work intercepting and translating radio messages and telephone calls, where his knowledge of Spanish and Basque was invaluable.

Because he was convinced on moral grounds that this was a war which had to be fought, he had on its outbreak volunteered for the Air Force; to his astonishment, he had been turned down because of a partially dislocated shoulder, the result of the bite he had received from a horse, as a boy, an event which he had totally forgotten.

Rosita and Ramon were a comfort to each other, as they took shelter under the cellar steps during air raids, and they gave thanks to God each time Manuel and Leo came home from sea.

Chapter Forty-six

With sorrow in his heart, Old Manuel tried to write something of the war for Lorilyn, to make her understand its personal impact, something separate from lists of battles. Just as Rosita used to do, he chewed his ballpoint pen, as he considered his healthy, lively granddaughter. She was not unlike her great-aunt Maria; she had the same dark colouring and vivacity, the same impatience with small obstacles in her life – dear Little Maria, who had had fifteen months of happy married life, before a direct hit in an air raid on Madeleine's house, so near the target of the docks, had killed not only Madeleine herself, but also Vicente and Maria, who were expecting their first baby.

He put down his pen, in order to rub his aching arthritic fingers. Thoughts of his sisters made him feel so lonely that he wanted to weep. The loss of Maria had broken his mother's heart, and Manuel himself had not been able to believe that someone so lively, so close to him, could possibly be dead. Francesca, too, had been stunned by it. She came down from Glasgow to comfort her mother; but wars were such that they took little note of personal grieving, and Francesca had had to return to her work, and leave Rosita and Ramon to comfort each other as best they could. That same night Manuel went back to sea – it was pure chance that he had been in dock on the night of the tragedy. There was no individual funeral because there was nothing much left to bury. A communal service was held for all the victims of the incident and the bits were buried in a communal grave.

The old man remembered all the fine women who had

filled his young life, Grandma Micaela, Rosita, Francesca and Maria, dear delicate Aunt Maria, Bridget Connolly, Peggy O'Brien, Effie Halloran, Madeleine Saitua and vague ghosts of his Bilbao cousins and his Echaniz grandmother.

With the weakness of great age, he let the tears run. Then, telling himself not to be an old fool, he took off his glasses and wiped them carefully. As he put them on again, he saw almost with shock, that he had not included Kathleen, his dear wife of many years, or Faith, who doggedly did her best for him even now, or Lorilyn, in whom he put his hopes for the future.

He sighed, as he leaned back in his swivel chair. He had loved, still loved, Kathleen, and Faith and Lorilyn, too. But they had understood little or nothing of the world from which he had come; they belonged in another place, nice, sanitized, wealthy ... But often dull, he considered suddenly.

He went to have his afternoon nap. Before lying down, he stopped in the kitchen to get a glass of water and take one of his pills. It seemed to him that, lately, his damaged legs had ached a lot more than they used to, though ever since the day he had been carried into the hospital at Halifax, he had had to take an occasional pill to ease the pain. As he stood leaning against the kitchen counter, waiting for the pill to do its work, he told himself he was lucky; he could easily have had to have his legs amputated.

After his nap, he made a cup of coffee and took it to his desk. He would tell Lorilyn how he met her grandmother.

I was torpedoed off the coast of Nova Scotia, he wrote. It was the second time – the first time was near the coast of Northern Ireland; but we managed to get the lifeboats off, that night. This time, we weren't so lucky and had to cling to a raft, with several men on it. The water was so cold, it was a miracle some of us survived – you probably know how the icebergs drift down from the North Pole in the western Atlantic; their chill seems to permeate the water all year. Some convoys had a rescue boat, to pick up men like us, after the convoy had extricated itself from the submarine attack. Ours did not, and, of a necessity, the convoy — what was left of it — had to continue on its way to Liverpool; otherwise they might lose more ships, while searching for men in the water. The last ship in the convoy passed right by us.

By chance, Joey Connolly was an able seaman on the same ship, and he, too, was clinging to the raft. Because he was obviously weakening, two of the men tried to heave him on to it. He was far gone, however, and he slipped into the sea and we lost him, young Joey who never learned to cheat at marbles.

Some fishermen risked their own lives to rescue the three of us still alive when they spotted the raft. They took us into a Newfoundland outport. The few inhabitants opened their doors and came running; they took blankets from their beds to wrap round us. We were nearly smothered in oil, and the women washed our faces as best they could, and then spooned hastily heated canned soup into us, while we waited for transport to Halifax, Nova Scotia. It seemed like eternity, waiting for medical help.

A team of doctors and nurses was ready for us, when we did arrive, and we were stripped and washed and the damage assessed. Though the doctors had by that time had a fair amount of experience of resuscitating patients like us, one died.

Thinking about it, Manuel mentally doffed his beret to the Halifax doctors and nurses. Thanks to them, he still had a pair of legs.

In the night, when the sedation was wearing off, I must have made some sort of a noise, because the night nurse left her desk and came to my bedside. Fair, brisk and capable, she arranged pillows round me to ease the weight on tender parts, and she sat a few minutes with me until I must have dozed off.

And that's how I met Grandma Kathleen. I fell in love at first sight — not that I expected to live to do anything about it — I was sure I was a goner — I hurt everywhere!

He did not write that he had cried that night for Joey and for Auntie Bridget Connolly, whose heart would be broken when she got the news.

Chapter Forty-seven

It was several months before he was passed as fit, plenty of time in which to woo his night nurse. It was with reluctance that he joined a British ship sailing from Halifax, in convoy, to Liverpool. As before, the convoy was attacked by German submarines. Two ships were lost, and one damaged, but he himself was lucky this time.

When he walked up the tree-lined street to his home, he found Uncle Leo sitting on the doorstep in the spring sunshine, reading the single sheet evening newspaper.

Manuel dropped the small suitcase given him in Halifax with a few clothing basics and some toiletries, and grasped his uncle's hand. They hugged each other until every distressed muscle and joint in Manuel's body began to ache all over again. Both of them had been under the same intolerable stress for months and months and did not need to say much to each other to understand. Leo had not actually lost a ship under him, but he had had a number of uncomfortable encounters with subs.

'We'd no means of knowing when you'd dock. There's never a word of shipping news in the paper. Come in, lad. I docked yesterday – real lucky to see you.'

As he took off his jacket, Manuel asked after the family and was assured that everyone was well, and that Arnador had left a telephone number with Rosita for him. 'He's gone to Manchester to be some sort of a back-room boy for the Government,' Leo explained.

'Any air raids?'

'Oh, aye. But not much up this end – the north end's taken a beating, though.'

After a long, Basque-speaking evening with the family, where he seemed to have held Rosita's hand for hours to reassure her that he was, indeed, there and was well again, Manuel said he thought he should go out to Norris Green, the next day, to see Bridget and Pat Connolly about the loss of Joey.

'Yes, you must go. She came to me when Maria and Vicente . . .' Words failed her, and she clutched Manuel's hand even harder. 'She's taking Joey's death very hard. She'd love to see you.'

The next morning, with a heavy heart, he made the long tram journey out to Norris Green, and did his best in a hopeless situation.

That afternoon, Ramon played truant from school to be with Manuel. They went down to the Mercantile Marine office, where he had to arrange for a new discharge book, and to inquire for a ship to Halifax, sailing fairly soon. He was told that it would be some days before he got his new book, and the clerk promised to bear him in mind for a likely ship.

Afterwards, they walked along the landing stage to look at the river, crowded with shipping, and to catch up on their news.

Kathleen was constantly at the forefront of Manuel's mind, and one problem in regard to her was troubling him; she was a Protestant and he was a Roman Catholic, a very serious matter in Liverpool.

After he had heard about Ramon's prowess in the school football team and how many pieces of shrapnel had just missed hitting him during the air raids, he asked the boy, 'Do the kids get at you for being Catholic or speaking Basque?'

Ramon laughed. 'I never tell them — they don't ask

anyway. If the class goes into church for something special, I go along. What does it matter?'

'I'm glad for you. Do you think you'll get a scholarship to the Institute? Mam said she thought it was possible.'

'I dunno. I'll try. Uncle Arnie says he'll coach me when I'm old enough.'

That evening, Manuel asked Rosita what the feeling was about Catholics in the city. She thought it was an odd question, but she answered, 'Well, for sure, you can get a job in a Prottie business now – and that wasn't always easy. They'll take anybody now. Remember when they used to ask what your religion was when you applied for a job? Well, not any more.'

She smiled up at him impishly, and added, 'When the bombs are dropping on you, Catholic and Prottie alike, you just think to comfort each other – you don't think, "Is she a good Catholic?"'

If anyone as devout as his mother could say that, Manuel decided, times were really changing. Perhaps there would no longer be bloody religious riots in Liverpool, as there had been before the war.

The whole family had a good laugh that evening, as Manuel collected every big copper penny that anybody had, so that he could telephone Arnador in Manchester and Francesca in Glasgow from the public telephone box at the end of the road.

Francesca was delighted to hear his voice, she said. She told him that, for once in her life, being trilingual was proving an asset. 'When the nuns realized that Maria and I could both speak a little Spanish – because we'd heard it at home and in the Church, like you did – they pushed us to take it as a subject. And I thought it was such waste of time! But nobody's interested in cosmetics at present, so it's a lifesaver for me.'

She sounded happy, and said she was sharing a flat with a Scottish lady, who had been the governess to a rich Egyptian family and had learned good Egyptian Arabic. 'She's a wonderful old bird – and she works in the same building as I do. We have a good time together.'

Arnador sounded lonely in his Manchester flat. He did not say exactly what he was doing, but told Manuel that he worked long hours – and that it was just as well. He would be glad when he could go back to his own kind of work, and get a decent post.

It was not like Arnie to complain, so Manuel stayed on the phone until the very last penny had been expended and he had been cut off. It was then that he thought of writing to Arnie once a month without fail, to keep his spirits up.

Arnador responded with alacrity, and they kept up the habit for the rest of their lives. We put the world to rights – by mail, thought Old Manuel with a wicked grin. And we're still doing it.

As he slit open Arnador's latest epistle, he chuckled to himself. Before he went back to sea, he told his mother about Kathleen. 'I'm going to ask her to marry me,' he told her.

They were sitting on the cellar steps, while outside an air raid raged noisily, and Ramon snuffled softly in his bed beneath the stone steps. Leo had already sailed.

Rosita did not answer immediately. She was glad enough that the boy had found someone at last, but a sharp fear pierced her, and she asked, 'Where will you live?'

'Probably in Halifax,' he replied. 'It depends on her. I've been earning better since the war began – things are more expensive there – but they've got everything, Mam – not like us here.'

She nodded. She felt suddenly old. With Little Maria gone and Francesca in Glasgow and now Manuel, it seemed as if there would be no family any more. And for what else had she struggled and fought?

She made a tremendous effort, as, in the candlelight, Manuel turned to look at her. She patted his hand, and said, 'She sounds a lovely girl, dear. I hope I shall be able to meet her.'

'Of course you will, Mam. When the war's over, you and Uncle Leo must come to stay with us. And probably I'll be docking in Liverpool regularly – and be able to see you.'

But Kathleen had other ideas. They were married while the war still raged; and she continued to nurse. But once peace was declared, she persuaded Manuel to move to Montreal, where he could go back to college to study – this time, marine architecture – while she continued to work.

It was the autumn of 1953, when he was already in a good post as a marine architect, before Rosita was able to come to see them. In the years immediately after the war, half the world was trying to get home again, and reasonably priced passages were hard to obtain. It was a stroke of luck that Arnador managed a visit before she did. He had been to a conference in Chicago, and returned to Britain via Montreal.

Faith was six, Manuel remembered, preparing to begin school that September. He took a week off to be with his friend. To give Kathleen some relief from the child, they took her up to Mount Royal, and she played with the dog, while they lay in the summer sunshine and poured out their souls in Basque.

It was then that Arnador told him that he had always loved Francesca and that they were going to be married shortly. 'Rosita seems very pleased,' he said. 'And my mother is delighted – she's expecting a few Basque grand-children. Neither Frannie nor I have the courage to tell her that we don't want any children. Frannie wants to continue with Pond's – she loves her job – selling Hope, as she calls it, to plain women.

'Neither of us is that young, anyway – I couldn't ask her until I had a tenured position – something to offer her.'

'I suspect she would have married you if you hadn't got a bean. Frannie's like that.'

'Well, I can take care of her, now.' He was sprawled on the grass, and he turned to face his friend. 'It'll be great being brothers-in-law!'

Manuel laughed. 'For sure. We're as good as brothers, anyway.'

After he sailed, Manuel missed him badly.

Kathleen looked forward to Rosita's visit with no little trepidation. She could not visualize what Rosita would be like.

She kept Faith with her in the car, while Manuel went down to the dock to meet his mother, having thought mother and son might appreciate being together for a few minutes.

When Manuel saw Rosita coming down the gangway of the liner, he had been shocked. Dressed in dead black, she looked like a small dark wraith. She looked elegant, as always, but under her hat, her pageboy hairstyle was snow white, and she peered at him through plastic-rimmed spectacles, her face wizened like a walnut shell.

'Mannie!' she exclaimed softly, and he took her in his arms. For a moment she murmured endearments in his ear in tremulous Basque, and then she asked, 'Where's Kathleen – and little Faith?'

'In the car,' he said. 'She was afraid of Faith getting knocked about in the rush to meet the boat.'

Though Rosita looked frail, she was very alert. When first meeting Kathleen she was kind but wary, concentrating on Faith, who, at first, clung to her mother; this grandma was not at all like the brightly clad grandma who came on the train from Vancouver.

Once they reached their apartment and she had carefully hung up her best black coat and hat and had drunk a dreadfully weak cup of tea with no milk in it, Rosita looked around the living-room. She was generous in her praise, as if no one else in the world had managed to produce such a pretty child or so cleverly arranged such a nice apartment. She finally succeeded in persuading Faith on to her knee, and slowly produced a whole family of tiny golliwogs out of her skirt pocket. They were beautifully made and just the right size to inhabit Faith's new doll's house. From the very bottom of the pocket she drew out an old-fashioned paper poke of dolly mixtures and handed them to the child. Together they spread out the tiny coloured sweets on the coffee table to be admired and tasted.

At the sight of the little bag of sweets, Manuel's throat contracted. He remembered two other little girls, long ago, kneeling on a rag rug and, regardless of dust, spreading out halfpennyworths of the same sweets, each trying to be first to claim the heart-shaped ones.

On the whole, the visit went very well. Kathleen learned to cook some good Basque dishes, and Rosita revelled in the plenitude of food in the shops.

At the end of a month, they saw Rosita on to her ship, promising to visit England soon, but Kathleen never did; she always seemed to have some good reason why she should not. So Manuel went over, shortly after Rosita's visit, to attend Arnador's and Frannie's wedding, and to be the best man.

A few months later, he went for his mother's funeral, five days in a ship, which seemed to crawl.

Ramon was in his last year at the Liverpool Institute. He had said firmly that he did not want to go to university, and, although Arnador thought he could do it if he wanted to, the boy said firmly that he would rather go to work.

One icy February day, in 1954, he came home from school, to find Rosita apparently asleep in Grandma Micaela's rocking chair. She had sewing resting on her lap, and the needle was dangling. Thinking that the needle might fall to the floor and that someone might tread on it, he went quietly towards her with the intention of pinning it back into the doll's dress she had been sewing. It was then that he discovered that she was not breathing.

He was a sensible youth, but he had never seen anyone dead before and he was afraid. Behind his first primeval fear was another terror – that of being alone, bereft.

He backed away, trying not to panic.

Francesca, that was it! He ran into the kitchen, and found Rosita's change purse in its usual place in the kitchen drawer. He took out all the pennies it contained, ran out of the house, forgetting to shut the front door, and went to the public phone box to call Francesca.

Because she was in town arranging a special promotion for her company, in Lewis's Store, there was no reply.

Ramon put down the phone and stood shivering. Then he picked up the battered telephone book and found the university number. He asked the telephonist who replied to his call if she could trace Dr Arnador Ganivet, Demography.

Mercifully, Arnador was not lecturing, so he came immediately, tearing down the street on his old bicycle, known to the family as the Flying Bedstead.

While Ramon dithered behind him, he checked that Rosita was indeed dead. Then he sent the lad with a written message to the doctor on Parliament Street with whom, Ramon said, Rosita was registered for health care. 'Not that we've ever had to call him,' Ramon assured Arnador.

The doctor was resting for a little while, before his evening surgery. He got up immediately, however, picked up his bag and bundled Ramon into his rusty Austin Seven, to drive the boy home.

While Ramon had been away, Arnador had picked up the thin shadow of a woman, who had been his friend since he was nine years old, and very gently taken her upstairs and laid her on her bed. As he stood panting by the bed, getting his breath back, a slow grief overwhelmed him, almost as if it were his own mother who was there. He bent and closed the already half-shut eyes, and then kissed her on the cheek.

Then he went downstairs to the kitchen to see if he could find some wine. When Ramon returned with the physician, he was slowly drinking a glass. The kettle was singing on the gas stove to make a strong cup of sugary tea for Ramon.

The doctor concluded that it had been, in layman's language, a silent heart attack which had caused such an obviously quiet death.

After he had gone and a very white Ramon had drunk the tea which his adopted uncle proffered, they went back to Arnador's house, to await the return of Francesca from work. To keep the boy busy, Arnador asked him to help to prepare the evening meal, and when Francesca opened the front door with her latchkey, she could smell fish frying.

Arnador handed the frying pan over to Ramon, and went to the hall to greet his wife and tell her the news.

She looked at him, stunned, and then burst into tears, to cry helplessly in his arms. Ramon turned off the gas ring on which he had been frying the fish, and came into the hall. When he saw his weeping cousin, he burst into tears himself, and Arnador, himself distressed, hardly knew which to deal with first.

Francesca turned to him and hugged him to her. 'You must stay with us, darling, until Uncle Leo comes home. Then we'll think what to do.'

It was comforting to Francesca to have Ramon with them, and even better when Manuel arrived.

When, six weeks later, Uncle Leo arrived, he had already received the news of his sister's death by cable, kindly sent through the office of his shipping company. He had had time to think what they should do, and he asked Ramon if he would come back and live in Rosita's house with him, if he got a job ashore.

Since to Ramon, Leo had always been his father, he agreed and they lived together until, at the age of twenty-one, he brought home a happy-go-lucky girl called Julie to be his wife and look after the pair of them.

After leaving school, he had obtained a job in the accounts department of an insurance company. He was quick at figures and had had a couple of promotions by the time he married, but he disliked the daily confinement in a tiny office.

On the first anniversary of his marriage, he took Julie to a Chinese restaurant for dinner. It was a beautiful place and not one that they would normally go to. Afterwards, while Julie went to the ladies' room, Ramon went to the cash desk to pay the bill.

It was presided over by a stout, elderly Chinese, who first glanced at the young man, and then stared at him, as he took his credit card. After saying that he hoped the young couple had enjoyed their meal and being assured that, indeed, they had, the Chinese said, 'I know you, don't I? But I don't think you've been here before?'

Ramon stared back at the amiable Chinese, and assured him that he had not seen him before.

They laughed, and the Chinese looked down at the credit card as he put it into his machine.

'Barinèta!' he exclaimed. 'I bet your grandpa lived by Wapping Dock! There's a real likeness – that's why I thought I knew you. Are you any relation to Manuel Echaniz? I used to play with him when I was a little boy. My name's Brian Wing.'

Ramon had never heard of Brian, but, when Julie rejoined her husband, she found herself invited to a table behind a fine ebony screen. Wine was brought, while Brian poured out the stories of Manuel and himself. Ramon's credit card was returned to him, with an absolute refusal of payment for their dinner, and anxious inquiries were made as to Manuel's whereabouts.

Brian was a widower with one son and two married daughters. He owned two restaurants and a small whole-sale fish business. Though his son managed the restaurants, his wife had always kept the company's books and he missed her help sorely.

After a most interesting hour together, the young couple went home. A few days later, Ramon went to see Brian again, to ask for a job as bookkeeper. The salary was not much more than he was getting, but he gradually under-took the supervision of the wholesale fish business.

When Brian died, Ramon bought the fish business from Brian's son, using the money which Rosita had saved for him and had left him on her death. At the time of Old Manuel's proposed visit to him, he had also established a retail outlet, which Julie helped him to run. Their one son helped to run the wholesale side. No matter how many baths the family took, they all smelled slightly of fish – but they were quite prosperous; and the odour from the source of their prosperity did not seem to worry them very much.

Chapter Forty-eight

Although he had been retired for many years, Arnador still belonged to the academic world; as Professor Emeritus, he could always go over to the university and find someone to discuss the latest trends in his discipline.

On the other hand, there were days when Old Manuel felt as if he had lost the art of intelligent verbal communication. Since Kathleen's death, he had, at times, been beside himself with mental loneliness. Though he had not been as close to his wife as Pedro had been to Rosita, they had managed to get along amiably when he was at home. Even as a marine architect, however, he had been away for protracted periods in various shipyards, and this had been her main complaint during their marriage. 'It's all very well for you. You've the company of men you work with. Unless I'm nursing, I can get quite lonesome,' she would say.

'But you do all kinds of things,' he would reply helplessly. 'You're hardly home when I'm home.' He would watch her go off to a tea party or to preside over a meeting of some kind, when all he longed to do was to take her to bed, before Faith got home.

It took him a long time to understand that her attitude to their sexual relationship was different from his, though he had, at times, from the beginning felt a stiffness in her response. Sex was way down at the bottom of the list of things to do as far as she was concerned.

Sometimes he laughed ruefully to himself. Was he any different, he wondered, from other men in that it was always at the *top* of his list.

When he went home to Liverpool, which he had done

from time to time, some of the tension and frustration which lay uncomfortably at the back of his life in Canada left him. He was more relaxed, though he was never unfaithful to his wife. It seemed to help him to speak Basque in a Roman Catholic world in Liverpool. Without effort, he understood the subtle nuances of tone and gesture.

He still enjoyed feminine company, he considered, as long as its name was not Veronica. He rather wished that he had not cut himself off from Kathleen's circle of friends immediately after her death; he could have visited them occasionally and enjoyed conversations with their husbands as well. It was too late, however, to do much about it now. And only this morning, he had collected his plane tickets from the pretty Pakistani girl in the travel agency. In two weeks' time he would be in Liverpool with Ramon and Arnador – and they would not stop talking for the whole month he proposed to stay there! Blessed thought!

Meanwhile it occurred to him that young Sharon had been looking a bit peaky last time she had popped in to see him. He wondered if she would like a day's sailing in the *Rosita*. On Sunday, if she were free, they could go up the coast and have lunch somewhere. And she, at least, would be interested in the details of his trip to England; she had urged him to take it. He would phone her this evening.

He chuckled to himself. He still had not told Faith that he was going. She was going to be so annoyed with him when she found out.

Sunday proved to be a perfect day for sailing; not too hot and with a steady gentle breeze. Sharon insisted on bringing a picnic basket as her share in the expedition, and they sat on the rocks in a tiny cove to eat their lunch, while they watched speedboats and other yachts taking advantage of the lovely day.

She was, as he had expected, enthusiastic about his proposed visit, and she asked him who looked after his house while he was away.

'Well, the post office holds my mail, and Jack Audley'll pick up the circulars from off the step – if he remembers. He's done the lawn for me once or twice, when I've been away.' He hesitated, and then told her, 'I'm not too happy about askin' him this time – he's been complaining of a pain in his chest lately, and I know his wife wants him to see the quack.'

'Oh, don't worry. I'll do your lawn for you. Would once a week be enough?'

He was embarrassed. 'I wasn't meaning to ask you,' he assured her. 'Doing lawns is a man's job. It can wait until I get back.'

She brushed back her hair from her face, and replied firmly, 'No, it can't. Unkept lawns are the first things looked for by thieves – a lawn that hasn't been cut signals that the owner is away. I'll do it. Your yard's a pleasure to be in.'

He grinned at the compliment to his garden, and shyly accepted her offer.

'I'll give you a key to the house, so you can go in and get a drink if you like. I keep the wine in a rack in a cupboard next to the fridge.'

She laughed. 'You'll probably find me flat on my back on the sofa, when you get back – dead drunk!'

He looked her up and down, pretty as a picture in her blue jeans and white T-shirt. 'That would be no hardship,' he said with one of his slow chuckles.

Her eyes twinkled as she accepted the implied compliment. She handed him another sandwich, and then asked, 'Have you told your daughter about your trip?'

He made a face. 'No. I'll phone her the day before I fly.'

'You are naughty!'

'I will not have her run my life,' he responded with

sudden fierceness. 'She means well – but it is very irritating to be lectured at my age.'

Sharon did not attempt to alter his decision. She suggested instead that he leave Faith's telephone number with her. 'So that I can give her a call if anything goes wrong in connection with your house – a break-in, for instance.' Inwardly, she thought it might be interesting to hear from Faith how she felt about her father some time.

'That's a good idea,' he agreed. 'Can I give her your name and number?'

'Sure.'

As he munched his sandwich, he ruminated over the arrangement, and then he said, 'You're a true friend.'

She lifted her glass of wine towards him. 'I hope so,' she said.

Chapter Forty-nine

It was with his usual sense of relaxation and freedom that Manuel emerged from Customs at Manchester Airport, to see Ramon running towards him, pushing his way rapidly through a straggling crowd of others on similar errands.

Now in his fifties, Ramon was a stout man with a mass of greying curls bouncing round a bald pate. His shabby, working macintosh ballooned behind him as he opened his arms to embrace Manuel. They hugged each other and got in the way of other, less demonstrative, passengers, and wiped tears from their eyes, as they climbed into the fishy aroma of Ramon's delivery van parked outside; the blue van had white frothing waves painted along its sides, and *Barinèta and Son Fresh Fish Daily* proudly above them.

During the drive to Liverpool they spoke Basque to each other, and the dear familiar idioms poured out, like water from a fireman's hose. There was a fine, warm affinity between them as if they were much closer in age than they actually were.

As the van bumped its way into Aigburth, the Liverpool suburb where Ramon had bought a little house, Manuel felt a surge of pure happiness, and he forgot the aching loneliness of his life in Victoria.

When Ramon's wife, Julie, heard the van pull up at the gate, she hurried to the door and flung it open. She was nearly as stout as her husband and, despite liberal applications of perfume and scented talcum powder, still smelled slightly of fish. Her tiny feet, in high-heeled patent-leather pumps, took her surprisingly quickly down the path to greet her guest, of whom she had long since grown very fond.

Again, he was hugged and kissed, then dragged into the little home, to be seated by the sitting-room electric fire, and have a glass of wine thrust into his hand, until the kettle had been boiled and tea made. 'Aye, it's good to see you,' Julie assured him.

Old Manuel leaned back in the small fireside chair, and looked around the comfortable room, with its bookshelf, its radio on a side table and television set in the corner. Without hesitation, he said, 'It's good to be home.'

He felt as if he had just docked after a long and tiring voyage.

Much later, when Julie had gone up to bed and he and Ramon were seated comfortably in the sitting-room finishing a cup of cocoa each, pressed upon them by Julie, he asked Ramon what he felt he was, now that he was older, Basque or English?

Ramon laughed. 'I'm not sure,' he said. 'I don't know any other place, except Liverpool. The wife and I did a bus tour of Spain once – but Bilbao wasn't on the itinerary, so I've never been there. Julie was tickled pink that I could speak some Spanish, though; learned it from Francesca. I've got one or two Basque friends – Uncle Arnador, for one – he comes regularly to see me, and we talk Basque together. The wife thinks we're *both* learned. Don't disillusion her!'

'What about your boy – young Leo?'

'Ha! Pure Scouse! I used to tell him about his grandfather, Quanito Barinèta, and how he avenged his grandmother's death. But the Spanish Civil War doesn't mean anything to him, any more than the Second World War does. They were just dates to learn in school. He's married now and off my hands, though he works for me.' In further

368

explanation of himself, he said, 'Being a Basque is like being a Welshman whose parents were born in Anglesey; he'll say, as I would, that he's a Liverpool man – but you can bet he'll belong to the Welsh Society – and sing like a lark! The Welsh is still there.'

Manuel laughed. 'How's your singing in Basque?'

'Lousy. The Basque may be still there, but . . . Uncle Leo was the last person I ever heard sing the old Basque songs – he could hold a tune well, God rest him. I can still put a beret on properly, though!'

Uncle Leo was the only person in our family who died in hospital, remembered Manuel suddenly, and he shuddered visibly; it was the last thing he wanted to happen to himself. Better to be run down and finished in one blow.

The mention of Uncle Leo brought to mind Rosita and his sisters, particularly Francesca, who had been the last of the three women to die. She had died from injuries sustained in a train accident, when, in 1963, she had been returning from a visit to her company's head office in London. As recorded in a long, heart-rending letter from Arnador, it was as well that she did die from her injuries within forty-eight hours of the accident. 'Not only was she badly crushed, but her lovely face was hopelessly disfigured,' he said.

It had taken old Arnie – and himself – a long time to get over that, if either of them ever really had. And, sometimes, considered Old Manuel sadly, another bright spirit, Little Maria, danced in the back of his memory, to haunt him through a sleepless night.

He and Ramon talked a little while longer, and then Ramon took him up to his bedroom, where Julie had turned on the electric fire in case he was cold.

When, afterwards, Ramon climbed into bed with his wife, she was still reading a novel, and he said regretfully to her,

'He's gone that thin; he looks as if a breath of wind would blow him away.'

Julie looked up from her love story, and said prosaically, 'He's feeling his age — like Uncle Arnie.'

Chapter Fifty

It was a joy to Manuel to walk into the spacious lobby of the Adelphi Hotel in Liverpool, to see his old friend waiting for him. Arnador was leaning on a walking-stick, but with such self-assurance that onlookers could be convinced that he did not really need such support. They greeted each other warmly. In some ways it was barely necessary to talk; after seventy-six years of friendship, carefully nursed through wars, depressions and uneasy peace, they knew each other more intimately than did men who lived closer to each other. Both Manuel and Arnador believed that you could express ideas and feelings in letters which you would never mention face to face.

They were to dine together, and, once they were seated in the restaurant, they spoke Basque, with old-fashioned idioms and exclamations no longer heard in the streets of Guernica or Bilbao or Pamplona. Although Arnador had had the advantage of speaking Basque with his wife, Francesca, and with his ancient sister, Josefa, his language was as outdated as was Manuel's.

Manuel inquired after Josefa's health, something he had forgotten to do when he had telephoned Arnador on his arrival at Ramon's. He was told that she was still quite spry. 'Her daughter – my niece, Josephine – you know her – keeps an eye on both of us, when she's not on tour with her Chamber Music Group.' He laughed when he added, 'She's not that young herself – must be over fifty now.'

'Does she speak Basque?'

'No, despite Grandma Ganivet's best efforts when she was small.'

371

'My Lorilyn's the same. I suppose it's the first thing that goes, with immigrants.'

Arnador carefully poised some green peas on his fork, and then, before he put them into his mouth, he replied philosophically, 'It has to go – children want to be like the others round them – and they know that they must speak English to get a job.'

After a good dinner, and a bottle of wine split between them, they retired to the lounge for coffee. It was a fine Edwardian room, full of gilt and mirrors. The coffee drinkers already there seemed small and insignificant, drowned in the room's huge proportions. After a while, Arnador began to fidget, and he remarked, 'It's too damned quiet. Let's go over to the Big House. We could have a drink there.' He put his coffee cup down and pushed it into the middle of the small table in front of him, as if to discard more than an empty cup.

Manuel hastily drained his cup, and got up. He beamed at Arnador, as he also rose, carefully using his stick to balance himself. In spite of being very bent, his head thrust forward from years of study, he still gave an impression of height. Manuel had always been shorter than him and was still fairly upright in his carriage, though half a bottle of wine and a liqueur had made his balance a trifle uncertain, and he held on to the back of a chair for a moment before setting out across the vast carpet to the door.

Arnador had insisted on paying the restaurant's bill and for the coffee.

They tottered down the marble steps and across the fine lobby, oblivious of the stifled giggles of the girls behind the reservation counter; berets were not seen too often in Liverpool any more.

Chattering expansively in Basque, they descended a series of front steps, once trodden by kings and princes, and walked slowly along the pavement, to cross a narrow street to The Vines, known to seamen as the Big House. It seemed a long way to both of them, and they sank thankfully into mahogany chairs in the bar, to sigh with satisfaction at a glittering array of bottles and mirrors and to notice and remark that the Victorian Walker paintings were still hanging there. This had been the haunt of seamen, flush with pay, since before they were born, and they opened their coats and settled back happily for a long session.

After a couple of measures of the best Jamaican rum that the house could provide, they fell into conversation with two retired excisemen, full of wild stories of their adventures in search of taxes. When the excisemen left they grinned at each other. The soft lighting glanced warmly off the fine wooden panelling; and the rise and fall of Liverpool voices around them added to their sense of well-being. Arnador said comfortably, as he looked around, 'Just like old times!'

'Remember when you were seventeen, and you bet you could get me and Joey Connolly into here and buy us both a drink?' Manuel asked. 'And we got kicked out in short order, because we were all too young – and you stood outside and called them everything you could think of – in Basque?'

Arnador giggled, like a young girl. 'Of course I remember. I'd more courage in those days!' He took another sip of his rum and savoured it, before letting it slide down his throat. 'I'm getting old, Mannie!'

'That's why I made this trip. Feeling old myself. Don't have the steam I used to have,' Manuel replied with studied solemnity. 'Felt I might not be able to do it – next year.' He ruminated on this sad fact, and then added dejectedly, 'Wish I'd never left Liverpool. Could've brought Kathleen here.'

'Come on. You live in a lovely place.'

'Boring. Full of old people,' Manuel announced with the certainty of the very drunk.

They had a heated and laborious argument about why one man's boredom was another man's paradise; and Manuel invited Arnador to come with him, when he returned to Victoria, to spend the rest of the summer with him. 'I've still got a car – take you all over the island,' he promised. 'Beautiful to look at – you're right there. And good fishing.'

Arnador considered this offer, and then responded dampeningly, 'We've already done it.' He stopped, to collect words which seemed to be fluttering disorientingly around his brain. Then he suggested, 'We could go to Vizcaya from here. Strange – but I've never been there – and, come to think of it, neither did Frannie.'

'Except when she was a baby.' Manuel drained his glass, as he remembered a little boy looking down into a flawless, fairytale valley, from a shepherd's hut. 'Most beautiful place I've ever seen. And I've seen most places.' He sighed heavily. 'Let's have another drink.'

While another two rums were ordered, the idea of going to Bilbao began to be discussed between them. 'We could stay in a hotel there,' suggested Arnador, 'and take bus tours wherever we wanted to go. Easier than trying to rent a car – I've not had a driving licence for years, anyway.'

And so the idea grew. They planned to meet the following day for lunch and then go together to Thomas Cook's to discuss the details of the journey.

'I want to go down to Wapping,' Manuel announced suddenly. 'Never seem to get there when I come on a visit. Ramon always wants to go to Wales or up to the Lakes, when I suggest it!'

'That's easy,' responded Arnador promptly, though his speech was slurred. 'Remember the Baltic Fleet? Josephine mentioned recently that it's a very nice restaurant, now. We could meet there for lunch, and you can see your old home.' He stopped to yawn mightily. 'And then we can go into town and see about going to Spain. Haven't been down to Wapping since your mother went to live in Toxteth.'

When the barman called, 'Time, gentlemen, please,' and put a white cloth over his beer pumps, they could barely stand on their feet as they got up from their seats.

'Like me to call you a taxi?' asked a barmaid as she quickly mopped their table.

They looked at each other, and giggled foolishly as they clung swaying to the edge of the bar.

'Yes, please,' Manuel said to the girl. 'Wanna go Aigburth – and then Grassendale, for this gentleman.'

That night, helped by a laughing Julie, it was with a huge sense of satisfaction that Manuel climbed the stairs to bed, while singing an unprintable song in Basque.

Around two in the morning, moonlight flooding into the room woke him.

Though his jacket and shoes had been removed, he still wore the rest of his clothes. An eiderdown had been tucked around him. He had no idea where he was.

Disoriented, he found it difficult to breathe, and his mouth was dry and foul. He felt he was suffocating, and he threw off the eiderdown.

It did not help.

He lay very still, taking short breaths, while his brain went round and round like a roundabout. Where was he? And why was there such a sense of weight on his chest – as if old Mr Wing was pressing his big iron down on him?

He began to be frightened and to sweat. Maudlin tears ran down his face.

'Drunk!' he suddenly recollected. 'Very tight!'

He must have made some slight noise, because a rumpled Ramon in striped pyjamas came quietly into the room, bringing with him the usual slight tang of fish. 'You all right, Mannie?' He came over to the bedside and peered down at the old man.

His presence was comforting. Manuel whispered, 'Could you open the window – and give me a drink of water?'

Ramon took a glass of water from the side table and Manuel sipped it eagerly, while Ramon steadied him with an arm round his back. Then he laid the old man back on his pillow, and went to open the window.

The cool night air flooded in, and Manuel immediately felt easier. 'Bevvied,' he announced carefully to the younger man, and closed his eyes.

'It were just like holding a bird,' Ramon told Julie the next morning. 'No weight in him at all.'

Resplendent in a red silky-looking dressing-gown, Julie woke Manuel about nine o'clock the next morning. She carried a steaming cup of tea.

He smiled weakly at her, as he eased himself slowly upright. He felt tremendously, overwhelmingly tired.

'How's your head?' There was a gurgle of laughter in her voice.

'Fine,' he answered truthfully, as with a trembling hand he took the cup of tea from her. 'We drank good stuff. I feel a bit tired, that's all.' The effects of the rum had not yet worn off.

While he drank the tea, she sat down on the bed. 'What do you want to do today?'

He grinned his wide, slow grin at her over his cup, as he told her about the luncheon engagement. 'Would you like to come?' he asked her.

'I can't. It's Friday,' she said regretfully. 'I've got to help Ramon and young Leo in the shop. Funny how a lot of people still eat fish on Fridays – but never go near a church! And we're one of the few places, now, that still sells really fresh fish – so we get a big crowd – I should be down there now.'

She made him promise to take a taxi down to Wapping. 'I'll leave the telephone number on the kitchen counter for you,' she said.

Manuel was resigned to the idea that Liverpool had altered greatly since the days of his youth; but he was ill-prepared for the shock, when his taciturn taxi driver drew up in Hurst Street at the entrance to the Baltic Fleet. Before descending, he paid the driver. When the man had left, he stood, bewildered and forlorn, with his back to the restaurant, surveying, with unbelieving eyes, the view across the narrow street.

He could not locate a single familiar landmark, except that at the side of a narrow road leading off Hurst Street to his right, a rusty street sign, hanging by a single bolt on a block of stone, declared *Sparling Street*. Other than that, there was nothing but rubble, which had been used to fill up the cellars of the demolished buildings. It was like the scene of an air raid, a tumbled sweep of brick, stone and concrete, through which a few blades of grass and dandelion leaves announced that, one day, nature would repair the damage.

His head bent towards the gusty wind, he slowly walked round the tiny Baltic Fleet, which stood alone beside the huge highway along which the taxi had brought him. He wanted to see what lay across the roaring river of traffic.

Where once had been the Salthouse Dock, there was a car park, and beyond it he could see the familiar bulk of the Albert Dock Warehouse. The great walls that had protected the docks had gone. Slightly to his left should have been the Wapping Basin. If it were still there, he could not see it through eyes blurred with tears.

Since he was early for his appointment with Arnador, he walked slowly back along Hurst Street and up and down the traces of the tiny side streets.

After carefully pacing distances, he saw what he had

been looking for; two steps leading from the narrow pavement up into the rubble — and, a foot or two away, two more steps.

He stood looking down at them, feeling dizzily confused and very tired. After a few moments of hesitation, he squatted down on one of the steps, and rested his arms on his knees. Then he put his head down and cried, cried on his mother's doorstep, and cried again because the next doorstep was that of Bridget, who had comforted them all.

Not a soul passed him, not a vehicle went up and down the narrow lanes which had been his childhood playground; the Baltic Fleet was locked in pre-lunchtime calm.

After a while, he took off his spectacles and wiped his eyes with a paper handkerchief, and then cleaned his glasses before putting them back on. He stared down at the street where he and Joey Connolly, Brian Wing and Andy Pilar had played at marbles or flicking ciggie cards, or, later with Arnador, had played cricket with a couple of beer bottles as stumps, much to the alarm of various beshawled housewives, who had visions of the ball going through their windows.

Except for the traffic roaring along the busy new road, which once had been the dock road, there was no noise, no thudding machinery, no horses' hooves, no clanging bell of the railway train that used to run along the other side of the street under the overhead railway — no overhead railway, either.

Old Manuel picked up from the side of the step on which he sat two tiny shattered pieces of brick. He looked at them in the palm of his hand, and then slowly slipped them into his pocket. Nothing left, he thought, except the memories in my head — and in Arnie's head.

He was thankful to see signs of life in the Baltic Fleet; a curtain was flicked straight; the door was set ajar. A taxi drew up and discharged Arnador, who, as the taxi left, went towards the restaurant's entrance. Then, spotting Manuel struggling to get up from his doorstep, he grinned and waved.

Manuel was truly glad to see him, but found it difficult to hurry amid the ghosts which swarmed around him.

They had an excellent lunch with a good wine, and Arnie listened attentively to Manuel's expression of shock at what he had seen. Arnador had taken one glance at the carnage wrought by time and city planning, and said he really did not want to walk around it.

They sat smoking for a while over a brandy each, Manuel still looking a little disconsolate. Anxious to cheer up his friend, Arnador suggested that before making their proposed visit to the travel agent, they should go across to the new Albert Dock complex to look at the Maritime Museum.

The brandy and the suggestion had their effect. 'All right. Let's go,' agreed Manuel. He was determined not to further spoil his time with Arnador by being depressed. He got up quickly and the room whirled around him. He shouldn't have taken the brandy, he decided ruefully. It took more time than you would think for rum to work its way out of your system, never mind downing brandy so soon after it. He unsteadily beckoned for the bill, and insisted that it was his turn to pay.

As they stood in the entrance, they both carefully put on their berets, last reminders of a once vibrant Basque community for whom the Baltic Fleet had been the great meeting place.

Teetering on the edge of the pavement, they viewed cautiously the fast-moving traffic, which lay between them and the Museum. Then, picking what seemed to be a quiet moment, they began carefully to cross the wide road, lane by lane.

*

'I never saw neither of them, I didn't,' cried an almost incoherent driver of a huge lorry laden with containers for Seaforth Dock. 'They was masked by another lorry,' he wailed, to a shaken young police constable not yet enured to the results of traffic accidents.

As the constable jotted down notes in his notebook, and another constable waved slowing traffic onwards, the driver tried not to look at the ambulance crew gently wrapping up the remains of a lifelong friendship.

He saw instead, two berets blown by the wind, scampering over the ruins at the side of the road, to come to rest on what must have been a doorstep. The wind whined, and it seemed, for a moment, to be the sound of the high-pitched laughter of old men enjoying a joke.

The frightened man shivered; the place felt haunted.

Selective Bibliography

Ancona, George, *Freighters* (Thomas Y. Crowell, New York, 1985).

Behrens, C. B. A., *History of the Second World War. Merchant Shipping and the Demands of War* (HMSO and Longman Green, London, 1955).

Carr, Raymond, *Modern Spain* (Oxford University Press, Oxford, 1980).

Collins, Roger, *The Basques* (Basil Blackwell Ltd, Oxford, 1986).

Forester, C. S., *Brown on Resolution* (Pan Books, London, 1963).

Keefe, Eugene K., *Area Handbook for Spain* (The American University, Washington, DC, 1976).

Lane, Tony, *Grey Dawn Breaking* (Manchester University Press, Manchester, 1986).

Lane, Tony, *Liverpool: Gateway of Empire* (Lawrence and Wishart, London, 1987).

Laxalt, Robert, *In a Hundred Graves* (University of Nevada Press, Reno, Nevada, 1972).

Laxalt, Robert, *Sweet Promised Land* (University of Nevada Press, Reno, Nevada, 1986).

Legarreta, Dorothy, *The Guernica Generation* (University of Nevada Press, Reno, Nevada, 1984).

Middlebrook, Martin, *Convoy* (Penguin Books, Harmondsworth, 1978).

O'Connor, Fred, *Liverpool: It All Came Tumbling Down* (Brunswick Printing and Publishing Co. Ltd, Liverpool, 1986).

Robinson, A. R. B., *Chaplain on the Mersey, 1859–67* (A. R. B. Robinson, York, 1987).

Scott, Dixon, *Liverpool* (Adam and Charles Black, London, 1907).

Spanish State Tourist Department, *Spain* (Spanish State Tourist Department, Madrid, date unknown).

Taylor, J. E., *Of Ships and Seamen* (Williams and Norgate Ltd, London, 1949).

Unwin, Frank, *Reflections on the Mersey* (Gallery Press, Neston, 1984).

Waters, John M., Jr., *Bloody Winter* (D. Van Nostrand Co., Inc, New York, 1967).

Whittington-Egan, Richard, *Liverpool: This Is My City* (Gallery Press, Liverpool, 1972).